NORTH AMERICA
PHYSICAL FEATURES

Alvin Miller's Road ....
(Wobbish Road)

Scale of Miles
0   50 100 150 200 250 300

HIGH WATER LAKE

LAKE MIZOGAN

HURON LAKE

L. IRRAKWA

LAKE CANADA

Fort Detroit

R. St. Denis

R. Rhone

R. Seine

Scoggin

Merrimack

Netticut River

Boston
Cape Faith

Mo-Hawk

Hudson River

River Thames

New Amsterdam

Philadelphia

Osh-Kontsy R.

Mizzipy R.

Paw-Nee River

Noisy River

St. Joseph

Tippy-Canoe Cr.

Maw-Mee

Dekane

Hatrack
Hatrack

Eight-face Mound

Algony R.

Suskwahenny

Mongoly

River Hio

Luther

Potomac

Vigor Church
Carthage City

My-Ammy

Pickawee

Virgin R.

Shenandoah

James River

Bay of St. Olaf

R. Mizeray

Wobbish River

Hio River

Kenituck R.

River

Cherriky

Cree-ek

Roanoke River

Yadkin River

APPALACHEE MOUNTAINS

Hot R.

Ozark R.

Ar-Kansas R.

Tennizy R.

Franklin

Smoky

Tennizy R.

Avon River

River Mersey

Camelot

Red River

Mizzipy River

Yazoo River

R. Santa Maria

R. Noche

Bammy River

Pearl River

River Tweed

Savannah River

Rio de Hispania

Santa Isabela

Alvin Wandering

Alvin Wandering

Alvin Journeyman
Heartfire

ORSON SCOTT CARD

FANTASY

Contents

Alvin Journeyman   1

Heartfire   343

Alvin Journeyman

To Jason Lewis,
long-legged wanderer,
walker through woods,
dreamer of true dreams.

Acknowledgments

For the past few years, at every book signing or speech I gave, I was asked one question more than any other: Will there be another Alvin Maker book? The answer was always, Yes, but I don't know when. My original outline for *The Tales of Alvin Maker* had long since been abandoned, and while I knew certain incidents that would happen in this book, I still did not know enough about what would happen to Alvin, Peggy, Taleswapper, Arthur Stuart, Measure, Calvin, Verily Cooper, and others to be able to start writing.

At last the logjam broke and the story came right, or as near right as I could get it. As I composed, I was constantly aware of those hundreds of readers who were waiting for *Alvin Journeyman*. It was encouraging to know that this book was much looked for; it was also frightening, because I knew that for some, at least, the expectations would be so high that any story I wrote would be bound to disappoint. To the disappointed I can only express my regret that the reality is never as good as the anticipation (cf. Christmas); and to all who hoped for this book, I give my thanks for your encouragement.

I thank the many readers on America Online who came to the Hatrack River Town Meeting and downloaded each chapter of the manuscript as I wrote it, responding with many helpful comments. These sharp-eyed readers caught inconsistencies and dangling threads—questions raised in earlier books that needed to be resolved. Newel Wright, Jane Brady, and Len Olen, in particular, won my undying gratitude: Jane, by preparing a chronology of the events in the previous books, Newel, by saving me from two ghastly continuity errors, and Len, by a thorough proofreading that caught several errors that all the editors and I had missed. Thanks also go to David Fox for an insightful reading of the first nine chapters at a key point in the composition of the book.

Quite without my planning it, a peculiar and delightful community has grown up within the Hatrack River Town Meeting on AOL; people began to arrive, not as themselves, but as characters living within Alvin's world, and set up in trade or farming in that fictional town. Thus Hatrack River has taken on a life of its own. The temptation was irresistible to include mention of as many of these characters as I could within this storyline; I only regret that I couldn't work them all into the plot. If you want to know more about the wonderful characters these good people have created, come visit us online (keyword: Hatrack).

The only active online character I made extensive use of in this book was one I devised myself as a fictional foil, whom Kathryn Kidd (town identity: GoodyTradr) and I (town identity: HoracGuest) referred to from time to time in a comical way as a notorious gossip: Vilate Franker. A couple of years after we invented her, along came a good friend, Melissa Wunderly, who volunteered to portray her in the online community; so it was Melissa who brought her to life, false teeth, hexes, and all. Vilate's "best friend," however, was mine, and Melissa is not to be blamed for Vilate's unpleasant behavior in this book. And I appreciate Kathryn Kidd's allowing me to use her character, Goody Trader, at a couple of key moments.

I must tip my hat to Graham Robb, whose excellent, well-written *Balzac: A Biography* (Norton, 1994) gave me not only respite from writing but also the foundation of a character I personally enjoy.

As with many previous novels, each chapter was read as it emerged from the printer or the fax machine by my wife, Kristine; my son Geoffrey; and my friend and sometime collaborator, Kathryn H. Kidd. Their responses have been of incalculable value.

My thanks also go to those who keep our office and household functioning when I'm (too rarely) in writer mode: Kathleen Bellamy, who tends to the business, and Scott Allen, who keeps the computers and the house itself in running order. A tip of the hat also goes to Jason, Adam, and (on one occasion) Michael Lewis, for holes dug and holes filled; and to Emily, Kathryn, and Amanda Jensen for giving us those nights out.

If it weren't for Kristine, Geoffrey, Emily, Charlie Ben, and Zina Meg, I doubt that I would ever write at all: They make the work worth doing.

Contents

1	I Thought I Was Done	11
2	Hypocrites	18
3	Watchers	29
4	Quest	55
5	Twist	62
6	True Love	73
7	Booking Passage	79
8	Leavetaking	89
9	Cooper	105
10	Welcome Home	121

11 Jail   136

12 Lawyers   155

13 Maneuvers   175

14 Witnesses   202

15 Love   251

16 Truth   271

17 Decisions   289

18 Journeys   317

19 Philadelphia   338

1

I Thought I Was Done

I thought I was done writing about Alvin Smith. People kept telling me I wasn't, but I knew why. It's because they'd all heard Taleswapper and the way he tells stories. When he's done, it's all tied up neat in a package and you pretty much know what things meant and why they happened. Not that he spells it all out, mind you. But you just have this feeling that it all makes sense.

Well I ain't Taleswapper, which some of you might already have guessed, seeing how we don't look much alike, and I don't plan on becoming Taleswapper anytime soon, or anything much like him, not cause I don't reckon him to be a fine fellow, worthy of folks emulating him, but mainly because I don't see things the way he sees them. Things don't all make sense to me. They just happen, and sometimes you can extract a bit of sense from some calamity and sometimes the happiest day is just pure nonsense. There's no predicting it and there's *sure* no making it happen. Worst messes I ever saw folks get into was when they was trying to make things go in a sensible way.

So I set down what I knew of the earliest beginnings of Alvin's life right up till he made him the golden plow as his journeyman project, and I told how he went back to Vigor and set to teaching folks how to be Makers and how things already wasn't right with his brother Calvin and I thought I was done, because anybody who cares was there from then on to see for themselves or you know somebody who was. I told you the truth of how Alvin came to kill a man, so as to put to rest all the vicious rumors told about it. I told you how he came to break the runaway slave laws and I told you how Peggy Larner's mama came to die and believe me, that was pretty much the end of the story as far as I could see it.

But the ending didn't make sense of it, I reckon, and folks have been pestering me more and more about the early days and didn't I know more I could tell? Well sure I know. And I got nothing against telling it. But I hope you don't think that when I'm done telling all I know it'll finally be clear to everybody what everything that's happened was all about, because I don't know myself. Truth is, the story ain't over yet, and I hope it never will be, so the most I can hope to do is set down the way it looks to this one fellow at this exact moment, and I can't even promise you that tomorrow I won't come to understand it much better than anything I'm writing now.

My knack ain't storytelling. Truth is, Taleswapper's knack ain't storytelling either, and he'd be the first to tell you that. He collects stories, all right, and the ones he gathers are important so you listen because the tale itself matters. But you know he don't do nothing much with his voice, and he don't roll his eyes and use them big gestures like the real orators use. His voice ain't strong enough to fill a good-size cabin, let alone a tent. No, the telling ain't his knack. He's a painter if anything, or maybe a woodcarver or a printer or whatever he can use to tell or show the story but he's no genius at any of them.

Fact is if you ask Taleswapper what his knack is, he'll tell you he don't have none. He ain't lying—nobody can ever lay that charge at Taleswapper's door. No, he just set his heart on one knack when he was a boy, and all his life that seemed to him the only knack worth having and since he never got it (he thinks) why then he must not have no knack at all. And don't pretend you don't know what knack it was he wanted, because he practically slaps you in the face with it whenever he talks for long. He wanted the knack of prophecy. That's why he's always been so powerful jealous of Peggy Larner, because she's a torch and from childhood on she saw all the possible futures of people's lives, and while that's not the same thing as

knowing *the* future—the way things will actually happen instead of
how they might happen—it's pretty close. Close enough that I think
Taleswapper would have been happy for five minutes of being a
torch. Probably would have grinned himself to death within a week
if such a thing happened.

When Taleswapper says he's got no knack, though, I'll tell you,
he's wrong. Like a lot of folks, he has a knack and doesn't even
know it because that's the way knacks work—it just feels as natural
as can be to the person who's got it, as easy as breathing, so you
don't think *that* could possibly be your unusual power because heck,
that's *easy*. You don't know it's a knack till other people around
you get all astonished about it or upset or excited or whatever feelings your knack seems to provoke in folks. Then you go, "Boy
howdy, other folks can't *do* this! I got me a knack!" and from then
on there's no putting up with you till you finally settle down and
get back to normal life and stop bragging about how you can do this
fool thing that you used to never be excited about back when you
still had sense.

Some folks never know they got them a knack, though, because
nobody else ever notices it either, and Taleswapper's that way. I
didn't notice it till I started trying to collect all my memories and
everything anybody ever told me about Alvin Maker's life. Pictures
of him working that hammer in the forge every chance he got in
case we ever forgot that he had an honest trade, hard come by with
his own sweat, and didn't just dance through life like a quadrille
with Dame Fortune as his loving partner—as if we ever thought
Dame Fortune did anything more than flirt with him, and likely as
not if he ever got close to her he'd find out she had the pox anyway;
Fortune has a way of being on the side of the Unmaker, when folks
start relying on her to save them. But I'm getting off the subject,
which I had to read back to the beginning of this paragraph to see
what in hell I was talking about (and I can hear you prickle-hearted
prudes saying, What's he doing putting down curses on paper, hasn't
he no sense of decent language? to which I say, When I curse it
don't harm nobody and it makes my language more colorful and
heaven knows I can use the color, and I can assure you I've studied
cussing from the best and I know how to make my language a whole
lot more colorful than it is right now, but I already tone myself down
so you don't have apoplexy reading my words. I wouldn't want to
spend half my life just going to the funerals of people who had a
stroke from reading my book, so instead of criticizing me for the
nasty words that creep into my writing why don't you praise me for

the really ugly stuff that I virtuously chose to leave out? It's all how you choose to look at it, I think, and if you have time to rail on about my language, then you don't have enough to do and I'll be glad to put you in touch with folks who need more hands to help with *productive* labor), so anyway I looked back to the beginning of this paragraph *again* to see what the hell I was talking about and my point is that when I gathered all these stories together, I noticed that Taleswapper seems to keep showing up in the oddest places at *exactly* the moment when something important was about to happen, so that he ended up being a witness or even a participant in a remarkable number of events.

Now, let me ask you plain, my friends. If a man seems to know, down in his bones, when something important's about to happen, and where, and enough in advance that he can get his body over there to be a witness of it before it even starts, now ain't that prophecy? I mean why was it William Blake ever left England and came to America if it wasn't because he *knew* that the world was about to be torn open to give birth to a Maker again after all these generations? Just cause he didn't know it out in the open didn't mean that he wasn't a prophet. He thought he had to be a prophet with his mouth, but I say he's a prophet in his bones. Which is why he just happened to be wandering back to the town of Vigor Church, to Alvin's father's mill, for no reason he was aware of, at exactly the day and hour that Alvin's little brother Calvin Miller decided to run off and go study trouble in faraway places. Taleswapper had no idea what was going to happen, but folks, I tell you, he was *there*, and anybody who tells you Taleswapper's got no knack, including Taleswapper himself, is a blame fool. Of course I mean that in the nicest possible way, as Horace Guester would tell you.

So as I pick up my tale again that's the day I choose to start with, mostly because I can tell you from experience that *nothing* interesting happened during those long months when Alvin was still trying to teach a bunch of plain folks how to be a Maker like him instead of . . . well, all in time. Let's just say that while some of you are bound to criticize me for *not* telling all of Alvin's lessons about Makering and every single boring moment of every class he held trying to teach fish to hop, I can promise you that leaving out those days from my tale is an act of charity.

There's a lot of people and a lot of confusion in the story, too, and I can't help that, because if I made it all clear and simple that would be a lie. It was a mess and there was a lot of different people involved and also, to tell you the truth, there's a lot of things that happened that I didn't know about then and still don't know much about now. I'd like to say that I'm telling you all the important parts of the story, telling about all the important people, but I know perfectly well that there might be important parts that I just don't know about, and important people that I didn't realize were important. There's stuff that *nobody* knows, and stuff that them as knows ain't telling, or them as knows don't know they know. And even as I try to explain things as I understand them I'm still going to leave things out without meaning to, or tell you things twice that you already know, or contradict something that you know to be a fact, and all I can say is, I ain't no Taleswapper, and if you want to know the deepest truth, get him to unseal that back two-thirds of his little book and read you what he's got in *there* and I bet, for all he claims to be no prophet, I bet you'll hear things as will curl your hair, or uncurl it, depending.

There's one mystery, though, that I plain don't know the answer to, even though everything depends on it. Maybe if I tell you enough you'll figure it out for yourself. But what I don't understand is why Calvin went the way he did. He was a sweet boy, they all say it. He and Alvin were close as boys can be, I mean they fought but there was never malice in it and Cally grew up knowing Al would die for him. So what was it made jealousy start to gnaw at Calvin's heart and turn him away from his own brother and want to undo all his work? I heard a lot of the tale I'm about to tell you from Cally's own mouth, but you can be sure he never sat down and explained to me or anybody why he changed. Oh, he told plenty of folks why he hated Alvin, but there's no ring of truth in what he says about that, since he always accuses his brother of doing whatever his audience hates the most. To Puritans he says he came to hate Alvin because he saw him trucking with the devil. To Kingsmen he says he hated Alvin because he saw how his brother went so far as to murder a man just to keep him from recovering his own property, a runaway slave baby named Arthur Stuart (and don't *that* set them Royalists' teeth on edge, to think of a half-Black boy having the same name as the King!). Calvin always has a tale that justifies himself in the eyes of strangers, but never a word of explanation does he ever have to those of us who know the truth about Alvin Maker.

I just know this: When I first set eyes on Calvin, in Vigor Church during that year when Alvin tried to teach Makering, that year before he left, I'll tell you, folks, Calvin was already gone. In his heart every word that Alvin said was like poison. If Alvin paid no attention to him, Calvin felt neglected and said so. Then if Alvin *did* pay attention to him, Calvin got surly and sullen and claimed Alvin wouldn't leave him alone. There was no pleasing him.

But to say he was "contrary" don't explain a thing. It's just a name for the way he was acting, not an answer to the question of why he acted that way. I have my own guesses, but they're just guesses and no more, not even what they call "educated guesses" because there's no such thing as education so good it makes one man's guess any better than another's. Either you know or you don't, and I don't know.

I don't know why people who got what they need to be happy don't just go ahead and be happy. I don't know why lonely people keep shoving away everybody as tries to befriend them. I don't know why people blame weak and harmless folks for their troubles while they leave their real enemy alone to get away with all his harm. And I sure don't know why I bother to go to the trouble to write all this down when I know you still won't be satisfied.

Let me tell you one little thing about Calvin. I saw him one day taking class with Alvin, and for once he was paying attention, real close attention, heeding every word that came from his brother's lips. And I thought: He's finally come around. He finally realized that if he really wants to be a seventh son of a seventh son, if he really wants to be a Maker, he has to learn from Alvin how it's done.

And then the class ended, and I sat there watching Calvin as everybody else went on out to get back to their chores, until only me and Calvin was left in the room, and Calvin actually talks to me—mostly he ignored me like I wasn't there—he talks to me and in a few seconds I realize what he's doing. He's imitating Alvin. Not Alvin's regular voice, but Alvin's schoolteachery voice. You all remember when he got that way—I remember he learned that flowery fancy talk when he was studying with Miss Larner, before she came out of disguise and he realized she was the same Peggy Guester who kept his birth caul and protected him through his growing-up years. The big five-dollar words she learned in Dekane or from them books she read. Alvin wanted to sound refined like her, or sometimes he wanted to, anyway, and so he'd learn them words and use them and talk so fine you'd have thought he learned English from an expert instead of just growing up with it like the rest of us. But he couldn't keep it up. He'd hear himself talking so high-toned and he'd just suddenly laugh or make some joke and then he'd go back to talking like folks. And there was Calvin talking that same high-toned way, only he didn't laugh. He just did all his imitating and when he was done, he looked at me and said, "Was that right?"

As if I'd know!

And I says back to him, "Calvin, *sounding* like an educated man don't make you educated," and he says back to me, "I'd rather be ignorant and sound educated than be educated and sound ignorant," and I said, "Why?" and he says to me, "Because if you sound educated then nobody ever tests you to find out, but if you sound ignorant they never stop."

Here's my point. Well, maybe it's not the point I started out to make, but I long since lost track of *that*. So here's the point I want to make *now:* I know more about what happened during Alvin's year of wandering than anybody else on God's green Earth. But I also am aware of how many questions I still can't answer. So I reckon I'm the one as knows but seems ignorant. Which kind are you?

If you already figure you know this story, for heaven's sake stop reading now and save yourself some trouble. And if you're going to criticize me for not finishing the whole thing and tying it up in a bow for you, why, do us both a favor and write your own damn book, only have the decency to call it a romance instead of a history, because history's got no bows on it, only frayed ends of ribbons and knots that can't be untied. It ain't a pretty package but then it's not your birthday that I know of, so I'm under no obligation to give you a gift.

2

Hypocrites

Calvin was about fed up. Just this close to walking up to Alvin and . . . and something. Punching him in the nose, maybe, only he'd tried that afore and Alvin just caught him by the wrist and gripped him with those damn blacksmith muscles and he says, "Calvin, you know I could always throw you, do we have to do this now?" Alvin could always do everything better, or if he couldn't then it must not be worth doing. Folks all gathered around and listened to Alvin's babbling like it all made sense. Folks watched every move he made like he was a dancing bear. Only time they noticed Calvin was to ask him if he would kindly step aside so they could see Alvin a little better.

Step aside? Yep, I reckon I can step aside. I can step right out the door and out into the hot sun and right out onto the path going up the hill to the tree line. And what's to stop me from keeping right on? What's to stop me from walking on to the edge of the world and then jumping right off?

But Calvin didn't keep walking. He leaned against a big old

maple and then hunkered down in the grass and looked out over Father's land. The house. The barn. The chicken coops. The pigpen. The millhouse.

Did the wheel ever turn in Father's mill anymore? The water passed useless through the chase, the wheel leaned forward but never moved, and so the stones inside were still, too. Might as well have left the huge millstone in the mountain, as to bring it down here to stand useless while big brother Alvin filled these poor people's minds with hopeless hopes. Alvin was grinding them up as surely as if he put their heads between the stones. Grinding them up, turning them to flour which Alvin himself would bake into bread and eat up for supper. He may have prenticed as a blacksmith all those years in Hatrack River, but here in Vigor Church he was a baker of brains.

Thinking of Alvin eating everybody's ground-up heads made Calvin feel nasty in a delicious kind of way. It made him laugh. He stretched his long thin legs out into the meadow grass and lay back against the trunk of the maple. A bug was scampering along the skin of his leg, up under his trousers, but he didn't bother to reach down and pull it out, or even to shake his leg to get it off. Instead, he got his doodlebug going, like a spare pair of eyes, like an extra set of fingers, looking for the tiny rapid flutter of the bug's useless stupid life and when he found it he gave it a little pinch, or really more like a squint, a tiny twitch of the muscles around his eyes, but that was all it took, just that little pinch and then the bug wasn't moving no more. Some days, little bug, it just don't pay to get up in the morning.

"That must be some funny story," said a voice.

Calvin fairly jumped out of his skin. How did somebody come on him unawares? Still, he didn't let himself show he'd been surprised. His heart might be beating fast inside his chest, but he still waited a minute before even turning around to look, and then he made sure to look about as uninterested as a fellow can look without being dead.

A bald fellow, old and in buckskins. Calvin knew him, of course. A far traveler and sometime visitor named Taleswapper. Another one who thought the world began with God and ended with Alvin. Calvin looked him up and down. The buckskins were about as old as the man. "Did you get them clothes off a ninety-year-old deer, or did your daddy and grandpa wear them all their lives to get them so worn out like that?"

"I've worn these clothes so long," said the old man, "that I sometimes send them on errands when I'm too busy to go, and nobody can tell the difference."

"I think I know you," said Calvin. "You're that old Taleswapper fellow."

"So I am," said the old man. "And you're Calvin, old Miller's youngest boy."

Calvin waited.

And here it came: "Alvin's little brother."

Calvin folded himself sitting down and then unfolded himself standing. He liked how tall he was. He liked looking down at the old man's bald head. "You know, old man, if we had another just like you, we could put your smooth pink heads together and you'd look like a baby's butt."

"Don't like being called Alvin's little brother, eh?" asked Taleswapper.

"You know where to go for your free meal," said Calvin. He started to walk away into the meadow. Having no destination in mind, of course, his walking pretty soon petered out, and he paused a moment, looking around, wishing there was something he wanted to do.

The old man was right behind him. Damn but the old boy was quiet! Calvin had to remember to keep a watch out for people. Alvin did it without thinking, dammit, and Calvin could do it too if he could just remember to remember.

"Heard you chuckling," said Taleswapper. "When I first walked up behind you."

"Well, then, I guess you ain't deaf yet."

"Saw you watching the millhouse and heard you chuckling and I thought, What does this boy see so funny in a mill whose wheel don't turn?"

Calvin turned to face him. "You were born in England, weren't you?"

"I was."

"And you lived in Philadelphia awhile, right? Met old Ben Franklin there, right?"

"What a memory you have."

"Then how come you talk like a frontiersman? You know and I know that it's supposed to be 'a mill whose wheel *doesn't* turn,' but here you are talking bad grammar as if you never went to school but I know you did. And how come you don't talk like other Englishmen?"

"Keen ear, keen eye," said Taleswapper. "A sharp one for details. Dull on the big picture, but sharp on details. I notice you talk worse than *you* know how, too.''

Calvin ignored the insult. He wasn't going to let this old coot distract him with tricks. ''I said how come you talk like a frontiers-man?''

''Spend a lot of time on the frontier.''

''I spend a lot of time in the chicken coop but that don't make me cluck.''

Taleswapper grinned. ''What do *you* think, boy?''

''I think you try to sound like the people you're telling your lies to, so they'll trust you, they'll think you're one of them. But you're not one of us, you're not one of anybody. You're a spy, stealing the hopes and dreams and wishes and memories and imaginings of everybody and leaving them nothing but lies in exchange.''

Taleswapper seemed amused. ''If I'm such a criminal, why ain't I rich?''

''Not a criminal,'' said Calvin.

''I'm relieved to be acquitted.''

''Just a hypocrite.''

Taleswapper's eyes narrowed.

''A hypocrite,'' Calvin said again. ''Pretending to be what you're not. So other people will trust you, but they're trusting in a bunch of pretenses.''

''That's an interesting idea, there, Calvin,'' said Taleswapper. ''Where do you draw the line between a humble man who knows his own weaknesses but tries to act out virtues he hasn't quite mastered yet, and a proud man who pretends to have those virtues without the slightest intention of acquiring them?''

''Listen to the frontiersman now,'' said Calvin scornfully. ''I knew you could shed that folksy talk the minute you wanted to.''

''Yes, I can do that,'' said Taleswapper. ''Just as I can speak French to a Frenchman and Spanish to a Spaniard and four kinds of Red talk depending on which tribe I'm with. But you, Calvin, do you speak Scorn and Mockery to everyone? Or just to your betters?''

It took Calvin a moment to realize that he had been put down, hard and low. ''I could kill you without using my hands,'' he said.

''Harder than you think,'' said Taleswapper. ''Killing a man, that is. Why not ask your brother Alvin about it? He's done it the once, for just cause, whereas you think of killing a man because he tweaks your nose. And then you wonder why I call myself your better.''

"You just want to put me down because I named you for what you are. Hypocrite. Like all the others."

"*All* the others?"

Calvin nodded grimly.

"*Everyone* is a hypocrite except Calvin Miller?"

"Calvin *Maker*," said Calvin. Even as he said it, he knew it was a mistake; he had never told anyone the name by which he thought of himself, and now he had blurted it out, a boast, a brag, a *demand*, to this most unsympathetic of listeners. This man who was most likely, of all men, to repeat Calvin's secret dream to others.

"Well, now it seems to be unanimous," said Taleswapper. "We're all pretending to be something that we're not."

"I *am* a Maker!" Calvin insisted, raising his voice, even though he knew he was making himself seem even weaker and more vulnerable. He just couldn't stop himself from talking to this slimy old man. "I've got all the knack for it that Alvin ever had, if anyone would bother to notice!"

"Made any millstones lately, without tools?" asked Taleswapper.

"I can make stones in a fence fit together like as if they growed that way out of the ground!"

"Healed any wounds?"

"I killed a bug crawling on my leg just a moment ago without so much as laying a hand on it."

"Interesting. I ask of healing and you answer with killing. Doesn't sound like a Maker to me."

"You said yourself that Alvin killed a man!"

"With his hands, not with his knack. A man who had just murdered an innocent woman who died to protect her son from captivity. The bug—was it going to harm you or anyone?"

"Yes, there you are, Alvin is always righteous and wonderful, while Calvin can't do nothing right! But Alvin hisself told me the story of how he caused a bunch of roaches to get theirselfs kilt when he was a boy and—"

"And you learned nothing from his story, except that you have the power to torment insects."

"*He* gets to do what he wants and then talks about how he's learned better now, but if *I* do the same things then I'm not worthy! I can't be taught any of his secrets because I'm not *ready* for them only I *am* ready for them, I'm just not ready to let Alvin decide *how* I'll use the knack I was born with. Who tells *him* what to do?"

"The inner light of virtue," said Taleswapper, "for lack of a clearer name."

"Well what about *my* inner light?"

"I imagine that your parents ask themselves this very question, and often."

"Why can't *I* be allowed to figure things out on my own like Alvin did?"

"But of course you *are* being allowed to do *exactly* that," said Taleswapper.

"No I'm not! He sits there trying to explain to those boneheaded no-knack followers of his how to get inside other things and learn what they are and how they're shaped inside and then ask them to take on new forms, as if that's a thing that folks can learn—"

"But they *do* learn it, don't they?"

"If you call an inch a year moving, then I guess you can call that learning," said Calvin. "But me, the one who actually understands everything he says, the one who could actually put it all to use, he won't even let me in the room. If I stay there he just tells stories and makes jokes and won't teach a *thing* until I leave, and why? I'm his best pupil, ain't I? I learn it all, I soak it in fast and I can use it on the instant, but he won't teach me! He calls them others 'apprentice Makers' but me he won't even take on for a single lesson, all because I don't bow down and worship whenever he starts talking about how a Maker can never use his power to destroy, but only to build, or he loses it, which is nonsense, since a man's knack is his knack and—"

"It seems to me," said Taleswapper, his voice sharp enough to cut through Calvin's raging, "that you are a singularly unteachable young man. You ask Alvin to teach you, and he tries to do it, but then you refuse to listen because *you* know what's nonsense and what matters, *you* know that a man doesn't have to make in order to be a Maker, *you* already know so much I'm surprised you still wait around here, wishing for Alvin to teach you things that you plainly have no desire to know."

"I want him to teach me how to get into the small of things!" cried Calvin. "I want him to teach me how to change people the way he changed Arthur Stuart so the Finders couldn't Find him anymore! I want him to teach me how to get inside bones and blood vessels, how to turn iron to gold! I want me a golden plow like his and he won't teach me *how*!"

"And it has never occurred to you," said Taleswapper, "that when he speaks of using the power of Making only to build things up, never to tear them down, he might be teaching you precisely the thing you are asking? Oh, Calvin, I'm so sorry to see that your mama did have one stupid child after all.''

Calvin felt the rage explode inside himself, and before he knew what he was doing he knocked the old man down and straddled his hips, pounding on his frail old ribs and belly. It took many blows before he realized that the old man wasn't fighting back. Have I killed him? Calvin wondered. What will I do if he's dead? They'll have me for murder, then. They won't understand how he provoked me, begging for a beating. It's not like I planned to kill him.

Calvin put his fingers to Taleswapper's throat, feeling for a pulse. It was there, feeble, but it probably was always feeble, given how old the fellow was.

"Didn't quite kill me, eh?" whispered Taleswapper.

"Didn't feel like it," said Calvin.

"How many men will you have to beat up before everyone agrees that you're a Maker?"

Calvin wanted to hit him again. Didn't this old man learn anything?

"You know, if you hurt people enough, eventually they'll all call you whatever you want. Maker. King. Captain. Boss. Master. Holy One. Pick your title, you can beat people into calling you that. But you don't change yourself a bit. All you do is change the meanings of those words, so they all mean the same thing: Bully.''

Calvin, hot with shame, got up and stood over him. He restrained himself from kicking the old man until his head was jelly. "You've got a knack for words," he said.

"True words in particular," said Taleswapper.

"Lies, from all I can see," said Calvin.

"A liar sees lies," said Taleswapper. "Even when they aren't there. Just as a hypocrite sees hypocrites whenever he runs across good people. Can't stand to think that anyone might *really* be what you only pretend to be."

"You did say one true thing," said Calvin. "About its making no sense me waiting around here for Alvin to teach me what he plainly means to keep secret. I should've realized that Alvin wasn't never going to teach me anything, because he's afraid if people see me doing all the things he can do, he won't be king of the hill anymore. I have to find it out on my own, just like he did."

"You have to find it out by learning the same things he did," said Taleswapper. "Alone or as his pupil, though, I don't think you're capable of learning those things."

"You're wrong," said Calvin. "I'll prove it to you."

"By learning to master your own will and use your power only to build things, only to help others?"

"By going out into the world and learning everything and coming back and showing Alvin who's got the real Maker's knack and who's just pretending."

Taleswapper propped himself up on one elbow. "But Calvin, your actions here today have made the answer to that question as plain as day."

Calvin wanted to kick him in his face. Silence that mouth. Break that shiny pate and watch the brains spill out into the meadow grass.

Instead he turned away and took a few steps toward the woods. He had a destination this time. East. Civilization. The cities, the lands where people lived together cheek by jowl. Among them there would be those who could teach him. Or, failing that, those he could experiment with until he learned all that Alvin knew, and more. Calvin was wrong to have stayed here so long. Foolish to have kept hoping that he'd ever get any love or help from Alvin. I worshipped him, that was my mistake, thought Calvin. It took this boneheaded old fool to show me the kind of contempt that people have for me. Always comparing me to Alvin, perfect Alvin, Alvin the Maker, Alvin the virtuous son.

Alvin the hypocrite. He does with his power just what I want to do—only he's so subtle about it that people don't even realize he's controlling them. Tell us what to do, Alvin! Teach us how to Make, Alvin! Does Alvin ever say, It's not your knack, you poor fool, I can't teach you how to do this any more than I can teach a fish to walk? No. He pretends to teach them, helps them get a few pathetic illusory successes so they stay with him, his obedient servants, his disciples.

Well, I'm not one of them. I'm my own man, smarter than he is, and more powerful, too, if I can just learn what I need to learn. After all, Alvin was only a seventh son for a couple of moments after he was born, until our oldest brother Vigor died. But I have been a seventh son my whole life, and still am one today. Before long I'm bound to surpass Alvin. I'm the real Maker. The real thing. Not a hypocrite. Not a pretender.

"When you see Alvin, tell him not to follow me. He won't see me again until I'm ready for him to square off against me, Maker against Maker."

"There can never be a battle of Maker against Maker," said Taleswapper.

"Oh?"

"Because if there's a battle," said Taleswapper, "it's because one of them, at least, is not a Maker at all, but rather its opposite."

Calvin laughed. "That old wives' tale? About some supposed Unmaker? Alvin tells the stories, but it's all a bunch of hogwash to make him look like more of a hero."

"I'm not surprised that you don't believe in the Unmaker," said Taleswapper. "The first lie the Unmaker always tells is that he doesn't exist. And his true servants always believe him, even as they carry out his work in the world."

"So I'm the Unmaker's servant?" asked Calvin.

"Of course," said Taleswapper. "I have the bruises on my body now to prove it."

"Those bruises prove you're a weak man with a big mouth."

"Alvin would have healed me and strengthened me," said Taleswapper. "That's what *Makers* do."

Calvin couldn't take any more of this. He kicked the man right in the face. He could feel Taleswapper's nose break under the ball of his foot; then the old man flopped back into the grass and lay there still. Calvin didn't even bother to check his pulse. If he was dead, so be it. The world would be a better place without his lies and rudeness.

Not until he was well into the woods, about five minutes later, did the enormity of what he had done flow over him. Killed a man! I might have killed a man, and left him to die!

I should have healed him before I left. The way Alvin healed people. Then he would have *known* that I'm truly a Maker, because I healed him. How could I have missed such an opportunity to show what I can do?

At once he turned and raced back through the forest, dodging the roots, skittering down a bank he had so eagerly climbed only moments before. But when, panting, he emerged into the meadow, the old man wasn't there, though bits of blood still clung to the grass and pooled where his head had lain. Not dead, then. He got up and walked, so he can't be dead.

What a fool I was, thought Calvin. Of course I didn't kill him. I'm a Maker. Makers don't destroy things, they build them. Isn't that what Alvin always tells me? So if I'm a Maker, nothing I do can possibly be destructive.

For a moment he almost headed down the hill toward the millhouse. Let Taleswapper accuse him in front of everybody. Calvin would simply deny it, and let them work out how to deal with the problem. Of course they'd all believe Taleswapper. But Calvin only needed to say, "That's his knack, to make people believe his lies. Why else would you trust in this stranger instead of Alvin Miller's youngest boy, when you all know I don't go around beating people up?" It was a delicious scene to contemplate, with Father and Mother and Alvin all frozen into inaction.

But a better scene was this: Calvin free in the city. Calvin out of his brother's shadow.

Best of all, they couldn't even get up a group of men to follow him. For here in the town of Vigor Church, the adults were all bound by Tenskwa-Tawa's curse, so that any stranger they met, they had to tell him the story of how they slaughtered the innocent Reds at Tippy-Canoe. If they didn't tell the story, their hands and arms would become covered with dripping blood, mute testimony of their crime. Because of that they didn't venture out into the world where they might run into strangers. Alvin himself might come looking for him, but no one else except those who had been too young to take part in the massacre would be able to join with him. Oh, yes, their brother-in-law Armor, he wasn't under the curse. And maybe Measure wasn't really under the curse, because he took it on himself, even though he wasn't part of the battle. So maybe he could leave. But that still wouldn't be much of a search party.

And why would they bother to search for him anyway? Alvin thought Calvin was a nothing. Not worth teaching. So how could he be worth following?

My freedom was always just a few steps away, thought Calvin. All it took was my realizing that Alvin was *never* going to accept me as his true friend and brother. Taleswapper showed me that. I should thank him.

Hey, I already gave him all the thanks he deserved.

Calvin chuckled. Then he turned and headed back into the forest. He tried to move as silently as Alvin always did, moving through the forest—a trick Al had learned from the wild Reds back before they either gave up and got civilized or moved across the Mizzipy into the empty country of the west. But despite all his efforts, Calvin always ended up making noise and breaking branches.

For all I know, Calvin told himself, Alvin makes just as much noise, and simply uses his knack to make us *think* he's quiet. Because if everybody *thinks* you're silent, you *are* silent, right? Makes no difference at all.

Wouldn't it be just like that hypocrite Alvin to have us all thinking he's in such harmony with the greenwood when he's really just as clumsy as everyone else! At least I'm not ashamed to make an honest noise.

With that reassuring thought, Calvin plunged on into the underbrush, breaking off branches and disturbing fallen leaves with every step.

3

Watchers

While Calvin was a-setting out on his journey to wherever, trying not to think about Alvin with every step, there was someone else already on a journey, also wishing she could stop thinking about Alvin. That's about where the semblance ends, though. Because this was Peggy Larner, who knew Alvin better and loved Alvin more than any living soul. She was riding in a coach along a country road in Appalachee, and she was at least as unhappy as Calvin ever was. Difference was, she blamed her woes on nary a soul but her own self.

In the days after her mother was murdered, Peggy Larner figured that she would stay in Hatrack River for the rest of her life, helping her father tend his roadhouse. She was done with the great matters of the world. She had set her hand to meddling in them, and the result had been that she didn't tend to her own backyard and so she failed to see her mother's death looming. Preventable, easily, it was so dependent upon merest chance; a simple word of warning and her mother and father would have known the Slave Finders were coming back that night, and how many of them there were, and how armed, and through what door coming. But Peggy had been watching the great matters of the world, had been minding her foolish love for the young journeyman smith named Alvin who had learned to make a plow of living gold and then asked her to marry him and go with him through the world to do battle with the Unmaker, and all the while the Unmaker was destroying her own life through the back door, with a shotgun blast that shredded her mother's flesh and gave Peggy the most terrible of burdens to carry all her life. What kind of child does not watch out to save her own mother's life?

She could not marry Alvin. That would be like rewarding herself for her own selfishness. She would stay and help her father in his work.

And yet she couldn't do even that, not for long. When her father looked at her—or rather, when he wouldn't look at her—she felt his grief stab to her heart. He knew she could have prevented it. And thought it was his great effort not to reproach her with it, she didn't need to hear his words to know what was in his heart. No, nor did she need to use her knack to see his heart's desire, his bitter memories. She knew without looking, because she knew him deep, as children know parents.

There came a day, then, when she could bear it no longer. She had left home once before, as a girl, with a note left behind. This time she left with more courage, facing her father and telling him that she couldn't stay.

"Have I lost my daughter then, as well as my wife?"

"Your daughter you have as well as ever," said Peggy. "But the woman who could have prevented your wife's death, and failed to do it—that woman can't live here anymore."

"Have I said anything? Have I by word or deed—"

"It's your knack to make folks feel welcome under your roof, Father, and you've done your best with me. But there's no knack can take away the terrible burden charged to my soul. There's no love or kindness you can show toward me that will hide—from *me*—what you suffer at the very sight of me."

Father knew he couldn't deceive his daughter any longer, her being a torch and all. "I'll miss you with all my heart," he said.

"And I'll miss you, Father," she answered. With a kiss, with a brief embrace, she took her leave. Once again she rode in Whitley Physicker's carriage to Dekane. There she visited with a family that had done her much kindness, once upon a time.

She didn't stay long, though, and soon she took the coach down to Franklin, the capital of Appalachee. She knew no one there, but she soon would—no heart could remain closed to her, and she quickly found those people who hated the institution of slavery as much as she did. Her mother had died for taking a half-black boy into her home, into her family as her own son, even though by law he belonged to some white man down in Appalachee.

The boy, Arthur Stuart, was still free, living with Alvin in the town of Vigor Church. But the institution of slavery, which had killed both the boy's birth mother and his adoptive mother, that lived on, too. There was no hope of changing it in the King's lands to the south and east, but Appalachee was the nation that had won its freedom by the sacrifice of George Washington and under the leadership of Thomas Jefferson. It was a land of high ideals. Surely she could have some influence here, to root out the evil of slavery from this land. It was in Appalachee that Arthur Stuart had been conceived by a cruel master's rape of his helpless slave. It was in Appalachee, then, that Peggy would quietly but deftly maneuver to help those who hated slavery and hinder those who would perpetuate it.

She traveled in disguise, of course. Not that anyone here would know her, but she didn't like being called by the name of Peggy Guester, for that was also her mother's name. Instead she passed as Miss Larner, gifted teacher of French, Latin, and music, and in that guise she went about tutoring, here a few weeks, there a few weeks. It was master classes that she taught, teaching the schoolmasters in various towns and villages.

Though her public lessons were conscientiously taught, what concerned her most was seeking out the heartfires of those who loathed slavery, or those who, not daring to admit their loathing, were at least uncomfortable and apologetic about the slaves they owned. The ones who were careful to be gentle, the ones who secretly allowed their slaves to learn to read and write and cipher. These good-hearted ones she dared to encourage. She called upon them and said words that might turn them toward the paths of life, however few and faint they were, in which they gained courage and spoke out against the evil of slavery.

In this way, she was still helping her father in his work. For hadn't old Horace Guester risked his life for many years, helping runaway slaves make it across the Hio and on north into French territory, where they would be no longer slaves, where Finders could not go? She could not live with her father, she could not remove any part of his burden of grief, but she could carry on his work, and might in the end make his work unnecessary, for it would have been accomplished, not a slave at a time, but all the slaves of Appalachee at once.

Would I then be worthy to return and face him? Would I be redeemed? Would Mother's death mean something then, instead of being the worthless result of my carelessness?

Here was the hardest part of her discipline: She refused to let any thought of Alvin Smith distract her. Once he had been the whole focus of her life, for she was present at his birth, peeled the birth caul from his face, and for years thereafter used the power of the dried-up caul to protect him against all the attacks of the Unmaker. Then, when he became a man and grew into his own powers enough that he could mostly protect himself, he was still the center of her heart, for she came to love the man he was becoming. She had come home to Hatrack River then, in disguise for the first time as Miss Larner, and there she gave him and Arthur Stuart the kind of book learning that they both hungered for. And all the time she was teaching him, she was hiding behind the hexes that hid her true face and name, hiding and watching him like a spy, like a hunter, like a lover who dared not be seen.

It was in that disguise that he fell in love with her, too. It was all a lie, a lie I told him, a lie I told myself.

So now she would not search for his bright heartfire, though she knew she could find it in an instant, no matter how far away he was. She had other work in her life. She had other things to achieve or to undo.

Here was the best part of her new life: Everyone who knew anything about slavery knew that it was wrong. The ignorant—children growing up in slave country, or people who had never kept slaves or seen them kept or even known a Black man or woman—they might fancy that there was nothing wrong with it. But those who knew, they all understood that it was evil.

Many of them, of course, simply told themselves lies or made excuses or flat-out embraced the evil with both arms—anything to keep their way of life, to keep their wealth and leisure, their prestige, their honor. But more were made miserable by the wealth that came from the labor and suffering of the blacks that had been stolen from their native land and brought against their will to this dark continent of America. It was these whose hearts Peggy reached for, especially the strong ones, the ones who might have the courage to make a difference.

And her labors were not in vain. When she left a place, people were talking—no, to be honest they were quarreling—over things that before had never been openly questioned. To be sure, there was suffering. Some of those whose courage she had helped awaken were tarred and feathered, or beaten, or their houses and barns burnt. But the excesses of the slavemasters served only to expose to others the necessity of taking action, of winning their freedom from a system that was destroying them all.

She was on this errand today. A hired carriage had come to fetch her to a town called Baker's Fork, and she was well on the way, already hot and tired and dusty, as summer travelers always were, when all of a sudden she felt curious to see what was up a certain road.

Now, Peggy wasn't one to be curious in any ordinary way. Having had, since childhood, the knack of knowing people's inmost secrets, she had learned young to shy away from simple curiosity. Well she knew that there were some things folks were better off not knowing. As a child she would have given much not to know what the children her age thought of her, the fear they had of her, the loathing because of her strangeness, because of the hushed way their parents talked of her. Oh, she would have been glad not to know the secrets of the men and women around her. Curiosity was its own punishment, when you were sure of finding the answer to your question.

So the very fact that she felt curious about, of all things, a rutted track in the low hills of northern Appalachee—that was the most curious thing of all. And so, instead of trying to follow the track, she looked inside her own heartfire to see what lay down that road. But every path she saw in which she called to the carriage driver and bade him turn around and follow the track, every one of those paths led to a blank, a place where what might happen there could not be known.

It was a strange thing for her, not to know at all what the outcome might be. Uncertainty she was used to, for there were many paths that the flow of time could follow. But not to have a glimmer, that was new indeed. New and—she had to admit—attractive.

She tried to warn herself off, to tell herself that if she couldn't see, it must be the Unmaker blocking her, there must be some terrible fate down that road.

But it didn't *feel* like the Unmaker. It felt right to follow the track. It felt *necessary*, though she tingled a bit with the danger of it. Is this how other people feel all the time? she wondered. Knowing nothing, the future all a blank, able to rely only on feelings like this? Is this tingling what George Washington felt just before he surren-

dered his army to the rebels of Appalachee and then turned himself
over to the king he had betrayed? Surely not, for old George was
certain enough of the outcome. Maybe it's what Patrick Henry felt
when he cried out, Give me liberty or give me death, having no
notion which of the two, if either, he might win. To act without
knowing . . .

"Turn around!" she called.

The driver didn't hear her over the clattering of the horses'
hooves, the rattling and creaking of the carriage.

She thumped on the roof of the carriage with her umbrella.
"Turn around!"

The driver pulled the horses to a stop. He slid open the tiny door
that allowed words to pass between driver and passengers. "What,
ma'am?"

"Turn around."

"I ain't took no wrong turn, ma'am."

"I know that. I want to follow that track we just passed."

"That just leads on up to Chapman Valley."

"Excellent. Then take me to Chapman Valley."

"But it's the school board in Baker's Fork what hired me to
bring you."

"We're going to stop the night anyway. Why not Chapman
Valley?"

"They got no inn."

"Nevertheless, either turn the carriage around or wait here while
I *walk* up that track."

The door slid shut—perhaps more abruptly than necessary—and
the carriage took a wide turn out into the meadow. It had been dry
these past few days, so the turn went smoothly, and soon they were
going up the track that had made her so curious.

The valley, when she saw it, was pretty, though there was nothing remarkable about its prettiness. Except for the rough woods at
the crests of the surrounding hills, the whole valley was tamed, the
trees all in the place where they were planted, the houses all built
up to fit the ever-larger families that lived there. Perhaps the walls
were more crisply painted, and perhaps a whiter white than other
places—or perhaps that was just what happened to Peggy's percep-
tions, because she was looking especially sharp to see what had
piqued her curiosity. Perhaps the orchard trees were older than usual,
more gnarled, as if this place had been settled long ago, the earliest
of the Appalachee settlements. But what of that? Everything in
America was newish; there was bound to be someone in this town

who still remembered its founding. Nothing west of the first range of mountains was any older than the lifespan of the oldest citizen.

As always, she was aware of the heartfires of the people dwelling here, like sparks of light that she could see even in the brightest part of noon, through all walls, behind all hills, in all attics or basements where they might be. They were the ordinary folk of any town, perhaps a bit more content than others, but not immune to the suffering of life, the petty resentments, the griefs and envies. Why had she come here?

They came to a house with no one home. She rapped on the roof of the carriage again. The horses were whoaed to a stop, and the little door opened. "Wait here," she said.

She had no idea why this house, the empty one, drew her curiosity. Perhaps it was the way it had obviously grown up around a tiny log cabin, growing first prosperous, then grand, and finally nothing more than large, as aesthetics gave way to the need for more room, more room. How, in such a large and well-tended place, could there be no one home?

Then she realized that she heard singing coming from the house. And laughter from the yard. Singing and laughter, and yet not a heartfire to be seen. There had never been such a strange thing in all her life. Was this a haint house? Did the restless dead dwell here, unable to let go of life? But who ever heard of a haint that laughed? Or sang such a cheery song?

And there, running around the house, was a boy not more than six, being chased by three older girls. Not one with a heartfire. But from the dirt on the boy's face and the rage in the eyes of the red-faced girls, these could not be the spirits of the dead.

"Hallo, there!" cried Peggy, waving.

The boy, startled, looked at her. That pause was his undoing, for the girls caught up to him and fell to pummeling him with much enthusiasm; his answer was to holler with equal vigor, cursing them roundly. Peggy didn't know them, but had little doubt that the boy, in the fashion of all boys, had done some miserable mischief which outraged the girls—his sisters? She also had little doubt that the girls, despite the inevitable protests of innocence, had no doubt provoked *him* before, but in subtle, verbal ways so that he could never point to a bruise and get his mother on his side. Such was the endless war between male and female children. Stranger or not, however, Peggy could not allow the violence of the girls to get out of hand, and it seemed they were not disposed to go lightly in their determined battering of the bellowing lad. They were pursuing the beating, not as a holiday, but as if it were their bread-and-butter labor, with an overseer who would examine their handiwork later and say, "I'd say the boy was well beaten. You get your day's pay, all right!"

"Let up now," she said, striding across the goat-cropped yard.

They ignored her until she was on them and had two of the girls by the collars. Even then, they kept swinging with their fists, not a few of the blows landing on Peggy herself, while the third girl took no pause. Peggy had no choice but to give the two girls she had hold of a stern push, sending them sprawling in the grass, while she dragged the third girl off the boy.

As she had feared, the boy hadn't done well under the girls' blows. His nose was bleeding, and he got up only slowly; when the girl Peggy was holding lunged at him, he scurried on all fours to evade her.

"Shame on you," said Peggy. "Whatever he did, it wasn't worth this!"

"He killed my squirrel!" cried the girl she held.

"But how can you have had a squirrel?" asked Peggy. "It would be cruel of *you* to pen one up."

"She was never penned," said the girl. "She was my friend. I fed her and these others saw it—she came to me and I kept her alive through the hard winter. He knew it! He was jealous that the squirrel came to me, and so he killed it."

"It was a squirrel!" the boy shouted—hoarsely and rather weakly, but it was clear he *meant* it to be a shout. "How should I know it was yours?"

"Then you shouldn't have killed any," said another of the girls. "Not till you were sure."

"Whatever he did to the squirrels," said Peggy, "even if he was malicious, it was wrong of you and unchristian to knock him down and hurt him so."

The boy looked at her now. "Are you the judge?" he asked.

"Judge? I think not!" said Peggy with a laugh.

"But you can't be the Maker, that one's a boy. I think you're a judge." The boy looked even more certain. "Aunt Becca said the judge was coming, and then the Maker, so you can't be the Maker because the judge ain't come yet, but you could be the judge because the judge comes first."

Peggy knew that other folks often took the words of children to be nonsense, if they didn't understand them immediately. But Peggy knew that the words of children were always related to their view of the world, and made their own sense if you only knew how to hear them. Someone had told them—Aunt Becca, it was—that a judge and a Maker were coming. There was only one Maker that Peggy knew of. Was Alvin coming here? What was this place, that the children knew of Makers, and had no heartfires?

"I thought your house was standing empty," said Peggy, "but I see that it is not."

For indeed there now stood a woman in the doorway, leaning against the jamb, watching them placidly as she slowly stirred a bowl with a wooden spoon.

"Mama!" cried the girl that Peggy still held. "She has me and won't let go!"

"It's true!" cried Peggy at once. "And I still won't let go, till I'm sure she won't murder the boy here!"

"He killed my squirrel, Mama!" cried the girl.

The woman said nothing, just stirred.

"Perhaps, children," said Peggy, "we should go talk to this lady in the doorway, instead of shouting like river rats."

"Mother doesn't like you," said one of the girls. "I can tell."

"That's a shame," said Peggy. "Because I like *her*."

"Do not," said the girl. "You don't know her, and if you did you *still* wouldn't like her because nobody does."

"What a terrible thing to say about your mother," said Peggy.

"I don't have to like her," said the girl. "I *love* her."

"Then take me to this woman that you love but don't like," said Peggy, "and let me reach my own conclusions about her."

As they approached the door, Peggy began to think that the girls might be right. The woman certainly didn't look welcoming. But for that matter, she didn't look hostile, either. Her face was empty of emotion. She just stirred the bowl.

"My name is Peggy Larner." The woman ignored her outstretched hand. "I'm sorry if I shouldn't have intervened, but as you can see the boy was taking some serious injury."

"Just my nose is bloody, is all," said the boy. But his limp suggested other less visible pains.

"Come inside," said the woman.

Peggy had no idea whether the woman was speaking just to the children, or was including her in the invitation. If it could be called an invitation, so blandly she spoke it, not looking up from the bowl she stirred. The woman turned away, disappearing inside the house. The children followed. So, finally, did Peggy.

No one stopped her or seemed to think her action strange. It was this that first made her wonder if perhaps she had fallen asleep in the carriage and this was some strange dream, in which unaccountable unnatural things happen which nevertheless excite no comment in the land of dreams, where there is no custom to be violated. Where I am now is not real. Outside waits the carriage and the team of four horses, not to mention the driver, as real and mundane a fellow as ever belched in the coachman's seat. But in here, I have stepped into a place beyond nature. There are no heartfires here.

The children disappeared, stomping somewhere through the wood-floored house, and at least one of them went up or down a flight of stairs; it had to be a child, there was so much vigor in the step. But there were no sounds that told Peggy where to go, or what purpose was being served by her coming here. Was there no order here? Nothing that her presence disrupted? Would no one but the children ever notice her at all?

She wanted to go back outside, return to the carriage, but now, as she turned around, she couldn't remember what door she had come through, or even which way was north. The windows were curtained, and whatever door she had come through, she couldn't see it now.

It was an odd place, for there was cloth everywhere, folded neatly and stacked on all the furniture, on the floors, on the stairs, as if someone had just bought enough to make a thousand dresses with and the tailors and seamstresses were yet to arrive. Then she realized that the piles were of one continuous cloth, flowing off the top of one stack into the bottom of the next. How could there be a cloth so long? Why would anyone make it, instead of cutting it and sending it out to get something made from it?

Why indeed. How foolish of her not to realize it at once. She knew this place. She hadn't visited it herself, but she had seen it through Alvin's heartfire, years ago.

He was still in Ta-Kumsaw's thrall in those days. The Red warrior took Alvin with him and brought him into his legend, so that those who now spoke of Alvin Smith the Finder-killer, or Alvin Smith and the golden plow, had once spoken of the same boy, little knowing it, when they spoke of the evil "Boy Renegado," the white boy who went with Ta-Kumsaw in all his travels in the last year before his defeat at Fort Detroit. It was in that guise that Alvin came here, and walked down this hall, yes, turning right here, yes, tracking the folded cloth into the oldest part of the house, the original cabin, into the slanting light that seems to have no source, as if it merely seeped in through the chinks between the logs. And here, if I open this door, I will find the woman with the loom. This is the place of weaving.

Aunt Becca. Of course she knew the name. Becca, the weaver who held the threads of all the lives in the White man's lands in North America.

The woman at the loom looked up. "I didn't want you here," she said softly.

"Nor did I plan to come," said Peggy. "The truth is, I had forgotten you. You slipped my mind."

"I'm supposed to slip your mind. I slip all minds."

"Except one or two?"

"My husband remembers me."

"Ta-Kumsaw? He isn't dead, then?"

Becca snorted. "My husband's name is Isaac."

That was Ta-Kumsaw's White name. "Don't quibble with me," said Peggy. "Something called me here. If it wasn't you, who was it?"

"My untalented sister. The one who breaks threads whenever she touches the loom."

Aunt Becca, the children had called the weaver. "Is your sister the mother of the children I met?"

"The murderous little boy who kills squirrels for sport? His brutal sisters? I think of them as the four horses of the apocalypse. The boy is war. The sisters are still sorting themselves out among the other forces of destruction."

"You speak metaphorically, I hope," said Peggy.

"I hope not," said Becca. "Metaphors have a way of holding the most truth in the least space."

"Why would your sister have brought me here? She didn't seem to know me at the door."

"You're the judge," said Becca. "I found a purple thread of justice in the loom, and it was you. I didn't want you here, but I knew that you'd come, because I knew my sister would have you here."

"Why? I'm no judge. I'm guilty myself."

"You see? Your judgment includes everyone. Even those who are invisible to you."

"Invisible?" But she knew before asking what it was that Becca meant.

"Your vision, your torching, as you quaintly call it—you see where people are in the many paths of their lives. But I am not on the path of time. Nor is my sister. We don't belong anywhere in your prophecies or in the memories of those who know us. Only in the present moment are we here.''

"Yet I remember your first word long enough to make sense of the whole sentence,'' said Peggy.

"Ah,'' said Becca. "The judge insists on correctness of speech. Boundaries are not so clear, Margaret Larner. You remember perfectly now; but what will you remember in a week from now? What you forget of me, you'll forget so completely that you won't remember that you once knew it. Then my statement will be true, but you'll forget that I said it.''

"I think not.''

Becca smiled.

"Show me the thread,'' said Peggy.

"We don't do that.''

"What harm can it do? I've already seen all the possible paths of my life.''

"But you haven't seen which one you'll choose,'' said Becca.

"And you have?''

"At this moment, no,'' said Becca. "But in the moment that contains all moments, yes. I've seen the course of your life. That isn't why you came, though. Not to find out something as stupid as whether you'll marry the boy you've nurtured all these years. You will or you won't. What is that to me?''

"I don't know,'' said Peggy. "I wonder why you exist at all. You change nothing. You merely see. You weave, but the threads are out of your control. You are meaningless.''

"So you say,'' said Becca.

"And yet you have a life, or had one. You loved Ta-Kumsaw— or Isaac, whatever name you use. So loving some boy, marrying him, that didn't always seem stupid to you.''

"So you say,'' said Becca.

"Or do you include yourself in that? Do you call yourself stupid in having loved and married? You can't pretend to be inhuman when you loved and lost a man.''

"Lost?'' she asked. "I see him every day.''

"He comes here? To Appalachee?''

Becca hooted. "I think not!''

"How many threads broke under your hand with that pass of the shuttlecock?'' asked Peggy.

"Too many,'' said Becca. "And not enough.''

"Did you break them? Or did they simply happen to break?''

"The thread grew thin. The life wore out. Or it was cut. It isn't the thread that cuts the life, it's the death that cuts the thread."

"So you keep a record, is that it? The weaving causes nothing, but simply records it all."

Becca smiled thinly. "Passive, useless creatures that we are, but we must weave."

Peggy didn't believe her, but there was no use in arguing. "Why did you bring me here?"

"I told you. I didn't."

"Why did *she* bring me here?"

"To judge."

"What is it that I'm supposed to judge?"

Becca passed the shuttlecock from her right hand to her left. The loom slammed forward, then dropped back. She passed the shuttlecock from her left hand to her right. Again, the frame slammed forward, weaving the threads tight.

This *is* a dream, thought Peggy. And not a very pleasant one. Why can't I ever wake up to escape from some foolish useless dream?

"Personally," said Becca, "I think you've already made your judgment. It's only my sister thinks that you deserve a second chance. She's very romantic. She thinks that you deserve some happiness. My own feeling is that human happiness is a very random thing, and bestows itself willy-nilly, and there's not much deserving about the matter."

"So it's myself that I'm supposed to judge?"

Becca laughed.

One of the girls stuck her head into the room. "Mother says it's nasty and uncompassionate when you laugh during the weaving," she said.

"Nanner nanner," said Becca.

The girl laughed lightly, and Becca did too.

"Mother mixed up something really vile for your supper. *With* dumplings."

"Vileness with dumplings," said Becca. "Do sup with me."

"Let the *judge* do that," said the girl. "She really *is* a bossy one. Telling *us* about right and wrong." With that the girl disappeared.

Becca clucked for a moment. "The children are so full of themselves. Still very impressed with the idea that they aren't part of the normal world. You must forgive them for being arrogant and cruel.

They couldn't have hurt their brother much, because they haven't the strength to strike a blow that will really harm him."

"He bled," said Peggy. "He limped."

"But the squirrel died," said Becca.

"You keep no threads for squirrels."

"*I* keep no threads for them. But that doesn't mean their threads aren't woven."

"Oh, tell me flat out. Don't waste my time with mysteries."

"I haven't been," said Becca. "No mysteries. I've told you everything that's useful. Anything else I told you might affect your judgment, and so I won't do it. I let my sister have her way, bringing you here, but I'm certainly *not* going to bend your life any more than that. You can leave whenever you want—that's a choice, and a judgment, and I'll be content with it."

"Will *I*?"

"Come back in thirty years and tell me."

"Will I be—"

"If you're still alive then." Becca grinned. "Do you think I'm so clumsy as to let slip your real span of years? I don't even know it. I haven't cared enough to look."

Two girls came in with a plate and a bowl and a cup on a tray. They set it on a small table near the loom. The plate was covered with a strange-smelling food. Peggy recognized nothing about it. Nor was there anything that she might have called a dumpling.

"I don't like it when people watch me eat," said Becca.

But Peggy was feeling very angry now, with all the elusiveness of Becca's conversation, and so she did not leave as courtesy demanded.

"Stay, then," said Becca.

The girls began to feed her. Becca did nothing to seek out the food. She kept up the perfect rhythm of her weaving, just as she had done throughout their conversation. The girls deftly maneuvered spoon or fork or cup to find their Aunt Becca's mouth, and then with a quick slurp or bite or sip she had the food. Not a drop or crumb was spilled on the cloth.

It could not always be like this, thought Peggy. She married Ta-Kumsaw. She bore a daughter to him, the daughter that went west to weave a loom among the Reds beyond the Mizzipy. Surely those things were not done with the shuttlecock flying back and forth, the loom slamming down to tamp the threads. It was deception. Or else it involved things Peggy was not going to understand however she tried.

She turned and left the room. The hall ended in a narrow stair. Sitting on the top step was, she assumed, the boy—she could see only his bare feet and trouser legs. "How's the nose?" she asked.

"Still hurts," said the boy. He scootched forward and dropped down a couple of steps by bouncing on his bottom.

"But not too bad," she said. "Healing fast."

"They was only *girls*," he said scornfully.

"You didn't think such scorn of them when they were pounding on you," she said.

"But you didn't hear me callin' uncle, did you? You didn't hear no uncle from me."

"No," said Peggy. "No uncle from you."

"I got me an uncle, though. Big Red man. Ike."

"I know of him."

"He comes most every day."

Peggy wanted to demand information from him. How does Ta-Kumsaw get here? Doesn't he live west of the Mizzipy? Or is he dead, and comes only in the spirit?

"Comes through the west door," said the boy. "We don't use that one. Just him. It's the door to my cousin Wieza's cabin."

"Her father calls her Mana-Tawa, I think."

The boy hooted. "Just giving her a Red name don't mean he can hold on to her. She don't belong to him."

"Whom does she belong to?"

"To the loom," he said.

"And you?" asked Peggy. "Do you belong to the loom?"

He shook his head. But he looked sad.

Peggy said it as she realized it: "You want to, don't you."

"She ain't going to have no more daughters. She don't stop weaving for him anymore. So she can't go. She'll just be there forever."

"And nephews can't take her place?"

"Nieces can, but my sisters ain't worth pigslime, in my opinion, which happens to be correck."

"Correct," said Peggy. "There's a *t* on the end."

"Correckut," the boy said. "But what I think is they ought to spell the words the way folks say 'em, stead of making us say 'em the way they're spelt."

Peggy had to laugh. "You have a point. But you can't just start spelling words any which way. Because you don't say them the same as someone from, say, Boston, and so pretty soon you and he would be spelling things so differently that you couldn't read each other's letters or books.''

"Don't want to read his damn old books," said the boy. "I don't even know no boys in Boston."

"Do you have a name?"

"Not for *you* to know," said the boy. "You think I'm stupid? You're so thick with hexes you think I'm going to give you power over my name?"

"The hexes are to hide me from others."

"What do you have to hide for? Ain't nobody looking for you."

The words struck her hard. Nobody looking for her. Well, there it was. Once she had hidden so she could return to her own house without her family knowing her. Whom was she hiding from now?

"Perhaps I'm hiding from myself. Perhaps I don't want to be what I'm supposed to be. Or perhaps I don't want to keep living the life I already started to live."

"Perhaps you don't know squat about it," he said.

"Perhaps."

"Oh, don't be so mysterious, you silly old lady."

Silly she might accept, but *old*? "I'm not that many years older than you."

"When people say *perhaps* it's cause they're lying. Either they don't believe the thing they're saying, or they *do* believe it only they don't want to admit they do."

"You're a very wise young man."

"And the *real* liars change the subject the minute the truth comes up."

Peggy regarded him steadily. "You were waiting for me, weren't you?"

"I knew what Aunt Becca would do. She don't tell nobody nothin'."

"And you're going to tell me?"

"Not me! That's trouble too deep for me to get into." He smiled. "But you did stop the three witches from making soup of me. So I got you thinking in the right direction, if you've got the brains to see it." With that he jumped up and she listened as his feet slapped up the stairs and he was gone.

The choice was for Peggy to be happy. Becca said that, or said that her sister said it—though it was hard to imagine that blank-faced woman caring a whit whether anybody was happy or not. And now the boy got her talking about why she was hiding behind hexes, and said that he had guided her. The choice she was being offered was obvious enough now. She had buried herself in her father's work of breaking the back of slavery, and had stopped looking out for Alvin. They wanted her to look back again. They wanted her to reach out for him.

She stormed back into the cabin. "I won't do it," she said. "Caring for that boy is what killed my mother."

"Excuse me but I think a shotgun is what did for her," said Becca.

"A shotgun I could have prevented."

"So you say," said Becca.

"Yes, I say so."

"Your mother's thread broke when she decided to pick up a shotgun and do some killing of her own rather than trust to Alvin. Her boy Arthur was safe. She didn't need to kill, but when she chose to do that, she chose to die. Do you think you could have changed her mind about that?"

"Don't expect me to accept easy answers."

"No, I expect you to make all the answers as hard as possible. But sometimes it's the easy answers that are true."

"So it's back to the old days? Watching Alvin? Am I supposed to fall in love with him? Marry him? Watch him die?"

"I don't much care either way. My sister thinks you'll be happier with him than without him, and he's dead either way, in the long run, but then aren't we all? Most women that aren't killed by having babies live to be widows. What of that?"

What *of* that? Just because she could foresee so many ways for Alvin to die didn't mean that she should avoid loving him. She knew that, rationally. But fear wasn't rational.

"You spend your whole life grieving for those that haven't died yet," said Becca. "What a waste of an interesting knack."

"Interesting?"

"You *could* have had the knack of making shoe leather supple. Just see how happy that would've made you."

Peggy tried to imagine herself as a cobbler and had to laugh. "I suppose that I'd rather know than not know, mostly."

"Exactly. Knowing hurts sometimes, especially when you can't do anything to change it."

But there was something furtive in her, the way she said that. "Can't do anything to change it my left eye!" said Peggy.

"Don't use curses you don't understand," said Becca.

"You *do* make changes. *You* don't think the loom is immutable, not one bit."

"It's dangerous to change. The consequences are unpredictable."

"You saw Ta-Kumsaw dead at Detroit. So you picked up Alvin's thread and you—"

"What do you know about the loom!" cried Becca. "What do you know about watching the threads flow under your hands and seeing all the grief and pain and suffering and thinking! It doesn't matter, they're God's cattle and he can herd them how he likes, only then you find the one you love more than life and God has him slaughtered by the treachery of the French and the hatred of the English and for *nothing*, his whole life meaningless and lost and nothing changed by it except a few legends and songs, and here I am, still loving him, a widow forever because he's gone! So yes, I found the one who could save him. I knew if they met, they'd love each other and save each other."

"But what you did caused the massacre at Tippy-Canoe," said Peggy. "The people of Vigor Church thought Alvin had been kidnapped and tortured to death, so they slaughtered Tenskwa-Tawa's people in vengeance. Now they have a curse on them, all because you—"

"Because Harrison took advantage of their rage. Do you think there wouldn't have been a massacre anyway?"

"But the blood wouldn't have been on the same hands, would it?"

Becca wept, and her tears fell onto the cloth.

"Shouldn't you dry those tears?" asked Peggy.

"If tears could mar this cloth, there'd be no cloth left."

"So you of all people know the cost of meddling with the course of others' lives."

"And you of all people know the cost of failing to meddle when the time was right." Becca raised her head and continued her work. "I saved him, and that was my goal. Those who died would have died anyway."

"Yet here I am because your sister wants me to look after Alvin."

"Here you are because we only see the threads and then half-guess as to what they mean and who they are. We know the young Maker's thread—there's no way to miss it in this cloth. Besides, I moved it once, I twined it with my Isaac's thread. Do you think I could lose track of it after that? I'll show you, if you promise not to look beyond the inch of cloth I show."

"I promise not to look. But I can't help what I chance to see."

"Chance to see this, then."

Peggy looked at the cloth, knowing that the sight of it was rarely given to those not of the loom. Alvin's thread was obvious, shimmering light, with all colors in it; but it was no thicker than any other, and it looked frail, easily snapped by careless handling. "You dared to move this one?"

"It returned of itself to its own place," said Becca. "I only borrowed it for a while. And he saved his brother Measure. Eight-face mound opened up for him. I tell you there are forces at work in his life far stronger than my power to move the threads."

"More powerful than me, too."

"You are one of the forces. Not all of them, not the greatest of them, but you are one. Look. See how the threads cross him. His brothers and sisters, I think. He is closely entwined with his family. And see how these threads are brightening, taking on more hues. He's teaching them to be Makers."

Peggy hadn't known that. "Isn't that dangerous?"

"He can't do his work alone," said Becca. "So he teaches others to help him in it. He's more successful at it than he knows."

"This one," said Peggy, pointing to the brightest of the other threads. It veered off widely, wandering through the cloth far from the rest of the family.

"His brother. Also a seventh son of a seventh son," said Becca. "Though the eighth, if you count the one who died."

"But the seventh of those alive when he was born," said Peggy.

"Yes, there's power in him."

"Look," said Becca. "See how he was at the beginning. Every bit as bright as Alvin's. There was near as much in him then as in Alvin. And no more forces working against him than Alvin overcame. Fewer, really, because by the time he came into his own you and Alvin between you had the Unmaker at bay. At least, all the killing tricks. But the Unmaker found another way to undo the boy. Hate and envy. If you love Alvin, Peggy, find his younger brother's heartfire. Somehow he must be brought back before it's too late."

"Why? I don't know anything about Calvin, except his name and Alvin's hopes for him."

"Because the way the threads are going now, when his rejoins Alvin's, Alvin's comes to an end."

"He kills him?"

"How should I know? We learn what we can learn, but the threads say little except by their movement through the cloth. You will know. That's why she called you. Not just for your own happiness, but because . . . as she said, because I owe it to the Maker. I used him once to save my love. Didn't I owe you the same chance? That's what she said. But we knew that if I showed you this at first, before you chose, you would help him out of duty. For the grand cause, not for love of him.''

"But I hadn't decided to watch him again.''

"So you say,'' said Becca.

"You're very smug,'' said Peggy, "for a woman who has made such a botch of things herself.''

"I inherited a botch,'' said Becca. "One day my mother, who crossed the ocean and brought us here, one day she took her hands from the loom and walked away. My sister and I came in with her supper and found her gone. We were both married, but I had borne a child for my husband, and in those days my sister had none. So I took the loom, and she went to her husband. And all the time, I was furious at my mother for going away like that. Fleeing her duty.'' Becca stroked the threads, gently, even gingerly. "Now I think I understand. The price of holding all these lives in our hands is that we scarcely have a life ourselves. My mother wasn't good at this, because her heart wasn't in it. Mine is, and if I made a mistake to save my husband's life, perhaps you can judge me more kindly knowing that I had already given up my life with my husband in order to fill my mother's place.''

"I didn't mean to condemn you,'' said Peggy, abashed.

"Nor did I mean to justify myself to you,'' said Becca. "And yet you did condemn me, and I did justify myself. I hold my mother's thread here. I know where she is. But I'll never know, really, why she did what she did. Or what might have happened if she stayed.'' Becca looked up at Peggy. "I don't know much, but what I know, I know. Alvin must go out into the world. He must leave his family—let them learn Making on their own now, as he did. He must rejoin Calvin before the boy has been completely turned by the Unmaker. Otherwise, Calvin may be not only his death, but also the undoing of all the Maker's works.''

"I have an easy answer,'' said Peggy. "I'll find Calvin and make sure he never comes home.''

"You think you have the power to control a Maker's life?''

"Calvin is no Maker. How could he be? Think what Alvin had to do, to come into his own.''

"Nevertheless, you never had the power to stand against Alvin, even when he was a child. And he was kind at heart. I think Calvin isn't governed by the same sense of decency.''

"So I can't stand against him," said Peggy. "Nor can I send Alvin out on errands. He's not mine to command."

"Isn't he?" asked Becca.

Peggy buried her face in her hands. "I don't want him to love me. I don't want to love him. I want to continue my struggle against slavery here in Appalachee."

"Oh, yes. Using your knack to meddle with the cloth, aren't you?" said Becca. "Do you know where it leads?"

"To liberty for the slaves, I hope."

"Perhaps," she said. "But the sure thing is this: It leads to war."

Peggy looked up grimly. "I see warsigns down all the paths. Before I started doing this, I saw those signs." Grieving mothers. The terror of battle in young men's lives.

"It begins as a civil war in Appalachee, but it ends as a war between the King on the one side and the United States on the other. Brutal, bloody, cruel . . ."

"Are you saying I should stop? That I should let these monsters continue to rule over the Blacks they kidnapped and all their children forever?"

"Not at all," said Becca. "The war comes because of a million different choices. Your actions push things that way, but you aren't the only cause. Do you understand? If war is the only way to free the slaves, then isn't the war worth all the suffering? Are lives wasted, when they end for such a cause?"

"I can't judge this sort of thing," said Peggy.

"But that's not true," said Becca. "Only you are fit to judge, because only you see the outcomes that might result. By the time I see things they've become inevitable."

"If they're inevitable, then why are you bothering to tell me to try to change them?"

"Almost inevitable. Again, I spoke imprecisely. I can't meddle with the threads on a grand scale. I can't foresee the consequences of change. But a single thread—sometimes I can move it without undoing the whole fabric. I didn't know a way to move Calvin that would make a difference. But I could move you. I could bring the judge here, the one who sees with the blindfold over her eyes. So I've done that."

"I thought you said your sister did it."

"Well, she's the one who decided it must be done. But only I could touch the thread."

"I think you spend a lot of your time lying and concealing things."

"Quite possibly."

"Like the fact that the western door leads into Ta-Kumsaw's land west of the Mizzipy."

"I never lied about that, or concealed it either."

"And the eastern door, where does that lead?"

"It opens in my auntie's house in Winchester, back in England. See? I conceal nothing."

"You have but one daughter," said Peggy, "and she's already got a loom of her own. Who will take your place here?"

"None of your business," said Becca.

"Nothing is none of my business now," said Peggy. "Not after you picked up my thread and moved it here."

"I don't know who will take my place. Maybe I'll be here forever. I'm not my mother. I won't quit and force this on an unwilling soul."

"When it comes time to choose, look at the boy," said Peggy. "He's wiser than you think."

"A boy's hands on the loom?" Becca's face bore an expression that suggested she had just tasted something awful.

"Before any talent for weaving," said Peggy, "doesn't the weaver have to care about the threads coming into the cloth? He may have killed a squirrel, but I don't think he loves death."

Becca regarded her steadily. "You take too much upon yourself."

"As you said. I'm a judge."

"You'll do it, then?"

"What, watch Alvin? Yes. Though I know I'll have a broken heart six times over before I bury him, yes, I'll turn my eyes back to that boy."

"That man."

"That Maker," said Peggy.

"And the other?"

"I'll meddle if I can find a way."

Becca nodded. "Good." She nodded again. "We're done, now. The doors will lead you out of the house."

That was all the good-bye that Peggy got. But what Becca said was true. Where once Peggy couldn't see a way out, now every corridor led to a door standing open, with the daylight outside. She didn't want to go through the doors back into her own world, though. She wanted to pass through the doors in the old cabin. The east door, into England. The west door, into Red country. Or the south door—where did it lead?

Nevertheless, it was this time and place where she belonged. There was a carriage waiting for her, and work to do, stirring up war by encouraging compassion for the slaves. She could live with that, yes, as Becca had said. Didn't Jesus himself say that he came to bring, not peace, but war? Turning brother against brother? If that's what it takes to remove the stain of slavery from this land, then so be it. I speak only of peaceful change—if others choose to kill or die rather than let the slaves go free, that is their choice, and I didn't cause it.

Just as I didn't cause my mother to take up the gun and kill the Finder who was, after all, only obeying the law, unjust as the law might be. He wouldn't have found Arthur Stuart, hidden as he was in my house, his very smell changed by Alvin's Making, and his presence hidden behind all the hexes Alvin had put there. I didn't kill her. And even if I could have prevented what she did, it wouldn't have changed who she was. She was the woman who would make such a choice as that. That was the woman I loved, her fierce angry courage along with everything else. I am not guilty of her death. The man who shot her was. And she was the one, not I, who placed her in harm's way.

Peggy strode out into the sunlight feeling invigorated, light of step. The air tasted sweet to her. The place with no heartfires had rekindled her own.

She got back into the carriage and it took her without further distractions to an inn well north of Chapman Valley. She spent the night there, and then the next day rode on to Baker's Fork. Once there, she held her master classes, teaching schoolmasters and gifted students, and in between conversing with this man or that woman about slavery, making comments, scorning those who mistreated slaves, declaring that as long as anyone had such power over other men and women, there would be mistreatment, and the only cure for it was for all men and women to be free. They nodded. They agreed. She spoke of the courage it would take, how the slaves themselves bore the lash and had lost all; how much would White men and women suffer in order to free them? What did Christ suffer, for the sake of others? It was a strong and measured performance that she gave. She did not retreat from it one bit, even though she knew now that it would lead to war. Wars have been fought for foolish causes. Let there be one, at last, in a good cause, if the enemies of decency refuse to soften their hearts.

Amid all the teaching and all the persuasion, she did find time, a scrap of an hour to herself, sitting at the writing desk in one old plantation widow's home. It was the very desk where, moments before, the woman had manumitted all her slaves and hired them on as free workingmen and workingwomen. Peggy saw in her heartfire when the choice was made that she would end up with her barns burnt and her fields spoiled. But she would lead these newfreed Blacks northward, despite all harassment and danger. Her courage would become legendary, a spark that would inspire other brave hearts. Peggy knew that in the end, the woman would not miss her fine house and lovely lands. And someday twenty thousand Black daughters would be given the woman's name. Why am I named Jane? they would ask their mothers. And the answer would come: Because once there was a woman by that name who freed her slaves and protected them all the way north, and then hired and looked after them until they learned the ways of free men and women and could stand on their own. It is a name of great honor. No one would know of the schoolteacher who came one day and gave open words to the secret longings of Jane's heart.

At that writing desk, Peggy took the time to write a letter and address it. Vigor Church, in the state of Wobbish. It would get to him, of course. As she sealed it, as she handed it over to the postal rider, she looked at long last toward the heartfire that she knew best, knew even better than her own. In it she saw the familiar possibilities, the dire consequences. But they were different now, because of the letter. Different . . . but better? She couldn't guess. She wasn't judge enough to know. Right and wrong were easy for her. But good and bad, better and worse, those were still too tricky. They kept sliding past each other strangely and changing before her eyes. Perhaps there was no judge who could know that; or if there was, he wasn't talking much about it.

The messenger took the letter and carried it north, where in another town he handed it to a rider who paid him what he thought the letter might be worth on delivery, minus half. The second rider took it on north, in his meandering route, and finally he stood in a store in the town of Vigor Church, where he asked about a man named Alvin Smith.

"I'm his brother-in-law," said the storekeeper. "Armor-of-God Weaver. I'll pay you for the letter. You don't want to go any farther into the town, or up there, either. You don't want to listen to the tale those people have to tell."

The tone of his voice convinced the rider. "Five dollars, then," he said.

"I'll wager you only paid the rider who gave it to you a single dollar, thinking the most you could get from me was two. But I'll pay you the five, if you still ask for it, because I'm willing to be cheated by a man who can live with himself after doing it. It's you that'll pay most, in the end."

"Two dollars, then," said the rider. "You didn't have to get personal about it."

Armor-of-God took out three silver dollars and laid them in the man's hand. "Thank you for honest riding, friend," he said. "You're always welcome here. Stay for dinner with us."

"No," the man said. "I'll be on my way."

As soon as he was gone, Armor-of-God laughed and told his wife, "He only paid fifty cents for that letter, I'll wager. So he still thinks he cheated me."

"You need to be more careful with our money, Armor," she answered.

"Two dollars to cause a man a little spiritual torment that perhaps could change his life for the better? Cheap enough bargain, I'd say. What is a soul worth to God? Two dollars, do you think?"

"I shudder to think what some men's souls will be marked down to when God decides to close the shop," said his wife. "I'll take the letter up to Mother's house. I'm going there today anyway."

"Measure's boy Simon comes down for the mail," said Armor-of-God.

She glared at him. "I wasn't going to read it."

"I didn't say you were." But still he didn't hand her the letter. Instead he laid it on the counter, waiting for Measure's oldest boy to come and fetch it up the hill to the house where Alvin was teaching people to be Makers. Armor-of-God still wasn't happy about it. It seemed unreligious to him, improper, against the Bible. And yet he knew Alvin was a good boy, grown to be a good man, and whatever powers of witchery he had, he didn't use them to do harm. Could it be truly against God and religion for him to have such powers, if he used them in a Christian way? After all, God created the world and all things in it. If God didn't want there to be Makers, he didn't have to create any of them. So what Alvin was doing must be in line with the will of God.

Sometimes Armor-of-God felt perfectly at peace with Alvin's doings. And sometimes he thought that only a devil-blinded fool would think even for a moment that God was happy with any sort of witchery. But those were all just thoughts. When it came to action, Armor-of-God had made his decision. He was with Alvin, and against whoever opposed him. If he was damned for it, so be it. Sometimes you just had to follow your heart. And sometimes you just had to make up your mind and stick with it, come hell or high water.

And nobody was going to mess with Alvin's letter from Peggy Larner. Especially not Armor-of-God's wife, who was a good deal too clever with hexery herself.

Far away in another place, Peggy saw the changes in the heart-fires and knew the letter was now in Alvin's family. It would do its work. The world would change. The threads in Becca's loom would move. It is unbearable to watch without meddling, thought Peggy. And then it is unbearable to watch what my meddling causes.

4

Quest

Even before Miss Larner's letter came, Alvin was feeling antsy. Things just wasn't going the way he planned. After months of trying to turn his family and neighbors into Makers, it was looking like a job for six lifetimes, and try as he might, Alvin couldn't figure out how he was going to have more than one lifetime to work with.

Not that the teaching was a failure—he couldn't call it an outright bust, not yet, considering that some of them really were learning how to do some small Makings. It's just that Making wasn't their knack. Alvin had figured out that there wasn't no knack that another person couldn't learn, given time and training and wit enough and plain old stick-to-it-iveness. But what he hadn't taken into account was that Making was like a whole bunch of knacks, and while some of them could grasp this or that little bit of it, there was hardly any who seemed to show a sign of grasping the whole of it. Measure sometimes showed a glimmer. More than a glimmer, really. He could probably be a Maker himself if only he didn't keep getting distracted. But the others—there was no way they were going

to be anything like what Alvin was. So if there was no hope of
success, what was the point of trying?

Whenever he got to feeling discouraged like that, though, he'd
just tell himself to shut his mouth and stick to his work. You don't
get to be a Maker by changing your plan every few minutes. Who
can follow you then? You stick to it. Even when Calvin, the only
natural born Maker among them, even when he refused to learn
anything and finally took himself off to do who knows what sort of
mischief in the wide world, even then you don't give up and go off
in search of him because, as Measure pointed out to the men who
wanted to get up a search party, "You can't force a man to be a
Maker, because forcing folks to do things is to Unmake them."

Even when Alvin's own father said, "Al, I marvel at what you
can do, but it's enough for me that you can do it. My part was done
when you were born, it seems to me. Ain't no man alive but what
he isn't proud to have his son pass him up, which you done handily,
and I don't aim to get back into the race." Even then, Alvin determined grimly to go on teaching while his father went back to the
mill and began to clean it up and get it ready to grind again.

"I can't figure out," said Father, "if my milling is Making or
Unmaking. The stones grind the grain and break it apart into dust,
so that's Unmaking. But the dust is flour, and you can use it to make
bread and cake that the maize or wheat can't be made into, so milling
might be just a step along the road to Making. Can you answer me
that, Alvin? Is grinding flour Making or Unmaking?"

Well, Alvin could answer it glib enough, that it was Making for
sure, but it kept nagging at him, that question. I set out to make
Makers out of these people, my family, my neighbors. But am I
really just grinding them up and Unmaking them? Before I started
trying to teach them, they were all content with their own knacks or
even their own lack of a knack, when you come down to it. Now
they're frustrated and they feel like failures and why? Is it Making
to turn people into something that they weren't born to be? To be a
Maker is good—I know it, because I am one. But does that mean
it's the only good thing to be?

He asked Taleswapper about it, of course. After all, Taleswapper
didn't show up for no reason, even if the old coot had no notion
what the reason was himself. Maybe he was there to give Alvin some
answers. So one day when the two of them were chopping wood out
back, he asked, and Taleswapper answered like he always did, with
a story.

"I heard a tale once about how a man who was building a wall as fast as he could, but somebody else was tearing it down faster than he could build it up. And he wondered how he could keep the wall from being torn down completely, let alone ever finish it. And the answer was easy: You can't build it alone.''

"I remember that tale," said Alvin. "That tale is why I'm here, trying to teach these folks Making."

"I just wonder," said Taleswapper, "if you might be able to stretch that story, or maybe twist it a little and wring a bit more useful truth out of it."

"Wring away," said Alvin. "We'll find out whether the story is a wet cloth or a chicken's neck when you're done wringing."

"Well maybe what you need isn't a bunch of other stonemasons, cutting the stone and mixing the mortar and plumbing the wall and all those jobs. Maybe what you need is just a lot of cutters, and a lot of mortar mixers, and a lot of surveyors, and so on. Not everybody has to be a Maker. In fact, maybe all you need is just the one Maker."

The truth of what Taleswapper was saying was obvious; it had already occurred to Alvin many times, in other guises. What took him by surprise was how tears suddenly came to his own eyes, and he said softly, "Why does that make me so desperate sad, my friend?"

"Because you're a good man," said Taleswapper. "An evil man would delight to find out that he was the only one who could rule over a great many people working in a common cause."

"More than anything I don't want to be alone anymore," said Alvin. "I've been alone. Almost my whole time as a prentice in Hatrack River, I felt like there was nobody to take my part."

"But you were never alone the whole time," said Taleswapper.

"If you mean Miss Larner looking out for me—"

"Peggy is who I meant. I can't see why you still call her by that false name."

"That's the name of the woman I fell in love with," said Alvin. "But she knows my heart. She knows I killed that man and I didn't have to."

"The man who murdered her mother? I don't think she holds it against you."

"She knows what kind of man I am and she doesn't love me, that's what," said Alvin. "So I *am* alone, the minute I leave this place. And besides, leaving here is like lining up all these people and slapping their faces and saying, You failed so I'm gone."

At that Taleswapper just laughed. "That is plain foolishness and you know it. Truth is you've already taught them everything, and now it's just a matter of practice. They don't need you here any-more.''

"But nobody needs me anywhere else," said Alvin.

Taleswapper laughed again.

"Stop laughing and tell me what's funny."

"A joke you have to explain isn't going to be funny anyway," said Taleswapper, "so there ain't no point in explaining it."

"You're no help," said Alvin, burying the head of his axe in the chopping stump.

"I'm a great help," said Taleswapper. "You just don't want to be helped yet."

"Yes I do! I just don't need riddles, I need answers!"

"You need somebody to tell you what to do? That's a surprise. Still an apprentice then, after all? Want to turn your life over to somebody else? For how long, another seven years?"

"I may not be a prentice anymore," said Alvin, "but that don't mean I'm a master. I'm just a journeyman."

"Then hire on somewhere," said Taleswapper. "You've still got things to learn."

"I know," said Alvin. "But I don't know where to go to learn it. There's that crystal city I saw in the twister with Tenskwa-Tawa. I don't know how to build it. I don't know *where* to build it. I don't even know *why* to build it, except that it ought to exist and I ought to make it exist."

"There you are," said Taleswapper. "Like I said, you've al-ready taught everybody here everything you know, twice over. All you're doing now is helping them practice—and cheating now and then by helping them, don't think I haven't noticed."

"When I use my knack to help them, I tell them I helped," said Alvin, blushing.

"And then they feel like failures anyway, figuring that your help was all that made anything happen, and nothing of their own doing. Alvin, I think I *am* giving you your answer. You've done what you can here. Leave Measure to help them, and the others who've learned a bit of it here and there. Let them work things out on their own, the way you did. Then you go out into the world and learn more of the things you need to know."

Alvin nodded, but in his heart he still refused to believe it. "I just can't see what good it is to go out to try to learn when you know as well as I do there's not another Maker in the world right now, unless you count Calvin which I don't. Who am I going to learn from? Where am I going to go?"

"So you're saying that there's no use in just wandering around, seeing what happens and learning as you can?"

Taleswapper's face was so wry as he said this that Alvin knew at once there was a double meaning. "Just because *you* learn that way doesn't mean *I* can. You're just collecting stories, and there's stories everywhere."

"There's Making almost everywhere, too," said Taleswapper. "And where there isn't Making, there's still old made things being torn down, and you can learn from them, too."

"I can't go," said Alvin. "I can't go."

"Which is to say, you're afraid."

Alvin nodded.

"You're afraid you'll kill again."

"I don't think so. I know I won't. Probably."

"You're afraid you'll fall in love again."

Alvin hooted derisively.

"You're afraid you'll be alone out there."

"How could I be alone?" he asked. "I'd have my golden plow with me."

"That's another thing," said Taleswapper. "That living plow. What did you make it for, if you keep it in darkness all the time and never use it?"

"It's gold," said Alvin. "People want to steal it. Many a man would kill for that much gold."

"Many a man would kill for that much tin, for that matter," said Taleswapper. "But you remember what happened to the man who was given a talent of gold, and buried it in the earth."

"Taleswapper, you're plumb full of wisdom today."

"Brimming over," said Taleswapper. "It's my worst fault, splashing wisdom all over other people. But most of the time it dries up real fast and doesn't leave a stain."

Alvin grimaced at him. "Taleswapper, I'm not ready to leave home yet."

"Maybe folks have to leave home *before* they're ready, or they never get ready at all."

"Was that a paradox, Taleswapper? Miss Larner taught me about paradox."

"She's a fine teacher and she knows all about it."

"All I know about paradox is that if you don't shovel it out of the stable, the barn gets to stinking real bad and fills up with flies."

Taleswapper laughed at that, and Alvin joined in laughing, and that was the end of the serious part of the conversation. Only it clung to Alvin, the whole thing, knowing that Taleswapper thought he should leave home, and him not having a clue where he would go if he did leave, and not being willing to admit failure, either. All kinds of reasons for staying. Most important reason of all was simply being home. He'd spent half his childhood away from his family, and it was good to sit down at his mother's table every day. Good to see his father standing at the mill. Hear his father's voice, his brothers' voices, his sisters' voices laughing and quarreling and telling and asking, his mother's voice, his mother's sharp sweet voice, all of them covering his days and nights like a blanket, keeping him warm, all of them saying to him, You're safe here, you're known here, we're your people, we won't turn on you. Alvin had never heard him a symphony in his life, or even more than two fiddles and a banjo at the same time, but he knew that no orchestra could ever make a music more beautiful than the voices of his family moving in and out of their houses and barns and the millhouse and the shops in town, threads of music binding him to this place so that even though he knew Taleswapper was right and he ought to leave, he couldn't bring himself to go.

How did Calvin ever do it? How did Calvin leave this music behind him?

Then Miss Larner's letter came.

Measure's boy Simon brought it, him being five now and old enough to run down to Armor-of-God's store to pick up the post. He could do his letters now, too, so he didn't just give the letter over to his grandma or grandpa, he took it right to Alvin himself and announced at the top of his lungs, "It's from a woman! She's called Miss Larner and she makes real purty letters!"

"*Pretty* letters," Alvin corrected him.

Simon wasn't to be fooled. "Oh, Uncle Al, you're the only person around here as says it like that! I'd be plumb silly to fall for a joke like that!"

Alvin pried up the sealing wax and unfolded the letter. He knew her handwriting from the many hours he had tried to imitate it, studying with her back in Hatrack River. His hand was never as smooth, could never flow the way hers did. Nor was he as eloquent. Words weren't his gift, or at least not the formal, elegant words Miss Larner—Peggy—used in writing.

> *Dear Alvin,*
>   *You've overstayed in Vigor Church. Calvin's a great danger to you, and you must go find him and reconcile with*

*him; if you wait for him to come back to you, he will bring
the end of your life with him.*

*I can almost hear you answer me: I ain't afraid to see
my life end. (I know you still say ain't, just to spite me.) Go
or stay, that's up to you. But I can tell you this. Either you
will go now, of your own free will, or you will go soon
anyway, but not freely. You're a journeyman smith—you will
have your journey.*

*Perhaps in your travels we shall encounter each other.
It would please me to see you again.*

Sincerely,
Peggy

Alvin had no idea what to make of this letter. First she bosses
him around like a schoolboy. Then she talks teasingly about how he
still says *ain't.* Then she as much as asks him to come to her, but
in such a cold way as to chill him to the bone—"It would please
me to see you again" indeed! Who did she think she was, the
Queen? And she signed the letter "sincerely" as if she was a
stranger, and not the woman that he loved, and that once said she
loved him. What was she playing at, this woman who could see so
many futures? What was she trying to get him to do? It was plain
there was more going on than she was saying in her letter. She
thought she was so wise, since she knew more about the future than
other folks, but the fact was that she could make mistakes like anybody else and he didn't want her telling him what to *do,* he wanted
her to tell him what she *knew* and let him make up his own mind.

One thing was certain. He wasn't going to drop everything and
take off in search of Calvin. No doubt she knew exactly where he
was and she hadn't bothered to tell him. What was *that* supposed to
accomplish? Why should he go off searching for Calvin when she
could send him a letter and tell him, not where Calvin was right
now, but where Calvin would *be* by the time Alvin caught up with
him? Only a fool takes off on foot trying to follow the flight of a
wild goose.

I know I've got to leave here sometime. But I'm not going to
leave in order to chase down Calvin. And I'm not going to leave
because the woman I almost married sends me a bossy letter that
doesn't even hint that she still loves me, if she ever really did. If
Peggy was so sure that he'd go soon anyway, because he had to,
well, then he might as well just wait around and see what it was that
would make him go.

5

Twist

America was too small a country for Calvin. He knew that now. It was all too new. The powers of a land took time to ripen. The Reds, they knew the land, but they were gone. And the Whites and Blacks who lived here now, they had only shallow powers, knacks and hexes, spells and dreams. Nothing like the ancient music that Alvin had talked about. The greensong of the living forest. Besides, the Reds were gone, so whatever it was they knew, it must have been weak. Failure was proof enough of that.

Even before Calvin knew in his mind where he was headed, his feet knew. East. Sometimes a bit north, sometimes a bit south, but always east. At first he thought he was just going to Dekane, but when he got there he just worked for a day or two to get a bit of coin and some bread in his belly, and then he was off over the mountains, following the new railroad into Irrakwa, where he could sneer a little at men and women who were Red in body but White in dress and speech and soul. More work, more coin, more practice at using his Making here and there. Pranks, mostly, because he didn't dare use his knack out in the open where folks would take notice and spread word of him. Just little favors for houses where they treated him good, like driving all the mice and roaches off their property. And a little bit of getting even with those who turned him away. Sending a rat to die in a well. Causing a leak in the roof over a flour barrel. That one was hard, making the wood swell and then shrink. But he could work with the water. The water lent itself to his use better than any other element.

Turned out that Irrakwa wasn't where his feet were taking him, either. He worked his way across Irrakwa to New Holland, where the farmers all spoke Dutch, and then down the Hudson to New Amsterdam.

He thought when he came to the great city on the tip of Manhattan Island that this might be the place he was looking for. Biggest city in the U.S.A. And it wasn't hardly Dutch anymore. Everybody spoke English for business, and on top of that Calvin counted a dozen languages before he stopped caring how many. Not to mention strange accents of English from places like York and Glasgow and Monmouth. Surely all the lores of the world were gathered here. Surely he could find teachers.

So he stayed for days, for a week. He tried the college farther up the island, but they wanted him to study intellectual things instead of the lore of power, and soon enough Calvin figured out that none of them high-toned professors knew anything useful anyhow. They treated him like he was crazy. One old coot with a white goat-beard spent half an hour trying to convince Calvin to let the man study *him*, like as if he was some strange specimen of bug. Calvin only stayed for the whole half hour so he'd have time to loosen all the bindings of all the books on the man's shelves. Let him wonder about Calvin's kind of madness as the pages of every book he picked up fell out and scattered on the floor.

If the professors weren't worth nothing, the street wasn't much better. Oh, he heard about loremasters and wizards and such. Gypsies bragged on some cursemonger. Irishmen knew of a priest who had special ways. Frenchmen and Spaniards heard of witches or child-saints or whatever. One Portugee told of a free Black woman who could make your enemy's crotch turn as smooth and blank as an armpit—which, according to the story, was how she got her freedom, after doing that to her master's firstborn son and threatening to do it next to him. But every one of them kept retreating out of sight. He'd find out who knew the loremaster, and then go to that person and find out that he only knew somebody else who knew the powerful one, and so on and so on, like constables searching through the night for a fugitive who kept slipping away into alleys.

In the meantime, though, Calvin learned to live in a city and he liked it. He liked the way that you could disappear right out in the open. Nobody knew you. Nobody expected anything from you. You were what you wore. When he arrived he dressed like a rube from the country, and so people expected him to be stupid and awkward and, what the hell, he was. But in a few days he realized how his clothes gave him away and he bought some city garb from a used-garment house. That was when people started being willing to talk to him. And he learned to change his speech a little, too. Talk faster, get rid of some of the drawl. Shake off the country twang. He knew he gave himself away with every word he said, but he was getting better. People didn't ask him to repeat himself as much. And by the end of the week, he was no more out of place than any of the other immigrants. That was as good as it got—it wasn't as if anybody was actually *from* New Amsterdam. Except maybe for some old Dutch landlords hiding in their mansions up-island.

Rumors of wisdom, but no wisdom to be had in this town. Well, what did he expect? Anybody who really knew the powers of the old world would hardly have to board some miserable boat and sail west at risk of life and limb in order to come live in some sinkhole of a slum in New Amsterdam. No, the people of Europe who understood power were still in Europe—because they were running things there, and didn't have no reason to leave.

And who was the most powerful one of all? Why, the man whose victories had caused all these people of the dozen languages to flock to American shores. The man who drove the aristocrats out of France, and then conquered Spain and the Holy Roman Empire and Italy and Austria and then for some reason stopped at the Russian border and the English Channel, declared peace and held on, iron-fisted but, as they said, tender-hearted, so that pretty soon nobody in Italy or Austria or the low countries or anywhere, really, was wishing for their old rulers to come back. That was the man who understood power. That was the man who was fit to teach Calvin what he needed to know.

Only trouble was, why would a man so powerful ever agree to speak to a poor farmboy from Wobbish? And how was that poor farmboy ever going to find passage across the ocean? If only Alvin had bothered to teach him how to turn iron into gold. Now *that* would be useful. Imagine a whole steam locomotive turned to solid gold. Fire up the engine and the whole damn thing would melt down—but it would melt down into pools of gold. Just put in a dipper and draw it out and there was passage to France, and not in no steerage, neither. First-class passage, and a fine hotel in Paris. Fine clothes, too, so that when he walked into the American embassy the flunkies would bow and scrape and take him straight to the ambassador and the ambassador would take him straight to the imperial palace where he would be presented to Napoleon himself and Napoleon would say, Why should I meet with you, an ordinary citizen of a second-rate country in the wild lands of the west? And Calvin would take three dipperfuls of gold out of his pockets and set them heavily in Napoleon's hands and say, How much of this do you want? I know how to make more. And Napoleon would say, I have all the taxes of Europe to buy me gold. What do I need with your pathetic handfuls? And Calvin would say, Now you have a bit more gold than you had before. Look at your buttons, sir. And Napoleon would look at the brass buttons on his coat and they would be gold, too, and he would say, What do you want from me, sir? That's right, he'd call Calvin "sir" and Calvin would say, All I want is for you to teach me the ways of power.

Only if Calvin knew how to turn iron or brass into gold, he sure as hell wouldn't need no help from Napoleon Bonaparte, Emperor of Earth or whatever fool title the man had given himself in his latest promotion. It was one of those circular dilemmas that he always kept running into. If he had enough power to attract Napoleon's attention, he wouldn't need Napoleon. And, because he needed Napoleon, there was no chance that any of his underlings would let Calvin come anywhere near him.

Calvin wasn't stupid. He wasn't no rube, whatever the city people thought. He knew that powerful men didn't let just anybody come in and chat.

But I do have some powers, thought Calvin. I do have some powers, and I can wangle a way, once I get across the pond. That's what the sophisticated people called the Atlantic Ocean—the pond. Once I get across the pond. Might have to learn French, but they say Napoleon speaks English, too, from his days as a general in Canada. One way or another, I'll get to see him and he'll take me on as his apprentice. Not apprenticed like to take over his empire after him, but instead to do the same thing in America. Bring the Crown Colonies and New England and the United States all under one flag. And Canada, too. And Florida. And then maybe he'd turn his eyes across the Mizzipy and see how good a job old Tenskwa-

Tawa would do at holding back a *Maker* who wanted to cross and conquer Red country.

All dreams. All stupid foolish dreams of a boy sleeping in a cheap boardinghouse and doing lousy odd jobs to earn a few cents a day. Calvin knew that, but he also knew that if he couldn't turn a knack like his into money and power he didn't deserve nothing better than those lousy beds and wormy meals and backbreaking jobs.

One thing, though. Folks on the street were getting used to the idea that Calvin was searching for something, and finally the old woman he bought apples from—the one who'd given him an apple his first day there when he was out of money, since she was a country girl herself, she said; the one who from that day to this found no more worms or flies in her fruit—she said to him, "Well I hope you've talked to the Bloody Man, he knows stuff."

"Bloody Man?"

"You know, the one as tells horrible stories or when he can't find nobody new to tell it to, his hands are dripping with blood. Everybody knows the Bloody Man. He come here because the curse on him is, he has to find new people every day to tell his story to, and where you going to find a good supply of new people all the time?"

Of course Calvin knew by now exactly who she was talking about. "Harrison is *here*?"

"You know him?"

"Know *of* him. He called hisself—himself—governer of Wob-bish for a while. Slaughtered Tenskwa-Tawa's people at Tippy-Canoe."

"That's the one. Dreadful story. Thank heaven I only had to hear it the once. But there's some kind of power in the fact that his hands get all bloody. I mean, that's strange, ain't it? All them other folks you hear about, you never actually see them do nothing, if you know what I mean. But you can see the blood. That's power, I reckon."

"Reckon so." Again he corrected himself. "I think so."

"Might as well say, 'I imagine so,' if you're trying to get all highfalutin."

"Just don't want to sound country, that's all."

"Then you'd better learn French. All the high-tone folks do. Here we are in a Dutch city where everybody speaks English, and they go into their toney restaurants and order their food in French! What did the *French* ever have to do with New Amsterdam? You want to eat in French, you go to Canada, that's what I say!"

He listened to her diatribe until he could finally get free—which meant when she finally got a customer—and then he set out to find Harrison. White Murderer Harrison. Calvin knew all about the curse on him, from the stories told by his own father and neighbors, and he'd sometimes imagined Harrison walking country roads from town to town, folks throwing him out before he could come in and start telling his awful tale. It never occurred to him that Harrison would come to the city, but it made sense, once you thought about it. Bloody Man.

He found him in an alleyway behind a restaurant where he got fed every night by a manager who didn't want him accosting his customers. "It's a stiff punishment," said the manager. "I had a landlord in Kilkenny who believed in that kind of justice. Punishments that went on forever. Permanent shame. I think it's wrong. I don't care much what the man did. Let him without sin among you, and all that. So he eats back of my restaurant. Long as he doesn't hurt trade."

"Aren't you the generous one," said Calvin.

"You got a mouth on you, boy. In fact I *am* generous, and open-minded, too, and just because I know it and take credit for it doesn't make it any less true. So you can take your little winking sort of wit and leave my establishment if you're going to eat my food and then sit in judgment on me."

"I haven't eaten your food."

"But you will," said the man, "because, as I said, I *am* generous, and you look hungry. Now get back to the kitchen and you can tell the cook to give you something for yourself and something for Bloody Man out in the alley. If you come with his food, he'll talk to you, right enough. He'll probably tell you his story, for that matter."

"I know his story."

"Everybody might know a story, but it's never the same story they know. Now get away from my door, you look like a street rat."

Calvin looked down at his clothes and realized, yes, he had bought clothing to blend in, but what he blended in with was the street, not the city. He'd have to do something about that before he went to Paris. Have to become, if not a gentleman, then at least a tradesman. Not a street rat.

He didn't like people who called themselves generous, but the fact was the food in the kitchen was good. The cook didn't give him no scraps or scrapings. He got food that was decent and there was plenty. How did this manager stay in business, being so generous to

the poor? No doubt he was cheating his boss. He could afford to be
generous, since he didn't have to pay for it himself. Most virtues
were like that. People could take pride in how virtuous they were,
but the fact was that as soon as virtue got expensive or inconvenient,
it was amazing how fast it gave way to practical concerns.

The man's generosity got him this much: No roaches or mice in
his kitchen.

Out in the alleyway, Bloody Man was sipping from a wine bottle. He saw Calvin and his eyes went hungry. Calvin laughed. "I
hear you've got a story to tell."

"They still sending boys like you to find me, as a prank?"

"No prank. I know your story, mostly. Just wanted to meet you
my own self, I guess."

Harrison offered him the wine bottle. "Best thing about this
place," he said. "Besides that they don't run me off in the first
place. When somebody opens a bottle of wine and doesn't finish it
at the table, the manager refuses to pour from that bottle to anyone
else. So it comes out into the alley."

"The big surprise," said Calvin, "is that there ain't ten dozen
other hungry drunks here."

Harrison laughed. "They used to. But they got sick of hearing
me tell my story and now I have the alley to myself. That's how I
like it."

But Calvin could hear it in his voice that it was a lie. He didn't
like it that way. He was hungry for company.

"Might as well start telling me the story. Between bites, if you
want," said Calvin.

Harrison started eating. Calvin could see a remnant of table manners. Once he had been a civilized man.

Between bites, Harrison told the tale. All of it: How he had some
Reds from south of the Hio come and kidnap two White boys in
order to blame it on Tenskwa-Tawa, the so-called Red Prophet. Only
the boys were rescued somehow and fell in with the Prophet's
brother, Ta-Kumsaw. But that didn't matter because Harrison still
used the kidnapping to rile up the White folks in the northern part
of Wobbish, the ones as lived nearest to the Prophet's village at
Tippy-Canoe. So Harrison was able to raise an army to go wipe out
Prophetstown. And then at the last minute, who shows up but one
of the kidnapped boys. Well, Harrison sees nothing for it but to have
the boy killed, and everything seems to be working. The Reds just
stand there, letting the musketfire and the grapeshot mow them down

until nine out of ten of them was dead, the whole meadow a sheet
of blood flowing down into the Tippy-Canoe, only it was too much
for those White men—they *called* themselves men—because they
all stopped shooting before the job was done, and then up comes
that boy who was supposed to be dead and he wasn't even injured,
and he tells the truth to everybody and then the Red Prophet puts a
curse on all of them there and the worst curse on Harrison, including
that he has to tell a new person every day and . . .

"You're telling it all wrong," said Calvin.

Harrison looked at him angrily. "You think after all these years
I don't know how to tell the tale? If I tell it any other way, I get
blood on my hands and believe me, it looks bad. People throw up
when they see me. Looks like I stuck my hands in a corpse up to
my elbows."

"Telling it *your* way has you living in an alley, eating from
charity and drinking leftover wine," said Calvin.

Harrison squinted at him. "Who *are* you?"

"The boy you tried to kill is my brother Measure. The other
boy you had them kidnap is my brother Alvin."

"And you came to gloat?"

"Do I look like I'm gloating? No, I left home because I got sick
of their righteousness, knowing everything and not having respect
for nobody else."

Harrison winked. "I never liked people like that."

"You want to hear how you *ought* to tell your tale?"

"I'm listening."

"The Reds were at war with the Whites. They weren't using the
land but they didn't want White farmers to use it, either. They just
couldn't share even though there was plenty of room. Tenskwa-Tawa
claimed to be peaceful, but you knew that he was gathering all those
thousands of Reds together in order to be Ta-Kumsaw's army. You
had to do *something* to rile up the Whites there to put a stop to this
menace. So yes, you had two boys kidnapped, but you never gave
orders for anybody to be killed—"

"If I say *that* the blood just leaps onto my hands on the spot—"

"I'm sure you've thought of all the possible lies, but hear me
out," said Calvin.

"Go on."

"You didn't order anybody killed. That was just lies your enemies told about you. Lies originating with Alvin Miller Junior, now
called Alvin Smith. After all, Alvin was the Boy Renegado, the

White boy who went everywhere with Ta-Kumsaw for a year. He was Ta-Kumsaw's friend—we'll use the word *friend* because we're in decent company—so of course he lied about you. It was your battle at Tippy-Canoe that broke the back of Ta-Kumsaw's plans. If you hadn't struck then and there, Ta-Kumsaw would have been victorious later at Fort Detroit, and Ta-Kumsaw would have driven all the civilized folks out of the land west of the Appalachees and Red armies would be descending on the cities of the east, raiding out of the mountains and—why, thanks to you and your courage at Tippy-Canoe, the Reds have been driven west of the Mizzipy. You opened up all the western lands to safe colonization."

"My hands would be dripping before I said all that."

"So what? Hold them up and say, 'Look what the Red Witch Tenskwa-Tawa did to punish me. He covered my hands with blood. But I'm glad to pay that price. The blood on my hands is the reason why White men are building civilization right to the shores of the Mizzipy. The blood on my hands is the reason why people in the east can sleep easy at night, without so much as a thought about Reds coming and raping and killing the way those savages always did.' "

Harrison chuckled. "Every word you've said is the profoundest bull hockey, my boy, I hope you know that."

"You just need to decide whether you're going to let Tenskwa-Tawa have the final victory over you."

"Why are you telling me this? What's in it for you?"

"I don't know. I came looking for you thinking you might know something of power, but when I heard you tell that weaselly weakling tale I knew that you didn't know nothing that a *man* could use. In fact, I knew more than *you*. So, seeing how I was going to ask you to share, it seemed only fair to share right back."

"How kind of you." His sarcasm was inescapable.

"I don't think so. I just picture the look on my brother Alvin's face when you tell everbody he was the Boy Renegado. You say *that*, and nobody'll believe him if he testifies against you. In fact, he'll have to hide himself, when you think of all the terrible things folks believe about the Boy Renegado. How he was the cruelest Red of them all, killing and torturing so even the Shaw-Nee puked."

"I remember those tales."

"You hold up those bloody hands, my friend, and then make them mean what *you* want them to mean."

Harrison shook his head. "I can't live with the blood."

"So you *have* a conscience, eh?"

Harrison laughed. "The blood gets in my *food*. It stains my clothes. It makes people sick."

"If I were you, I'd eat with gloves on and I'd wear dark clothes."

Harrison was through eating. So was Calvin.

"So you want me to do this to hurt your brother."

"Not hurt him. Just keep him silent and out of sight. You've spent, what, eight years living like a dog. Now it's his turn."

"There's no going back," said Harrison. "Once I tell lies, I'll have bloody hands till the day I die."

Calvin shrugged. "Harrison, you're a liar and a murderer, but you love power more than life. Unfortunately you're piss-poor at getting it and keeping it. Ta-Kumsaw and Alvin and Tenskwa-Tawa played you for a sucker. I'm telling you how to undo what they done to you. How to set yourself free. I don't give a rat's front teeth whether you do what I said or not." He got up to go.

Harrison half-rose and clutched at Calvin's pantlegs. "Someone told me that Alvin, he's a Maker. That he has real power."

"No he doesn't," said Calvin. "Not for you to worry about. Because, you see, my friend, he can only use his power for *good*, never to harm nobody."

"Not even me?"

"Maybe he'll make an exception for you." Calvin grinned wickedly. "I know *I* would."

Harrison withdrew his hands from Calvin's clothing. "Don't look at me like that, you little weasel."

"Like what?" asked Calvin.

"Like I'm scum. Don't *you* judge *me*."

"Can you tell me a single good reason why not?"

"Because whatever else I did, boy, I never betrayed my own brother."

Now it was Calvin's turn to look into the face of contempt. He spat on the ground near Harrison's knees. "Eat pus and die," he said.

"Was that a curse?" asked Harrison jeeringly as Calvin walked away. "Or merely a friendly warning?"

Calvin didn't answer him. He was already thinking of other things. How to raise the money to get passage east, for one thing. First class. He was going to go first class. Maybe what he needed to do was see if his knack extended to causing money to fall out of some shopkeeper's moneybag as he carried his earnings to the bank. If he did it right, no one would see. He wouldn't get caught. And even if someone saw the money fall out and him pick it up, they could only accuse him of finding dropped money, since he never laid a hand on the bag. That would work. It would be easy enough. So easy that it was stupid that Alvin had never done it before. The family could have used the money. There were some hard years. But Alvin was too selfish ever to think of anybody but himself, or anything but his stupid plan of trying to teach Making to people with no knack for it.

First-class passage to England, and from there across the channel to France. New clothes. It wouldn't take much to get that kind of money. A lot of money changed hands in New Amsterdam, and there was nothing to stop some of it from falling onto the street at Calvin's feet. God had given him the power, and that meant that it must be the will of God for him to do it.

Wouldn't it be a hoot if Harrison actually took Calvin's advice?

6

True Love

Amy Sump didn't care what her friends or anybody said. What she felt for Alvin Maker was love. Real love. True, deep, abiding love that would withstand the test of time.

If only he would pay any attention to her openly, so others could see it. Instead all he ever did was give her those glances that made her heart flutter so within her. She worried sometimes that maybe it was just his Makerness, his knack or whatever it was. Worried that he was somehow reaching inside her chest and making her heart turn over and her whole body quiver. But no, that wasn't the sort of thing that Makers did. In fact maybe he didn't even *know* about her love for him. Maybe his glances were really searching looks, hoping to see in her face some sign of her love. That was why she no longer tried to hide her maidenly blushes when her heart beat so fast and her face felt all hot and tingly. Let him see how his gaze transforms me into a quivering mass of devoted worshipfulness.

How Amy longed to go to the teaching sessions where Alvin worked with a dozen or so grownups at once, telling them how a

Maker had to see the world. How she would love to hear his voice for hours on end. Then she would discover the true knack within her, and both she and her beloved Alvin would rejoice to discover that she was secretly a Maker herself, so that the two of them together would be able to remake the world and fight off the evil nasty Unmaker together. Then they would have a dozen babies, all of them Makers twice over, and the love of Alvin and Amy Maker would be sung for a thousand generations throughout the whole world, or at least America, which was pretty much the same thing as far as Amy cared.

But Amy's parents wouldn't let her go. "How could Alvin possibly concentrate on teaching anybody anything with you making cow-eyes at him the whole time?" her mother said, the heartless old hag. Not as cruel as her father, though, telling her, "Get some control over yourself, girl! Or I'm going to have to get you some love diapers to keep you from embarrassing yourself in public. Love diapers, do you understand me?" Oh, she understood him, the nasty man. Him of the cranks and pulleys, pipes and cables. Him of pumps and engines and machinery, who had no understanding of the human heart. "The heart's just a pump itself, my girl," he said, which showed him to be a deeply totally impossibly eternally abysmally ignorant machine of a man his own self but said nothing about the truth of the universe. It was her beloved Alvin who understood that all things were alive and had feelings—all things *except* her father's hideous dead machines, chugging away like walking corpses. A steam-powered lumbermill! Using fire and water to cut wood! What an abomination before the Lord! When she and Alvin were married, she'd get Alvin to stop her father from making any more machines that roared and hissed and chugged and gave off the heat of hell. Alvin would keep her in a sylvan wonderland where the birds were friends and the bugs didn't bite and they could swim naked together in clear pools of water and he would swim to her in real life instead of just in her dreams and he would reach out and embrace her and their naked bodies would touch under the water and their flesh would meet and join and . . .

"No such thing," said her friend Ramona.

Amy felt herself grow hot with anger. Who was Ramona to decide what was real and what wasn't? Couldn't Amy tell her dreams to *somebody* without having to keep saying it was just a dream instead of pretending that it was real, that his arms had been around her? Didn't she remember it as clearly—no, far *more* clearly—than anything that had ever happened to her in real life?

"Did so happen. In the moonlight."

"When!" said Ramona, her voice dripping with contempt.

"Three nights ago. When Alvin *said* he was going out into the woods to be alone. He was really going to be with me."

"Well where is there a pool of clear water like that? Nothing like that around here, just rivers and streams, and you *know* Alvin never goes into the Hatrack to swim or nothing."

"Don't you know *anything*?" said Amy, trying to match her best friend's disdain. "Haven't you heard of the greensong? How Alvin learned from them old Reds how to run through the forest like the wind, silent and not even so much as bending a branch? He can run a hundred miles in an hour, faster than any railroad train. It wasn't any kind of pool around *here*, it was so far away that it would take anybody from Vigor Church three days to get there on a good horse!"

"Now I know you're just lying," said Ramona.

"He can do that *any day*," insisted Amy hotly.

"*He* can, but *you* can't. You screech when you brush up into a spiderweb, you dunce."

"I'm not a dunce I'm the best student in the school *you're* the dunce," said Amy all in a breath—it was an epigram she had often used before. "I held Alvin's *hand* is what, and he carried me along, and then when I got tired he picked me up in those blacksmith's arms of his and carried me."

"And then I'm *sure* he really took off all his clothes and you took off all of yours, like you was a couple of weasels or something."

"Muskrats. Otters. Creatures of water. It wasn't nakedness, it was naturalness, the freeness of two kindred souls who have no secrets from each other."

"Well, what a bunch of beautifulness," said Ramona. "Only I think if it really happened it would be *disgustingness* and *revolting-ness*, him coming up and hugging you in your complete and utter *starkersness*."

Amy knew that Ramona was making fun of her but she wasn't sure why making up words like *disgustingness* made the idiotic girl laugh and almost fall off the tree branch where they were sitting.

"You have no appreciation of beauty."

"You have no appreciation of *truth*," said Ramona. "Or should I say, of 'truthfulness.' "

"You calling me a liar?" said Amy, giving her a little push.

"Hey!" cried Ramona. "No fair! I'm farther out on the branch so there's nothing for me to grab onto."

Amy pushed her again, harder, and Ramona wobbled, her eyes growing wide as she clutched at the branch.

"Stop it you little liar!" cried Ramona. "I'll tell what lies you've been saying."

"They *aren't* lies," said Amy. "I remember it as clearly as . . . as clearly as the sunlight over the fields of green corn."

"As clearly as the grunting of the hogs in my father's sty," said Ramona, in a voice that matched Amy's for dreaminess.

"Of course true love would be beyond your ability to imagine."

"Yes, my imaginingness is the epitaph of feebleness."

"Epitome, not epitaph," Amy said.

"Oh, if only I could have your sublimeness of correctness, your wiseness."

"Stop *ness*ing all the time."

"*You* stop."

"I don't do that."

"Do so."

"Do not."

"Eat worms," said Ramona.

"On brain salad," said Amy. And now that they were back to familiar playful argument, they both broke into laughter and talked about other things for a while.

And if things had stayed that way, maybe nothing would have happened. But on the way back home in the gathering dusk, Ramona asked one last time, "Amy, telling truth, cross your heart, friend to friend, swear to heaven, remember forever, tell me that you didn't really actually with your own flesh and blood go swimming naked with Alvin Smith—"

"Alvin *Maker.*"

"Tell me it was a dream."

Almost Amy laughed and said, Of course it was a dream, you silly girl.

But in Ramona's eyes she saw something: wide-eyed wonder at the idea that such things were possible, and that someone Ramona actually knew might have done something so wicked and wonderful. Amy didn't want to see that look of awe change to a look of knowing triumph. And so she said what she knew she shouldn't say. "I wish it was a dream, I honestly do, Ramona. Because when I think back on it I long for him all the more and I wonder when he'll dare to speak to my father and tell him that he wants me for his wife. A man who's done a thing like that with a girl—he's got to marry her, doesn't he?''

There. She had said it. The most secret wonderful dream of her heart. Said it right out.

"You've got to tell your papa," said Ramona. "He'll see to it Alvin marries you."

"I don't want him to be forced," said Amy. "That's silly. A man like Alvin can only be enticed into marriage, not pushed into it."

"Everybody thinks you're all goo-goo over Alvin and he doesn't even see you," said Ramona. "But if he's going off with you a swimming starkers in some faraway pond that only he can get to, well, I don't think that's right. I honestly don't."

"Well, I don't care what you think," said Amy. "It *is* right and if you tell I'll cut off all your hair and tat it into a doily and *burn* it."

Ramona burst out laughing. "Tat it into a *doily?* What kind of power does *that* have?"

"A six-sided doily," said Amy portentously.

"Oh, I'm trembling. Made out of my own hair, too. Silly, you can't do things like that, that's what Black witches do, make things out of hair and burn them or whatever."

As if that was an argument. Alvin did Red magic; why couldn't Amy learn to do Black magic, when her Makering knack was finally unlocked? But there was no use arguing about that sort of thing with Ramona. Ramona thought she knew better than anybody. It was a marvel that Amy even bothered to keep her as a best friend.

"I'm going to tell," said Ramona. "Unless you tell me right now that it's all a lie."

"If you tell I'll kill you," said Amy.

"Tell me it's a lie, then."

Tears sprang unbidden to Amy's eyes. It was *not* a lie. It was a dream. A true dream, of true love, a dream that came from the paths of secretness within her own and Alvin's hearts. He dreamed the same dream at the same time, she knew it, and he felt her flesh against his as surely as she felt his against hers. That made it true, didn't it? If a man and a woman both remembered the realness of each other's bodies pressing against each other, then how was that anything but a true experience? "I love Alvin too much to lie about such a thing. Cut my tongue out if any part of it is false!"

Ramona gasped. "I never believed you till now."

"But you tell *no* one," said Amy. Her heart swelled with satisfaction over her victory. Ramona finally believed her. "Swear."

"I swear," said Ramona.

"Show me your fingers!" cried Amy.

Ramona brought her hands out from behind her. The fingers weren't crossed, but that didn't prove they weren't crossed a few moments ago.

"Swear again now," said Amy. "When I can see your hands."

"I *swear*," said Ramona, rolling her eyes.

"It's our beautiful secret," said Amy, turning and walking away.

"Ours and Alvin's," said Ramona, uncrossing her ankles and following her.

7

Booking Passage

It didn't take Calvin too long to figure out that it was going to take a powerful long time to earn enough money to buy passage to Europe as a gentleman. A long time and a lot of work. Neither idea sounded attractive.

He couldn't turn iron into gold, but there was plenty of things he *could* do, and he thought about them long and hard. He wasn't sure, but he didn't reckon them banks could keep him out of their vaults for long if he got to working on what all was holding them together. Still, there was a chance of being caught, and that would be the ruination of all his dreams. He thought of putting out his shingle as a Maker, but that would bring a kind of fame and attention that wouldn't stand in his favor later, not to mention all the accusations of charlatanry that would be bound to come. He was already hearing rumors of Alvin—or rather, of some prentice smith out west who turned an iron plow into gold. Half those who told the tale did it with rolled eyes, as if to say, I'm sure some western farmboy has a Maker's knack, that's likely, yes!

Sometimes Calvin wished it was a different knack he had. For instance, he could do with a torch's knack about now. Seeing the future—why, he could see which property to buy, or which ship to invest in! But even then he'd have to have a partner to put up the money, since he had nothing now. And hanging around New Amsterdam getting rich wasn't what he wanted. He wanted to learn Makering, or whatever it was that Napoleon could teach him. Having set his sights so high, the petty businessmen of Manhattan were hardly the partners he wanted.

There's more than one way to skin a cat, as the saying went. If he couldn't easily get the money for his first-class voyage, why not go direct to the source of all voyages? So it was that he found himself walking the wharfs of Manhattan, along the Hudson and the East River. It was entertaining in its own right, the long, sleek sailing ships, the clunky, smoky steamers, the stevedores shouting and grunting and sweating, the cranes swinging, the ropes and pulleys and nets, the stink of fish and the bawling of the gulls. Who would have guessed, when he was a boy rowdying in a millhouse in Vigor Church, that one day he would be here on the edge of the land, drinking in the liquorous scents and sounds and sights of the life of the sea.

Calvin wasn't one to get lost in reverie and contemplation, though. He had his eye out for the right ship, and from time to time stopped to ask a stevedore of a loading ship what the destination might be. Those as were bound for Africa or Haiti or the Orient were no use to him, but them with European destinations got a thorough looking-over. Until at last he found the right one, a bright and tall-masted English ship with a captain of some breeding who didn't seem to raise his voice at all, though all the men did his will, working hard and working smart under his eye. Everything was clean, and the cargo included trunks and parcels carefully loaded up the ramp instead of being tossed around carelesslike.

Naturally, the captain wouldn't think of talking to a boy Calvin's age, wearing Calvin's clothes. But it wasn't hard for Calvin to think of a plan to get the captain's attention.

He walked up to one of the stevedores and said, "Scuse me, sir, but there's a sharp leak a-going near the back of the boat, on the further side."

The stevedore looked at him oddly. "I'm not a sailor."

"Neither am I, but I think the captain'll thank them as warns him of the problem."

"How can you see it, if it's under the water?"

"Got a knack for leaks," said Calvin. "I'd hurry and tell him, if I were you."

Saying it was a knack was enough for the stevedore, him being an American, even if he *was* a Dutchman by his accent. The captain, of course, wouldn't care diddly about knacks, being an Englishman, which under the Protectorate had a law against knacks. Not against having them, just against believing they existed or attempting to use them. But the captain was no fool, and he'd send somebody to check, knack or no knack.

Which is how it happened. The stevedore talking to his foreman; the foreman to some ship's officer; each time there was a lot of pointing at Calvin and staring at him as he nonchalantly whistled and looked down at the waterline of the ship. To Calvin's disappointment, the officer didn't go to the captain, but instead sent a sailor downstairs into the dark cellar of the ship. Calvin had to provide something for him to see, so now he sent out his doodlebug and got into the wood, right where he'd said the leak was. It was a simple thing to let the planks get just a little loose and out of position under the waterline, which sent a goodly stream of water spurting into the cellar of the ship. Just for the fun of it, when he figured the sailor must be down there looking at it, Calvin opened and closed the gap, so the leak was sometimes a fine spray, sometimes a gush of water, and sometimes just a trickle. Like blood seeping from a wound with an intermittent tourniquet. But he never saw no leak like that before, thought Calvin.

Sure enough, in a few minutes the sailor was back, acting all agitated, and now the officer barked orders to several seamen, then went straight to the captain. This time, though, there wasn't no finger-pointing. The officer wasn't going to give Calvin none of the credit for finding the leak. That really got Calvin's goat, and for a minute he thought of sinking the boat then and there. But that wouldn't do him no good. Time enough to put that greedy ambitious officer in his place.

When the captain went below, Calvin put on a fine show for him. Instead of causing one leak to spurt and pulse, Calvin shifted the leak from one place to another—a gush here, a gush there. By now it had to be obvious that there wasn't nothing natural about that leak. There was a good deal of stirring on the deck, and a lot of sailors started rushing below. Then, to Calvin's delight, a fair number started rushing back onto the deck and onto the gangplank, heading for dry land where there wasn't no strange powers causing leaks in the boat.

Finally the captain came on deck, and this time the officer wasn't taking all the credit for himself. He pointed to the foreman, who pointed to the stevedore, and pretty soon they were all pointing at Calvin.

Now, of course, Calvin could stop fiddling with the leak. He stopped it cold. But he wasn't done. As the captain headed for the gangplank, Calvin sent his bug to seek out all the nearby rats that he could sense lurking under the wharf and among the crates and barrels and on the other ships. By the time the captain got halfway down the gangplank, a couple of dozen rats were racing up the very same bridge, heading for the ship. The captain tried in vain to shoo them back, but Calvin had filled them with courage and grim determination to reach the deck—food, food, Calvin was promising them—and they merely dodged and went on. Dozens more were streaming across the planking of the pier, and the captain was fairly dancing to avoid tripping on rats and falling on his face. On deck, sailors with mops and bowling pins were striking at the rats, trying to knock or sweep them off into the sea.

Then, as suddenly as he had launched the rats, Calvin sent them a new message: Get off this ship. Fire, fire. Leaks. Drowning. Fear.

Squealing and scurrying, all the rats that he had sent aboard came rushing back down the gangplank and all the lines and cables connecting the ship to the shore. And all the rats that had already been aboard, lurking in the cargo hold and in the dark wet cellar and in the hidden caves in the joints and beams of the ship, they also gushed up out of the hatches and portholes like water bubbling out of a new spring. The captain stopped cold to watch them leave. Finally, when all the rat traffic had disappeared into their hiding places on the wharf and the other ships, the captain turned toward Calvin and strode to him. Through it all the man had never lost his dignity—even while dancing to avoid the rats. My kind of man, thought Calvin. I must watch him to learn how gentlemen behave.

"How did you know there was a leak on my ship?" asked the captain.

"You're an Englishman," said Calvin. "You don't believe in what I can see and do."

"Nevertheless, I believe in what *I* can see, and there was nothing natural about that leak."

"I'd say them rats might have been doing it. Good thing for you they all left your ship."

"Rats and leaks," said the captain. "What do you want, boy?"

"I want to be called a man, sir," said Calvin. "Not a boy."

"Why do you wish harm to me and my ship? Has someone of my crew done you an offense?"

"I don't know what you're talking about," said Calvin. "I reckon you're not such a fool as to blame the one as told you you had a leak."

"I'm also not such a fool as to think you knew of anything you didn't have the power to cause or cure at will. Were the rats your doing as well?"

"I was as surprised as you were by their behavior," said Calvin. "Didn't seem natural, all them rats rushing *onto* a sinking ship. But then they seemed to come to their senses and leave again. Every single rat, I daresay. Now, that would be an interesting voyage, wouldn't it—to cross the ocean without any loss of your food supply to the nibbling of rats."

"What do you want from me?" asked the captain.

"I stopped to do you a favor, with no thought of benefit to my own self," said Calvin, trying to sound like an educated Englishman and knowing from the expression on the captain's face that he was failing pathetically. "But it happens that I am in need of first-class passage to Europe."

The captain smiled thinly. "Why in the world would you want to book passage on a leaking ship?"

"But sir," said Calvin, "I've got a sort of knack for spotting leaks. And I can promise you that if I were aboard your ship, during the whole voyage there'd be not a single leak, even in the stoutest storm." Calvin had no idea whether he could keep a ship tight during all the stresses of a storm at sea, but odds were that he'd never have to find out, either.

"Correct me if I'm wrong," said the captain, "but am I to guess that if I take you on my ship, first class, without your paying a farthing, I'll find no problem with leaks and not a rat on my ship? While if I refuse, I'll find my ship at the bottom of the harbor?"

"That would be a rare disaster," said Calvin. "How could such a well-made ship possibly sink faster than your boys could pump?"

"I saw how the leak moved from place to place. I saw how strangely the rats behaved. I may not believe in your American knacks, but I know when I'm in the presence of unaccountable power."

Calvin felt pride flush through his body like ale.

Suddenly he felt the barrel of a pistol just under his breastbone. He looked down to see that the captain had somehow come up with a weapon.

"What's to stop me from blowing a hole in your belly?" asked the captain.

"The likelihood of your dancing on the end of an American rope," said Calvin. "There ain't no law against knacks here, sir, and saying that somebody was doing witchery ain't cause enough to kill him the way it is in England."

"But it's to England you're going," said the captain. "What's to stop me from taking you on my ship, then having you arrested the moment you step ashore?"

"Nothing," said Calvin. "You could do that. You could even kill me in my sleep during the voyage and cast my body overboard into the sea, telling all the others that you had to dispose of the body of a plague victim as quickly as possible. You think I'm a fool, not to think of that stuff?"

"So go away and leave me and my ship alone."

"If you killed me, what would keep the planks from pulling free of the beams of your boat? What would stop your boat from turning into scraps of lumber bobbing on the water?"

The captain eyed him curiously.

"First-class passage is ludicrous for you. The other first-class passengers would snub you at once, and no doubt they'd assume I'd brought you aboard as my catamite. It would ruin my career anyway, to permit an uncouth, unlettered ruffian like you to sail among my gentle passengers. To put it plainly, young master, you may have power over rats and planks, but you have none over rich men and women."

"Teach me," said Calvin.

"There aren't enough hours in the day or days in the week."

"Teach me," said Calvin again.

"You come here threatening me with destruction of my ship by the evil powers of Satan, and then dare to ask me to teach you to be a gentleman?"

"If you believed my powers were from the devil," said Calvin, "then why didn't you once say a prayer to ward me off?"

The captain glared at him for a moment, then smiled, grimly but not without genuine mirth. "Touché," he said.

"Whatever the devil *that* means," said Calvin.

"It's a fencing term," said the captain.

"I must've put up ten miles of fences in my life," said Calvin. "Post and rail, stone, wire, and picket, every kind, and I never heard of no tooshay."

The captain's smile broadened. "There is something attractive in your challenge. You may have some interesting . . . what do you call them . . . knacks? But you're still a poor boy from the farm. I've taken many a peasant lad and turned him into a first-rate seaman. But I've never taken a boy who wasn't a gentleman born and turned him into something that could pass for civilized."

"Consider me the challenge of your life."

"Oh, believe me, I already do. I haven't altogether decided not to kill you, of course. But it seems to me that since you mean to cause me trouble anyway, why not accept the challenge and see if I can work a miracle just as inexplicable and impossible as any of the nasty pranks you've played on me this morning?"

"First class, not steerage," Calvin insisted.

The captain shook his head. "Neither one. You'll travel as my cabin boy. Or rather, my cabin boy's boy. Rafe is a good three years younger than you, I imagine, but he knows from birth all that you are so desperate to learn. With you to help him, perhaps he'll have enough free time to teach you. And I'll oversee you both. On several conditions, though."

Calvin didn't see as how the captain was in much of a position to set conditions, but he listened civil-like all the same.

"No matter what powers you have, survival at sea depends on instant and perfect obedience from everyone on board the ship. Obedience to *me*. You know nothing of the sea and I gather you don't care about learning seamanship, either. So you will do nothing that interferes with my authority. And you will obey me yourself. That means that when I say piss, you don't even look for a pot, you just whip it out and pee."

"In front of others, I'll do a fine show of obedience, unless you command me to kill myself or some such foolishness."

"I'm not a fool," said the captain.

"All right, I'll do like you say."

"And you'll keep your mouth shut until you learn—in *private*— to talk in some way approximating gentlemanly speech. Right now if you open your mouth you confess your low origins and you will embarrass yourself and me in front of my crew and the other officers and passengers."

"I know how to keep my mouth shut when I need to."

"And when you reach England, our deal is done and you leave no curse on my ship."

"Now you've asked too much," said Calvin. "What I need is your introduction to other high-class people. And passage to France."

"To France! Aren't you aware that England is at war with France?"

"You *have* been ever since Napoleon conquered Austria and Spain. What's that to me?"

"In other words, reaching England doesn't mean I'll be rid of you."

"That's right," said Calvin.

"So why don't I just kill myself now and spare myself all this adventure before you send me to an early grave?"

"Because them as is my friends will prosper in this world and there ain't nothing much bad that can happen to them."

"And all I have to do is maintain my status as your friend, is that it?"

Calvin nodded.

"But someday, isn't it going to occur to you that if the only reason I'm kind to you is out of terror that you'll destroy my ship, I'm not really your friend at all?"

Calvin smiled. "That just means you'll have to try extra hard to convince me that you really mean it."

The officer who had first heard Calvin's message now approached the captain diffidently. "Captain Fitzroy," he said. "The leaking seems to have stopped, sir."

"I know," said the captain.

"Thank you sir," said the officer.

"Get everyone back to work, Benson," said the captain.

"Some of the American stevedores and sailors won't get back on that ship no matter what we say, sir."

"Pay them off and hire others," said the captain. "That will be all, Benson."

"Yes sir." Benson turned around and headed back toward the gangplank.

Calvin, in the meantime, had heard the air of crisp command in Captain Fitzroy's voice and wondered how a man could learn to use his voice like a sharp hot knife, slicing through other men's will like warm butter.

"I would say you've already caused me more trouble than you're worth," said Captain Fitzroy. "And I personally doubt that you have it in you to learn to be a gentleman, though heaven knows there are plenty that have the title who are every bit as ignorant and boorish as you. But I will accept your coercive agreement, in part because I find you fascinating as well as despicable."

"I don't know what all them words mean, Captain Fitzroy, but

I know this—Taleswapper once told us how when kings have bastards, the babies get the last name 'Fitzroy.' So no matter what I am, your name says you're a son of a bitch."

"In my case, the great-great-grandson of a bitch. The second Charles sowed his wild oats. My great-great-grandmother, a noted actress of semi-noble origins, entered into a liaison with him and managed to get her child recognized as royal before the parliament deprived him of his head. My family has had its ups and downs since the end of the monarchy, and there have been Lords Protector who thought that our association with the royal family made us dangerous. But we managed to survive and even, in recent years, prosper. Unfortunately, I'm the younger son of a younger son, so I had the choice of the church or the army or the sea. Until meeting you, I did not regret my choice. Do you have a name, my young extortionist?"

"Calvin," he said.

"And are you of such a benighted family that you have but the one name to spend as your patrimony?"

"Maker," said Calvin. "Calvin Maker."

"How deliciously vague. Maker. A general term that can be construed in many ways while promising no particular skill. A Calvin of all trades. And master of none?"

"Master of rats," said Calvin, smiling. "And leaks."

"As we have seen," said Captain Fitzroy. "I will have your name enrolled as part of the ship's company. Have your gear aboard by nightfall."

"If you have someone follow me to kill me, your ship—"

"Will dissolve into sawdust, yes, the threat has already been made," said Fitzroy. "Now you only have to worry about how much I actually care for my ship."

With that, Fitzroy turned his back on Calvin and headed up the gangplank. Calvin almost made him slip and take a pratfall, just to pierce that dignity. But there was a limit, he knew, to how far he could push this man. Especially since Calvin hadn't the slightest idea how to carry out his threat to make the ship fall apart if they killed him. Either he could make the ship leak or stop leaking, but either way he had to be there and alive to do it. If Fitzroy ever realized that his worst threats were pure bluff, how long would he let Calvin live?

Get used to it, Calvin, he told himself. Plenty of people have wanted Alvin dead, too, but he got through it all. We Makers must have some kind of protection, it's as simple as that. All of nature is looking out for us, to keep us safe. Fitzroy won't kill me because I can't be killed.

I hope.

8

Leavetaking

For some reason Alvin's classroom of grownup women just wasn't going well today. They were distracted, it seemed like, and Goody Sump was downright hostile. It finally came to a head when Alvin started working with their herb boxes. He was trying to help them find their way into the greensong, the first faintest melody, by getting their sage or sorrel or thyme, whatever herb they chose, to grow one specially long branch. This was something Alvin reckoned to be fairly easy, but once you mastered it, you could pretty much get into harmony with any plant. However, only a couple of the women had had much success, and Goody Sump was not one of them. Maybe that was how come she was so testy—her laurel wasn't even thriving, let alone showing lopsided growth on one branch.

"The plants don't make the same music they did back when the Reds were tending the woods," Alvin said. He was going to go on and explain how they could do, in a small way, what the Reds did large, but he didn't get a chance, because that was the moment Goody Sump chose to erupt.

She leapt from her chair, strode over to the herb table, and brought her fist right down on top of her own laurel, capsizing the pot and spattering potting soil and laurel leaves all over the table and her own dress. "If you think them Reds was so much better why don't you just go live with *them* and carry off *their* daughters to secret randy views!"

Alvin was so stunned by her unprovoked rage, so perplexed by her inscrutable words, that he just looked at her gape-mouthed as she pulled what was left of her laurel out of what was left of the soil, pulled off a handful of leaves, and threw them in his face, then turned and stalked out of the room.

As soon as she was gone, Alvin tried to make a joke out of it. "I reckon there's some folks as don't take natural to agriculture." But hardly anybody laughed.

"You got to overlook her behavior, Al," said Sylvy Godshadow. "A mother's got to believe her own daughter, even if everybody else knows she's spinning moonbeams."

Since Goody Sump had five daughters, and Alvin had heard nothing significant about any of them lately, this information wasn't much help. "Is Goody Sump having some trouble at home?" he asked.

The women all looked around at each other, but not a one would meet his eyes.

"Well, it looks to me like everybody here knows somewhat as hasn't yet found its way to my ears," said Alvin. "Anybody mind explaining?"

"We're not gossips," said Sylvy Godshadow. "I'm surprised you'd think to accuse us." With that, she stood up and started for the door.

"But I didn't call nobody a gossip," said Alvin.

"Alvin, I think before you criticize others, you'd comb the lice out of your own hair," said Nana Pease. And she was up and off, too.

"Well, what are the rest of you waiting for?" said Alvin. "If you all wanted a day off of class, you only had to ask. It's a sure thing *I'm* done for the day."

Before he could even get started sweeping up the spilt soil, the other ladies had all flounced out.

Alvin tried to console himself by muttering things he'd heard his own father mutter now and then over the years, things like "Women" and "Can't do nothing to please 'em" and "Might as well shoot yourself first thing in the morning." But none of that helped, because this *wasn't* just some normal display of temper. These were levelheaded ladies, every one of them, and here they were up in arms over plain nothing, which wasn't natural.

It wasn't till afternoon that Alvin realized something serious was wrong. A couple of months ago, Alvin had asked Clevy Sump, Goody Sump's husband, to teach them all how to make a simple one-valve suction pump. It was part of Alvin's idea to teach folks that making is making, and everybody ought to know everything they can possibly learn. Alvin was teaching them hidden powers of Making, but they ought to be learning how to make with their hands as well. Secretly Alvin also hoped that when they saw how tricky and careful it was to make fine machinery like Clevy Sump did, they'd realize that what Alvin was teaching wasn't much harder if it was harder at all. And it was working well enough.

Except that today, after the noon bread and cheese, he went on out to the mill to find the men gathered around the wreckage of the pumps they'd been making. Every one of them was broke in pieces. And since the fittings were all metal, it must have took some serious work to break it all up. "Who'd do a thing like this?" Alvin asked. "There's a lot of hate goes into something like *this*." And thinking of hate, it made Alvin wonder if maybe Calvin hadn't come back secretly after all.

"There's no mystery who done it," said Winter Godshadow. "I reckon we ain't got us a pump-making teacher no more."

"Yep," said Taleswapper. "This looks like a specially thorough way of telling us, 'Class dismissed.' "

Some of the men chuckled. But Alvin could see that he wasn't the only one angry at the destruction. After all, these pumps were nearly completed, and all these men had put serious work into making them. They counted on them at their own houses. For many of them, it meant the end of drawing water, and Winter Godshadow in particular had got him a plan to pipe the water right into the kitchen, so his wife wouldn't even have to go outdoors to fetch it. Now their work was undone, and some of them weren't taking kindly to it.

"Let me talk to Clevy Sump about this," said Alvin. "I can't hardly believe it was him, but if it was, whatever's the problem I bet it can be set to rights. I don't want none of you getting angry at him before he's had his say."

"We ain't angry at *Clevy*," said Nils Torson, a burly Swede. His heavy-lidded gaze made it clear who he *was* angry at.

"Me?" said Alvin. "You think *I* done this?" Then, as if he

could hear Miss Larner's voice in his ear, he corrected himself: "*Did this?*"

Murmurs from several of the men assented to the proposition.

"Are you crazy? Why would I go to all this trouble? I'm not an Unmaker, boys, you know that, but if I was, don't you think I could tear up these pumps a lot more thoroughly without taking half so much trouble?"

Taleswapper cleared his throat. "Perhaps you and I ought to talk alone about this, Alvin."

"They're accusing me of wrecking all their hard work and it ain't so!" said Alvin.

"Ain't nobody accusin' nobody of nothin'," said Winter Godshadow. "God follows all. God sees all deeds."

Usually when Winter got into his God-talking moods, the others would sort of back off and pretend to be busy paring their nails or something. But not this time—this time they were nodding and murmuring their agreement.

"Like I said, Alvin, let's you and me have a word. In fact, I think we ought to go on up to the house and talk to your father and mother."

"Talk to me right here," said Alvin. "I'm not some little boy to be taken out behind the woodshed and given a licking in private. If I stand accused of something that everybody knows about except me . . ."

"We ain't accusing," said Nils. "We're pondering."

"Pondering," echoed a couple of the others.

"Tell me here and now what you're pondering," said Alvin. "Because whatever I'm accused of, if it's true I want to make it right, and if it's false I want to set it straight."

They looked at each other back and forth, until finally Alvin turned to Taleswapper. "*You* tell me."

"I only repeat tales that I believe to be true," said Taleswapper. "And this one I believe to be a flat-out lie told by a dreamy-hearted girl."

"Girl? What girl?" and then, putting together Goody Sump's behavior and what Clevy Sump had done to the pumps, and remembering the dreamy expression in one girl's eyes when she sat there in the children's class paying no intelligent attention to a thing that Alvin said, he jumped to a certain conclusion and whispered her name. "Amy."

To Alvin's consternation, some of the men took the fact that he came up with her name as proof that Amy was telling the truth about whatever it was she had said. "See?" they murmured. "See?"

"I'm done with this," said Nils. "I'm done. I'm a farmer. Corn and hogs, that's my knack if I have me any." When he left, several other men went with him.

Alvin turned to the others. "I *don't* know what I'm accused of, but I can promise you this, I've done nothing wrong. In the meantime, it's plain there's no use in holding class today, so let's all go home. I reckon there's a way to salvage every one of these pumps, so your work isn't lost. We'll get back to it tomorrow."

As they left, some of the men touched Alvin's shoulder or punched his arm to show their support. But some of the support was of a kind he didn't much like. "Can't hardly blame you, pretty little calf-eyed thing like that." "Women is always reading more into things than a man means."

Finally Alvin was alone with Taleswapper.

"Don't look at me," said Taleswapper. "Let's go on up to the house and see if your father's heard the stories yet."

When they got there, it was like a family council was already in session. Measure, Armor-of-God, and Father and Mother were all gathered around the kitchen table. Arthur Stuart was kneading dough—small as he was, he was good with bread and liked doing it, so Mother had finally given in and admitted that a woman could still be mistress of her own house even if somebody else made the bread.

"Glad you're here, Al," said Measure. "You'd think a piece of silliness like this would just get laughed out of town. I mean, these folks should *know* you."

"Why should they?" asked Mother. "He's been gone most of the past seven years. When he left he was a scrub-size boy who'd just spent a year running around the countryside with a Red warrior. When he come back he was full of power and majesty and scared the pellets out of all the bunny-hearts around here. What do they know of his character?"

"Would somebody please tell me what this is *about*?" Alvin said.

"You mean they haven't?" asked Father. "They were powerful quick to tell your mother and Measure and Armor-of-God."

Taleswapper chuckled. "Of course they didn't tell Alvin. Those who believe the tale assume he already knows. And those who don't believe it are plain ashamed that anyone could say such silly slander."

Measure sighed. "Amy Sump told her friend Ramona, and Ramona told her mama, and her mama went straight to Goody Sump, and she went straight to her husband, and he like to went crazy because he can't conceive that every male creature larger than a mouse isn't hottin' up after his nubian daughter."

"Nubile," Alvin corrected him.

"Yeah yeah," said Measure. "I know, you're the one who reads the books, and now's *sure* the time to correct my grammar."

"Nubians are Black Africans," said Alvin. "And Amy ain't no Black near as I can figure."

"This might be a good time to shut up and listen," said Measure.

"Yes *sir*," said Alvin.

"If only you had left when that torch girl sent you that warning," said Mother. "It's a plain fool who stays inside a burning house because he wants to see the color of the flames."

"What's Amy saying about me?" asked Alvin.

"Pure nonsense," said Father. "About you running off in the Red way, a hundred miles in a night through the woods, taking her to a secret lake where you swum nekkid and other such indecencies."

"With *Amy*?" asked Alvin, incredulous.

"Meaning that you'd do it with someone else?" asked Measure.

"I'd do such a thing with nobody," said Alvin. "Ain't decent, and besides, there ain't enough unbroken living forest these days to *get* a hundred miles in a night. I can't make half so good a speed through fields and farms. The greensong gets noisy and busted up and I get too tired trying to hear it and *why* is anybody believing such silliness?"

"Because they think you can do anything," said Measure.

"And because a good number of these men have noticed Amy filling out of late," said Armor-of-God, "and they know that if *they* had the power, and if Amy was as moony toward them as she plainly is toward you, they'd have her naked in a lake in two seconds flat."

"You're too cynical about human nature," said Taleswapper. "Most of these fellows are the wishing kind. But they know Alvin is a doer, not just a wisher."

"I hardly noticed her except to think she was sure slow to learn, considering how tight she seemed to pay attention," said Alvin.

"To *you* she was paying attention. Not to what you said or taught," said Measure.

"Well it ain't so. I didn't do anything to her or with her, and . . ."

"And even if you did it would be plain disaster if you married her," said Mother.

"*Married* her!" cried Alvin.

"Well of course if it was true, you'd have to marry her," said Father.

"But it *ain't* true."

"You got any witnesses of that?" asked Measure.

"Witnesses of what? How can I have witnesses that it didn't happen? Everybody's my witness—everybody didn't see any such thing."

"But she says it happened," said Measure. "And you're the only other one who knows whether she's lying or not. So either she's a plain liar and you're innocently accused, or she's a brokenhearted lied-to seduced girl and you're the cad who got the use of her and now won't do the decent thing, and nobody can prove either way."

"So *you* don't even believe me?"

"Of course we believe you," said Father. "Do you think we're insane? But our believing you ain't any kind of evidence. Measure's been reading law, and he explained it to us."

"Law?" asked Alvin.

"Well, afore you come home from Hatrack River, anyway. And now and then since. I reckon somebody in the family ought to know something about the law."

"But you mean you think this might come to court?"

"Might," said Measure. "That's what the Sumps were saying. Get them a lawyer from Carthage City instead of one of the frontier lawyers as has a shingle out here in Vigor Church. Lots of publicity."

"But they can't convict me of anything!"

"Breach of promise. Indecent liberties with a child. All depends on how many jurors think that where there's smoke, there's fire."

"Indecent liberties with a . . ."

"That one's a hanging offense, all right," said Measure. "But I hear that's the charge that Clevy wants to bring."

"Doesn't matter if they convict you or not," said Taleswapper.

"Matters to *me*," said Mother.

"Either way, the tale will spread. Alvin the so-called Maker, taking advantage of young girls. You can't let this go to trial," said Taleswapper.

Alvin saw at once how such rumors, such publicity as a trial would bring, it would bring down his work, make it impossible to attract others to come and learn Making at Vigor Church.

Not that he was doing much good teaching Making anyway.

"Miss Larner," murmured Alvin.

"Yep," said Taleswapper. "She warned you. Leave now freely, or leave later because you have to."

"Why should he be driven from his own home just because a horny lying little . . ." Mother's voice trailed off.

Alvin sat in the ensuing silence, recognizing his foolishness. "I spose I'm a plain fool for not heeding Miss Larner." And then, stiffening his back, he closed his eyes and said, "There's another way. So I don't have to leave at all."

"What's that?" asked Measure.

"I could marry her."

"No!" cried Mother and Father at once.

"Why not just sign a confession?" asked Armor-of-God.

"You can't marry her," said Measure.

"It's what she wants," said Alvin. "You can bet she'd say yes, and her father and mother would have to agree to it."

"Agree to it—and then despise you ever after," said Father.

"Doesn't matter about his reputation or what people think of him or anything, compared to this," said Measure. "Waking up every morning and seeing Amy Sump in bed next to you, and knowing the only reason she's there is because she slandered you—tell me what kind of home you'll make, the two of you, for your babies?"

Alvin thought about that for a moment and nodded. "I guess marriage ain't much of a solution. More like starting a whole new set of problems."

"Ah, good," said Father. "I was afraid we'd raised us a fool."

"So I sneak off like a thief, and everybody reckons Amy was telling the truth and I ran off."

"Not likely," said Measure. "We'll let it be known that you left because your work is too important to be distracted by this nonsense. You'll be back when Amy starts telling the truth, and in the meantime, you'll be studying up on . . . whatever. Learning something."

"Learning how to build the Crystal City," murmured Taleswapper.

They all looked at him.

"You don't know how, do you, Alvin?" asked Taleswapper. "While you're busy trying to make Makers out of these people, you don't even know yourself what the Crystal City really is, or how to make it.''

Alvin nodded. ''That's right.''

''So . . . it isn't even a lie,'' said Taleswapper. ''You *do* have much to learn, and you're overdue to learn it. Why, you're even grateful to Amy for showing you that you've been hanging around here far too long. Measure's been learning right good. He's far enough ahead of the others that he can go on teaching in your absence. And him being a married man, no schoolgirl's going to get some foolish notion about *him*.''

''I don't know,'' said Measure. ''I'm pretty cute.''

''You have my bags packed yet, Taleswapper?'' asked Alvin.

''Ain't as if you need much luggage,'' said Taleswapper. ''You're going to be traveling small and fast. I reckon there's only one burden that will weigh you down much. A certain farm implement.''

''I couldn't leave it here?'' asked Alvin.

''Not safe,'' said Taleswapper. ''Not safe for your family, to have the rumor get about that the Maker is gone but he left the golden plow behind.''

''Not safe for *him* to have the rumor say he took it with him,'' said Mother.

''Nobody on this planet is safer than Alvin, if he wants to be,'' said Measure.

''So I just pick up the plow, put it in a gunnysack, and head on out?'' asked Alvin.

''That's about the best plan,'' said Armor-of-God. ''Though I bet your ma will insist on you taking some salt pork with you, and a change of clothes.''

''And me.''

They all turned to the source of the small piping voice.

''He's taking me with him,'' said Arthur Stuart.

''You'd only slow him down, boy,'' said Father. ''You got a good heart, but short legs.''

''He ain't in no hurry,'' said Arthur, ''specially figuring as he don't know where he's going.''

''The point is you'd be in the way,'' said Armor-of-God. ''He'd always have to be thinking of you, trying to keep you out of harm's way. There's plenty of places in this land where a free half-Black boy is going to get folks' dander up, and that won't be much help to Alvin either.''

''You're talking like you think you got a choice,'' said Arthur.

"But if Alvin goes, I go, and that's it. You can lock me in a closet, but someday I'll get out and then I'll follow him and find him or die trying."

They all looked at him in consternation. Arthur Stuart had been near silent since coming to Vigor after his adopted mother was murdered back in Hatrack River. Silent but hardworking, cooperative, obedient. This was a complete surprise, this attitude from him.

"And besides," said Arthur Stuart, "while Alvin's busy looking after the whole world, I'll be there to look after *him*."

"I think the boy should go," said Measure. "The Unmaker plainly ain't done with Alvin yet. He needs somebody to watch his back. I think Arthur's got it in him."

And that was pretty much it. Nobody could size up a fellow like Measure could.

Alvin walked to the hearth and pried up four stones. Nobody would have guessed that anything was hid under them, because until he raised the stones there wasn't so much as a crack in the mortar. He didn't dig in the earth under the stones; the plow was buried eight feet deep, and shoveling would have taken all day, not to mention the dismantling of the entire hearth. No, he just held out his hands and called to the plow, and willed the earth to float it up to him. A moment later, the plow bobbed to the surface of the soil like a cork on a still pond. Alvin could hear a couple of sharp breaths behind him—it still got to folks, even his own family, when he showed his knack so openly. Also, the gold had such a luster to it. As if, even in the pitch black of the darkest moonless stormy night, that plow would still be visible, the gold burning its way even through your closed eyelids to imprint its shining life straight onto your eyes, straight into your brain. The plow trembled under Alvin's hand.

"We got us a journey to take," Alvin murmured to the warm gold. "And maybe along the way we'll figure out what I made you for."

An hour later, Alvin stood at the back door of the house. Not that it took him an hour to pack—he'd spent most of the time down at the mill, fixing the pumps. Nor had he spent any of the time on farewells. They hadn't even sent word to any of the family that he was going, because word would get out and the last thing Alvin needed was for folks to be lying in wait for him when he headed into the forest. Mother and Father and Measure and Armor would have to carry his words of love and Godblessyou to his brothers and sisters and nieces and nephews.

Alvin hitched the bag with the plow and his change of clothes in it over his shoulder. Arthur Stuart took his other hand. Alvin scanned the hexes he'd laid in place around the house and made sure they were still perfect in their sixness, undisturbed by wind or meddling. All was in order. It was the only thing he could do for his family in his absence, was to keep wardings about to fend off danger.

"Don't you worry about Amy, neither," said Measure. "Soon as you're gone, she'll notice some other strapping boy and pretty soon the dreams and stories will be about *him* and folks'll realize that you never done nothing wrong."

"Hope you're right," said Alvin. "Because I don't intend to stay away for long."

Those words hung in the silence for a moment, because they all knew it was quite possible that this time Alvin might be gone for good. Might never come home. It was a dangerous world, and the Unmaker had plainly gone to some trouble to get Alvin out of here and onto the road.

He kissed and hugged all around, taking care not to let the heavy plow smack into anybody. And then he was off for the woods behind the house, sauntering so as to give anyone watching him the impression that this was just a casual errand he was on, and not some life-changing escape. Arthur Stuart had ahold of his left hand again. And to Alvin's surprise, Taleswapper fell into step right beside him.

"You coming with me, then?" asked Alvin.

"Not far," said Taleswapper. "Just to talk a minute."

"Glad to have you," said Alvin.

"I just wondered if you've given any thought to finding Peggy Larner," said Taleswapper.

"Not even for a second," said Alvin.

"What, are you mad at her? Hell, boy, if you'd just listened to her . . ."

"You think I don't know that? You think I haven't been thinking of that this whole time?"

"I'm just saying that you two was on the verge of marrying back there in Hatrack River, and you could do with a good wife, and she's the best you'll ever find."

"Since when do you meddle?" asked Alvin. "I thought you just collected stories. I didn't think you made them happen."

"I was afraid you'd be angry at her like this."

"I'm not angry at her. I'm angry at myself."

"Alvin, you think I don't know a lie when I hear it?"

"All right, I *am* angry. She knew, right? Well, why didn't she just *tell* me? Amy Sump is going to tell lies about you and force you to leave, so get out now before her childish imaginings ruin everything.''

"Because if she said that, you wouldn't have left, would you, Alvin? You would have stayed, figuring you could make everything work out fine with Amy. Why, you would have taken her aside and told her not to love you, right? And *then* when she started talking about you, there'd be witnesses who remembered how she stayed after class one day and was alone with you, and then you *would* be in trouble because even *more* people would believe her story and—''

"Taleswapper, I wish you sometime would learn the knack of shutting up!''

"Sorry," said Taleswapper. "I just don't have any gift for that. I just blather on, annoying people. The fact is that Peggy told you as much as she could without making things worse.''

"That's right. In her judgment, she decided how much I was entitled to know, and that's all she told me. And then you have the gall to tell me I should go *marry* her?''

"I'm not following your logic here, Al," said Taleswapper.

"What kind of marriage is it, when my wife knows *everything* but she never tells me enough to make up my own mind! Instead she always makes up my mind for me. Or tells me exactly what she needs to tell me in order to get me to do what *she* thinks I ought to do.''

"But you didn't do what she said you ought to do. You stuck around.''

"So that's the life you want for me? Either to obey my wife in everything, or wish I had!''

Taleswapper shrugged. "I'm still not getting your objection.''

"It's this simple: A grownup man doesn't want to be married to his mother. He wants to make his own decisions.''

"I'm sure you're right," said Taleswapper. "And who's this grownup man you're talking about?''

Alvin refused to be baited. "I hope someday it's me. But it'll never be me if I tie myself to a torch. I owe much to Miss Larner. And I owe even more to the girl she was before she became a teacher, the girl who watched over me and saved my life again and again. No wonder I loved her. But marrying her would have been the worst mistake of my life. It would have made me weak. Dependent. My knack might have remained in my hands, but it would be entirely at her service, and that's no way for a man to live.''

"A *grownup* man, you mean.''

"Mock me all you want, Taleswapper. I notice *you* got no wife."

"I must be a grownup, then," said Taleswapper. But now there was an edge to his voice, and after gazing at Alvin for just another moment, he turned and walked back the way they'd come together.

"I never seen Taleswapper mad like that before," said Arthur Stuart.

"He doesn't like it when folks throw his own advice back in his face," said Alvin.

Arthur Stuart said nothing. Just waited.

"All right, let's go."

At once Arthur turned and started walking.

"Well, wait for me," said Alvin.

"Why?" said Arthur Stuart. "You don't know where we're going, either."

"Reckon not, but I'm bigger, so I get to choose which nowhere we head for."

Arthur laughed a little. "I bet there's not a single direction you can choose where there isn't *somebody* standing in your road, somewhere. Even if it's halfway around the world."

"I don't know about that," said Alvin. "But I know for sure that no matter which way we go, eventually we'll run into the ocean. Can you swim?"

"Not an ocean's worth I can't."

"So what good are *you*, then?" said Alvin. "I was counting on you to tow me across."

Hand in hand they plunged deeper into the woods. And even though Alvin didn't know where he was going, he did know this: The greensong might be weak and jumbled these days, but it was still there, and he couldn't help but fall into it and start moving in perfect harmony with the greenwood. The twigs leaned out of his way; the leaves were soft under his feet, and soon he was soundless, leaving no trail behind him and making no disturbance as he went.

That night they camped on the shore of Lake Mizogan. If you could call it camping, since they made no fire and built no shelter. They broke out of the woods late in the afternoon and stood there on the shore. Alvin remembered being at this lake—not quite this spot, but not far off either—when Tenskwa-Tawa had called a whirlwind and cut his feet and walked out on the bloody water, taking Alvin with him, drawing him up into the whirlwind and showing him visions. It was then that Alvin first saw the Crystal City and knew that he would build it someday, or rather rebuild it, since it

had existed once before, or maybe more than once. But the storm
was gone, a distant memory; Tenskwa-Tawa and his people were
gone, too, most of them dead and the rest of them in the west. Now
it was just a lake.

Once Alvin would have been afraid of the water, for it was water
that the Unmaker had used to try to kill him, over and over, when
he was a child. But that was before Alvin grew into his knack and
became a true Maker that night in the forge, turning iron into gold.
The Unmaker couldn't touch him through water anymore. No, the
Unmaker's tool would be more subtle now. It would be people.
People like Amy Sump, weak-willed or greedy or dreamy or lazy,
but all of them easily used. It was people who held danger for him
now. Water was safe enough, for them as could swim, and that was
Alvin.

"How about a dip in the water?" Alvin asked.

Arthur shrugged. It was when they dipped together in the water
of the Hio that the last traces of Arthur's old self got washed away.
But there'd be none of that now. They just stripped down and swam
in the lake as the sun set, then lay down in the grass to dry off, the
moonlight making the water shine, a breeze making the humid air
cool enough for sleeping. In the whole journey they hadn't said a
word till they got to the shore of the lake, just moved in perfect
harmony through the wood; even now as they swam, they still said
nothing, and hardly splashed they were so much in harmony with
everything, with each other. So it startled Alvin when Arthur spoke
to him, lying there in the dark.

"This is what Amy dreamed of, ain't it?"

Alvin thought of that for a moment. Then he got up and put on
his clothes. "I reckon we're dry now," he said.

"You think maybe she had a true dream? Only it wasn't her, it
was me?"

"I didn't do no hugging or unnatural things when we was naked
in the water," said Alvin.

Arthur laughed. "Ain't nothin' unnatural about what *she*
dreamed of."

"It wasn't no true dream."

Arthur got up and put his clothes on, too. "I heard the greensong
this time, Alvin. Three times I let go of your hand, and I still heard
it for the longest time before it started fading and I had to catch
your hand or get left behind."

Alvin nodded as if that was what he expected. But it wasn't. In
all his teaching of the folks of Vigor Church, he hadn't even *tried*

to teach Arthur Stuart much, sending him instead to the schoolhouse to learn reading and ciphering. But it was Arthur who might well be his best student after all.

"You going to become a Maker?" asked Alvin.

Arthur shook his head. "Not me," he said. "Just going to be your friend."

Alvin didn't say aloud the thought of his heart: To be my friend, you might just have to be a Maker. He didn't have to say it. Arthur already understood.

The wind rose a little in the night, and far away, out over the lake, lightning brightened the underside of distant clouds. Arthur breathed softly in his sleep; Alvin could hear him in the stillness, louder than the whisper of distant thunder. It should have made him feel lonely, but it didn't. The breaths in the darkness beside him could have been Ta-Kumsaw on their long journey so many years ago, when Alvin had been called the Boy Renegado and the fate of the world seemed to hang in the balance. Or it might have been his brother Calvin when as boys they shared a room; Alvin remembered him as a baby in a cradle, then in a crib, the child's eyes looking up to him as if he were God, as if he knew something no other human knew. Well, I did know it, but I lost Calvin anyway. And I saved Ta-Kumsaw's life, but couldn't do a thing to save his cause, and he is lost to me also, across the river in the fog of the Red west.

And the breathing could have been a wife, instead of just a dream of a wife. Alvin tried to imagine Amy Sump there in the darkness, and even though Measure was right that it would have been a miserable marriage, the fact was that her face was pretty, and in this moment of solitary wakefulness Alvin could imagine that her young body was sweet and warm to the touch, her kiss eager and full of life and hope.

Quickly he shrugged off that image. Amy was not for him, and even to imagine her like that felt akin to some kind of awful crime. He could never marry someone who worshipped him. Because his wife would not be married to the Maker named Alvin; his wife would be married to the man.

It was Peggy Larner he thought of then. He imagined leaning up on one elbow and looking at her when the low distant lightning cast a brush of light across her face. Her hair loose and tousled in the grass. Her ladylike hands no longer controlled and graceful with studied gestures, but now casually flung out in sleep.

To his surprise tears came to his eyes. In a moment he realized why: She was as impossible for him as Amy, not because she would worship him, but because she was more committed to his cause than he was. She loved, not the Maker, and certainly not the man, but rather the Making and the thing made. To marry her would be a kind of surrender to fate, for she was the one who saw futures that might arise out of all possible present choices, and if he married her he would be no man at all, not because she would mean to unman him, but because he himself would not be so stupid as not to follow her advice. Freely he would follow her, and thus freely lose his freedom.

No, it was Arthur lying there beside him, this strange boy who loved Alvin beyond all reason and yet demanded nothing from him; this boy who had lost a part of himself in order to be free, and had replaced it with a part of Alvin.

The parallel was suddenly obvious to Alvin, and for a moment he was ashamed. I did to Arthur just what I fear that Peggy Larner might do to me. I took away a part of him and replaced it with myself. Only he was so young and his danger so great that I didn't ask him or explain, nor could he have understood me if I tried. He had no choice. I still have one.

Would I be as content as Arthur, if once I gave myself to Peggy?

Perhaps someday, Alvin thought. But not now. I'm not ready yet to give myself to someone, to surrender my will. The way Arthur has to me. The way parents do to their children, giving their lives over to the needs of helpless selfish little ones. The road is open before me, all roads, all possibilities. From this grassy bed beside Lake Mizogan I can go anywhere, find all that is findable, do all that is doable, make all that can be made. Why should I build a fence around myself? Leash myself to one tree? Not even a horse, not even a dog was loyal enough to do such a mad thing to itself.

From infancy on his knack had captured him. Whether as a child in his family, as Ta-Kumsaw's traveling companion, as a prentice smith, or as a teacher of would-be Makers, he had been hobbled by his knack. But not now.

The lightning flashed again, farther off this time. There would be no rain here tonight. And tomorrow he would get up and go south, or north, or west, or east, as the idea struck him, seeking whatever goal seemed desirable. He had left home to get away, not to go toward anything. There was no greater freedom than that.

9

Cooper

Peggy Larner kept watch on both of those bright heartfires: Alvin as he wandered through America, Calvin as he made his way to England and prepared for his audience with Napoleon. There was little change in the possible futures that she saw, for neither man's plan was one whit altered.

Alvin's plan, of course, was no plan at all. He and Arthur Stuart, traveling afoot, made their way westward from Mizogan, past the growing town of Chicago and on until the dense fogs of the Mizzipy turned them back. Alvin had entertained a vague hope that he, at least, would be permitted to pass to the Mizzipy and beyond, but if such a thing would ever be possible, it certainly was not possible now. So he went north all the way to High Water Lake, where he boarded one of the new steamboats that was carrying iron ore to Irrakwa, where it would be loaded on trains and carried the rest of the way to the coal country of Suskwahenny and Pennsylvania, to feed into the new steel mills. "Is that Making?" asked Arthur Stuart, when Alvin explained the process to him. "Turning iron into steel?"

"It's a sort of Making," said Alvin, "where earth is forced by fire. But the cost is high, and the iron aches when it's been transformed like that. I've seen some of the steel they've made. It's in the rails. It's in the locomotives. The metal screams all the time, a soft sound, very high, but I can hear it."

"Does that mean it's evil to use steel?" asked Arthur Stuart.

"No," said Alvin. "But we should only use it when it's worth the cost of such suffering. Maybe someday we'll find a better way to bring the iron up to strength. I *am* a smith. I won't deny the forgefire or refuse the hammer and the anvil. Nor will I say that the foundries of Dekane are somehow worse than my small forge. I've been inside the flame. I know that the iron can live in it too, and come out unhurt."

"Maybe that's what we're wandering for," said Arthur Stuart. "For you to go to the foundries and help them make steel more kindly."

"Maybe," said Alvin, and they rode the train to Dekane and Alvin applied for work in a foundry and learned by watching and doing all the things there was to know about the making of steel, and in the end he said, "I found a way, but it takes a Maker to do it, or pretty close." And there it was: If Alvin was to change the world, it required him to do what he had already half-failed at doing back in Vigor Church, which was to make more Makers. They left the steeltowns and went on east and as Peggy watched Alvin's heartfire she saw no change, no change, no change. . . .

And then one day, of a sudden, for no reason she could see in Alvin's life, a thousand new roads opened up and down every one of them was a man that she had never seen before. A man who called himself Verily Cooper and spoke like a book-learned Englishman and walked beside Alvin every step of his life for years. Down that path the golden plow was fixed with a perfect handle and leapt to life under human hands. Down that path the Crystal City rose skyward and the fog at the Mizzipy shore cleared for a few miles and Red folk stood on the western shore and gladly greeted White folk come on coracles and rafts to trade with them and speak to them and learn from them.

But where did this Verily Cooper come from, and why had he now so suddenly appeared in Alvin's life?

Only later in the day did it occur to Peggy that it was none of Alvin's doing that brought this man to him, but rather someone else. She looked to Calvin's heartfire—so far away she had to look deep through the ground to see him in England, around the curve of the

Earth—and there she saw that it was he who had made the change, and by the simplest of choices. He took the time to charm a Member of Parliament who invited him to tea, and even though Calvin knew that this man had nothing for him, on a whim, the merest chance, he decided he would go. That decision transformed Calvin's own futures only slightly. Nothing much was changed, except this: Down almost every road, Calvin spent an hour at the tea sitting beside a young barrister named Verily Cooper, who listened avidly to all that Calvin had to say.

Was it possible, then, that Calvin was part of Alvin's making after all? He went to England with the undoing of all of Alvin's works in his heart; and yet, by whim, by chance—if there was such a thing as chance—he would have an encounter that would almost surely bring Verily Cooper to America. To Alvin Smith. To the golden plow, the Crystal City, the opening of the Mizzipy fog.

Arise Cooper was an honest hardworking Christian. He lived his life as close to purity as he could, given the finite limits of the human mind. Every commandment he learned of, he obeyed; every imperfection he could imagine, he purged from his soul. He kept a detailed journal every day, tracking the doings of the Lord in his life.

For instance, on the day his second son was born, he wrote: "Today Satan made me angry at a man who insisted on measuring the three kegs I made him, sure that I had given him short measure. But the Spirit of God kindled forgiveness within my heart, for I realized that a man might become suspicious because he had been so often cheated by devilish men. Thus I saw that the Lord had trusted me to teach this man that not all men will cheat him, and I bore his insult with patience. Sure enough, as Jesus taught, when I answered vileness with kindness the stranger did part from my coopery as my friend instead of my enemy, and with a wiser eye about the workings of the Lord among men. Oh how great thou art, my beloved God, to turn my sinful heart into a tool to serve thy purposes in this world! At nightfall entered into the world my second son, whom I name Verily, Verily, I Say Unto You, Except Ye Become As A Little Child Ye Shall In No Wise Enter Into The Kingdom Of Heaven."

If anyone thought the name a bit excessive, they said nothing to Arise Cooper, whose own name was also a bit of scripture: Arise And Come Forth. Nor did the child's mother, whose own name was the shortest verse in scripture: He Wept. They all knew that the baby's whole name would almost never be used. Instead he was

known as Verily, and as he grew up the name would often be short-
ened to Very.

It was not the name that was Verily Cooper's heaviest burden.
No, there was something much darker that cast its shadow upon the
boy very early in his life.

Arise's wife, Wept, came to him one day when Verily was only
two years old. She was agitated. "Arise, I saw the boy playing with
scraps today, building a tower of them."

Arise cast his mind through all the evil that one might do with
wood scraps from the cooper's trade and could think of only one.
"Was it a representation of the tower of Babel?"

Wept looked puzzled. "It might be, or might not. What would
I know of that, since the boy speaks not a word yet?"

"What, then?" asked Arise, impatient now because she had not
got straight to the point. No, no, he was impatient because he had
guessed wrong and now was a bit ashamed of himself. It was a sin
to try to put the blame on her for ill feelings of his own causing. In
his heart he prayed for forgiveness even as she went on.

"Arise, he built high with the scraps, but they fell over, again
and again. I saw him and thought, The Lord of heaven teaches our
little one that the works of man are all futility, and only the works
of God can last. But then he gets on his face this look of grim
determination, and now he studies each scrap of wood as he builds
with it, laying it in place all careful-like. He builds and he builds
and he builds, until the last scrap is higher than his own head, and
still it stands."

Arise was uncertain what she meant by this, or why it troubled
her.

"Come, husband, and see the working of our baby's hand."

Arise followed her into the kitchen. No one else was there,
though this was the busiest cooking time of the day. Arise could see
why they had all fled. For the pile of scrap wood rose higher than
reason or balance should have allowed. The blocks lay every which
way, balanced perfectly no matter how odd or precarious the fit with
the blocks above and below.

"Knock it down at once," said Arise.

"Do you think that didn't occur to me?" asked Wept. She flung
out her arm and dashed the tower to the ground. It fell, but all in
one motion, and even lying on the ground the blocks remained attached to each other as surely as if they were glued.

"He must have been playing with the mucilage," said Arise,
but he knew even as he said it that it wasn't so.

He knelt beside the supine tower and tried to separate a block from the end. He couldn't pry it away. He picked up the whole tower and dashed it across his knee. It bruised him but did not break. Finally, by standing on the middle of it and lifting one end with all his strength, he broke the tower, but it took as much force as if he were breaking a sturdy plank. And when he examined the torn ends, he saw that the tower had broken in the middle of a block, and not at the joint between them.

He looked at his wife, and knew what he should say to her. He should tell her that it was obvious her son had been possessed by Satan, to such a point that the lad was now fully empowered with extraordinary witchery. When such a word was said, there would be no choice but to take the boy to the magistrate, who would administer the witch tests. The boy, being too young and speechless to confess or recant, would burn as the court's sentence, if he did not drown during the trial.

Arise had never questioned the rightness of the laws that kept England pure of witchery and the other dark doings of Satan. No more would they exile witches to America—the only result of that old policy had been a nation possessed by the Devil. The scripture was clear, and there was no room for mercy: Thou shalt not suffer a witch to live.

And yet Arise did not say to his wife the words that would force them to give their baby to the magistrate for discipline. For the first time in his life, Arise Cooper, knowing the truth, did not act upon it.

"I say we burn this odd-shaped board," said Arise. "And forbid the child to play with blocks. Watch him close, and teach him to live each moment in close obedience to the laws of God. Until he has learned, let no other woman look after him out of your presence."

He looked his wife in the eye, and Wept looked back at him. At first her eyes were wide with surprise at his words; then surprise gave way to relief, and then to determination. "I will watch him so close that Satan will have no opportunity to whisper in his ear," she said.

"We can afford to have a cook to supervise the work of the serving girls from now on," said Arise. "The raising of this most difficult son is in our hands. We *will* save him from the Devil. No other work is more important than this."

Thus it was that Verily Cooper's upbringing became difficult and interesting. He was beaten more than any other child in the

family, for his own good, for Arise well knew that Satan had made
an inroad in the child's heart at an early age. Thus all signs of
rebellion, disrespect, and sin must be driven out vigorously.

If little Verily was resentful of the special discipline he received
compared to his older brother and his younger sisters, he said nothing of it—perhaps because complaint always resulted in swift blows
from a birch rod. He learned to live with such punishment and even,
after a little while, to take some pride in it, for the other children
looked at him in awe, seeing how much beating he took without so
much as crying—and for offenses which, in them, would have
brought no more than a sharp look from their parents.

Verily was quick to learn. The birch rod taught him which of
his actions were merely the normal mischief of a growing boy, and
which were regarded as signs that Satan was laboring mightily for
possession of his soul. When the neighborhood boys were building
a snow fort, for instance, if he built sloppily and carelessly like they
did, there was no punishment. But when he took special care to make
the blocks fit smoothly and seamlessly together, he got such a caning
that his buttocks bled. Likewise, when he helped his father in the
shop, he learned that if he joined the staves of a barrel loosely, as
other men did it, barely holding them together inside the hoops,
relying on the liquid the barrel would eventually hold to swell the
wood and make the joints truly airtight, then it was all right. But if
he chose the wood carefully and concentrated to fit them so the wood
joined perfectly, and the barrel held air as tight as a pig's bladder,
his father beat him with the sizing tool and drove him from the shop.

By the time he was ten, Verily no longer went openly into his
father's shop, and it seemed that his father didn't mind having him
stay away. Yet still it galled him to see the work that the shop turned
out without his help, for Verily could sense the roughness, the loose-
ness of the fit between the staves of the kegs and the barrels and the
butts. It grated on him. It made him tingle between the shoulder
blades just to think of it, until he could hardly stand it. He took to
rising in the middle of the night and going into the shop and re-
building the worst of the barrels. No one guessed what he had done,
for he left no scraps behind. All he did was unhoop the barrel, refit
the staves, and draw the hoops back on, more tightly than before.

The result was, first, that Arise Cooper got a name for making
the best barrels in the midlands; second, that Verily was often sleepy
and lazy-seeming during the day, which led to more beatings, though
nothing like as severe as the ones he got when he really concentrated
on making things fit together; and third, that Verily learned to live

with constant deception, hiding what he was and what he saw and what he felt and what he did from everyone around him. It was only natural that he should be drawn to the study of law.

Lazy as Verily sometimes seemed, he had a sharp mind with his studies—Arise and Wept both saw it, and instead of contenting themselves with the local taxpaid teacher, they sent him to an academy that was normally only for the sons of squires and rich men. The taunting and mockery that Verily endured from the other boys because of his rough accent and homely clothing was hardly noticeable to Very—such poundings as the boys inflicted on him were nothing compared to the beatings he was inured to, and any abuse that didn't cause physical pain didn't even enter Very's consciousness. All he cared about was that at school he didn't have to live in fear all the time, and the teachers loved it when he studied carefully and saw how ideas fit together. What he could only do in secret with his hands, he could do openly with his mind.

And it wasn't just ideas. He began to learn that if he concentrated on the boys around him, really listening to them, watching how they acted, he could see them as clearly as he saw bits of wood, seeing exactly where and how each boy might fit well with each other boy. Just a word here and there, just an idea tossed into the right mind at the right time, and he made the boys of his dormitory into a cohesive band of loving friends. As much as they were willing, that is. Some were filled with deep rage that made it so that the better they fit, the more surly and suspicious they became. Verily couldn't help that. He couldn't change a boy's heart—he could only help him find where his natural inclinations would make him fit most comfortably with the others.

No one saw it, though—no one saw that it was Verily who made these boys into the tightest group of friends that had ever passed through this school. The masters saw that they were friends, but they also saw that Verily was the one misfit who never quite belonged. They could not have imagined that he was the cause of the others' extraordinary closeness. And that was fine with Very. He suspected that if they knew what he was doing, it would be like being home with Father again, only now it wouldn't be birch rods.

For in his studies, particularly in religion class, Verily finally came to understand what the beatings were all about. Witchery. Verily Cooper had been born a witch. No wonder his father looked haunted all the time. Arise Cooper had suffered a witch to live, and those canings, far from being an act of rage or hatred, were really designed to help Verily learn to disguise the evil born in him so that no one would ever know that Arise and Wept Cooper had concealed a witchchild in their own home.

But I'm not a witch, Verily finally told himself. Satan never came to me. And what I do causes no harm. How can it be against God to make barrels tight, or help boys find the best chance of friendship between them? How have I ever used my powers except to help others? Was that not what Christ taught? To be the servant of all?

By the time Verily was sixteen, a sturdy and rather good-looking young man of some education and impeccable manners, he had become a thoroughgoing skeptic. If the dogmas about witchery could be so hopelessly wrong, how could any of the teachings of the ministers be relied upon? It left Verily Cooper at loose ends, intellectually speaking, for all his teachers spoke as if religion were the cornerstone of all other learning, and yet all of Very's actual studies led him to the conclusion that sciences founded upon religion were uncertain at best, utterly bogus at worst.

Yet he breathed no word of these conclusions. You could be burned as an atheist just as fast as you could be burned as a witch. And besides, he wasn't sure he didn't believe in *anything*. He just didn't believe in what the ministers said.

If the preachers had no idea of what was good or evil, where could he turn to learn about right and wrong? He tried reading philosophy at Manchester, but found that except for Newton, the best the philosophers had to offer was a vast sea of opinion with a few blocks of truth floating here and there like wreckage from a sunken ship. And Newton and the scientists who followed him had no soul. By deciding that they would study only that which could be verified under controlled conditions, they had merely limited their field of endeavor. Most truth lay outside the neat confines of science; and even within those boundaries, Verily Cooper, with his keen eye for things which did not fit, soon found that while the pretense of impartiality was universal, the fact of it was very rare. Most scientists, like most philosophers and most theologians, were captives of received opinion. To swim against the tide was beyond their powers, and so truth remained scattered, unassembled, waterlogged.

At least lawyers knew they were dealing with tradition, not truth; with consensus, not objective reality. And a man who understood how things fit together might make a real contribution. Might save a few people from injustice. Might even, in some far distant year, strike a blow or two against the witchery laws and spare those few dozen souls a year so incautious as to be caught manipulating reality in unapproved ways.

As for Arise and Wept, they were deeply gratified when their son Verily left home expressing no interest in the family business. Their oldest child, Mocky (full name: He Will Not Be Mocked Cooper) was a skilled barrelmaker and popular both inside and outside the family. He would inherit everything. Verily would go to London and Arise and Wept would no longer be responsible for him. Verily even gave them a quit-claim against the family estate, though they hadn't asked for it. When Arise accepted the document, twenty-one-year-old Verily took the birch rod from where it hung on the wall, broke it over his knee, and fed it into the kitchen fire. There was no further discussion of the matter. All understood: What Verily chose to do with his powers was his own business now.

Verily's talents were immediately noticed. He was invited to join several law firms, and finally chose the one that gave him the greatest independence to choose his own clients. His reputation soared as he won case after case; but what impressed the lawyers who truly understood these things was not the number of victories, but rather the even larger number of cases that were settled—justly—without even going to trial. By the time Verily turned twenty-five, it was becoming a custom several times a month for both parties in hotly contested lawsuits to come to Verily and beg him to be their arbiter, completely sidestepping the courts: such was his reputation as a wise and just man. Some whispered that in due course he would become a great force in politics. Some dared to wish that such a man might someday be Lord Protector, if that office were only filled by election, like the presidency of the United States.

The United States of America—that motley, multilingual, mongrel, mossbacked republic that had somehow, kingless and causeless, arisen by accident between the Crown Lands and New England. America, where men wearing buckskin were said to walk the halls of Congress along with Reds, Dutchmen, Swedes, and other semi-civilized specimens who would have been ejected from Parliament before they could speak a word aloud. More and more Verily Cooper turned his eyes to that country; more and more he yearned to live in a place where his gift for making things fit together could be used to the fullest. Where he could join things together with his hands, not just with his mind and with his words. Where, in short, he could live without deception.

Maybe in such a land, where men did not have to lie about who they were in order to be granted the right to live, maybe in such a land he could find his way to some kind of truth, some kind of understanding about what the universe was for. And, failing that, at least Verily could be free there.

The trouble was, it was English law that Verily had studied, and it was English clients who were on the way to making him a rich man. What if he married? What if he had children? What kind of life would he make for them in America, amid the forest primeval? How could he ask a wife to leave civilization and go to Philadelphia?

And he wanted a wife. He wanted to raise children. He wanted to prove that goodness wasn't beaten into children, that fear was not the fount from which virtue flowed. He wanted to be able to gather his family in his arms and know that not one of them dreaded the sight of him, or felt the need to lie to him in order to have his love.

So he dreamed of America but stayed in London, searching in high society to find the right woman to make a family with. By now his homely manners had been replaced by university fashion and finally with courtliness that made him welcome in the finest houses. His wit, never biting, always deep, made him a popular guest in the great salons of London, and if he was never invited to the same dinners or parties as the leading theologians of the day, it was not because he was thought to be an atheist, but rather because there were no theologians regarded as his equal in conversation. One had to place Verily Cooper with at least one who could hold his own with him—everyone knew that Very was far too kindhearted to destroy fools for public entertainment. He simply fell silent when surrounded by those of dimmer wit; it was a shameful thing for a host when word spread that Verily Cooper had been silent all night long.

Verily Cooper was twenty-six years old when he found himself at a party with a remarkable young American named Calvin Miller.

Verily noticed him at once, because he didn't fit, but it wasn't because of his Americanness. In fact, Verily could see at once that Calvin had done a good job of acquiring a veneer of manners that kept him from the most egregious faux pas that bedevilled most Americans who attempted to make their way in London. The boy was going on about his effort to learn French, joking about how abominably untalented he was at languages; but Verily saw (as did many others) that this was all pretense. When Calvin spoke French each phrase came out with splendid accents, and if his vocabulary was lacking, his grammar was not.

A lady near Verily murmured to him, "If he's bad at languages, I shudder to imagine what he's *good* at."

Lying, that's what he's good at, thought Verily. But he kept his mouth shut, because how could he possibly know that Calvin's every word was false, except because he knew that nothing fit when Calvin was speaking? The boy was fascinating if only because he seemed to lie when there was no possible benefit from lying; he lied for the sheer joy of it.

Was this what America produced? The land that in Verily's fantasies was a place of truth, and this was what was spawned there? Maybe the ministers were not wholly wrong about those with hidden powers—or "knacks," as the Americans quaintly called them.

"Mr. Miller," said Verily. "I wonder, since you're an American, if you have any personal knowledge of knacks."

The room fell silent. To speak of such things—it was only slightly less crude than to speak of personal hygiene. And when it was rising young barrister Verily Cooper doing the asking . . .

"I beg your pardon?" asked Calvin.

"Knacks," said Verily. "Hidden powers. I know that they're legal in America, and yet Americans profess to be Christian. Therefore I'm curious about how such things are rationalized, when here they are considered to be proof of one's enslavement to Satan and worthy of a sentence of death."

"I'm no philosopher, sir," said Calvin.

Verily knew better. He could tell that Calvin was suddenly more guarded than ever. Verily's guess had been right. This Calvin Miller was lying because he had much to hide. "All the better," said Verily. "Then there's a chance that your answer will make sense to a man as ignorant of such matters as I am."

"I wish you'd let me speak of other things," said Calvin. "I think we might offend this company."

"Surely you don't imagine you were invited here for any reason other than your Americanness," said Verily. "So why do you resist talking about the most obvious oddity of the American people?"

There was a buzz of comment. Who had ever seen Verily be openly rude like this?

Verily knew what he was doing, however. He hadn't interviewed a thousand witnesses without learning how to elicit truth even from the most flagrant habitual liar. Calvin Miller was a man who felt shame sharply. That was why he lied—to hide himself from anything that would shame him. If provoked, however, he would respond with heat, and the lies and calculation would give way to bits of honesty now and then. In short, Calvin Miller had a dander, and it was up.

"Oddity?" asked Calvin. "Perhaps the odd thing is not having knacks, but rather denying that they exist or blaming them on Satan.''

Now the buzz was louder. Calvin, by speaking honestly, had shocked and offended his pious listeners more than Verily's rudeness had. Yet this *was* a cosmopolitan crowd, and there *were* no ministers present. No one left the room; all watched, all listened with fascination.

"Take that as your premise, then," said Verily. "Explain to me and this company how these occult knacks came into the world, if not caused by the influence of the Devil. Surely you won't have us believe that we Englishmen burn people to death for having powers given to them by God?"

Calvin shook his head. "I see that you want merely to provoke me, sir, into speaking in ways that are against the law here."

"Not so," said Verily. "There are three dozen witnesses in this salon right now who would testify that far from initiating this conversation, you were dragged into it. Furthermore, I am not asking you to preach to us. I'm merely asking you to tell us, as scientists, what Americans believe. It is no more a crime to tell about American beliefs concerning knacks than it is to report on Muslim harems and Hindu widow-burning. And this is a company of people who are eager to learn. If I'm wrong, please, let me be corrected."

No one spoke up to correct him. They were, in fact, dying to hear what the young American would say.

"I'd say there's no consensus about it," said Calvin. "I'd say that no one knows what to think. They just use the knacks that they have. Some say it's against God. Some say God made the world, knacks included, and it all depends on whether the knacks are used for righteousness or not. I've heard a lot of different opinions."

"But what is the wisest opinion that you've heard?" insisted Verily.

He could feel it the moment Calvin decided on his answer: It was a kind of surrender. Calvin had been flailing around, but now he had given in to the inevitable. He was going to tell, if not the truth, then at least a true reporting of somebody else's truth.

"One fellow says that knacks come because of a natural affinity between a person and some aspect of the world around him. It's not from God *or* Satan, he says. It's just part of the random variation in the world. This fellow says that a knack is really a matter of winning the trust of some part of reality. He reckons that the Reds, who don't believe in knacks, have found the truth behind it all. A White man gets it in his head he has a knack, and from then on all he works

on is honing that particular talent. But if, like the Reds, he saw
knacks as just an aspect of the way all things are connected together,
then he wouldn't concentrate on just one talent. He'd keep working
on all of them. So in this fellow's view, knacks are just the result
of too much work on one thing, and not enough work on all the rest.
Like a hodsman who carries bricks only on his right shoulder. His
body's going to get twisted. You have to study it all, learn it all.
Every knack is within our power to acquire it, I reckon, if only
we . . ."

His voice trailed off.

When Calvin spoke again, it was in the crisp, clear, educated-
sounding way he must have learned since reaching England. Only
then did Verily and the others realize that his accent had changed
during that long speech. He had shed the thin coating of Englishness
and shown the American.

"Who is this man who taught you all this lore?" asked Verily.

"Does it matter? What does such a rough man know of nature?"
Calvin spoke mockingly; but he was lying again, Verily knew it.

"This 'rough man,' as you call him. I suspect he says a great
deal more than the mere snippet you've given us today."

"Oh, you can't stop him from talking, he's so full of his own
voice." The bitterness in Calvin's tone was a powerful message to
Verily: This is sincere. Calvin resents whoever this frontier philosopher is, resents him deeply. "But I'm not about to bore this company with the ravings of a frontier lunatic."

"But you don't think he's a lunatic, do you, Mr. Miller?" said
Verily.

A momentary pause. Think of your answer quickly, Calvin Miller. Find a way to deceive me, if you can.

"I can't say, sir," said Calvin. "I don't think he knows half as
much as he lets on, but I wouldn't dare call my own brother a liar."

There was a sudden loud eruption of buzzing. Calvin Miller had
a brother who philosophized about knacks and said they weren't
from the Devil.

More important to Verily was the fact that Calvin's words obviously didn't fit in with the world he actually believed in. Lies, lies.
Calvin obviously believed that his brother was very wise indeed;
that he probably knew *more* than Calvin was willing to admit.

At this moment, without realizing it himself, Verily Cooper
made the decision to go to America. Whoever Calvin's brother was,
he knew something that Verily wanted desperately to learn. For there
was a ring of truth in this man's ideas. Maybe if Verily could only

meet him and talk to him, he could make Verily's own knack clear to him. Could tell him why he had such a talent and why it persisted even though his father tried to beat it out of him.

"What's your brother's name?" asked Verily.

"Does that matter?" asked Calvin, a faint sneer in his voice. "Planning a visit to the backwoods soon?"

"Is that where you're from? The backwoods?" asked Verily.

Calvin immediately backtracked. "Actually, no, I was exaggerating. My father was a miller."

"How did the poor man die?" asked Verily.

"He's not dead," said Calvin.

"But you spoke of him in the past tense. As if he were no longer a miller."

"He still runs a mill," said Calvin.

"You still haven't told me your brother's name."

"Same as my father's. Alvin."

"Alvin Miller?" asked Verily.

"Used to be. But in America we still change our names with our professions. He's a journeyman smith now. Alvin Smith."

"And you remain Calvin Miller because . . ."

"Because I haven't chosen my life's work yet."

"You hope to discover it in France?"

Calvin leapt to his feet as if his most terrible secret had just been exposed. "I have to get home."

Verily also rose to his feet. "My friend, I fear my curiosity has made you feel uncomfortable. I will stop my questioning at once, and apologize to this whole company for having broached such difficult subjects tonight. I hope you will all excuse my insatiable curiosity."

Verily was at once reassured by many voices that it had been most interesting and no one was angry with or offended by anyone. The conversation broke into many smaller chats.

In a few moments, Verily managed to maneuver himself close to the young American. "Your brother, Alvin Smith," he said. "Tell me where I can find him."

"In America," said Calvin; and because the conversation was private, he did not conceal his contempt.

"Only slightly better than telling me to search for him on Earth," said Verily. "Obviously you resent him. I have no desire to trouble you by asking you to tell me any more of his ideas. It will cost you nothing to tell me where he lives so I can search him out myself."

"You'd make a voyage across the ocean to meet with a boy who talks like a country bumpkin in order to learn what he thinks about knacks?"

"Whether I make such a voyage or merely write him a letter is no concern of yours," said Verily. "In the future I'm bound to be asked to defend people accused of witchery. Your brother may have the arguments that will allow me to save a client's life. Such ideas can't be found here in England because it would be the ruin of a man's career to explore too assiduously into the works of Satan."

"So why aren't you afraid of ruining your own career?" said Calvin.

"Because whatever he knows, it's true enough to make a liar like you run halfway around the world to get away from the truth."

Calvin's expression grew ugly with hate. "How dare you speak to me like that! I could . . ."

So Verily had guessed right about the way Calvin fit into his own family back home. "The name of the town, and you and I will never have to speak again."

Calvin paused for a moment, weighing the decision. "I take you at your word, Mr. Rising Young Barrister Esquire. The town is Vigor Church, in Wobbish Territory. Near the mouth of Tippy-Canoe Creek. Go find my brother if you can. Learn from him—if you can. Then you can spend the rest of your life wondering if maybe you wouldn't have been better off trying to learn from *me*."

Verily laughed softly. "I don't think so, Calvin Miller. I already know how to lie, and alas, that's the only knack you have that you've practiced enough to be truly accomplished at it."

"In another time I would have shot you dead for that remark."

"But this is an age that loves liars," said Verily. "That's why there are so many of us, acting out lives of pretense. I don't know what you're hoping to find in France, but I can promise you, it will be worthless to you in the long run, if your whole life up to that moment is a lie."

"Now you're a prophet? Now you can see into a man's heart?" Calvin sneered and backed away. "We had a deal. I told you where my brother lives. Now stay away from me." Calvin Miller left the party, and, moments later, so did Verily Cooper. It was quite a scandal, Verily's acting so rudely in front of the whole company like that. Was it quite safe to invite him to dinners and parties anymore?

Within a week that question ceased to matter. Verily Cooper was gone: resigned from his law firm, his bank accounts closed, his apartment rented. He sent a brief letter to his parents, telling them only that he was going to America to interview a fellow about a case he was working on. He didn't add that it was the most important case of his life: his trial of himself as a witch. Nor did he tell them when, if ever, he meant to return to England. He was sailing west, and would then take whatever conveyance there was, even if it was his own feet on a rough path, to meet this fellow Alvin Smith, who said the first sensible thing about knacks that Verily had ever heard.

On the very day that Verily Cooper set sail from Liverpool, Calvin Miller stepped onto the Calais ferry. From that moment on, Calvin spoke nothing but French, determined to be fluent before he met Napoleon. He wouldn't think of Verily Cooper again for several years. He had bigger fish to fry. What did he care about what some London lawyer thought of him?

10

Welcome Home

Left to himself, Alvin likely wouldn't have come back to Hatrack River. Sure, it was his birthplace, but since his folks moved on before he was even sitting up by himself he didn't have no memories of the way it was then. He knew that the oldest settlers in that place were Horace Guester and Makepeace Smith and old Vanderwoort, the Dutch trader, so when he was born the roadhouse and the smithy and the general store must have been there already. But he couldn't conjure up no pictures in his memory of such a little place.

The Hatrack River he knew was the village of his prenticeship, with a town square and a church with a preacher and Whitley Physicker to tend the sick and even a post office and enough folks with enough children that they got them up a subscription and hired them a schoolteacher. Which meant it was a real town by then, only what difference did that make to Alvin? He was stuck there from the age of eleven, bound over to a greedy master who squeezed the last ounce of work out of "his" boy while teaching him as little as possible, as late as possible. There was scarce any money, and nei-

ther time to get any pleasure from it nor pleasures to be bought if
you had the time.

Even so, miserable as his prenticeship was, he might have
looked back on Hatrack River with some fondness. There was Makepeace's shrewish wife Gertie, who nevertheless was a fine cook and
had a spot of kindness for the boy now and then. There was Horace
and Old Peg Guester, who remembered his birth and made him feel
welcome whenever he had a moment to visit with them or do some
odd job to help them out. And as Alvin got him a name for making
perfect hexes and doing better ironwork than his master, there was
plenty of visits from all the other folks in town, asking for this,
asking for that, and all sort of pretending they didn't know Alvin
was the true master in that smithy. Wouldn't want to rile up old
Makepeace, cause then he'd take it out on the boy, wouldn't he?
But he was a good one with his hands, that boy Alvin.

So Alvin might have made him some happy memories of the
place, the way folks always finds a way to dip into their own past
and draw out wistful moments, even if those very moments was
lonely or painful or downright hellish to live through at the time.

For Alvin, though, all those childish and youthish memories was
swallowed up in the way it ended. Right at the happiest time, when
he was falling in love with Miss Larner while trying to pick up some
decent book learning, them Slave Finders came for little Arthur Stuart and everything went ugly. They even forced Alvin to make the
manacles that Arthur would wear back into slavery. Then Alvin and
Horace Guester took their life in their hands and went to fetch back
the boy, and Alvin changed Arthur Stuart deep inside and washed
away his old self in the Hio, so the Finders could never match him
up with the bits of hair and flesh in their cachet. So even then, it
might have still been hopeful, a good memory of a bad time that
turned out fine.

Then that last night, standing in the smithy with Miss Larner,
Alvin told her he loved her and asked her to marry him and she
might have said yes, she had a look in her eyes that said yes, he
thought. But at that very moment Old Peg Guester killed one Finder
and got herself killed by the other. Only then did Alvin find out that
Miss Larner was really Little Peggy, Peg's and Horace's long-lost
daughter, the torch girl who saved Alvin's life when he was a little
baby. What a thing to find out about the woman you love, in the
exact moment that you're losing her forever.

But he wasn't really thinking of losing Miss Larner then. All he
could think of was Old Peg, gruff and sharp-tongued and loving old

Peg, shot dead by a Slave Finder, and never mind that she shot one of them first, they was in her house without leave, trespassing, and even if the law gave them the right to be there, it was an evil law and they was evil to make their living by it and it didn't none of it matter then, anyway, because Alvin was so angry he wasn't thinking straight. Alvin found the one as killed Old Peg and snapped his neck with one hand, and then he beat his head against the ground until the skull inside the skin was all broke up like a pot in a meal sack.

When Alvin's fury died, when the white-hot rage was gone, when deep justice stopped demanding the death of the killer of Old Peg, all that was left was the broken body in his arms, the blood on his apron, the memory of murder. Never mind that nobody in Hatrack River would ever call him a killer for what he done that night. In his own heart he knew that he had Unmade his own Making. For that moment he had been the Unmaker's tool.

That dark memory was why none of the other memories could ever turn light in Alvin's heart. And that's why Alvin probably wouldn't never have come back to Hatrack River, left to himself.

But he wasn't left to himself, was he? He had Arthur Stuart with him, and to that little boy the town of Hatrack River was nothing but pure golden childhood. It was setting and watching Alvin work in the smithy, or even pumping the bellows sometimes. It was listening to the redbird song and knowing the words. It was hearing all the gossip in the town and saying it back all clever so the grown-ups clapped their hands and laughed. It was being the champion speller of the whole town even though for some reason they wouldn't let him into the school proper. And yes, sure, the woman he called Mother got herself killed, but Arthur didn't see that with his own eyes, and anyway, he *had* to go back, didn't he? Old Peg his adopted mother who killed a man to save him and died her own self, she lay buried on a hill behind the roadhouse. And in a grave on the same hill lay Arthur's true mother, a little Black slavegirl who used her secret African powers to make wings for herself so she could fly with the baby in her arms, she could fly all the way north to where her baby would be safe, even though she herself died from the journey. How could Arthur Stuart not return to that place?

Don't go thinking that Arthur Stuart ever asked Alvin to go there. That wasn't the way Arthur thought about things. He was going along with Alvin, not telling Alvin where to go. It was just that when they talked, Arthur kept going on about this or that memory from Hatrack River until Alvin reached his own conclusion. Alvin reckoned that it would make Arthur Stuart happy to go back to Hatrack River, and then it never crossed Alvin's mind that his own sadness might outweigh Arthur's happiness. He just up and left Irrakwa, where they happened to be that week in late August of 1820. Up and left that land of railroads and factories, coal and steel, barges and carriages and men on horseback going back and forth on urgent errands. Left that busy place and came through quiet woods and across whispering streams, down deer paths and along rutted roads until the land started looking familiar and Arthur Stuart said, "I've been here. I know this place." And then, in wonder: "You brung me home, Alvin."

They came from the northeast, passing the place where the railroad spur was fixing to pass near Hatrack River and cross the Hio into Appalachee. They came across the covered bridge over the Hatrack that Alvin's own father and brothers built, like a monument to their dead oldest brother Vigor, who got mashed by a tree carried on a storm flood while he was crossing the river. They came into town on the same road his family used. And, just like Alvin's family, they passed the smithy and heard the ringing of hammer on iron on anvil.

"Ain't that the smithy?" asked Arthur Stuart. "Let's go see Makepeace and Gertie!"

"I don't think so," said Alvin. "In the first place, Gertie's dead."

"Oh, that's right," said the boy. "Blew out a blood vein screaming at Makepeace, didn't she?"

"How'd you hear that?" asked Alvin. "You don't miss much gossip, do you, boy?"

"I can't help what people talk about when I'm right there," said Arthur Stuart. And then, back to his original idea: "I reckon it wouldn't be proper anyway, to visit Makepeace before seeing Papa."

Alvin didn't tell him that Horace Guester hated it when Arthur called him Papa. Folks got the wrong impression, like maybe Horace himself was the White half of that mixup boy, which wasn't so at all but folks will talk. When Arthur got older, Alvin would explain to him that he ought to not call Horace Papa anymore. For now, though, Horace was a man and a man would have to bear the innocent offense of a well-meaning boy.

The roadhouse was twice as big as before. Horace had built on a new wing that doubled the front, with the porch continuing all along it. But that wasn't hardly the only difference—the whole thing was faced with clapboards now, whitewashed and pretty as you could imagine against the deep green of the forest that still snuck as close to the house as it dared.

"Well, Horace done prettied up the place," said Alvin.

"It don't look like itself no more," said Arthur Stuart.

"Anymore," Alvin corrected him.

"If you can say 'done prettied up' then I can say 'no more,' " said Arthur Stuart. "Miss Larner ain't here to correct us no more anyhow."

"That should be 'no more nohow,' " said Alvin, and they both laughed as they walked up onto the porch.

The door opened and a somewhat stout middle-aged woman stepped through it, almost running into them. She carried a basket under one arm and an umbrella under the other, though there wasn't a sign of rain.

"Excuse me," said Alvin. He saw that she was hedged about with hexes and charms. Not many years ago, he would have been fooled by them like any other man (though he would always have seen where the charms were and how the hexes worked). But he had learned to see past hexes of illusion, and that's what these were. These days, seeing the truth came so natural to him that it took real effort to see the illusion. He made the effort, and was vaguely saddened to see that she was almost a caricature of feminine beauty. Couldn't she have been more creative, more *interesting* than this? He judged at once that the real middle-aged woman, somewhat thick-waisted and hair salted with grey, was the more attractive of the two images. And it was a sure thing she was the more interesting.

She saw him staring at her, but no doubt she assumed it was her beauty that had him awed. She must have been used to men staring at her—it seemed to amuse her. She stared right back at him, but *not* looking for beauty in him, that was for sure.

"You were born here," she said, "but I've never seen you before." Then she looked at Arthur Stuart. "But you were born away south."

Arthur nodded, made mute by shyness and by the overwhelming force of her declaration. She spoke as if her words were not only true, but superseded all other truth that had ever been thought of.

"He was born in Appalachee, Missus. . . ." In vain Alvin waited for her reply. Then he realized that he was supposed to assume, seeing her young beautiful false image, that she was a Miss rather than a Missus.

"You're bound for Carthage City," said the woman, speaking to Alvin again, and rather coldly.

"I don't think so," said Alvin. "Nothing for me there."

"Not yet, not yet," she said. "But I know you now. You must be Alvin, that prentice boy old Makepeace is always going on about."

"I'm a journeyman, ma'am. If Makepeace isn't saying that part, I wonder how much of what he says *is* true."

She smiled, but her eyes weren't smiling. They were calculating. "Aha. I think there's the makings of a good story in that. Just needs a bit of stirring."

At once Alvin regretted having said so much to her. Why *had* he spoken up so boldly, anyway? He wasn't a one to babble on to strangers, especially when he was more or less calling another fellow a liar. He didn't want trouble with Makepeace, but now it looked pretty sure he was going to get it anyway. "I wish you'd tell me who you are, ma'am."

It wasn't *her* voice that answered. Horace Guester was in the doorway now. "She's the postmistress of Hatrack River, on account of her uncle's brother-in-law being the congressman from some district in Susquahenny and he had some pull with the president. We're all hoping to find a candidate in the election this fall who'll promise to throw her out so we can vote for him for president. Failing that, we're going to have to up and hang her one of these days."

The postmistress got a sort of half-smile on her face. "And to think Horace Guester's knack is to make folks feel welcome!"

"What would the charge be, in the hanging?" asked Alvin.

"Criminal gossip," said Horace Guester. "Rumor aforethought. Sniping with malice. Backbiting with intent to kill. Of course I mean all that in the nicest possible way."

"I do no such thing," said the postmistress. "And my name, since Horace hasn't deigned to utter it yet, is Vilate Franker. My grandmother wasn't much of a speller, so she named my mother Violet but spelled it Vilate, and when my mother grew up she was so ashamed of grandmama's illiteracy that she changed the pronunciation to rhyme with 'plate.' However, I am *not* ashamed of my grandmother, so I pronounce it 'Violet,' as in the delicate flower."

"To rhyme," said Horace, "with Pilate, as in Pontius the hand-washer."

"You sure talk a lot, ma'am," said Arthur Stuart. He spoke in all innocence, simply observing the facts as he saw them, but Horace hooted and Vilate blushed and then, to Alvin's shock, clicked with her tongue and opened her mouth wide, letting her upper row of teeth drop down onto the lower ones. False teeth! And such a horrible image—but neither Arthur nor Horace seemed to see what she had done. Behind her wall of illusion, she apparently thought she could get away with all kinds of ugly contemptuous gestures. Well, Alvin wasn't going to disabuse her. Yet.

"Forgive the boy," said Alvin. "He hasn't learned when's the right time to speak his mind."

"He's right," she said. "Why shouldn't he say so?" But she dropped her teeth at the boy again. "I find it irresistible to tell stories," she went on. "Even when I know my listeners don't care to hear them. It's my worst vice. But there are worse ones—and I thank the good Lord I don't have *those*."

"Oh, I like stories, too," said Arthur Stuart. "Can I come listen to you talk some more?"

"Any time you like, my boy. Do you have a name?"

"Arthur Stuart."

It was Vilate's turn to hoot with laughter. "Any relation to the esteemed king down in Camelot?"

"I was named after him," he said, "but far as I know we ain't no kin."

Horace spoke up again. "Vilate, you won yourself a convert cause the poor boy's got no guile and less sense, but kindly stand aside of this door and let me welcome in this man who was born in my house and this boy who grew up in it."

"There's obviously parts of this story that I haven't heard yet," said Vilate, "but don't trouble yourself on my account—I'm sure I'll get a much fuller version from others than I would ever get from you. Good day, Horace! Good day, Alvin! Good day, my young kingling. Do come see me, but don't bring me any of Horace's cider, it's sure to be poisoned if he knows it's for me!" With that she bustled off the porch and out onto the hard-packed dirt of the road. Alvin saw the illusions dazzle and shimmer as she went. The hexes weren't quite so perfect from the rear. He wondered if others ever saw through her when she was going away.

Horace watched her grimly as she walked up the road. "We pretend that we're only pretending to hate each other, but in fact we really do. The woman's evil, and I mean that serious. She has this knack of knowing where something or somebody's from and where they're bound to end up, but she uses that to piece together the nastiest sort of gossip and I swear she reads other people's mail."

"Oh, I don't know," said Alvin.

"That's right, my boy, you ain't been here for the past year and you *don't* know. A lot of changes since you left."

"Well, let me in, Mr. Guester, so I can set down and maybe eat some of today's stew and have a drink of something—even poisoned cider sounds good about now."

Horace laughed and embraced Alvin. "Have you been gone so long you forgot my name is Horace? Come in, come in. And you too, young Arthur Stuart. You're always welcome here."

To Alvin's relief, Arthur Stuart said nothing at all, and so naturally among the things he didn't say was "papa."

They followed him inside and from then on till they laid down for naps in the best bedroom, they were in Horace's hospitable care. He fed them, gave them hot water for washing their hands and feet and faces, took their dirty clothes for laundering, stuffed more food in them, and then personally tucked them into bed after making them watch him put clean sheets on the bed "just so you *know* I still keep my dear Peg's high standards of cleanliness even if I am just an old widower living alone."

The mention of his late wife was all it took, though, to bring memory flooding back. Tears came into Arthur Stuart's eyes. Horace at once began to apologize, but Alvin stilled him with a smile and a gesture. "He'll be all right," he said. "It's coming home, and her not here. Those are good tears and right to shed them."

Arthur reached out and patted Horace's hand. "I'll be all right, Papa," he said.

Alvin looked at Horace's face and was relieved to see that instead of annoyance, his eyes showed a kind of rueful gladness at hearing the name of Papa. Maybe he was thinking of the one person who had the true right to call him that, his daughter Peggy, who had come home in disguise and was too soon gone, and who knew if he'd ever see her again. Or maybe he was thinking of the one who taught Arthur Stuart to call him Papa, the dear wife whose body lay in the hilltop plot behind the roadhouse, the woman who was always faithful to him even though he never deserved her goodness, being (as only he in all the world believed) a man of evil.

Soon Horace backed on out of the room and closed the door, and Arthur Stuart quietly cried himself to sleep in Alvin's arms. Alvin lay there, wanting to doze, too, for a little while. It was good to be home, or as near to home as Alvin could figure in these days when he wondered what home even was. Carthage City was where he was bound to end up, eh? Why would he go there to live? Or would he only go there to die? What did this Vilate Franker actually know, anyway? He lay there, sleepless, wondering about her, wondering if she could really be as evil as Horace Guester said. Alvin had met true evil in his life, but he still persisted in thinking it was awful rare, and the word was bandied about too much by those who didn't understand what real badness was.

What he could not let himself think of was the only other woman he had known who fenced herself around with hexes. Rather than remember Miss Larner, who was really little Peggy, he finally drifted into sleep.

What an interesting boy, thought Vilate as she walked away from the roadhouse. Not at all like the shifty little weasel I expected after the things Makepeace Smith has said. But then, nobody trusts shifty little weasels well enough to be betrayed by them—it's strong, fine-looking men as tricks folks into thinking they're as open-hearted as they are open-faced. So maybe every word Makepeace said was true. Maybe Alvin did steal some precious hoard of gold that he found while digging a well. Maybe Alvin did fill up the well where the gold was found and dig another a few yards off, hoping nobody'd notice. Maybe he did shape it like a plow and pretend that he had turned iron into gold so he could run off with Makepeace's treasure trove. What's that to me? thought Vilate. It wasn't my gold, and never could be, as long as Makepeace had it. But if it happens to be a golden plow that Alvin has in that bag he carries over his shoulder, why, then it might end up being anybody's gold.

Anybody strong enough might take it away by brute force, for instance. Anybody cruel enough might kill Alvin and take it from the corpse. Anybody sneaky enough could take it out of Alvin's room as he slept. Anybody rich enough could hire lawyers to prove something against Alvin in court and take it away by force of law. All kinds of ways to get that plow, if you want it bad enough.

But Vilate would never stoop to coercion. She wouldn't even *want* that golden plow, if it existed, unless Alvin gave it to her of his own free will. As a gift. A love-gift, perhaps. Or . . . well, she'd settle for a guilt gift, if it came to that. He looked like a man of honor, but the way he was staring at her . . . well, she knew that look. The man was smitten. The man was hers, if she wanted him.

Play this right, Vilate, she told herself. Set the stage. Make *him* come after you. Let no one say you set your cap for him.

Her best friend was waiting for her in the kitchen shed back of the post office when she got there. "So what do you think of that Alvin?" she asked, before Vilate even had time to greet her.

"Trust you to get the news before I can tell you myself." Vilate set to work stoking up the fine cast-iron stove with a bread oven in it that made her the envy of the women in Hatrack River.

"Five people saw you on the roadhouse porch greeting him, Vilate, and the word reached me before your foot touched the street, I'm sure."

"Then those are idle people, I'd say, and the devil has them."

"No doubt you'd know—I'm sure the devil gives you a new list every time he makes another recruit."

"Of course he does. Why, everyone knows the devil lives right here in my fancy oven." Vilate cackled with glee.

"So . . ." said her best friend impatiently. "What do you think of him?"

"I don't think he's that much," said Vilate. "Workingman's arms, of course, and tanned like any low-class boy. His talk is rather coarse and country-like. I wonder if he can even read."

"Oh, he can read all right. Teacher lady taught him when he lived here."

"Oh, yes, the fabled Miss Larner who was so clever she got her prize student to win a spelling bee, which caused the slave finders to get wind of a half-Black boy and ended up killing Horace Guester's wife, Miss Larner's own mother. A most unnatural woman."

"You do find a way to make the story sound right ugly," said her friend.

"Is there a pretty version of it?"

"A sweet love story. Teacher tries to transform the life of a half-Black boy and his rough-hewn friend, a prentice smith. She falls in love with the smith boy, and turns the half-Black lad into a champion speller. Then the forces of evil take notice—"

"Or God decides to strike down her pride!"

"I do think you're jealous of her, Vilate. I do think that."

"Jealous?"

"Because she won the heart of Alvin Smith, and maybe she still owns it."

"Far as I can tell, his heart's still beating in his own chest."

"And is the gold still shining in his croker sack?"

"You talk sweet about Miss Larner, but you always assume *I* have the worst motives." Vilate had the stove going nicely now, and put on a teapot to boil as she began cutting string beans and dropping them in a pan of water.

"Because I know you so well, Vilate."

"You *think* you know me, but I'm full of surprises."

"Don't you drop your teeth at *me*, you despicable creature."

"They dropped by themselves," said Vilate. "I never do it on purpose."

"You're such a liar."

"But I'm a beautiful liar, don't you think?" She flashed her best smile at her friend.

"I don't understand what men see in women anyway," her friend answered. "Hexes or no hexes, as long as a woman has her clothes on a man can't see what he's interested in anyhow."

"I don't know about *all* men," said Vilate. "I think some men love me for my character."

"A character of sterling silver, no doubt—never mind a little tarnish, you can wipe *that* off with a little polish."

"And some men love me for my wit and charm."

"Yes, I'm sure they do—if they've been living in a cave for forty years and haven't seen a civilized woman in all that time."

"You can tease me all you want, but I know you're jealous of me, because Alvin Smith is already falling in love with me, the poor hopeless boy, while he'll never give a look at you, not a single look. Eat your heart out, dear."

Her best friend just sat there with a grumpy face. Vilate had really hit home with that last one. The teapot sang. As always, Vilate set out two teacups. But, as always, her best friend sniffed the tea but never drank it. Well, so what? Vilate never failed in her courtesy, and that's what mattered.

"Makepeace is going to take him to court."

"Ha," said Vilate. "You heard *that* already, too?"

"Oh, no. I don't know if Makepeace Smith even knows his old prentice is back in town—though you can bet that if the word reached *me* that fast, it got to him in half the time! I just know that Makepeace has been bragging so much on how Alvin robbed him that if he don't serve papers on the boy, everybody's going to know it was just empty talk. So he's *got* to bring the boy to trial, don't you see?"

Vilate smiled a little smile to herself.

"Already planning what you're going to bring to him in jail?" asked her friend.

"Or something," said Vilate.

Alvin woke from his nap to find Arthur Stuart gone and the room half-dark. The traveling must have taken more out of him than he thought, to make him sleep the afternoon away.

A knock on the door. "Open up, now, Alvin," said Horace. "The sheriff's just doing his job, he tells me, but there's no way out of it."

So it must have been a knock on the door that woke him in the first place. Alvin swung his legs off the bed and took the single step that got him to the door. "It wasn't barred," he said as he opened it. "You only had to give it a push."

Sheriff Po Doggly looked downright sheepish. "Oh, it's just Makepeace Smith, Alvin. Everybody knows he's talking through his hat, but he's gone and got a warrant on you, to charge you with stealing his treasure trove."

"Treasure?" asked Alvin. "I never heard of no treasure."

"Claims you dug up the gold digging a well for him, and moved the well so nobody'd know—"

"I moved the well cause I struck solid stone," said Alvin. "If I found gold, why would that make me move the well? That don't even make sense."

"And that's what you'll say in court, and the jury will believe you just fine," said Sheriff Doggly. "Everybody knows Makepeace is just talking through his hat."

Alvin sighed. He'd heard the rumors flying hither and yon about the golden plow and how it was stolen from a blacksmith that Alvin prenticed with, but he never thought Makepeace would have the face to take it to court, where he'd be proved a liar for sure. "I give you my word I won't leave town till this is settled," said Alvin. "But I've got Arthur Stuart to look after, and it'd be right inconvenient if you locked me up."

"Well, now, that's fine," said Doggly. "The warrant says you have a choice. Either you surrender the plow to me for safekeeping till the trial, or you sit in jail *with* the plow."

"So the plow is the only bail I can pay, is that it?" asked Alvin.

"Reckon that's the long and short of it."

"Horace, I reckon you'll have to look after the boy," said Alvin to the innkeeper. "I didn't bring him here to put him back in your charge, but you can see I got small choice."

"Well, you could put the plow in Po's keeping," said Horace. "Not that I mind keeping the boy."

"No offense, Sheriff, but you wouldn't keep the plow safe a single night," said Alvin, smiling wanly.

"Reckon I could do just fine," said Po, looking a mite offended. "I mean, even if I lock you up, you don't think I'd let you keep the plow in the cell with you, do you?"

"Reckon you *will*," said Alvin mildly.

"Reckon not," said Po.

"Reckon you think you could keep it safe," said Alvin. "But what you don't know is how to keep folks safe from the plow."

"So you admit you have it."

"It was my journeypiece," said Alvin. "There are witnesses of that. This whole charge is nonsense, and you and everybody else knows it. But what'll the charge be if I give you this plow and somebody opens the sack and gets struck blind? What's the charge then?"

"Blind?" asked Po Doggly, glancing at Horace, as if his old friend the innkeeper could tell him whether he was having his leg pulled.

"You think you can tell your boys not to look in the sack, and that's going to be enough?" said Alvin. "You think they won't just try to take a peek?"

"Blind, eh?" said Po.

Alvin picked up the sack from where it had lain beside him on the bed. "And who's going to carry the plow, Po?"

Sheriff Doggly reached out to take it, but no sooner had his hands closed around the sack than he felt the hard metal inside shift and dance under his hands, sliding away from him. "Stop doing that, Alvin!" he demanded.

"I'm just holding the top of the sack," said Alvin. "What shelf you going to keep this on?"

"Oh, shut up, boy," said Doggly. "I'll let you keep it in the cell. But if you plonk somebody over the head with that thing and make an escape, I'll find you and the charge won't be no silly tale from Makepeace Smith, I promise you."

Alvin shook his head and smiled.

Horace laughed out loud. "Po, if Al wanted to escape from your jail, he wouldn't have to do no head plonking."

"I'm just telling you, Al," said the sheriff. "Don't push your luck with me. There's a outstanding extradition order from Appalachee about standing trial for the death of a certain dead Slave Finder."

Suddenly Horace's genial manner changed, and in a quick movement he had the sheriff pressed into the doorjamb so tight it looked like it might make a permanent difference in his posture. "Po," said Horace, "you been my dearest friend for many a year. We done in the dark of night what would get us kilt for doing in daylight, and trusted each other's life through it all. If you ever bring a charge or even *try* to extradite this boy for killing the *Slave Finder* who killed my Margaret in my own house, I will do a little justice on you with my own two hands.''

Po Doggly squinted and looked the innkeeper in the eye. "Is that a threat, Horace? You want me to break my oath of office for you?''

"How can it be a threat?'' said Horace. "You know I meant it in the nicest possible way.''

"Just come along to jail, Alvin,'' said Doggly. "I reckon if the town ladies don't have meals for you, Horace here will bring you roadhouse stew every night.''

"I keep the plow?'' asked Alvin.

"I ain't coming near that thing,'' said the sheriff. "*If* it's a plow. *If* it's gold.'' Doggly gestured him to pass through the door and come into the hall. Alvin complied. The sheriff followed him down the narrow hall to the common room, where about two dozen people were standing around waiting to see what the sheriff had been after. "Alvin, nice to see you,'' several of them greeted him. They looked kind of embarrassed, seeing how Alvin was in custody. "Not much of a welcome, is it?'' said Ruthie Baker, her face grim. "I swan, that Makepeace Smith has bit himself a tough piece of gristle with this mischief.''

"Just bring me some of them snickerdoodles in jail,'' said Alvin. "I been hankering for them the whole way here.''

"You can bet the ladies'll be quarreling all day about who's to feed you,'' said Ruth. "I just wish dear old Peg had been here to greet you.'' And she burst into quick, sentimental tears. "Oh, I wish I didn't cry so easy!''

Alvin gave her a quick hug, then looked at the sheriff. "She ain't passing me no file to saw the bars with,'' he said. "So is it all right if I . . .''

"Oh, shut up, Alvin,'' said Sheriff Doggly. "Why the hell did you even come back here?''

At that moment the door swung open and Makepeace Smith himself strode in. "There he is! The thief has been apprehended at last! Sheriff, make him give me my plow!''

Po Doggly looked him in the eye. Makepeace was a big man, with massive arms and legs like tree trunks, but when the sheriff faced him Makepeace wilted like a flower. "Makepeace, you get out of my way right now.''

"I want my plow!'' Makepeace insisted—but he backed out the door.

"It ain't your plow till the court says it's your plow, if it ever does," said the sheriff.

Horace Guester chimed in. "It ain't your plow till you show you know how to make one just like it."

But Alvin himself said nothing to Makepeace. He just walked on out of the roadhouse, pausing in the doorway only to tell Horace, "You let Arthur Stuart visit me all he wants, you hear?"

"He'll want to sleep right in the cell with you, Alvin, you know that!"

Alvin laughed. "I bet he can fit right through the bars, he's so skinny."

"I made those bars!" Makepeace Smith shouted. "And they're too close together for anyone to fit through!"

Ruth Baker shouted back, just as loudly. "Well, if you made those bars, little Arthur can no doubt *bend* them out of the way!"

"Come on now, folks," Sheriff Doggly said. "I'm just making a little arrest here, so stand clear and let me bring the prisoner on through. While you, Makepeace, are exactly three words away from being arrested your own self for obstructing justice and disturbing the peace."

"Arrest *me!*" cried Makepeace.

"Now you're just *one* word away," said Sheriff Doggly. "Come on, any word will do. Say it. Let me lock you up, Makepeace. You know I'm dying to."

Makepeace knew he was. He clamped his mouth shut and took a few steps away from the roadhouse porch. But then he turned to watch, and let himself smile as he saw Alvin getting led away down the street toward the courthouse, and the jail out back.

11

Jail

Calvin's French was awful—but that was hardly his worry. Talking he had done in England, and plenty of it, until he learned to imitate the cultured accents of a refined gentleman. But here in Paris, talking was useless—harmful, even. One did not become a figure of myth and rumor by chatting. That's one thing Calvin had learned from Alvin, all right, even though Alvin never meant to teach it. Alvin never tooted his own horn. So every Tom, Dick, and Sally tooted it for him. And the quieter he got, the more they bragged on him. That was what Calvin did from the moment he arrived in Paris, kept his silence as he went about healing people.

He had been working on healing—like Taleswapper said, that was a knack people would appreciate a lot more than a knack for killing bugs. No way could Calvin do the subtle things that Alvin talked about, seeing the tiny creatures that spread disease, understanding the workings of the little bits of life out of which human bodies were built. But there *were* things within Calvin's grasp. Gross things, like bringing the edges of open wounds together and getting the skin to scar over—Calvin didn't rightly understand how he did it, but he could sort of squinch it together in his mind and the scar-stuff would grow.

Getting skin to split, too, letting the nasty fluids spew out—that was impressive indeed, especially when Calvin did it with beggars on the city streets. Of course, a lot of the beggars had phony wounds. Calvin could hardly heal *those*, and he wouldn't make himself many friends by making the painted scars slide off beggars' faces. But the real ones—he could help some of them, and when he did, he was careful to make sure plenty of people could see exactly what happened. Could see the healing, but could not hear him brag or boast, or even promise in advance what would happen. He would make a great show of it, standing in front of the beggar, ignoring the open hand or the proffered cup, looking down instead at the wound, the sore, the swelling. Finally the beggar would fall silent, and so would the onlookers, their attention at last riveted on the spot that Calvin so intently watched. By then, of course, Calvin had the wound clearly in mind, had explored it with his doodling bug, had thought through what he was going to do. So in that exact moment of silence he reached out with his bug and gave the new shape to the skin. The flesh opened or the wound closed, whatever was needed.

The onlookers gasped, then murmured, then chattered. And just when someone was about to engage him in conversation, Calvin turned and walked away, shaking his head and refusing to speak.

The silence was far more powerful than any explanation. Rumors of him spread quickly, he knew, for in the cafe where he supped (but did no healing) he heard people speaking of the mysterious silent healer, who went about doing good as Jesus did.

What Calvin hoped would not get spread about was the fact that he wasn't exactly healing people, except by chance. Alvin could get into the deep hidden secrets of the body and do real healing, but Calvin couldn't see that small. So the wound might drain and close, but if there was a deep infection it would come right back. Still, some of them might be healed, for all he knew. Not that it would really help them—how would they beg, without a wound? If they were smart, they'd get away from him before he could take away the coin they used to buy compassion. But no, the ones with real injury wanted to be healed more than they wanted to eat. Pain and suffering did that to people. They could be wise and careful when they felt fine. Add a little pain to the mix, though, and all they wanted was whatever would make the pain go away.

It took a surprisingly long time before one of the Emperor's secret police came to see him. Oh, a gendarme or two had witnessed what he did, but since he touched no one and said nothing, they also did nothing, said nothing to him. And soldiers—they were beginning to seek him out, since so many veterans had injuries from their days in service, and half the cripples Calvin helped had old companions from the battle lines they went to see, to show the healing miracle that Calvin had brought them. But no one with the furtive wariness of the secret police was ever in the crowd, not for three long weeks—weeks in which Calvin had to keep moving his operation from one part of the city to another, lest someone he had already healed come back to him for a second treatment. What good would all this effort do if the rumor began to get about that the ones he healed didn't stay healed?

Then at last a man came, a middle-sized man of bourgeois clothing and modest demeanor, but Calvin saw the tension, the watchfulness—and, most important, the brace of pistols hidden in the pockets of his coat. This one would report to the Emperor. So Calvin made quite sure that the secret policeman was in a good position to see all that transpired when he healed a beggar. Nor did it hurt that even before the silence fell and he did the healing, everyone was murmuring things like, "Is he the one? I heard he healed that one-legged beggar near Montmartre," though of course Calvin had never even attempted to heal someone with a missing limb. Even Alvin might not be able to do something as spectacular as *that*. But it didn't hurt that such a rumor was about. Anything to get him into the presence of the Emperor, for everyone knew that he suffered agonies from the gout. Pain in the legs—he will bring me to him to end the pain in his legs. For the pain, he'll teach me all he knows. Anything to remove the pain.

The healing ended. Calvin walked away, as usual. To his surprise, however, the secret policeman left by quite another route. Shouldn't he follow me? Whisper to me that the Emperor needs me? Would I come and serve the Emperor? Oh, but I'm not sure I can be of help. I do what I can, but many wounds are stubborn and refuse to be fully healed. Oh, that's right, Calvin meant to promise *nothing*. Let his deeds speak for themselves. He would make the Emperor's leg feel better for a while—he was sure he could do that—but no one would ever be able to say that Calvin Miller had promised that the healing would be permanent, or even that there would be any kind of healing at all.

But he had no chance to say these things, for the secret policeman went another way.

That evening, as he waited for his supper at the cafe, four gendarmes came into the cafe, laughing as if they had just come off duty. Two went toward the kitchen—apparently they knew someone there—while the other two jostled, clumsy and laughing, among the tables. Calvin smiled a moment and then looked out the window.

The laughing stopped. Harsh hands seized his arms and lifted him out of his chair. All four gendarmes were around him now, not laughing at all. They bound his wrists together and hobbled his legs. Then they half-dragged him from the cafe.

It was astonishing. It was impossible. This had to be a response to the report of the secret policeman. But why would they arrest him? What law had he broken? Was it simply that he spoke English? Surely they understood the difference between an Englishman and an American. The English were still at war with France, or something like war, anyway, but the Americans were neutral, more or less. How dare they?

For a moment, painfully hobbling along with the gendarmes at the too-brisk pace they set for him, Calvin toyed with the idea of using his Makering power to loose the bonds and stand free of them. But they were all armed, and Calvin had no desire to tempt them to use their weapons against an escaping prisoner.

Nor did he waste effort, after the first few minutes, trying to persuade them that some terrible mistake was underway. What was the point? They knew who he was; someone had told them to arrest him; what did they care whether it was a mistake or not? It wasn't *their* mistake.

Half an hour later, he found himself stripped and thrown into a miserable stinking cell in the Bastille.

"Welcome to the Land of the Guillotine!" croaked someone farther up the corridor. "Welcome, O pilgrim, to the Shrine of the Holy Blade!"

"Shut up!" cried another man.

"They sliced through another man's neck today, the one who was in the cell you're in now, new boy! That's what happens to Englishmen here in Paris, once somebody decides that you're a spy."

"But I'm not English!" Calvin cried out.

This was greeted with gales of laughter.

Peggy set down her pen in weariness, closed her eyes in disgust. Wasn't there some kind of plan here? The One who sent Alvin into the world, who protected him and prepared him for the great work of building the Crystal City, didn't that One have some kind of plan? Or was there no plan? No, there had to be some meaning in the fact that this very day, in Paris, Calvin was locked up in prison, just as Alvin was in prison in Hatrack River. The Bastille, of course, was a far cry from a second-story room in the back of the courthouse, but jail was jail—they were both locked in, for no good reason, and with no idea of how it would all come out.

But Peggy knew. She saw all the paths. And, finally, she closed up her pen, put away the papers she had been writing on, and got up to tell her hosts that she would have to leave earlier than she expected. "I'm needed elsewhere, I think."

Bonaparte's nephew was a weasel who thought he was an ermine. Well, let him have his delusion. If men didn't have delusions, Bonaparte wouldn't be Emperor of Europe and Lawgiver of Mankind. Their delusions were his truth; their hungers were his heart's desire. Whatever they wanted to believe about themselves, Bonaparte helped them believe it, in exchange for control over their lives.

Little Napoleon, the lad called himself. Half of Bonaparte's nephews had been named Napoleon, in an effort to curry favor, but only this one had the effrontery to use the name in court. Bonaparte wasn't quite sure if this meant that Little Napoleon was bolder than the others, or simply too stupid to realize how dangerous it was to dare to use the Emperor's own name, as if to assert one's claim to succeed him. Seeing him now, marching in here like a mechanical soldier—as if he had some secret military accomplishment that no one knew about but which entitled him to strut about playing the general—Bonaparte wanted to laugh in his face and expose in front of all the world Little Napoleon's dreams of sitting on the throne, ruling the world, surpassing his uncle's accomplishments. Bonaparte wanted to look him in the eye and say, "You couldn't even fill my pisspot, you vainglorious mountebank."

Instead he said, "What good wind blows you here, my little Napoleon?"

"Your gout," said the lad.

Oh, no. Another cure. Cures found by fools usually did more harm than good. But the gout was a curse, and . . . let's see what he has.

"An Englishman," said Little Napoleon. "Or, to speak more accurately, an American. My spies have watched him—"

"*Your* spies? These are different spies from the spies I pay?"

"The spies you assigned to me for supervision, Uncle."

"Ah, those spies. They do still remember they work for me, don't they?"

"Remember it so well that instead of simply following orders and watching for enemies, they have also watched for someone who might help you."

"Englishmen in Europe are all spies. Someday after some notable achievement when I'm very very popular I will round them all up and guillotine them. Monsieur Guillotin—now *that* was a useful fellow. Has he invented anything else lately?"

"He's working on a steam-powered wagon, Uncle."

"They already exist. We call them locomotives, and we're laying track all over Europe."

"Ah, but *he* is working on one that doesn't have to run on rails."

"Why not a steam-powered balloon? I can't understand why that has never worked. The engine would propel the craft, and the steam, instead of being wastefully discharged into the atmosphere, would fill the balloon and keep the craft aloft."

"I believe the problem, Uncle, is that if you carry enough fuel to travel more than twenty or thirty feet, the whole thing weighs too much to get off the ground."

"That's why inventors exist, isn't it? To solve problems like that. Any fool could come up with the basic idea—*I* came up with it, didn't I? And when it comes to such matters I'm plainly a fool, as most men are." Bonaparte had long since learned that such modest remarks always got repeated by onlookers in the court and did much to endear him to the people. "It's Monsieur Guillotin's job to ... well, never mind, the machine that bears his name is enough of a contribution to mankind. Swift, sure, and painless executions—a boon to the unworthiest of humans. A very Christian invention, showing kindness to the least of Jesus' brethren." The priests would repeat that one, and from the pulpit, too.

"About this Calvin Miller," said Little Napoleon.

"And my gout."

"I've seen him drain a swollen limb just by standing on the street staring at a beggar's pussing wound."

"A pussing wound isn't the gout."

"The beggar had his trousers ripped open to show the wound, and this American stood there looking for all the world as if he were dozing off, and then suddenly the skin erupted with pus and all of it drained out, and then the wound closed without a single stitch. Neither he nor any man touched the leg. It was quite a demonstration of remarkable healing powers."

"You saw this yourself?"

"With my own eyes. But only the once. I can hardly go about secretly, Uncle. I look too much like your esteemed self."

No doubt Little Napoleon imagined that this was flattery. Instead it sent a faint wave of nausea through Bonaparte. But he let nothing show in his face.

"You now have this healer under arrest?"

"Of course. Waiting for your pleasure."

"Let him sweat."

Little Napoleon cocked his head a moment, studying Bonaparte, probably trying to figure out what plan his uncle had for the healer, and why he didn't want to see him right away. The one thing he would never think of, Bonaparte was quite sure, was the truth: that Bonaparte hadn't the faintest idea what to do about a healer who actually had power. It made him uneasy thinking about it. And he remembered the young white boy who had come with the Red general, Ta-Kumsaw, to visit him in Fort Detroit. Could this American be the same one?

Why should he even make such a connection? And why would that boy in Detroit matter, after all these years? Bonaparte was uncertain about what it all meant, but it felt to him as if forces were at work, as if this American in the Bastille were someone of great importance to him. Or perhaps not to him. To someone, anyway.

Bonaparte's leg throbbed. Another episode of gout was starting. "Go away now," he said to Little Napoleon.

"Do you want information from the American?" asked Little Napoleon.

"No," said Bonaparte. "Leave him alone. And while you're at it, leave *me* alone, too."

Alvin had a steady stream of visitors in the courthouse jail. It seemed like they all had the same idea. They'd sidle right up to the bars, beckon him close, and whisper (as if the deputy didn't know right well what they was talking about), "Don't you have some way to slip on out of here, Alvin?"

What, they believed he hadn't thought of it? Such a simple matter, to soften the stone and pull one of the bars out. Or, for that matter, he could make the metal of a bar flow away from the stone it was embedded in. Or dissolve the bar entirely. Or push against the stone and press on through, walking through the wall into freedom. Such things would be easy enough for Alvin. As a child he had played with stone and found softness and weakness in it; as a prentice blacksmith, he had come to understand iron from the heart out. Hadn't he crawled into the forgefire and turned an iron plow-share to living gold?

Now, locked in this prison, he thought of leaving, thought of it all the time. Thought of hightailing it off into the woods, with or without Arthur Stuart—the boy was happy here, so why take him away? Thought of the sun on his back, the wind in his face, the greensong of the forest now so faint to him through stone and iron that he could hardly hear it.

But he told himself what he told those friendly folk who meant so well. "I need to be shut of this whole affair before I go off. So I mean to stand trial here, get myself acquitted, and then go on without fear of somebody tracking me down and telling the same lies on me again."

And then they always did the same thing. Having failed to persuade him to escape, they'd eye his knapsack and whisper, "Is it in there?"

And the boldest of them would say what they were all wishing. "Can I see it?"

His answer was always the same. He'd ask about the weather. "Think it's a hard winter coming on?" Some picked up slower than others, but after a while they all realized he wasn't going to answer a blame thing about the golden plow or the contents of his knapsack, not a word one way or the other. Then they'd make some chat or take up his used dishes, them as brought food, but it never took long and soon they was on their way out of the courthouse to tell their friends and family that Alvin was looking sad kind of but he still wasn't saying a thing about that gold plow that Makepeace claimed was his own gold treasure stolen by the boy back in his prentice days.

One day Sheriff Doggly brought in a fellow that Alvin recognized, sort of, but couldn't remember why or who. "That's the one," said the stranger. "Got no respect for any man's knack except his own." Then Alvin recollected well enough—it was the dowser who picked the spot for Alvin to dig a well for Makepeace Smith. The spot where Alvin dug right down to a sheet of thick hard rock, without finding a drop of water first. No doubt Makepeace meant to use him as a witness that Alvin's well wasn't in the spot the dowser chose. Well, that was true enough, no disputing it. The dowser fellow wasn't going to testify to anything that Alvin wouldn't have admitted freely his own self. So let them plot their plots. Alvin had the truth

with him, and that was bound to be enough, with twelve jurors of
Hatrack River folk.

The visits that really cheered him were Arthur's. Two or three
times a day, the boy would blow in from the square like a leaf getting
tucked into an open door by a gust of wind. "You just got to meet
that feller John Binder," he'd say. "Ropemaker. Some folks is joking how if they decide to hang you, he'll be the one as makes the
rope, but he just shuts 'em right up, you should hear him, Alvin.
'No rope of mine is going to hang no Maker,' he says. So even
though you never met him I count him as a friend. But I tell you,
they say his ropes *never* unravel, never even *fray*, no matter where
you cut em. Ain't that some knack?"

And later in the same day, he'd be on about someone else. "I
was out looking for Alfreda Matthews, Sophie's cousin, she's the
one lives in that shack down by the river, only the river's a long
windy thing and I couldn't find her and in fact it was getting on
toward dark and I couldn't rightly find myself, and then here I am
face to face with this Captain Alexander, he's a ship's captain only
who knows what he's doing so far from the sea? But he lives around
here doing tinkering and odd fixing, and Vilate Franker says he must
have done some terrible crime to have to hide from the sea, or maybe
there was some great sea beast that swallowed up his ship and left
only him alive and now he daresn't go back to sea for fear the
beast—she calls it La Vaya Than, which Goody Trader says is Spanish for 'Ain't this a damn lie,' do you know Goody Trader?"

"Met her," says Alvin. "She brung me some horehound drops.
Nastiest candy I ever ate, but I reckon for them as loves horehound
they were good enough. Strange lady. Squatted right outside the door
here pondering for the longest time until she finally gets up and says
'Humf, you're the first man I ever met what didn't need *nothing* and
here you are in jail.' "

"They say that's her knack, knowing what a body needs even
when he don't know himself," said Arthur. "Though I *will* say that
Vilate Franker says that Goody Trader is a humbug just like the
alligator boy in the freak show in Dekane, which you wouldn't take
me to see cause *you* said if he was real, it was cruel to gawk at him,
and—"

"I remember what I said, Arthur Stuart. You don't have to gossip to me about *me*."

"Anyway, what was I talking about?"

"Lost in the woods looking for old drunken Freda."

"And I bumped into that sea captain, anyway, and he looks me in the eye and he says, 'Follow me,' and I go after him about ten paces and he sets me right in the middle of a deer track and he says, 'You just go along this way and when you reach the river again, you go upstream about three rods.' And you know what? I did what he said and you know what?''

"You found Freda.''

"Alfreda Matthews, and she was stone drunk of course but I splashed her face with some water and I done what you said folks ought to do, I emptied her jug out and boy howdy, she was spitting mad, I like to had to out-dance the devil just to keep from getting hit by them rocks she threw!''

"Poor lady," said Alvin. "But it won't do no good as long as there's folks to give her another jug.''

"Can't you do like you did with that Red Prophet?''

Alvin looked at him sharp. "What do you think you know about *that*?''

"Just what your own mama told me back in Vigor Church, about how you took a drunken one-eyed Red and made a prophet out of him.''

Alvin shook his head. "No sir, she got it wrong. He was a prophet all along. And he wasn't a drunk the way Freda's a drunk. He took the likker into him to drown out the terrible black noise of death. That's what I fixed, and then he didn't need that likker no more. But Freda—there's something else in her that hungers for it, and I don't understand it yet.''

"I told her to come to you though, so I reckon you oughta know and that's why I told you she's a-coming to get healed.''

Alvin shook his head.

"Did I do wrong?''

"No, you done right," said Alvin. "But there's nothing I can do for her beyond what she oughta do for herself. She knows the likker's eating her up, stealing her life away from her. But I'll talk to her and help her if I can.''

"They say she can tell you when rain's coming. If she's sober.''

"Then how would anybody know she has such a knack?'' asked Alvin.

Arthur just laughed and laughed. "I reckon she must have been sober *once*, anyway. And it was raining!''

When Arthur Stuart left, Alvin pondered the tales he told. Some of Arthur's chat was just gossip. There was some powerful gossips in Hatrack River these days, and the way Alvin figured it, the two biggest gossips was Vilate Franker, who Alvin had met and knew she was living inside a bunch of lying hexes, and Goody Trader, who he didn't really know yet except for what he gleaned from her visit. Her real name was either Chastity or Charity—Vilate said it was Chastity, but other folks said the other. She went by Goody, short for Goodwife, seeing how she'd been married three times and kept all them husbands happy till they croaked, accidental every time, though again Vilate managed to give Arthur the impression that they wasn't truly accidental. Them two women was at war all the time, that much was plain—hardly a word one said as wasn't contradicted flat out by the other. Now, neither one of these ladies invented gossip, nor was it so that Hatrack River didn't have rumors and tales before the two of them moved here. But it was plain that Arthur was visiting both of them every day, and both of them was filling him full of tales until Alvin could hardly make sense of it and it was a sure thing that Arthur didn't really understand the half of what he'd been told.

Alvin knew for himself that Vilate was deceptive and spiteful. But Goody might be just the same or worse, only she was better at it so Alvin couldn't see it so plain. Hard to tell. And that business with Goody Trader saying Alvin didn't need nothing—well, what was *that*?

But behind all the gossip and quarreling, there was something else that struck Alvin as pretty strange. Mighty knacks was thick underfoot in Hatrack River. Most towns might have somebody with something of a knack that you might notice. Most knacks, though, was pretty plain. A knack for soup. A knack for noticing animal tracks. Useful, but nothing to write a letter to your daddy about. A lot of folks had no idea what their own knack was, because it was so easy for them and not all that remarkable in the eyes of other folks. But here in Hatrack River, the knacks was downright astonishing. This sea captain who could help you find your way even when you didn't know you was lost. And Freda—Alvin pooh-poohed it to Arthur Stuart, but there was folks in town as swore she didn't just *predict* rain, if you sobered her up in a dry season she could *bring* it. And Melyn, a Welsh girl who can harp and sing so you forget everything while she's doing it, forget it all and just sit there with a stupid smile on your face because you're so happy—she came and played for Alvin and he could feel how the sound that flowed from her could reach inside him like a doodlebug scooting through the earth, reach inside and find all the knots and loosen them up and just make him feel good.

It was power like he'd been trying to teach the folks back in

Vigor, only they could hardly understand it, could hardly get but a glimmer of it now and then, and here it was so thick on the ground you could rake it up like leaves. Maggie who helped out in Goody Trader's store, she could ride any horse no matter how wild, plenty of witnesses of that. And one who scared Alvin a little, a girl named Dorcas Bee who could draw portraits of folks that not only looked like their outward face, but also showed everything that was inside them—Alvin didn't know what to make of her, and even with his eyes he couldn't rightly understand how she did it.

Any one of these folks would be remarkable in whatever town they lived in, no matter if it was as big as New Amsterdam or Philadelphia. Yet here they were living in the middle of nowhere, Hatrack River of all places, swelling the numbers of the town but yet nobody seemed to find it remarkable at all that so many knacks was gathered here.

There's a reason for it, Alvin thought. Got to be a reason for it. And I have to know it, because there's going to be a jury of these knacky folks, and they're going to decide whether Makepeace Smith is a plain liar—or I am. Only this town is full of lies, since the things Vilate Franker says and the things Goody Trader says can't all be true at the same time. Full of lies and, yes, miseries. Alvin could feel that there was something of the Unmaker going on, but couldn't lay hands on it or find who it was. Hard to find the Unmaker when the Unmaker didn't want to be found. Especially hard from a jail cell, where all you got was rumor and brief visits.

Well, they wasn't *all* brief. Vilate Franker herself came and stayed sometimes half an hour at a time, even though there wasn't no place to sit down. Alvin couldn't figure what she wanted. She didn't gossip with him, rightly speaking—all of *her* gossip Alvin got secondhand from Arthur Stuart. No, Vilate came to him to talk about philosophy and poetry and such, things that no man or woman had talked to him about since Miss Larner. Alvin wondered if maybe Vilate was trying to charm him, but since he couldn't see the beauty-image from her hexes, he didn't rightly know. She sure wasn't pretty to *him*. But the more she talked, the more he liked her company, till he found himself looking forward to her coming every day. More than anybody except Arthur Stuart, truth be known, and as they talked, Alvin would lie down on the cot in the cell and he'd close his eyes and then he didn't have to see either her unprettiness *or* her hexery, he could just hear the words and think the ideas and see the visions that she conjured in him. She'd say poetry and the words had music inside him. She'd talk of Plato and Alvin understood and it made him feel wise in a way that the adulation of folks back in Vigor Church never did.

Was this some knack of hers? Alvin didn't know, just plain couldn't tell. He only knew that it was only during her visits that he could completely forget that he was in jail. And it dawned on him, after a week or so, that he might just be falling in love. That the feelings that he had only ever had toward Miss Larner were getting waked up, just a little, by Vilate Franker. Now wouldn't that beat all? Miss Larner had been pretty and young, using knacks to make herself look plain and middle-aged. Now here was a woman plain and middle-aged using knacks that made other folks think she was pretty and young. How opposite could you be? But in both cases, it was the mature woman without obvious beauties that he delighted in.

And yet, even as he wondered if he was falling in love with Vilate, every now and then, in his lonely hours especially after dark, he would think of another face entirely. A young girl back in Vigor, the girl whose lies had driven him from home in the first place, the girl who claimed he had done forbidden things with her. He found himself thinking of those forbidden things, and there was a place in his heart where he wished he *had* done them. If he had, of course he would have married her. In fact, he would have married her before doing them, because that was right and the law and Alvin wasn't no kind of man to do wrong by a woman or break no law if he could help it. But in his imaginings in the dark there wasn't no law nor right and wrong neither, he just woke up sweating from a dream in which the girl wasn't no liar after all, and then he was plain ashamed of himself, and couldn't figure out what was wrong with him, to be falling in love with a woman of words and ideas and experience during the day, but then to be hot with passion for a stupid lying girl who just happened to be pretty and flat-out in love with him once upon a time back home.

I am an evil man, thought Alvin at times like that. Evil and unconstant. No better than them faithless fellows who can't leave women alone no matter what. I am the kind of man that I have long despised.

Only even that wasn't true, and Alvin knew it. Because he hadn't done a blamed thing wrong. Hadn't *done* anything. Had only imagined it. Imagined . . . and enjoyed. Was that enough to make him evil? "As a man thinketh in his heart, so is he," said the scripture. Alvin remembered it because his mother quoted it all the time till his father barked back at her, "That's just your way of saying that all men are devils!'' and Alvin wondered if it was true—if all men had evil in their hearts, and those men as were good, maybe they were simply the ones who controlled theirselves so well they could act contrary to their heart's desire. But if that were so, then no man was good, not one.

And didn't the Holy Book say that, too?

No man good, not one. Not me, neither. Maybe me least of all.

And that was his life in that jail in Hatrack River. Darker and darker thoughts about his own worthiness, falling in love with two women at once, caught up in the gossip of a town where the Unmaker was surely at work, and where knacks abounded.

Calvin was pretty good with stone—he always did all right with that. Well, not always. He wasn't *born* finding the natural weaknesses of stone. But after Alvin went off to be a prentice to a smith, Calvin started trying to do what he saw or heard of his big brother doing. In those days he was still hoping to show Alvin how good he was at Makering when he got back, to hear his brother say to him, "Calvin, why, you're most as good as I am!" Which Alvin never said, nor even close to it. But it was true, at least about stone. Stone was easy, really, not like flesh and bone. Calvin could find his way into the stone, part it, shift it.

Which is what he started doing right away with the Bastille, of course. He didn't know why the secret police had put him inside those walls, clammy and cold. It wasn't a dungeon, not like in those stories, where the prisoner never sees any light except when a guard comes down with a torch, so he can go blind without knowing it. There was light enough, and a chair to sit on and a bed to lie on and a chamber pot that got emptied every day, once he figured out he was supposed to leave it by the door.

It was still a prison, though.

It took Calvin about five minutes to figure out that he could pretty much dissolve the whole locking mechanism, but he remembered just in time that getting out of his cell wasn't exactly the same thing as getting out of the Bastille. He couldn't make himself invisible, and Maker or not, a musket ball would knock him down or maim him or kill him like any other man.

He'd have to find another way out. And that meant going right through the wall, right through stone. Trouble was, he didn't have any idea whether he was forty feet up or twenty feet under the street level. Or if the wall at the back of his cell opened on the outside or into an inner courtyard. Who might see if a gap appeared in the wall? He couldn't just remove a stone—he had to remove it in once piece, so he could put it back after if he had to.

He waited till night, then began working on a stone block right near floor level. It was heavy, and he didn't know of any way to make it lighter. Nor was there some subtle way to make stone move across stone. Finally he just softened the stone, plunged his fingers into it, then let it harden around his fingers, so he had a grip right in the middle of the stone block. Now, as he pulled on it, he made a thin layer of the stone turn liquid on the bottom and sides, so it was easier to pull it out, once he got it moving. It also made it silent as rock slid across rock. Except for the loud thud as the back of the stone dropped out of the hole and fell the few inches to the floor.

A breeze came through the cell, making it all the cooler. He slid the stone out of the way and then lay down and thrust his head and shoulders into the gap.

He was maybe twelve feet above the ground and directly over the head of a group of a dozen soldiers marching from somewhere to somewhere. Fortunately, they didn't look up. But that didn't keep Calvin's heart from beating halfway out of his chest. Once they were past, though, he figured he could go feetfirst through the hole and drop safely down to the ground and just walk away into the streets of Paris. Let them wonder how he got a stone out of the wall. That'd teach them to lock up folks who heal beggars.

He was all set to go, his feet already going into the hole, when it suddenly dawned on him that escaping was about as dumb a thing as he could do. Wasn't he here to see the Emperor? If he became a fugitive, that wasn't going to be too helpful. Bonaparte had powers that even Alvin didn't know about. Calvin *had* to learn them, if he could. The smart thing to do was sit tight here and see if somehow, someone in the chain of command might realize that a fellow who could heal beggars might be able to help with Bonaparte's famous gout.

So he got his back into it and hefted the stone back up into the gap and shoved it into place. He left the finger holes in it—it was dark at the back of the cell and besides, maybe if they noticed those holes in the stone they'd have more respect for his powers.

Or maybe not. How could he know? Everything was out of his control now. He hated that. But if you want to get something, you got to put yourself in the way of getting it.

Now that he wasn't trying to escape—but knew that he could if he wanted to—Calvin spent the days and nights lying on his cot or pacing his cell. Calvin wasn't good at being alone. He'd learned that on his trek through the woods after leaving Vigor. Alvin might be happy running along like a Red, but Calvin soon abandoned the forest tracks and got him on a road and hitched a ride on a farmer's wagon and then another and another, making friends and talking for company the whole way.

Now here he was stuck again, and even if the guards had been willing to talk to him, he didn't know the language. It hadn't bothered him that much when he was free to walk the streets of Paris and feel himself surrounded by the bustle of busy city life. Here, though, his inability to so much as ask a guard what day it was . . . it made him feel crippled.

Finally he began to amuse himself with mischief. It was no trouble at all to get his doodle bug inside the lock mechanism and ruin the guard's key by softening it when he inserted it. When the guard took the key back out, it had no teeth and the door was still locked. Angry, the guard stalked off to get another key. This time Calvin let him open the door without a problem—but what was it that made the first key lose its teeth?

And it wasn't just his own lock. He began to search far and wide with his doodle bug until he located the other occupied cells. He played games with their locks, too, including fusing a couple of them shut so no key could open them, and ruining a couple of others so they couldn't be locked at all. The shouting, the stomping, the running, it kept Calvin greatly entertained, especially as he imagined what the guards must be thinking. Ghosts? Spies? Who could be doing these strange things with the locks in the Bastille?

He also learned a few things. Back in Vigor, whenever he sat down for long he'd either get impatient and get up and move again, or he'd start thinking about Alvin and get all angry. Either way, he didn't spend all that much time testing the limits of his powers, not since Alvin came home. Now, though, he found that he could send his doodle bug right far, and into places that he'd never seen with his own eyes. He began to get used to moving his bug through the stone, feeling the different textures of it, sensing the wooden frames to the heavy doors, the metal hinges and locks. Damn, but he was good at this!

And he explored his own body with that doodle bug, and the bodies of the other prisoners, trying to find what it was that Alvin saw, trying to see deep. He experimented a little on the other prisoners' bodies, too, making changes in their legs the way he'd have to change Bonaparte's leg. Not that any of them had gout, of course—that was a rich man's disease, and nobody in prison was rich, even if they had money on the outside. Still, he could get a mental chart of what a more-or-less healthy leg looked like, on the inside. Get some idea of what he needed to do to get the Emperor's leg back in good shape.

Truth to tell, though, he didn't understand much more about legs after a week of this than he did at the beginning.

A week. A week and a half. Every day, more and more often, he'd walk to the wall, squat down, and put his fingers into those finger holes. He'd pull the stone a little bit, or maybe sometimes more, and once or twice all the way out of the wall, wanting to slide through the hole and walk away to freedom. Always, after a little thought, he put it back. But it took more thought every day. And the longing to be gone got stronger and stronger.

It was a blame fool plan anyway, like all his plans, when you came right down to it. Calvin was a fool to think they'd let some unknown American boy have access to the Emperor.

He had the stone out of the wall for what he thought might well be the last time, when he heard the steps in the corridor. Nobody ever came along here this late at night! No time to get the stone back in place, either. So . . . was it go, or stay? They'd see the stone out of the wall no matter what he did. So did he want to face the consequences, which might include seeing the Emperor, but might just as easy mean facing the guillotine; or did he duck through the hole and get out into the street before they got the door open?

Little Napoleon grumbled to himself. All these days, the Emperor could have asked about the American healer any time. But no, it had to be in the middle of the night, it had to be *tonight*, when Little Napoleon had reserved the best box for the opening of a new opera by some Italian, what's-his-name. He wanted to tell the Emperor that tonight was *not* convenient, he should find another toady to do his bidding. But then the Emperor smiled at him and suggested that he had others who could do such a menial job, and he shouldn't waste his nephew's time on such unimportant matters . . . and what could Little Napoleon do? He couldn't let the Emperor realize that he could be replaced by some flunky. No, he insisted, No, Uncle, I'll go myself, it'll be my pleasure.

"I just hope he can do what you promised," Bonaparte said.

The bastard was playing with him, that was the truth. He knew as well as Little Napoleon did that there was no promise of anything, just a report. But if it pleased the Emperor to make his nephew sweat with fear that maybe he'd be made a fool of, well, Emperors were allowed to toy with other people's feelings.

The guard made a great noise about marching down the stone corridor and fumbling a long time with the keys.

"What, fool, are you giving the prisoner time to stop digging his tunnel and hide the evidence?"

"There be no tunnels from this floor, my lord," the turnkey said.

"I know that, fool. But what's all the fumble with the keys?"

"Most of them are new, my lord, and I don't recognize which one opens which door, not as easy as I used to."

"Then get the old keys and don't waste my time!"

"The old keys been stripped, or the locks was broken, my lord. It's been crazy, you wouldn't believe it."

"I *don't* believe it," said Little Napoleon grumpily. But he did, really—he had heard something about some sabotage or some kind of rare lock rust or something in the Bastille.

The key finally slid into the lock, and the door creaked open. The turnkey stepped in and shone his lantern about, to make sure the prisoner was in his place and not poised to jump him and take the keys. No, this one, the American boy, he was sitting far from the door, leaning against the opposite wall.

Sitting on what? The turnkey took a step or two closer, held the lantern higher.

"Mon dieu," murmured Little Napoleon.

The American was sitting on a large stone block from the wall, with a gap that led right out to the street. No man could have lifted such a block out of the wall with his bare hands—how could he even get hold of it? But having moved it somehow, what did this American fool do but sit down and wait! Why didn't he escape?

The American grinned at him, then stood up, still smiling, still looking at Little Napoleon—and then plunged his hands into the stone right up to his elbows, as easy as if the stone had been a water basin.

The turnkey screeched and ran for the door.

The American pulled his hands back out of the stone—except that one of them was in a fist now. He held out the stone to Little Napoleon, who took it, hefted it. It was stone, as hard as ever—but it was shaped with the print of the inside of a man's palms and fingers. Somehow this fellow could reach into solid rock and grab a lump of stone as if it were clay.

Little Napoleon reached into his memory and pulled out some English from his days in school. "What are your name?" he asked.

"Calvin Maker," said the American.

"Speak you the French?"

"Not a word," said Calvin Maker.

"Go *avec* me," said Little Napoleon. *"Avec . . ."*

"With," said the boy helpfully. "Go with you."

"Oui. Yes."

The Emperor had finally asked for the boy. But now Little Napoleon had serious misgivings. There was nothing about the healing of beggars to suggest the boy might have power over solid stone. What if this Calvin Maker did something to embarrass him? What if—it was beyond imagining, but he had to imagine it—what if he killed Uncle Napoleon?

But the Emperor had asked for him. There was no undoing *that.* What was he going to do, go tell Uncle that the boy he'd brought to heal his gout just *might* decide to plunge his hands into the floor and pull up a lump of marble and brain him with it? That would be political suicide. He'd be living on Corsica tending sheep in no time. If he didn't get to watch the world tumble head over heels as his head rolled down into the basket from the guillotine.

"Go go go," said Little Napoleon. "Wiss me."

The turnkey was huddled in a far corner of the corridor. Little Napoleon aimed a kick in his direction. The man was so far gone that he didn't even dodge. The kick landed squarely, and with a whimper the turnkey rolled over like a cabbage.

The American boy laughed out loud. Little Napoleon didn't like his laugh. He toyed with the idea of drawing his knife and killing the boy on the spot. But the explanation to the Emperor would be dangerous. "So you tried for weeks to get me to see him, and he was an assassin all along?" No, whatever happened, the American would see the Emperor.

Calvin Maker would see Napoleon Bonaparte . . . while Little Napoleon would see if God would answer a most fervent prayer.

12

Lawyers

"You know the miller's boy, Alvin, is in jail up in Hatrack River." The stranger leaned on the counter and smiled.

"I reckon we heard about it," said Armor-of-God Weaver.

"I'm here to help get the truth about Alvin, so the jury can make the right judgment up in Hatrack. They don't know Alvin as well as folks around here are bound to. I just need to get some affidavits about his character." The stranger smiled again.

Armor-of-God nodded. "I reckon this is the place for affidavits, if the truth about Alvin is what you're after."

"That I am. I take it you know the young man yourself?"

"Well enough." Armor-of-God figured if he was going to find out what this fellow was doing, it was best not to say he was married to Alvin's sister. "But I reckon you don't know what you're getting into up here, friend. You'll get more than the affidavits you're after."

"Oh, I've heard tell about the massacre at Tippy-Canoe, and the curse that folks here are under. I'm a lawyer. I'm used to hearing grim stories from people I'm defending."

"Defending, eh?" asked Armor. "You a lawyer as defends people, is that it?"

"That's what I'm best known for, in my home in Carthage City."

Armor nodded again. He might live in Carthage City now, but his accent said New England. And he might try some folksy talk, but it was a lawyer's version of it, to put folks off guard. This man could talk like the Bible if he wanted to. He could talk like Milton. But Armor didn't let on that he didn't trust the man. Not yet. "So when folks here tell you how they slaughtered Reds what never done nobody no harm, you can hear that without batting an eye, is that it?"

"I can't guarantee I won't do any eye-batting, Mr. Weaver. But I'll listen, and when it's done, I'll get on with the business that brought me here."

Now it's time. "And what business is that?" asked Armor.

The man blinked. Already batting an eye, thought Armor. That was right quick.

"I told you, Mr. Weaver. Getting affidavits about Alvin the miller's son."

"In order to tell people in Hatrack River about his true character, I remember. The thing is, out of the last eight years, Alvin spent seven in Hatrack, and only one here in Vigor Church. We knowed him as a child, you bet, but lately I'd say it's the people of Hatrack River as knows him best. So the way I see it, you're here to get a picture of Alvin that folks in Hatrack *don't* know. And the only reason for that is because you need to change their point of view about the boy. And since I know for a fact that Alvin is respected in Hatrack, you can only be here to try to dig up some dirt on the boy in order to do him harm. Have I just about got it? Friend?"

The lawyer's sudden lack of a cheerful smile was all the confirmation Armor needed. "Dirt is the farthest thing from my mind, Mr. Weaver. I come here with an open mind."

"An open mind, and free talk about how you defend people and all so as to make folks think you're on Alvin's side, instead of being hired to do your best to destroy folks' good opinion of him. So I reckon the fact that you're here means that Alvin's friends better get somebody else to go around collecting affidavits in his favor, since you won't be satisfied until you dig up some lies."

The man stiffened and stepped back. "I see that you're rather a partisan about the matter. I hope you can tell me what I said to give offense."

"Why, the only offense you gave was thinking that because I'm not a lawyer I must be dumb as a dog's butt."

"Well, no matter what conclusion you have reached, I assure you that as an officer of the court I seek nothing more than the simple truth."

"Officer of the court, is it? Well, I happen to know that *all* lawyers is called officers of the court. Even when they're hired by a private party to do mischief, because you sure as God lives wasn't hired by the county attorney down in Hatrack, because *he* would've give you a letter of introduction and you wouldn't have tried none of these pussyfooting prevaricating misrepresenting shenanigans."

The stranger put his hat back on his head and pushed it down right firm. Armor suppressed the impulse to reach out and push it down still firmer. As the stranger reached the door, Armor called out one last question. "Do you have a name, so we can inquire with the state bar association about any outstanding actions against you?"

The lawyer turned and smiled, even broader than when he was trying to fool Armor. "My name is Daniel Webster, Mr. Weaver, and my client is truth and justice."

"Truth and justice must pay a damn sight better in New England than it does out here," said Armor. "You *are* from New England, aren't you?"

"I was born there, and raised there, but saw no future for myself in that benighted backward place. So I came to the United States, where the laws are founded on the rights of man instead of the dynastic claims of monarchs or the worn-out theology of Puritans."

"Ah. So nobody's paying you?"

"I didn't say that, Mr. Weaver."

"Who's paying you, then? Ain't the county, and it ain't the state. And it sure can't be Makepeace Smith, since he's got him hardly four bits to rub together."

"I'm representing a consortium of concerned citizens of Carthage City, who are determined to see that justice prevails even in the benighted backwaters of the state of Hio."

"A consortium. That anything like a public house? Or a brothel?"

"How amusing."

"Name me a name, Mr. Webster. I happen to be mayor of this town, such as it is, and you're here practicing law, after a fashion, and I think I have a right to know who's sending lawyers up here to collect lies about our respected citizens."

"Do you own a gun of any kind, Mr. Weaver?"

"I do, friend."

"Then why should I reveal the names of my clients to an armed and angry man of a town that is so proud of being a nest of murderers that they brag out the whole story to any unfortunate visitor who happens by? Also, mayors have no right to inquire about anything from an attorney about his relations with his clients. Good day, Mr. Weaver."

Armor watched the Webster fellow out the door, then put on his hat, called out to his oldest boy to leave off soapmaking and watch the store, and took off at a jog up and over the hill to his in-laws' house. His wife would be there, since she was the best of the women at doing Alvin's Makery stuff and so was in much demand as a teacher and a fashioner of—much as Armor hated it—hexes. The family needed to know what was going on, that Alvin had enemies from the capital who were spending money on a lawyer to come dig up dirt about the boy. There was no way around it now—they had to get them a lawyer for Alvin, somehow. And not no country cousin, either. It had to be a city lawyer who knew all the same tricks as this Webster fellow. Armor vaguely remembered having heard of this man somewhere. He was spoke of with awe in some circles, and having talked to him and heard his golden voice and his quick answers and the way he made a lie sound like the natural truth even to someone who knew it was deception—well, Armor knew it would take some finding to get them a lawyer who could best him. And finding was going to be complicated by another problem— paying.

Calvin had no idea what he was supposed to do upon meeting the Emperor. The man's title was a throwback to ancient Rome, to Persia, to Babylon. But there he sat in a straight-back chair instead of a throne, his leg up on a cushioned bench; and instead of courtiers there were only secretaries, each scribbling away on a writing desk until an order or letter or edict was finished, then leaping to his feet and rushing from the room as the next secretary began to scribble furiously as Bonaparte dictated in a continuous stream of biting, lilting, almost Italian-sounding French.

As the dictation proceeded, Calvin, with guards on either side of him (as if that could stop him from making the floor collapse under the Emperor if he felt like it), watched silently. Of course they did not invite him to sit down; even Little Napoleon, the Emperor's nephew, remained standing. Only the secretaries could sit, it seemed, for it was hard to imagine how they could write without a lap.

At first Calvin simply took in the surroundings; then he studied the face of the Emperor, as if that slightly pained expression contained some secret which, if only examined long enough, would yield the secrets of the sphinx. But soon Calvin's attention drifted to the leg. It was the gout that he had to cure, if he was to make any headway. And Calvin had no idea what caused the gout or even how to figure it out. That was Alvin's province.

For a moment it occurred to Calvin that maybe he ought to beg permission to write to his brother so he could get Alvin over here to cure the Emperor and win Calvin's freedom. But he immediately despised himself for the cowardly thought. Am I a Maker or not? And if a Maker, then Alvin's equal. And if Alvin's equal, why should I summon him to bail me out of a situation which, for all I know right now, might need no bailing?

He sent his doodling bug into Napoleon's leg.

It wasn't the sort of swelling that Calvin was used to in the festering sores of beggars. He didn't understand what the fluids were—not pus, that was certain—and he dared not simply make them flow back into the blood, for fear that they might be poisons that would kill the very man he came to learn from.

Besides, was it really in Calvin's best interests to cure this man? Not that he knew how to do it—but he wasn't sure he really ought to try. What he needed was not the momentary gratitude of a cured man, but the continuing dependence of a sufferer who needed Calvin's ministration for relief. Temporary relief.

And this was something Calvin *did* understand, to a point. He had learned long ago how to find the nerves in a dog or squirrel and give them a sort of tweak, an invisible pinch. Sometimes it set the animal to squealing and screeching till Calvin almost died from laughing. Other times the creature didn't show pain, but limped along as if that pinched limb didn't even exist. One time a perfectly healthy dog dragged around its hindquarters till its belly and legs were rubbed raw in the dirt and Father was all set to shoot the poor thing to put it out of its misery. Calvin took mercy on the beast then and unpinched the nerve so it could walk again, but after that it never did walk right, it sort of sidled, though whether that was from the pinch Calvin gave it or from the damage caused by dragging its butt through the dirt for most of a week Calvin had no way to guess.

What mattered was that pinching of the nerve, to remove all feeling—Bonaparte might limp, but it would take away the pain. Relief, not a cure.

Which nerve? It wasn't like Calvin had them all charted out. That sort of methodical thinking was Alvin's game. In England, Calvin had realized that this was one of the crucial differences between him and his brother. There was a new word a fellow just coined at Cambridge for people who were ploddingly methodical like Alvin: *scientist*. While Calvin, with dash and flair and verve and, above all, the spirit of improvisation, *he* was an artist. Trouble was, when it came to getting at the nerves in Bonaparte's leg, Calvin couldn't very well experiment. He didn't think a strong friendship would develop between the Emperor and him if it began with the Emperor squealing and screeching like a tortured squirrel.

He pondered that for a while until, watching a secretary rise up and rush from the room, it occurred to him that Bonaparte's weren't the only legs around. Now that it mattered that Calvin find out exactly which nerve did what, and that his pinch deadened pain instead of provoking it, he had to play the scientist and test many legs until he got it right.

He started with the secretary who was next in line, a shortish fellow (smaller even than the Emperor, who was a man of scant stature) who fidgeted a little in his chair. Uncomfortable? Calvin asked him silently. Then let's see if we can find you some relief. He sent his bug into the man's right leg, found the most obvious nerve, and pinched.

Not a wince, not a grimace. Calvin was annoyed. He pinched harder. Nothing.

Then the current secretary jumped to his feet and rushed from the room. It was now the turn of the short fellow Calvin had pinched. The man tried to shift his body in his chair, to adjust the position of the lapdesk, but to Calvin's delight a look of astonishment came over the man's face, followed by a blush as he had to reach down and move his right leg with his hands. So. That large nerve—or was it a bundle of very fine nerves?—had nothing to do with feeling. Instead they seemed to control movement. Interesting.

The fellow wrote in silence, but Calvin knew that all he was really thinking about was what would happen when he had to jump up and run from the room. Sure enough, when the edict ended—it was about the granting of a special tax exemption to certain vintners in southern France because of a bad harvest—the man leapt up, spun around, and sprawled on the floor, his right leg tangled with his left like the fishing lines of children.

Every eye turned to the poor fellow, but not a word was spoken. Calvin watched with amusement as he got up on his hands and his left knee, while the right leg hung useless. The knee bent well enough, of course, and the man got it under his body so it *looked* like it might work, but twice he tried to put weight on it and twice he fell again.

Bonaparte, looking annoyed, finally spoke to him. "Are you a secretary, sir, or a clown?"

"My leg, sir," said the miserable clerk. "My right leg seems not to work just now."

Bonaparte turned sharply to the guards detaining Calvin. "Help him out of here. And fetch someone to clean up the spilled ink."

The guards hauled the man to his feet and started to move him toward the door. Now it was time for Little Napoleon to assert himself. "Take his desk, fools," said the Emperor's nephew. "And the inkwell, and the quill, and the edict, if it isn't spoiled."

"And how will they do all that?" asked Bonaparte testily. "Seeing they have to hold up this one-legged beggar?" Then he looked expectantly at Little Napoleon's face.

It took a moment for Little Napoleon to realize what the Emperor wanted of him, and an even longer moment for him to swallow his pride enough to do it. "Why, of course, Uncle," he said, with careful mildness. "I shall gladly pick it up myself, sir."

Calvin suppressed a smile as the proud man who had arrested him now knelt down and gathered up papers, lapdesk, quill, and inkwell, carefully avoiding getting a single drop of ink on himself. By now the secretary Calvin had pinched was out of the room. He thought of sending out his bug to find the man and unpinch the nerve, but he wasn't sure where he had gone and anyway, what did it matter? It was just a secretary.

When Little Napoleon was gone, Bonaparte resumed dictating, but now his delivery was not rapid and biting. Rather he halted, corrected himself now and then, and sometimes lapsed into silence for a time, as the secretary sat with pen poised. At such moments Calvin would cause the ink on the quill to flow to the tip and drop off suddenly onto the paper—ah, the flurry of blotting! And of course this only served to distract the Emperor all the more.

There remained, however, the matter of legs. Calvin explored each secretary in turn, finding other nerves to pinch, ever so slightly. He left the nerves of movement alone now; it was the nerves of pain that he was finding now, charting his progress by the widened eyes, flushed faces, and occasional gasps of the unfortunate secretaries. Bonaparte was not unaware of their discomfort—it distracted him all the more. Finally, when a man gasped at a particularly sharp pinch—Calvin's touch was not always precise with such slender things as nerves—Bonaparte turned himself in his chair, wincing at the pain in his own leg, and said, as best Calvin could understand his French, "Do you mock me with these pains and moans? I sit here in agony, making no sound, while you, with no more pain than that of sitting too long to take letters, moan and gasp and wince and sigh until I can only imagine I am trapped with a choir of hyenas!"

At that moment Calvin finally got it right, giving just the right amount of pressure to a secretary's pain nerve that all feeling vanished, and instead of the man wincing, his face relaxed in relief. That's it, thought Calvin. That's how it's done.

He almost sent his bug right into Bonaparte's leg to do that same little twist and make the Emperor's pain go away. Fortunately he was distracted by the opening of the door. It was a scullery maid with a bucket and rags to clean up the ink from the marble floor. Bonaparte glared at her, and she almost dropped her things and fled, except that he at once softened his expression. "My rage is at my pain, girl," he said to her. "Come in and do your work, no one minds."

With that she gathered her courage, scurried to the drying ink, set down the bucket with a clank and a slosh, and set to work scrubbing.

By now Calvin had come to his senses. What good would it do to take away Bonaparte's pain if the Emperor didn't *know* that it was Calvin doing it? Instead he practiced the soothing twist of the nerves on all the secretaries, to their undoubted relief, and as he did he began to sense a sort of current, a humming, a vibration on the nerves that were actually carrying pain at the instant he twisted them, so that he could get even more precise, taking away not all the feeling in a leg, but just the pain itself. Finally he got to the scullery maid, to the pain she always felt in her knees as she knelt on hard cold floors to do her work. So sudden was the relief, and so sharp and constant had been the pain, that she cried aloud, and again Bonaparte glared at the interruption.

"Oh sir," she said, "forgive me, but I suddenly felt no pain in my knees."

"Lucky you," said Bonaparte. "Along with this miracle, do you also find that you see no ink on the floor?"

She looked down. "Sir, with all my scrubbing, I can't get up the whole stain. I'm afraid it's gone down into the stone, sir."

Calvin at once sent his doodling bug into the surface of the marble and discovered that the ink had, indeed, penetrated beyond the reach of her scrubbing. Now was the chance to have Bonaparte notice him, not as a prisoner—even his guards were gone—but as a man of power. "Perhaps I can help," he said.

Bonaparte looked at him as if seeing him for the first time, though Calvin was quite aware that the Emperor had sized him up several times over the past half-hour. Bonaparte spoke to him in accented English. "Was it for scullery work you came to Paris, my dear American friend?"

"I came to serve you, sir," said Calvin. "Whether with a stained floor or a pained leg, I care not."

"Let's see you with floors first," said Bonaparte. "Give him the rags and bucket, girl."

"I don't need them," said Calvin. "I've already done it. Have her scrub again, and this time the stain will come right up."

Bonaparte glowered at the idea of serving as interpreter for an American prisoner and a scullery maid, but his curiosity got the better of his dignity and he gave the girl the order to scrub again. This time the ink came right up, and the stone was clean again. It had been child's play for Calvin, but the awe in the girl's face was the best possible advertisement for his wondrous power. "Sir," she said, "I had only to pass the rag over the stain and it was gone!"

The secretaries were eyeing Calvin carefully now—they weren't fools, and they clearly suspected him of causing both their discomfort and their relief, though some of them were pinching the legs to try to restore feeling after Calvin's first, clumsier attempts at numbing pain. Now Calvin went back into their legs, restored feeling, and then gave the more delicate twist that removed pain. They watched him warily, as Bonaparte looked back and forth between his clerks and his prisoner.

"I see you have been busy playing little jokes on my secretaries."

Without an answer, Calvin reached into the Emperor's leg and, for just a moment, removed all pain. But only for a moment; he soon let it come back.

Bonaparte's face darkened. "What kind of man are you, to take away my pain for a moment and then send it back to me?"

"Forgive me, sir," said Calvin. "It's easy to cure the pain I caused myself, in your men. Or even the pain from hours of kneeling, scrubbing floors. But the gout—that's hard, sir, and I know of no cure, nor of any relief that lasts more than a little while."

"Longer than five seconds, though—I'll wager you know how to do *that*."

"I can try."

"You're the clever one," said Bonaparte. "But I know a lie. You can take away the pain and yet you choose not to. How dare you hold me hostage to my pain?"

Calvin answered in mild tones, though he knew he took his life in his hands to say such a bold thing in *any* tone: "Sir, you have held my whole body prisoner this whole time, when I was free before. I come here and find you already a prisoner of pain, and you complain to *me* that I do not set *you* free?"

The secretaries gasped again, but not in pain this time. Even the scullery maid was shocked—so much so that she knocked her bucket over, spilling soapy, inky water over half the floor.

Calvin quickly made the water evaporate from the floor, then made the residue of ink turn to fine, invisible dust.

The scullery maid went screaming from the room.

The secretaries, too, were on their feet. Bonaparte turned to them. "If I hear any rumor of this, you will all go to the Bastille. Find the girl and silence her—by persuasion or imprisonment, she deserves no torture. Now leave me alone with this extortionist, while I find out what he wants to get from me."

They left the room. As they were going, Little Napoleon and the guards returned, but Bonaparte sent them away as well, to his nephew's ill-concealed fury.

"All right, we're alone," said Bonaparte. "What do you want?"

"I want to heal your pain."

"Then heal it and have done."

Calvin took the challenge, twisted the nerves just right, and saw Bonaparte's face soften, losing the perpetual wince. "Such a gift as that," murmured the Emperor, "and you spend it cleaning floors and taking stones from prison walls."

"It won't last," said Calvin.

"You mean you choose not to make it last," said Bonaparte.

Calvin took the unusual step of telling the plain truth, sensing that Bonaparte would know if anything he said was a lie. "It's not a cure. The gout is still there. I don't understand the gout and I can't cure it. I can take away the pain."

"But not for long."

Truthfully, Calvin answered, "I don't know how long."

"And for what payment?" asked Bonaparte. "Come on, boy, I know you want something. Everyone does."

"But you're Napoleon Bonaparte," said Calvin. "I thought you knew what every man wanted."

"God doesn't whisper it in my ear, if that's what you think. And yes, I know what you want but I have no idea why you've come to me for it. You're hungry to be the greatest man on Earth. I've met men with ambition like yours before—and women, too. Unfortunately I can't easily bend such ambition into subservience to my interests. Generally I have to kill them, because they're a danger to me."

Those words went like a knife through Calvin's heart.

"But you're different," said Bonaparte. "You mean me no harm. In fact, I'm just a tool to you. A means of gaining advantage. You don't want my kingdom. I rule all of Europe, northern Africa, and much of the ancient East, and yet you want me only to tutor you in preparation for a much greater game. What game, on God's green Earth, might that be?"

Calvin never meant to tell him, but the words came blurting out. "I have a brother, an older brother, who has a thousand times my power." The words galled him, burned his throat as he said them.

"And a thousand times your virtue, too, I think," said Bonaparte. But those words had no sting for Calvin. Virtue, as Alvin defined it, was waste and weakness. Calvin was proud to have little of it.

"Why hasn't your brother challenged me?" asked Bonaparte. "Why hasn't he shown his face to me in all these years?"

"He's not ambitious," said Calvin.

"That is a lie," said Bonaparte, "even though in your ignorance you believe it. There is no such thing as a living human being without ambition. St. Paul said it best: Faith, ambition, and love, the three driving forces of human life."

"I believe it was hope," said Calvin. "Hope and charity."

"Hope is the sweet weak sister of ambition. Hope is ambition wishing to be liked."

Calvin smiled. "That's what I've come for," he said.

"Not to heal my gout."

"To ease your pain, as you ease my ignorance."

"With powers like yours, what do you need with my small world-conquering gifts?" Bonaparte's irony was plain and painful.

"My powers are nothing compared to my brother's, and he is the only teacher I can learn them from. So I need other powers that he doesn't have."

"Mine."

"Yes."

"Then how do I know that you won't turn on me and try to take my empire?"

"If I wanted it I could have it now," said Calvin.

"It's one thing to terrify people with displays of power," said Bonaparte. "But terror only gets you obedience when you're there. I have the power to hold men obedient to me even when my back is turned, even when there's no chance I'd ever catch them in wrongdoing. They love me, they serve me with their whole hearts. Even if you sent every building in Paris crashing to the street, it wouldn't win the people's loyalty."

"That's why I'm here, because I know that."

"Because you want to win the loyalty of your brother's friends," said Bonaparte. "You want them to spurn your brother and put you in his place."

"Call me Cain if you want, but yes," said Calvin. "Yes."

"I can teach you that," said Bonaparte. "But no pain. And no little games with the pain, either. If the pain comes back, I'll have you killed."

"You can't even hold me in a prison if I don't want to stay there."

"When I decide to kill you, boy, you won't even see it coming."

Calvin believed him.

"Tell me, boy—"

"Calvin."

"Boy, don't interrupt me, don't correct me." Bonaparte smiled sweetly. "Tell me, Calvin, weren't you afraid that I would win *your* loyalty and put your gifts to use in my service?"

"As you said," Calvin answered, "your powers have scant effect on people with ambition as great as your own. It's only really the goodness in people that you turn against them to control them. Their generosity. Isn't that right?"

"In a sense, though it's much more complicated than that. But yes."

Calvin smiled broadly. "Well, then, you see? I knew I was immune."

Bonaparte frowned. "Are you so sure of that? So proud to be a man utterly devoid of generosity?"

Calvin's smile faded just a little. "Old Boney, the terror of Europe, the toppler of empires—Old Boney is shocked at *my* lack of compassion?"

"Yes," said Bonaparte. "I never thought I'd see the like. A man I'll never have power over . . . and yet I will let you stay with me, for the sake of my leg, and I'll teach you all that can be taught. For the sake of my leg.''

Calvin laughed and nodded. ''Then you've got a deal.''

Only later, as he was being shown to a luxurious apartment in the palace, did it occur to Calvin to wonder if, perhaps, Bonaparte's admission that Calvin could not be controlled might not be just a ploy; if, perhaps, Bonaparte already had control over Calvin but, like all the Emperor's other tools, Calvin continued to think that he was free.

No, he told himself. Even if it's true, what good will it do me to think about it? The deed's done or it's not done, and either way I'm still myself and still have Alvin to deal with. A thousand times more powerful than me! A thousand times more virtuous! We'll see about that when the time comes, when I take your friends away from you, Alvin, the way you stole my birthright from *me*, you thieving Esau, you pit-digging Reuben, you jealous taunting Ishmael. God will give me my birthright, and has given me Bonaparte to teach me how to accomplish something with it.

Alvin didn't realize he was doing it. Daytimes he thought he was bearing his imprisonment right well, putting on a cheerful face for his visitors, singing now and then—harmonizing with the jailors when they knew the song and joined in. It was a jaunty sort of imprisonment, and everyone was saying that it was a shame for Alvin to be all cooped up, but wasn't he taking it like a soldier?

In his sleep, though, his hatred for the jail walls, for the sameness and lifelessness of the place, it came out in another kind of song, an inward music that harmonized with the greensong that once had filled this part of the world. It was the music of the trees and the lesser plants, of the insects and spiders, of the furred and finny creatures that dwelt in the leaves, on the ground, in the earth, or in the cold streams and unstoppable rivers. And Alvin's inner voice was tuned to it, knew all the melodies, and instead of harmonizing with jailors his heart sang with free creatures.

And they heard his song that went unheard by human ears. In the tattered remnants of the ancient woods, in the new growth where a few abandoned fields were four or ten years fallow, they heard him, the last few bison, the still deer, the hunting cats and the sociable coyotes and the timber wolves. The birds above all heard him, and they came first, in twos, in tens, in flocks of hundreds, visiting the town and singing with his music for a while, daybirds coming in the nighttime, until the town was wakened by the din of so many songs all at once. They came and sang an hour and left again, but the memory of their song lingered.

First the birds, and then the song of coyotes, the howl of wolves, not so near as to be terrifying, but near enough to fill the untuned hearts of most folks with a kind of dread, and they woke with night-sweats. Raccoon prints were all over, and yet there was no tearing or thievery, and no more than the usual number of chickens were taken, though foxfeet had trodden on every henhouse roof. Squirrels a-gathering their nuts ran fearlessly through the town to leave small offerings outside the courthouse. Fish leapt in the Hatrack and in other nearby streams, a silver dance in the sparkling moonlit water, the drops like stars falling back into the stream.

Through it Alvin slept, and most folks also slept, so only grad-ually did the word spread that the natural world was all a-flutter, and then only a few began to link it with Alvin being in jail. Logical folks said there couldn't be no connection. Dr. Whitley Physicker boldly said, when asked (and sometimes when no one asked at all), "I'm the first to say it's wrong to have that boy locked up. But that doesn't imply that the swarming of harmless unstinging bees through the town last night meant anything at all except that perhaps this will be a hardish winter. Or perhaps a mild one. I'm not a great reader of bees. But it's *nothing* to do with Alvin in jail because nature hardly concerns itself with the legal disputes of human be-ings!"

True enough, but, as a lawyer might say, irrelevant. It wasn't Alvin in jail that disturbed nature, it was Alvin singing in his dreams that drew them. And those few in town who could hear some faint echo of his song—ones like John Binder, for instance, and Captain Harriman, who had heard such silent stirrings all their lives—why, they didn't wake up to the birdsong and the coyotes yipping and the wolves howling and the patter of squirrel feet on shingles. Those things just fit into their own dreams, for to them it all belonged, it all fit, and Alvin's song and the natural greensong of the world spoke peace to them deep in their hearts. They heard the rumors but didn't understand the fuss. And if Drunken Freda drank a little less and slept a little better, who would notice it besides herself?

Verily Cooper came to Vigor Church the hard way, but then every-body did. What with the town's reputation for making travelers listen to a hard dark story, it's no wonder nobody put a stagecoach route there. The railroad wasn't out that far west yet, but even if it was, it wasn't likely there'd be a Vigor Station or even a spur. The town that Armor-of-God Weaver once expected to be the gateway to the west was now a permanent backwater.

So it was railroad—shaky and stinky, but fast and cheap—to Dekane, and stagecoach from there. By sheerest chance, Verily's route took him right through the town of Hatrack River, where the man he was coming to meet, Calvin's brother Alvin, was locked up. But this was the express coach and it didn't stop in Hatrack for a leisurely meal at Horace Guester's roadhouse, where no doubt Verily would have heard talk that stopped his journey right there. Instead he rode on to Carthage City, changed to a slow coach heading northwest into Wobbish, and then got out at a sleepy little ferry town and bought him a horse and a saddle and a pack mule for his luggage, which wasn't all that much but more than he wanted to have on the horse he was riding. From there it was a simple matter of riding north all day, stopping at a farmhouse at night, and riding another day until, late in the afternoon, just as the sun was setting, he came to Armor's general store, where lamps were lit and Verily hoped he might find a night's lodging.

"I'm sorry," said the man at the door. "We don't take in lodgers—not much call for them in this town. The miller's family up the road takes in such lodgers as we get, but . . . well, friend, you might as well come in. Because most of the miller's family is right here in my store, and besides, there's a tale they have to tell you before you or they can go to bed tonight."

"I've been told of it," said Verily Cooper, "and I'm not afraid to hear it."

"So you came here on purpose?"

"With those signs on the road, warning travelers away?" Verily stepped through the doorway. "I have a horse and a mule to attend to—"

His words were heard by the people gathered on stools and chairs and leaning on the store counter. Immediately two young men with identical faces swung themselves over the counter. "I've got the horse," said one.

"Which gives me the mule—and his baggage, no doubt."

"And I've got the saddle," said the first. "I think it comes out even."

Verily Cooper stuck out his hand in the forthright American manner he had already learned. "I'm Verily Cooper," he said.

"Wastenot Miller," said one of the boys.

"And I'm Wantnot," said the other.

"Puritans, from the naming of you," said Verily.

"Not on a bet," said a thick-bodied middle-aged man who was sitting on a stool in the corner. "Naming babies for virtues ain't no monopoly of religious fanatics from New England."

For the first time Verily felt suspicion in the air, and he realized that they had to be wondering who he was and what his business was here. "There's not more than one miller in town, is there?" he asked.

"Only me," said the thickset man.

"Then you must be Alvin Miller, Senior," said Verily, striding up to him and thrusting out his hand.

The miller took it warily. "You've got me pegged, young feller, but all I know about you is that you come here late in the day, nobody knew you was coming, and you talk like a highfalutin Englishman with a lot of education. Had us a preacher here for a while who talked like you. Not anymore though." And from the tone of his voice, Verily gathered that the parting hadn't been a pleasant one.

"My name is Verily Cooper," he said. "My father's trade is barrelmaking, and I learned the trade as a boy. But you're right, I did get an education and I'm now a barrister."

The miller looked puzzled. "Barrelmaker to barrister," he said. "I got to say I don't rightly know the difference."

The man who greeted him at the door helped out. "A barrister is an English lawyer."

The dry tone of his voice and the way everyone stiffened up told Verily that they had something against lawyers here. "Please, I assure you, I left that profession behind when I left England. I doubt that I'd be allowed to practice law here in the United States, at least not without some kind of examination. I didn't come here for that, anyway."

The miller's wife—or so Verily guessed from her age, for she wasn't sitting by the man—spoke up, and with a good deal less hostility in her voice than her husband had had. "A man comes from England especially to come to the town in America that lives every day in shame. I admit I'm curious, lawyer or no lawyer. What *is* your business here?"

"Well, I met a son of yours, I think. And what he told me—"

It was almost comic, the way they all suddenly leaned forward. "You saw Calvin?"

"The very one," said Verily. "An interesting young man."

They reserved comment.

Well, if there was one thing Verily had learned as a lawyer, it was that he didn't have to fill every silence with his own speech. He couldn't be sure of this family's attitude toward Calvin—after all, Calvin was such an accomplished liar he must have practiced the art here at home before trying to use it to make his way in the world. So he might be hated. Or he might be loved and yearned for. Verily didn't want to make a mistake.

Finally, predictably, it was Calvin's mother who spoke up. "You saw my boy? Where was he? How was he?"

"I met him in London. He has the language and bearing of quite a clever young man. Seems to be in good health, too."

They nodded, and Verily saw that they seemed to be relieved. So they did love him, and had feared for him.

A tall, lanky man of about Verily's age stretched out his long legs and leaned back on his stool. "I'm pretty near certain that you didn't come all this way just to tell us Calvin was a-doing fine, Mr. Cooper."

"No, indeed not. It was something Calvin said." Verily looked around at them again, this large family that was at once welcoming and suspicious of a stranger, at once concerned and wary about a missing son. "He spoke of a brother of his." At this Verily looked at the lanky one who had just spoken. "A son with talents that exceeded Calvin's own."

The lanky one hooted and several others chuckled. "Don't go telling us no stories!" he said. "Calvin wouldn't never speak of Alvin that way!"

So the lanky one wasn't Alvin Junior after all. "Well, let's just say that I read between the lines, so to speak. You know that in England, the use of hidden powers and arcane arts is severely punished. So we Englishmen remain quite ignorant of such matters. I gathered, however, that if there was one person in the world who could teach me how to understand such things, it might well be Calvin's brother Alvin."

They all agreed with that, nodding, some even smiling.

But the father remained suspicious. "And why would an English lawyer be looking to learn more about such things?"

Verily, to his own surprise, was at a loss for words. All his thought had been about finding Alvin the miller's son—but of course they would have to know why he cared so much about hidden powers. What could he say? All his life he had been forced to hide his gift, his curse; now he found he couldn't just blurt it out, or even hint.

Instead, he strode to the counter and picked up a couple of large wooden spools of thread that were standing there, presumably so that customers could reel off the length of thread they wanted and wind it onto a smaller spool. He put the ends of the spools together, and then found the perfect fit for them, so that no man could pull them apart.

He handed the joined spools to the miller. At once the man tried to pull them apart, but he didn't seem surprised when he failed. He looked at his wife and smiled. "Lookit that," he said. "A lawyer who knows how to do something useful. That's a miracle."

The spools got passed around, mostly in silence, until they got to the lanky young man leaning back on his stool. Without a moment's reflection, he pulled the spools apart and set them on the counter. "Spools ain't no damn good stuck together like that," he said.

Verily was stunned. "You *are* the one," he said. "You *are* Alvin."

"No, sir," said the young man. "My name is Measure, but I've been learning somewhat of my brother's skill. That's his main work these days, is teaching folks how to do the same Makering stuff that he does, and I reckon I'm learning it about as good as anybody. But you—I *know* he'd want to meet you."

"Yes," said Verily, making no effort to hide his enthusiasm. "Yes, that's what I've come for. To learn from him—so I'm glad to hear that he wants to teach."

Measure grinned. "Well, he wants to teach, and you want to learn. But I got a feeling you two are going to have to do each other a different kind of service before that can happen."

Verily was not surprised. Of course there would be some kind of price, or perhaps a test of loyalty or trustworthiness. "I'll do whatever it takes to have a Maker teach me what my gift is for and how to use it well."

Mrs. Miller nodded. "I think you just might do," she said. "I think perhaps God brought you here."

Her husband snorted.

"It would be enough if he brought you to teach my husband manners, but I fear that may be beyond even the powers of a benevolent God," she said.

"I hate it when you talk like old Reverend Thrower," said the miller grumpily.

"I know you do, dear," said his wife. "Mr. Cooper, suppose you *did* need to practice law, not in Wobbish, but in the state of Hio. How long would it take you to prepare to take the test?"

"I don't know," he said. "It depends on how far American legal practice has diverged from English common law and equity. Perhaps only a few days. Perhaps much longer. But I assure you, I didn't come here to practice law, but rather to study higher laws."

"You want to know why you found us all down here at Armor's store?" asked the miller. "We were having a meeting, to try to figure out how to raise the money to hire us a lawyer. We knew we needed a good one, a first-rate one, but we also knew that some rich and secret group in Carthage had already hired them the best lawyers in Hio to work against us. So the question was, who could we hire, and how in the world could we pay him? My wife thinks God brung you, but my own opinion is that you brung your own self, or in another way of looking at it, my boy Alvin brung you. But who knows, I always say. You're here. You're a lawyer. And you want something from Alvin."

"Are you proposing an exchange of services?" asked Verily.

"Not really," Measure interrupted, rising from his stool. Verily had always thought of himself as rather a tall man, but this young farmer fairly towered over him. "Alvin would teach you for free, if you want to learn. The thing is, you pretty much *got* to do us that legal service before Alvin can take you on as a pupil. That's just the way it is."

Verily was baffled. Either it was barter or it wasn't.

The storekeeper spoke up from behind him, laughing. "We're all talking at each other every whichaway. Mr. Cooper, the legal service we need from you is to defend Alvin Junior at his trial. He's in jail over in Hatrack River, charged with stealing a man's gold and my guess is they're going to pile on a whole bunch of other charges, too. They're out to put that boy in prison for a long time, if not hang him, and you coming along here just now—well, you got to see that it looks mighty fortunate to us."

"In jail," Verily said.

"In Hatrack River," said Armor.

"I just rode through there not a week ago."

"Well, you passed by the courthouse where they got him locked up."

"Yes, I'll do it. When is the trial?"

"Oh, pretty much whenever you want. The judge there is a friend of Alvin's, as are most of the townfolk, or most of them as amount to much, anyway. They can't just let him go, much as they'd like to. But they'll delay the trial as long as you need to get admitted to the bar."

Verily nodded. "Yes, I'll do it. But . . . I'm puzzled. You have
no idea whether I'm a *good* lawyer or not."

Measure hooted with laughter. "Come on, friend, you think
we're blind? Look at your clothes! You're rich, and you didn't get
that way from barrelmaking."

"Besides," said Armor, "you have that English accent, those
gentlemanly airs. The jury in Hatrack River will mostly be on Alvin's side. Everything you say is going to sound powerful clever to
them."

"You're saying that I don't actually have to be very good. I just
have to be English, an attorney-at-law, alive, and present in the
courtroom."

"Pretty much, yep," said Armor.

"Then you have an attorney. Or rather, your son does. If he
wants me, that is."

"He wants to get out of jail and have his name cleared," said
Measure solemnly. "And he wants to teach folks how to be Makers.
I think you'll fit right in with what he wants."

"Come here!" The command came from Mrs. Miller, and Verily obediently walked to her. She reached out and took his right hand
and held it in both of hers. "Mr. Verily Cooper," she said, "will
you be a true friend to my son?"

He realized that it was an oath she was asking for, an oath with
his whole heart in it. "Yes, ma'am. I will be his true friend."

It wasn't quite silence that followed his promise. There was the
sound of breaths long pent being released. Verily had never been
the answer to anyone's heartfelt wish before. It was rather exhilarating. And a bit terrifying, too.

Wastenot and Wantnot came back in. "Horse and mule are un-
loaded, fed, watered, and stabled."

"Thank you," said Verily.

The twins looked around. "What's everybody grinning for?"

"We got us a lawyer for Alvin," said Measure.

Wastenot and Wantnot grinned, too. "Well, heck, then let's go
home to bed!"

"No," said the miller. "One more item of business we got to
do."

At once the cheerful mood faded.

"Have a seat, Mr. Cooper," said the miller. "We have a tale to
tell you. A sad one, and it ends with all the men of this town, except
Armor here, and Measure—it ends with all of us in shame."

Verily sat down to listen.

13

Maneuvers

Vilate brought him another pie. "I couldn't finish the last one," Alvin said. "You think my stomach is a bottomless pit?"

"A man of your size and strength needs something to keep the meat on his bones," said Vilate. "And I haven't figured out yet how to make half a pie."

Alvin chuckled. But as she slid the pie under the iron-barred door of the cell, Alvin noticed that she had some new hexes on her, not to mention a come-hither and a beseeching. Most hexes he recognized right off—he'd made a few of them in his own time, for protection or warding, and even for concealment and mildness of heart, which made for a deeper kind of safety but were much harder to make. What Vilate had today, though, was beyond Alvin's ken. And since they probably wouldn't work on him, or not too well, he couldn't rightly tell what they'd be for. Nor could he ask her.

Some kind of concealment, maybe. It seemed related to an over-look-me hex, which was always very subtle and usually worked only in one direction.

Alvin bent down, picked up the pie, and set it on the small table they'd allowed him.

"Alvin," she said softly.

"Yes?" he answered.

"Sh."

He looked up, wondering what the secrecy was about.

"I don't want to be heard," she said. She glanced toward the half-open door leading to the sheriff's office, where the guard was no doubt eavesdropping. She beckoned to Alvin.

What went through his mind then made him a little shy. Was she perhaps thinking some of the same romantic thoughts about him that he had thought about her on some of these lonely nights? Maybe she knew somehow that he alone could see past her false charms of beauty and liked her for who she really was. Maybe she thought of him as someone she could come to love, as he had wondered sometimes about her, seeing as how his first love was lost to him.

He came closer. "Alvin, do you want to escape from here?" she whispered. She leaned her forehead on the bars. Her face was so close. Was she, in some shy way, offering a kiss?

He reached down and touched her chin, lifted her face. Did she want him to kiss her? He smiled ruefully. "Vilate, if I wanted to escape, I—"

He didn't get to finish his sentence, didn't get to say, I reckon I could walk on out of here any old day. Because at that moment the deputy swung the door open and looked into the jail. He immediately got a frantic look on his face, and scanned right past them as if he didn't see them at all. "How in the hell!" he cried, then rushed from the jail. Alvin heard his feet pounding down the hall as he called out, "Sheriff! Sheriff Doggly!"

Alvin looked down at Vilate. "What was *that* all about?" he asked.

Vilate dropped her teeth at him, then smiled. "How should I know, Alvin? But I reckon this is a dangerous time to be talking about what I come to talk about." She picked up her skirts and rushed from the jail.

Alvin had no idea what her visit had been about, but he knew this much: Whatever her new hexes did, they were involved with the deputy and what he saw when he came in. And since there was a come-hither and a beseeching, Vilate might well have been the reason the deputy came into the room in the first place, and the reason he panicked so fast and rushed out without investigating any further.

She dropped the upper plate of her teeth to show contempt for me, thought Alvin. Just like she did to Horace, her enemy. Somehow I've become her enemy.

He looked at the pie sitting on the cot. He picked it up and slid it back under the door.

Five minutes later, the deputy came back with the sheriff and the county attorney. "What the hell was this all about!" Sheriff Doggly demanded. "There he is, just like always! Billy Hunter, you been drinking?"

"I swear there wasn't a soul here," said the deputy. "I saw Vilate Franker go in with a pie—"

"Sheriff, what's he talking about?" said Alvin. "I saw him come in here not five minutes ago and start yelling and running down the hall. It scared poor Vilate so she took on out of here like she had a bear after her."

"He was *not* here, I'd swear to that before God and all the angels!" said Billy Hunter.

"I was right here by the door," said Alvin.

"Maybe he was bending over to get the pie and you didn't see him," said the sheriff.

"No sir," said Alvin, unwilling to lie. "I was standing right up. There's the pie—you can have it if you want, I told Miz Vilate that I didn't finish the last one."

"I don't want none of your pie," said Billy. "Whatever you did, you made me look like a plain fool."

"It don't take no help from Alvin to make you look that way," said Sheriff Doggly. Marty Laws, the county attorney, hooted at the joke. Marty had a way of laughing at just the right time to make everything worse.

Billy glared at Alvin.

"Now, Alvin, we got to put you on your parole," said Marty. "You can't just go taking jaunts out of the jail whenever you feel like it."

"So you *do* believe me," said the deputy.

Marty Laws rolled his eyes.

"*I* don't believe nobody," said Sheriff Doggly. "And Alvin ain't taking no jaunts, are you, Alvin?"

"No sir," said Alvin. "I have not stirred from this cell."

None of them bothered to pretend that Alvin *couldn't* have escaped whenever he wanted.

"You calling me a liar?" asked Billy.

"I'm calling you mistaken," said Alvin. "I'm thinking maybe

somebody fooled you into thinking what you thought and seeing what you saw.''

''Somebody's fooling somebody,'' said Billy Hunter.

They left. Alvin sat on the cot and watched as an ant canvassed the floor of the jail, looking for something to eat. There's a pie right there, just a little that way . . . and sure enough, the ant turned, heeding Alvin's advice though of course the words themselves were just too hard a thing to fit into an ant's tiny mind. No, the ant just got the message of food and a direction, and in a minute or two it was up the pie dish and walking around on the crust. Then it headed out to find its friends and bring them for lunch. Might as well somebody get some good out of that pie.

Vilate's hexes were for concealment, all right, and they were aimed at the door. She had got him to stand close so that he'd be included in her strong overlook-me, so Billy Hunter had looked and couldn't see that anybody was there.

But why? What possible good could she accomplish from such a bit of tomfoolery as that?

Underneath all his puzzlement, though, Alvin was mad. Not so much at Vilate as he was mad at himself for being such a plain fool. Getting all moony-eyed about a woman with false teeth and vanity hexes, for pete's sake! Liking her even when he knew she was a plain gossip and suspected that half the tales she told him weren't true.

And the worst thing was, when he saw Peggy again—*if* he saw Peggy again—she'd know just how stupid he was, falling for a woman that he knew was all tricks and lies.

Well, Peggy, when I fell in love with *you* you were all tricks and lies, too, you know. Remember *that* when you're thinking I'm the biggest fool as ever lived.

The door opened and Billy Hunter came back in, stalked over to the cell door, and picked up the pie. ''No sense this going to waste even if you are a liar,'' said Billy.

''As I said, Billy, you're welcome to it. Though I sort of half-promised it to an ant a minute ago.''

Billy glared at him, no doubt thinking that Alvin was making fun of him instead of telling the plain truth. Well, Alvin was, kind of. Making fun out of the situation, anyway. He'd have to talk this over with Arthur Stuart when the boy came back, see if he had any idea what Vilate might have meant by this charade.

The ant came back, leading a line of her sisters. All they found was a couple of crumbs of crust. But those were something, weren't they? Alvin watched as they struggled to maneuver the big chunks of pastry. To help them out, he sent his doodlebug to break the pieces into smaller loads. The ants made short work of them then, carrying out the crumbs in a line. A feast in the anthill tonight, no doubt.

His stomach growled. Truth to tell, he could have used that pie, and might not have left much behind, neither. But he wasn't eating nothing that came from Vilate Franker, never again. That woman wasn't to be trusted.

Dropped her teeth at me, he thought. Hates me. Why?

There was no way around it. Even with the best possible luck in choosing a jury, even with this new English fellow as Alvin's lawyer, Little Peggy saw no better than a three-in-four chance of him being acquitted, and that wasn't good enough odds. She would have to go to him. She would have to be available to testify. Even with all the newcomers in Hatrack, one thing was certain: If Peggy the torch said a thing was true, she would be believed. The people of Hatrack knew that she saw the truth, and they also knew—sometimes to their discomfiture—that she never said what wasn't true, though they were grateful enough that she didn't tell every truth she knew.

Only Peggy herself could count how many terrible or shameful or mournful secrets she had left unmentioned. But that was neither here nor there. She was used to carrying other people's secrets around inside her, used to it from the earliest time of her life, when she had to face her father's dark secret of adultery. Since then she had learned not to judge. She had even come to love Mistress Modesty, the woman with whom her father, old Horace Guester, had been unfaithful. Mistress Modesty was like another mother to her, giving her, not the life of the body, but the life of the mind, the life of mannered society, the life of grace and beauty that Peggy valued perhaps too highly.

Perhaps too highly, because there wasn't going to be too much of grace and beauty in Alvin's future, and like it or not, Peggy was tied to that future.

What a lie I tell myself, she thought. "Like it or not" indeed. If I chose to, I could walk away from Alvin and not care whether he stayed in jail or got himself drowned in the Hio or whatnot. I'm tied to Alvin Smith because I love him, and I love what he can be, and I want to be part of all that he will do. Even the hard parts. Even the ungraceful, unmannered, stupid parts of it.

So she headed for Hatrack River, one stage at a time.

On a certain day she passed through the town of Wheelwright in northern Appalachee. It was on the Hio, not far upriver from where the Hatrack flowed into it. Close enough to home that she might have hired a wagon and taken the last ferry, trusting that the moonlight and her ability as a torch would get her home safely. Might have, except that she stopped for dinner at a restaurant she had visited before, where the food was fresh, the flavors good, and the company reputable—a welcome change in all three categories, after long days on the road.

While she was eating, she heard some kind of tumult outside—a band playing, rather badly but with considerable enthusiasm; people shouting and cheering. "A parade?" she asked her waiter.

"You know the presidential election's only a few weeks off," said the waiter.

She knew, but had scarcely paid attention. Somebody was running against somebody else for some office or other in every town she passed through, but it hardly mattered, compared to the matter of stopping slavery, not to mention her concerns about Alvin. It made no difference to her, up to now, who won these elections. In Appalachee, as in the other slave states, there wasn't a soul dared to run openly as an anti-slavery candidate—that would be a ticket for a free suit of tar and feathers and a rail ride out of town, if not worse, for those as loved slavery were violent at heart, and those as hated it were mostly timid, and wouldn't stand together. Yet.

"Some sort of stump speech?" she asked.

"I reckon it's old Tippy-Canoe," said the waiter.

She blanched, knowing at once whom the man referred to. "Harrison?"

"Reckon he'll carry Wheelwright. But not farther south, where the Cherriky tribe is right numerous. They figure him to be the man to try take away their rights. Won't amount to much in Irrakwa, neither, that being Red country. But, see, White folks isn't too happy about how the Irrakwa control the railroads and the Cherriky got them toll roads through the mountains."

"They'd vote for a murderer, out of nothing more than envy?"

The waiter smiled thinly. "There's them as says just because a Red witch feller put a spell on Tippy-Canoe don't mean he did nothing wrong. Reds get mad over any old thing."

"Slaughtering thousands of innocent women and children—silly of them to take offense."

The waiter shrugged. "I can't afford to have strong opinions on politics, ma'am."

But she saw that he *did* have strong opinions, and they were not the same as hers.

Paying for the meal—and leaving two bits on the table for the waiter, for she saw no reason to punish a man in his livelihood because of his political views—she made haste outside to see the fuss. A few rods up the street, a wagon had been made over into a sort of temporary rostrum, decked out with the red, white, and blue bunting of the flag of the United States. Not a trace of the red and green colors of the old flag of independent Appalachee, before it joined the Union. Of course not. Those had been the Cherriky colors—red for the Red people, green for the forest. Patrick Henry and Thomas Jefferson had adopted them as the colors of a free Appalachee; it was for that flag that George Washington died. But now, though other politicians still invoked the old loyalties, Harrison could hardly want to bring to mind the alliance between Red and White that won freedom for Appalachee from the King at Camelot. Not with those bloody hands.

Hands that even now dripped blood as they gripped the podium. Peggy, standing on the wooden sidewalk across the street, looked over the heads of the cheering crowd to watch William Henry Harrison's face. She looked in his eyes first, as any woman might study any man, to see his character. Quickly enough, though, she looked deeper, into the heartfire, seeing the futures that stretched out before him. He had no secrets from her.

She saw that every path led to victory in the election. And not just a slight victory. His leading opponent, a hapless lawyer named Andrew Jackson from Tennizy, would be crushed and humiliated—and then suffer in the ignominious position of vice-president into which the leading loser in each election was always forced. A cruel system, Peggy had always thought, the political equivalent of putting a man in the stocks for four years. It was significant that both candidates were from the new states in the west; even more significant that both were from territories that permitted slavery. Things were taking a dark turn indeed. And darker yet were the things she saw in Harrison's mind, the plans he and his political cronies meant to carry out.

Their most extravagant ideas had little hope of success—only a few paths in Harrison's heartfire led to the union with the Crown Lands that he hoped for; he would never be a duke; what a pathetic dream, she thought. But he would certainly succeed in the political destruction of the Reds in Irrakwa and Cherriky, because the Whites, especially in the west, were ready for it, ready to break the power of a people that Harrison dared to speak of as savages. "God didn't bring the Christian race to this land in order to share it with heathens and barbarians!" cried Tippy-Canoe, and the people cheered.

Harrison would also succeed in spreading slavery beyond its present locale, permitting slave owners to bring slaves to property in the free states and continue to own them and force them to serve on such property—as long as the slave owner continued to own any amount of land in a slave state and cast his vote there. It was precisely to achieve this end that most of Harrison's backers were behind him. It was the matter of Reds that would sweep Tippy-Canoe into office, but once there, it was the matter of slavery that would give him his power base in Congress.

This was unbearable. Yet she bore it, watching on into the afternoon as he ranted and exhorted, periodically lifting his bloody hands skyward to remind the crowd. "*I* have tasted the treacherous wrath of the secret powers of the Red man, and I'll tell you, if this is all they can do, well, that's good, because it ain't much! Sure, I can't keep a shirt clean"—and they laughed at that, over and over, each variation on the tedious details of life with bloody hands— "and ain't a soul willing to lend me a hankie"—laughter again— "but they can't stop me from telling you the plain truth, and they can't stop a Christian people from electing the one man proven to be willing to stand up against the Red traitors, the barbarians who dress like White men but secretly plan to own everything the way they own the railroads and the mountain toll roads and . . ."

And on and on. Confounded nonsense, all of it, but the crowd only grew as the afternoon passed, and by dark, when Harrison finally climbed down from his pulpit, he was carried away on the shoulders of his supporters to be watered with beer and stuffed with some sort of rough food, whatever would make the crowd think of him as one of them, while Peggy Larner stood gripping the rail on the sidewalk, seeing down every path that this man was the undoing of all her work, that this man would be the cause of the death and suffering of countless more Reds than had already died or suffered at his hands.

If she had had a musket in her hands at that moment, she might have gone after him and put a ball through his heart.

But the murderous rage passed quickly and shamefully. I am not a one who kills, she thought. I am one who frees the slave if I can, not one who murders the master.

There had to be a way to stop him.

Alvin would know. She had to get to Hatrack River all the more urgently, not just to help with Alvin's trial, but to get his help in stopping Harrison. Perhaps if he went to Becca's house and used the doorways in her ancient cabin to let him visit with Tenskwa-Tawa— surely the Red Prophet would do something to make his curse against White Murderer Harrison more effective. Though she didn't see such an outcome down any of the paths in Alvin's heartfire, she never knew when some act of hers or of someone else's might open up new paths that led to better hopes.

It was too late that day, though. She would have to spend the night in Wheelwright and finish her journey to Hatrack River the next day.

"I come to you, sir, with the good wishes of your family," said the stranger.

"I confess I didn't catch your name," said Alvin, unfolding himself from his cot. "It's pretty late in the evening."

"Verily Cooper," said the stranger. "Forgive my late arrival. I thought it better that we speak tonight, since the first matter of your defense before the court is in the morning."

"I know the judge is finally going to start choosing him a jury."

"Yes, that's important, of course. But under the advice of an outside lawyer, a Mr. Daniel Webster, the county attorney has introduced some unpleasant motions. As, for instance, a motion requiring that the contested property be placed under the control of the court."

"The judge won't go for that," said Alvin. "He knows that the second this plow is out of my hands, some rough boys from the river, not to mention a few greedier souls from town, will move heaven and earth to get their hands on it. The thing's made of gold— that's all they know and care about it. But who are you, Mr. Cooper, and what does all this have to do with you?"

"I'm your attorney, Mr. Smith, if you'll have me." He handed Alvin a letter.

Alvin recognized Armor-of-God's handwriting at once, and the signatures of his parents and his brothers and sisters. They all signed, affirming that they found Mr. Cooper to be a man of good character and assuring him that someone was paying a high-powered lawyer from New England named Daniel Webster to sneak around and collect lies from anyone as had a grievance against him in Vigor Church. "But I've done no harm to anyone there," said Alvin, "and why would they lie?"

"Mr. Smith, I have to—"

"Call me Alvin, would you? 'Mr. Smith' always sounds to me

like my old master Makepeace, the fellow whose lies got me into this fix.''

''Alvin,'' said Cooper again. ''And you must call me Verily.''

''Whatever.''

''Alvin, it has been my experience that the better a man you are, the more folks there are who resent you for it, and find occasion to get angry at you no matter how kindly meant your deeds may be.''

''Well then, I'm safe enough, not being such a remarkable good man.''

Cooper smiled. ''I know your brother Calvin,'' he said.

Alvin raised an eyebrow. ''I'd like to say that any friend of Calvin's is a friend of mine, but I can't.''

''Calvin's hatred of you is, I believe, one of the best recommendations of your character that I could think of. It's because of his account of you that I came to meet you. I met him in London, you see, and determined then and there to close my legal practice and come to America and see the man who can teach me who and what I am, and what it's for.''

With that, Cooper bent down and took up Alvin's Testament, the book that lay open on the floor beside his cot. He closed it, then handed it back to Alvin.

Alvin tried to thumb it open, but the pages were fused shut as tight as if the book were one solid block of wood with a leather cover.

Verily took it back from him for only a moment, then returned it yet again. This time the book fell open to the exact page that Alvin had been reading. ''I could have died for that in England,'' said Verily. ''It was the wisdom of my parents and my own ability to learn to hide these powers that kept me alive all these years. But I have to know what it is. I have to know why God lets some folks have such powers. And what to do with them. And who you are.''

Alvin lay back on his cot. ''Don't this beat all,'' he said. ''You crossed an ocean to meet me?''

''I had no idea at the time that I might be of service to you. In fact, I must say that it occurs to me that perhaps some providential hand led me to the study of law instead of following my father's trade as a cooper. Perhaps it was known that one day you would face the silver tongue of Daniel Webster.''

''You got you a tongue of gold, then, Verily?'' asked Alvin.

''I hold things together,'' said Verily. ''It's my . . . knack, as you Americans call it. That is what the law does. I use the law to hold things together. I see how things fit.''

"This Webster fellow—he's going to use the law to try to tear things apart."

"Like you and the plow."

"And me and my neighbors," said Alvin.

"Then you understand the dilemma," said Verily. "Up till now you've been known as a man of generosity and kindness to all. But you have a plow made of gold that you won't let anyone see. You have fantastic wealth which you share with no one. This is a wedge that Webster will attempt to use to split you from your community like a rail from a log."

"When gold comes into it," said Alvin, "folks start to finding out just how much love and loyalty is worth to them, in cash money."

"And it's rather shameful, don't you think, how cheap the price can be sometimes." Verily smiled ruefully.

"What's *your* price?"

"When you get free of this place, you let me go with you, to learn from you, to watch you, to be part of all you do."

"You don't even know me, and you're proposing marriage?"

Verily laughed. "I suppose it sounds like that, doesn't it."

"Without none of the benefits, neither," said Alvin. "I'm right comfortable taking Arthur Stuart along with me because he knows when to keep silent, but I don't know if I can take having a fellow who wants to pick my brains tagging along with me every waking minute."

"I'm a lawyer, so my trade is talk, but I promise you that if I didn't know when and how to keep silence, I'd never have lived to adulthood in England."

"I can't give you no promises," said Alvin. "So I reckon you ain't my attorney after all, since I can't make your fee."

"There's one promise you can make me," said Verily. "To give me an honest chance."

Alvin studied the man's face and decided he liked the look of him, though he wished as more than once before that he had Peggy's knack of seeing inside a fellow's mind instead of just being able to check out the health of his organs.

"Yes, I reckon I can make that promise, Verily Cooper," said Alvin. "An honest chance you'll have, and if that's fee enough for you, then you're my attorney."

"Then the deed is done. And now I'll let you go back to sleep, excepting only for one question."

"Ask it."

"This plow—how vital is it to you that the plow remain in your hands, and no one else's?"

"If the court demands that I give it up, I'll buck this jail and live in hiding the rest of my days before I'll let any other hand touch the plow."

"Let's be precise. Is it the possession of it that matters, or the very seeing and touching of it?"

"I don't get your question."

"What if someone else could see and touch it in your presence?"

"What good would that do?"

"Webster will argue that the court has the right and duty to determine that the plow exists and that it's truly made of gold, in order to make just compensation possible, if the court should determine that you need to pay Mr. Makepeace Smith the cash value of the plow."

Alvin hooted. "It never crossed my mind, in all this time in jail, that maybe I could buy old Makepeace off."

"I don't think you can," said Verily. "I think it's the plow he wants, and the victory, not the money."

"True enough, though I reckon if the money's all he can get . . ."

"So tell me, as long as the plow is in your possession . . ."

"I guess it depends on who's doing the looking and the touching."

"If you're there, nobody can steal it, am I right?" asked Verily.

"Reckon that's true," said Alvin.

"So how free a hand do I have?"

"Makepeace can't be the one to touch it," said Alvin. "Not out of any meanness on my part, but here's the thing: The plow's alive."

Verily raised an eyebrow.

"It don't breathe and it don't eat or nothing like that," said Alvin. "But the plow is alive under a man's hand. Depending on the man. But for Makepeace to touch the plow while he's living in the midst of a black lie—I don't know what would happen to him. I don't know if it'd be safe for him ever to touch metal again. I don't know what the hammer and anvil would do to him, if his hands touched the plow with his heart so black."

Verily leaned his face against the bars, closed his eyes.

"Are you unwell?" asked Alvin.

"Sick with the thrill of at last staring knowledge in the face," said Verily. "Sick with it. Faint with it."

"Well, don't puke on the floor, I'll have to smell it all night."
Then Alvin grinned.

"I was thinking more of fainting," said Verily. "Not Makepeace, or anyone else who's living in a . . . black lie. Makes me
wonder about my opponent, Mr. Daniel Webster."

"Don't know him," said Alvin. "Might be an honest man, for
all I know. A lying man might have an honest attorney, don't you
think?"

"He might," said Verily. "But such a combination would only
work to destroy the lying man in the end."

"Well hell, Verily, a lying man destroys himself in the end every
time anyway."

"Do you know that? I mean, the way you know the plow is
alive?" asked Verily.

"I reckon not," said Alvin. "But I have to believe it's true, or
how could I trust anybody?"

"I think you're right, in the long run," said Verily. "In the long
run, a lie ties itself in knots and eventually people come to see that
it's a lie. But the long run is very, very long. Longer than life. You
could be long dead before the lie dies, Alvin."

"You warning me of something in particular?" asked Alvin.

"I don't think so," said Verily. "The words just sounded like
something I had to say and you had to hear."

"You said them. I heard them." Alvin grinned. "Good night,
Verily Cooper."

"Good night, Alvin Smith."

Peggy Larner got to the ferry bright and early in the morning, wearing her urgency like a tight corset so she could hardly breathe. White
Murderer Harrison was going to be president of the United States.
She had to talk to Alvin, and this river, this Hio, was standing in
her way.

But the ferry was on the other side of the river, which made
perfect sense, since the farmers on the other side would need to have
it earliest, to bring their goods to market. So she had to wait, urgency
or not. She could see the ferry already being poled along, tied to a
metal ring that slid along the cable that crossed the river some forty
feet overhead. Only that frail connection kept the whole thing from
being washed downriver; and she imagined that when the river was
in flood they didn't run the ferry at all some days, since even if the
cable were strong enough, and the ring, and the rope, there'd be no
trees strong enough to tie the ends to without fear of one or the other

of them pulling out of the ground. Water was not to be tamed by cables, rings, or ropes, any more than dams or bridges, hulls or rafts, pipes or gutters, roofs or windows or walls or doors. If she had learned anything in her early years of looking out for Alvin, it was the untrustworthiness of water, the sneakiness of it.

There was the river to be crossed, though, and she would cross it.

As so many others had crossed. She thought of how many times her father had snuck down to the river and taken a boat across to rescue some runaway slave and bring him north to safety. She thought of how many slaves had come without help to this water, and, not knowing how to swim, had either despaired and waited for the Finders or the dogs to get them, or struck out anyway, breasting the water until their feet found no purchase on the bottom mud and they were swept away. The bodies of such were always found on some downriver bank or bar or snag, made white by the water, bloated and horrible in death; but the spirit, ah, the spirit was free, for the owner who thought he owned the woman or the man, that owner had lost his property, for his property would not be owned whatever it might cost. So the water killed, yes, but just reaching this river meant freedom of one kind or another to those who had the courage or the rage to take it.

Harrison, though, would take away all meaning from this river. If his laws came to be, the slave who crossed would still be a slave no matter what; only the slave who died would be free.

One of the ferrymen, the one poling on this side, he looked familiar to her. She had met him before, though he'd not been missing an ear then, nor had he any kind of scar on his face. Now a gash marked him with a faint white line, a little puckering and twisting at the eyebrow and the lip. It had been a wicked fight. Once no one had been able to lay a hand of harm on this rough man, and in the sure knowledge of that he had been a bully. But someone took that lifelong hex away from him. Alvin had fought this man, fought him in defense of Peggy herself, and when the fight was done, this river rat had been undone. But not completely; and he was alive still, wasn't he?

"Mike Fink," she said softly when he stepped ashore.

He looked sharp at her. "Do I know you, ma'am?"

Of course he didn't. When they met before, not two years ago, she was covered in hexes that made her look many years older. "I don't expect you to remember me," she said. "You must take many thousands of people a year across the river."

He helped her hoist her traveling bags onto the ferry. "You'll want to sit in the middle of the raft, ma'am." She sat down on the bench that ran the middle of the raft. He stood near her, waiting, while another couple of people sauntered over to the ferry—locals, obviously, since they had no luggage.

"A ferryman now," she said.

He looked at her.

"When I knew you, Mike Fink, you were a full-fledged river rat."

He smiled wanly. "You was that lady," he said. "Hexed up six ways to Tuesday."

She looked at him sharply. "You saw through them?"

"No ma'am. But I could feel them. You watched me fight that Hatrack River boy."

"I did."

"He took away my mother's hex," said Mike.

"I know."

"I reckon you know damn near everything."

She looked at him again. "You seem to be abundant in knowledge yourself, sir."

"You're Peggy the torch, of Hatrack River town. And the boy as whupped me and stole my hex, he's in jail in Hatrack now, for stealing gold off'n his master when he was a prentice smith."

"And I suppose that pleases you?" asked Peggy.

Mike Fink shook his head. "No ma'am."

And in truth, as she looked into his heartfire, she saw no future in which he harmed Alvin.

"Why are you still here? Not ten miles from Hatrack Mouth, where he shamed you?"

"Where he made a man of me," said Mike.

She was startled then, for sure. "That's how you think of it?"

"My mother wanted to keep me safe. Tattooed a hex right into my butt. But what she never thought of was, what kind of man does it make a fellow, to never get hurt no matter what harm he causes to others? I've killed folks, some bad, but some not so bad. I've bit off ears and noses and broken limbs, too, and all the time I was doing it, I never cared a damn, begging your pardon, ma'am. Because nothing ever hurt me. Never touched me."

"And since Alvin took away your hex, you've stopped hurting people?"

"Hell no!" Mike Fink said, then roared with laughter. "Why, you sure don't know a thing about the river, do you! No, every last man I ever beat in a fight had to come find me, soon as word spread that a smith boy whupped me and made me howl! I had to fight every rattlesnake and weasel, every rat and pile of pigshit on the river all over again. You see this scar on my face? You see where my hair hangs straight one side of my head? That's two fights I damn near lost. But I won the rest! Didn't I, Holly!''

The other ferryman looked over. ''I wasn't listening to your brag, you pitiful scab-eating squirrel-fart,'' he said mildly.

''I told this lady I won every fight, every last one of them.''

''That's right enough,'' said Holly. ''Course, mostly you just shot them dead when they made as if to fight you.''

''Lies like that will get you sent to hell.''

''Already got me a room picked out there,'' said Holly, ''and you to empty my chamberpot twice't a day.''

''Only so's you can lick it out after!'' hooted Mike Fink.

Peggy felt repulsed by their crudity, of course; but she also felt the spirit of camaraderie behind their banter.

''What I don't understand, Mr. Fink, is why you never sought vengeance against the boy who beat you.''

''He wasn't no boy,'' said Fink. ''He was a man. I reckon he was probably born a man. *I* was the boy. A bully boy. He knew pain, and I didn't. He was fighting for right, and I wasn't. I think about him all the time, ma'am. Him and you. The way you looked at me, like I was a crusty toad on a clean bedsheet. I hear tell he's a Maker.''

She nodded.

''So why's he letting them hold him in jail?''

She looked at him quizzically.

''Oh, come now, ma'am. A fellow as can wipe the tattoo off my butt without touching it, he can't be kept in no natural jail.''

True enough. ''I imagine he believes himself to be innocent, and therefore he wants to stand trial to prove it and clear his name.''

''Well he's a damn fool, then, and I hope you'll tell him when you see him.''

''And why will I give him this remarkable message?''

Fink grinned. ''Because I know something he don't know. I know that there's a feller lives in Carthage City who wants Alvin dead. He plans to get Alvin exerdited to Kenituck—''

''Extradited?''

''That means one state tells another to give them up a prisoner.''

''I know what it means,'' said Peggy.

''Then what was you asking, ma'am?''

"Go on with your story."

"Only when they take Alvin in chains, with guards awake and watching him day and night, they'll never take him to Kenituck for no trial. I know some of the boys they hired to take him. They know that on some signal, they're to walk away and leave him alone in chains."

"Why haven't you told the authorities?"

"I'm telling *you*, ma'am," said Mike Fink, grinning. "And I already told myself and Holly."

"Chains won't hold him," said Peggy.

"You reckon not?" said Mike. "There was some reason that boy took the tattoo off my butt. If hexes had no power over him, I reckon he never would've had to clean mine off, do you think? So if he needed to get rid of my hex, then I reckon them as understands hexes right good might be able to make chains that'd hold him long enough for somebody to come with a shotgun and blow his head off."

But she had seen nothing of the kind in his future.

"Course it'll never happen," said Mike Fink.

"Why not?" she asked.

"Cause I owe that boy my life. My life as a man, anyway, a man worth looking at in the mirror, though I ain't half so pretty as I was before he dealt with me. I had a grip on that boy in my arms, ma'am. I meant to kill him, and he knowed it. But he didn't kill me. More to the point, ma'am, he broke both my legs in that fight. But then he took pity on me. He had mercy. He must've knowed I wouldn't live out the night with broke legs. I had too many enemies, right there among my friends. So he laid hands on my legs and he fixed them. Fixed my legs, so the bones was stronger than before. What kind of man does that to a man as tried to kill him not a minute before?"

"A good man."

"Well, many a good man might wish to, but only one good man had the power," said Mike. "And if he had the power to do that, he had the power to kill me without touching me. He had the power to do whatever he damn well pleased, begging your pardon. But he had mercy on me, ma'am."

That was true—the only surprise to Peggy was that Mike Fink understood it.

"I aim to pay the debt. As long as I'm alive, ma'am, ain't no harm coming to Alvin Smith."

"And that's why you're here," she said.

"Came here with Holly as soon as I found out what was getting plotted up."

"But why here?"

Mike Fink laughed. "The portmaster at Hatrack Mouth knows me real good, and he don't trust me, I wonder why. How long you reckon it'd be afore the Hatrack County sheriff was on my back like a sweaty shirt?"

"I suppose that also explains why you haven't made yourself known to Alvin directly."

"What's he going to think when he sees me, but that I've come to get even? No, I'm watching, I'm biding my time, I ain't showing my hand to the law nor to Alvin neither."

"But you're telling me."

"Because you'd know it anyway, soon enough."

She shook her head. "I know this: There's no path in your future that has you rescuing Alvin from thugs."

His face grew serious. "But I got to, ma'am."

"Why?"

"Because a good man pays his debts."

"Alvin won't think you're in his debt, sir."

"Don't matter to me what he thinks about it, I feel the debt so the debt's going to be paid."

"It's not just debt, is it?"

Mike Fink laughed. "Time to push this raft away and get it over to the north shore, don't you think?" He hooted twice, high, as if he were some kind of steam whistle, and Holly hooted back and laughed. They set their poles against the floating dock and pushed away. Then, smooth as if they were dancers, he and Holly poled them across the river, so smoothly and deftly that the line that tied them to the cable never even went taut.

Peggy said nothing to him as he worked. She watched instead, watched the muscles of his arms and back rippling under the skin, watched the slow and graceful up-and-down of his legs as he danced with the river. There was beauty in it, in him. It also made her think of Alvin at the forge, Alvin at the anvil, his arms shining with sweat in the firelight, the sparks glinting from the metal as he pounded, the muscles of his forearms rippling as he bent and shaped the iron. Alvin could have done all his work without raising a hand, by the use of his knack. But there was a joy in the labor, a joy from making with his own hands. She had never experienced that—her life, her labors, all were done with her mind and whatever words she could think of to say. Her life was all about knowing and teaching. Alvin's life was all about feeling and making. He had more in common with this one-eared scar-faced river rat than he had with her. This dance of the human body in contest with the river, it was a kind of wrestling, and Alvin loved to wrestle. Crude as Fink was, he was Alvin's natural friend, surely.

They reached the other shore, bumping squarely against the floating dock, and the shoreman lashed the upstream corner of the raft to the wharf. The men with no luggage jumped ashore at once. Mike Fink laid down his pole and, sweat still dripping down his arms and from his nose and grizzled beard, he made as if to pick up her bags.

She laid a hand on his arm to stop him. "Mr. Fink," she said. "You mean to be Alvin's friend."

"I had in mind more along the lines of being his champion, ma'am," he said softly.

"But I think what you really want is to be his friend."

Mike Fink said nothing.

"You're afraid that he'll turn you away, if you try to be his friend in the open. I tell you, sir, that he'll *not* turn you away. He'll take you for what you are."

Mike shook his head. "Don't want him to take me for that."

"Yes you do, because what you are is a man who means to be good, and undo the bad he's done, and that's as good as any man ever gets."

Mike shook his head more emphatically, making drops of sweat fly a little; she didn't mind the ones that struck on her skin. They had been made by honest work, and by Alvin's friend.

"Meet him face to face, Mr. Fink. Be his friend instead of his rescuer. He needs friends more. I tell you, and you know that I know it: Alvin will have few true friends in his life. If you mean to be true to him, and never betray him, so he can trust you always, then I can promise you he may have a few friends he loves as much, but none he loves more than you."

Mike Fink knelt down and turned his face away toward the river. She could see from the glinting that his eyes were awash with tears. "Ma'am," he said, "that's not what I was daring to hope for."

"Then you need more courage, my friend," she said. "You need to dare to hope for what is good, instead of settling for what is merely good enough." She stood up. "Alvin has no need of your violence. But your honor—that he can use." She lifted both her bags herself.

At once he leapt to his feet. "Please ma'am, let me . . ."

She smiled at him. "I saw you take such joy from wrestling with the river just now. It made me want to do a little physical work myself. Will you let me?"

He rolled his eyes. "Ma'am, in all the tales of you I've heard around here, I never heard you was *crazy*."

"You have something to add to the legend, then," she said, winking. She stepped onto the floating dock, bags in hand. They were heavy, and she almost regretted turning down his help.

"I heard all you said," Mike told her, coming up behind her. "But please don't shame me by letting me be seen empty-handed while a fine lady carried her own luggage."

Gratefully she turned and handed the bags to him. "Thank you," she said. "I think some things must be built up to."

He grinned. "Maybe I'll build up to going to see Alvin face to face."

She looked into his heartfire. "I'm sure of it, Mr. Fink."

As Fink put her bags into the carriage in which the men who had crossed with them impatiently waited for her, she wondered: I just changed the course of events. I brought Mike Fink closer than he would ever have come on his own. Have I done something that will save Alvin in the end? Have I given him the friend that will confound his enemies?

She found Alvin's heartfire almost without trying. And no, there was no change, no change, except for a day when Mike Fink would go away from a prison cell in tears, knowing that Alvin would surely die if he wasn't there, but knowing also that Alvin refused to have him, refused to let him stand guard.

But it was not the jail in Hatrack River. And it was not anytime soon. Even if she hadn't changed the future much, she'd changed it a little. There'd be other changes, too. Eventually one of them would make the difference. One of them would turn Alvin away from the darkness that would engulf the end of his life.

"God be with you, ma'am," said Mike Fink.

"Call me Miss Larner, please," said Peggy. "I'm not married."

"So far, anyway," he said.

Even though he hardly slept the night before, Verily was too keyed up to be sleepy as he entered the courtroom. He had met Alvin Smith, after all these weeks of anticipation, and it was worth it. Not because Alvin had overawed him with wisdom—time enough to learn from him later. No, the great and pleasant surprise was that he liked the man. He might be a bit rough-hewn, more American and more countrified than Calvin. What of that? He had a glint of humor in his eyes, and he seemed so direct, so open . . .

And I am his attorney.

The American courtroom was almost casual, compared to the English ones in which Verily had always litigated up to now. The judge had no wig, for one thing, and his robe was a little threadbare. There could hardly be any majesty of law here; and yet law was law, and justice was not utterly unconnected to it, not if the judge was honest, and there was no reason to think he wouldn't be.

He called the court into session and asked for motions. Marty Laws rose quickly. "Motion to have the golden plow removed from the prisoner and placed into the custody of the court. It doesn't make any sense for the very item in question to remain in the possession of the prisoner when . . ."

"Didn't ask for arguments," said the judge. "I asked for motions. Any others?"

"If it please the court, I move for dismissal of all charges against my client," said Verily.

"Speak up, young man, I couldn't hear a word you said."

Verily repeated himself, more loudly.

"Well, wouldn't that be nice," said the judge.

"When the court is ready for argument, I'll be glad to explain why."

"Explain now, please," said the judge, looking just a little annoyed.

Verily didn't understand what he had done wrong, but he complied. "The point at issue is a plow that all agree is made of solid gold. Makepeace Smith has not a scintilla of evidence that he was ever in possession of such a quantity of gold, and therefore he has no standing to bring a complaint."

Marty Laws pounced at once. "Your Honor, that's what this whole trial is designed to prove, and as for evidence, I don't know what a scintilla is, unless it has something to do with *The Odyssey*—"

"Amusing reference," said the judge, "and quite flattering to me, I'm sure, but please sit back down on your chairybdis until I ask for rebuttal, which I won't have to ask for because the motion to dismiss is denied. Any other motions?"

"I've got one, your honor," said Marty. "A motion to postpone the matter of extradition until after—"

"Extradition!" cried the judge. "Now what sort of nonsense is this!"

"It was discovered that there was an outstanding warrant of extradition naming the prisoner, demanding that he be sent to Kenituck to stand trial for the murder of a Slave Finder in the act of performing his lawful duty."

This was all news to Verily. Or was it? The family had told him some of the tale—how Alvin had changed a half-Black boy so the Finders could no longer identify him, but in their search for the boy they got into the roadhouse where his adopted parents lived, and there the boy's mother had killed one of the Finders, and the other had killed her, and then Alvin had come up and killed the one that killed her, but not until after the Finder had shot him, so it was obviously self-defense.

"How can he be tried for this?" asked Verily. "The determination of Pauley Wiseman, who was sheriff at the time, was that it was self-defense."

Marty turned to the man sitting, up to now silently, beside him. The man arose slowly. "My learned friend from England is unaware of local law, Your Honor. Do you mind if I help him out?"

"Go ahead, Mr. Webster," said the judge.

So . . . the judge had already had dealings with Mr. Webster, thought Verily. Maybe that meant he was already biased; but which way?

"Mr.—Cooper, am I right?—Mr. Cooper, when Kenituck, Tennizy, and Appalachee were admitted to the union of American states, the Fugitive Slave Treaty became the Fugitive Slave Law. Under that law, when a Slave Finder engaged in his lawful duty in one of the free states is interfered with, the defendant is tried in the state where the owner of the slave being pursued has his legal residence. At the time of the crime, that state was Appalachee, but the owner of the slave in question, Mr. Cavil Planter, has relocated in Kenituck, and so that is where by law Mr. Smith will have to be extradited to stand trial. If it is found there that he acted in self-defense, he will of course be set free. Our petition to the court is to set aside the matter of extradition until after the conclusion of this trial. I'm sure you'll agree that this is in the best interests of your client."

So it seemed, on the surface. But Verily was no fool—if it *was* in the best interest of Alvin Smith, Daniel Webster would not be so keen on it. The most obvious motive was to influence the jury. If people in Hatrack, who mostly liked Alvin, came to believe that by convicting him of stealing Makepeace's plow they might keep him from being extradited to a state where he would surely be hanged, they might convict him for his own good.

"Your Honor, my client would like to oppose this motion and demand an immediate hearing on the matter of extradition, so it may be cleared up before he stands trial on the charges here."

"I don't like that idea," said the judge. "If we have the hearing and approve the extradition, then this trial takes second place and off he goes to Kenituck."

Marty Laws whispered to Verily, "Don't be daft, boy! I'm the one as pushed Webster into agreeing to this, it's crazy to send him to Kenituck."

For a moment Verily wavered. But by now he had some understanding of how Webster and Laws fit together. Laws might believe that he had persuaded Webster to put off the extradition, but Verily was pretty sure the reality went the other way. Webster wanted extradition postponed. Therefore Verily didn't.

"I'm quite aware of that," said Verily, a statement that had become true not five seconds before. "Nevertheless, we wish an immediate hearing on the matter of extradition. I believe that is my client's right. We don't wish the jury to be aware of a matter of extradition hanging over him."

"But *we* don't want the defendant leaving the state while still in possession of Makepeace Smith's gold!" cried Webster.

"We don't know whose gold it is yet," said the judge. "This is all pretty darn confusing, I must say. Sounds to me like the prosecution is pleading the defense's cause, and vice-versa. But on general principles I'm inclined to give the capital charge precedence over a matter of larceny. So the extradition hearing will be—how long do you boys need?"

"We could be ready in this afternoon," said Marty.

"No you can't," said Verily. "Because you have to obtain evidence that at present is almost certainly in Kenituck."

"Evidence!" Marty looked genuinely puzzled. "Of what? All the witnesses of Alvin's killing that Finder fellow live right here in town."

"The crime for which extradition is mandatory is not killing a Finder, plain and simple. It's interfering with a Finder who is in pursuit of his lawful duty. So you must not only prove that my client killed the Finder—you must prove the Finder was in lawful pursuit of a particular slave." The thread that Verily was holding to was what the Miller family back in Vigor had told him about Alvin changing the half-Black boy so the Finders couldn't find him anymore.

Marty Laws leaned close to Daniel Webster and they conferred for a moment. "I believe we'll have to bring us a Slave Finder over the river from Wheelwright," said Laws, "and fetch the cachet. Only that's in Carthage City, so . . . by horse and then by train . . . day after tomorrow?"

"That works for me," said the judge.

"If it please the court," said Webster.

"Nothing has pleased me much so far today," said the judge. "But go ahead, Mr. Webster."

"Since there is some considerable history of people hiding the slave in question, we'd like him taken into custody immediately. I believe the boy is in this courtroom right now." He turned and looked straight at Arthur Stuart.

"On the contrary," said Verily Cooper. "I believe the boy Mr. Webster is indicating is the adopted son of Mr. Horace Guester, the owner of the roadhouse in which I have taken lodging, and therefore he has presumptive rights as a citizen of the state of Hio, which decrees that he is presumed to be a free man until and unless it is proven otherwise."

"Hell's bells, Mr. Cooper," said Marty Laws, "we all know the Finders picked the boy out and took him back across the river in chains."

"It is my client's position that they did so in error, and a panel of impartial Finders will be unable, using only the cachet, to pick the boy out from a group of other boys if his race is concealed from them. We propose this as the first matter for the court to demonstrate. If the panel of Finders cannot pick out the boy, then the Finders who died in this town were *not* pursuing their lawful business, and therefore Kenituck has no jurisdiction because the Fugitive Slave Law does not apply."

"You're from England and you don't know diddly about what these Finders can do," said Marty, quite upset now. "Are you trying to get Arthur Stuart sent off in chains? And Alvin hanged?"

"Mr. Laws," said the judge, "you are the state's attorney in this matter, not Mr. Smith's or Mr. Stuart's."

"For crying out loud," said Marty.

"And if the Fugitive Slave Law does not apply, then I submit to the court that Alvin Smith has already been determined by the sheriff and attorney of Hatrack County to have acted in self-defense, and therefore to bring charges now would put him in double jeopardy, which is forbidden by—"

"I know exactly who and what forbids double jeopardy," said the judge, now getting a little edgy with Verily.

What am I doing wrong? Verily wondered.

"All right, since it's Mr. Smith's neck that's on the line, I'll deny the prosecution's motion and grant the defense motion to set up a blind test of a panel of Finders. Let's add another day—we'll meet on Friday to see if they can identify Arthur Stuart. As for putting Arthur in custody, I'll ask the boy's adopted father—is old Horace in the court today?"

Horace stood up. "Here I am, sir," he said.

"You going to make my life difficult by hiding this boy, so I have to lock you up for the rest of your natural life for contempt of court? Or are you going to keep him in plain sight and bring him to court for that test?"

"I'll bring him," said Horace. "He ain't going nowheres as long as Alvin's in jail, anyhow."

"Don't get cute with me, Horace, I'm just warning you," said the judge.

"Got no intention of being cute, dammit," murmured Horace as he sat back down.

"Don't curse in my courtroom, either, Mr. Guester, and don't insult me by assuming that my grey hair means I'm deaf." The judge rapped with his gavel. "Well, that does it for motions and—"

"Your Honor," said Verily.

"That's me," said the judge. "What, you got another motion?"

"I do," said Verily.

"And there's the matter of arguments on the motion to produce the plow," offered Marty Laws helpfully.

"Dammit," muttered the judge.

"I heard that, judge!" cried Horace Guester.

"Bailiff, put Mr. Guester outside," said the judge.

They all waited while Horace Guester got up and hurried out of the courtroom.

"What's your new motion, Mr. Cooper?"

"I respectfully request to know the position of Mr. Webster in this courtroom. He seems not to be an official of the county of Hatrack or the state of Hio."

"Ain't you co-counsel or some other fool thing?" asked the judge of Daniel Webster.

"I am," said Webster.

"Well, there you have it."

"Begging your pardon, Your Honor, but it seems plain to me that Mr. Webster's fees are not being paid by the county. I respectfully request to know who *is* paying him, or if he is acting out of the goodness of his heart.''

The judge leaned on his desk and cocked his head to look at Daniel Webster. ''Now that you mention it, I do recall never seeing you represent anybody as wasn't either very rich or very famous, Mr. Webster. I'd like to know myself who's paying you.''

''I'm here volunteering my services,'' said Webster.

''So if I put you under oath and ask you to tell me if your time and expenses here are or are not being paid by someone other than your own self, you would say that you are receiving no payment? Under oath?''

Webster smiled faintly. ''I'm on retainer, and so my expenses are paid, but not for this case specifically.''

''Let me ask it another way. If you don't want the bailiff to put you out with Mr. Guester, tell me who's paying you.''

''I am on retainer with the Property Rights Crusade, located at 44 Harrison Street in the city of Carthage in the state of Wobbish.'' Webster smiled thinly.

''Does that answer your respectful request, Mr. Cooper?'' the judge asked.

''It does, Your Honor.''

''Then I'll declare this—''

''Your Honor!'' cried Marty Laws. ''The matter of possession of the plow.''

''All right, Mr. Laws,'' said the judge. ''Time for brief arguments.''

''It's absurd for the defendant to remain in possession of the property in question, that's all,'' said Marty.

''Since the defendant himself is in the custody of the county jail,'' said Verily Cooper, ''and the plow is in his possession, then, like his clothing and his pen and ink and paper and everything else in his possession, the plow is obviously in the custody of the county jail as well. The state's motion is moot.''

''How do we know that the defendant even *has* the plow?'' asked Marty Laws. ''Nobody's seen it.''

''That's a point,'' said the judge, looking at Verily.

''Because of special properties of the plow,'' said Verily, ''the defendant feels it unwise to let it out of his sight. Nevertheless, if the state wishes to designate three officers of the court to see it . . .''

''Let's keep it simple,'' said the judge. ''Mr. Laws, Mr. Cooper, and I will go see this plow today, as soon as we finish here.''

Verily noticed with pleasure that Daniel Webster flushed with anger as he realized he was not going to be treated as an equal and invited along. Webster tugged at Laws' coat and then whispered in his ear.

"Um, Your Honor," said Laws.

"What message are you delivering for Mr. Webster?" asked the judge.

"We can't exactly call me, you, and Mr. Cooper as witnesses, us being, um, what we are," said Laws.

"I thought the point of this was to make sure the plow existed," said the judge. "If you and me and Mr. Cooper see it, then I think we can fairly well assure everybody it exists."

"But in the trial, we'll want people other than the defendant and Mr. Makepeace Smith to be able to testify about the plow."

"Plenty of time for worrying about that later. I'm sure we can get a few witnesses to see it by then, too. How many do you want?"

Another whispered conference. "Eight will do fine," said Laws.

"You and Mr. Cooper get together in the next while and decide which eight people you'll settle on as witnesses. In the meantime, the three of us will go visit Mr. Alvin Smith in prison and get an eyeful of this marvelous legendary mythical golden plow that has— how did you put it, Mr. Cooper?"

"Special properties," said Verily.

"You Englishmen have such a fine way with words."

Once again, Verily could sense some kind of nastiness directed toward him from the judge. As before, he had no idea what he had done to provoke it.

Still, the judge's inexplicable annoyance aside, things had gone rather well.

Unless, of course, the Millers had been all wrong and the Slave Finders *could* identify Arthur Stuart as the wanted runaway. Then there'd be problems. But . . . the nicest thing about this case was that if Verily performed quite badly, making it certain that Alvin would be hanged or Arthur Stuart returned to slavery, Alvin, being a Maker, could always just take the boy and go away; and not a soul could stop them if Alvin didn't want to be stopped, or find them if Alvin didn't want to be found.

Still, Verily had no intention of doing badly. He intended to win spectacularly. He intended to clear Alvin's name of all charges so the Maker would be free to teach him all that he wanted to know. And another, deeper motive, one which he did not try to hide from himself though he would never have admitted it to another: He wanted the Maker to respect him. He wanted Alvin Smith to look him in the eye and say, "Well done, friend."

That would be good. Verily Cooper wanted that good thing.

14

Witnesses

All the time of waiting hadn't been so bad, really. Nothing was happening in the jail, but Alvin didn't mind being alone and doing nothing. It gave him thinking time. And thinking time was making time, he reckoned. Not like he used to do as a boy, making bug baskets out of pulled-up grass to keep the Unmaker back. But making things in his head. Trying to remember the Crystal City as he saw it in the waterspout with Tenskwa-Tawa. Trying to figure how such a place was made. Can't teach folks how to make it if I don't know what it is myself.

Outside the jail he knew that the Unmaker was moving in the world, tearing down a little here, knocking over a little there, setting a wedge in every tiny crack it found. And there were always people searching for the Unmaker, for some awful destructive power outside themselves. Poor fools, they always thought that Destruction was merely destruction, they were using it and when they were done with it, they'd set to building. But you don't build on a foundation of destruction. That's the dark secret of the Unmaker, Alvin thought.

Once he sets you to tearing down, it's hard to get back to building, hard to get your own self back. The digger wears out the ground *and* the spade. And once you let yourself be a tool in the Unmaker's hand, he'll wear you out, he'll tear you down, he'll dull you and hole you and all the time you'll be thinking you're so sharp and fine and bright and whole, and you never know till he lets go of you, lets you drop and fall. What's that clatter? Why, that was me. That was me, sounding like a wore-out tool. What you leaving me for? I still got use left in me!

But you don't, not when the Unmaker's got you.

What Alvin figured out was that when you're Making, you don't use people like tools. You don't wear them out to achieve *your* purpose. You wear yourself out helping them achieve *theirs*. You wear yourself out teaching and guiding, persuading and listening to advice and letting folks persuade *you*, when it happens they're right. So instead of one ruler and a bunch of wore-out tools, you got a whole city of Makers, all of them free fellow-citizens, hard workers every one . . .

Except for one little problem. Alvin couldn't teach Making. Oh, he could get people to sort of set their minds right and their work would be enhanced a little. And a few people, like Measure, mostly, and his sister Eleanor, they learned a thing or two, they caught a glimmer. But most was in the dark.

And then there comes a one like this lawyer from England, this Verily Cooper, and he was just born knowing how to do in a second what Measure could only do after a whole day's struggle. Sealing a book shut like it was a single block of wood and cloth, and then opening it again with no harm to any of the pages and the letters still stuck on the surfaces. That was some Making.

What did he have to teach Verily? He was born knowing. And how could he hope to teach those as wasn't born knowing? And anyway how could he teach anything when he didn't know how to make the crystal out of which the city would be made?

You can't build a city of glass; it'll break, it can't hold weight. You can't build out of ice, either, because it ain't clear enough and what about summer? Diamonds, they're strong enough, but a city made of diamond, even if he could find or make so much of it—no way would they be allowed to use such rich stuff for building, there'd be folks to tear it down in no time, each one stealing a bit of wall to make hisself rich, and pretty soon the whole thing would be like a Swiss cheese, more hole than wall.

Oh, Alvin could spin himself through these thoughts and wonderings, through memories and words of books he read when Miss Larner—when Peggy—was teaching him. He could keep his mind occupied in solitude and not mind it a bit, though he also sure didn't mind when Arthur Stuart came to talk to him about goings on.

Today, though, things were happening. Verily Cooper would be fending off motions for this and that, and even if he was a good lawyer, he was from England and he didn't know the ways here, he could make mistakes, but there wasn't a blame thing Alvin could do about it even if he did. He just had to put his trust in other folks and Alvin hated that.

"Everyone hates it," said a voice, a so-familiar voice, a dreamed-of, longed-for voice with which he had had many a debate in his memory, many a quarrel in his imagination; a voice that he dreamed of whispering gently to him in the night and in the morning.

"Peggy," he whispered. He opened his eyes.

There she was, looking just as she would if he had conjured her up, only she was real, he hadn't done no conjuring.

He remembered his manners and stood up. "Miss Larner," he said. "It was kind of you to come and visit me."

"Not so much kind as necessary," she said, her tone businesslike.

Businesslike. He sighed inwardly.

She looked around for a chair.

He picked up the stool that stood inside the cell and impulsively, thoughtlessly handed it right through the bars to her. He hardly even noticed how he made the bits of iron bar and the strands of woodstuff move apart to let each other through; only when he saw Peggy's wide, wide eyes did he realize that of course she'd never seen anybody pass wood and iron right through each other like that.

"Sorry," he said. "I've never done that before, I mean without warning or nothing."

She took the stool. "It was very thoughtful of you," she said. "To provide me with a stool."

He sat down on his cot. It creaked under him. If he hadn't toughened up the material, it would have given way under his weight days ago. He was a big man and he used furniture kind of rough; he didn't mind if it complained out loud now and then.

"They're doing pretrial motions in court today, I understand."

"I watched part of it. Your lawyer is excellent. Verily Cooper?"

"I think he and I ought to be friends," Alvin said. He watched for her reaction.

She nodded, smiled thinly. "Do you really want me to tell you what I know about the possible courses your friendship might take?"

Alvin sighed. "I do, and I don't, and you know it."

"I'll tell you that I'm glad he's here. Without him you'd have no chance of getting through this trial."

"So now I'll win?"

"Winning isn't everything, Alvin."

"But losing is nothing."

"If you lost the case but kept your life and your life's work, then losing would be better than winning, and dying for it, don't you think?"

"I'm not on trial for my life!"

"Yes you are," said Peggy. "Whenever the law gets its hands on you, those who use the law to their own advantage will also turn it against you. Don't put your trust in the laws of men, Alvin. They were designed by strong men to improve their power over weaker ones."

"That's not fair, Miss Larner," said Alvin. "Ben Franklin and them others as made the first laws—"

"They meant well. But the reality for you is that whenever you put yourself in jail, Alvin, your life is in grave danger every moment."

"You came to tell me that? You know I can walk out of here whenever I want."

"I came so I could tell you when to walk away, if the need comes."

"I want my name cleared of Makepeace's lies."

"I also came to help with that," she said. "I'm going to testify."

Alvin thought of that night when Goody Guester died, Peggy's mother, though he hadn't known that Miss Larner was really Peggy Guester until she knelt weeping over her mother's ruined body. Right till the moment they heard the first gunshot, he and Peggy had been on the verge of declaring their love for each other and deciding to marry. And then her mother killed the Finder, and the other Finder killed her, and Alvin got there way too late to heal her from the shotgun blast, and all he could do was kill the man that shot her, kill him with his bare hands, and what did that do? What good did that do? What kind of Making was that?

"I don't want you to testify," he said.

"I wasn't looking forward to it myself," she said. "I won't do it if it's not needed. But you have to tell Verily Cooper what and

who I am, and tell him that when he's all done with his other witnesses, he's to look to me, and if I nod, he's to call me as a witness,
no arguments. Do you understand me? I'll know better than either
of you whether my testimony is necessary or not.''

Alvin heard what she said and knew he'd go along, but there
was a part of him that was seething with anger even though he didn't
know why—he'd been longing to see her for more than a year now,
and suddenly she was here and all he wanted to do was yell at her.

Well, he didn't yell. But he did speak up in a voice that sounded
less than kind. "Is that what you come back for? To tell poor stupid
Alvin and his poor stupid lawyer what to do?''

She looked sharp at him. "I met an old friend of yours at the
ferry.''

For a moment his heart leapt within him. "Ta-Kumsaw?'' he
whispered.

"Goodness no,'' she said. "He's out west past the Mizzipy for
all I know. I was referring to a fellow who once had a tattoo on an
unmentionable part of his body, a Mr. Mike Fink.''

Alvin rolled his eyes. "I guess the Unmaker's assembling all
my enemies in one place.''

"On the contrary,'' said Peggy. "I think he's no enemy. I think
he's a friend. He swears he means only to protect you, and I believe
him.''

He knew she meant him to take that as proof that the man could
be trusted, but he was feeling stubborn and said nothing.

"He came to the Wheelwright ferry in order to be close enough
to keep an eye on you. There's a conspiracy to get you extradited
to Kenituck under the Fugitive Slave Law.''

"Po Doggly told me he wasn't going to pay no mind to that.''

"Well, Daniel Webster is here precisely to see to it that whether
you win or lose here, you get taken to Kenituck to stand trial.''

"I won't go,'' said Alvin. "They'd never let me get to trial.''

"No, they never would. That's what Mike Fink came to watch
out for.''

"Why is he on my side? I took away his hex of protection. It
was a strong one. Near perfect.''

"And he's suffered a few scars and lost an ear since then. But
he's also learned compassion. He values the exchange. And you
healed his legs. You left him with a fighting chance.''

Alvin thought about that. "Well, you never know, do you. I
thought of him as a stone killer.''

"I think that a good person can sometimes do wrong out of

ignorance or weakness or wrong thinking, but when hard times come, the goodness wins out after all. And a bad person can often seem good and trustworthy for a long time, but when hard times come, the evil in him gets revealed.''

"So maybe we're just waiting for hard enough times to come in order to find out just how bad I am.''

She smiled thinly. "Modesty is a virtue, but I know you too well to think for a minute you believe you're a bad man.''

"I don't think much about whether I'm good or bad. I think a lot about whether I'm going to be worth a damn or not. Right now I reckon myself to be worth about six bits.''

"Alvin," she said, "you never used to swear in front of me.''

He felt the rebuke but he rather liked the feeling of annoying her. "It's just the bad in me coming out.''

"You're very angry with me.''

"Yes, well, you know all, you see all.''

"I've been busy, Alvin. You've been doing your life's work, and I've been doing mine.''

"Once upon a time I hoped it might be the same work," said Alvin.

"It will never be the same work. Though our labors may complement each other, I will never be a Maker. I only see what is there to be seen. While you imagine what might be made, and then make it. Mine is by far the lesser gift, and mostly useless to you.''

"That's the purest nonsense I ever heard.''

"I don't speak nonsense," she said sharply. "If you don't think my words sound true, then think again until you understand them.''

He imagined her as he used to see her, the severe-looking teacher lady at least ten years older than Peggy really was; she still knew how to use her voice like a rap across the knuckles. "It ain't useless to me to know what's coming in the future.''

"But I don't *know* what's coming. I only know what *might* come. What seems likely to come. There are so many paths the future might take. Most people stumble blindly along, plunging into this or that path that I see in their heartfire, heading for disaster or delight. Few have your power, Alvin, to open up a new path that did not exist. There was no future in which I saw you push that stool through the bars of the cell. And yet it was an almost inevitable act on your part. A simple expression of the impulsiveness of a young man. I see in people's heartfires the futures that are possible for them in the natural course of events. But you can set aside the laws of nature, and so you can't be properly accounted for. Sometimes I can see clearly; but there are deep gaps, dark and wide.''

He got up from the cot and came to the bars, held them, knelt down in front of her. "Tell me how I find out how to make the Crystal City.''

"I don't know how you do it. But I've seen a thousand futures in which you do.''

"Tell me where I look then, in order to learn!''

"I don't know. Whatever it is, it doesn't follow the laws of nature. Or at least I think that's why I can't see it.''

"Vilate Franker says my life ends in Carthage City," said Alvin. She stiffened. "How does she know such a thing?''

"She knows where things come from and where they'll end up.''

"Don't go to Carthage City. Never go there.''

"So she's right.''

"Never go there," she whispered. "Please.''

"I got no plans for it," he said. But inside his heart he thought: She cares for me after all. She still cares for me.

He might have said something about it, or she might have talked a bit more tenderly and less businesslike. *Might* have, but then the door opened and in trooped the sheriff and the judge and Marty Laws and Verily Cooper.

"Scuse us," said Sheriff Doggly. "But we got us a courtroom thing to do here.''

"I'm at your service, gentlemen," said Alvin, rising at once to his feet. Peggy also rose, then stooped to move the stool out of the way of the door.

The sheriff looked at the stool.

"It was so kind of you to allow Alvin's stool to be placed outside the bars for me," said Peggy.

Po Doggly looked at her. He hadn't given any such order, but he decided not to argue the point. Alvin was Alvin.

"Explain things to your client," said the judge to Verily Cooper.

"As we discussed last night," said Verily, "we'll need to have various witnesses view the plow. The three of us will be enough to ascertain that the plow exists, that it appears to be made of gold, and . . .''

"That's all right," said Alvin.

"And we've agreed that after the jury is empaneled, we'll select eight more witnesses who can testify to the existence and nature of the plow in open court.''

"As long as the plow stays in here with me," said Alvin. He glanced toward Sheriff Doggly.

"The sheriff already knows," said the judge, "that he is *not* one of the designated witnesses."

"Blame it all, Your Honor!" said Doggly. "It sets in here for weeks in my jail and I can't even *see* it?"

"I don't mind if he stays," said Alvin.

"I do," said the judge. "It's better if he doesn't regale his deputies with tales of how big and how gold the thing is. I know we can trust Mr. Doggly. But why exacerbate the temptation that must already afflict at least some of his deputies?"

Alvin laughed.

"What's so funny, Mr. Smith?" asked the judge.

"How everybody's all pretending they know what in hell the word *exacerbate* means." They all joined him in laughter.

When it died down, Sheriff Doggly was still in the room. "I'm waiting to escort the lady out," he said.

Alvin rolled his eyes. "She saw the plow on the night that it was made."

"Nevertheless," said the judge, "three witnesses on this official occasion. You can show it to every visitor in the jail if you want to, but on this occasion, we have agreed to three, and three it is."

Peggy smiled at the judge. "You are a man of extraordinary integrity, sir," she said. "I'm glad to know you're presiding at this trial."

When she was gone and the sheriff had closed the door to the jail, the judge looked at Alvin. "That was Peggy Guester? The torch girl?"

Alvin nodded.

"She grew up prettier than I ever expected," said the judge. "I just wish I knew whether she was being sarcastic."

"I don't think so," said Alvin. "But you're right, she has a way of saying even nice things as if she's only barely holding back from telling a bunch of stuff that ain't so nice."

"Whoever marries that one," said the judge, "he better have a thick skin."

"Or a stout stick," said Marty Laws, and then he laughed. But he laughed alone, and soon fell silent, vaguely embarrassed, uncertain why his joke had fallen so flat.

Alvin reached under the cot and slid out the burlap bag that held the plow. He pulled back the mouth of the sack, so the plow sat exposed, surrounded by burlap, shining golden in the light from the high windows.

"I'll be damned," said Marty Laws. "It really is a plow, and it really is gold."

"*Looks* gold," said the judge. "I think if we're to be honest witnesses, we have to touch it."

Alvin smiled. "I ain't stopping you."

The judge sighed and turned to the county attorney. "We forgot to get the sheriff to open the cell door."

"I'll fetch him," said Marty.

"Please cover the plow, Mr. Smith," said the judge.

"Don't bother," said Alvin. He reached over and opened the cell door. The latch didn't even so much as make a sound; nor did the hinges squeak. The door just opened, silent and smooth.

The judge looked down at the latch and lock. "Is this broken?" he asked.

"Don't worry," said Alvin. "It's working fine. Come on in and touch the plow, if you want."

Now that the door was open, they hung back. Finally Verily Cooper stepped in, the judge after him. But Marty held back. "There's something about that plow," he said.

"Nothing to be worried about," said Alvin.

"You're just bothered because the door opened so easy," said the judge. "Come on in, Mr. Laws."

"Look," said Marty. "It's trembling."

"Like I told you," said Alvin, "it's alive."

Verily knelt down and reached out a hand toward the plow. With no one touching it yet, the plow slid toward him, dragging the burlap with it.

Marty yelped and turned his back, pressing his face into the wall opposite the cell door.

"You can't be much of a witness with your back turned," said the judge.

The plow slid to Verily. He laid his hand on the top of it. It slowly turned under his hand, turned and turned, around and around, smooth as an ice skater.

"It *is* alive," he said.

"After a fashion," said Alvin. "But it's got a mind of its own, so to speak. I mean, it's not like I've tamed it or nothing."

"Can I pick it up?" asked Verily.

"I don't know," said Alvin. "Nobody but me has ever tried."

"It would be useful," said the judge, "if we could heft it to see if it weighs like gold, or if it's some other, lighter alloy."

"It's the purest gold you'll ever see in your life," said Alvin, "but heft it if you can."

Verily squatted, got his hands under the plow, and lifted. He grunted at the weight of it, but it stayed in his hands as he lifted it. Still, there was some struggle with it. "It wants to turn," said Verily.

"It's a plow," said Alvin. "I reckon it wants to find good soil."

"You wouldn't actually plow with this, would you?" said the judge.

"I can't think why else I made it, if it ain't for plowing. I mean, if I was making a bowl I got the shape wrong, don't you think?"

"Can you hand it to me?" asked the judge.

"Of course," said Verily. He stepped close to the judge and held the plow as the older man wrapped his hands around it. Then Verily let go.

At once the plow began to buck in the judge's hands. Before the judge could drop it, Alvin reached out and rested his right hand on the plow's face. Immediately it went still.

"Why didn't it do that with Mr. Cooper?" asked the judge, his voice trembling a little.

"I reckon it knows Verily Cooper is my attorney," said Alvin, grinning.

"While I am impartial," said the judge. "Perhaps Mr. Laws is correct not to handle it."

"But he has to," said Verily. "He's the most important one to see it. He has to assure Mr. Webster and Makepeace Smith that it's the real plow, the gold plow, and that it's safe here in the jailhouse."

The judge handed the plow to Alvin, then left the cell and put his hand on Marty Laws' shoulder. "Come now, Mr. Laws, I've handled it, and even if it bucks a bit, it won't harm you."

Laws shook his head.

"Marty," said Alvin. "I don't know what you're afraid of, but I promise you that the plow won't hurt you, and you won't hurt it."

Marty turned sideways. "It was so bright," he said. "It hurt my eyes."

"Just a glint of sunlight," said the judge.

"No sir," said Marty. "No, your honor. It was bright. It was bright from way down deep inside itself. It shone right into me. I could feel it."

The judge looked at Alvin.

"*I* don't know," said Alvin. "It's not like I've been showing it to folks."

"I know what he means," said Verily. "I didn't see it as light. But I felt it as warmth. When the bag fell open, the whole place felt warmer. But there's no harm in it, Mr. Laws. Please—I'll hold it with you."

"As will I," said the judge.

Alvin held the plow out to them.

Marty slowly turned so he could watch, his head partly averted, as the other two witnesses got their hands on and under the plow. Only then did he sidle forward and gingerly lay his fingertips on and under the golden plowshare. He was sweating something awful, and Alvin felt plain sorry for him, but couldn't begin to understand what the man was going through. The plow had always felt comfortable and friendly-like to him. What did it mean to Marty?

When the thing didn't hurt him, Marty gained confidence, and shifted his hands to get some of the weight of the plow. Still his eyes were squinted and he looked sidelong, as if to protect one eye in case the other one was suddenly blinded. "I can hold it alone, I guess," he said.

"Let Mr. Smith keep his hand on it, so it doesn't buck," said the judge.

Alvin left his hand, but the others took their hands away, and Marty held the plow alone.

"I reckon it weighs like gold," said Marty.

Alvin reached under the plow and got hold of it. "I got it now, Marty," he said.

Marty let go—reluctantly, it seemed to Alvin.

"Anyway, I reckon you can see why I don't just let anyone have a grab at it," said Alvin.

"I'd hate to think what shape I'd be in if I dropped it on my toe," said the judge.

"Oh, it lands easy," said Alvin.

"It really is alive," said Verily softly.

"You're a bold fellow," said the judge to Alvin. "Your attorney was quite adamant about having a hearing on the extradition matter before we even empanel a jury about the larceny business."

Alvin looked at Verily. "I reckon my attorney knows what he's doing."

"I told them," said Verily, "that my defense would be that the Finder was not engaged in lawful business, since by the cachet they carried, Arthur Stuart could not possibly be identified."

Alvin knew that this was more a question than a statement. "They walked right by Arthur Stuart that night," said Alvin.

"We are going to bring a group of Slave Finders from Wheelwright to see if they can pick Arthur Stuart from a group of boys about his age," said Verily. "Their faces and hands will be hidden, of course."

"Make sure," said Alvin, "to get a couple of Mock Berry's boys in the group, along with whatever White boys you settle on. I reckon those as spends their whole lives looking for Black folks might have some ways of spotting which is which, even if they got gloves on and bags over their heads."

"Mock Berry?" asked the judge.

"He's a Black fellow," explained Marty. "Free Black, mind you. Him and Anga his wife, they've got a passle of young folks in a cabin in the woods not far from the roadhouse."

"Well, that's a good idea, to have some Black boys in the mix," said the judge. "And maybe I'll see to a few others things to make things stay fair." He reached out to the plow, which Alvin still held in his hands. "Mind if I touch it one more time?"

He did; the plow trembled under his hand.

"If the jury should decide that this is truly Makepeace Smith's gold," said the judge, "I wonder how he's going to get it home?"

"Your Honor," Marty protested.

The judge glared at him. "Don't you even for a *moment* imagine that I'm going to be anything but completely fair and impartial in the conduct of this trial."

Marty shook his head and held out his hands as if to ward off the very *thought* of impartiality.

"Besides," said the judge. "You saw what you saw, too. You going to turn the trial over to Mr. Webster, now that you seen it move and shine and whatnot?"

Marty shook his head. "The point at issue is whether Alvin Smith made the plow with gold that belonged to Makepeace. What the plow is like, its other properties—I don't see but what that's completely irrelevant."

"Exactly," said the judge. "All we needed to verify right now is that it exists, it's gold, and it should remain in Alvin's custody while Alvin remains in the custody of the sheriff. I think we've determined all three points to everyone's satisfaction. Right, gentlemen?"

"Right," said Marty.

Verily smiled.

Alvin put the plow back in the burlap bag.

As they left the cell, the judge carefully closed the door until the latch clicked. Then he tried to open it and couldn't. "Well, I'm glad to see the jail is secure." He didn't grin when he said it. He didn't have to.

Po Doggly looked beside himself with curiosity as they emerged from the jail into the outer office. In moments he was inside the jail, looking through bars at Alvin, hoping to catch a glint of gold.

"Sorry, Sheriff," said Alvin. "All put away."

"You got no sense of sport, Alvin," said Doggly. "You couldn't even leave the top open a little bit?"

"I won't mind a bit if you're one of the eight," said Alvin. "Let's see what happens."

"Not a bad idea," said Doggly. "And thank you for not minding. I won't do that, though. Better to use eight ordinary citizens, instead of a public official. I'm just curious, you know. Never saw that much gold in all my life, and I'd like to be able to tell my grandchildren."

"So would I," said Alvin. And then: "Sheriff Doggly, Peggy Larner wouldn't still be out there, would she?"

"No. Sorry, Al. She's gone. Reckon she went on home to say howdy to her pa."

"Reckon so," said Alvin. "No matter."

Arthur Stuart would never have called himself a spy. He couldn't help it that he was short. He couldn't help it that his skin was dark and that, being shy, he tended to stand in shadows and hold very, very still so people overlooked him quite easily. He wasn't aware that some of the greensong from his long journeys with Alvin still lingered with him, a melody in the back of his mind, so that his step was unusually quiet, twigs tended to bend out of his way, and boards didn't often squeak under his step.

But when it came to his visit to Vilate's house, well, it wasn't no accident she didn't see him. In fact, he made it a point not to step on the porch of the post office, so he couldn't very well walk through the front door and make the bell ring. Nor, when he got around to the back of Vilate Franker's house, did he knock on her back door or ask her permission before climbing up on her rain barrel and leaning over to look through her window into her kitchen, where the teapot simmered on the stove and Vilate sat drinking tea and carrying on quite a lively conversation with . . .

With a salamander.

Not a lizard—even from the window, Arthur Stuart could see there were no scales. Besides, you didn't have to be some kind of genius to know a salamander from a lizard at five paces. Arthur Stuart was a boy, and boys tended to know such things. Moreover, Arthur Stuart had been an unusually solitary and inquisitive boy, and he had a way with animals, so even if some other boy might make a mistake, Arthur Stuart never would. It was a salamander.

Vilate would say something, and then sip her tea, glancing up from the cup now and then to nod or murmur something—"Mm-hm"; "I know"; "Isn't it just awful?"—as if the salamander was saying something.

But the salamander didn't say nothing. Didn't even look at her, most of the time, though truth to tell you never quite knew for sure what a salamander was looking at, because if one eye was looking there, the other might be looking here and how would you know? Still and all, Arthur was pretty sure it looked right at him. Knew he was there. But didn't seem to get alarmed or nothing, so Arthur just kept on looking and listening.

"A man shouldn't trifle with a lady's affections," she was saying. "Once a man goes down that road, the lady has a right to protect herself as best she can."

Another sip. Another nod.

"Oh, I know. And the worst of it is, people are going to think so badly of me. But everyone knows that Alvin Smith has hidden powers. Of course I couldn't help myself."

Another sip. And then, abruptly, tears streamed out of her eyes.

"Oh, my dear, dear soul, my friend, my beloved trusted friend, how can I do this? I really do care for the boy. I really do care for him. Why oh why couldn't he have loved me? Why did he have to spurn me and make me do this?"

And so it went. Arthur wasn't no dummy. He knew right off that Vilate Franker was planning some kind of devilment against Alvin, and he sort of hoped she might mention what it was, though that wasn't too likely, since all she talked about was how bad she felt and how she hated to do it but it was a lady's right to defend her honor even though it might involve giving the appearance of having *no* honor but that's why it was so good having such a good, true, wonderful *friend*.

Ah, the tears that flowed. Ah, the sighs. Ah, the quart of tea she consumed while Arthur leaned on the sill, watching, listening.

Oddly, though, as soon as the tears were done, her face just went clean. Not a streak. Not a trace of redness around the eyes. Not a sign that she had even shed a tear.

The tea eventually took its toll. Vilate slid her chair back and rose to her feet. Arthur knew where the privy was; he immediately jumped from the rain barrel and ran around the front of the house before the door even opened leading out to the back. Then, knowing she couldn't possibly hear the bell, he opened the post office door, went inside, clambered over the counter, and made his way into the kitchen from the front of the house. There was the salamander, licking a bit of tea that had spilled from the saucer. As Arthur entered, the salamander lifted its head. Then it scurried back and forth, making a shape on the table. One triangle. Another triangle crossing it.

A hex.

Arthur moved to the chair where Vilate had been sitting. Standing, his head was just about at the height her head was at when she was seated. And as he leaned over her chair, the salamander changed.

No, not really. No, the salamander disappeared. Instead, a woman was sitting in the chair across from him.

"You're an evil little boy," the woman said with a sad smile.

Arthur hardly even noticed what she said. Because he knew her. It was Old Peg Guester. The woman he called Mother. The woman who was buried under a certain stone marker on the hill behind the roadhouse, near his real mother, the runaway slave girl he never met. Old Peg was there.

But it wasn't Old Peg. It was the salamander.

"And you imagine things, you nasty boy. You make up stories."

Old Peg used to call him her "nasty boy," but it was a tease. It was when he repeated something someone else had said. She would laugh and call him nasty boy and give him a hug and tell him not to repeat *that* remark to anyone.

But this woman, this pretend Old Peg, she meant it. She thought he was a nasty boy.

He moved away from the chair. The salamander was back on the table and Old Peg was gone. Arthur knelt by the table to look at the salamander at eye level. It stared into his eyes. Arthur stared back.

He used to do this for hours with animals in the forest. When he was very little, he understood them. He came away with their story in his mind. Gradually that ability faded. Now he caught only glimmers. But then, he didn't spend as much time with animals anymore. Maybe if he tried hard enough . . .

"Don't forget me, salamander," he whispered. "I want to know your story. I want to know who taught you how to make them hexes on the table."

He reached out a hand, then slowly let a single finger come to rest on the salamander's head. It didn't recoil from him; it didn't move even when his finger made contact. It just looked at him.

"What are you doing indoors?" he whispered. "You don't like it indoors. You want to be outside. Near the water. In the mud. In the leaves. With bugs."

It was the kind of thing Alvin did, murmuring to animals, suggesting things to them.

"I can take you back to the mud if you want. Come with me, if you want. Come with me, if you can."

The salamander raised a foreleg, then slowly set it down. One step closer to Arthur.

And from the salamander he thought he felt a hunger, a desire for food, but more than that, a desire for . . . for freedom. The salamander didn't like being a prisoner.

The door opened.

"Why, Arthur Stuart," said Vilate. "Imagine you coming to visit."

Arthur had sense enough not to jump to his feet as if he was doing something wrong. "Any letters for Alvin?" he asked.

"Not a one."

Arthur didn't even mention the salamander, which was just as well, because Vilate never even looked at it. You'd think that if a lady was caught with a live salamander—or even a dead one, for that matter—on her kitchen table, she'd at least offer some explanation.

"Want some tea?" she asked.

"Can't stay," said Arthur.

"Oh, next time then. Give Alvin my love." Her smile was sweet and beautiful.

Arthur reached out his hand, right in front of her, and touched the salamander's back.

She didn't notice. Or at least she gave no sign of noticing.

He moved away, backed out of the room, hopped the counter, and ran out the front door, hearing the bell ring behind him as he went.

If the salamander was a prisoner, who had captured it? Not Vilate—the salamander was making hexes to fool her into seeing somebody there. Though Arthur was willing to bet that it wasn't Old

Peg Guester that Vilate saw. But the salamander wasn't fooling her out of its own free will, because all it wanted was to be free to go back to being an ordinary salamander again.

He'd have to tell Alvin about this, that was sure. Vilate was planning to do something rotten to him, and the salamander that walked out hexes on the kitchen table, it had something to do with the plot.

How could Vilate be so stupid that she didn't even see me touching her salamander? Why didn't she get upset when she saw me in the kitchen when she got back from the privy?

Maybe she wanted me to see the salamander. Or maybe someone else wanted me to see it.

Wanted me to see Mother.

For a moment, walking along the dusty main street of Hatrack River, he lost control of himself, almost let himself cry thinking about Mother, thinking about seeing her sitting across from him.

It wasn't real, he told himself. It was all fakery. Humbug. Hoax- ification. Whoever was behind all this was a liar, and a mean liar at that. Nasty boy indeed. Evil boy. He wasn't no evil boy. He was a good boy and the real Peg Guester would know that, she wouldn't say nothing like that to him. The real Peg Guester would hug him up tight and say, "My good boy, Arthur Stuart, you are my own good boy."

He walked it off. He walked the tears right out of his eyes, and when the sad feelings went away, another feeling came in its place. He was plain mad. Got no right making him see Mama. Got no right. I hate you, whoever you are, making me see my Mama calling me names like that.

He trotted up the stairs into the courthouse. The only good thing about Alvin being in jail was that Arthur Stuart always knew where he was.

It was hard for Napoleon to believe that he had once come *this* close to killing the American boy Calvin. Hard to remember how fright- ened he had been to see the boy's power. How for the first few days, Napoleon had watched him closely, had hardly slept for fear that the boy would do something to him in the night. Remove his legs, for instance. That would be a cure for the gout! It only occurred to him because of the number of times he had wished, in the throes of agony, that in one of his battles a cannonball had severed his leg. Stumping around on sticks couldn't be worse than this. And the boy brought such relief. Not a cure . . . but a cessation of the pain.

In exchange for that, Napoleon was content to let Calvin manipulate him. He knew who was really in control, and it wasn't an upstart, ignorant American boy. Who cared if Calvin thought he was clever, doling out a day's relief from pain in exchange for another lesson on how to govern men? Did he really imagine Napoleon would teach him anything that would give him the upper hand? On the contrary, with every hour, every day they spent together, Napoleon's control over a boy who *could* have been uncontrollable grew stronger, deeper. And Calvin had no idea.

They never understood, none of them. They all thought they served Napoleon out of love and admiration, or out of greed and self-interest, or out of fear and discretion. Whatever motive drove them, Napoleon fed it, got control of it. Some were impelled by shame, and some by guilt; some by ambition, some by lust, some even by their excess of piety—for when the occasion demanded, Napoleon could convince some spiritually starved soul that he was God's chosen servant on Earth. It wasn't hard. None of it was hard, when you understood other people the way Napoleon did. They gave off their desires like sweat, like the smell of an athlete after the contest or a soldier after a battle, like the smell of a woman—Napoleon didn't even have to think, he simply said the word, the exact words they needed to hear to win them to him.

And on those rare occasions when someone was immune to his words, when they had some sort of protective amulet or hex, each one more clever than the last—well, that's what guards were for. That's why there was a guillotine. The people knew that Napoleon was not a cruel man, that few indeed were ever punished under his rule. They knew that if a man was sent to the guillotine, it was because the world would be better off with that particular mouth detached from those lungs, with those hands unconnected to that head.

Calvin? Ah, the boy could have been dangerous. The boy had the power to save himself from the guillotine, to stop the blade from striking his neck. The boy might have been able to prevent anything that didn't come as a complete surprise. How would the Emperor have defeated him? Perhaps a little opium to dull him; he had to sleep sometime. But it didn't matter. No need to kill after all. Only a little study, a little patience, and Napoleon had him.

Not as his servant—no, this American boy was clever, he was watching for that, he was careful not to allow himself to succumb to any attempt by Napoleon to turn him into a slave, into one of those servants who looked at their Emperor with adoring eyes. Now and then Napoleon made a remark, a sort of feint, so Calvin would *think* he was fending off the Emperor's best strokes. But in fact, Napoleon had no need for this boy's loyalty. Just his healing touch.

This boy was driven by envy. Who would have guessed it? All that innate power, such gifts from God or Nature or whatever, and the boy was wasting it all because of envy for his older brother Alvin. Well, he wasn't about to tell Calvin he had to stop letting those feelings control him! On the contrary, Napoleon fed them, subtly, with little queries now and then about how Alvin might have done this or that, or comments about how awful it was having to put up with younger brothers who simply haven't the ability to measure up to one's own ability. He knew how this would rankle, how it would fester in Calvin's soul. A worm, twisting its way through the boy's judgment, eating tunnels in it. I have you, I have you. Look across the ocean, your gaze fixed upon your brother; you might have challenged me for the empire here, for half the world, but instead all you can think about is some useless fellow in homespun or deerskin or whatever who can make polished stone with his bare hands and heal the sick.

Heal the sick. That's the one that Napoleon was working on now. He knew perfectly well that Calvin was deliberately not healing him; he also knew that if Calvin ever got the idea that Napoleon was really in command, he'd probably flee and leave him with the gout again. So he had to keep a delicate balance: Taunt him because his brother could heal and he couldn't; at the same time, convince him that he'd already learned all the Emperor had to teach, that it was just a matter of practice now before he was as good at controlling other men.

If it worked out well, the boy, filled with confidence that he had squeezed the last drop of knowledge from Napoleon's mind, would finally show off that he was a match for his brother after all. He would heal the Emperor, then leave the court at once and sail back to America to challenge his brother—to attempt, using Napoleon's teachings, to get control over him.

Of course, if he got there and nothing he learned from the Emperor worked, well, he'd be back for vengeance! But Napoleon really was teaching him. Enough to play on the weaknesses of weak men, the fears of fearful men, the ambitions of proud men, the ignorance of stupid men. What Calvin didn't notice was that Napoleon wasn't teaching him any of the truly difficult arts: how to turn the virtues of good men against them.

The most hilarious thing was that Calvin was surrounded by the

very best men, the most difficult ones that Napoleon had won over.
The Marquis de La Fayette, for instance—he was the servant who
bathed the boy, just as he bathed the Emperor. It would never occur
to Calvin that Napoleon would keep his most dangerous enemies
near him, oblivious to how he humiliated them. If Calvin only understood, he would realize that this was *real* power. Evil men, weak
men, fearful men—they were so easy to control. It was only when
men of virtue fell under Napoleon's control that he felt at last the
confidence to reach for power, to unseat the king and take his place,
to conquer Europe and impose his peace upon the warring nations.

Calvin never sees that, because he is himself a fearful and ambitious man, and does not realize that others might be fearless and
generous. No wonder he resents his older brother so much! From
what Calvin said of him, it seemed to Napoleon that Alvin would
be a very difficult case indeed, a very hard one to break. In fact,
knowing that Calvin's brother existed was enough to cause Napoleon
to hold off on his plan of building up his armies in Canada with an
eye to conquering the three English-speaking nations of America.
No reason to do anything to make Alvin Smith turn his eyes east-
ward. That was a contest Napoleon did not want to embark on.

Instead he would send Calvin home, armed with great skill at
subversion, deception, corruption, and manipulation. He'd have no
control over Alvin, of course, but he would surely be able to deceive
him, for Napoleon well knew that just as evil, weak, and fearful
people saw their own base motives in other people's actions, so also
the virtuous tended to assume the noblest of motives for other people's acts; why else were so many awful liars so successful at bilking
others? If good people weren't so trusting of bad ones, the human
race would have died out long ago— most women never would have
let most men near them.

Let the brothers battle it out. If anyone can get rid of the threat
of this Alvin Smith, it's his own brother, who can get close to him—
not me, with all my armies, with all my skill. Let them fight.

But not until my leg is healed.

"My dear Leon, you mustn't drift off with the covers down like
that."

It was La Fayette, checking on him before sleep. Napoleon let
the fellow pull his blanket up. It was a coolish night; it was good to
have such tender concern from a loving man of great responsibility,
dependability, creativity. I have in my hands the best of men, and
under my thumb the worst of them. My record is much better than
God's. Clearly the old fellow chose the wrong son to make his only

begotten. If I'd been in Jerusalem in the place of that dullard Jesus, I'd never have been crucified. I would have had Rome under my control in no time, and the whole world converted to my doctrine.

Maybe that's what this Alvin was—God's second try! Well, Napoleon would help with the script. Napoleon would send Alvin Smith his Judas.

"You need your sleep, Leon," said La Fayette.

"My mind is so full," said Napoleon.

"Of happy things, I pray."

"Happy indeed."

"No pain in your leg? It's good to have that American boy here, if he keeps you from that dreadful suffering."

"I know that when I'm in pain I'm so difficult to live with," said Napoleon.

"Not at all, never. Don't even think it. It's a joy to be with you."

"Do you ever miss it, my Marquis? The armies, the power? Government, politics, intrigues?"

"Oh, Leon! How could I miss it? I have it all through you. I watch what you do and I marvel. I never could have done so well. I'm at school with you every day; you are the superb master."

"Am I?"

"The master. The master of all is my dear Leon. How truly they named your house in Corsica, my dear. Buona Parte. Good parts. You are truly the lion of good parts."

"How sweet of you to say so, my Marquis. Good night."

"God bless you."

The candle retreated from the room, and moonlight returned its dim light through the curtains.

I know you're studying me, Calvin. Sending your doodling bug, as you so quaintly call it, into my legs, to find the cause of the gout. Figure it out. Be as smart as your brother about this one thing, so I can finally get rid of you and the pain both.

Verily had known debased men in his life; he had been offered large sums of money to defend one now and then, but his conscience was not for sale. He remembered one of them who, thinking that his minions had not been clear about just how *much* money he was offering, came to see Verily in person. When he finally realized that Verily was not simply holding out for a higher price, he looked quite hurt. "Really, Mr. Cooper, why isn't my money as good as anyone else's?"

"It isn't your money, sir," said Verily.

"What, then? What is your objection?"

"I keep imagining: What if, through some gross miscarriage of justice, I won?"

Livid, the man hurled vile threats at him and left. Verily never knew whether it was this man or another who sent an assassin after him—a pathetic attempt, knifework in the dark. Verily saw the blade and the assassin's vicious smile—obviously the fellow had chosen a profession that allowed him to satisfy his own predilections—and caused the blade to drop off the knife and shatter at the man's feet. The man couldn't have looked more crestfallen if Verily had made a cunuch of him.

Debased men, but they all had something in common: They showed a keen regard for virtue, and tried to dress themselves in that costume. Hypocrisy, for all its bad reputation, at least showed a decent respect for goodness.

These Slave Finders, however, were not noble enough to be hypocrites. Not having risen above the level of reptiles and sharks, they showed no awareness of their own despicableness, and thus made no attempt to hide what they were. One was almost tempted to admire their brazenness, until one remembered what callous disregard for decency they must have in order to spend their lives, in exchange for mere money, chasing down the most helpless of their fellow-beings and returning them to lives of bondage, punishment, and despair.

Verily was pleased that Daniel Webster seemed to be almost as repulsed by these men as he was. Fastidiously the New England lawyer disdained to shake their hands, managing to be busy with his papers as each one arrived. Nor did he even bother to learn their names; having once ascertained that the entire group contracted for was properly assembled, he then addressed them only as a group, and without quite looking any of them in the eye. If they noticed his aloofness, they made no remark and showed no resentment. Perhaps this is how they were always treated. Perhaps those who hired them always did so with distaste, washing their hands after passing them the cachet of the slave they were to hunt down, washing again after giving them their Finder's fee. Didn't they understand that it is the murderer who is filthy, and not the knife?

It was ten-thirty in the morning before the Finders, seated at a single long table before the judge's bench, were satisfied that they had got the information they needed from the cachet belonging to a certain Cavil Planter of Oily Spring, Kenituck. The judge had the

deposition, carefully taken by Mr. Webster at Mr. Planter's home in
Carthage City, Wobbish. Planter had attempted to assert that the
cachet was a collection of nail and hair clippings and a bit of dried
skin taken from one Arthur Stuart of Hatrack River; but Webster
insisted that he state the exact legal situation, which was that the
items in the cachet were taken from an unnamed baby born on his
farm in Appalachee to a slave woman belonging to Mr. Planter at
the time, who had shortly afterward escaped—with, as Planter insisted on adding, the help of the devil, who gave her the power to
fly, or so it was rumored among the ignorant and superstitious slaves.

The Finders were ready; the boys were led in, one at a time,
and lined up in a row in front of them. All the boys were dressed
in ordinary clothing, and all were more or less of a size. Their hands
were covered, not with gloves, but with burlap bags tied above their
elbows; a finer sacking material also covered their heads with loose-
fitting hoods. No scrap of skin was visible; care had even been taken
to make sure there was no gap between the buttons of their shirts.
And just in case, a large placard with a number on it hung from
each boy's neck, completely covering his shirtfront.

Verily watched carefully. Was there some difference between
the Black sons of Mock Berry and the White boys? Something about
their walk, their stance? Indeed, there were differences among the
boys—this one's pose of insouciance, that one's nervous fidgeting—
but Verily could not tell which were White and which were Black.
Certainly he could not tell which one was Arthur Stuart, the boy
who was not fully of either race. This did not mean, however, that
the Finders did not know or could not guess.

Alvin assured him, though, that their knack would be useless to
them, since Arthur Stuart was no longer a fair match for the cachet.

And Alvin was right. The Finders looked puzzled when the last
boy was brought in and the judge said, "Well, which of them
matches the cachet?" Clearly they had expected to know instantly
which of them was their prey. Instead, they began to murmur.

"No conference," said the judge. "Each of you must reach his
conclusion independently, write down the number of the boy you
think matches the cachet, and have done with it."

"Are you sure someone hasn't held out the boy in question?"
asked one Slave Finder.

"What you are asking me," said the judge, "is if I am either
corrupt or a fool. Would you care to specify which accusation you
are inquiring about?"

After that the Finders puzzled in silence.

"Gentlemen," said the judge—and was his tone somewhat dry when he called them that? "You have had three minutes. I was told your identification would be instant. Please write and have done."

They wrote. They signed their papers. They handed them to the judge.

"Please, return to your seats while I tabulate the results," said the judge.

Verily had to admire the way the judge showed no expression as he sorted through the papers. But it also frustrated him. Would there be *no* hint of the outcome?

"I'm disappointed," said the judge. "I had expected that the much-vaunted powers and the famous integrity of the Slave Finders would give me unanimous results. I had expected that you would either unanimously point the finger at one boy, or unanimously declare that the boy could not be one of this group. Instead, I find quite a range of answers. Three of you did declare under penalty of perjury that none of these boys matched the cachet. But four of you have named various boys—again, under penalty of perjury. Specifically, the four of you named three different boys. The only two who seemed to be in agreement both happened to be seated together, at my far right. Since you are the only two who agree in accusing one of the boys, I think we'll check your assertion first. Bailiff, please remove the hood from the head of boy number five."

The bailiff did as he was asked. The boy was Black, but he was not Arthur Stuart.

"You two—are you certain, do you swear before God, that this is the boy who matches the cachet? Remember please that it is your license to practice your profession in the state of Wobbish that hangs in the balance, for if you are found to be unreliable or dishonest, you will never be permitted to bring a slave back across the river again."

What they also knew, however, was that if they now backed down, they would be liable for charges of perjury. And the boy *was* Black.

"No sir, I am certain this is the boy," said one. The other nodded emphatically.

"Now, let's look at the other two boys that were named. Take the hoods from numbers one and two."

One of them was Black, the other White.

The Finder who named a White boy covered his face with his hands. "Again, knowing that your license is at stake, are you both prepared to swear that the boy you named is an exact match?"

The Finder who named the White boy began to stammer, "I don't know, I just don't, I was sure, I thought it was . . ."

"The answer is simple—do you continue to swear that this boy is an exact match, or did you lie under oath when you named him?"

The Finders who had sworn that the cachet matched no one were smiling now—they knew, obviously, that the others had lied, and were enjoying their torment.

"I did not lie," said the Finder who named the White boy.

"Neither did I," said the other defiantly. "And I *still* think I'm right. I don't know how these other boys could get it so wrong."

"But you—*you* don't think you're right, do you? You don't think some miracle turned that slave baby White, do you?"

"No, sir. I must be . . . mistaken."

"Give me your license. Right now."

The miserable Finder stood up and handed the judge a leather case. The judge took from the case a piece of paper with an official seal on it. He wrote in the margin and then on the back; then he signed it and crimped it with his own seal. "There you go," he said to the Finder. "You understand that if you're ever caught attempting to practice the profession of Slave Finding in the state of Hio, you will be arrested and tried and, when convicted, you will face at least ten years in prison?"

"I understand," said the humiliated man.

"And you are also aware that Hio maintains a reciprocity arrangement with the states of Huron, Suskwahenny, Irrakwa, Pennsylvania, and New Sweden? So that the same or similar penalties will apply to you there if you attempt to practice this profession?"

"I understand," he said again.

"Thank you for your help," said the judge. "You should only be grateful that you were incompetent, for if I had cause to suspect you of perjury, it would have been prison *and* the lash, I assure you, for if I thought that you had willfully named this boy falsely, I would have no mercy on you. You may go."

The others obviously got the message. As the unfortunate man fled the courtroom, the other three who had named one boy or another steeled themselves for what was to come.

"Sheriff Doggly," said the judge, "would you kindly inform us of the identity of these two boys who stand identified by three of our panel of Finders?"

"Sure, Your Honor," said Doggly. "These two is Mock Berry's boys, James and John. Peter's near growed and Andrew and Zebedee was too small."

"You're sure of their identity?"

"They've lived here in Hatrack all their lives."

"Any chance that either of them is, in fact, the child of a runaway slave?"

"No chance. For one thing, the dates are all wrong. They're both way too old—the Berry boys is always short for their age, kind of late-blooming roses if you know what I mean, then they just shoot up like spring grass, cause Peter's about the tallest fellow around here. But these boys, they was already clever little tykes well known around town before ever the slave that cachet belongs to was born."

The judge turned to the Finders. "Well, now. I wonder how it happens that you appointed for slavery these two freeborn Black children."

One of them spoke up immediately. "Your Honor, I will protest this whole procedure. We were not brought here to be placed on trial ourselves, we were brought here to practice our profession and—"

The gavel slammed down on the desk. "You were brought here to practice your profession, that is true. Your profession requires that when you make an identification, it must be assumed by all courts of law to be both honest and accurate. Whenever you practice your profession, here or in the field, your license is on the line, and you know it. Now, tell me at once, did you lie when you identified these boys, or were you merely mistaken?"

"What if we was just guessing?" one of them asked. Verily almost laughed out loud.

"Guessing, in this context, would be lying, since you were swearing that the boy you named was a match for the cachet, and if you had to guess, then he was not a match. Did you guess?"

The man thought about it for a moment. "No sir, I didn't lie. I was just plain wrong I reckon."

Another man tried a different tack. "How do we know this sheriff isn't lying?"

"Because," said the judge, "I already met all these boys, and their parents, and saw their birth records in the county archive. Any more questions before you decide whether you'll lose your license or be bound over for trial as perjurers?"

The two remaining Finders quickly agreed that they had been mistaken. Everyone waited while the judge signed and sealed the limitation on their licenses. "You gentlemen may also go."

They went.

Verily rose to his feet. "Your Honor, may I request that these young men who were not identified be allowed to remove their hoods? I fear that they may be growing quite uncomfortable.''

"By all means. Bailiff, it's certainly time.''

The hoods came off. The boys all looked relieved. Arthur Stuart was grinning.

To the three remaining Finders, the judge said, "You are under oath. Do you swear that none of these boys matches the cachet belonging to Mr. Cavil Planter?''

They all swore to it.

"I commend you for having the honesty to admit to not finding a match, when others were clearly tempted to find a match no matter what. I find your profession loathsome, but at least the three of you practice it honestly and with reasonable competence.''

"Thank you, Your Honor,'' said one of them; the others, however, seemed to know they had just been insulted.

"Since this proceeding is a legal hearing under the Fugitive Slave Law, I don't have to have your signatures on anything, but I'd prefer it if you'd stay long enough to sign your names to an affirmation that specifically states that this young man, the mixup boy named Arthur Stuart, is definitely not a match with the cachet. Can you sign such a statement under oath before God?''

They could. They did. They were dismissed.

"Mr. Webster, I can't think what in the world you'd have to say, but since you represent Mr. Cavil Planter in this matter, I must ask you for any statement you'd like to make on this matter before I issue my finding.''

Webster rose slowly to his feet. Verily wondered what the man could have the audacity to say, in the face of such evidence—what whining, sniveling complaint or protest he might utter.

"Your Honor,'' said Webster, "it is obvious to me that my client is the victim of fraud. Not today, your honor, for these proceedings have clearly been honest. No, the fraud was more than a year ago, when two Finders, hoping to collect a fee they had not earned, named this boy as Mr. Planter's property and proceeded to commit murder and get themselves killed in the effort to enslave a free boy. My client, believing them to be honest, naturally proceeded to secure the redress to which he would have been entitled by law; but now, I can assure you that as soon as my client learns that he was put upon most sorely by those Finders, he will be as horrified as I am by how close he came to enslaving a free child and, what is worse, extraditing for prosecution the young man named Alvin Smith, who it now seems was acting in proper self-defense when he

killed the second of those malicious, lying, fraudulent men pretending to be Finders.'' Webster sat back down.

It was a pretty speech. Webster's voice was lovely to hear. The
man should go into politics, Verily thought. His voice would be a
noble addition to the halls of Congress in Philadelphia.

"You pretty much summed up my summing up," said the judge.
"It is the finding of this court that Arthur Stuart is not the property
of Mr. Cavil Planter, and therefore the Finders who were trying to
take him back to Appalachee were not acting lawfully, and therefore
the interference Margaret Guester and Alvin Smith offered them was
legal and appropriate under the circumstances. I declare Alvin Smith
to be absolved of all responsibility, criminal or civil, in the deaths
of these Finders, and I declare Margaret Guester to be posthumously
absolved in like manner. Under the terms of the Fugitive Slave Law,
there may be no further attempt by anyone under any circumstances
to bring Arthur Stuart into slavery regardless of any additional evidence—this action is final. Likewise there may be no further attempt
to try Alvin Smith on any charges arising out of the illegal expedition
undertaken by those fraudulent Finders, including their death. This
action, likewise, is final.''

Verily loved hearing those words, for all that language insisting
that such actions were final had been placed in the law for the purpose of blocking any effort on the part of anti-slavery forces to
interfere with the recapture of a slave or the punishment of those
who helped a runaway. This time, at least, that finality would work
against the proponents of slavery. Hoist on their own petard.

The bailiff took the burlap bags off the boys' hands. The judge,
the sheriff, Verily, and Marty Laws all shook the boys' hands and
gave them—except Arthur, of course—the two bits they were entitled to for their service to the court. Arthur got something more
precious. Arthur got a copy of the judge's decision making it illegal
for him to be accosted by anyone searching for runaway slaves.

Webster shook Verily's hand, quite warmly. "I'm glad things
worked out this way," he said. "As you know, in our profession we
are sometimes called upon to represent clients in actions that we
wish they would not pursue.''

Verily held his silence—he supposed that for most lawyers this
was probably true.

"I'm glad that my presence here will not result in anyone en-
tering a life of slavery, or of your client being extradited under false
charges.''

Verily couldn't leave that statement alone. "And you would

have been sad to see him extradited, if this hearing had turned out otherwise?''

"Oh, not at all," said Webster. "If the Finders had identified young Mr. Stuart, then justice would have demanded that your client be tried in Kenituck for murder."

"Justice?" Verily didn't try to keep the contempt from his voice.

"The law *is* justice, my friend," said Webster. "I know of no other measure available to us as mortal men. God has a better justice than ours, but until angels sit upon the bench, the justice of law is the best justice we can have, and I, for one, am glad we have it."

If Verily had been tempted to feel even a glimmer of guilt over the fact that Arthur Stuart really was Cavil Planter's slave, by law, and that, again by law, Alvin Smith really should have been extradited, there was no chance of it now. Webster's narrow view of justice was just as truly satisfied by this outcome as Verily's much broader perspective. By God's justice, Arthur should be free and Alvin held to no penalty, and so the outcome had been just. But Webster's justice was as well served, for the letter of the law required the matching of the cachet to the slave, and if it so happened that Arthur Stuart had been changed somehow by a certain Maker so the cachet no longer matched—well, the law made no provision for exceptions, and so, as Webster had said, the law being satisfied, justice must also have been done.

"I'm grateful to know your mind upon the matter," said Verily. "I look forward to discovering, in my client's trial for larceny, precisely what your commitment to justice is."

"And so you shall," said Webster. "The gold belongs to Makepeace Smith, not his former apprentice. So when justice is done, Makepeace Smith will have his gold."

Verily smiled at him. "It shall be a contest, then, Mr. Webster."

"When two giants meet in battle," said Webster, "one giant will fall."

"And loud shall be the noise thereof," said Verily.

Webster took only a moment to realize that Verily was teasing him about his golden-voiced oratory; and when he did, instead of being insulted, he threw back his head and laughed, warmly, loudly, cheerfully. "I like you, Mr. Cooper! I shall enjoy all that lies ahead of us!"

Verily let him have the last word. But in his own mind, he answered, Not all, Mr. Webster. You shall not enjoy it all.

*   *   *

No one planned a meeting, but they arrived at Alvin's cell that evening almost at the same time, as if someone had summoned them. Verily Cooper had come to discuss what would happen during the selection of the jury and perhaps gloat a little over the easy victory in the hearing that morning; he was joined by Armor-of-God Weaver, who brought letters from family and wellwishers in Vigor Church; Arthur Stuart of course was there, as he was most evenings; Horace Guester had brought a bowl of roadhouse stew and a jug of the fresh cider—Alvin wouldn't take the cider that had turned, it dulled his mind; and no sooner were they all assembled in and around the open cell than the outer door opened and the deputy showed in Peggy Larner and a man that none but Alvin recognized.

"Mike Fink, as I live and breathe," said Alvin.

"And you're that smithy boy who bent my legs and broke my nose." Mike Fink smiled, but there was pain in the smile, and no one was sure but what there might not be a quarrel here.

"I see some scars and marks on you, Mr. Fink," said Alvin, "but I reckon from the fact you're standing here before us that those are marks of fights you won."

"Won fair and square, and hard fought," said Fink. "But I killed no man as didn't require me to, on account of trying to stick a knife in me and there being no other way to stop them."

"What brings you here, Mr. Fink?" asked Alvin.

"I owe you," said Fink.

"Not that I know of," said Alvin.

"I owe you and I mean to repay."

Still his words were ambiguous, and Arthur Stuart noticed how Papa Horace and Armor-of-God braced themselves to take on the powerful body of the riverman, if need arose.

It was Peggy Larner who made it clear. "Mr. Fink has come to give us information about a plot against Alvin's life. And to offer himself as a bodyguard, to make sure no harm comes to you."

"I'm glad to know you wanted to give me warning," said Alvin. "Come on in and sit down. You can share the floor with me, or sit on my cot—it's stronger than it looks."

"Don't have much to tell. I think Miss Larner already told you what I learned before, about a plot to kill you as they took you back for trial in Kenituck. Well, the men I know—if you can rightly call them men—haven't been fired from the plan. In fact what I heard this very afternoon was to pay no nevermind to how the extradition was squished—"

"Quashed," offered Verily Cooper helpfully.

"Mashed," said Fink. "Whatever. They got to pay no heed to it, because they'll still be needed. The plan is for you not to leave the town of Hatrack River alive."

"And what about Arthur Stuart?" asked Alvin.

"Not a word about no mixup boy," said Fink. "The way I see it, they don't give a damn about the boy, he's just an excuse for them to get you kilt."

"Please watch . . ." Alvin began, mildly enough, but Mike Fink didn't need to hear him finish saying "your language with the lady."

"Beg your pardon, Miss Larner," he said.

"Don't that beat all," said Alvin admiringly. "He's already beginning to sound like one of your students." But was there a bite in his tone?

There was certainly a bite in Peggy's answer. "I'd rather hear him swear than hear you say 'don't' for 'doesn't.' "

Alvin leaned close to Mike Fink to explain, though he never took his eyes from Peggy's face. "You see, Miss Larner knows all the words, and she knows just where they ought to be."

Arthur Stuart could see the fury in her face, but she held her tongue. It was some kind of fight going on between the two of them; but what was it about? Miss Larner had *always* corrected their grammar, ever since she tutored Alvin and Arthur together when she was the schoolteacher in Hatrack River.

What puzzled Arthur Stuart all the more was the way the older men—not Verily, but Horace and Armor-of-God and even Mike Fink—sort of glanced around at each other and half-smiled like they all understood *exactly* what was going on between Alvin and Peggy, understood it better than those two did their own selves.

Mike Fink spoke up again. "Getting back to matters of life and death instead of grammar . . ."

At which point Horace murmured under his breath, "And lovers' spats."

"I'm sorry to say I can't learn no more of their plans than that," said Fink. "It's not like we're dear friends or nothing—more like they'd be as happy to stab me in the back as pee on my boots, depending on whether their knife or their . . . whatever . . . was in their hands." He glanced again at Peggy Larner and blushed. Blushed! That grizzled face, scarred and bent by battle, that missing ear, but still the blood rushed into his face like a schoolboy rebuked by his schoolmarm.

But before the blush could even fade, Alvin had his hand on Fink's arm and pulled him down to sit beside him on the floor, and

Alvin threw an easy arm over his shoulder. "You and me, Mike, we just can't remember how to talk fine in front of some folks and plain in front of others. But I'll help you if you'll help me."

And there, in one easy moment, Alvin had put Mike Fink back to rights. There was just a kind of plain sincerity in Alvin's way of speaking that even when you knew he was trying to make you feel better, you didn't mind. You knew he cared about you, cared enough to try to make you feel better, and so you *did* feel better.

Thinking of Alvin making folks feel better made Arthur Stuart remember something that Alvin did to make *him* feel better. "Why don't you sing that song, Alvin?"

Now it was Alvin's turn to blush in embarrassment. "You know I ain't no singer, Arthur. Just because I sung it to you . . ."

"He made up a song," said Arthur Stuart. "About being locked up in here. We sung it together yesterday."

Mike Fink nodded. "Seems like a Maker got to keep making something."

"I got nothing to *do* but think and sing," said Alvin. "*You* sing it, Arthur Stuart, not me. You've got a good singing voice."

"I'll sing it if you want," said Arthur. "But it's your song. You made it up, words and tune."

"You sing it," said Alvin. "I don't even know if I'd remember all the words."

Arthur Stuart dutifully stood up and started to sing, in his piping voice:

> *I meant to be a journeyman,*
> *To wander on the earth.*
> *As quick as any fellow can*
> *I left the country of my birth—*
> *It's fair to say I ran.*

Arthur Stuart looked over at Alvin. "You got to sing the chorus with me, anyway."

So together they sang the rollicking refrain:

> *At daybreak I'll be risin',*
> *For never will my feet be still,*
> *I'm bound for the horizon—oh!*
> *I'm bound for the horizon.*

Then Arthur went back to the verse, but now Alvin joined him in a kind of tenor harmony, their voices blending sweetly to each other.

> *Till I was dragged from bed*
> *And locked inside a little cell.*
> *My journeys then were in my head*
> *On all the roads of hell.*

With the next verse, though, when Arthur began it, Alvin didn't join in, he just looked confused.

> *Alone with my imagining*
> *I dreamt the darkest dream—*

"Wait a minute, Arthur Stuart," said Alvin. "That verse isn't really part of this song."

"Well it fits, and you sung it to this tune your own self."

"But it's a nonsense dream, it don't mean a thing."

"I like it," said Arthur. "Can't I sing it?"

Alvin waved him to go ahead, but he still looked embarrassed.

> *Alone with my imagining*
> *I dreamt the darkest dream,*
> *Of tiny men, a spider's sting,*
> *And in a land of smoke and steam*
> *An evil golden ring.*

"What does that *mean?*" asked Armor-of-God.

"I don't know," said Alvin. "I wonder if sometimes I don't accidentally end up with somebody else's dream. Maybe that was a dream that belonged to somebody of ancient days, or maybe somebody who ain't even been born yet. Just a spare dream and I chanced to snag on it during my sleep."

Verily Cooper said, "When I was a boy, I wondered if the strange people in my dreams might not be just as real as me, and I was in *their* dreams sometimes too."

"Then let's just hope they don't wake up at a inconvenient moment," said Mike Fink dryly.

Arthur Stuart went on with the last verse.

> *The accusations all were lies*
> *And few believed the tale,*

So I was patient, calm and wise.
But legs grow weak inside a jail
And something in you dies.

"This song may be the saddest one I ever heard," said Horace
Guester. "Don't you *ever* have a cheerful thought in here?"

"The chorus is pretty sprightly," said Arthur Stuart.

"I had cheerful thoughts today," said Alvin, "thinking of four
Slave Finders losing their license to carry off free men and put them
into bondage in the south. And now I'm cheerful again, knowing
that the strongest man I ever fought is now going to be my bodyguard. Though the sheriff may not take kindly to it, Mr. Fink, since
he thinks I'm safe enough as long as I'm in the care of him and his
boys."

"And you are safe," said Peggy. "Even those deputies that
don't like you would never raise a hand against you or allow you
to be less than safe."

"There's no danger, then?" asked Horace Guester.

"Grave danger," said Peggy. "But not from the deputies, and
most particularly not till the trial is over, and Alvin prepares to leave.
That's when we'll need more than a bodyguard to die along with
Alvin. We'll need subterfuge to get him out of town in one piece."

"Who says I'll die?" asked Fink.

Peggy smiled thinly. "Against any five men I think you two
would do well."

"So there'll be more than five?" asked Alvin.

"There may be," said Peggy. "Nothing is clear right now.
Things are in flux. The danger is real, though. The plot's in place
and men have been paid. You know when money's involved, even
assassins feel obliged to fulfill their contracts."

"But for the nonce," said Verily Cooper, "we're not to worry
about our safety, or Alvin's?"

"Prudence is all that's needed," said Peggy.

"I don't know why we're putting our trust in knackery," said
Armor-of-God. "Our Savior is guard enough for us all."

"Our Savior will resurrect us," said Peggy, "but I haven't noticed that Christians end up any less dead at the end of life than
heathens."

"Well, one thing's sure," said Horace Guester. "If it wasn't for
knackery Alvin wouldn't be in this blamed fix."

"Did you like the song?" asked Alvin. "I mean, I thought Ar-

thur sung it real good. Real well. Very well." Each correction won
a bit more of a smile from Miss Larner.

"*Sang* it very well," said Peggy. "But each version of the sentence was better than the one before!"

"I got another verse," said Alvin. "It's not really part of the
song, on account of it isn't true yet, but do you want to hear it?"

"You got to sing it alone, I don't know another verse," said
Arthur Stuart.

Alvin sang:

> *I trusted justice not to fail.*
> *The jury did me proud.*
> *Tomorrow I will hit the trail*
> *And sing my hiking song so loud*
> *It's like to start a gale!*

They all laughed, and allowed as how they hoped he could soon
sing it for real. By the time the meeting ended, they'd decided that
Armor-of-God, with Mike Fink to watch his back and keep him safe,
would head for Carthage City and learn all he could about the men
who were paying Daniel Webster's salary and see for sure if they
were the same ones paying the river rats and other scoundrels to lie
in wait to take Alvin's life. Other than that, everything was in Verily
Cooper's hands. And to hear him tell it, it was up to the witnesses
and the jury. Twelve good men and true.

There was a long line at the county clerk's office as Peggy came in
for the first day of Alvin's trial. "Early voters," Marty Laws explained. "Folks that worry maybe the weather will keep them from
casting their ballot election day. This Tippy-Canoe campaign has
folks pretty riled up."

"Do you think they're voting for or against?"

"I'm not sure," said Marty. "You're the one who'd know,
aren't you?"

Peggy didn't answer. Yes, she *would* know, if she cared to look.
But she feared what she'd see.

"It's Po Doggly who knows about politics around here best. He
says that if it was all up or down on the whole Red business, Tippy-
Canoe wouldn't get him a vote. But he's also been playing on the
western pride thing. How Tippy-Canoe is from our side of the Appalachee Mountains. Which don't make much sense to me, seeing
as how Old Hickory—Andy Jackson—he's every bit as western as

Harrison. I think folks worry about how Andy Jackson, being from Tennizy, he's probably too much for slavery. Folks around here don't want to vote in somebody who'll make the slavery thing any worse than it is.''

Peggy smiled thinly. "I wish they knew Mr. Harrison's real position on slavery.''

Marty cocked an eyebrow. "You know something I don't know?''

"I know that Harrison is the candidate that those who wish to expand slavery into the northern states will want to support.''

"Ain't a soul here who wants to see that happen.''

"Then they shouldn't vote for Harrison—if he becomes president, it *will* happen.''

Marty stared long and hard at her. "Do you know this the way most folks know their political opinions, or do you know it as . . . as . . .''

"I know it,'' said Peggy. "I don't say that of mere opinions.''

Marty nodded and looked off into space. "Well damn. Wouldn't you know it.''

"You have a habit of betting on the wrong horse lately,'' said Peggy.

"You can say that again,'' said Marty. "I kept telling Makepeace for years that there wasn't a case against Alvin and I wasn't going to get him extradited from Wobbish. But then he showed up here, and what could I do? I had Makepeace, and he had him a witness besides himself. And you never know what juries are going to do. I think it's a bad business.''

"Then why don't you move to dismiss the charges?'' asked Peggy.

Marty glowered. "I can't do that, Miss Peggy, for the plain good reason that there *is* a case to be made. I hope this English lawyer Alvin's folks found for him can win him free. But I'm not going to roll over and play dead. What you got to understand, Miss Peggy, is I like most of the people in this county, and most of the time the folks I got to prosecute, they're people that I like. I don't prosecute them because I don't like them. I prosecute them because they done wrong, and the people of Hatrack County elected me to set things right. So I hope Alvin gets off, but if he does, it won't be because I failed to fulfill my responsibilities.''

"I was there on the night the plow was made. Why don't you call *me* as a witness?''

"Did you see it made?'' asked Marty.

"No. It was already finished when I saw it."

"Then what exactly are you a witness *of?*"

Peggy didn't answer.

"You want to get on that stand because you're a torch, and the people of Hatrack know you're a torch, and if you say Makepeace is lying, they'll believe you. But here's the thing I worry about, Miss Peggy. I know you and Alvin was once sweet for each other, and maybe still are. So how do I know that if you get on the stand, you won't commit some grievous sin against the God of truth in order to win the freedom of this boy?"

Peggy flushed with anger. "You know because you know my oath is as good as anyone's and better than most."

"If you get on the stand, Miss Peggy, I will rebut you by bringing up witnesses to say you lived in Hatrack for many months in complete disguise, lying to everyone that whole time about who you were. Covered with hexes, pretending to be a middle-aged spinster schoolteacher when the whole time you were seeing the smith's prentice boy under the guise of tutoring him. I know you had your reasons for doing all those things. I know there was a reason why on the night the plow was supposedly made, the same night your mother was killed, you and Alvin were seen running from the smithy together, only Alvin was stark naked. Do you get my drift, Miss Peggy?"

"You're advising me not to testify."

"I'm telling you that while some folks will believe you, others will be sure you're just helping Alvin as his co-conspirator. My job is to make sure every possible doubt of your testimony is introduced."

"So you *are* Alvin's enemy, and the enemy of truth." Peggy hurled the words, meaning them to bite.

"Accuse me all you like," said Marty, "but my job is to make the case that Alvin stole that gold. I don't think your testimony, based entirely on your unverifiable claim as a torch that Makepeace is a liar, should be allowed to stand unchallenged. If it did stand that way, then every half-baked dreamspeaker and soothsayer in the country would be able to say whatever he pleased and juries would believe them, and then what would happen to justice in America?"

"Let me understand you," said Peggy. "You plan to discredit me, destroy my reputation, and convict Alvin, all for the sake of justice in America?"

"As I said," Marty repeated, "I hope your lawyer can do as good a job defending Alvin as I'm going to do prosecuting him. I hope he can find as much damning evidence against my witnesses as Mr. Webster and I have found concerning Alvin. Because, frankly, I don't *like* my witnesses much, and I think Makepeace is a greedy lying bastard who should go to jail himself for perjury but I can't prove it.''

''How can you live with yourself, then, working in the service of evil when you know so clearly what is good?''

''It's also good for the public prosecutor to prosecute, instead of setting himself up as judge.''

Peggy nodded gravely. ''As so often is the case, there is no clear choice that has all the good on its side, opposed to one that is nothing but bad.''

''That's the truth, Peggy. That's God's honest truth.''

''You advise me not to testify.''

''Nothing of the kind. I just warned you of the price you'd pay for testifying.''

''It's unethical for us to have had this conversation, isn't it?''

''A little bit,'' said Marty. ''But your pa and I go back a long way.''

''He'd never forgive you if you discredited me.''

''I know, Miss Peggy. And that would break my heart.'' He nodded his good-bye, touching his forehead as if to tip the hat he wasn't wearing indoors. ''Good day to you.''

Peggy followed him into the courtroom.

That first morning was spent questioning the eight witnesses who had been shown the golden plow. First was Merlin Wheeler, who rolled in on his wheelchair. Peggy knew that Alvin had offered once, years ago, to heal him so he could walk again. But Merlin just looked him in the eye and said, ''I lost the use of my legs to the same men who killed my wife and child. If you can bring them back, then we'll see about my legs.'' Alvin didn't understand then, and truth to tell, Peggy didn't really understand now. How did it help his wife and children for Merlin to go around in a wheelchair all the time? But then, maybe it helped Merlin himself. Maybe it was like wearing widow's weeds. A public symbol of how he was crippled by the loss of those he loved best. Anyway, he made a sturdy witness, mostly because people knew he had a knack for seeing what was fair and right, making him a sort of informal judge, though it wasn't all that common for both parties in a dispute to agree to get him to arbitrate for him. One or the other of them, it seemed, always felt it somehow inconvenient to have the case decided by a man who was truly evenhanded and fair. Anyway, the jury was bound to listen when Wheeler said, "I ain't saying the plow's bewitched cause I don't know how it got to be the way it is. I'm just saying that it appears to be gold, it hefts like gold, and it moves without no hand touching it."

Wheeler set the tone for all the others. Albert Wimsey was a clockmaker with a knack for fine metalwork, who fled to America when his business rivals accused him of using witchery in making his clocks—when *he* said the plow was gold, he spoke with authority, and the jury would entertain no further doubt about the metal it was made of. Jan Knickerbacker was a glassmaker who was said to have an eye to see things more clearly than most folks. Ma Bartlett was a frail old lady who once was a schoolteacher but now lived in the old cabin in the woods that Po Doggly built when he first settled in the area; she got a small pension from somewhere and mostly spent her days under an oak tree by Hatrack River, catching catfish and letting them go. People went to her to find out if they could trust other folks, and she was always right, which made it so many a budding romance got nipped in the bud, until folks sort of shied away from asking certain questions of her.

Billy Sweet made candy, a young and gullible young fellow that nobody took all that seriously, but you couldn't help but like him no matter how foolish the things he said and did. Naomi Lerner made a little money tutoring, but her knack was ignorance, not teaching— she could spot ignorance a mile away, but wasn't much good at alleviating it. Joreboam Hemelett was a gunsmith, and he must have had a touch of fire knackery because it was well known that no matter how damp a day it might be, the powder in a Hemelett gun always ignited. And Goody Trader—whose first name was rumored to be either Chastity or Charity, both names used ironically by those who didn't like her—kept a general store on the new end of Main Street, where she was well known to stock her shelves, not just with the things folks wanted, but also with the things they needed without knowing it.

All through their testimony, about hefting the plow, about how it moved, or hummed, or trembled, or warmed their hands, the jurors' eyes were drawn again and again to the burlap sack under Alvin's chair. He never touched it or did anything to call attention to it, but his body moved as if the plow inside the sack were the fulcrum of his balance. They wanted to see for themselves. But they knew, from Alvin's posture, that they would not see it. That these eight had seen for them. It would have to be enough.

The eight witnesses were well known to the people in town, all of them trusted (though Billy Sweet was only trusted *this* far, seeing as how he was so trusting himself that any liar could get him to believe any fool thing) and all of them well enough liked, apart from the normal quarrels of small-town life. Peggy knew them all, better than they knew each other, of course, but perhaps it was that very knowledge of them that blinded her to a thing that only Arthur Stuart seemed to notice.

Arthur was sitting beside her in the courtroom, watching the testimony, wide-eyed. It was only when all eight of the witnesses were done testifying that he leaned up to Peggy and whispered, "Sure are a lot of folks with sharp knacks here in Hatrack, aren't there?"

Peggy grew up around here, and for all that a lot of folks had moved in after she left, she always felt that she pretty much knew everybody. But was that so? She had run off the first time just before Alvin got to Hatrack to start his prenticeship with Makepeace Smith, and in the more than eight years since then, she had only spent that single year in Hatrack—less than a year, really—when she was in disguise. During those eight years a lot of people had moved in. More, in fact, by twice, than had lived here at the time she left. She had scanned their heartfires, routinely, because she wanted to get a sense of who lived in this place.

But she hadn't realized until Arthur's whispered remark that of the newcomers, an unusual number had quite remarkable knacks. It wasn't that the eight witnesses were different from the rest of the town. Knacks were thick on the ground here, much more so than any other place that Peggy had visited.

Why? What brought them here?

The answer was easy and obvious—so obvious that Peggy doubted it at once. Could they really have been drawn here because Alvin was here? It was in Hatrack that the prentice learned to hone his knack until it became an all-encompassing power of powers. It was here that Alvin made the living plow. Was there something about his Making that drew them? Something that kindled a fire inside them and set their feet to wandering until they came to rest in this place, where Making was in the air?

Or was it more than that? Was there Someone perhaps guiding them, so it wasn't just the makery in Hatrack that drew them, but rather the same One who had brought Alvin to this town? Did it mean there was purpose behind it all, some master plan? Oh, Peggy longed to believe *that*, for it would mean she was not responsible for making things turn out all right. If God is tending to things here, then I can put away my broom and set aside my needle and thread, I have neither cleaning nor stitchery to do. I can simply be about my business.

One way or the other, though, it was plain that Hatrack River was more than just the town where Alvin happened to be in jail right now. It was a place where people of hidden powers congregated in goodly numbers. Just as Verily Cooper had crossed the sea to meet Alvin, perhaps unwittingly all these others had also crossed sea or mountains or vast reaches of prairie and forest to find the place where the Maker Made his golden plow. And now these eight had handled the plow, had seen it move, knew it was alive. What did it mean to them?

For Peggy, to wonder was to find out: She looked at their heart-fires and found something startling. On past examination, none of them had shown paths in their future that were closely tied to Alvin's. But now she found that their lives were bound up in his. All of them showed many paths into the future that led to a crystal city by the banks of a river.

For the first time, the Crystal City of Alvin's vision in the tornado was showing up in someone else's future.

She almost fainted from the relief of it. It wasn't just a formless dream in Alvin's heart, with no path guiding her as to how he would get there. It could be a reality, and if it was, all of these eight souls would be a part of it.

Why? Just because they had touched the living plow? Was that what the thing was? A tool to turn people into citizens of the Crystal City?

No, not that. No, it would hardly be the free place Alvin dreamed of, if folks were forced to be citizens because of touching some powerful object. Rather the plow opened up a door in their lives so they could enter into the future they most longed for. A place, a time where their knacks could be brought to full fruition, where they could be part of something larger than any of them were capable of creating on their own.

She had to tell Alvin. Had to let him know that after all that trying in Vigor Church to teach those of feeble knack how to do what they could not really do, or not easily, here in his true birthplace his citizens were already assembling, those who had the natural gifts and inclinations that would make them co-Makers with him.

Another thought struck her, and she began to look into the heart-fires of the jurors. Another group of citizens, randomly chosen—and again, while not all had spectacular knacks, they were all people whose knacks defined them, people who might well have been searching for what their gifts might mean, what they were *for*. People who, consciously or not, might well have found themselves gravitating toward the place where a Maker had been born. A place where iron was turned to gold, where a mixup boy had been changed so a cachet no longer named him as a slave. A place where people with knacks and talents and dreams might find purpose, might build something together, might become Makers.

Did they know how much they needed Alvin? How much their hopes and dreams depended on him? Of course not. They were jurors, trying to stay impartial. Trying to judge according to the law. And that was good. That was a kind of Making, too—keeping to the law even when it hurt your heart to do it. Maintaining good order in the community. If they showed favoritism to one person just because they admired him or needed him or liked him or even loved him, that would be the undoing of justice, and if justice were ever undone, were ever openly disdained, then that would be the end of good order. To corrupt justice was the Unmaker's trick. Verily Cooper would have to prove his case, or at least disprove Makepeace Smith's assertions; he would have to make it *possible* for the jury to acquit.

But if they did acquit, then the paths that opened in their heartfire were like the paths of the witnesses: They would be with Alvin one day, building great towers of shimmering crystal rising into the sky, catching light and turning it into truth the way it had happened when Tenskwa-Tawa took Alvin up into the waterspout.

Should I tell Alvin that his fellow-Makers are here around him in this courtroom? Would it help his work or make him overconfident to know?

To tell or not to tell, the endless question that Peggy wrestled with. Next to that one, Hamlet's little quandary was downright silly. Contemplations of suicide were always the Unmaker's work. But truth-telling and truth-hiding—it could go either way. The consequences were unpredictable.

Of course, for ordinary people consequences were *always* unpredictable. Only torches like Peggy were burdened by having such a clear idea of the possibilities. And there weren't many torches like Peggy.

Makepeace wasn't a very good witness in his own cause. Surly and nervous—not a winning combination, Verily knew. But that was why Laws and Webster had put him on first, so that his negative

impression would be forgotten after the testimony of more likable—
and believable—witnesses.

The best thing Verily could do, in this case, was to let Makepeace have his say—as memorably as possible, as negatively as
possible. So he made no objection when Makepeace peppered his
account with slurs on Alvin's character. "He was always the laziest
prentice I ever had." "I never could get the boy to do nothing
without standing over him and yelling in his ear." "He was a slow
learner, everybody knowed that." "He ate like a pig even on days
when he didn't lift a finger." The onslaught of slander was so re-
lentless that everyone was getting uncomfortable with it—even
Marty Laws, who was starting to glance at Verily to see why he
wasn't raising any objections. But why should Verily object, when
the jurors were shifting in their seats and looking away from Makepeace with every new attack on Alvin? They all knew these were
lies. There probably wasn't a one of them that hadn't come to the
smithy hoping that Alvin rather than his master would do the work.
Alvin's skill was famous—Verily had learned that from overhearing
casual conversation in the roadhouse at evening meals—so all Makepeace was doing was damaging his own credibility.

Poor Marty was trapped, however. He couldn't very well cut
short Makepeace Smith's testimony, since it was the foundation of
his whole case. So the questioning went on, and the answering, and
the slander.

"He made a plow out of plain iron. I saw it, and so did Pauley
Wiseman who was sheriff then, and Arthur Stuart, and the two dead
Finders. It was setting on the workbench when they come by to get
me to make manacles for the boy. But I wouldn't make no manacles,
no sir! That's not decent work for a smith, to make the chains to
take a free boy into slavery! So what do you know but Alvin himself,
who *said* he was such a friend to Arthur Stuart, *he* up and says he'll
make the manacles. That's the kind of boy he was and is today—
no loyalty, no decency at all!"

Alvin leaned over to Verily and whispered in his ear. "I know
it's wicked of me, Verily, but I want so bad to give old Makepeace
a bad case of rectal itch."

Verily almost laughed out loud.

The judge shot him a glare, but it wasn't about his near laughter.
"Mr. Cooper, aren't you going to object to any of these extraneous
comments upon your client's character?"

Verily rose slowly to his feet. "Your Honor, I am sure the jury
will know *exactly* how seriously to take all of Mr. Makepeace

Smith's testimony. I'm perfectly content for them to remember both his malice and his inaccuracy.''

"Well, maybe that's how it's done in England, but I will instruct the jury to *ignore* Mr. Smith's malice, since there's no way to know whether his malice came as a result of the events he has recounted, or predated them. Furthermore, I will instruct Mr. Smith to make no more aspersions on the defendant's character, since those are matters of opinion and not of fact. Did you understand me, Makepeace?''

Makepeace looked confused. "I reckon so.''

"Continue, Mr. Laws.''

Marty sighed and went on. "So you saw the iron plow, and Alvin made the manacles. What then?''

"I told him to use the manacles as his journeyman piece. I thought it would be fitting for a traitorous scoundrel to go through his whole life knowing that the manacles he made for his friend were the—''

The judge interrupted, again glaring at Verily. "Makepeace, it's words like 'traitorous scoundrel' that's going to get you declared in contempt of court. Do you understand me now?''

"I been calling a spade a spade all my life, Your Honor!'' Makepeace declared.

"At this moment you're digging a very deep hole with it,'' said the judge, "and I'm the man to bury you if you don't watch your tongue!''

Cowed, Makepeace put on a very solemn look and faced forward. "I apologize, Your Honor, for daring to live up to my oath to speak the truth, the whole truth, and nothing but the—''

The gavel came down.

"Nor will I allow sarcasm directed at this bench, Mr. Smith. Continue, Mr. Laws.''

And so it went, till Makepeace had finished with his tale. It truly was a weak and whining little complaint. First there was an iron plow, made of the very iron Makepeace had provided for the journeyman piece. Then there was a plow made of solid gold. Makepeace could only think of two possibilities. First, that Alvin had somehow used some sort of hexery to change the iron into gold, in which case it was made from the iron Makepeace had given him and, according to time-honored tradition and the terms of Alvin's prentice papers, the plow belonged to Makepeace. Or it was a different plow, not made from Makepeace's iron, in which case where did Alvin get such gold? The only time Alvin had ever done enough digging to bring up buried treasure like that was when he was digging a well for Makepeace, which he dug in the wrong place. Makepeace was betting Alvin had dug in the right place first, found the gold, and then hid it by digging in another spot for the actual well. And if the gold was found on Makepeace's land, well, it was Makepeace's gold that way, too.

Verily's cross-examination was brief. It consisted of two questions.

"Did you see Alvin take gold or anything like gold out of the ground?"

Angry, Makepeace started to make excuses, but Verily waited until the judge had directed him to answer the question yes or no.

"No."

"Did you see the iron plow transformed into a golden plow?"

"Well so what if I didn't, the fact is there *ain't* no iron plow so where *is* it then?"

Again, the judge told him to answer the question yes or no.

"No," said Makepeace.

"No more questions for this witness," said Verily.

As Makepeace got up and left the witness box, Verily turned to the judge. "Your Honor, the defense moves for immediate dismissal of all charges, inasmuch as the testimony of this witness is not sufficient to establish probable cause."

The judge rolled his eyes. "I hope I'm not going to have to listen to motions like that after *every* witness."

"Just the pathetic ones. Your Honor," said Verily.

"Your point is made. Your motion is denied. Mr. Laws, your next witness?"

"I would like to have called Makepeace's wife, Gertie, but she passed away more than a year ago. Instead, with the court's permission, I will call the woman who was doing kitchen help for her the day the golden plow was first . . . evidenced. Anga Berry."

The judge looked at Verily. "This will make her testimony hearsay, after a fashion. Do you have any objection, Mr. Cooper?"

Alvin had already assured Verily that nothing Anga could say would do him any possible harm. "No objection, Your Honor."

Alvin listened as Anga Berry testified. She didn't really witness to anything except that Gertie told her about Makepeace's accusations the very next morning, so the charge wasn't one he dreamed up later. On cross-examination, Verily was kind to her, only asking her whether Gertie Smith had said anything to lead Anga to believe she thought Alvin was as bad a boy as Makepeace said.

Marty rose to his feet. "Hearsay, Your Honor."

Impatiently the judge replied, "Well, Marty, we *know* it's hearsay. It was for hearsay that *you* called her in the first place!"

Abashed, Marty Laws sat back down.

"She never said nothing about his smithery or nothing," said Anga. "But I know Gertie set quite a store by the boy. Always helped her out, toted water for her whenever she asked—that's the *worst* job—and he was good with the children and just . . . always helping. She never said a bad word about him, and I reckon she had a high opinion of his goodness."

"Did Gertie ever tell you he was a liar or deceiver?" asked Verily.

"Oh, no, unless you count hiding some job he was doing till it was done, so as to surprise her. If *that's* deception, then he done that a couple of times."

And that was it. Alvin was relieved to know that Gertie hadn't been unkind to him behind his back, that even after her death she was a friend to him. What surprised Alvin was how glum Verily was when he sat down at the table next to him. Marty was busy calling his next witness, a fellow named Hank Dowser whose tale Alvin could easily guess—this was a man who *did* have malice and it wouldn't be pleasant to hear him. Still, he hadn't seen anything either, and in fact the well-digging had nothing to do with the plow so what did it matter? Why did Verily look so unhappy?

Alvin asked him.

"Because there was no reason for Laws to call that woman. She worked against his case and he had to know that in advance."

"So why did he call her?"

"Because he wanted to lay the groundwork for something. And since she didn't say anything new during his examination of her, it must have been during the cross-examination that the new groundwork was laid."

"All you asked Anga was whether Gertie had the same low opinion of me that her husband had."

Verily thought for a moment. "No. I also asked her if you had ever deceived Gertie. Oh, I'm such a fool. If only I could recall those words from my lips!"

"What's wrong with that?" asked Alvin.

"He must have some witness that calls you a deceiver, a witness who is otherwise irrelevant to this case."

In the meantime, the dowser, in a state of high dudgeon, was speaking of how uppity Makepeace's prentice was, how he dared to tell a dowser how to dowse. "He's got no respect for any man's knack but his own!"

Verily spoke up. "Your Honor, I object. The witness is not competent to testify concerning my client's respect or lack of it toward other people's knacks in general."

The objection was sustained. Hank Dowser was a quicker learner than Makepeace; there was no more problem with him. He quickly established that the prentice had obviously dug the well in a different place from the place where Hank had declared water could be found.

Verily had only one question for him. "Was there water in the place where he dug the well?"

"That's not the question!" declared Hank Dowser.

"I'm sorry to have to tell you, Mr. Dowser, that I am the one authorized by this court to ask questions at this time, and I tell you that it *is* the question that I would like you to answer. At this time."

"What was the question?"

"Did my client's well reach water?"

"It reached a *kind* of water. But compared to the pure water *I* found, I'm sure that what he got was a sludgy, scummy, foul-tasting brew."

"Do I take it that your answer is yes?"

"Yes."

And that was that.

For his next witness, Marty called a name that sent a shiver down Alvin's spine. "Amy Sump."

A very attractive girl arose from the back of the courtroom and walked down the aisle.

"Who is *she?*" asked Verily.

"A girl from Vigor with a *very* active imagination."

"About what?"

"About how she and I did what a man has no business doing with a girl so young."

"Did you?"

Alvin was annoyed by the question. "Never. She just started telling stories and it grew from there."

"Grew?"

"That's why I took off from Vigor Church, to give her lies a chance to settle down and die out."

"So she started telling stories about you and you *fled?*"

"What does it have to do with the plow and Makepeace Smith?"

Verily grimaced. "A certain matter of whether you deceive people or not. Marty Laws roped me in."

Marty was explaining to the judge that, because he had had no chance to talk with this witness himself beforehand, his illustrious co-counsel would conduct the examination. "The girl is young and fragile, and they have established a rapport."

Verily thought that the idea of Webster and Amy having rapport wasn't very promising when it came to getting honest testimony from her, but he had to tread carefully. She was a child, and a girlchild at that. He couldn't seem to be hostile or fearful of her before she spoke, and in cross-examination he'd have to proceed delicately lest he seem to be a bully.

Unlike Makepeace Smith and Hank Dowser, who were obviously angry and malicious, Amy Sump was absolutely believable. She spoke shyly and reluctantly. "I don't want to get Alvin in no trouble, sir," she said.

"And why not?" asked Daniel Webster.

Her answer came in a whisper. "Because I still love him."

"You . . . you still love him?" Oh, Webster was a fine actor, worthy of the boards in Drury Lane. "But how can you—why do you still love him?"

"Because I am with child," she whispered.

A buzzing arose through the courtroom.

Again, Webster feigned grieved surprise. "You are with . . . Are you married, Miss Sump?"

She shook her head. Glistening tears flew from her eyes onto her lap.

"Yet you are with child. The child of some man who didn't even have the decency to make an honest woman of you. *Whose* child, Miss Sump?"

This was already out of control. Verily leapt to his feet. "Your Honor, I object on the grounds that this can have *no* conceivable connection with—"

"It goes to the issue of deception, Your Honor!" cried Daniel Webster. "It goes to the issue of a man who will say whatever it takes to get his way, and then absconds without so much as a farewell, having taken away that which is most precious from the very one who trusted him!"

The judge smacked down his gavel. "Mr. Webster, that was such a fine summing up that I'm inclined to charge the jury and end the trial. Unfortunately this is *not* the end of the trial and I'd appreciate it if you'd refrain from jumping up on a stump and making a speech when it ain't speechifying time."

"I was responding to my worthy opponent's objection."

"Well, you see, Daniel, that's where you made your mistake. Because his objection was addressed to me, me being the judge here, and I didn't really need your help at that moment. But I'm grateful to know that your help is right there, ready for me, if ever I *do* need it."

Webster answered the sarcasm with a cheerful smile. What did he care? His point was already made.

"The objection is overruled, Mr. Cooper," said the judge. "Who is the father of your child, Miss Sump?"

She burst into tears—still on cue, despite the interruption. "Alvin," she said, sobbing. Then she looked up and gazed soulfully across the court into Alvin's eyes. "Oh, Al, it ain't too late! Come back and make a wife of me! I love you so!"

15

Love

Verily Cooper, doing his best to hide his astonishment, turned languidly to look at Alvin. Then he raised an eyebrow.

Alvin looked vaguely sad. "It's true she's pregnant," he whispered. "But it ain't true I'm the father."

"Why didn't you tell me if you knew?" Verily whispered.

"I didn't know till she said it. Then I looked and yes, there's a baby growing in her womb. About the size of a nib. No more than three weeks along."

Verily nodded. Alvin had been in jail for the past month, and traveling far from Vigor Church for several months before that. The question was whether he could get the girl to admit under crossexamination that she was barely a month along in her pregnancy.

In the meantime, Daniel Webster had gone on, eliciting from Amy a lurid account of Alvin's seduction of her. No doubt about it, the girl told a convincing story, complete with all kinds of details that made it sound true. It seemed to Verily that the girl wasn't lying, or if she was, she believed her own lies. For a few moments he had doubts about Alvin. Could he have done this? The girl was pretty and desirable and from the way she talked, she was certainly willing. Just because Alvin was a Maker didn't mean he wasn't a man all the same.

He quickly shook off such thoughts. Alvin Smith was a man with self-control, that was the truth. And he had honor. If he really did such things with this child, he'd certainly marry her and not leave her to face the consequences alone.

It was a measure of how dangerous the girl's testimony was, if she could get Alvin's own attorney to doubt him.

"And then he left you," said Daniel Webster.

Verily thought of objecting, but figured there was no point.

"It was my own fault, I know," said Amy, breaking down— again—into pathetic tears. "I shouldn't have told my best friend Ramona about Alvin and me, because she mouthed it around to everybody and they didn't understand about our true love and so of course my Alvin had to leave because he has great works to do in the world, he can't be tied down to Vigor Church just now. I didn't want to come here and testify! I want him to be free to do whatever he needs to do! And if my baby grows up without a pa, at least I can tell my child that she comes of noble blood, with Makery as her heritage!"

Oh, that was a nice touch, making her the suffering saint who is content that "her" Alvin is a lying seducing deceiving abandoning bastard-making cradle-robber, because she loves him so.

It was time for cross-examination. This had to proceed delicately indeed. Verily couldn't give a single hint that he believed her; at the same time, he didn't dare to be seen to attack her, because the jury's sympathy was all with the girl right now. The seeds of doubt had to be planted gently.

"I'm sorry you had to come all the way down here. It must be a hard journey for a young lady in your delicate condition."

"Oh, I'm doing all right. I just puke once in the morning and then I'm fine for the rest of the day."

The jury laughed. A friendly, sympathetic, believing laugh. Heaven help me, thought Verily.

"How long have you known you were going to have a baby?"

"A long time," she said.

Verily raised an eyebrow. "Now, that's a pretty vague answer. But before you hear my next question, I just want you to remember that we can bring your mother and father down here if need be, to establish the exact time this pregnancy began."

"Well I didn't tell them till just a few days ago," said Amy. "But I've been pregnant for—"

Verily raised his hand to silence her, and shook his head. "Be careful, Miss Sump. If you think for just a minute, you'll realize that your mother certainly knows and your father probably knows that you couldn't possibly have been pregnant for more than a few weeks."

Amy looked at him in a puzzled way for a long moment. Then dawning realization came across her face. She finally realized: Her mother would know, from washing rags, when she last menstruated. And it wasn't months and months ago.

"Like I was going to say all along, I got pregnant in the last month. Sometime in the last month."

"And you're sure that Alvin is the father?"

She nodded. But she was no fool. Verily knew she was doing the math in her head. She obviously had counted on being able to lie and say she'd been pregnant for months, since before Alvin left Vigor; when the baby was born she could say it had taken so long because it was a Maker's child, or some such nonsense. But now she had to have a better lie.

Or else she'd been planning this lie all along. That, too, was possible.

"Of course he is," she said. "He comes to me in the night even now. He's really excited about the baby."

"What do you mean by 'even now'?" asked Verily. "You know that he's in jail."

"Oh, posh," said Amy. "What's a jail to a man like him?"

Once again, Verily realized that he'd been playing into Webster's hands. Everybody knew Alvin had hidden powers. They knew he worked in stone and iron. They knew he could get out of that jail whenever he wanted.

"Your Honor," said Verily, "I reserve the right to recall this witness for further cross-examination."

"I object," said Daniel Webster. "If he recalls Miss Sump then she's *his* witness, it won't be cross-examination, and she's not a hostile witness."

"I need to lay the groundwork for further questioning," said Verily.

"Lay all you want," said the judge. "You'll have some leeway, but it won't be cross. The witness may step down, but don't leave Hatrack River, please."

Webster stood again. "Your Honor, I have a few questions on redirect."

"Oh, of course. Miss Sump, I beg your pardon. Please remain seated and remember you're still under oath."

Webster leaned back in his chair. "Miss Sump, you say that Alvin comes to you in the night. How does he do that?"

"He slips out of his cell and right through the walls of the jail and then he runs like a Red man, all caught up in . . . in . . . Redsong, so he reaches Vigor Church in a single hour and he ain't even tired. No, he is *not* tired!" She giggled.

Redsong. Verily had had enough conversation with Alvin by now to know that it was greensong, and if he'd really had any intimacy with this girl she'd know that. She was remembering things she'd heard from his lessons months and months ago in Vigor Church, when she went to class with people trying to learn to be Makers. That's all this was—the imaginings of a young girl combined with scraps of things she learned about Alvin. But it might take the golden plow away from him, and perhaps more important, it might send him to jail and destroy his reputation forever. This was not an innocent fib, and for all her pretense at loving Alvin, she knew exactly what she was doing to him.

"Does he come to you every night?"

"Oh, he can't do that. Just a couple of times a week."

Webster was done with her, but now Verily had a couple more questions. "Miss Sump, *where* does Alvin visit you?"

"In Vigor Church."

"You're only a girl, Miss Sump, and you live with your parents. Presumably you are supervised by them. So my question is quite specific—where are you when Alvin visits you?"

She was momentarily flustered. "Different places."

"Your parents let you go about unchaperoned?"

"No, I mean—we always start out at home. Late at night. Everybody's asleep."

"Do you have a room of your own?"

"Well, no. My sisters sleep in the same room with me."

"So where do you meet Alvin?"

"In the woods."

"So you deceive your parents and sneak into the woods at night?"

The word *deceive* was a red flag to her. "I don't deceive nobody!" she said, with some heat.

"So they know you're going to the woods alone to meet Alvin."

"No. I mean—I know they'd stop me, and it's true love between us, so—I don't sneak out, because Papa bars the door and he'd hear me so I—at the county fair I was able to slip away and—"

"The county fair was in broad daylight, not at night," said Verily, hoping he was right.

"Argumentative!" shouted Webster. But his interruption served not to help the girl but fluster her more.

"If this happens a couple of times a week, Miss Sump, you surely don't depend on the county fair to provide you with opportunities, do you?" asked Verily.

"No, that was just the once, just the one time. The other times . . ."

Verily waited, refusing to ease her path by filling her long silence with words. Let the jury see her making things up as she went along.

"He comes into my room, all silent. Right through the walls. And then he takes me out the same way, silent, through the walls. And then we run with the Redsong to the place where he gives me his love by moonlight."

"It must be an amazing experience," said Verily. "To have your lover appear at your bedside and raise you up and carry you through the walls and take you silently across miles and miles in an instant to an idyllic spot where you have passionate embraces by moonlight. You're in your nightclothes. Doesn't it get cold?"

"Sometimes, but he can make the air warm around me."

"And what about moonless nights? How do you see?"

"He . . . makes it light. We can always see."

"A lover who can do the most miraculous things. It sounds quite romantic, wouldn't you say?"

"Yes, it is, very very romantic," said Amy.

"Like a dream," said Verily.

"Yes, like a dream."

"I object!" cried Webster. "The witness is a child and doesn't realize the way the defense attorney can misconstrue her innocent simile!"

Amy was quite confused now.

"What did I say?" she asked.

"Let me ask it very clearly," said Verily Cooper. "Miss Sump, isn't it possible that your memories of Alvin come from a dream? That you dreamed all this, being in love with a strong and fascinating young man who was too old even to notice you?"

Now she understood why Webster had objected, and she got a

cold look in her eye. She knows, thought Verily. She knows she's
lying, she's not deceived, she knows exactly what she's doing and
hates me for tripping her up, even a little. "My baby ain't no dream,
sir," she said. "I never heard of no dream as gives a girl a baby."

"No, I've never heard of such a dream, either," said Verily.
"Oh, by the way, how long ago was the county fair?"

"Three weeks ago," she said.

"You went with your family?"

Webster interrupted, demanding to know the relevance.

"She gave the county fair as a specific instance of meeting Alvin," explained Verily, when the judge asked. The judge told him
to proceed. "Miss Sump," said Verily, "tell me how you got off
by yourself to meet Alvin at the fair. Had you already arranged to
meet him there?"

"No, it was—he just showed up there."

"In broad daylight. And no one recognized him?"

"Nobody saw him but me. That's a fact. That's—it's a thing he
can do."

"Yes, we're beginning to realize that when it comes to spending
time with you, Alvin Smith can and will do the most amazing, miraculous things," said Verily.

Webster objected, Verily apologized, and they went on. But Verily suspected that he was on a good track here. The way Amy made
her story so believable was by adding detail. When it came to the
events that didn't happen, the details were all dreamy and beautiful—but she wasn't just making them up, it was clear she had really
had such dreams, or at least daydreams. She was speaking from
memory.

But there must be another memory in her mind—the memory
of her time with the man who was the true father of the child she
carried. And Verily's hunch was that her mention of the county fair,
which didn't fit in at all with the pattern she had established for her
nighttime assignations with Alvin, was tied in with that real encounter. If he could get her drawing on memory with this one . . .

"So only you could see him. I imagine that you went off with
him? May I ask you where?"

"Under the flap of the freak show tent. Behind the fat lady."

"Behind the fat lady," said Verily. "A private place. But . . .
why there? Why didn't Alvin whisk you away into the forest? To
some secluded meadow by a crystal stream? I can't imagine it was
very comfortable for you—in the straw, perhaps, or on the hard
ground, in the dark . . ."

"That's just the way Alvin wanted it," she said. "I don't know why."

"And how long did you spend there behind the fat lady?"

"About five minutes."

Verily raised an eyebrow. "Why so hasty?" Then, before Webster could object, he plunged into his next question. "So Alvin escaped from the Hatrack County jail in broad daylight, journeyed all the way to Vigor Church on the far side of the state of Wobbish from here, in order to spend five minutes with you behind the fat lady?"

Webster spoke up again. "How can this young girl be expected to know the defendant's motivations for whatever bizarre acts he performs?"

"Was that an objection?" asked the judge.

"It doesn't matter," said Verily. "I'm through with her for now." And this time he let a little contempt into his voice. Let the jury see that he no longer had any regard for this girl. He hadn't destroyed her testimony, but he had laid the groundwork for doubt.

It was three in the afternoon. The judge adjourned them for the day.

Alvin and Verily had supper in his cell that night, conferring over what was likely to happen the next day, and what had to happen in order to acquit him. "They actually haven't proved anything about Makepeace," said Verily. "All they're doing is proving you're a liar in general, and then hoping the jury will think this removes all reasonable doubt about you and the plow. The worst thing is that every step of the way, Webster and Laws have played me like a harp. They set me up, I introduced an idea they were hoping I'd bring up in my cross-examination, and presto! There's the groundwork for the next irrelevant, character-damaging witness."

"So they know the legal tricks in American courts better than you do," said Alvin. "You know the law. You know how things fit together."

"Don't you see, Alvin? Webster doesn't care whether you're convicted or not—what he loves is the stories the newspapers are writing about this trial. Besmirching your reputation. You'll never recover from that."

"I don't know about never," said Alvin.

"Stories like this don't disappear. Even if we manage to find the man who impregnated her—"

"Oh, I know who it was," said Alvin.

"What? How could you—''

"Matt Thatcher. He's a couple of years younger than me, but all us boys knew him in Vigor. He was always a rapscallion of the first stripe, and when I was back there this past year he was always full of brag about how no girl could resist him. Every now and then some fellow'd have to beat him up cause of something he said about the fellow's sister. But after last year's county fair, he was talking about how he drove his tent spike into five different girls in the freak show tent behind the fat lady.''

"But that was more than a year ago.''

"A boy like Matt Thatcher don't got much imagination, Verily. If he found himself a spot that worked once, he'll be back there. For what it's worth, though, he never did name any of the girls he supposedly got last year, so we all figured he just found the spot and *wished* he could get himself some girl to go with him there. I just figure that this year he finally succeeded.''

Verily leaned back on his stool, sipping his mug of warm cider. "The thing that puzzles me is, Webster must have found Amy Sump when he visited in Vigor Church long before I got there. *Before* the county fair, too. She must not have been pregnant when he found her.''

Alvin smiled and nodded. "I can just imagine him telling Amy's parents, 'Well it's a good thing she's not with child. Though if she were, I dare say Alvin's wandering days would be over.' And she listens and goes and gets herself pregnant with the most willing but stupid boy in the county.''

Verily laughed. "You imitate his voice quite well, sir!''

"Oh, I'm nothing at imitations. I wish you could have heard Arthur Stuart back in the old days. Before . . .''

"Before?''

"Before I changed him so the Finders couldn't identify him.''

"So you didn't just subvert their cachet. You changed the boy himself.''

"I made him just a little bit less Arthur and a little bit more Alvin. I'm not glad of it. I miss the way he could make hisself sound like anybody. Even a redbird. He used to sing right back to the redbird.''

"Can't you change him back? Now that he has the official court decision, he can never be hauled into court again.''

"Change him back? I don't know. It was hard enough changing him the first time. And I don't think I remember well enough how he used to be.''

"The cachet has the way he used to be, doesn't it?"

"But I don't have the cachet."

"Interesting problem. Arthur doesn't seem to mind the change, though, does he?"

"Arthur's a sweet boy, but what he doesn't mind now he might well come to mind later, when he's old enough to know what I done to him." Alvin was drumming on his empty dish now. Clearly his mind kept going back to the trial. "I got to tell you, it's only going to get worse tomorrow, Verily."

"How so?"

"I didn't understand it till now, till what Amy said about me sneaking out of jail and all. But now I know what the plan is. Vilate Franker came in here covered with hexes, maneuvered me close enough to her that the same hex worked on me, too—an overlook-me, and a right good one. Then in comes Billy Hunter, one of the deputies, and when he looks in the cell, he doesn't see anybody at all. He runs off and gets the sheriff, and when he comes back, Vilate's gone but here *I* am, and I tell them I been nowhere, but Billy Hunter knows what he saw—or didn't see—and they're going to bring him into court, and Vilate too. Vilate too."

"So they'll have a witness to corroborate that you have indeed left your cell during your incarceration here."

"And Vilate's likely to say anything. She's a notorious gossip. Goody Trader plain hates her, and so does Horace Guester. She also thinks of herself as quite a beauty, though those particular hexes don't work on me no more. Anyway Arthur Stuart saw her . . ."

"I was here when Arthur told you about her. About the salamander."

"That ain't no regular salamander, Verily. That's the Unmaker. I've met it before. Used to come on me more directlike. A shimmering in the air, and there it was. Trying to take me over, rule me. But I wouldn't have it, I'd make something—a bug basket—and he'd go away. Nowadays I'd be more likely to make up some silly rhyme or song and commit it to memory to drive him back. But here's the thing—the Unmaker has a way of being different things to different people. There was a minister in Vigor Church, Reverend Philadelphia Thrower; he saw the Unmaker as an angel, only it was a kind of terrible angel, and one time—well, it doesn't matter. Armor-of-God saw it, not me. With Vilate the Unmaker's got that salamander doing some kind of hexery that makes Vilate see . . . somebody. Somebody who talks to her and tells her things. Only that somebody is really speaking the words of the Unmaker. You know what Arthur Stuart saw. Old Peg Guester, the woman who was the only mother he knew. The Unmaker appears as somebody you can trust, somebody who fulfills your most heartfelt dream, but in the process he perverts everything so that without quite realizing it, you start destroying everything and everybody around you. This whole thing, you don't have to look toward Webster to find the conspiracy. The Unmaker is all the connection they need. Putting together Amy Sump and Vilate Franker and Makepeace Smith and Daniel Webster and . . . not one of them thinks he's doing something all that awful. Amy probably thinks she really loves me. Maybe so does Vilate. Makepeace has probably talked himself into believing the plow really belongs to him. Daniel Webster probably believes I really am a scoundrel. But . . .''

"But the Unmaker makes everything work together to undo you.''

Alvin nodded.

"Alvin, that makes no sense," said Verily. "If the Unmaker's really out to Unmake everything, then how can he put together such an elaborate plan? That's a kind of Making, too, isn't it?''

Alvin lay back on the cot and whistled for a moment. "That's right," he said.

"The Unmaker sometimes Makes things, then?''

"No," said Alvin. "No, the Unmaker can't Make nothing. Can't. He just takes what's already there in twists and bends and breaks it. So I was wrong. The Unmaker's working on all these people, but if it's all fitting together into a plan, then somebody's planning it. Some person.''

Verily chuckled. "I think we already have the answer," he said. "Your speculation about Daniel Webster. He discovers Amy Sump as he searches in Vigor Church for any kind of dirt about you. She wasn't part of any plan, just a girl who started pretending that her daydreams were true. But then he puts into her head the idea of getting pregnant and the idea of testifying against you to clip your wings and force you to come home. She works out the rest herself, her own plan—the Unmaker doesn't have to teach her anything. Then Daniel Webster comes here to Hatrack and of course he meets the town gossip as he searches for dirt about you here. Vilate Franker barely knows you, but she *does* know everybody else's story, and they converse many times. He happens to let slip how Amy Sump's story will just sound like the imaginings of a dreamy but randy young girl unless they can get some kind of evidence that you actually do leave your cell. And then Vilate comes up with her *own* plan and the Unmaker just sits back and encourages her.''

''So the plan is all coming from Daniel Webster, only he doesn't even know it,'' said Alvin. ''He wishes for something, and then it just happens to come true.''

''Don't give him too much credit for integrity,'' said Verily. ''I suspect this is a method he's been using for a long time, wishing for some key piece of evidence, and then trusting in his client or one of his client's friends to come up with the testimony that he needs. He never quite soils his hands, but the effect is the same. Yet nothing can ever be proven—''

The outer door opened, and Po Doggly came in with Peggy Larner. ''Sorry to interrupt your supper and confabulation, gentlemen,'' said the sheriff, ''but something's come up. You got you a visitor with special circumstances, he's come a long way but he can only come in and see you after dark and I'm the only guard as can let him in, on account of he already sat me down and told me a tale.''

Alvin turned to Verily. ''That means it's someone from home. Someone besides Armor-of-God. Someone who's under the curse.''

''He shouldn't be under it,'' said Peggy. ''If it weren't for his grand gesture of including himself in a curse he didn't personally deserve.''

''Measure,'' said Alvin. To Verily he explained, ''My older brother.''

''He's coming,'' said the sheriff. ''Arthur Stuart's leading him in with his hat low and his eyes down so he won't see anybody who doesn't already know the story. Doesn't want to spend all night telling folks about the massacre at Tippy-Canoe. So the doors will be open here, but I'll still be outside, watching. Not that I think you'd try to escape, Alvin.''

''You mean you don't think I've been making twice-a-week trips to Vigor Church?''

''For *that* girl? I don't think so.'' With that, Doggly walked out, leaving the outer door open.

Peggy came on in and joined Alvin and Verily inside Alvin's cell. Verily stood up to offer her his stool, but with a gesture she declined to sit.

''Howdy, Peggy,'' said Alvin.

''I'm fine, Alvin. And you?''

''You know I never did any of those things she said,'' he told her.

"Alvin," she said, "I know that you *did* find her attractive. She saw that you paid her a little special attention. She began to dream and wish."

"So you're saying it's my fault after all?"

"It's her fault that dreams turned into lies. It's your fault that she had hopeless dreams like that in the first place."

"Well why don't I just shoot myself before I ever look at a woman with desire? It always seems to turn out pretty lousy when I do."

She looked as if he slapped her. As usual, Verily felt a keen sense of being left out of half of what went on in Alvin's life. Why should it bother him so much? He wasn't here, and they were under no obligation to explain. Still, it was embarrassing. He got up. "Please, I'll step outside so you can have this conversation alone."

"No need," said Peggy. "I'm sure Arthur is almost here with Measure by now."

"She doesn't want to talk to me," said Alvin to Verily. "She'll try to get me acquitted because she wants to see the Crystal City get built, only she can't offer me a lick of help in trying to figure out how to build it, seeing as how I don't know and she seems to know everything. But just cause she wants me acquitted doesn't mean she actually likes me or thinks I'm worth spending time with."

"I don't like being in the middle of this," said Verily.

"You're not," said Peggy. "There's no 'this' to be in the middle of."

"There never *was* no 'this,' either, was there?" asked Alvin.

Verily was quite sure he had never heard a man sound so miserable.

Peggy took a moment to answer. "I'm not—there was and is a—it hasn't a thing to do with you, Alvin."

"What doesn't have a thing to do with me? My still being crazy in love with you after a whole year with only one letter from you, and that one as cold as you please, like I was some kind of scoundrel you still had to do business with or something? Is that the thing that doesn't have anything to do with me? I asked you to marry me once. I understand that things have been pretty bleak since then, your mother getting killed and all, that was terrible, and I didn't press you, but I did write to you, I did think about you all the time, and—"

"And I thought of you, Alvin."

"Yes, well, *you're* a torch, so you *know* I'm thinking about you, or you do if you care to look, but what do *I* know when there's no sign from you? What do I know except what you tell me? Except what I see in your face? I know I looked in your face that night in the smithy, I looked in your eyes and I thought I saw love there, I thought I saw you saying yes to me. Did I make that up? Is that the 'this' that there isn't one of?''

Verily was thoroughly miserable, being forced to be a witness of this scene. He had tried to make his escape before; now it was clear they didn't want him to go. If only he knew how to disappear. How to sink through the floor.

It was Arthur who saved him. Arthur, with Measure in tow; and, just as the sheriff had said, Measure had his hat so low and his head bent so far down that he really did need Arthur Stuart to lead him by the hand. "We're here," said Arthur. "You can look up now."

Measure looked up. "Al," he said.

"Measure!" Alvin cried. It took about one stride each, with those two long-legged men, for them to be in each other's embrace. "I've missed you like my own soul," said Alvin.

"I've missed you too, you ugly scrawny jailbird," said Measure. And in that moment, Verily felt such a pang of jealousy that he thought his heart would break. He was ashamed of the feeling as soon as he was aware of it, but there it was: He was jealous of that closeness between brothers. Jealous because he knew that he would never be that close to Alvin Smith. He would always be shut out, and it hurt so deeply that for a moment he thought he couldn't breathe.

And then he did breathe, and blocked that feeling away in another part of himself where he didn't have to stare it in the face.

In a few minutes the greetings were over, and they were down to business. "We found out Amy was gone and it didn't take no genius to figure out where she went. Oh, at first the rumor was she got pregnant at the county fair and was sent off to have the baby somewhere, but we all remembered the tales she told about Alvin and Father and I went to her pa and got it out of him right quick, that she was off to testify in Hatrack. He didn't like it much, but they're paying them and he needs the money and his daughter swears it's true but you could tell looking at him that he don't believe her lies either. And in fact as we were leaving he says, When I find out who it was got my daughter pregnant I'm going to kill him. And Pa says, No you ain't. And Mr. Sump he says, I am so because I'm a merciful man, and killing him's kinder than making him marry Amy.''

They all laughed at that, but in the end they knew it wasn't exactly funny.

"Anyhow, Eleanor says, Amy's best friend is that mouse of a girl Ramona and I'm going to get the truth out of her."

Alvin turned to Verily. "Eleanor's our sister, Armor-of-God's wife."

Another reminder that he wasn't inside this circle. But also a reminder that Alvin thought of him and wanted to include him.

"So Eleanor gets Ramona and sets her down inside that hex you made for her in the shop, Alvin, the one that makes liars get so nervous, only I don't know as how it was really needed. Eleanor says to her, Who's the father of Amy's baby, and Ramona says, How should I know? only it's a plain lie, and finally when Eleanor won't let up, Ramona says, Last time I told the truth it only caused Alvin Maker to have to run away cause of Amy's lies, but she *swore* it was true, she *swore* it and so I believed her but now she's saying it was Alvin got her pregnant and I know that's not true cause she got into the freak show tent with—"

Alvin held up his hand. "Matt Thatcher?"

"Of course," said Measure. "Why we didn't just castrate him along with the pigs I don't know."

"She *saw* them or is it hearsay?" asked Verily.

"Saw them and stood guard where they went under the tent and heard Amy cry out once and heard Matt panting and then it was done and she asked Amy what it was like and Amy looked positively stricken and says to her, It's awful and it hurts. Ramona's got no doubt Amy was a virgin up till then, so all the other stories is lies."

"She's not competent to testify about Amy's virginity," said Verily, "but she'd still be a help. It would take care of the pregnancy and make it plain that Amy is something of a liar. Reasonable doubt. How long will it take to get her down here?"

"She's here," said Peggy. "I got her to the roadhouse and Horace Guester's feeding her."

"I'll want to talk to her tonight," said Verily. "This is good. This is something. And until now, we had nothing."

"*They* have nothing," said Peggy. "And yet . . ."

"And yet they'd convict me if they voted right now, wouldn't they?" Alvin asked.

Peggy nodded. "I thought they knew you better."

"This is all so extraneous to Makepeace's assertions," said Verily. "None of this would have been permitted in an English court."

"Next time somebody tries to get me arrested for larceny and a crazy girl claims to be pregnant by me, I'll arrange to have it tried in London," said Alvin, grinning.

"Good idea," said Verily. "Besides, we have a much higher grade of crazy girls in England."

"I'm going to testify," said Peggy.

"I don't think so," said Alvin.

"You aren't a witness of anything," said Verily.

"You saw how the rules go in this court," said Peggy. "You can work me in."

"It won't help," said Verily. "They'll chalk it up to your being in love with Alvin."

Alvin sighed and lay back on his cot.

"No they won't," said Peggy. "They know me."

"They know Alvin, too," said Verily.

"Don't mean to contradict you, sir," said Arthur Stuart, "but everybody knows Miss Larner here is a torch, and everybody knows that before she tells a lie, you can boil an egg in a pan of snow."

"If I testify, he won't be convicted," said Peggy.

"No," said Alvin. "They'll drag you through the mud. Webster doesn't care about convicting me, you know that. He only wants to destroy me and everybody near me, because that's what the people who hired him want."

"We don't even know who they are," said Verily.

"I don't know their names, but I know who they are and what they want. To you it looks as though Amy's testimony is a sidetrack, but it's Amy's testimony they wanted. And if they could get testimony about me and Peggy in the smithy on the night the plow was made—"

"I'm not afraid of their calumnies," said Peggy.

"It ain't calumnies I'm talking about, it's the plain truth," said Alvin. "I was naked, we was alone in the smithy. Can't help what conclusions folks draw from that, and so I won't have you getting on the stand and all that story coming out in the papers in Carthage and Dekane and heaven knows where else. We'll do it another way."

"Ramona will be a help," said Verily.

"Not Ramona either," said Alvin. "It does no good to have one friend betray another for my sake."

The others were flabbergasted.

"You got to be joking!" cried Measure. "After I brought her all the way here? And she wants to testify."

"I'm sure she does," said Alvin. "But after the papers are through hacking at Amy, how will Ramona feel *then*? She'll always remember that she betrayed a friend. That's a hard one. It'll hurt her. Won't it, Peggy?"

"Oh, you actually want my advice about something?"

"I want the truth. I've been telling the truth, and so have you, so just say it."

"Yes," said Peggy. "It would hurt Ramona greatly to testify against Amy."

"So we won't do it," said Alvin. "Nor do I want to see Vilate humiliated by having her hexes removed. She sets a store by being taken for beautiful."

"Alvin," said Verily, "I know you're a good man and wiser than me, but surely you can see that you can't let courtesy to a few individuals destroy all that you were put here on this earth to do!"

The others agreed.

Alvin looked as miserable as Verily had ever seen a man look, and Verily had seen men condemned to hang or burn. "Then you *don't* understand," he said. "It's true that sometimes people have to suffer to make something good come to be. But when I have it in my power to save them from suffering it, and bear it myself, well then that's part of what I do. That's part of Making. If I have it in my power, then I bear it. Don't you see?"

"No," said Peggy. "You *don't* have it in your power."

"Is that the honest torch talking? Or my friend?"

She hesitated only a moment. "Your friend. This passage in your heartfire is dark to me."

"I figured it was. And I think the reason is because I got to do some Making. I got to do something that's never been done before, to Make something new. If I do it, then I can go on. If I don't, then I go to jail and my path through life takes another course."

"*Would* you go to jail?" asked Arthur Stuart. "Would you really stay in prison for years and years?"

Alvin shrugged. "There are hexes I can't undo. I think if I was convicted, they'd see to it that I was bound about like that. But even if I could get away, what would it matter? I couldn't do my work here in America. And I don't know that my work could be done anywhere else. If there's any reason to my life at all, then there's a reason I was born here and not in England or Russia or China or something. Here's where my work's to be done."

"So you're saying that I can't use the two best witnesses to defend you?" asked Verily.

"My best witness is the truth. Somebody's going to speak it, that's for sure. But it won't be Miss Larner, and it won't be Ramona."

Peggy leaned down and looked Alvin in the eye, their faces not six inches apart. "Alvin Smith, you wretched boy, I gave my childhood to you, to keep you safe from the Unmaker, and now you tell me I have to stand by and watch you throw all that sacrifice away?"

"I already asked you for the whole rest of your life," said Alvin. "What do I want with your ruin? You lost your childhood for me. You lost your mother for me. Don't lose any more. I would have taken everything, yes, and given you everything too, but I won't take less because I can't give less. You'll take nothing from me, so I'll take nothing from you. If that don't make sense to you then you ain't as smart as you let on, Miss Larner."

"Why don't those two just get married and make babies?" said Arthur Stuart. "Pa said that."

Her face stony, Peggy turned away from them. "It has to be on *your* terms, doesn't it, Alvin. Everything on your terms."

"*My* terms?" said Alvin. "It wasn't my terms to say these things to you in front of others, though at least it's my friends and not strangers who have to hear them. I love you, Miss Larner. I love you, Margaret. I don't want you in that courtroom, I want you in my arms, in my life, in all my dreams and works for all time to come."

Peggy clung to the bars of the jail, her face averted from the others.

Arthur Stuart walked around to the outside of the cell and looked guilelessly up into her face. "Why don't you just marry him instead of crying like that? Don't you love him? You're real pretty and he's a good-looking man. You'd have damn cute babies. Pa said that."

"Hush, Arthur Stuart," said Measure.

Peggy slid down until she was kneeling, and then she reached through the bars and took Arthur Stuart's hands. "I can't, Arthur Stuart," she said. "My mother died because I loved Alvin, don't you see? Whenever I think of being with him, it just makes me feel sick and . . . guilty . . . and angry and . . ."

"My mama's dead too, you know," said Arthur Stuart. "My Black mama and my White mama both. They both died to save me from slavery. I think about that all the time, how if I'd never been born they'd both still be alive."

Peggy shook her head. "I know you think of that, Arthur, but you mustn't. They want you to be happy."

"I know," said Arthur Stuart. "I ain't as smart as you, but I know *that*. So I do my best to be happy. I'm happy most of the time, too. Why can't you do that?"

Alvin whispered an echo to his words. "Why can't you do that, Margaret?"

Peggy raised her chin, looked around her. "What am I doing here on the floor like this?" She got to her feet. "Since you won't take my help, Alvin Smith, then I've got work to do. There's a war in the future, a war over slavery, and a million boys will die, in America and the Crown Colonies and even New England before it's done. My work is to make sure those boys don't die in vain, to make sure that when it's over the slaves are free. That's what my mother died for, to free one slave. I'm not going to pick just one, I'm going to save them all if I can." She looked fiercely at the men who watched her, wide-eyed. "I've made my last sacrifice for Alvin Smith—he doesn't need my help anymore."

With those words she strode to the outer door.

"I do so," murmured Alvin, but she didn't hear him, and then she was gone.

"If that don't beat all," said Measure. "I ask you, Alvin, why didn't you just fall in love with a thunderstorm? Why don't you just go propose to a blizzard?"

"I already did," said Alvin.

Verily walked to the door of the cell. "I'm going to interview Ramona tonight in case you change your mind, Alvin," he said.

"I won't," said Alvin.

"I'm quite sure, but other than that there's nothing else I *can* do." He debated saying the next words, but decided that he might as well. What did he have to lose? Alvin was going to go to prison and Verily's journey to America was going to turn out to have been in vain. "I must say that I think you and Miss Larner are a perfect match. The two of you together must have more than seventy percent of the world's entire store of stupid bullheadedness."

It was Verily's turn to head for the outer door. Behind him as he left, he heard Alvin say to Measure and Arthur: "That's my lawyer." He wasn't sure if Alvin spoke in pride or mockery. Either way, it only added to his despair.

Billy Hunter's testimony was pretty damaging. It was plain that he liked Alvin well enough and had no desire to make him look bad. But he couldn't change what he saw and had to tell the truth—he'd looked into the jail and there was nowhere Alvin and Vilate could have hidden.

Verily's cross-examination consisted merely of ascertaining that when Vilate entered the cell, Alvin was definitely there, and that the pie she left behind tasted right good. "Alvin didn't want it?" asked Verily.

"No sir. He said . . . he said he sort of promised it to an ant."

Some laughter.

"But he let you have it anyway," said Verily.

"I guess so, yes."

"Well, I think that shows that Alvin is unreliable indeed, if he can't keep his word to an ant!"

There were some chuckles at Verily's attempt at humor, but that did nothing to ameliorate the fact that the prosecution had cut into Alvin's credibility, and rather deeply at that.

It was Vilate's turn then. Marty Laws laid the groundwork, and then came to the key point. "When Mr. Hunter looked into the jail and failed to see you and Alvin, where were you?"

Vilate made a great show of being reluctant to tell. He was relieved to see, however, that she was quite the actress Amy Sump had been, perhaps because Amy half-believed her own fantasies, while Vilate . . . well, this was no schoolgirl, and these were no fantasies of love. "I should never have let him talk me into it, but . . . I've been alone too long."

"Just answer the question, please," asked Laws.

"He took me through the wall of the jail. We passed through the wall. I held his hand."

"And where did you go?"

"Fast as the wind we went—I felt as though we were flying. For a time I ran beside him, taking strength from his hand as he held mine and led me along; but then it became too much for me, and I, fainting, could not go on. He sensed this in that way of his and gathered me into his arms. I was quite swept away."

"Where did you go?"

"To a place where I've never been."

There were some titters at that, which seemed to fluster her a little. Apparently she was not aware of her own double entendre— or perhaps she was a better actress than Verily thought.

"By a lake. Not a large one, I suppose—I could see the far shore. Waterbirds were skimming the lake, but on the grassy bank where we . . . reclined . . . we were the only living things. This beautiful young man and I. He was so full of promises and talk of love and . . ."

"Can we say he took advantage of you?" asked Marty.

"Your Honor, he's leading the witness."

"He did *not* take advantage of me," Vilate said. "I was a willing participant in all that happened. The fact that I regret it now does not change the fact that he did *not* force me in any way. Of course, if I had known then how he had said the same things, done the same things with that girl from Vigor Church . . ."

"Your Honor, she has no personal knowledge of—"

"Sustained," said the judge. "Please limit your responses to the questions asked."

Verily had to admire her skill. She managed to sound as if she were defending Alvin rather than trying to destroy him. As if she loved him.

16

Truth

When it came Verily's turn to question Vilate, he sat for a moment contemplating her. She was the picture of complacent confidence, with her head just slightly cocked to the left, as if she were somewhat—but not very—curious to hear what he would ask of her.

"Miss Franker, I wonder if you can tell me—when you passed through the wall from the jail, how did you get up to ground level?"

She looked momentarily confused. "Oh, is the jail below ground? Well, I suppose when we went through the wall, we—no, of course we didn't. The jail is on the second floor of the courthouse, and it's about a ten-foot drop to the ground. That was mean of you, to try to trick me."

"My question still stands," said Verily. "That must have been quite a drop, coming through the wall into nothing."

"We handled it gently. We . . . floated to the ground. It was part of the remarkable experience. If I had known you wanted so much detail, I'd have said so from the start."

"So Alvin . . . floats."

"He *is* a remarkable young man."

"I imagine so," said Verily. "In fact, one of his extraordinary talents is the ability to see through hexes of illusion. Did you know that?"

"No, I . . . no." She looked puzzled.

"For instance, he sees through the hex you use to keep people from seeing that little trick you play with your false teeth. Did you know that?"

"Trick!" She was mortified. "False teeth! What a terrible thing to say!"

"Do you or do you not have false teeth?"

Marty Laws was on his feet. "Your Honor, I can't see what relevancy false teeth have to the case at hand."

"Mr. Cooper, it does seem a little extraneous," said the judge.

"Your Honor has allowed the prosecution to cast far afield in trying to impugn the veracity of my client. I think the defense is entitled to the same latitude in impugning the veracity of those who claim my client is a deceiver."

"False teeth is a bit personal, don't you think?" asked the judge.

"And accusing my client of seducing her *isn't*?" asked Verily.

The judge smiled. "Objection overruled. I think the prosecution opened the door wide enough for such questions."

Verily turned back to Vilate. "Do you have false teeth, Miss Franker?"

"I do not!" she said.

"You're under oath," said Verily. "For instance, didn't you waggle your upper plate at Alvin when you said that he was a beautiful young man?"

"How can I waggle an upper plate that I do not have?" she said.

"Since that is your testimony, Miss Franker, would you be willing to appear in court without those four amulets you're wearing, and without the shawl with the hexes sewn in?"

"I don't have to sit here and . . ."

Alvin leaned over and tugged at Verily's coattail. Verily wanted to ignore him, because he knew that Alvin was going to forbid him to pursue this line any further. But there was no way he could pretend that he didn't notice a movement so broad that the whole court saw it. He turned back to Alvin, ignoring Vilate's remonstrances, and let Alvin whisper in his ear.

"Verily, you know I didn't want—"

"My duty is to defend you as best I—"

"Verily, ask her about the salamander in her handbag. Get it out in the open if you can."

Verily was surprised. "A salamander? But what good will that do?"

"Just get it out in the open," said Alvin. "On a table in the open. It won't run away. Even with the Unmaker possessing it, salamanders are still stupid. You'll see."

Verily turned back to face the witness. "Miss Franker, will you kindly show us the lizard in your handbag?"

Alvin tugged on his coat again. Mouth to ear, he whispered, "Salamanders ain't lizards. They're amphibians, not reptiles."

"Your pardon, Miss Franker. Not a lizard. An amphibian. A salamander."

"I have no such—"

"Your Honor, please warn the witness about the consequences of lying under—"

"If there's such a creature in my handbag, I don't have any idea who put it there or how it got there," said Vilate.

"Then you won't object if the bailiff looks in your bag and removes any amphibious creatures he might find?"

Overcoming her uncertainty, Vilate replied, "No, not at all."

"Your Honor, who is on trial here?" asked Marty Laws.

"I believe the issue is truthfulness," said the judge, "and I find this exercise fascinating. We've watched you come up with scandal. Now I'll be interested to see an amphibian."

The bailiff rummaged through the handbag, then suddenly hooted and jumped back. "Excuse me, Your Honor, it's up my sleeve!" he said, trying to maintain his composure as he wriggled and danced around.

With a flamboyant gesture, Verily swept his papers off the defense table and pulled it out into the middle of the courtroom. "When you retrieve the little fellow," he said, "set him here, please."

Alvin leaned back on his chair, his legs extended, his ankles crossed, looking for all the world like a politician who just won an election. Under his chair, the plow lay still inside its sack.

Alone of all the people in the court, Vilate paid no attention whatever to the salamander. She simply sat as if in a trance; but no, that wasn't it. No, she sat as if she were at a soiree where something slightly rude was being said, and she was pretending to take no notice of it.

Verily had no idea what would come of this business with the salamander, but since Alvin wouldn't let him try any other avenue to discredit Vilate or Amy, he'd have to make it do.

Alvin had been watching Vilate during her testimony—watching close, not just with his eyes, but with his inner sight, seeing the way the material world worked together. One of the first things he marked was the way Vilate cocked her head just a little before answering. As if she were listening. So he sent out his doodlebug and let it rest in the air, feeling for any tremors of sound. Sure enough, there *were* some, but in a pattern Alvin had never seen before. Usually, sound spread out from its source like waves from a rock cast into a pond, in every direction, bouncing and reverberating, but also fading and growing weaker with distance. This sound, however, was channeled. How was it done?

For a while he was in danger of becoming so engrossed in the scientific question that he might well forget that he was on trial here and this was the most dangerous but possibly the weakest witness against him. Fortunately, he caught on to what was happening very quickly. The sound was coming from two sources, very close together, moving in parallel. As the sound waves crossed each other, they interfered with each other, turning the sound into mere turbulence in the air. When Alvin listened closely, he could hear the faint hiss of the chaotic noise. But in the direction where the sound waves were perfectly parallel, they not only didn't interfere with each other, but rather seemed to increase the power of the sound. The result was that for someone sitting exactly in Vilate's position, even the faintest whisper would be audible; but for anyone anywhere else in the courtroom, there would be no sound at all.

Alvin found this curious indeed. He hadn't known that the Unmaker actually used sound to talk to his minions. He had supposed that somehow the Unmaker spoke directly into their minds. Instead, the Unmaker spoke from two sound sources, close together. Then Alvin had to smile. The old saying was true: The liar spoke out of both sides of his mouth.

Looking with his doodlebug into Vilate's handbag, Alvin soon found the source of the sound. The salamander was perched on the top of her belongings, and the sound was coming from its mouth—though salamanders had no mechanism for producing a human voice. If only he could hear what the salamander was saying.

Well, if he wasn't mistaken, that could be arranged. But first he needed to get the salamander out into the open, where the whole court could see where its speech was coming from. That was when he began to pay attention to the proceedings again—only to discover, to his alarm, that Verily was about to defy him and try to take away Vilate's beautiful disguise. He reached out and tugged on Verily's coat, and whispered a rebuke that was as mild as he could make it. Then he told him to get the salamander out of the bag.

Now, with the salamander in a panic, trapped in the bailiff's dark sleeve, it took Alvin a few moments to get his doodlebug inside the creature and start to help it calm down—to slow the heartbeat, to speak peace to it. Of course he could feel no resistance from the Unmaker. That was no surprise to Alvin. The Unmaker was always driven back by his Making. But he could sense the Unmaker, lurking, shimmering in the background, in the corners of the court, waiting to come back into the salamander so it could speak to Vilate again.

It was a good sign, the fact that the Unmaker needed the help of a creature in order to speak to Vilate. It suggested that she was not wholly consumed by the lust for power or Unmaking, so that the Unmaker could not speak to her directly.

Alvin didn't really know that much about the Unmaker, but with years in which to speculate and reason about it, he had come to a few conclusions. He didn't really think of the Unmaker as a person anymore, though sometimes he still called it "him" in his own thoughts. Alvin had always seen the Unmaker as a shimmering of air, as something that retreated toward his peripheral vision; he believed now that this was the true nature of the Unmaker. As long as a person was engaged in Making, the Unmaker was held at bay; and, in fact, most people weren't particularly attractive to it. It was drawn only to the most extraordinary of Makers—and the most prideful destroyers (or destructively proud; Alvin wasn't sure if it made a difference). It was drawn to Alvin in the effort to undo him and all his works. It was drawn to others, though, like Philadelphia Thrower and, apparently, Vilate Franker, because they provided the hands, the lips, the eyes that would allow the Unmaker to do its work.

What Alvin guessed, but could not know, was that the people to whom the Unmaker appeared most clearly had a kind of power over it. That the Unmaker, having been drawn into relations with them, could not suddenly free itself. Instead, it acted out the role that its human ally had prepared for it. Reverend Thrower needed an angelic visitor that was ripe with wrath—so that was what the Unmaker became for him. Vilate needed something else. But the Unmaker could not withhold itself from her. It could not sense that there was danger in being exposed, unless Vilate sensed that danger herself. And since Vilate was unable to be rational enough to know there even *was* a salamander—something Alvin had learned from Arthur Stuart's report—there was a good chance that the Unmaker could be led to expose itself to the whole courtroom, as long as Alvin worked carefully and took Vilate by surprise.

So he watched as the bailiff finally took the calm—well, calmer, anyway—salamander from the collar of his shirt, whither it had fled, and set it gently on the table. Gradually Alvin withdrew his doodle-bug from the creature, so that the Unmaker could come back into possession of it. Would it come? Would it speak again to Vilate, as Alvin hoped?

It did. It would.

The column of sound arose again.

Everyone could see the salamander's mouth opening and closing, but of course they heard nothing and so it looked like the random movements of an animal.

"Do you see the salamander?" asked Verily.

Vilate looked quizzical. "I don't understand the question."

"On this table in front of you. Do you see the salamander?"

Vilate smiled wanly. "I think you're trying to play with me now, Mr. Cooper."

A whisper arose in the courtroom.

"What I'm trying to do," said Verily, "is determine just how reliable an observer you are."

Daniel Webster spoke up. "Your Honor, how do we know there isn't some trick going on that the defense is playing? We already know that the defendant has remarkable hidden powers."

"Have patience, Mr. Webster," said the judge. "Time enough for rebuttal on redirect."

In the meantime, Alvin had been playing with the double column of sound coming from the salamander and leading straight to Vilate. He tried to find some way to bend it, but of course could not, since sound must travel in a straight line—or at least to bend it was beyond Alvin's power and knowledge.

What he could do, though, was set up a counterturbulence right at the source of one of the columns of sound, leaving the other to be perfectly audible, since there would be no interference from the column Alvin had blocked. The sound would still be faint, however; Alvin had no way of knowing whether it could be heard well enough for people to understand it. Only one way to find out.

Besides, this might be the new thing he had to Make in order to get past the dark place in his heartfire where Peggy couldn't see.

He blocked one of the columns of sound.

* * *

Verily was saying, "Miss Franker, since everyone in the court but you is able to see this salamander—"

Suddenly, a voice from an unexpected source became audible, apparently in midsentence. Verily fell silent and listened.

It was a woman's voice, cheery and encouraging. "You just sit tight, Vilate, this English buffoon is no match for you. You don't have to tell him a single thing unless you want to. That Alvin Smith had his chance to be your friend, and he turned you down, so now you'll show him a thing or two about a woman scorned. He had no idea of your cleverness, you sly thing."

"Who is that!" demanded the judge.

Vilate looked at him, registering nothing more than faint puzzlement. "Are you asking me?" she said.

"I am!" the judge replied.

"But I don't understand. Who is what?"

The woman's voice said, "Something's wrong but you just stay calm, don't admit a thing. Blame it on Alvin, whatever it is."

Vilate took a deep breath. "Is Alvin casting some kind of spell that affects everyone but me?" she asked.

The judge answered sharply. "Someone just said, 'Blame it on Alvin, whatever it is.' Who was it that said that?"

"Ah! Ah! Ah!" cried the woman's voice—which was obviously coming from the salamander's mouth. "Ah! How could he hear me? I talk only to you! I'm *your* best friend, Vilate, nobody else's! They're trying to trick you! Don't admit a thing!"

"I . . . don't know what you mean," said Vilate. "I don't know what you're hearing."

"The woman who just said, 'Don't admit a thing,' " said Verily. "Who is that? Who is this woman who says she's your best friend and no one else's?"

"Ah! Ah! Ah! Ah!" cried the salamander.

"My best friend?" asked Vilate. Suddenly her face was a mask of terror—except for her mouth, which still wore a pretty grin. Sweat beaded on her forehead.

On impulse, Verily strode to her and took hold of her shawl. "Please, Miss Franker, you seem overwarm. Let me hold your shawl for you."

Vilate was so confused she didn't realize what he was doing until it was done. The moment the shawl came from her shoulders, the smile on her mouth disappeared. In fact, the face that everyone knew so well was gone, replaced by the face of a middle-aged woman, somewhat wrinkled and sunburnt; and most remarkable of all, her mouth was wide open and inside it, the upper plate of her false teeth were clicking up and down, as if she were raising and lowering it with her tongue.

The buzz in the courtroom became a roar.

"Verily, dammit," said Alvin. "I told you not to—"

"Sorry," said Verily. "I see you need that shawl, Miss Franker." Quickly he replaced it.

Aware now of what he had done to her, she snatched the shawl close to her. The clicking false teeth were immediately replaced by the same lovely smile she had worn before, and her face was again thin and young.

"I believe we have some idea of the reliability of this witness," said Verily.

The salamander cried out, "They're winning, you foolish ninny! They trapped you! They tricked you, you silly twit!"

Vilate's face lost its composure. She looked frightened. "How can you talk like that to me," she whispered.

Vilate wasn't the only one who looked frightened. The judge himself had shrunk back into the far corner of his space behind the bench. Marty Laws was sitting on the back of his chair, his shoes on the seat.

"To whom are you speaking?" asked the judge.

Vilate turned her face away from judge and salamander both. "My friend," she said. "My best friend, I thought." Then she turned to the judge. "All these years, no one else has ever heard her voice. But you hear her now, don't you?"

"I do," said the judge.

"You're telling them too much!" cried the salamander. Was its voice changing?

"Can you see her?" asked Vilate, her voice thin and quavering. "Do you see how beautiful she is? She taught me how to be beautiful, too."

"Shut up!" cried the salamander. "Tell them nothing, you bitch!"

Yes, the voice was definitely lower in pitch now, thick in the throat, rasping.

"I can't see her, no," said the judge.

"She's not my friend, though, is she," said Vilate. "Not really."

"I'll rip your throat out, you . . ." The salamander let fly with a string of expletives that made them all gasp.

Vilate pointed at the salamander. "She made me do it! She told me to tell those lies about Alvin! But now I see she's really hateful! And not beautiful at all! She's not beautiful, she's ugly as a . . . as a newt!"

"Salamander," said the judge helpfully.

"I hate you!" Vilate cried at the salamander. "Get away from me! I don't want to see you ever again!"

The salamander seemed poised to move—but not away from her. It looked more as if it meant to spring from the table, leap the distance between it and Vilate, and attack her as its hideous voice had threatened.

Alvin was searching carefully through the salamander's body, trying to find where and how the Unmaker had control of it. But however it was done, it left no physical evidence that Alvin could see.

He realized, though, that it didn't matter. There were ways to get a person free of another person's control—an off-my-back hex. Couldn't it work for the salamander, if it was perfectly done? Alvin marked out in his mind the exact spots on the table where the hex would need to be marked, the order of the markings, the number of loops that would have to be run linking point to point.

Then he sent his doodlebug into that part of the salamander's brain where such sense as it had resided. Freedom, he whispered there, in the way he had that animals could understand. Not words, but feelings. Images. The salamander seeking after food, mating, scampering over mud, through leaves and grass, into cool mossy stone crevices. Free to do that instead of living in a dry handbag. The salamander longed for it.

Just do this, said Alvin silently into the salamander's mind. And he showed it the loops to make to get to the first mark.

The salamander had been poised to leap from the table. But instead it ran the looping pattern, touched one toe on the exact point; Alvin made it so the toe penetrated the wood just enough to make a mark, though no human eye could have seen it, the mark was so subtle. Scamper, loop, mark, and mark again. Six tiny prickings of the table's surface, and then a bound into the middle of the hex.

And the Unmaker was gone.

The salamander raced in a mad pattern, too fast to follow clearly; ran, then stopped stockstill in the middle of the table.

And then, suddenly, the intelligence seemed to go out of its movements. It no longer looked at Vilate. No longer looked at anyone in particular. It nosed across the table. Not certain yet whether the spell that bound the creature was done or not, no one moved toward it. It ran down the table leg, then scurried straight toward Alvin. It nosed the sack under his chair that contained the plow. It ran inside the sack.

Consternation broke out in the courtroom. "What's happening!" cried Marty Laws. "Why did it go in that sack!"

"Because it was spawned in that sack!" cried Webster. "You can see now that Alvin Smith was the source of all this mischief! I have seen the face of the devil and he sits cocky as you please in yonder chair!"

The judge banged with his gavel.

"He's not the devil," said Vilate. "The devil wears a much more lovely face than that." Then she burst into tears.

"Your honor," said Webster, "the defendant and his lawyer have turned this court into a circus!"

"Not until after you turned it into a cesspool of scandalous lies and filthy innuendoes!" Verily roared back at him.

And as he roared, the spectators burst into applause.

The judge banged the gavel again. "Silence! Come to order, or I'll have the bailiff clear the court! Do you hear me?"

And, after a time, silence again reigned.

Alvin bent over and reached into the sack. He took out the limp body of the salamander.

"Is it dead?" asked the judge.

"No, sir," said Alvin. "She's just asleep. She's very, very tired. She's been rode hard, so to speak. Rode hard and given nothing to eat. It ain't evidence of nothing now, Your Honor. Can I give her to my friend Arthur Stuart to take care of till she has her strength back?"

"Does the prosecution have any objection?"

"No, Your Honor," said Marty Laws.

At the same time, Daniel Webster rose to his feet. "This salamander never *was* evidence of anything. It's obvious that it was introduced by the defendant and his lawyer and was always under their command. Now they've taken possession of an honest woman and broken her! Look at her!"

And there sat beautiful Vilate Franker, tears streaming down her smooth and beautiful cheeks.

"An honest woman?" she said softly. "You know as well as I do how you hinted to me about how you needed corroboration for that Amy Sump girl, how if you just had some way of proving that

Alvin did *indeed* leave the jail, then she would be believed and no one would believe Alvin. Oh, you sighed and pretended that you weren't suggesting anything to me, but I knew and you knew, and so I learned the hexes from my friend and we did it, and now there you sit, lying again.''

"Your Honor," said Webster, "the witness is clearly distraught. I can assure you she has misconstrued the brief conversation we had at supper in the roadhouse.''

"I'm sure she has, Mr. Webster," said the judge.

"I have not misconstrued it," said Vilate, furious, whirling on the judge.

"And I'm sure you have not," said the judge. "I'm sure you're both completely correct.''

"Your Honor," said Daniel Webster, "with all due respect, I don't see—''

"No, you don't see!" cried Vilate, standing up in the witness box. "You claim to see an honest woman here? I'll show you an honest woman!''

She peeled her shawl off her shoulders. At once the illusion of beauty about her face disappeared. Then she reached down and pulled the amulets out of her bodice and lifted their chains from around her neck. Her body changed before their eyes: Now she was not svelte and tall, but of middle height and a somewhat thickened middle-aged body. There was a stoop to her shoulders, and her hair was more white than gold. "*This* is an honest woman," she said. Then she sank down into her seat and wept into her hands.

"Your Honor," said Verily, "I believe I have no more questions for this witness.''

"Neither does the prosecution," said Marty Laws.

"That's not so!" cried Webster.

"Mr. Webster," said Marty Laws quietly, "you are discharged from your position as co-counsel. The testimony of the witnesses you brought me now seems inappropriate to use in court, and I think it would be prudent of you to retire from this courtroom without delay.''

A few people clapped, but a glare from the judge quieted them.

Webster began stuffing papers into his briefcase. "If you are alleging that I behaved unethically to any degree—''

"Nobody's alleging anything, Mr. Webster," said the judge, "except that you have no further relationship with the county attorney of Hatrack County, and therefore it's appropriate for you to step to the other side of the railing and, in my humble opinion, to the other side of the courtroom door.''

Webster rose to his full height, tucked his bag under his arm, and without another word strode down the aisle and out of the court-room.

On his way out, he passed a middle-aged woman with brown-and-grey hair who was moving with some serious intent toward the judge's bench. No, toward the witness stand, where she stepped into the box, put her arm around Vilate Franker's shoulders, and helped the weeping woman rise to her feet. "Come now, Vilate, you did very bravely, you did fine, we're right proud of you.''

"Goody Trader,'' Vilate murmured, "I'm so ashamed.''

"Nonsense,'' said Goody Trader. "We all want to be beautiful, and truth to tell, I think you still are. Just—mature, that's all.''

The spectators watched in silence as Goody Trader led her erst-while rival from the courtroom.

"Your Honor,'' said Verily Cooper, "I think it should be clear to everyone that it is time to return to the real issue before the court. We have been distracted by extraneous witnesses, but the fact of the matter is that it all comes down to Makepeace Smith and Hank Dowser on one side, and Alvin Smith on the other. Their word against his. Unless the prosecution has more witnesses to call, I'd like to begin my defense by letting Alvin give his word, so the jury can judge between them at last.''

"Well said, Mr. Cooper,'' said Marty Laws. "That's the real issue, and I'm sorry I ever moved away from it. The prosecution rests, and I think we'd all like to hear from the defendant. I'm glad he's going to speak for himself, even though the constitution of the United States allows him to decline to testify without prejudice.''

"A fine sentiment,'' said the judge. "Mr. Smith, please rise and take the oath.''

Alvin bent over, scooped up the sack with the plow in it, and hoisted it over his shoulder as easy as if it was a loaf of bread or a bag of feathers. He walked to the bailiff, put one hand on the Bible and raised the other, sack and all. "I do solemnly swear to tell the truth, the whole truth, and nothing but the truth so help me God,'' he said.

"Alvin,'' said Verily, "just tell us all how this plow came to be.''

Alvin nodded. "I took the iron my master gave me—that's Makepeace, he was my master in those days—and I melted it to the right hotness. I'd already made my plow mold, so I poured it in and let it cool enough to strike off the mold, and then I shaped and hammered and scraped all the imperfections out of it, till near as I could tell it had the shape of a plow as perfect as I could do it."

"Did you use any of your knack for Making as you did it?" asked Verily.

"No sir," said Alvin. "That wouldn't be fair. I wanted to earn the right to be a journeyman smith. I did use my doodlebug to inspect the plow, but I made no changes except with my tools and my two hands."

Many of the spectators nodded. They knew something of this matter, of wanting to do something with their hands, without the use of the extraordinary knacks that were so common in this town these days.

"And when it was done, what did you have?"

"A plow," said Alvin. "Pure iron, well shaped and well tempered. A good journeyman piece."

"Whose property was that plow?" asked Verily. "I ask you not as an expert on law, but rather as the apprentice you were at the time you finished it. Was it your plow?"

"It was mine because I made it, and his because it was his iron. It's custom to let the journeyman keep his piece, but I knew it was Makepeace's right to keep it if he wanted."

"And then you apparently decided to change the iron."

Alvin nodded.

"Can you explain to the court your reasoning on the matter?"

"I don't know that it could be called reasoning, rightly. It wasn't rational, as Miss Larner would have defined it. I just knew what I wanted it to be, really. This had nothing to do with going from prentice to journeyman smith. More like going from prentice to journeyman Maker, and I had no master to judge my work, or if I do, he's not yet made hisself known to me."

"So you determined to turn the plow into gold."

Alvin waved off the idea with one hand. "Oh, now, that wouldn't be hard. I've known how to change one metal to another for a long time—it's easier with metals, the way the bits line up and all. Hard to change air, but easy to change metal."

"You're saying you could have turned iron to gold at any time?" asked Verily. "Why didn't you?"

"I reckon there's about the right amount of gold in the world, and the right amount of iron. A man doesn't need to make hammers and saws, axes and plowshares out of gold—he needs iron for that. Gold is for things that need a soft metal."

"But gold would have made you rich," said Verily.

Alvin shook his head. "Gold would have made me famous. Gold would have surrounded me with thieves. And it wouldn't have got me one step closer to learning how to be a proper Maker."

"You expect us to believe that you have no interest in gold?"

"No sir. I need money as much as the next fellow. At that time I was hoping to get married, and I hardly had a penny to my name, which isn't much in the way of prospects. But for most folks gold stands for their hard labor, and I don't see how I should have gold that didn't come from *my* hard labor, too. It wouldn't be fair, and if it's out of balance like that, then it ain't good Making, if you see my point."

"And yet you *did* transform the plow into gold, didn't you?"

"Only as a step along the way," said Alvin.

"Along the way to what?"

"Well, you know. To what the witnesses all said they seen. This plow ain't common gold. It moves. It acts. It's alive."

"And that's what you intended?"

"The fire of life. Not just the fire of the forge."

"How did you do it?"

"It's hard to explain to them as don't have the sight of a doodlebug to get inside things. I didn't create life inside it—that was already there. The bits of gold *wanted* to hold the shape I'd given them, that plow shape, so they fought against the melting of the fire, but they didn't have the strength. They didn't know their *own* strength. And I couldn't teach them, either. And then all of a sudden I thought to put my own hands into the fire and *show* the gold how to be alive, the way I was alive."

"Put your hands into the fire?" asked Verily.

Alvin nodded. "It hurt something fierce, I'll tell you—"

"But you're unscarred," said Verily.

"It was hot, but don't you see, it was a Maker's fire, and finally I understood what I must have known all along, that a Maker is part of what he Makes. I had to be in the fire along with the gold, to show it how to live, to help it find its own heartfire. If I knew exactly how it works I could do a better job of teaching folks. Heaven knows I've tried but ain't nobody learned it aright yet, though a couple or so is getting there, step by step. Anyway, the plow came to life in the fire."

"So now the plow was as we have seen it—or rather, as we have heard it described here."

"Yes," said Alvin. "Living gold."

"And in your opinion, whom does that gold belong to?"

Alvin looked around at Makepeace, then at Marty Laws, then at the judge. "It belongs to itself. It ain't no slave."

Marty Laws rose to his feet. "Surely the witness isn't asserting the equal citizenship of golden plows."

"No sir," said Alvin. "I am not. It has its own purpose in being, but I don't think jury duty or voting for president has much to do with it."

"But you're saying it doesn't belong to Makepeace Smith and it doesn't belong to you either," said Verily.

"Neither one of us."

"Then why are you so reluctant to yield possession of it to your former master?" asked Verily.

"Because he means to melt it down. He said as much that very next morning. Of course, when I told him he couldn't do that, he called me thief and insisted that the plow belonged to him. He said a journeyman piece belongs to the master unless he gives it to the journeyman and, I think he said, 'I sure as hell don't!' Then he called me thief."

"And wasn't he right? Weren't you a thief?"

"No sir," said Alvin. "I admit that the iron he gave me was gone, and I'd be glad to give that iron back to him, fivefold or tenfold, if that's what the law requires of me. Not that I stole it from him, mind you, but because it no longer existed. At the time, of course, I was angry at him because I was ready to be a journeyman years before, but he held me to all the years of the contract anyway, pretending all the time that he didn't know I was already the better smith—"

Among the spectators, Makepeace leapt to his feet and shouted, "A contract is a contract!"

The judge banged the gavel.

"I kept the contract, too," said Alvin. "I worked the full term, even though I was kept as a servant, there wasn't a thing he could teach me after the first year or so. So I figured at the time that I had more than earned the price of the iron that was lost. Now, though, I reckon that was just an angry boy talking. I can see that Makepeace was within his rights, and I'll be glad to give him the price of the iron, or even make him another iron plow in place of the one that's gone."

"But you won't give him the actual plow you made."

"If he gave me gold to make a plow, I'd give him back as much gold as he gave me. But he gave me iron. And even if he had a right to that amount of gold, he doesn't have the right to *this* gold, because if it fell into his hands, he'd destroy it, and such a thing as this shouldn't be destroyed, specially not by them as has no power to make it again. Besides, all his talk of thief was before he saw the plow move.''

"He saw it move?'' asked Verily.

"Yes sir. And then he said to me, 'Get on out of here. Take that thing and go away. I never want to see your face around here again.' As near as I can recall them, those were his exact words, and if he says otherwise then God will witness against him at the last day, and he knows it.''

Verily nodded. "So we have your view on it,'' he said. "Now, as to Hank Dowser, what about the matter of digging somewhere other than the place he said?''

"I knew it wasn't a good place,'' said Alvin. "But I dug where he said, right down till I reached solid stone.''

"Without hitting water?'' asked Verily.

"That's right. So then I went to where I knew I should have dug in the first place, and I put the well there, and it's drawing pure water even today, I hear tell.''

"So Mr. Dowser was simply wrong.''

"He wasn't wrong that there was water there,'' said Alvin. "He just didn't know that there was a shelf of rock and the water flowed under it. Bone dry above. That's why it was a natural meadow—no trees grew there, then or now, except some scrubby ones with shallow roots.''

"Thank you very much,'' said Verily. Then, to Marty Laws: "Your witness.''

Marty Laws leaned forward on his table and rested his chin on his hands. "Well, I can't say as how I have much to ask. We've got Makepeace's version of things, and we've got your version. I might as well ask you, is there any chance that you didn't actually turn iron into gold? Any chance that you *found* the gold in that first hole you dug, and then shaped it into a plow?''

"No chance of that, sir,'' said Alvin.

"So you didn't hide that old iron plow away in order to enhance your reputation as a Maker?''

"I never looked for no reputation as a Maker, sir,'' said Alvin. "And as for the iron, it ain't iron anymore.''

Makepeace nodded. "That's all the questions I've got.''

The judge looked back at Verily. "Anything more from you?''

"Just one question,'' said Verily. "Alvin, you heard the things

Amy Sump said about you and her and the baby she's carrying. Any truth to that?''

Alvin shook his head. ''I never left the jail cell. It's true that I left Vigor Church at least partly because of the stories she was putting out about me. They were false stories, but I needed to leave anyway, and I hoped that with me gone, she'd forget about dreaming me into her life and fall in love with some fellow her own age. I never laid a hand on her. I'm under oath and I swear it before God. I'm sorry she's having trouble, and I hope the baby she's carrying turns out fine and strong and makes a good son for her.''

''It's a boy?'' asked Verily.

''Oh yes,'' said Alvin. ''A boy. But not my son.''

''Now we're finished,'' said Verily.

It was time for final statements, but the judge didn't give the word to begin. He leaned back in his chair and closed his eyes for a long moment. ''Folks, this has been a strange trial, and it's taken some sorry turns along the way. But right now there's only a few points at issue. If Makepeace Smith and Hank Dowser are right, and the gold was found not made, then I think it's fair to say the plow is flat out Makepeace's property.''

''Damn straight!'' cried Makepeace.

''Bailiff, take Makepeace Smith into custody please,'' said the judge. ''He's spending the night in jail for contempt of court, and before he can say another word I'll inform him that every word he says will add another night to his sentence.''

Makepeace nearly burst, but he didn't say another word as the bailiff led him from the courtroom.

''The other possibility is that Alvin made the gold out of iron, as he says, and that the gold is something called 'living gold,' and therefore the plow belongs to itself. Well, I can't say the law allows any room for farm implements to be self-owning entities, but I will say that since Makepeace gave Alvin a certain weight of iron, then if Alvin made that iron disappear, he owes Makepeace the same weight of iron back again, or the monetary equivalent in legal tender. This is how it seems to me at this moment, though I know the jury may see other possibilities that escape me. The trouble is that right now I don't know how the jury can possibly make a fair decision. How can they forget all the business about Alvin maybe or maybe not having scandalous liaisons? A part of me says I ought to declare a mistrial, but then another part of me says, that wouldn't be right, to make this town go through yet another round of this trial. So here's what I propose to do. There's one fact in all of this that we can actually test. We can go out to the smithy and have Hank Dowser show us the spot where he called for the well to be dug. Then we can dig down and see if we find either the remnants of some treasure chest—and water—or a shelf of stone, the way Alvin said, and not a drop of water. It seems to me then we'll at least know something, whereas at the present moment we don't know much at all, except that Vilate Franker, God bless her, has false teeth.''

Neither the defense nor the prosecution had any objections.

''Then let's convene this court at Makepeace's smithy at ten in the morning. No, not tomorrow—that's Friday, election day. I see no way around it, we'll have to do it Monday morning. Another weekend in jail, I'm afraid, Alvin.''

''Your Honor,'' said Verily Cooper. ''There's only the one jail in this town, and with Makepeace Smith forced to share a cell in the same room with my client—''

''All right,'' said the judge. ''Sheriff, you can release Makepeace when you get Alvin back over there.''

''Thank you, Your Honor,'' said Verily.

''We're adjourned till ten on Monday.'' The gavel struck and the spectacle ended for the day.

17

Decisions

Because Calvin used to keep to himself so much in Vigor Church, he always thought of himself as a solitary sort of fellow. Everybody in Vigor who wasn't besotted with Alvin turned out to be pretty much of an idiot, when it came down to it. What did Calvin want with pranks like luring skunks under porches or pushing over outhouses? Alvin had him cut out of anything that mattered, and any other friends he might have had didn't amount to much.

In New Amsterdam and London, Calvin was even more alone, being concentrated as he was on the single-minded goal of getting to Napoleon. It was the same on the streets of Paris, when he was going around trying to get a reputation as a healer. And once he got the Emperor's attention, it was all study and work.

For a while. Because after a few weeks it became pretty clear that Napoleon was going to stretch out his teaching as long and slow as possible. Why should he do otherwise? As soon as Calvin was satisfied that he had learned enough, he'd leave and then Napoleon would be the victim of gout. Calvin toyed with the idea of putting on some pressure by increasing Napoleon's pain, and with that in mind he went and found the place in the Emperor's brain where pain was registered. He had some idea of using his doodling bug to poke directly into that place of pure agony, and then see if Napoleon didn't suddenly remember to teach Calvin a few things that he'd overlooked till now.

That was fine for daydreaming, but Calvin wasn't no fool. He could do that agony trick once, and get one day's worth of teaching, but then before he next fell asleep, he'd better be long gone from Paris, from France, and from anywhere on God's green Earth where Napoleon's agents might find him. No, he couldn't force Napoleon. He had to stay and put up with the excruciatingly slow pace of the lessons, the sheer repetitiveness. In the meantime, he observed carefully, trying to see what it was Napoleon was doing that Calvin didn't understand. He never saw a thing that made sense.

What was left for him, then, but to try out the things Napoleon *had* taught him about manipulating other people, and see if he could figure out more by pure experimentation? That was what finally brought him into contact with other people—the desire to learn how to control them.

Trouble was, the only people around were the staff, and they were all busy. What's worse, they were also under Napoleon's direct control, and it wouldn't do to let the Emperor see that somebody else was trying to win control of his toadies. He might get the wrong idea. He might think Calvin was trying to undermine his power, which wasn't true—Calvin didn't care a hoot about taking Napoleon's place. What was a mere Emperor when there was a Maker in the world?

Two Makers, that is. Two.

Who could Calvin try out his new-learned powers on? After a little wandering around the palace and the government buildings, he began to realize that there was another class of person altogether. Idle and frustrated, they were Calvin's natural subjects: the sons of Napoleon's clerks and courtiers.

They all had roughly the same biography: As their fathers rose to positions of influence, they got sent away to steadily better boarding schools, then emerged at sixteen or seventeen with education, ambition, and no social prestige whatsoever, which meant that most doors were closed to them except to follow in their fathers' footsteps and become completely dependent upon the Emperor. For some of them, this was perfectly all right; Calvin left those hardworking, contented souls alone.

The ones he found interesting were the desultory law students, the enthusiastically untalented poets and dramatists, the gossiping seducers looking around for women rich enough to be desirable and stupid enough to be taken in by such pretenders. Calvin's French improved greatly the more he conversed with them, and even as he followed Napoleon's lessons and learned to find what vices drove these young men, so he could flatter and exploit and control them, he also discovered that he enjoyed their company. Even the fools among them were entertaining, with their lassitude and cynicism, and now and then he found some truly clever and fascinating companions.

Those were the most difficult to win control of, and Calvin told himself that it was the challenge rather than the pleasure of their company that kept him coming back to them again and again. One of them most of all: Honoré. A skinny, short man with prematurely rotten teeth, he was a year older than Calvin's brother Alvin. Honoré was without manners; Calvin soon learned that it wasn't because he didn't know how to behave, but rather because he wished to shock people, to show his contempt for their stale forms, and most of all because he wished to command their attention, and being faintly repulsive all the time had the desired effect. He might start with their contempt or disgust, but within fifteen minutes he always had them laughing at his wit, nodding at his insights, their eyes shining with the dazzlement of his conversation.

Calvin even allowed himself to think that Honoré had some of the same gift Napoleon had been born with, that by studying him Calvin might learn a few of the secrets the Emperor still withheld.

At first Honoré ignored Calvin, not in particular but in the general way that he ignored everyone who had nothing to offer him. Then he must have heard from someone that Calvin saw the Emperor every day, that in fact the Emperor used him as his personal healer. At once Calvin became acceptable, so much so that Honoré began inviting him along on his nighttime jaunts.

"I am studying Paris," said Honoré. "No, let me correct myself—I am studying humankind, and Paris has a large enough sampling of that species to keep me occupied for many years. I study all people who depart from the norm, for their very abnormalities teach me about human nature: If the actions of this man surprise me, it is because I must have learned, over the years, to expect men to behave in a different way. Thus I learn not only the oddity of the one, but also the normality of the many."

"And how am I odd?" asked Calvin.

"You are odd because you actually listen to my ideas instead of my wit. You are an eager student of genius, and I half suspect that you may have genius yourself."

"Genius?" asked Calvin.

"The extraordinary spirit that makes great men great. It is perfect piety that turns men into saints or angels, but what about men who are indifferently pious but perfectly intelligent or wise or perceptive? What do they become? Geniuses. Patron saints of the mind, of the eye, of the mind's eye! I intend, when I die, to have my name invoked by those who pray for wisdom. Let the saints have the prayers of those who need miracles." He cocked his head and looked up at Calvin. "You're too tall to be honest. Tall men always tell lies, since they assume short men like me will never see clearly enough to contradict them."

"Can't help being tall," said Calvin.

"Such a lie," said Honoré. "You wanted to be tall when you were young, just as I wanted to be closer to the earth, where my eye could see the details large men miss. Though I do hope to be fat someday, since fatness would mean I had more than enough to eat, and that, my dear Yankee, would be a delicious change. It's a commonplace idea that geniuses are never understood and therefore never become popular or make money from their brilliance. I think this is pure foolishness. A true genius will not only be smarter than everyone else, but will be *so* clever that he'll know how to appeal to the masses without compromising his brilliance. Hence: I write novels."

Calvin almost laughed. "Those silly stories women read?"

"The very ones. Fainting heiresses. Dullard husbands. Dangerous lovers. Earthquakes, revolutions, fires, and interfering aunts. I write under several *noms de plume*, but my secret is that even as I master the art of being popular and therefore rich, I am also using the novel to explore the true state of humankind in this vast experimental tank known as Paris, this hive with an imperial queen who surrounds himself with drones like my poor stingless unflying father, the seventh secretary of the morning rotation—you gave him a hotfoot once, you miserable prankster, he wept that night at the humiliation of it and I vowed to kill you someday, though I think I probably won't—I have never kept a promise yet."

"When do you write? You're here all the time." Calvin gestured to include the environs of the government buildings.

"How would you know, when you *aren't* here all the time? By night I pass back and forth between the grand salons of the cream of society and the finest brothels ever created by the scum of the earth. And in the mornings, when you're taking emperor lessons from M. Bonaparte, I hole up in my miserable poet's garret—where my mother's housekeeper brings me fresh bread every day, so don't weep for me yet, not until I get syphilis or tuberculosis—and I write furiously, filling page after page with scintillating prose. I tried my hand at poetry once, a long play, but I discovered that by imitating Racine, one learns primarily to become as tedious as Racine, and by studying Molière, one learns that Molière was a lofty genius not to be trifled with by pathetic young imitators."

"I haven't read either of them," said Calvin. In truth he had never heard of either one and only deduced that they were dramatists from the context.

"Nor have you read my work, because in fact it is not yet genius, it is merely journeyman work. In fact I fear sometimes that I have the ambition of a genius, the eye and ear of a genius, and the talent of a chimneysweep. I go down into the filthy world, I come up black, I scatter the ashes and cinders of my research onto white papers, but what have I got? Paper with black marks all over it." Suddenly he gripped Calvin's shirtfront and pulled him down until they were eye to eye. "I would cut off my leg to have a talent like yours. To be able to see *inside* the body and heal or harm, give pain or relieve it. I would cut off both legs." Then he let go of Calvin's shirt. "Of course, I wouldn't give up my more fragile parts, for that would be too great a disappointment to my dear Lady de Berny. You will be discreet, of course, and when you gossip about my affair with her you will never admit you heard about it from me."

"Are you really jealous of me?" asked Calvin.

"Only when I am in my right mind," said Honoré, "which is rare enough that you don't yet interfere with my happiness. You are not yet one of the major irritations of my life. My mother, now—I spent my early childhood pining for some show of love from her, some gentle touch of affection, and instead was always greeted with coldness and reproof. Nothing I did pleased her. I thought, for many years, that it was because I was a bad son. Then, suddenly, I realized that it was because she was a bad mother! It wasn't me she hated, it was my father. So one year when I was away at school, she took a lover—and she chose well, he is a very fine man whom I respect greatly—and got herself impregnated and gave birth to a monster."

"Deformed?" asked Calvin, curious.

"Only morally. Otherwise he is quite attractive, and my mother dotes on him. Every time I see her fawning on him, praising him, laughing at his clever little antics, I long to do as Joseph's brothers did and put him in a pit, only *I* would never be softhearted enough to pull him out and sell him into mere slavery. He will also probably be tall and she will see to it he has full access to her fortune, unlike myself, who am forced to live on the pittance my father can give me, the advances I can extort from my publishers, and the generous impulses of the women for whom I am the god of love. After careful contemplation, I have come to the conclusion that Cain, like Prometheus, was one of the great benefactors of humankind, for which of course he must be endlessly tortured by God, or at least given a very ugly pimple in his forehead. For it was Cain who taught us that some brothers simply cannot be endured, and the only solution is to kill them or have them killed. Being a man of lazy disposition, I lean toward the latter course. Also one cannot wear fine clothes in prison, and after one is guillotined for murder, one's collars never stay on properly; they're always sliding off to one side or the other. So I'll either hire it done or see to it he gets employed in some miserable clerical post in a faroff colony. I have in mind Reunion in the Indian Ocean; my only objection is that its dot on the globe is large enough that Henry may not be able to see the entire circumference of his island home at once. I want him to feel himself in prison every waking moment. I suppose that is uncharitable of me.''

Uncharitable? Calvin laughed in delight, and regaled Honoré in turn with tales of his own horrible brother. ''Well, then,'' said Honoré, ''you must destroy him, of course. What are you doing here in Paris, with a great project like that in hand!''

''I'm learning from Napoleon how to rule over men. So that when my brother builds his Crystal City, I can take it away from him.''

''Take it away! Such shallow aims,'' said Honoré. ''What good is taking it away?''

''Because he built it,'' said Calvin, ''or he *will* build it, and then he'll have to see me rule over all that he built.''

''You think this because you are a nasty person by nature, Calvin, and you don't understand nice people. To you, the end of existence is to control things, and so you will never build anything, but rather will try to take control of what is already in existence. Your brother, though, is by nature a Maker, as you explain it; therefore he cares nothing about who rules, but only about what exists. So if you take away the rule of the Crystal City—when he builds it—you have accomplished nothing, for he will still rejoice that the thing exists at all, regardless of who rules it. No, there is nothing else for you to do but let the city rise to its peak—and then tear it down into such a useless heap of rubble that it can never rise again.''

Calvin was troubled. He had never thought this way, and it didn't feel good to him. "Honoré, you're joking, I'm sure. *You* make things—your novels, at least.''

"And if you hated me, you wouldn't just take away my royalties—my creditors do that already, thank you very much. No, you would take my very books, steal the copyright, and then revise them and revise them until nothing of truth or beauty or, more to the point, my genius remained in them, and then you would continue to publish them under my name, causing me to be shamed with every copy sold. People would read and say, 'Honoré de Balzac, such a fool!' That is how you would destroy me.''

"I'm not a character in one of your novels.''

"More's the pity. You would speak more interesting dialogue if you were.''

"So you think I'm wasting my time here?''

"I think you're *about* to waste your time. Napoleon is no fool. He's never going to give you tools powerful enough to challenge his own. So leave!''

"How can I leave, when he depends on me to keep his gout from hurting? I'd never make it to the border.''

"Then heal the gout the way you used to heal those poor beggars—that was a cruel thing for you to do, by the way, a miserable selfish thing, for how did you think they were going to feed their children without some suppurating wound to excite pity in passersby and eke out a few sous from them? Those of us who were aware of your one-man messianic mission had to go about after you, cutting off the legs of your victims so they'd be able to continue to earn their livelihood.''

Calvin was appalled. "How could you do such a thing!''

Honoré roared with laughter. "I'm joking, you poor literalminded American simpleton!''

"I can't heal the gout," said Calvin, coming back to the subject that interested him: his own future.

"Why not?''

"I've been trying to figure out how diseases are caused. Injuries are easy. Infections are, too. If you concentrate, anyway. Diseases have taken me weeks. They seem to be caused by tiny creatures, so small I can't see them individually, only *en masse*. Those I can destroy easily enough, and cure the disease, or at least knock it back a little and give the body a chance to defeat it on its own. But not all diseases are caused by those tiny beasts. Gout baffles me completely. I have no idea what causes it, and therefore I can't cure it."

Honoré shook his oversized head. "Calvin, you have such native talents, but they have been bestowed unworthily upon you. When I say you must heal Napoleon, of course I don't care whether you actually cure the gout. It isn't the gout that bothers him. It's the *pain* of the gout. And you already cure that every day! So cure it once and for all, thank Napoleon kindly for his lessons, and get out of France as quickly as possible! Have done with it! Get back about your life's work! I'll tell you what—I'll even pay your passage to America. No, I'll do more. I'll come with you to America, and add the study of that astonishingly crude and vigorous people to my vast store of knowledge about humankind. With your talent and my genius, what is there we couldn't accomplish?"

"Nothing," said Calvin happily.

He was especially happy because not five minutes before, Calvin had decided that he wanted Honoré to accompany him to America, and so by the tiniest of gestures, by certain looks and signs that Honoré was never aware of, he caused the young novelist to like him, to be excited by the work that Calvin had to do, and to want so much to be a part of it that he would come home to America with him. Best of all, Calvin had brought it off so skillfully that Honoré obviously had no idea that he had been manipulated into it.

In the meantime, Honoré's idea of curing Napoleon's pain once and for all appealed to him. That place in the brain where pain resided still waited for him. Only instead of stimulating it, all he had to do was cauterize it. It would not only cure Napoleon's gout, but would also cure all other pains he might feel in the future.

So, having thought of it, having decided to do it, that night Calvin acted. And in the morning, when he presented himself to the Emperor, he saw at once that the Emperor knew what he had done.

"I cut myself this morning, sharpening a pen," said Napoleon. "I only knew it when I saw the blood. I felt no pain at all."

"Excellent," said Calvin. "I finally found the way to end your pain from gout once and for all. It involved cutting off *all* pain for the rest of your life, but it's hard to imagine you'd mind."

Napoleon looked away. "It was hard for Midas to imagine that he would not want *everything* he touched to turn to gold. I might have bled to death because I felt no pain."

"Are you rebuking me?" said Calvin. "I give you a gift that millions of people pray for—to live a life without pain—and you're rebuking me? You're the Emperor—assign a servant to watch you day and night in order to make sure you don't unwittingly bleed to death.''

"This is permanent?'' asked Napoleon.

"I can't cure the gout—the disease is too subtle for me. I never pretended to be perfect. But the pain I could cure, and so I did. I cured it now and forever. If I did wrong, I'll restore the pain to you as best I can. It won't be a pleasant operation, but I think I can get the balance back to about what it was before. Intermittent, wasn't it? A month of gout, and then a week without it, and then another month?''

"You've grown saucy.''

"No sir, I merely speak French better, so my native sauciness can emerge more clearly.''

"What's to stop me from throwing you out, then? Or having you killed, now that I don't need you anymore?''

"Nothing has ever stopped you from doing those things,'' said Calvin. "But you don't needlessly kill people, and as for throwing me out—well, why go to the trouble? I'm ready to leave. I'm homesick for America. My family is there.''

Napoleon nodded. "I see. You decided to leave, and then finally cured my pain.''

"My beloved Emperor, you wrong me,'' said Calvin. "I found I could cure you, and then decided to leave.''

"I still have much to teach you.''

"And I have much to learn. But I fear I'm not clever enough to learn from you—the last several weeks you have taught me and taught me, and yet I keep feeling as if I have learned nothing new. I'm simply not a clever enough pupil to master your lessons. Why should I stay?''

Napoleon smiled. "Well done. Very well done. If I weren't Napoleon, you would have won me over completely. In fact, I would probably be paying your passage to America.''

"I was hoping you would, anyway, in gratitude for a painfree life.''

"Emperors can't afford to have petty emotions like gratitude. If I pay your passage it's not because I'm grateful to you, it's because I think my purpose will be better served with you gone and alive than with you, say, here and alive or, perhaps, here and dead, or the most difficult possibility, gone and dead.'' Napoleon smiled.

Calvin smiled back. They understood each other, the Emperor

and the young Maker. They had used each other and now were done
with each other and would cast each other aside—but with style.

"I'll take the train to the coast this very day, begging your
consent, sir."

"My consent! You have more than my consent! My servants
have already packed your bags and they are doubtless at the station
as we speak." Napoleon grinned, touched his forelock in an imaginary salute, and then watched as Calvin rushed from the room.

Calvin the American Maker and Honoré Balzac the annoyingly
ambitious young writer, both gone from the country in the same day.
And the pain of the gout now gone from him.

I'll have to be careful getting into the bath. I might scald myself
to death without knowing it. I'll have to get someone else to climb
into the water before me. I think I know just the young servant girl
who should do it. I'll have to have her scrubbed first, so she doesn't
foul the water for me. It will be interesting to see how much of the
pleasure of the bath came from the slight pain of hot water. And
was pain a part of sexual pleasure? It would be infuriating if the boy
had interfered with *that*. Napoleon would have to have him hunted
down and killed, if the boy had ruined that sport for him.

It didn't take long for the ballots to be counted in Hatrack River—
by nine P.M. Friday, the elections clerk announced a decisive victory
countywide for Tippy-Canoe, old Red Hand Harrison. Some had
been drinking all through the election day; now the likker began to
flow in earnest. Being a county seat, Hatrack drew plenty of farmers
from the hinterland and smaller villages, for whom Hatrack was the
nearest metropolis, having near a thousand people now; it was swollen to twice that number by ten in the evening. As word came in
from each of the neighboring counties and from some across river
that Tippy-Canoe was winning there, too, guns were shot off and so
were mouths, which led to fisticuffs and a lot of traffic into and out
of the jail.

Po Doggly came in about ten-thirty and asked Alvin if he'd mind
too much being put on his own parole to go spend the night in the
roadhouse—Horace Guester was standing bail for him, and did he
give his solemn oath etcetera etcetera because the jail was needed
to hold drunken brawlers ten to a cell. Alvin took the oath and
Horace and Verily escorted him through back lots to the roadhouse.
There was plenty of drinking and dancing downstairs in the common
room of the roadhouse, but not the kind of rowdiness that prevailed
at rougher places and out in the open, where wagons filled with

likker were doing quite a business. Horace's party, as always, was for locals of the more civilized variety. Still, it wouldn't do no good for Alvin to show his face there and get rumors going, especially since there was bound to be some in the crowds infesting Hatrack River as wasn't particular friends of Alvin's—and a few that *was* particular friends of Makepeace's. Not to mention them as was always a particular friend of any amount of gold that might be obtained by stealth or violence. It was up the back stairs for Alvin, and even then he stooped and had his face covered and said nary a word the whole jaunt.

Up in Horace's own bedroom, where Arthur Stuart and Measure already had cots, Alvin paced the room, touching the walls, the soft bed, the window as if he had never seen such things before. "Even cooped up in here," said Alvin, "it's better than a cell. I hope never to be back in such a place again."

"Don't know how you've stood it this far," said Horace. "I'd go plain bonkers in a week."

"Who's to say he didn't?" said Measure.

Alvin laughed and agreed with him. "I was crazy not to let Verily go with his plans, I know that," said Alvin.

"No, no," said Verily. "You were right, you came through in your own defense."

"But what if I hadn't figured out how to let the salamander's voice be heard? I've been thinking about that ever since yesterday. What if I hadn't done it? They was all talking like I could do anything, like I could fly or do miracles on the moon just by thinking about it. I wish I could. Sometimes I wish I could. It's still nip and tuck with the jury, ain't it, Verily?"

Verily agreed that it was. But they all knew that he wasn't likely to get convicted of anything now—assuming, of course, that the shelf of rock was still there in the spot Hank Dowser marked for a well. The real damage was to his good name. The real damage was to the Crystal City, which now would be harder to build because of all them stories going around about how Alvin Smith seduced young girls and old women and walked through walls to get to them. Never mind that the story had turned out to be lies and foolishness—there was always folks stupid enough to say, "Where there's smoke there's fire," when the saying should have been, "Where there's scandalous lies there's always malicious believers and spreaders-around, regardless of evidence."

The whooping and hollering in the street, with youngsters or drunken oldsters riding their horses at a breakneck speed up and

down until Sheriff Doggly or some deputy could either stop the horse
or shoot it, that guaranteed no sleep for anyone, not early, anyway.
So they were all still awake, even Arthur Stuart, when two more
men came into the common room of the roadhouse, looking wore
out and dirty from hard travel. They waited at the counter, nursing
a mug of cider each, till Horace came downstairs to check on things
and recognized them at once. "Come on up, he's here, he's upstairs," whispered Horace, and the three of them was up the stairs
in a trice.

"Armor," said Alvin, greeting him with a brotherly hug.
"Mike." And Mike Fink got him a hug as well. "You picked a
good night to return."

"We picked a *damn* good night," said Fink. "We was afraid
we might be too late. The plan was to take you out of the jail and
hang you as part of the election night festivities. Glad the sheriff
thought ahead."

"He just needed the space for drunk and disorderly," said Alvin.
"I don't think he had any inkling about no plot."

"There's twenty boys here," said Fink. "Twenty at least, all of
them well paid and likkered up. I hope well enough paid that they're
really likkered up so they'll just fall down, puke, and go to sleep,
and then slink off home to Carthage in the morning."

"I doubt it," said Measure. "I been caught up in plots against
Alvin before. Somebody once pretty much took me apart."

Fink looked at him again. "You wasn't so tall then," he said.
"I was plain ashamed of what I done to you," he said. "It was the
worst thing I ever done."

"I didn't die," said Measure.

"Not for lack of trying on my part," said Fink.

Verily was baffled. "You mean this man tried to kill you, Measure?"

"Governor Harrison ordered it," said Measure. "And it was
years ago. Before I was married. Before Alvin came here to Hatrack
River as a prentice boy. And if I recall aright, Mike Fink was a little
prettier in those days."

"Not in my heart," said Frank. "But I bore you no malice,
Measure. And after Harrison had me do that to you, I left him, I
wanted no truck with him. It don't make up for nothing, but it's the
truth, that I'm not a man who'd let such as him boss me around, not
anymore. If I thought you was the type of man to get even, I
wouldn't run, I'd let you do it. But you ain't that kind of man."

"Like I said," Measure answered, "no harm done. I learned

some things that day, and so did you. Let's have done with that now. You're Alvin's friend now, and that makes you my friend as long as you're loyal and true.''

There were tears in Mike Fink's eyes. ''Jesus himself couldn't be more kind to me, and me less deserving.''

Measure held out his hand. Mike took and held it. Just for a second. Then it was done, and they set it behind them and went on.

''Found out a few things,'' said Armor-of-God. ''But I'm glad Mike was with me. Not that he had to do any violence, but there was a couple of times that some fellows didn't take kindly to the questions I was asking.''

''I did throw a fellow into a horsetrough,'' said Fink, ''but I didn't hold him under or nothing so I don't think that counts.''

Alvin laughed. ''No, I reckon that was just playing around.''

''It's some old friends of yours behind all this, Alvin,'' said Armor-of-God. ''The Property Rights Crusade is mostly Reverend Philadelphia Thrower and a couple of clerks opening letters and mailing out letters. But there's some money people behind him, and he's behind other people who need money.''

''Like?'' asked Horace.

''Like one of his first and longest and loyalest contributors is a fellow name of Cavil Planter, who once owned him a farm in Appalachee and still clings to a certain cachet like it was gold bullion,'' said Armor-of-God, with a glance at Arthur Stuart.

Arthur nodded. ''You're saying that's the white man as raped my mama to make me.''

''Most likely,'' said Armor-of-God.

Alvin stared at Arthur Stuart. ''How do you know about such things?''

''I hear everything,'' said Arthur Stuart. ''I don't forget none of it. People said things about that stuff when I was too young to understand it, but I remembered the words and said them to myself when I was older and *could* understand them.''

''Damn,'' said Horace. ''How was Old Peg and me supposed to know he'd be able to figure it out later?''

''You did nothing wrong,'' said Verily. ''You can't help the knacks your children have. My parents couldn't predict what I'd do, either, though heaven knows they tried. If Arthur Stuart's knack let him learn things that were painful to know, then I'd also have to say his inward character was strong enough to deal with it and let him grow up untroubled by it.''

''I ain't troubled by it, that's true,'' said Arthur Stuart. ''But I'll never call him my pa. He hurt my mama and he wanted to make a slave of me, and that's no pa." He looked at Horace Guester. "My own Black mama died trying to get me here, to a real pa and to a ma who'd take her place when she died."

Horace reached out and patted the boy's hand. Alvin knew how Horace had never liked having the boy call him his father, but it was plain Horace had reconciled himself to it. Maybe it was because of what Arthur just said, or maybe it was because Alvin had taken the boy away for a year and Horace was realizing now that his life was emptier without this half-Black mixup boy as his son.

"So this Cavil Planter is one of the money men behind Thrower's little group," said Verily. "Who else?"

"A lot of names, we didn't get but a few of them but it's prominent people in Carthage, and all of them from the pro-slavery faction, either openly or clandestine," said Armor. "And I'm pretty sure about where most of the money's going *to*."

"We know some of it went to pay Daniel Webster," said Alvin.

"But a lot more of it went to help with White Murderer Harrison's campaign for president," said Armor.

They fell silent, and in the silence more gunshots went off, more cheering, more galloping of horses and whooping and hollering. "Tippy-Canoe just carried him another county," said Horace.

"Maybe he won't do so well back east," said Alvin.

"Who knows?" said Measure. "I can guarantee you he didn't get a single vote in Vigor Church. But that ain't enough to turn the tide."

"It's out of our hands for now," said Alvin. "Presidents ain't forever."

"I think what's important here," said Verily, "is that the same people whose candidate for president just won the election are also out to get you killed, Alvin."

"I'd think about lying low for a while," said Measure.

"I *been* lying low," said Alvin. "I had about all the low-lying I can stand."

"Being in jail so's they know right where you be ain't lying low," said Mike Fink. "You got to be where they don't think to look for you, or where if they do find you they can't do nothing to hurt you."

"The first place I can think of that fills those requirements is the grave," said Alvin, "but I reckon I don't want to go there yet."

There was a soft rap on the door. Horace went to it, whispered, "Who's there?"

"Peggy," came the answer.

He opened the door and she came in. She looked around at the assembled men and chuckled. "Planning the fate of the world here?"

Too many of them remembered what happened the last time they met together for her casual tone to be easily accepted. Only Armor and Fink, who weren't there in Alvin's cell that night, greeted her with good cheer. They filled her in on all that had happened, including the fact that Harrison's election was taken for a sure thing all along the route from Carthage City to Hatrack.

"You know what I don't think is fair?" said Arthur Stuart. "That old Red Hand Harrison is walking around with blood dripping off'n him and they made him president, while Measure here has to stay half-hid and all them other good folks daresn't leave Vigor Church cause of that curse. It seems to me like the good folks is still punished and the worsest one got off scot-free."

"Seems the same to me," said Alvin. "But it ain't my call."

"Maybe it ain't and maybe it is," said Arthur Stuart.

They all looked at him like he was a mess on the floor. "How is it Alvin's call?" asked Verily.

"That Red chief ain't dead, is he?" said Arthur Stuart. "That Red prophet what put the curse on, right? Well, him as puts on a curse can take it off, can't he?"

"Nobody can talk to them wild Reds no more," said Mike Fink. "They fogged up the river and nobody can get across. There ain't even no trade with New Orleans no more, damn near broke my heart."

"Maybe nobody can get across the river," said Arthur Stuart. "But Alvin can."

Alvin shook his head. "I don't know," he said. "I don't think so. Besides, I don't know if Tenskwa-Tawa's going to see things the same way as us, Arthur. He might say, The White people of America are bringing destruction on themselves by choosing White Murderer Harrison to be their leader. But the people of Vigor Church will be saved from that destruction because they respected the curse I gave them. So he'll say the curse is really a blessing."

"If he says that," said Measure, "then he ain't as good a man as I thought."

"He sees things a different way, that's all," said Alvin. "I'm just saying you can't be sure what he'll say."

"Then *you* can't be sure either," said Armor-of-God.

"I'm thinking something, Alvin," said Measure. "Miss Larner

here told me somewhat about how she and Arthur figured out there's a lot of people with sharp knacks in this place. Maybe drawn here cause you was born here, or cause you made the plow here. And there's all them people you've been teaching up in Vigor, folks who maybe don't got so sharp a knack but they know the things you taught them, they know the way to live. And I also have my own idea that maybe the curse forced us all to live together there, so we had to get along no matter what, we had to learn to make peace among ourselves. If the curse was lifted from the folks of Vigor Church, them as wanted to could come here and teach them as has the knacks. And teach them meantime how to live together in harmony.''

''Or folks from here could go there,'' said Alvin. ''Even if the curse ain't lifted.''

Measure shook his head. ''There's like a hundred people or more in Vigor Church who's already trying to follow the Maker way. Nobody here even knows about it, really. So if you said to the folks in Vigor, please come to Hatrack, they'd come; but if you said to the folks in Hatrack, please come to Vigor, they'd laugh.''

''But the river's still fogged up,'' said Mike Fink, ''and the curse is still on.''

''If it comes to that,'' said Miss Larner, ''there might be another way to talk to Tenskwa-Tawa without crossing the river.''

''You got a pigeon knows the way to the Red Prophet's wigwam?'' asked Horace, scoffing.

''I know a weaver,'' said Miss Larner, ''who has a door that opens into the west, and I know of a man named Isaac who uses that door.'' She looked at Alvin, and he nodded.

''I don't know what you're talking about,'' said Measure, ''but if you think you can talk to Tenskwa-Tawa, then I hope you'll do it. I hope you will.''

''I will for you,'' said Alvin. ''For your sake and the sake of my family and friends in Vigor Church, I'll ask even though I fear the answer will be worse than no.''

''What could be worse than no?'' asked Arthur Stuart.

''I could lose a friend,'' said Alvin. ''But when I weigh that friend against the people of Vigor and the hope that they might help teach other folks to be Makers and help build the Crystal City—then I don't see as how I've got no choice. I was a child when I went there, though, to that weaver's house.'' He was silent for a moment. ''Miss Larner knows the way, if she'll guide me there.'' It was his turn to look at her, waiting. After a moment's hesitation, she nodded.

"One way or another, though," said Verily Cooper, "you *will* leave this place as soon as the trial's over."

"Win or lose," said Alvin. "Win or lose."

"And if anybody tries to stop him or harm him, they'll have to deal with me first," said Mike Fink. "I'm going with you, Alvin, wherever you go. If these people have the president in their pocket, they're going to be all the more dangerous and you ain't going nowhere without me to watch your back."

"I wish I was younger," said Armor-of-God. "I wish I was younger."

"I don't want to travel alone," said Alvin. "But there's work to be done here, especially if the curse is lifted. And you have responsibilities, too, you married men. It's only the single ones, really, who are free to wander as I'll have to wander. Whatever I find out at the weaver's house, whatever happens when and if I talk to Tenskwa-Tawa, I still have to learn how to build the Crystal City."

"Maybe Tenskwa-Tawa can tell you," said Measure.

"If he knows, then he could have told me back when you and I was boys and in his company," said Alvin.

"I'm unmarried," said Arthur Stuart. "I'm coming with you."

"I reckon so," said Alvin. "And Mike Fink, I'll be glad of your company, too."

"I'm not married either," said Verily Cooper.

Alvin looked at him oddly. "Verily, you're already a dear friend, but you're a lawyer, not a woodsman or a wandering tradesman or a river rat or whatever the rest of us are."

"All the more reason you need me," said Verily. "There'll be laws and courts, sheriffs and jails and writs wherever you go. Sometimes you'll need what Mike Fink has to offer. And sometimes you'll need me. You can't deny me, Alvin Smith. I came all this way to learn from you."

"Measure knows all I know by now. He can teach you as well as I can, and you can help him."

Verily looked at his feet for a moment. "Measure's learned from you, and you from him, since you're brothers and have been for a long time. May it not be taken as an offense, I beg you, if I say that I'd be glad of a chance to learn from you directly for a while, Alvin. I mean to belittle no one else by saying that."

"No offense taken," said Measure. "If you hadn't said it, I would have."

"These three then to go with me on the long road," said Alvin. "And Miss Larner to go with me as far as Becca Weaver's house."

"I'll go too," said Armor-of-God. "Not the whole road, but as far as the weavers. So I can bring back word about what Tenskwa-Tawa says. I hope you'll forgive my presumption, but I crave the chance to be the one as brings the good news to Vigor Church, if they're set free."

"And if they're not?"

"Then they need to learn that too, and from me."

"Then our plans are laid, such as they are," said Alvin.

"All except how to get out of Hatrack River alive, with all these thugs and ruffians about," said Verily Cooper.

"Oh, me and Armor already got that figured out," said Mike Fink with a grin. "And we pretty much won't have to beat nobody to a pulp to do it, neither, if we're lucky."

There was such glee in Mike Fink's face when he said it, though, that more than one of the others wondered whether Mike really thought it would be *good* luck not to have to pulverize somebody. Nor were a few of them altogether sure that they didn't wish to do a little pulp-beating themselves, if push came to shove.

Fink and Armor-of-God were about to head downstairs with Horace then, to freshen up from their journey before he put them to bed in his attic, a good clean space but one he never rented out, just in case of late-night sudden visitors like these, when Measure called out, "Mike Fink."

Fink turned around.

"There's a story I got to tell you before I go to sleep tonight," he said.

Fink looked puzzled for a moment.

"Measure's under the curse," said Armor-of-God. "He's got to tell you or he'll go to bed with bloody hands."

"I came this close to being under the curse myself," said Fink. "But you? How did you get under it?"

"He took it on himself," said Miss Larner. "But that doesn't mean the same rules don't apply."

"But I already know the story."

"That'll make the telling of it easier," said Measure. "But I got to do it."

"I'll come back up when I've peed and et," said Fink. "Begging your pardon, ma'am."

There they were, then, looking at each other, Alvin and Peggy— but once again with Verily Cooper, Arthur Stuart, and Measure looking on.

"Don't the two of you get tired of playing out your scenes in front of an audience?"

"There's no scene to play," said Miss Larner.

"Too bad," said Alvin. "I thought this was the part of the play where I says to you, 'I'm sorry,' and you says to me—"

"I say to you, There is nothing to be sorry for."

"And I say to you, Is so. And you say, Is not. Is so, Is not, Is so, back and forth till we bust out laughing."

At which she burst out laughing.

"I was right, you didn't need to testify," Alvin said.

Her face went stern at once.

"Hear me out, for pete's sake, cause you were right too, if it came right down to it, it wasn't my place to tell you whether or not you could testify. It's not my decision whether you get to make this sacrifice or that one, or whether it's worth it. You decide your own sacrifices, and I decide mine. Instead of me bossing you about it, I should have just asked you to hold off and see if I could manage without. And you would have said yes. Wouldn't you."

She looked him in the eye. "Probably not," she said. "But I *should* have."

"So maybe we ain't so bullheaded after all."

"The day after—no, two days later—that's when we're not so bullheaded."

"That'll do, if we just stay friends till we soften up a little."

"You're not ready for married life, Alvin," said Miss Larner. "You still have many leagues to travel, and until you're ready to build the Crystal City, you have no need of me. I'm not going to sit home and pine for you, and I'm not going to try to tag along with you when the companions you need are men like these. Speak to me when your journey's done. See if we still need each other then."

"So you admit we need each other now."

"I'm not debating with you now, Alvin. I concede no points to you, and petty contradictions will not be explained or reconciled."

"These men are my witnesses, Margaret. I will love you forever. The family we make together, that will be our best Making, better than the plow, better than the Crystal City."

She shook her head. "Be honest with yourself, Alvin. The Crystal City will stand forever, if you build it right. But our family will be gone in a few lifetimes."

"So you admit we'll have a family."

She grinned. "You should run for office, Alvin. You'd lose, but the debates would be entertaining." She was turning toward the door when it opened without a knock. It was Po Doggly, his eyes wide. He scanned the room till he saw Alvin. "What are you doing sitting there like that, and not a gun in the room!"

"I wasn't robbing any of them, and they wasn't robbing me," said Alvin. "We didn't think to bring guns along."

"There was a break-in at the jail. A man claiming to be Amy Sump's father riled up the crowd and about thirty men broke into the courthouse and overpowered Billy Hunter and took away his keys. They hauled every damn prisoner out of there and started beating on them till they told which one of them was you. I got there before they killed anybody and I run them off all right, but they can't get far from town in one night and I don't know but what somebody's going to tell them where you are so I want you to sleep with guns tonight."

"Don't worry about it," said Miss Larner. "They won't come here tonight."

Po looked at her, then at Alvin. "You sure?"

"Don't even post a guard, Po," said Miss Larner. "It will only draw attention to the roadhouse. The men hired to kill Alvin are all cowards, really, so they had to get drunk in order to make the attempt. They'll sleep it off tonight."

"And go away after that?"

"Make sure the trial is well guarded, and after that if Alvin is acquitted he'll leave Hatrack and your nightmares will be over."

"They broke into my jail," said Doggly. "I don't know who your enemies are, boy, but if I was you I'd get rid of that golden plow."

"It ain't the plow," said Alvin. "Though some of them probably thinks it is. But plow or no plow, the ones as want me dead would be sending boys like those after me."

"And you really don't want my protection?" asked Doggly.

Both Alvin and Miss Larner agreed that they did not.

When Po made his good-byes and was ready to leave, Miss Larner slipped her arm through his. "Take me downstairs, please, and on to the room I'm sharing with my new friend Ramona." She gave not so much as a backward glance at Alvin.

Measure hooted once—after the door was closed. "Alvin, is she testing you? Just to make sure that you'll *never* turn wife-beater, no matter what the provocation?"

"I got a feeling I ain't seen provocation yet." But Alvin was smiling when he said it, and the others got the idea he didn't mind the idea of sparring with Miss Larner now and then—sparring with words, that is, words and looks and winks and nasty grins.

After the candles were doused and the room was dark and still, with all of them in bed and wishing to sleep, Alvin murmured: "I wonder what they meant to do to me."

Nobody asked who he meant; Measure didn't have to. "They meant to kill you, Alvin. Does it matter what method they used? Hanging. Burning alive. A dozen musket balls. Do you really care which way you die?"

"I'd like to have a corpse decent-looking enough that the coffin can be open and my children can bear to look at me and say good-bye to me."

"You're dreaming then," said Measure. "Cause even right now I don't know how no wife and children could bear to look at you, though I daresay they'll say good-bye readily enough."

"I expect they were going to hang me," said Alvin. "If you ever see folks about to hang me, don't waste your time or risk your life trying to save me. Just come along after they've given up on me so you can get me on home."

"So you got no fear of the rope," said Measure.

"Nor fear of drowning or suffocation," said Alvin. "Nor falling—I can fix up breaks and make the rocks soft under me. But fire, now. Fire and beheading and too many bullets, those can take me right off. I could use some help if you see them going at me like that."

"I'll try to remember that," said Measure.

Monday morning behind the smithy, everyone was gathered by ten o'clock; but from dawn onward, heavily armed deputies were on guard all around the site. The judge arranged things so the whole jury could see, as well as Marty Laws, Verily Cooper, Alvin Smith, Makepeace Smith, and Hank Dowser. "This court is now in session," said the judge loudly. "Now, Hank Dowser, you show us the exact place you marked."

Verily Cooper spoke up. "How do we know he'll mark the same place?"

"Cause I'll dowse it again," said Hank Dowser, "and the same spot will still be best."

Alvin spoke up then. "There's water everywhere here. There's not a place you can pick where there won't be water if you just go far enough down."

Hank Dowser whirled on him and glared. "There it is! He's got no respect for any man's knack except his own! You think I don't know there's water most everywhere? The question is, is the water pure? Is it close to the surface? That's what I find—the easy dig, the clean water. And I'll tell you, by the use of hickory and willow wands, that the water is purest here, and closest to the surface here, and so I mark this spot, as I would have more'n a year ago! Tell me, Alvin Journeyman, if you're so clever, is this or is it not the same spot I marked, exactly?"

"It is," said Alvin, sounding a little abashed. "And I didn't mean to imply that you weren't a real dowser, sir."

"You didn't exactly mean *not* to imply it either, though, did you!"

"I'm sorry," said Alvin. "The water is purest here, and closest to the surface, and you truly found it twice the same, the exact spot."

The judge intervened. "So after this unconventional courtroom exchange, which seems appropriate to this unconventional courtroom, you both agree that this is the spot where Alvin says he dug the first well and found nothing but solid impenetrable stone, and where it is Makepeace's contention that there was no such stone, but rather a buried treasure which Alvin stole and converted to his own use while telling a tale of turning iron into gold."

"For all we know he hid my iron underground here!" cried Makepeace.

The judge sighed. "Makepeace, please, don't make me send you to jail again."

"Sorry," muttered Makepeace.

The judge beckoned to the team of workingmen he'd arranged to come do the digging. Paying them would come out of the county budget, but with four diggers it couldn't take long to prove one or the other right.

They dug and dug, the dirt flying. But it was a dryish dirt, a little moist from the last rain which was only a week ago, but no hint of a watery layer. And then: *chink*.

"The treasure box!" cried Makepeace.

A few moments later, after scraping and prying, the foreman of the diggers called out, "Solid stone, your honor! Far as we can reach. Not no boulder, neither—feels like bedrock if'n I ever saw it."

Hank Dowser's face went scarlet. He muscled his way to the hole and slid down the steep side. With his own handkerchief he brushed away the soil from the stone. After a few minutes of examination, he stood up. "Your Honor, I apologize to Mr. Smith, as graciously, I hope, as he just apologized to me a moment ago. Not only is this bedrock—which I did not see, for I have never found such a sheet of water *under* solid stone like this—but also I can see old scrape marks against the stone, proving to me that the prentice boy *did* dig in this spot, just as he said he did, and reached stone, just as he said he did.''

"That don't prove he didn't find gold along the way!" cried Makepeace.

"Summations to the jury!" the judge called out.

"In every particular that we could test," said Verily Cooper, "Alvin Smith has proven himself to be truthful and reliable. And all the county has to assail him is the unproven and unprovable speculations of a man whose primary motive seems to be to get his hands upon gold. There are no witnesses but Alvin himself of how the gold came to be shaped like a plow, or the plow came to be made of gold. But we have eight witnesses, not to mention His Honor, myself, and my respected colleague, not to mention Alvin himself, all swearing to you that this plow is not just gold, but also alive. What possible property interest can Makepeace Smith have in an object which clearly belongs to itself and only keeps company with Alvin Smith for its own protection? You have more than a reasonable doubt—you have a certainty that my client is an honest man who has committed no crime, and that the plow should stay with him.''

It was Marty Laws' turn then. He looked like he'd had sour milk for breakfast. "You've heard the witnesses, you've seen the evidence, you're all wise men and you can figure this out just fine without my help," said Laws. "May God bless your deliberations.''

"Is that your summing up?" demanded Makepeace. "Is that how you administer justice in this county? I'll support your opponent in the next local election, Marty Laws! I swear you haven't heard the end of this!''

"Sheriff, kindly arrest Mr. Makepeace Smith again, three days this time, contempt of court and I'll consider a charge of attempted interference with the course of justice by offering a threat to a sitting judge in order to influence the outcome of a case.''

"You're all ganging up against me! All of you are in this together! What did he do, Your *Honor*, bribe you? Offer to share some of that gold with you?''

"Quickly, Sheriff Doggly," said the judge, "before I get angry with the man.''

When Makepeace's shouting had died down enough to proceed, the judge asked the jury, "Do we need to traipse on back to the

courtroom for hours of deliberation? Or should we just stand back
and let you work things out right here?''

The foreman whispered to his fellow jurors; they whispered
back. ''We have a unanimous verdict, Your Honor.''

''What say you, etcetera etcetera?''

''Not guilty of all charges,'' said the foreman.

''We're done. I commend both attorneys for fine work in a difficult case. And to the jury, my commendation for cutting through
the horse pucky and seeing the truth. Good citizens all. This court
stands adjourned until the next time somebody brings a blame fool
charge against an innocent man, at least that's what I'm betting on.''
The judge looked around at the people, who were still standing there.
''Alvin, you're free to go,'' he said. ''Let's all go home.''

Of course they didn't all go; nor, strictly speaking, was Alvin free.
Right now, surrounded by a crowd and with a dozen deputies on
guard, he was safe enough. But as he gripped the sack with the plow
inside, he could almost feel the covetings of other men directed
toward that plow, that warm and trembling gold.

He wasn't thinking of that, however. He was looking over at
Margaret Larner, whose arm was around young Ramona's waist.
Someone was speaking to Alvin—it was Verily Cooper, he realized,
congratulating him or something, but Verily would understand. Alvin
put a hand on Verily's shoulder, to let him know that he was a good
friend even though Alvin was about to walk away from him. And
Alvin headed on over to Miss Larner and Ramona.

At the last moment he got shy, and though he had his eyes on
Margaret all the way through the crowd, it was Ramona he spoke
to when he got there. ''Miss Ramona, it was brave of you to come
forward, and honest too.'' He shook her hand.

Ramona beamed, but she was also a little upset and nervous.
''That whole thing with Amy was my fault I think. She was telling
me those tales about you, and I was doubting her, which only made
her insist more and more. And she stuck to it so much that for a
while I believed maybe it *was* true and that's when I told my folks
and that's what started all the rumors going, but then when she went
with Thatch under the freak show tent and she comes out pregnant
but babbling about how it was you got her that way, well, I had my
chance then to set things straight, didn't I? And then I didn't get to
testify!''

''But you told my friends,'' said Alvin, ''so the people who
matter most to me know the truth, and in the meantime you didn't

have to hurt your friend Amy." In the back of his mind, though, Alvin couldn't shake the bitter certainty that there would always be some who believed her charges, just as he was sure that she would never recant. She would go on telling those lies about him, and some folks at least would go on believing them, and so he would be known for a cad or worse no matter how clean he lived his life. But that was spilled milk.

Ramona was shaking her head. "I don't reckon she'll be my friend no more."

"But you're *her* friend whether she likes it or not. So much of a friend that you'd even hurt her rather than let her hurt someone else. That's something, in my book."

At that moment, Mike Fink and Armor-of-God came up to him. "Sing us that song you thought up in jail, Alvin!"

At once several others clamored for the song—it was that kind of festive occasion.

"If Alvin won't sing it, Arthur Stuart knows it!" somebody said, and then there was Arthur tugging at his arm and Alvin joined in singing with him. Most of the jury was still there to hear the last verse:

> *I trusted justice not to fail.*
> *The jury did me proud.*
> *Tomorrow I will hit the trail*
> *And sing my hiking song so loud*
> *It's like to start a gale!*

Everybody laughed and clapped. Even Miss Larner smiled, and as Alvin looked at her he knew that this was the moment, now or never. "I got another verse that I never sung to anybody before, but I want to sing it now," he said. They all hushed up again to hear:

> *Now swiftly from this place I'll fly,*
> *And underneath my boots*
> *A thousand lands will pass me by,*
> *Until we choose to put down roots,*
> *My lady love and I.*

He looked at Margaret with all the meaning he could put in his face, and everybody hooted and clapped. "I love you, Margaret Larner," he said. "I asked you before, but I'll say it again now. We're about to journey together for a ways, and I can't think of a good reason

why it can't be our honeymoon journey. Let me be your husband,
Margaret. Everything good that's in me belongs to you, if you'll
have me.''

She looked flustered. "You're embarrassing me, Alvin," she
murmured.

Alvin leaned close and spoke into her ear. "I know we got
separate work to do, once we leave the weavers' house. I know we
got long journeys apart.''

She held his face between her hands. "You don't know what
you might meet on that road. What woman you might meet and love
better than me.''

Alvin felt a stab of dread. Was this something she had seen with
her torchy knack? Or merely the worry any woman might feel? Well,
it was *his* future, wasn't it? And even if she saw the possibility of
him loving somebody else, that didn't mean he had to let it come
true.

He wrapped his long arms around her waist and drew her close,
and spoke softly. "You see things in the future that I can't see. Let
me ask you like an ordinary man, and you answer me like a woman
that knows only the past and the present. Let my promise to you
now keep watch over the future.''

She was about to raise another objection, when he kissed her
lightly on the lips. "If you're my wife, then whatever there is in the
future, I can bear it, and I'll do my best to help you bear it too. The
judge is right here. Let me begin my life of new freedom with you.''

For a moment, her eyes looked heavy and sad, as if she saw
some awful pain and suffering in his future. Or was it in her own?

Then she shook it off as if it was just the shadow of a cloud
passing over her and now the sun was back. Or as if she had decided
to live a certain life, no matter what the cost of it, and now would
no longer dread what couldn't be helped. She smiled, and tears ran
down her cheeks. "You don't know what you're doing, Alvin, but
I'm proud and glad to have your love, and I'll be your wife.''

Alvin turned to face the others, and in a loud voice he cried,
"She said yes! Judge! Somebody stop the judge from leaving! He's
got him one more job to do!'' While Peggy went off to find her
father and drag him back so he could give her away properly, Verily
Cooper fetched the judge.

On the way over to where Alvin waited, the judge put a kindly
arm across Verily's back. "My lad, you have a keen mind, a lawyer's mind, and I approve of that. But there's something about you
that sets a fellow's teeth on edge.''

"If I knew what it was, sir, you may be sure that I'd stop."

"Took me a while to figure it out. And I don't know what you can do about it. What makes folks mad at you right from the start is you sound so damnably English and educated and fine."

Verily grinned, then answered in the vernacular accent he had grown up with, the one he had spent so many years trying to lose. "You mean, sir, that if I talks like a common feller, I'll be more likable?"

The judge whooped with laughter. "That's what I mean, lad, though I don't know as how *that* accent is much better!"

And with that they reached the spot where the wedding party was assembled. Horace stood beside his daughter, and Arthur Stuart was there as Alvin's best man.

The judge turned to Sheriff Doggly. "Do the banns, my good sir."

Po Doggly at once cried out, "Is there a body here so foolish as to claim there's any impediment to the marriage of this pair of good and godly citizens?" He turned to the judge. "Not a soul as I can see, Judge."

So Alvin and Peggy were married, Horace Guester on one side, Arthur Stuart on the other, all standing there in the open on the grounds of the smithy where Alvin had served his prenticehood. Just up the hill was the springhouse where Peggy had lived in disguise as a schoolteacher; the very springhouse where twenty-two years before, as a five-year-old girl, she had seen the heartfires of a family struggling across the Hatrack River in flood, and in the womb of the mother of that family there was a baby with a heartfire so bright it dazzled her, the like of which she'd never seen before or since. She ran, then, ran down this hill, ran to this smithy, got Makepeace Smith and the other men gathered there to race to the river and save the family. All of it began here, within sight of this place. And now she was married to him. Married to the boy whose heartfire shone like the brightest star in her memory, and in all her life since then.

There was dancing that night at Horace's roadhouse, you can bet, and Alvin had to sing his song five more times, and the last verse thrice each time through. And that night he carried his Margaret—his now, and he was hers—in those strong blacksmith's arms up the stairs to the room where Margaret herself had been conceived twenty-eight years before. He was awkward and they both were shy and it didn't help that half the town was charivareeing outside the roadhouse halfway till dawn, but they were man and wife, made one flesh as they had so long been one heart even though she had tried to deny it and he had tried to live without her. Never mind that she had seen his grave in her mind, and herself and their children standing by it, weeping. That scene was possible in every wedding night; and at least there would be children; at least there would be a loving widow to grieve him; at least there would be memory of this night, instead of regretful loneliness. And in the morning, when they awoke, they were not quite so shy, not quite so awkward, and he said such things to her as made her feel more beautiful than anyone who had ever lived before, and more beloved, and I don't know who would dare to say that in that moment it wasn't the pure truth.

18

Journeys

Two days later they were ready to light out. They made no secret about the carriage Armor-of-God hired in Wheelwright, ready to take them off the ferry as soon as they crossed the Hio. That would be enough to decoy the stupid ones. As for the clever ones, well, Mike Fink had his own plan, and even Margaret allowed as how it might well work.

Friends came to the roadhouse all that evening to bid good-bye. Alvin and Peggy and Arthur were well known to them all; Armor-of-God had a few friends here, from business traveling; and Verily had made some new friends, having been the spokesman for the winning side in a highly emotional trial. If Mike Fink had local friends, they weren't the sort to show up in Horace Guester's road-house; as Mike confided to Verily Cooper, his friends were most of them the very men Alvin's enemies had hired to kill him and take the plow once he got out on the road tomorrow.

When the last soul had left, Horace embraced his daughter and his new son-in-law and the adopted son he had helped to raise, shook hands with Verily, Armor, and Mike, and then went about as he always did, dousing the candles, putting the night log on the fire, checking to make sure all was secure. As he did, Measure helped the travelers make their way, lightly burdened, quietly down the stairs and out the back, finding the path with only the faintest sliver of moon. Even at that, they walked at first toward the privy, so that anyone casually glancing wouldn't think a thing amiss, unless they noticed the satchel or bag each one carried. Meantime, Measure kept watch, in case someone else was thinking to snatch Alvin that night while he was relieving himself. He kept watch even though Peggy Larner—or was it Goody Smith now?—assured him that not a soul was watching the back of the house.

"All my teaching is in your hands now, Measure," Alvin whispered as he was about to step off the back porch into the night. "I leave you behind this time again, but you know that we set out on the real journey together as true companions, and always will be to the end."

Measure heard him, and wondered if Peggy maybe whispered to him something she had seen in his heartfire, that Measure worried lest Alvin forget how much Measure loved him and wanted to be on this journey by his side. But no, Alvin didn't need Peggy to tell him he had a brother who was more loyal than life and more sure than death. Alvin kissed his brother's cheek and was gone, the last to go.

They met up again in the woods behind the privy. Alvin went about among them, calming them with soft words, touching them, and each time he touched them they could hear it just a little clearer, a kind of soft humming, or was it the soughing of the wind, or the call of a far-off bird too faint to hear, or perhaps a distant coyote mumbling in its sleep, or the soft scurry of squirrel feet on a tree on the next rise? It was a kind of music, and finally it didn't matter what it was that produced the sound, they fell into the rhythm of it, all holding each other's hands, and at the head of the line, Alvin. They moved swift and sure, keeping step to the music, sliding easily among the trees, making few sounds, saying nothing, marveling at how they could have walked past these woods before and never guessed that such a clear and well-marked path was here; except when they looked back, there was no path, only the underbrush closed off again, for the path was made by Alvin's progress in the midst of the greensong, and behind his party the forest relaxed back into its ordinary shape.

They came to the river, where Po Doggly waited, watching over two boats. "Mind you," he whispered, "I'm not sheriff tonight. I'm only doing what Horace and I done so many times in the past, long before I had me a badge—helping folks as ought to be free get safe across the river." Po and Alvin rowed one of them and Mike and Verily the other, for though he was unaccustomed to such labor, no wooden oar would ever leave a blister on Verily's hands. Silently they moved out across the Hio. Only when they got to the middle did anyone speak. Peggy, controlling the tiller, whispered to Alvin, "Can we talk a little now?"

"Soft and low," said Alvin. "And no laughing."

How had he known she was about to laugh? "We passed a dozen of them as we walked through the woods, all of them asleep, waiting for first light. But there's none on the opposite shore, except the heartfire we're looking for."

Alvin nodded, and gave a thumbs up to the men in the other boat.

They skirted the shore on the Appalachee side for about a quarter mile before coming to the landing site they looked for. Once it had been a putting-in place for flatboats, before the Red fog on the Mizzipy and the new railroad lines slowed and then stopped most of the flatboat traffic. Now an elderly couple lived there mostly from fishing and an orchard that still produced, poorly, but enough for their needs.

Dr. Whitley Physicker was waiting in the front yard of that house with his carriage and four saddled horses; he had insisted on buying or lending them himself, and refused any thought of reimbursement. He also paid the old folks who lived there for the annoyance of having visitors arrive so late at night.

He had a man with him—Arthur Stuart recognized him at once and called him by name. John Binder smiled shyly and shook hands all around, as did Whitley Physicker. "I'm not much for rowing, at my age," Dr. Physicker explained. "So John, being as trustworthy a man as ever there was, agreed to come along, asking no questions. I suppose all the questions he *didn't* ask are answered now."

Binder smiled and chuckled. "Reckon so, all but one. I heard about how you was teaching folks about Makery away out there in Vigor Church, and I hoped you might teach some of it here. Now you're going."

Alvin reassured him. "My brother is holed up in the roadhouse. Nobody's to know he's there, but if you go to Horace Guester and tell him I sent you, he'll let you go up and talk to Measure. There's a hard tale he'll have to tell you—"

"I know about the curse."

"Well good," said Alvin. "Cause once that's done, he can teach you just what I was teaching in Vigor Church."

Po Doggly and John Binder pushed the boats off the shore before the others were even mounted on their horses or properly seated in the carriage; Whitley Physicker waved from Binder's boat. Alvin shook hands with the old couple, who had got up from their beds to see them off. Then he climbed up into the front seat of the carriage with Margaret; Verily and Arthur sat behind. Armor and Mike rode two of the horses; Verily's horse and the horse that Alvin and Arthur would ride together were tied to the back of the carriage.

As they were about to leave, Mike brought his horse—stamping and fuming, since Mike was a sturdy load and not much of a horseman—beside the carriage and said to Alvin, "Well this plan worked too well! I was looking forward to scaring some poor thug half to death before the night was through!"

Peggy leaned over from the other side of the front seat and said, "You'll get your wish about a mile up the road. There's two fellows there who saw Dr. Physicker's carriage come here this afternoon and wondered what he was doing with four horses tied behind. They're just keeping watch on the road, but even if they don't stop us, they'll give the alarm and then we'll be chased instead of getting away clean."

"Don't kill them, Mike," said Alvin.

"I won't unless they make me," said Mike. "Don't worry, I ain't loose with other folks' lives no more." He rode to Armor, gave him the reins, and said, "Here, bring this girl along with you. I do better on my feet for this kind of work." Then he dismounted and took off running.

Near as I can gather from Mike Fink's tale of the event—and you got to understand that a fellow who wants his story to be truthful has to allow for a lot of brag before deciding what's true in a tale of Mike Fink's heroic exploits—those two smarter-than-normal thugs was dozing while sitting with their backs to opposite sides of the same stump when all of a sudden they both felt their arms pretty near wrenched right out of their sockets and then they were dragged around, grabbed by the collars, and smacked together so hard their noses bled and they saw stars.

"You're lucky I took me a vow of nonviolence," said Mike Fink, "or you'd be suffering some pain right now."

Since they were already suffering something pretty excruciating, they didn't want to find out what this night-wandering fellow thought of as pain. Instead, they obeyed him and held very still as he tied their hands to a couple of lengths of rope, so that the one man's right hand was tied on one end of a rope that held the other man's left, with about two feet of rope between them; and the same with their other two hands. Then Fink made them kneel, picked up a huge log, and laid it down across the two lengths of rope that joined them. What he could lift alone they couldn't lift together. They just knelt there as if they were praying to the log, their hands too far apart even to dream of untying their bonds.

"Next time you want gold," said Fink, "you ought to get yourself a pick and shovel and dig for it, stead of lying in wait in the night for some innocent fellow to come by and get himself robbed and killed."

"We wasn't going to rob nobody," burbled one of the men.

"It's a sure thing you wasn't," said Fink, "cause any man ever wants to get at Alvin Smith has to go through me, and I make a better wall than window, I'll tell you that right now."

Then he jogged back to the road, waved to the others, and waited for them to come alongside so he could mount his horse. In a couple of minutes it was done, and they rode briskly south along a lacework of roads that would completely bypass Wheelwright—including the fancy carriage waiting all day empty by the river, until Horace Guester crossed over, got in the carriage, and used it to shop for groceries in the big-city market that was Wheelwright's pride and joy. That's when the ruffians knew they had been fooled. Oh, some of them lit out in search of Alvin's group, but they had a whole day's head start, or nearly so, and not a one of them found anything except a couple of men kneeling before a log with their butts in the air.

All the way to the coast, Calvin expected to be accosted by Napoleon's troops, the carriage blown to bits with grapeshot or set afire or some other grisly end. Why he expected Napoleon to be ungrateful he didn't know. Perhaps it was simply a feeling of general unease. Here he was, not yet twenty years old, and already he had moved through the salons of London and Paris, had spent hours alone discussing a thousand different things with the most powerful man in the world, had learned as many of the secrets of that powerful man as he was likely ever to tell, spoke French if not fluently then competently, and through it all had remained aloof, untouched, his life's dream unchanged. He was a Maker, far more so than Alvin, who remained at the rough frontier of a crude upstart country that couldn't properly call itself a nation; who had Alvin known, except other homespun types like himself? Yet Calvin felt vaguely afraid at the thought of going back to America. Something was trying to stop him. Something didn't want him to go.

"It is nerves," said Honoré. "You will face your brother. You know now that he is a provincial clown, but still he remains your nemesis, the stick against which you must measure yourself. Also you are traveling with me, and you are constantly aware of the need to make a good impression."

"And why would I need to impress *you*, Honoré?"

"Because I am going to write you into a story someday, my friend. Remember that the ultimate power is mine. You may decide what you will do in this life, up to the point. But I will decide what others think of you, and not just now but long after you're dead."

"If anyone still reads your novels," said Calvin.

"You don't understand, my dear bumpkin. Whether they read my novels or not, my judgment of your life will stand. These things take on a life of their own. No one remembers the original source, or cares either."

"So people will only remember what you say about me—and you they won't remember at all."

Honoré chuckled. "Oh, I don't know about that, Calvin. I intend to be memorable. But then, do I care whether I'm remembered? I think not. I have lived without the affection of my own mother; why should I crave the affection of strangers not yet born?"

"It's not whether you're remembered," said Calvin. "It's whether you changed the world."

"And the first change I will make is: They must remember me!" Honoré's voice was so loud that the coachman slid open the panel and inquired whether they wanted something from him. "More speed," cried Honoré, "and softer bumps. Oh, and when the horses relieve themselves: Less odor."

The coachman growled and closed the panel shut.

"Don't you intend to change the world?" asked Calvin.

"Change it? A paltry project, smacking of weak ambition and much self-contempt. Your brother wants to build a city. You want to tear it down before his eyes. *I* am the one with vision, Calvin. I intend to *create* a world. A world more fascinating, engrossing, spellbinding, intricate, beautiful, and real than this world."

"You're going to outdo God?"

"He spent far too much time on geology and botany. For him, Adam was an afterthought—oh, by the way, is man found upon the Earth? I shall not make that mistake. I will concentrate on people, and slip the science into the cracks."

"The difference is that your people will all be confined to tiny black marks on paper," said Calvin.

"My people will be more real than these shallow creatures God has made! I, too, will make them in my own image—only taller— and mine will have more palpable reality, more inner life, more connection to the living world around them than these mud-covered peasants or the calculating courtiers of the palace or the swaggering soldiers and bragging businessmen who keep Paris under their thumbs."

"Instead of worrying about the emperor stopping us, perhaps I should worry about lightning striking us," said Calvin.

It was meant as a joke, but Honoré did not smile. "Calvin, if God was going to strike you dead for anything, you'd already be dead by now. I don't pretend to know whether God exists, but I'll tell you this—the old man is doddering now! The old fellow talks rough but it's all a memory. He hasn't the stuff anymore! He can't stop us! Oh, maybe he can write us out of his will, but we'll make our own fortune and let the old boy stand back lest he be splashed when we hurtle by!"

"Do you ever have even a moment of self-doubt?"

"None," said Honoré. "I live in the constant certainty of failure, and the constant certainty of genius. It is a species of madness, but greatness is not possible without it. Your problem, Calvin, is that you never really question yourself about anything. However you feel, that's the right way to feel, and so you feel that way and everything else better get out of your way. Whereas I endeavor to change my feelings because my feelings are always wrong. For instance, when approaching a woman you lust after, the foolish man acts out his feelings and clutches at an inviting breast or makes some fell invitation that gets him slapped and keeps him from the best parties for the rest of the year. But the wise man looks the woman in the eye and serenades her about her astonishing beauty and her great wisdom and his own inadequacy to explain to her how much she deserves her place in the exact center of the universe. No woman can resist this, Calvin, or if she can, she's not worth having."

The carriage came to a stop.

Honoré flung open the door. "Smell the air!"

"Rotting fish," said Calvin.

"The coast! I wonder if I shall throw up, and if I do, whether the sea air will have affected the color and consistency of my vomitus."

Calvin ignored his deliberately crude banter as he reached up for their bags. He well know that Honoré was only crude when he didn't much respect his company; when with aristocrats, Honoré never uttered anything but bon mots and epigrams. For the young novelist to speak that way to Calvin was a sign, not so much of intimacy, but of disrespect.

When they found an appropriate ship bound for Canada, Calvin showed the captain the letter Napoleon had given him. Contrary to his worst fears, after seeing a production of a newly revised and prettied-up script of *Hamlet* in London, the letter did not instruct the captain to kill Calvin and Honoré at once—though there was no guarantee that the fellow didn't have orders to strangle them and pitch them into the sea when they were out of sight of land.

Why am I so afraid?

"So the Emperor's treasurer will reimburse me for all expenses out of the treasury when I come back?"

"That's the plan," said Honoré. "But here, my friend, I know how ungenerous these imperial officials can be. Take this."

He handed the captain a sheaf of franc notes. Calvin was astonished. "All these weeks you've pretended to be poor and up to your ears in debt."

"I *am* poor! I *am* in debt. If I didn't owe money, why would I ever steel myself to write? No, I simply borrowed the price of my passage from my mother *and* my father—they never talk, so they'll never find out—and from two of my publishers, promising each of them a completely exclusive book about my travels in America."

"You borrowed to pay our passage, knowing all along that the Emperor would pay it?"

"A man has to have spending money, or he's not a man," said Honoré. "I have a wad of it, with which I have every intention of being generous with you, so I hope you won't condemn my methods."

"You're not terribly honest, are you?" said Calvin, half appalled, half admiring.

"You shock me, you hurt me, you offend me, I challenge you to a duel and then take sick with pneumonia so that I can't meet you, but I urge you to go ahead without me. Keep in mind that *because* I had that money, the captain will now invite us into his cabin for dinner every night of the voyage. And in answer to your question, I am perfectly honest when I am creating something, but otherwise words are mere tools designed to extract what I need from the pockets or bank accounts of those who currently but temporarily possess it. Calvin, you've been too long among the Puritans. And I have been too long among the Hypocrites."

*   *   *

It was Peggy who found the turnoff to Chapman Valley, found it easily though there was no sign and she was coming this time from the other direction. She and Alvin left the others with the carriage under the now-leafless oak out in front of the weavers' house. For Peggy, coming to this place now was both thrilling and embarrassing. What would they think of the way things had turned out since they set her on this present road?

Then, just as she raised her hand to knock on the door, she remembered something.

"Alvin," she said. "It slipped my mind, but something Becca said when I was here a few months ago—"

"If it slipped your mind, then it was supposed to slip your mind."

"You and Calvin. You need to reclaim Calvin, find him and reclaim him before he turns completely against the work you're doing."

Alvin shook his head. "Becca doesn't know everything."

"And what does that mean?"

"What makes you think Calvin wasn't already the enemy of our work before he was born?"

"That's not possible," said Peggy. "Babies are born innocent and pure."

"Or steeped in original sin? Those are the choices? I can't believe that you of all people believe either idea, you who put your hands on the womb and see the futures in the baby's heartfire. The child is already himself then, the good and bad, ready to step into the world and make of himself whatever he wants most to be."

She squinted at him. "Why is it that when we're alone, talking of something serious, you don't sound so much the country bumpkin?"

"Because maybe I learned everything you taught me, only I also learned that I don't want to lose touch with the common people," said Alvin. "They're the ones who are going to build the city with me. Their language is my native language—why should I forget it, just because I learned another? How many educated folks do you think are going to come away from their fine homes and educated friends and roll up their sleeves to make something with their own hands?"

"I don't want to knock on this door," said Peggy. "My life changes when I come into this place."

"You don't have to knock," said Alvin. He reached out and turned the knob. The door opened.

When he made as if to step inside, Peggy took his arm. "Alvin, you can't just walk in here!"

"If the door wasn't locked, then I can walk in," said Alvin. "Don't you understand what this place is? This is the place where things are as they must be. Not like the world out there, the world you see in the heartfires, the world of things that can be. And not like the world inside my head, the world as it might be. And not like the world as it was first conceived in the mind of God, which is the world as it should be."

She watched him step over the threshold. There was no alarum in the house, nor even a sound of life. She followed him. Young as he was, this man she had watched over from his infancy, this man whose heart she knew more intimately than her own, he could still surprise her by what he did of a sudden without thought, because he simply knew it was right and had to be this way.

The endless cloth still lay folded in piles, linked each to each, winding over furniture, through halls, up and down stairs. They stepped over the spans and reaches of it. "No dust," said Peggy. "I didn't notice that the first time. There's no dust on the cloth."

"Good housekeepers here?" asked Alvin.

"They dust all this cloth?"

"Or maybe there's simply no passage of time within the cloth. Always and forever it exists in that one present moment in which the shuttlecock flew from side to side."

As he said these words, they began to hear the shuttlecock. Someone must have opened a door.

"Becca?" called Peggy.

They followed the sound through the house to the ancient cabin at the house's heart, where an open door led into the room with the loom. But to Peggy's surprise, it wasn't Becca seated there. It was the boy. Her nephew, the one who had dreamed of this. With practiced skill he drove the shuttlecock back and forth.

"Is Becca . . ." Peggy couldn't bring herself to ask about the weaver's death.

"Naw," said the boy. "We changed the rules a little here. No more pointless sacrifice. You done that, you know. Came here as a judge—well, your judgment was heeded. I take my shift for a while, and she can go out a little."

"So is it you we talk to now?" asked Alvin.

"Depends on what you want. I don't know nothing about nothing, so if you want answers, I don't think I'm it."

"I want to use the door that leads to Ta-Kumsaw."

"Who?" the boy asked.

"Your uncle Isaac," said Peggy.

"Oh, sure." He nodded with his head. "It's that one."

Alvin strode toward it.

"You ever used one of these doors before?" asked the boy.

"No," said Alvin.

"Well then ain't you the stupid one, heading right for it like it was some ordinary door."

"What's different? I know it leads to the Red lands. I know it leads to the house where Ta-Kumsaw's daughter weaves the lives of the Reds of the west."

"Here's the tricky part. When you pass through the door, you can't have no part of yourself touching anything here but air. You can't brush up against the doorjamb. You can't let a foot linger on the floor. It's not a step throught the door, it's a leap."

"And what happens if some part of me *does* touch?"

"Then that part of this place drags you down just a little, slows you, lowers you, and so instead of you passing through the door in one smooth motion, you go through in a couple of pieces. Ain't nobody can put you together after that, Mr. Maker."

Peggy was appalled. "I never realized it was so dangerous."

"Breathing's dangerous too," said the boy, "if'n you breathe in something to make you sick." He grinned. "I saw you two get all twined up together here. Congratulations."

"Thanks," said Alvin.

"So what do they call you now, judge woman?" the boy asked Peggy. "Goody Smith?"

"Most still call me Peggy Larner. Only they say Miz Larner now, and not Miss."

"I call her Margaret," said Alvin.

"I reckon you'll really be married when she starts to think of herself by the name you call her, instead of the name her parents called her by." He winked at Peggy. "Thanks for getting me my job. My sisters are glad, too, they had nightmares, I'll tell you. There ain't no love of the loom in them." He turned back to Alvin. "So are you going or what?"

At that moment the door flew open and a tied-up bundle flew through it.

"Uh-oh," said the boy. "Best turn your back. Becca's coming through, and she travels stark nekkid, seeing as how women's clothing can't fit through that door without touching."

Alvin turned his back, and so did Peggy, though unlike Alvin she cheated and allowed herself to watch anyway. It was not Becca who came through the door first, however. It was Ta-Kumsaw, a man Peggy had never met, though she had seen him often enough in Alvin's heartfire. He was not naked, but rather clothed in buckskins that clung tightly to his body. He saw them standing there and grunted. "Boy Renegado comes back to see the most dangerous Red man who ever lived."

"Howdy, Ta-Kumsaw," said Alvin.

"Hi, Isaac," said the boy. "I warned him about the door like you said."

"Good boy," said Ta-Kumsaw. He turned his back on them then, just in time for Becca to leap through the door wearing only thin and clinging underwear. He gathered her at once into his arms. Then together they untied the bundle and unfolded it into a dress, which she drew down over her head. "All right," said Ta-Kumsaw. "She's dressed enough for a White woman now."

Alvin turned around and greeted her. There were handshakes, and even a hug between women. They talked about what had happened in Hatrack River over the past few months, and then Alvin explained his errand.

Ta-Kumsaw showed no emotion. "I don't know what my brother will say. He keeps his own counsel."

"Does he rule there in the west?" asked Alvin.

"Rule? That's not how we do things. There are many tribes, and in each tribe many wise men. My brother is one of the greatest of them, everyone agrees to that. But he doesn't make law just by deciding what it should be. We don't do anything as foolish as you do, electing one president and concentrating too much power in his hands. It was good enough when good men held the office, but always when you create an office that a man can lay hands on, an evil man will someday lay hands on it."

"Which is going to happen on New Year's day when Harrison—"

Ta-Kumsaw glowered. "Never say that name, that unbearable name."

"Not saying it won't make him go away."

"It will keep his evil out of this house," said Ta-Kumsaw. "Away from the people I love."

In the meantime, Becca had finished dressing. She came to the boy and bumped him with her hip. "Move over, stubby-fingers. That's my loom you're tangling."

"Tightest weave ever," the boy retorted. "People will always know which spots I wove."

Becca settled onto the chair and then began to make the shuttle-cock dance. The whole music of the loom changed, the rhythm of it, the song. "You came for a purpose, Maker? The door's still open for you. Do what you came to do."

For the first time Peggy really looked at the door, trying to see what lay beyond it; and what lay beyond was nothing. Not blackness, but not daylight either. Just . . . nothing. Her eyes couldn't look at it; her gaze kept shifting away.

"Alvin," she said. "Are you sure you want to—"

He kissed her. "I love it when you worry about me."

She smiled and kissed him back. As he took off his cap and his boots, and his long coat that might flap against the doorjamb, he couldn't see how she reached into the small box she kept in a pocket of her skirt; how she held the last scrap of his birth caul between her fingers and then watched his heartfire, ready to spring into action the moment he needed her, to use his power to heal him even if he, in some dire extremity, could not or dared not or would not use it himself.

He ran for the door, leapt toward it left-foot-first, his right foot leaving the ground before any part of him broke the plane of the door. He sailed through with his head ducked down; he missed the top of the door by an inch.

"I don't like it when people leap through all spread out like that," said Ta-Kumsaw. "Better to spring from both feet at once, and curl up into a ball as you go."

"You athletic men can do that," said Becca. "But I can't see myself hitting the floor like that and rolling. Besides, you leap half the time yourself."

"I'm not as tall as Alvin," said Ta-Kumsaw. He turned to Peggy. "He grew to be very tall."

But Peggy didn't answer him.

"She's watching his heartfire," said Becca. "Best leave her alone till he comes back."

Alvin tumbled and fell when he hit the floor on the other side; he sprawled into a pile of cloth and heard the sound of laughter. He got up and looked around. Another cabin, but a newish one, and the girl at the loom was scarcely older than he was. She was a mixup like Arthur, only half-Red instead of half-Black, and the combination of Ta-Kumsaw and Becca was becoming in her.

"Howdy, Alvin," she said. He had expected her voice to sound like Ta-Kumsaw's and Tenskwa-Tawa's, accented when she spoke in English, but she spoke like Becca, a bit old-fashioned sounding but like a native speaker of the tongue.

"Howdy," he said.

"You sure came through like a ton of bricks," she said.

"Made a mess of the piles of cloth here."

"Don't fret," she said. "That's why they're there. Papa always smacks into them when he comes through like a cannonball."

With that he ran out of conversation, and so did she, so he stood there watching as she ran her loom.

"Go find Tenskwa-Tawa. He's waiting for you."

Alvin had heard so much about the fog on the Mizzipy that he had halfway got it into his head that the whole of the western lands was covered with fog. When he opened the cabin and stepped outside, though, he found that far from being foggy, the sky was so clear it felt like he could see clear into heaven in broad daylight. There were high mountains looming to the east, and he could see them so crisp and clear that he felt as though he could trace the crevices in the bare granite near the top, or count the leaves on the oak trees halfway up their craggy flanks. The cabin stood at the brow of a hill separating two valleys, both of which contained lakes. The one to the north was huge, the far reaches of it invisible because of the curve of the Earth, not because of any haze or thickness of the air; the lake to the south was smaller, but it was even more beautiful, shining like a blue jewel in the cold sunlight of late autumn.

"The snow is late," said a voice behind him.

Alvin turned. "Shining Man," he said, the name slipping from his lips before he could think.

"And you are the man who learned how to be a man when he was a boy," said Tenskwa-Tawa.

They embraced. The wind whistled around them. When they parted, Alvin glanced around again. "This is a pretty exposed place to build a cabin," he said.

"Had to be here," said Tenskwa-Tawa. "The valley to the south is Timpa-Nogos. Holy ground, where there can be no houses and no wars. The valley to the north is grazing land, where the deer can be hunted by families that run out of food in the winter. No houses either. Don't worry. Inside a weaver's house is always warm." He smiled. "I'm glad to see you."

Alvin wasn't sure if he could remember Tenskwa-Tawa ever smiling before. "You're happy here?"

"Happy?" Tenskwa-Tawa's face went placid again. "I feel as though I stand with one foot on this earth and the other foot in the place where my people wait for me."

"Not all died that day at Tippy-Canoe," said Alvin. "You still have people here."

"They also stand with one foot in one place, one foot in the other." He glanced toward a canyon that led up into a gap between the impossibly high mountains. "They live in a high mountain valley. The snow is late this year, and they're glad of that, unless it means poor water for next year, and a poor crop. That's our life now, Alvin Maker. We used to live in a place where water leapt out of the ground wherever you struck it with a stick."

"But the air is clear. You can see forever."

Tenskwa-Tawa put his fingers to Alvin's lips. "No man sees forever. But some men see farther. Last winter I rode a tower of water into the sky over the holy lake Timpa-Nogos. I saw many things. I saw you come here. I heard the news you told me and the question you asked me."

"And did you hear your answer?"

"First you must make my vision come true," said Tenskwa-Tawa.

So Alvin told him about Harrison being elected president by bragging about his bloody hands, and how they wondered if Tenskwa-Tawa might release the people of Vigor Church from their curse, so they could leave their homes, those as wanted to, and become part of the Crystal City when Alvin started to build it. "Was that what you heard me ask you?"

"Yes," said Tenskwa-Tawa.

"And what was your answer?"

"I didn't see my answer," said Tenskwa-Tawa. "So I have had all these months to think of what it was. In all these months, my people who died on that grassy slope have walked before my eyes in my sleep. I have seen their blood again and again flow down the grass and turn the Tippy-Canoe Creek red. I have seen the faces of the children and babies. I knew them all by name, and I still remember all the names and all the faces. Each one I see in the dream, I ask them, Do you forgive these White murderers? Do you understand their rage and will you let me take your blood from their hands?"

Tenskwa-Tawa paused. Alvin waited, too. One did not rush a shaman as he told of his dreams.

"Every night I have had this dream until finally last night the last of them came before me and I asked my question."

Again, a silence. Again, Alvin waited patiently. Not patiently the way a White man waits, showing his patience by looking around or moving his fingers or doing something else to mark the passage of time. Alvin waited with a Red man's patience, as if this moment were to be savored in itself, as if the suspense of waiting was in itself an experience to be marked and remembered.

"If even one of them had said, I do not forgive them, do not lift the curse, then I would not lift the curse," said Tenskwa-Tawa. "If even one baby had said, I do not forgive them for taking away my days of running like a deer through the meadows, I would not lift the curse. If even one mother had said, I do not forgive them for the baby that was in my womb when I died, who never saw the light of day with its beautiful eyes, I would not lift the curse. If even one father had said, The anger still runs hot in my heart, and if you lift the curse I will still have some hatred left unavenged, then I would not lift the curse."

Tears flowed down Alvin's face, for he knew the answer now, and he could not imagine himself ever being so good that even in death he could forgive those who had done such a terrible thing to him and his family.

"I also asked the living," said Tenskwa-Tawa. "Those who lost father and mother, brother and sister, uncle and aunt, child and friend, teacher and helper, hunting companion, and wife, and husband. If even one of these living ones had said, I cannot forgive them yet, Tenskwa-Tawa, I would not lift the curse."

Then he fell silent one last time. This time the silence lasted and lasted. The sun had been at noon when Alvin arrived; it was touching the tops of the mountains to the west when at last Tenskwa-Tawa moved again, nodding his head. Like Alvin, he, too, had wept, and then had waited long enough for the tears to dry, and then had wept again, all without changing the expression on his face, all without moving a muscle of his body as the two of them sat facing each other in the tall dry autumn grass, in the cold dry autumn wind. Now he opened his mouth and spoke again. "I have lifted the curse," he said.

Alvin embraced his old teacher. It was not what a Red man would have done, but Alvin had acted Red all afternoon, and so Tenskwa-Tawa accepted the gesture and even returned it. Touched by the Red Prophet's hands, his cheek against the old man's hair, the old man's face against his shoulder, Alvin remembered that once he had thought of asking Tenskwa-Tawa to strengthen the curse on Harrison, to stop him from misusing his bloody hands. It made him ashamed. If the dead could forgive, should not the living? Harrison would find his own way through life, and his own path to death. Judgment would have to come, if it came at all, from someone wiser than Alvin.

When they arose from the grass, Tenskwa-Tawa looked north toward the larger lake. "Look, a man is coming."

Alvin saw where he was looking. Not far off, a man was jogging lightly along a path through the head-high grass. Not running in the Red man's way, but like a White man, and not a young one. His hatless bald head glinted momentarily in the sunset.

"That ain't Taleswapper, is it?" asked Alvin.

"The Sho-sho-nay invited him to come and trade stories with them," said Tenskwa-Tawa.

Instead of asking more questions, Alvin waited with Tenskwa-Tawa until Taleswapper came up the long steep path. He was out of breath when he arrived, as might have been expected. But as Alvin sent his doodlebug through Taleswapper's body, he was surprised at the old man's excellent health. They greeted each other warmly, and Alvin told him the news. Taleswapper smiled at Tenskwa-Tawa. "Your people are better than you thought they were," he said.

"Or more forgetful," said Tenskwa-Tawa ruefully.

"I'm glad I happened to be here, to hear this news," said Taleswapper. "If you're going back through the weaver's house, I'd like to go with you."

When Alvin and Taleswapper returned to Becca's cabin within the heart of the weaver's house, it had been dark for two hours. Ta-Kumsaw had gone outside and invited Peggy's and Alvin's friends to come in and eat with his family. Becca's sister and her daughters and her son joined them; they ate a stew of bison meat, Red man's food cooked the White man's way, a compromise like so much else in this house. Ta-Kumsaw had introduced himself by the name of Isaac Weaver, and Peggy was careful to call him by no other name.

Alvin and Taleswapper found them all lying on their bedrolls on the floor of the parlor, except for Peggy, who was sitting on a chair, listening as Verily Cooper told them tales of his life in England, and all the subterfuges he had gone through in order to conceal his knack from everyone. She turned to face the door before her husband and their old friend came through it; the others also turned, so all eyes were on them. They knew at once from the joy on Alvin's face what Tenskwa-Tawa's answer had been.

"I want to ride out tonight and tell them," said Armor-of-God. "I want them to know the good news right *now*."

"Too dark," said Ta-Kumsaw, who came in from the kitchen where he had been helping his sister-in-law wash the dishes from supper.

"There's no more rules, now, the curse is lifted free and clear," said Alvin. "But he asks that we do something all the same. That everyone who used to be under the curse gather their family together once a year, on the anniversary of the massacre at Tippy-Canoe, and on that day eat no food, but instead tell the story as it used to be told to all strangers who came through Vigor Church. Once a year, our children and our children's children, forever. He asks that we do that, but there'll be no punishment if we don't. No punishment except that our children will forget, and when they forget, there's always the chance that it might happen again."

"I'll tell them that too," said Armor. "They'll all take a vow to do that, you can be sure, Alvin." He turned to Ta-Kumsaw. "You can tell your brother that for me when next you see him, that they'll all take that vow."

Ta-Kumsaw grunted. "So much for calling myself Isaac in order to conceal from you who I really am."

"We've met before," said Armor, "and even if we hadn't, I know a great leader when I see one, and I knew who it was Alvin came to see."

"You talk too much, Armor-of-God, like all White men," said Ta-Kumsaw. "But at least what you say isn't always stupid."

Armor nodded and smiled to acknowledge the compliment.

Alvin and Peggy were given a bedroom and a fine bed, which Peggy suspected was Ta-Kumsaw's and Becca's own. The others slept on the floor in the parlor—slept as best they could, which wasn't well, what with all the excitement and the way Mike Fink snored so loud and the way Armor had to get up to pee about three times an hour it seemed like, till Peggy heard the activity, woke Alvin up, and Alvin *did* something with his doodlebug inside Armor's body so he didn't feel like his bladder was about to bust all the time. When morning came the men in the parlor slept a little late, and woke to the smell of a country breakfast, with biscuits and gravy and slabs of salted ham fried with potatoes.

Then it was time for parting. Armor-of-God was like an eager horse himself, stamping and snorting till they finally told him to go *on*. He mounted and rode out of Chapman Valley, waving his hat and whooping like those damn fools on election night the week before.

Alvin's and Peggy's parting was harder. She and Taleswapper would take Whitley Physicker's carriage and drive it to the next town of any size, where she'd hire another carriage and Taleswapper would drive this one north to Hatrack River to return it to the good doctor. From there Peggy intended to go to Philadelphia for a while. "I hope that I might turn some hearts against Harrison's plans, if I'm there where Congress meets. He's only going to be president, not king, not emperor—he has to win the consent of Congress to do anything, and perhaps there's still hope." But Alvin knew from her voice that she had little hope, that she knew already along what dark roads Harrison would lead the country.

Alvin felt nearly as bleak about his own prospects. "Tenskwa-Tawa couldn't tell me a thing about how to make the Crystal City, except to say a thing I already knew: The Maker is a part of what he Makes."

"So . . . you will search," said Peggy, "and I will search."

What neither of them said, because both of them knew that they both knew, was that there was a child growing already in Margaret's womb; a girl. Each of them could calculate nine months as well as the other.

"Where will you be next August?" asked Alvin.

"Wherever I am, I'll make quite sure you know about it."

"And wherever you are, I'll make quite sure I'm there."

"I think the name should be Becca," said Peggy.

"I was thinking to call her after you. Call her Little Peggy."

Peggy smiled. "Becca Margaret, then?"

Alvin smiled back, and kissed her. "People talk about fools counting chickens before they hatch. That's nothing. We name them."

He helped her up into the carriage, beside Taleswapper, who already had the reins in hand. Arthur Stuart led Alvin's horse to him, and as he mounted, the boy said, "We made up a song about us last night, while you two was upstairs!"

"A song?" said Alvin. "Let's hear it then."

"We made it up like as if it was you singing it," said Arthur Stuart. "Come on, you all got to sing! And at the end I made up a chorus all by myself, I made up the last part *alone* without *no help* from *nobody*."

Alvin reached down and hauled the boy up behind him. Arthur Stuart's arms went around his middle. "Come on," the boy shouted. "Let's all sing."

As they began the song, Alvin reached down and took hold of the

harness of the carriage's lead horse, starting the parade up the road
leading out of Chapman Valley.

> *A young man startin' on his own*
> *Must leave his home so fair.*
> *Better not go wand'rin' all alone*
> *Or you might get eaten by a bear!*
>
> *I'm wise enough to heed that song,*
> *But who'll make up my pair?*
> *If I choose my boon companion wrong*
> *Then I might get eaten by a bear!*
>
> *I'll take a certain mixup lad—*
> *He's small, but does his share—*
> *And I'll watch him close, cause I'd be sad*
> *If the boy got eaten by a bear!*
>
> *I'll take along this barrister*
> *With lofty learned air,*
> *And I'll make of him a forester*
> *So he won't get eaten by a bear!*
>
> *Behold this noble river rat*
> *With brag so fine and rare!*
> *He's as dangerous as a mountain cat—*
> *He will not get eaten by a bear!*
>
> *Now off we go, where'er we please.*
> *We're heroes, so we dare*
> *To defy mosquitoes, wasps, and fleas,*
> *And we won't get eaten by a bear!*

They reached the main road and Peggy turned right, heading
north, while the men took their horses south. She waved from the
driver's seat, but did not look back. Alvin stopped to watch her, just
for a moment, just for a lingering moment, as Arthur Stuart behind
him shouted, "Now I get to sing the last part that I made up all by
myself! I get to!"

"So sing it," said Alvin.

So Arthur Stuart sang.

Grizzly bear, grizzly bear,
Run and hide, you sizzly bear!
We'll take away your coat of hair
And roast you in your underwear!

Alvin laughed till tears streamed down his face.

19

Philadelphia

When Calvin's and Honoré's ship arrived in New Amsterdam, the newspapers were full of chat about the inauguration, which was only a week away in Philadelphia. Calvin remembered Harrison's name at once—how many times had he listened to the tale of the massacre at Tippy-Canoe? He remembered meeting the bloody-handed bum on the streets of New Amsterdam, and told the tale to Honoré.

"So you created him."

"I helped him make the best of his limited possibilities," said Calvin.

"No, no," said Honoré. "You are too modest. This man created himself as a monster who killed people for political gain. Then this Red prophet destroyed him with a curse. Then, from the hopeless ruin of his life, you turned his path upward again. Calvin, you finally impress me. You have achieved, in life, that infinite power which is usually reserved to the novelist."

"The power to use up enormous amounts of paper and ink to no avail?"

"The power to make people's lives take the most illogical turns. Parents, for instance, have no such power. They can help their children along, or, more likely, shatter their lives as someone's mother once did with her casual adultery even as she abandoned her child to the tender mercies of the boarding school. But such parents have no power then to heal the child they have injured. Having brought the child low, they cannot raise the child up. But *I* can bring a man low, then raise him up, then bring him low again, all with a stroke of the pen.''

"And so can I," said Calvin thoughtfully.

"Well, to a degree," said Honoré. "To be honest, however, you did not bring him low, and now, having raised him up, I doubt you can bring him low again. The man has been elected president, even if his domain consists primarily of trees and tree-dwelling beasts.''

"There's several million people in the United States," said Calvin.

"It was to them that I referred," said Honoré.

The challenge was too much for Calvin to resist. Could he bring down the president of the United States? How would he do it? This time there could be no scornful words that would provoke him into self-destruction, as Calvin's words had helped the man resurrect himself from shameful oblivion. But then, Calvin had learned to do much more subtle things than mere talk in the many months since then. It would be a challenge. It was almost a dare.

"Let's go to Philadelphia," said Calvin. "For the inauguration.''

Honoré was perfectly happy to board the train and go along. He was amused by the size and newness of the tiny towns that Americans referred to as "cities," and Calvin constantly had to watch out for him as he practiced his feeble English with the kind of rough American who was likely to pick up the little Frenchman and toss him into a river. Honoré, armed only with an ornate cane he had purchased from a fellow-voyager, had fearlessly walked through the most wretched immigrant districts of New Amsterdam and now of Philadelphia. "These men aren't characters in novels," said Calvin, more than once. "If they break your neck, it'll really be broken!''

"Then you'll have to fix me, my talented knackish friend." He said the word *knackish* in English, though truth to tell no one would have understood the word but Calvin himself.

"There's no such word as *knackish* in the English language," Calvin said.

"There is now," said Honoré, "because I put it there.''

As Calvin awaited the inauguration, he considered many possible plans. Nothing with mere words would do the job. Harrison's election had been so openly based on lies that it was hard to imagine how anything could now be revealed about Harrison that would shock or disappoint anyone. When the people elected a president like this one, who ran a campaign like the one he ran, it was hard to imagine what kind of scandal might bring him down.

Besides, Calvin's knack was now way beyond words. He wanted to get inside Harrison's body and do some mischief. He remembered Napoleon and how he suffered from the gout; he toyed with the idea of giving Harrison some debilitating condition. Regretfully he concluded that this was beyond his power, to fine-tune such a thing so that it would cause pain without killing. No doubt Calvin would have to wait around to watch, to make sure that whatever he did wasn't cured. And besides, pain wouldn't bring Harrison low any more than gout had stopped Napoleon from fulfilling all his ambitions.

Pain without killing. Why had he put such a ridiculous limitation on himself? There was no reason not to kill Harrison. Hadn't the man ordered the death of Calvin's own brother Measure? Hadn't he slaughtered all those Reds and caused all of Calvin's family and neighbors to be under a curse for most of Calvin's life? Nothing brought a man lower than dying. Six feet under the ground, that was as low as a body ever got.

The day of the inauguration, the first day of the new year, was bitterly cold, and as Harrison walked through the streets of Philadelphia to the temporary stand where he would take the oath in front of several thousand spectators, it began to snow. Proudly he refused even to put on a hat—what was cold weather to a man from the west?—and when he reached the platform to give his speech, Calvin was delighted to see that the new president's throat was already sore, his chest already somewhat congested. It was really a simple matter of Calvin to send his doodling bug inside the chest of White Murderer Harrison and encourage the little animals inside his lungs to grow, to multiply, to spread throughout his body. Harrison, you're going to be one very, very sick man.

The speech lasted an hour, and Harrison didn't cut out a single word, though by the end he was coughing thickly into his handkerchief after every sentence. "Philadelphia is colder to hell," Honoré said in his feeble English as they finally left the square. "And your President he is one dammit long talker." Then, in French, Honoré asked, "Did I say it right? Did I swear properly?"

"Like a stevedore," said Calvin. "Like a river rat. I was proud of you."

"I was proud of you too," said Honoré. "You looked so serious, I thought maybe you were paying attention to his speech. Then I thought, No, the lad is using his powers. So I hoped you might sever his head as he stood there and make it roll down splat on his speech. Let him put his hands on *that* to take his oath of office."

"That would have been a memorable inauguration," said Calvin.

"But it wouldn't be good for you to take another man's life," said Honoré. "All joking aside, my friend, it isn't good for a man to get a taste for blood."

"My brother Alvin killed a man," said Calvin. "He killed a man who needed killing, and nobody said boo to him about it."

"Dangerous for him, but perhaps more dangerous for you," said Honoré. "Because you are already filled with hate—I say this not as criticism, it's one of the things I find most attractive about you— you are filled with hate, and so it is dangerous for you to open the faucet of murder. That is a stream you may not be able to damp."

"Not to worry," said Calvin.

They lingered in Philadelphia for several more weeks, as Harrison's bad cold turned into pneumonia. He struggled on, being something of a tough old nut, but in the end he died, scarcely a month after his inauguration, having never been healthy enough even to name a cabinet.

This being the first time a president of the United States had died in office, there was some unresolved ambiguity in the Constitution about whether the vice-president merely acted as president or actually took the office. Andrew Jackson neatly resolved the issue by walking into Congress and placing his hand on the Bible they kept there as a reminder of all the virtues they worked so hard to get the voters to believe they possessed. In a loud voice he took the oath of office in front of all of them, daring them to deny him the right to do so. There were jokes about "His Accidency the President" for a while, but Jackson wasn't a man to be trifled with. All of Harrison's cronies found themselves with sore backsides from bouncing down the steps of the George Washington Building where the executive branch of the government had its offices. Whatever Harrison had planned for America would never happen now, or at least not in the way that he had planned it. Jackson was in nobody's pocket but his own.

Calvin and Honoré agreed that they had done a great service for the nation. "Though my part of it was very small," said Honoré. "A mere word. A suggestion." Calvin knew, however, that in his own heart Honoré undoubtedly took credit for the whole thing, or at least for everything beneficial that resulted from it. That knowledge scarcely bothered Calvin, though. Nothing really bothered him now, for his power had been confirmed in his own heart. I brought down a president and no one knew that I did it. Nothing messy or awkward like Alvin's killing of that Finder with his own bare hands. I learned more than the honing of my knack on the continent. I acquired finesse. Alvin will never have that, crude frontiersman that he is and always will be.

How easy it had been. Easy and free of risk. There was a man who needed to die, and all it took was a little maneuvering in his lungs and it was done. Well, that plus a few adjustments as the man lay in his sickbed in the presidential mansion. It wouldn't do to have his body fight off the infection and recover, would it? But I never had to touch him. Never even had to speak to him. Didn't even have to get ink on my fingers, like poor Honoré, whose characters never really breathe despite all his skill, and so never really die.

Calvin allowed himself, on the last night he and Honoré spent in Philadelphia, to lie in bed imagining Alvin's death. A slow agonizing death from some miserable disease like lockjaw. I could do that, thought Calvin.

Then he thought, No I couldn't, and went to sleep.

Heartfire

To Mark and Margaret,
for whom all heartfires
burn bright

Acknowledgments

Several books were of incalculable value in developing the story of Alvin's search through America for patterns he might use to build a community that is both strong and free. Most important was David Hackett Fischer's *Albion's Seed: Four British Folkways in America* (Oxford University Press, 1989, 946 pp.), a brilliant, well-defended exposition of a non-reductionist theory of the origins of American culture; in its pages I found both detail and rich causal reasoning, greatly helping me take this book from plan to page. William W. Freehling's *Road to Disunion: Secessionists at Bay, 1776–1854* (Oxford University Press, 1990, 640 pp.) gave me details of life, obscure historical characters, and the economic and political realities of Charleston in the 1820s, which I could then distort into my American "Camelot." Carl J. Richard's *Founders and the Classics: Greece, Rome, and the American Enlightenment* (Harvard University Press, 1994, 295 pp.) provided me with the attitudes of educated American leaders toward the Greek and Roman classics that were a part of traditional education at the time.

As so often before, I thank Clark and Kathy Kidd for providing me with a retreat where I could jump-start this book.

Thanks also to Kathleen Bellamy and Scott J. Allen for help above and beyond the call of duty; to Jane Brady and Geoffrey Card for their collection of data from the earlier books.

As Alvin wanders through the world, it is his wife who provides his harbor; this my wife, Kristine, also provides for me. All my stories are told first to her.

Contents

1	Gooses	351
2	A Lady of the Court	371
3	Painted Birds	386
4	Stirred-Up	399
5	Purity	412
6	Names	431
7	Accusation	451
8	Basket of Souls	474
9	Witch Hunt	489
10	Captivity	511

11   Decent Men   529

12   Slaves   548

13   Judgment Day   568

14   Revolt   588

15   Fathers and Mothers   608

1

Gooses

Arthur Stuart stood at the window of the taxidermy shop, rapt. Alvin Smith was halfway down the block before he realized that Arthur was no longer with him. By the time he got back, a tall White man was questioning the boy.

"Where's your master, then?"

Arthur did not look at him, his gaze riveted on a stuffed bird, posed as if it were about to land on a branch.

"Boy, answer me, or I'll have the constable . . ."

"He's with me," said Alvin.

The man at once became friendly. "Glad to know it, friend. A boy this age, you'd think if he was free his parents would have taught him proper respect when a White man—"

"I think he only cares about the birds in the window." Alvin laid a gentle hand on Arthur's shoulder. "What is it, Arthur Stuart?"

Only the sound of Alvin's voice could draw Arthur out of his reverie. "How did he see?"

"Who?" asked the man.

"See what?" asked Alvin.

"The way the bird pushes down with his wings just before roosting, and then poses like a statue. Nobody sees that."

"What's the boy talking about?" asked the man.

"He's a great observer of birds," said Alvin. "I think he's admiring the taxidermy work in the window."

The man beamed with pride. "I'm the taxidermist here. Almost all of those are mine."

Arthur finally responded to the taxidermist. "Most of these are just dead birds. They looked more alive when they lay bloody in the field where the shotgun brought them down. But this one. And that one. . . ." He pointed to a hawk, stooping. "Those were done by someone who knew the living bird."

The taxidermist glowered for a moment, then put on a tradesman's smile. "Do you like those? The work of a French fellow goes by the name 'John-James.' " He said the double name as if it were a joke. "Journeyman work, is all. Those delicate poses—I doubt the wires will hold up over time."

Alvin smiled at the man. "I'm a journeyman myself, but I do work that lasts."

"No offense meant," the taxidermist said at once. But he also seemed to have lost interest, for if Alvin was merely a journeyman in some trade, he wouldn't have enough money to buy anything; nor would an itinerant workman have much use for stuffed animals.

"So you sell this Frenchman's work for less?" asked Alvin.

The taxidermist hesitated. "More, actually."

"The price falls when it's done by the master?" asked Alvin innocently.

The taxidermist glared at him. "I sell his work on consignment, and he sets the price. I doubt anyone will buy it. But the fellow fancies himself an artist. He only stuffs and mounts the birds so he can paint pictures of them, and when he's done painting, he sells the bird itself."

"He'd be better to talk to the bird instead of killing it," said Arthur Stuart. "They'd hold still for him to paint, a man who sees birds so true."

The taxidermist looked at Arthur Stuart oddly. "You let this boy talk a bit forward, don't you?"

"In Philadelphia I thought all folks could talk plain," said Alvin, smiling.

The taxidermist finally understood just how deeply Alvin was mocking him. "I'm not a Quaker, my man, and neither are you."

With that he turned his back on Alvin and Arthur and returned to his store. Through the window Alvin could see him sulking, casting sidelong glances at them now and then.

"Come on, Arthur Stuart, let's go meet Verily and Mike for dinner."

Arthur took one step, but still couldn't tear his gaze from the roosting bird.

"Arthur, before the fellow comes out and orders us to move along."

Even with that, Alvin finally had to take Arthur by the hand and near drag him away. And as they walked, Arthur had an inward look to him. "What are you brooding about?" asked Alvin.

"I want to talk to that Frenchman. I have a question to ask him."

Alvin knew better than to ask Arthur Stuart what the question was. It would spare him hearing Arthur's inevitable reply: "Why should I ask *you*? *You* don't know."

Verily Cooper and Mike Fink were already eating when Alvin and Arthur got to the rooming house. The proprietor was a Quaker woman of astonishing girth and very limited talents as a cook—but she made up for the blandness of her food with the quantities she served, and more important was the fact that, being a Quaker in more than name, Mistress Louder made no distinction between half-Black Arthur Stuart and the three White men traveling with him. Arthur Stuart sat at the same table as the others, and even though one roomer moved out the day Arthur Stuart first sat at table, she never acted as if she even noticed the fellow was gone. Which was why Alvin tried to make up for it by taking Arthur Stuart with him on daily forays out into the woods and meadows along the river to gather wild ginger, wintergreen, spearmint, and thyme to spice up her cooking. She took the herbs, with their implied criticism of her kitchen, in good humor, and tonight the potatoes had been boiled with the wintergreen they brought her yesterday.

"Edible?" she asked Alvin as he took his first bite.

Verily was the one who answered, while Alvin savored the mouthful with a beatific expression on his face. "Madame, your generosity guarantees you will go to heaven, but it's the flavor of tonight's potatoes that assures you will be asked to cook there."

She laughed and made as if to hit him with a spoon. "Verily Cooper, thou smooth-tongued lawyer, knowest thou not that Quakers have no truck with flattery?" But they all knew that while she didn't believe the flattery, she did believe the warmheartedness behind it.

While the other roomers were still at table, Mike Fink regaled them all with the tale of his visit to the Simple House, where Andrew Jackson was scandalizing the elite of Philadelphia by bringing his cronies from Tennizy and Kenituck, letting them chew and spit in rooms that once offered homesick European ambassadors a touch of the elegance of the old country. Fink repeated a tale that Jackson himself told that very day, about a fine Philadelphia lady who criticized the behavior of his companions. "This is the Simple House," Jackson declared, "and these are simple people." When the lady tried to refute the point, Jackson told her, "This is *my* house for the next four years, and these are my friends."

"But they have no manners," said the lady.

"They have excellent manners," said Jackson. "Western manners. But they're tolerant folks. They'll overlook the fact that you ain't took a bite of food yet, nor drunk any good corn liquor, nor spat once even though you always look like you got a mouth full of *somethin'*." Mike Fink laughed long and hard at this, and so did the roomers, though some were laughing at the lady and some were laughing at Jackson.

Arthur Stuart asked a question that was bothering Alvin. "How does Andy Jackson get anything done, if the Simple House is full of river rats and bumpkins all day?"

"He needs something done, why, one of us river rats went and done it for him," said Mike.

"But most rivermen can't read or write," Arthur said.

"Well, Old Hickory can do all the readin' and writin' for his-self," said Mike. "He sends the river rats to deliver messages and persuade people."

"Persuade people?" asked Alvin. "I hope they don't use the methods of persuasion you once tried on *me*."

Mike whooped at that. "Iffen Old Hickory let the boys do *those* old tricks, I don't think there'd be six noses left in Congress, nor twenty ears!"

Finally, though, the tales of the frolicking at the Simple House—or degradation, depending on your point of view—wound down and the other roomers left. Only Alvin and Arthur, as latecomers, were still eating as they made their serious reports on the day's work.

Mike shook his head sadly when Alvin asked him if he'd had a chance to talk to Andy Jackson. "Oh, he included me in the room, if that's what you mean. But talking alone, no, not likely. See, Andy Jackson may be a lawyer but he knows river rats, and my name rang a bell with him. Haven't lived down my old reputation yet, Alvin. Sorry.''

Alvin smiled and waved off the apology. "There'll come a day when the president will meet with us.''

"It was premature, anyway,'' said Verily. "Why try for a land grant when we don't even know what we're going to use it for?''

"Do so,'' said Alvin, playing at a children's quarrel.

"Do not,'' said Verily, grinning.

"We got a city to build.''

"No sir,'' said Verily. "We have the *name* of a city, but we don't have the *plan* of a city, or even the idea of the city—''

"It's a city of Makers!''

"Well, it would have been nice if the Red Prophet had told you what that means,'' said Verily.

"He showed it to me inside the waterspout,'' said Alvin. "He doesn't know what it means any more than I do. But we both saw it, a city made of glass, filled with people, and the city itself taught them everything.''

"Amid all that seeing,'' said Verily, "did you perhaps hear a hint of what we're supposed to tell people to persuade them to come and help us build it?''

"I take it that means you didn't accomplish what you set out to do, either,'' said Alvin.

"Oh, I perused the Congressional Library,'' said Verily. "Found many references to the Crystal City, but most of them were tied up with Spanish explorers who thought it had something to do with the fountain of youth or the Seven Cities of the Onion.''

"Onion?'' asked Arthur Stuart.

"One of the sources misheard the Indian name 'Cibola' as a Spanish word for 'onion,' and I thought it was funny,'' said Verily. "All dead ends. But there *is* an interesting datum that I can't readily construe.''

"Wouldn't want to have anything constroodled redly,'' said Alvin.

"Don't play frontiersman with me,'' said Verily. "Your wife was a better schoolteacher than to leave you that ignorant.''

"You two leave off teasing,'' demanded Arthur Stuart. "What did you find out?''

"There's a post office in a place that calls itself Crystal City in the state of Tennizy.''

"There's probably a place called Fountain of Youth, too,'' said Alvin.

"Well, I thought it was interesting," said Verily.

"Know anything else about it?"

"Postmaster's a Mr. Crawford, who also has the titles Mayor and—I think you'll like this, Alvin—White Prophet."

Mike Fink laughed, but Alvin didn't like it. "White Prophet. As if to set himself against Tenskwa-Tawa?"

"I just told you all I know," said Verily. "Now, what did *you* accomplish?"

"I've been in Philadelphia for two weeks and I haven't accomplished a thing," said Alvin. "I thought the city of Benjamin Franklin would have something to teach me. But Franklin's dead, and there's no special music in the street, no wisdom lingering around his grave. Here's where America was born, boys, but I don't think it lives here anymore. America lives out there where I grew up— what we got in Philadelphia now is just the *government* of America. Like finding fresh dung on the road. It ain't a horse, but it tells you a horse is somewhere nearby."

"It took you two weeks in Philadelphia to find *that* out?" said Mike Fink.

Verily joined in. "My father always said that government is like watching another man piss in your boot. Someone feels better but it certainly isn't you."

"If we can take a break from all of this philosophy," said Alvin, "I got a letter from Margaret." He was the only one who called his wife by that name—everyone else called her Peggy. "From Camelot."

"She's not in Appalachee anymore?" asked Mike Fink.

"All the agitation for keeping slavery in Appalachee is coming from the Crown Colonies," said Alvin, "so there she went."

"King ain't about to let Appalachee close off slavery, I reckon," said Mike Fink.

"I thought they already settled Appalachee independence with a war back in the last century," said Verily.

"I reckon some folks think they need another war to settle whether Black people can be free," said Alvin. "So Margaret's in Camelot, hoping to get an audience with the King and plead the cause of peace and freedom."

"The only time a nation ever has both at the same time," said Verily, "is during that brief period of exhilarated exhaustion after winning a war."

"You're sure grim for a man what's never even killed anybody," said Mike Fink.

"Iffen Miz Larner wants to talk to Arthur Stuart, I'm right here," said Arthur with a grin. Mike Fink made a show of slapping him upside the head. Arthur laughed—it was his favorite joke these days, that he'd been given the same name as the King of England, who ruled in exile in the slave shires of the South.

"And she also has reason to believe that my younger brother is there," said Alvin.

At that news Verily angrily looked down and played with the last scraps of food on his plate, while Mike Fink stared off into space. They both had their opinions of Alvin's little brother.

"Well, I don't know," said Alvin.

"Don't know what?" asked Verily.

"Whether to go there and join her. She told me not to, of course, because she has some idea that when Calvin and I get together, then I'll die."

Mike grinned nastily. "I don't care what that boy's knack is, I'd like to see him try."

"Margaret never said he'd kill me," said Alvin. "In fact she never said I'd die, exactly. But that's what I gather. She doesn't want me there until she can assure me that Calvin is out of town. But I'd like to meet the King my own self."

"Not to mention seeing your wife," said Verily.

"I could use a few days with her."

"And nights," murmured Mike.

Alvin raised an eyebrow at him and Mike grinned stupidly.

"Biggest question is," Alvin went on, "could I safely take Arthur Stuart down there? In the Crown Colonies it's illegal to bring a free person of even one-sixteenth Black blood into the country."

"You could pretend he's your slave," said Mike.

"But what if I died down there? Or got arrested? I don't want any chance of Arthur getting confiscated and sold away. It's too dangerous."

"So don't go there," said Verily. "The King doesn't know a thing about building the Crystal City, anyway."

"I know," said Alvin. "But neither do I, and neither does anyone else."

Verily smiled. "Maybe that's not true."

Alvin was impatient. "Don't play with me, Verily. What do you know?"

"Nothing but what you already know yourself, Alvin. There's two parts to building the Crystal City. The first part is about Makering and all that. And I'm no help to you there, nor is any mortal soul, as far as I can see. But the second part is the word *city*. No matter what else you do, it'll be a place where people have to live together. That means there's got to be government and laws.''

"Does there *have* to be?'' asked Mike wistfully.

"Or something to do the same jobs,'' said Verily. "And land, divided up so people can live. Food planted and harvested, or brought in to feed the population. Dry goods to make or buy, houses to build, clothes to make. There'll be marrying and giving in marriage, unless I'm mistaken, and people will have children so we'll need schools. No matter how visionary this city makes the people, they still need roofs and roads, unless you expect them all to fly.''

Alvin leaned back in his chair with his eyes closed.

"Have I put you to sleep, or are you thinking?'' asked Verily.

Alvin didn't open his eyes when he answered. "I'm just thinking that I really don't know a blame thing about what I'm doing. White Murderer Harrison may have been the lowest man I ever knowed, but at least he could build a city in the wilderness.''

"It's easy to build a city when you arrange the rules so that bad men can get rich without getting caught,'' said Verily. "You build such a place and greed will bring you your citizens, if you can stand to live with them.''

"It ought to be possible to do the same for decent folks,'' said Alvin.

"It ought to be and is,'' said Verily. "It's been done, and you can learn from the way they did it.''

"Who?'' asked Mike Fink. "I never heard of such a town.''

"A hundred towns at least,'' said Verily. "I'm speaking of New England, of course. Massachusetts most particularly. Founded by Puritans to be their Zion, a land of pure religion across the western ocean. All my life, growing up in England, I heard about how perfect New England was, how pure and godly, where there were neither rich nor poor, but all partakers of the heavenly gift, and where they were free of distraction from the world. They live in peace and equity, in the land most just of all that have ever existed on God's Earth.''

Alvin shook his head. "Verily, if Arthur can't go to Camelot, it's a sure bet you and I can't go to New England.''

"There's no slavery there,'' said Verily.

"You know what I mean,'' said Alvin. "They hang witches.''

"I'm no witch,'' said Verily. "Nor are you.''

"By their lights we are.''

"Only if we do any hexery or use hidden powers,'' said Verily.

"Surely we can restrain ourselves long enough to learn how they created such a large country free of strife and oppression, and filled with the love of God."

"Dangerous," said Alvin.

"I agree," said Mike. "We'd be insane to go there. Isn't that where that lawyer fellow Daniel Webster came from? He'll know about you, Alvin."

"He's in Carthage City making money from corrupt men," said Alvin.

"Last you heard of him, maybe," said Mike. "But he can write letters. He can come home. Things can go wrong."

Arthur Stuart looked up at Mike Fink. "Things can go wrong lying in your own bed on Sunday."

Alvin at last opened his eyes. "I have to learn. Verily's right. It's not enough to learn Makering. I have to learn governing, too, and city building, and everything else. I have to learn everything about everything, and I'm just getting farther behind the longer I sit here."

Arthur Stuart looked glum. "So I'm never going to meet the King."

"Far as I'm concerned," said Mike Fink, "you *are* the real Arthur Stuart, and you've got as much right as he has to be king in this land."

"I want him to make me a knight."

Alvin sighed. Mike rolled his eyes. Verily put a hand on Arthur's shoulder. "The day the King knights a half-Black boy . . ."

"Can't he knight the White half?" asked Arthur Stuart. "If I do something real brave? That's how a fellow gets hisself knighted, I hear."

"Definitely time to go to New England," said Alvin.

"I tell you I got misgivings," said Mike Fink.

"Me too," said Alvin. "But Verily's right. They built a good place and got good people to come to it."

"Why not go to that Tennizy place as calls itself Crystal City?" asked Mike.

"Maybe that's where we'll go after we get run out of New England," said Alvin.

Verily laughed. "You're an optimist, aren't you."

They mostly packed before they went to bed that night. Not that there was that much to put in their satchels. When a man is traveling with only a horse to carry himself and his goods, he gets a different idea of what he needs to carry from place to place than does a man riding a coach, or followed by servants and pack animals. It's not much more than a walking man would be willing to tote, lest he wear down the horse.

Alvin woke early in the morning, before dawn, but it took him no more than two breaths to notice that Arthur Stuart was gone. The window stood open, and though they were on the top floor of the house, Alvin knew that wouldn't stop Arthur Stuart, who seemed to think that gravity owed him a favor.

Alvin woke Verily and Mike, who were stirring anyway, and asked them to get the horses saddled and loaded up while he went in search of the boy.

Mike only laughed, though. "Probably found him some girl he wants to kiss good-bye."

Alvin looked at him in shock. "What are you talking about?"

Mike looked back at him, just as surprised. "Are you blind? Are you deaf? Arthur's voice is changing. He's one whisker from being a man."

"Speaking of whiskers," said Verily, "I think the shadow on his upper lip is due to become a brush pretty soon. In fact, I daresay his face grows more hair on it already than yours does, Alvin."

"I don't see your face flowing with moustachery, either," said Alvin.

"I shave," said Verily.

"But it's a long time between Christmases," said Alvin. "I'll see you before breakfast is done, I wager."

As Alvin went downstairs, he stopped into the kitchen, where Mistress Louder was rolling out the dough for morning biscuits. "You didn't happen to see Arthur Stuart this morning?" asked Alvin.

"And when wast thou planning to tell me ye were leaving?"

"When we settled up after breakfast," said Alvin. "We wasn't trying to slip out, it was no secret we were packing up."

Only then did he notice the tears running down her cheeks. "I hardly slept last night."

Alvin put his hands on her shoulders. "Mistress Louder, I never thought you'd take on so. It's a rooming house, ain't it? And roomers come and go."

She sighed loudly. "Just like children," she said.

"And don't children come back to the nest from time to time?"

"If that's a promise, I won't have to turn these into salt biscuits with my silly tears," she said.

"I can promise that I'll never pass a night in Philadelphia anywhere other than your house, lessen my wife and I settle down here someday, and then we'll send our children to your house for breakfast while we sleep lazy."

She laughed outright. "The Lord took twice the time making thee, Alvin Smith, cause it took that long to put the mischief in."

"Mischief sneaks in by itself," said Alvin. "That's its nature."

Only then did Mistress Louder remember Alvin's original question. "As for Arthur Stuart, I caught him climbing down the tree outside when I went out to bring in firewood."

"And you didn't wake me? Or stop him?"

She ignored the implied accusation. "I forced some cold johnnycake into his hands before he was out the door again. Said he had an errand to run before ye boys left this morning."

"Well, at least that sounds like he means to come back," said Alvin.

"It does," said Mistress Louder. "Though if he didn't, thou'rt not his master, I think."

"Just because he's not my property don't mean I'm not responsible for him," said Alvin.

"I wasn't speaking of the law," said Mistress Louder, "I was speaking the simple truth. He doesn't obey thee like a boy, but like a man, because he wants to please thee. He'll do nowt because thou commandest, but does it only when he agrees he ought to."

"But that's true of all men and all masters, even slaves," said Alvin.

"What I'm saying is he doesn't act in fear of thee," said Mistress Louder. "And so it won't do for thee to be hot with him when thou find him. Thou hast no right."

Only then did Alvin realize that he was a bit angry with Arthur Stuart for running off. "He's still young," said Alvin.

"And thou'rt what, a greybeard with a stoop in his back?" she laughed. "Get on and find him. Arthur Stuart never seems to know the danger a lad of his tribe faces, noon and night."

"Nor the danger that sneaks up behind," said Alvin. He kissed her cheek. "Don't let all those biscuits disappear before I get back."

"It's thy business, not mine, what time thou'lt choose to come back," she said. "Who can say how hungry the others will be this morning?"

For that remark, Alvin dipped his finger into the flour and striped her nose with it, then headed for the door. She stuck her tongue out at him but didn't wipe the flour away. "I'll be a clown if thou want me to," she called after him.

It was far too early in the morning for the shop to be open, but Alvin went straight for the taxidermist's anyway. What other business could Arthur Stuart have? Mike's guess that Arthur had found a girl was not likely to be right—the boy almost never left Alvin's side, so there'd been no chance for such a thing, even if Arthur was old enough to want to try.

The streets were crowded with farmers from the surrounding countryside, bringing their goods to market, but the shops in buildings along the streets were still closed. Paperboys and postmen made their rounds, and dairymen clattered up the alleys, stopping to leave milk in the kitchens along the way. It was noisy on the streets, but it was the fresh noise of morning. No one was shouting yet. No neighbors quarreling, no barkers selling, no driver shouting out a warning to clear the way.

No Arthur at the front door of the taxidermy shop.

But where else would he have gone? He had a question, and he wouldn't rest until he had the answer. Only it wasn't the taxidermist who had the answer, was it? It was the French painter of birds, John-James. And somewhere inside the shop, there was bound to be a note of the man's address. Would Arthur really be so foolhardy as to . . .

There was indeed an open window, with two crates on a barrel stacked beneath it. Arthur Stuart, it's no better to be taken for a burglar than to be taken for a slave.

Alvin went to the back door. He twisted the knob. It turned a little, but not enough to draw back the latch. Locked, then.

Alvin leaned against the door and closed his eyes, searching with his doodlebug till he found the heartfire inside the shop. There he was, Arthur Stuart, bright with life, hot with adventure. Like so many times before, Alvin wished he had some part of Margaret's gift, to see into the heartfire and learn something of the future and past, or even just the thoughts of the present moment—that would be convenient.

He dared not call out for Arthur—his voice would only raise an alarm and almost guarantee that Arthur would be caught inside the shop. For all Alvin knew the taxidermist lived upstairs or in an upper floor of one of the nearby buildings.

So now he put his doodlebug inside the lock, to feel out how the thing was made. An old lock, not very smooth. Alvin evened out the rough parts, peeling away corrosion and dirt. To change the shape of it was easier than moving it, so where two metal surfaces pressed flat against each other, keeping the latch from opening, Alvin changed them both to a bevel, making the metal flow into the new shapes, until the two surfaces slid easily across each other. With that he could turn the knob, and silently the latch slid free.

Still he did not open the door, for now he had to turn his attention to the hinges. They were rougher and dirtier than the lock. Did the man even use this door? Alvin smoothed and cleaned them also, and now, when he turned the knob and pushed open the door, the only sound was the whisper of the breeze passing into the shop.

Arthur Stuart sat at the taxidermist's worktable, holding a blue-jay between his hands, stroking the feathers. He looked up at Alvin and said, softly, "It isn't even dead."

Alvin touched the bird. Yes, there was some warmth, and a heartbeat. The shot that stunned it was still lodged in its skull. The brain was bruised and the bird would soon die of it, even though none of the other birdshot that had hit it would be fatal.

"Did you find what you were looking for?" asked Alvin. "The address of the painter?"

"No," said Arthur bleakly.

Alvin went to work on the bird, quickly as he could. It was more delicate than metal work, moving his doodlebug through the pathways of a living creature, making tiny alterations here and there. It helped him to hold the animal, to touch it while he worked on it. The blood in the brain was soon draining into the veins, and the damaged arteries were closed. The flesh healed rapidly under the tiny balls of lead, forcing them back out of the body. Even the ball lodged in the skull shrank, loosened, dropped out.

The jay rustled its feathers, struggled in Alvin's grasp. He let it loose.

"They'll just kill it anyway," said Alvin.

"So we'll let it out," said Arthur.

Alvin sighed. "Then we'd be thieves, wouldn't we?"

"The window's open," said Arthur. "The blue jay can leave after the man comes in this morning. So he'll think it escaped on its own."

"And how will we get the bird to do that?"

Arthur looked at him like he was an idiot, then leaned close to the bluejay, which stood still on the worktable. Arthur whispered so softly that Alvin couldn't hear the words. Then he whistled, several sharp birdlike sounds.

The jay leapt into the air and flapped noisily around the room. Alvin ducked to avoid it.

"He's not going to hit you," said Arthur, amused.

"Let's go," said Alvin.

He took Arthur through the back door. When he drew it closed, he stayed for just a moment longer, his fingers lingering on the knob, as he returned the pieces of the lock to their proper shape.

"What are you doing here!" The taxidermist stood at the turn of the alley.

"Hoping to find you in, sir," said Alvin calmly, not taking his hand off the knob.

"With your hand on the knob?" said the taxidermist, his voice icy with suspicion.

"You didn't answer to our knock," said Alvin. "I thought you might be so hard at work you didn't hear. All we want is to know where we might find the journeyman painter. The Frenchman. John-James."

"I know what you wanted," said the taxidermist. "Stand away from the door before I call the constable."

Alvin and Arthur stepped back.

"That's not good enough," said the taxidermist. "Skulking at back doors—how do I know you don't plan to knock me over the head and steal from me as soon as I have the door unlocked?"

"If that was our plan, sir," said Alvin, "you'd already be lying on the ground and I'd have the key in my hand, wouldn't I?"

"So you *did* have it all thought out!"

"Seems to me *you're* the one who has plans for robbing," said Alvin. "And then you accuse others of wanting to do what only you had thought of."

Angrily the man pulled out his key and slid it into the lock. He braced himself to twist hard, expecting the corroded metal to resist. So he visibly staggered when the key turned easily and the door slipped open silently.

He might have stopped to examine the lock and the hinges, but at that moment the bluejay that had spent the night slowly dying on his worktable fluttered angrily in his face and flew out the door. "No!" the man shouted. "That's Mr. Ridley's trophy!"

Arthur Stuart laughed. "Not much of a trophy," he said. "Not if it won't hold still."

The taxidermist stood in the doorway, looking for the bird. It was long gone. He then looked back and forth from Alvin to Arthur.

"I know you had something to do with this," he said. "I don't know what or how, but you witched up that bird."

"No such thing," said Alvin. "When I arrived here I had no idea you kept living birds inside. I thought you only dealt with dead ones."

"I do! That bird was dead!"

"John-James," said Alvin. "We want to see him before we leave town."

"Why should I help you?" said the taxidermist.

"Because we asked," said Alvin, "and it would cost you nothing."

"Cost me nothing? How am I going to explain to Mr. Ridley?"

"Tell him to make sure his birds are dead before he brings them to you," said Arthur Stuart.

"I won't have such talk from a Black boy," said the taxidermist. "If you can't control your boy, then you shouldn't bring him out among gentlemen!"

"Have I?" asked Alvin.

"Have you what?"

"Brought him out among gentlemen?" said Alvin. "I'm waiting to see the courtesy that would mark you as such a one."

The taxidermist glowered at him. "John-James Audubon is staying in a room at the Liberty Inn. But you won't find him there at this time of day—he'll be out looking at birds till midmorning."

"Then good day to you," said Alvin. "You might oil your locks and hinges from time to time. They'll stay in better condition if you do."

The taxidermist got a quizzical look on his face. He was still opening and closing his silent, smooth-hinged door as they walked back down the alley to the street.

"Well, that's that," said Alvin. "We'll never find your John-James Audubon before we have to leave."

Arthur Stuart looked at him in consternation. "And why won't we?" He whistled a couple of times and the bluejay fluttered down to alight on his shoulder. Arthur whispered and whistled for a few moments, and the bird hopped up onto Arthur's head, then (to Alvin's surprise) Alvin's shoulder, then Alvin's head, and only then launched itself into the air and flew off up the street.

"He's bound to be near the river this morning," said Arthur Stuart. "Geese are feeding there, on their way south."

Alvin looked around. "It's still summer. It's hot."

"Not up north," said Arthur Stuart. "I heard two flocks yesterday."

"I haven't heard a thing."

Arthur Stuart grinned at him.

"I thought you stopped hearing birds," said Alvin. "When I
changed you, in the river. I thought you lost all that."

Arthur Stuart shrugged. "I did. But I remembered how it felt. I
kept listening."

"It's coming back?" asked Alvin.

Arthur shook his head. "I have to figure it out. It doesn't just
come to me, the way it used to. It's not a knack anymore. It's . . ."

Alvin supplied the word. "A skill."

"I was trying to decide between 'a wish' and 'a memory.' "

"You heard geese calling, and I didn't. My ears are pretty good,
Arthur."

Arthur grinned at him again. "There's hearing and there's listening."

There were several men with shotguns stalking the geese. It was
easy enough to guess which was John-James Audubon, however.
Even if they hadn't spotted the sketchpad inside the open hunter's
sack, and even if he hadn't been oddly dressed in a Frenchman's
exaggerated version of an American frontiersman's outfit—tailored
deerskin—they would have known which hunter he was, by one
simple test: He was the only one who had actually found the geese.

He was aiming at a goose floating along the river. Without thinking, Alvin called out, "Have you no shame, Mr. Audubon?"

Audubon, startled, half-turned to look at Alvin and Arthur.
Whether it was the sudden movement or Alvin's voice, the lead
goose honked and rose dripping from the water, staggering at first
from the effort, then rising smoothly with great beats of his wings,
water trailing behind him in a silvery cascade. In a moment, all the
other geese also rose and flew down the river. Audubon raised his
shotgun, but then cursed and rounded on Alvin, the gun still leveled.
"Pour quoi, imbecile!"

"You planning to shoot me?" asked Alvin.

Reluctantly, Audubon lowered the gun and remembered his English, which at the moment wasn't very good. "I have the beautiful
creature in my eye, but you, man of the mouth open!"

"Sorry, but I couldn't believe you'd shoot a goose on the water
like that."

"Why not?"

"Because it's—not sporting."

"Of course it's not sporting!" His English was getting better as he warmed to the argument. "I'm not here for sport! Look everywhere, Monsieur, and tell me the very important thing you do *not* see."

"You got no dog," said Arthur Stuart.

"Yes! Le garçon noir comprend! I cannot shoot the bird in the air because how do I collect the bird? It falls, the wing breaks, what good is it to me now? I shoot on the water, then splash splash, I have the goose."

"Very practical," said Alvin. "*If* you were starving, and needed the goose for food."

"Food!" cried Audubon. "Do I look like a hungry man?"

"A little lean, maybe," said Alvin. "But you could probably fast for a day or two without keeling over."

"I do not understand you, Monsieur Americain. Et je ne veux pas te comprendre. Go away." Audubon started downstream along the riverbank, the direction the geese had gone.

"Mister Audubon," Arthur Stuart called out.

"I must shoot you before you go away?" he called out, exasperated.

"I can bring them back," said Arthur.

Audubon turned and looked at him. "You call geese?" He pulled a wooden goose call from the pocket of his jacket. "I call geese, too. But when they hear this, they think, Sacre Dieu! That goose is dying! Fly away! Fly away!"

Arthur Stuart kept walking toward him, and instead of answering, he began to make odd sounds with his throat and through his nose. Not goose calls, really, or not that anyone would notice. Not even an imitation of a goose. And yet there was something gooselike about the babble that came from his mouth. And it wasn't all that loud, either. But moments later, the geese came back, skimming over the surface of the water.

Audubon brought the shotgun to his shoulder. At once Arthur changed his call, and the geese flew away from the shore and settled far out on the water.

In an agony of frustration, Audubon whirled on Arthur and Alvin. "When did I insult you or the cauliflower face of your ugly mother? Which clumsy stinking Philadelphia prostitute was your sister? Or was it le bon Dieu that I offended? Notre Pere Celeste, why must I do this penance?"

"I'm not going to bring the geese back if you're just going to shoot them," said Arthur.

"What good are they if I don't shoot one!"

"You're not going to eat it, you're just going to paint it," said Arthur Stuart. "So it doesn't have to be dead."

"How can I paint a bird that will not stand in one place!" cried Audubon. Then he realized something. "You know my name. You know I paint. But I do not know *you*."

"I'm Alvin Smith, and this is my ward, Arthur Stuart."

"Wart? What kind of slave is that?"

"Ward. He's no slave. But he's under my protection."

"But who will protect *me* from the two of you? Why could you not be ordinary robbers, taking my money and run away?"

"Arthur has a question for you," said Alvin.

"Here is my answer: Leave! Departez!"

"What if I can get a goose to hold still for you without killing it?" asked Arthur Stuart.

Audubon was on the verge of a sharp answer when it finally dawned on him what he had just seen Arthur do, summoning the geese. "You are, how do you say, a knack person, a caller of gooses."

"Geese," Alvin offered helpfully.

Arthur shook his head. "I just like birds."

"*I* like birds too," said Audubon, "but they don't feel the same about me."

"Cause you kill 'em and you ain't even hungry," said Arthur Stuart.

Audubon looked at him in utter consternation. At last he made his decision. "You can make a goose hold still for me?"

"I can ask him to. But you got to put the gun away."

Audubon immediately leaned it against a tree.

"Unload it," said Arthur Stuart.

"You think I break my promise?"

"You didn't make no promise," said Arthur Stuart.

"All right!" cried Audubon. "I promise upon the grave of my grandmother." He started unloading the gun.

"You promise *what*?" demanded Arthur.

Alvin almost laughed aloud, except that Arthur Stuart was so grim about it, making sure there were no loopholes through which Audubon could slip once Arthur brought the geese back.

"I promise, I shoot no gooses! Pas de shooting of gooses!"

"Not even powder shooting, whatever that is. No shooting *any* birds *all day*," Arthur said.

"Not 'powder,' you ignorant boy. J'ai dit 'pas de.' *Rien! No* shooting of gooses, that's what I say!" In a mutter, he added, "Tous les sauvages du monde sont ici aujourd'hui."

Alvin chuckled. "No shooting savages, either, if you don't mind."

Audubon looked at him, furious and embarrassed. "Parlez-vous français?" "Je ne parle pas français," said Alvin, remembering a phrase from the few halting French lessons Margaret tried before she finally gave up on getting Alvin to speak any language other than English. Latin and Greek had already been abandoned by then. But he did understand the word *sauvage,* having heard it so often in the French fort of Detroit when he went there as a boy with Ta-Kumsaw.

"C'est vrai," muttered Audubon. Then, louder: "I make the promise you say. Bring me a goose that stand in one place for my painting."

"You going to answer my questions?" asked Arthur Stuart.

"Yes of course," said Audubon.

"A real answer, and not just some stupid nothing like adults usually say to children?"

"Hey," said Alvin.

"Not you," said Arthur Stuart quickly. But Alvin retained his suspicions.

"Yes," said Audubon in a world-weary voice. "I tell you all the secret of the universe!"

Arthur Stuart nodded, and walked to the point where the bank was highest. But before calling the geese, he turned to face Audubon one last time. "Where do you want the bird to stand?"

Audubon laughed. "You are the very strange boy! This is what you Americans call 'the brag'?"

"He ain't bragging," said Alvin. "He really has to know where you want the goose to stand."

Audubon shook his head, then looked around, checked the angle of the sun, and where there was a shady spot where he could sit while painting. Only then could he point to where the bird would have to pose.

"All right," said Arthur Stuart. He faced the river and babbled again, loudly, the sound carrying across the water. The geese rose from the surface and flew rapidly to shore, landing in the water or on the meadow. The lead goose, however, landed near Arthur Stuart, who led it toward the spot Audubon had picked.

Arthur looked at the Frenchman impatiently. He was just standing there, mouth agape, watching the goose come into position and then stop there, standing still as a statue. "You gonna draw in the mud with a stick?" asked Arthur.

Only then did Audubon realize that his paper and colors were still in his sack. He jogged briskly to the bag, stopping now and then to look back over his shoulder and make sure the goose was still there. While he was out of earshot, Alvin asked Arthur, "You forget we were leaving Philadelphia this morning?"

Arthur looked at him with the expression of withering scorn that only the face of an adolescent can produce. "You can go anytime you like."

At first Alvin thought he was telling him to go on and leave Arthur behind. But then he realized that Arthur was merely stating the truth: Alvin could leave Philadelphia whenever he wanted, so it didn't matter if it was this morning or later. "Verily and Mike are going to get worried if we don't get back soon."

"I don't want no birds to die," said Arthur.

"It's God's job to see every sparrow fall," said Alvin. "I didn't hear about him advertising that the position was open."

Arthur just clammed up and said no more. Soon Audubon was back, sitting in the grass under the tree, mixing his colors to match the exact color of the goosefeathers.

"I want to watch you paint," said Arthur.

"I don't like having people look over my shoulder."

Arthur murmured something and the goose started to wander away.

"All right!" said Audubon frantically. "Watch me paint, watch the bird, watch the sun in the sky until you will be blind, whatever you want!"

At once Arthur Stuart muttered to the goose, and it waddled back into place.

Alvin shook his head. Naked extortion. How could this be the sweet-tempered child Alvin had known for so long?

2

A Lady of the Court

Peggy spent the morning trying not to dread her meeting with Lady Guinevere Ashworth. As one of the senior ladies-in-waiting to Queen Mary she had some influence in her own right; more importantly, she was married to the Lord Chancellor, William Ashworth, who might have been born the third son of a schoolteacher, but by wit, dazzle, and enormous energy had clawed his way to a fine education, a good marriage, and a high office. Lord William had no illusions about his own parentage: He took his wife's family's name upon marrying her.

A woman is a woman, regardless of her parents' rank or her husband's office, Peggy reminded herself. When Lady Ashworth's bladder was full, angels didn't miraculously turn it into wine and bottle it, though from the way her name was spoken throughout Camelot, one might have thought so. It was a level of society Peggy had never aspired to or even been interested in. She hardly knew the proper manner of address to a daughter of a marquis—and whenever Peggy thought that she ought to make inquiries, she forced herself to remember that as a good Republican, she *should* get it wrong, and ostentatiously so. After all, both Jefferson and Franklin invariably referred to the King as "Mr. Stuart," and even addressed him as such on official correspondence between heads of state—though the story was that clerks in the ministry of state "translated" all such letters so that proper forms of address appeared on them, thus avoiding an international incident.

And if there was any hope of averting the war that loomed among the American nations, it might well rest on her interview with Lady Ashworth. For along with her lofty social position—some said the Queen herself consulted Lady Ashworth for advice on how to dress—Lady Ashworth was also leader of the most prominent anti-slavery organization in the Crown Colonies: Ladies Against Property Rights in Persons. (According to the fashion in the Crown Colonies, the organization was commonly called Lap-Rip, from the initials of its name—a most unfortunate acronym, Peggy thought, especially for a ladies' club.)

So much might be riding on this morning's meeting. Everything else had been a dead end. After all her months in Appalachee, Peggy had finally realized that all the pressure for maintaining slavery in the New Counties was coming from the Crown Colonies. The King's government was rattling sabers, both figuratively and literally, to make sure the Appalachian Congress understood exactly what abolition of slavery would cost them in blood. In the meantime, union between Appalachee and the United States of America was impossible as long as slavery was legal anywhere within Appalachee. And the simplest compromise, to allow the pro-slavery New Counties of Tennizy, Cherriky, and Kenituck to secede from Appalachee, was politically impossible in Appalachee itself.

The outcome Peggy most feared was that the United States would give in and admit the New Counties as slaveholding States. Such a pollution of American freedom would destroy the United States, Peggy was sure of it. And secession of the New Counties was only slightly more acceptable to her, since it would leave most of the Blacks of Appalachee under the overseer's lash. No, the only way to avoid war while retaining a spark of decency among the American people was to persuade the Crown Colonies to allow the whole of Appalachee, New Counties and all, to form a union with the United States of America—with slavery illegal throughout the nation that would result.

Her abolitionist friends laughed when Peggy broached this possibility. Even her husband, Alvin, sounded doubtful in his letters, though of course he encouraged her to do as she thought right. After hundreds of interviews with men and women throughout Appalachee and for the last few weeks in Camelot, Peggy had plenty of doubts of her own. And yet as long as there was a thread of hope, she would try to tat it into some sort of bearable future. For the future she saw in the heartfires of the people around her could not be borne, unless she knew she had done her utmost to prevent the war that threatened to soak the soil of America in blood, and whose outcome was by no means certain.

So, dread it as she might, Peggy had no choice but to visit with Lady Ashworth. For even if she could not enlist Lady Ashworth and her Lap Rip club in the cause of emancipation, she might at least win an introduction to the King, so she could plead her cause with the monarch directly.

The idea of meeting with the King frightened her less than the prospect of meeting Lady Ashworth. To an educated man Peggy could speak directly, in the language they understood. But Southern ladies, Peggy already knew, were much more complicated. Everything you said meant something else to them, and everything they said meant anything but the plain meaning of the words. It was a good thing they didn't let Southern ladies go to college. They were far too busy learning arcane languages much more subtle and difficult to master than mere Greek and Latin.

Peggy slept little the night before, ate little that morning, and kept down even less. The most acute nausea from her pregnancy had passed, but when she was nervous, as she was this morning, it returned with a vengeance. The spark of life in the baby in her womb was just beginning to be visible to her. Soon she would be able to see something of the baby's future. Mere glimpses, for a baby's heartfire was chaotic and confusing, but it would become real to her then, a life. Let it be born into a better world than this one. Let my labors change the futures of all the babies.

Her fingers were weak and trembly as she tried to fasten her buttons; she was forced to ask the help of the slavegirl who was assigned to her floor in the boardinghouse. Like all slaves in the Crown Colonies, the girl would not meet Peggy's gaze or even face her directly, and while she answered softly but clearly every question Peggy asked, what passed between them could hardly be called a conversation. "I'm sorry to trouble you, but will you help me fasten my buttons?"

"Yes ma'am."

"My name is Peggy. What's yours?"

"I's Fishy, ma'am."

"Please call me Peggy."

"Yes ma'am."

Don't belabor the point. "Fishy? Really? Or is that a nickname?"

"Yes ma'am."

"Which?"

"Fishy, ma'am."

She must be refusing to understand; let it go. "Why would your mother give you such a name?"

"I don't know, ma'am."

"Or was it your mother who named you?"

"I don't know, ma'am."

"If I give you a tip for your service, do you get to keep it?"

"No tips please, ma'am."

"But if you were to find a penny in the street, would you be permitted to keep it as your own?"

"Never found no penny, ma'am. All done now, ma'am." And Fishy was out the door in a heartbeat, pausing in the doorway only long enough to say, "Anything else, ma'am?"

Peggy knew the answers to her questions, of course, for she saw into the woman's heartfire. Saw how Fishy's mother had shunted her off on other slavewomen, because she could hardly attract the master's lust with a baby clinging to her thighs. And when the woman grew too slack-bellied from her repeated pregnancies, how the master began to share her with his White visitors, and finally with the White overseers, until the day the master gave her to Cur, the Black foreman of the plantation craftsmen. The shame of being reduced to whoring with Blacks was too much for Fishy's mother and she hanged herself. It was Fishy who found her. Peggy saw all of that flash through Fishy's mind when Peggy asked about her mother. But it was a story Fishy had never told and would never tell.

Likewise, Peggy saw that Fishy got her name from the son of the first owner she was sold to after her mother's suicide. She was assigned to be his personal maid, and the senior maid in the plantation house told her that meant that she must do *whatever* the master's son told her to do. What that might have meant Fishy never knew. The boy took one look at her, declared that she smelled fishy, and wouldn't let her in his room. She was reassigned to other duties for the months that she remained in the house, but the name Fishy stuck, and when she was sold into a household in the city of Camelot, she took the name Fishy with her. It was better than the one her mother had given her: Ugly Baby.

As for tipping, if any slave in this house were found with money, it was assumed that it had been stolen and the slave would be stripped and branded and chained in the yard for a week. Slaves might walk with their heads downcast, but in this house, at least, they saw no pennies on the ground.

The worst frustration for Peggy, though, was that she couldn't say to the slave, "Fishy, do not despair. You feel powerless, you *are* powerless except for your sullen contempt, your deliberate sloth-fulness, the tiny rebellions that you can carry out and still survive. But there are some of us, many of us working to try to set you free." For even if Peggy said it, why should Fishy believe a White woman? And if she did believe, what should she do then? If her behavior changed one iota from this obsequiousness, she would suffer for it, and emancipation, when and if it came, was still many years away.

So Peggy bore Fishy's unspoken scorn and hatred, though she knew she did not deserve it. Her black skin makes her a slave in this country; and therefore my white skin makes me her enemy, for if she took the slightest liberty with me and addressed me with any-thing like friendship or equality, she would risk terrible suffering.

It was at moments like these that Peggy thought that her fire-eating abolitionist friends in Philadelphia might be right: Only blood and fire could purge America of this sin.

She shrugged off the thought, as she always did. Most of the people who collaborated in the degradation of Blacks did so because they knew no better, or because they were weak and fearful. Igno-rance, weakness, and fear led to great wrongs, but they were not in themselves sins, and could often be more profitably corrected than punished. Only those whose hearts delighted in the degradation of the helpless and sought out opportunities to torment their Black cap-tives deserved the blood and horror of war. And war was never so careful as to inflict suffering only where it was merited.

Buttoned now, Peggy would go to meet Lady Ashworth and see if the light of Christianity burned in the heartfire of a lady-in-waiting.

There were carriages for hire in the streets of Camelot, but Peggy had no money to spare for such luxury. The walk wasn't bad, as long as she stayed away from King's Street, which had so much horse traffic that you couldn't tell there were cobbles under the dung, and flecks of it were always getting flipped up onto your clothes. And of course she would never walk along Water Street, because the smell of fish was so thick in the air that you couldn't get it out of your clothes for days afterward, no matter how long you aired them out.

But the secondary streets were pleasant enough, with their well-tended gardens, the flamboyant blooms splashing everything with color, the rich, shiny green of the leaves making every garden look like Eden. The air was muggy but there was usually a breeze from the sea. All the houses were designed to capture even the slightest breeze, and porches three stories high shaded the wealthier houses along their longest face. It gave them deep shade in the heat of the afternoons, and even now, a bit before noon, many a porch already had slaves setting out iced lemonade and preparing to start the shoo-flies a-swishing.

Small children bounced energetically on the curious flexible benches that were designed for play. Peggy had never seen such devices until she came here, though the bench was simple enough to make—just set a sturdy plank between two end supports, with nothing to brace it in the middle, and a child could jump on it and then leap off as if launched from a sling. Perhaps in other places, such an impractical thing, designed only for play, would seem a shameful luxury. Or perhaps in other places adults simply didn't think of going to so much trouble merely to delight their children. But in Camelot, children were treated like young aristocrats—which, come to think of it, most of them were, or at least their parents wished to pretend they were.

As so often before Peggy marveled at the contradictions: People so tender with their children, so indulgent, so playful, and yet they thought nothing of raising those same children to order that slaves who annoyed them be stripped or whipped, or their families broken up and sold off.

Of course, here in the city few of the mansions had large enough grounds to allow a proper whipping on the premises. The offending slave would be taken to the market and whipped there, so the moaning and weeping wouldn't interfere with conversations in the sitting rooms and drawing rooms of the beautiful houses.

What was the truth of these people? Their love for their children, for king and country, for the classical education at which they excelled, all these were genuine. By every sign they were educated, tasteful, generous, broad-minded, hospitable—in a word, civilized. And yet just under the surface was a casual brutality and a deep shame that poisoned all their acts. It was as if two cities sat on this place. Camelot, the courtly city of the king-in-exile, was the land of dancing and music, education and discourse, light and beauty, love and laughter. But by coincidence, the old city of Charleston still existed here, with buildings that corresponded with Camelot wall for wall, door for door. Only the citizenry was different, for Charleston was the city of slave markets, half-White babies sold away from their own father's household, lashings and humiliations, and, as seed and root and leaf and blossom of this evil town, the hatred and fear of both Blacks and Whites who lived at war with each other, the one doomed to perpetual defeat, the other to perpetual fear of . . .

Of what? What did they fear?

Justice.

And it dawned on her for the first time what she had *not* seen in Fishy's heartfire: the desire for revenge.

And yet that was impossible. What human being could bear such constant injustice and not cry out, at least in the silence of the soul, for the power to set things to rights? Was Fishy so meek that she forgave all? No, her sullen resistance clearly had no piety in it. She was filled with hate. And yet not one thought or dream or plan for retribution, either personal or divine. Not even the hope of emancipation or escape.

As she walked along the streets under the noonday sun, it made her almost giddy to realize what must be going on, and not just with Fishy, but with every slave she had met here in Camelot. Peggy was not able to see everything in their heartfires. They were able to conceal a part of their feelings from her. For it was impossible to imagine that they *had* no such feelings, for they were human beings, and all the Blacks she met in Appalachee had yearnings for retribution, manumission, or escape. No, if she didn't see those passions among the slaves of Camelot, it wasn't because they didn't feel them, it was because they had somehow learned to lie a lie so deep that it existed even in their heartfires.

And that threw everything in doubt. For if there was one thing Peggy had always counted on, it was this: No one could lie to her without her knowing it. It had been that way with her almost since birth. It was one of the reasons people didn't usually like to spend much time around a torch—though few of them could see even a fraction of what Peggy saw. There was always the fear of their secret thoughts being known and exposed.

When Peggy was a child, she did not understand why adults became so upset when she responded to what was in their heartfire rather than the words they were saying to her. But what could she do? When a traveling salesman patted her on her head and said, "I

got something for this little girl, I wager!'' she hardly noticed his
words, what with all that his heartfire was telling her, not to mention
her father's heartfire and everybody else nearby. She just naturally
had to answer, "My papa's not a fool! He knows you're cheating
him!''

But everybody got so upset with her that she learned to keep
silent about all lies and all secrets. Her response was to hold her
tongue and say nothing at all. Fortunately, she learned silence before
she was old enough to understand the truly dark secrets that would
have destroyed her family. Silence served her well—so well that
some visitors to her father's inn took her for a mute.

Still, she had to converse with local people, and with other children her age. And for a long time it made her angry, how people's
words never matched up very well with their desires or memories,
and sometimes were the flat opposite. Only gradually did she come
to see that as often as not, the lies people told were designed to be
kind or merciful or, at the very least, polite. If a mother thought her
daughter was plain, was it bad that she lied to the child and told her
that she loved how her face brightened up when she smiled? What
good would it have done to give her true opinion? And the lie helped
the child grow up more cheerful, and therefore more attractive.

Peggy began to understand that what made a statement good
was rarely dependent on whether it was true. Very little human
speech was truthful, as she knew better than anyone else. What mattered was whether the deception was kindly meant or designed to
take advantage, whether it was meant to smooth a social situation
or aggrandize the speaker in others' eyes.

Peggy became a connoisseur of lies. The good lies were motivated by love or kindness, to shield someone from pain, to protect
the innocent, or to hide feelings that the speaker was ashamed of.
The neutral lies were the fictions of courtesy that allowed conversations to proceed smoothly without unnecessary or unproductive
conflict. How are you? Just fine.

The bad lies were not all equal, either. Ordinary hypocrisy was
annoying but did little harm, unless the hypocrite went out of his
way to attack others for sins that he himself committed but concealed. Careless liars seemed to have no regard for truth, and lied
from habit or for sport. Cruel liars, though, sought out their target's
worst fears and then lied to make them suffer or to put them at a
disadvantage; or they gossiped to destroy people they resented, often
accusing them falsely of the sins the gossips themselves most wished

to commit. And then there were the professional liars, who said whatever was necessary to get others to do their will.

And despite Peggy's gifts as a torch—and no ordinary torch at that, able merely to catch a glimpse of a child inside the womb— even she often had trouble discerning the motive behind a lie, in part because there were often many motives in conflict. Fear, weakness, a desire to be liked—all could produce lies that in someone else might come from ruthlessness or cruelty; and within their heartfire, Peggy could not easily see the difference. It took time; she had to understand the pattern of their lives to find out what sort of soul they had, and where the lies all seemed to lead.

So many questions were posed by every lie she was told that she despaired of answering any but the most obvious. Even when she knew the truth that someone was lying to conceal, what was that truth? The mother who thought her daughter was ugly might be lying when she told the girl that her smile made her pretty—but in fact the mother might be wrong, and in fact her lie might be true in the eyes of another observer. Most "truths" that people believed in, and therefore which they contradicted with their lies, were not objectively true at all. The *real* truth—how things are or were or would become—was almost unknowable. That is, people often knew the truth, but they just as often "knew" things that were not true, and had no reliable way to tell the difference. So while Peggy could always see what the person believed was true while they told their lies, this did not mean that Peggy therefore knew the *real* truth.

After years of sorting out the lies and realizing that the lies often told more truth than the "truth" that the lies concealed, Peggy finally came to the conclusion that what she needed was not a better sense of truth, but simply the skill to hear a lie and react to it as if she knew nothing else.

It was after she ran away from home and went to Dekane that, under the tutelage of Mistress Modesty, she learned the balancing act of hearing both the words and the heartfire, and yet letting her voice, her face, her gestures show only the response that was appropriate for the words. She might sometimes make use of the hidden knowledge she saw in their heartfires, but never in such a way that they would realize she knew their deepest secrets. "Even those of us who are not torches have to learn those skills," said Mistress Modesty. "The ability to act as if you did not know what you know perfectly well is the essence of courtesy and poise." Peggy learned them right along with music, geography, history, grammar, and the classics of philosophy and poetry.

But there was no balancing act with the slaves here. They were able to hide their hearts from her.

Did they know she was a torch, and so hid deliberately? That was hardly likely—they could not *all* have such a sense of her hidden powers. No, their secret dreams were hidden from her because they were also hidden from the slaves themselves. It was how they survived. If they did not know their own rage, then they could not inadvertently show it. Slave parents must teach this to their children, to hide their rage so deeply that they couldn't even find it themselves.

And yet it was there. It was there, burning. Does it turn their hearts to ash, gradually growing cold? Or to lava, waiting to erupt?

The Ashworth house wasn't the largest or the most elegantly finished, but then it didn't need to be, since they could take up residence on at least a half-dozen huge estates all over the Crown Colonies. So the house in town could be relatively modest without loss of prestige.

Even so, the signs of true wealth were there. Everything was perfectly maintained. The bell gave off a musical tone. The street door opened noiselessly on its hinges. The floor of the lower porch did not creak, it was that solidly built—even the porch! And the furniture showed no sign of weathering—obviously it must be carried in whenever the weather went bad, either that or replaced every year. The perfection of detail. The ostentation of people with unlimited money and impeccable taste.

The slave who opened the door for her and ushered her into the room was a wiry, middle-aged man who fit his livery as if he had been born in it and it had grown along with him. Or perhaps he shed it from time to time like a snake, revealing a perfect new costume underneath. He said nothing and never looked at her. She spoke her own name when he opened the door; he stepped back and let her in. By his manner, by the most subtle of gestures, he showed her when she should follow him, and where she should wait.

In his wordlessness she was free to search his heartfire without distraction, and now that she was aware, she could search for the missing part. For it *was* missing: the offended dignity, the anguish, the fear, the rage. All gone. Only service was in his thoughts, only the jobs he had to do, and the manner in which he had to do them. Intense concentration on the routine of the house.

But it was impossible. He could not conduct his life with such intense singularity of thought. No one could. Where were the distractions? Where were the people he liked, or loved? Where was his humanity?

Had the slaveowners succeeded in this place? Had they torn the very life out of the hearts of the slaves? Had they succeeded in making these people what they always claimed they were—animals?

He was gone, and so dim was his heartfire that she had trouble tracking him through the house. What was his name? Was even his name hidden? No, there it was—Lion. But that was only a house name, given to him when he arrived here. Apparently it pleased Lord and Lady Ashworth to name their slaves for noble animals. How could such a transient name be the one contained in his heartfire?

There was a deep name hidden somewhere in him. As there must be in Fishy, too—some name deeper than Ugly Baby. And where the deep name was hidden, there she would find the true heartfire. In Fishy, in Lion, in all the Blacks whose hands did the labor of this city.

"Miz Larner," said a soft voice. A woman this time, old and wrinkled, her hair steel-gray. *Her* costume hung on her like a sack on a fencepost, but that did not reflect ill on the house—no clothing could look right on such a wizened frame. Peggy wasn't sure whether it spoke well of the family that they kept such an old slave as part of the household, or whether it suggested that they were squeezing the last ounce of service out of her.

No, no, don't be cynical, she told herself. Lady Ashworth is the president of Lap-Rip, publicly committed to putting limits on slavery. She would hardly let this old woman guide company through the house if she thought anyone could possibly find a negative implication in it.

The old woman moved with excruciating slowness, but Peggy followed patiently. She was called Doe in this house, but to Peggy's great relief, there seemed to be no dimming or hiding of her heartfire, and it was easy to find her true name, an African word that Peggy could hear in her mind but wouldn't know how to form with her lips. But she knew what the name meant: It was a kind of flower. This woman had been kidnapped by raiders from another village only days before her planned wedding, and was sold three times in as many days before seeing her first White face, a Portuguese ship captain. Then the voyage, her first owner in America, her struggle to learn enough English to understand what she was being commanded to do. The times she was slapped, starved, stripped, whipped. None of her White masters had ravished her, but she had been bred like a mare, and of the nine children she bore, only two had been left with her past their third birthday. Those were sold locally, a girl and a boy, and she saw them now and then, even today. She even knew of three of her grandchildren, for her daughter had been a virtual concubine to her master, and . . .

And all three of the grandchildren were free.

Astonishing. It was illegal in the Crown Colonies, yet in this woman's heartfire Peggy could see that Doe certainly believed that it was true.

And then an even bigger surprise. Doe herself was also free, and had been for five years. She received a wage, in addition to a tiny rent-free room in this house.

That was why her heartfire was so easily found. The memory of bitterness and anger was there, but Lord Ashworth had freed her on her seventieth birthday.

How wonderful, thought Peggy. After fewer than six decades of slavery, when she had already lived longer than the vast majority of slaves, when her body was shriveled, her strength gone, *then* she was set free.

Again, Peggy forced herself to reject cynicism. It might seem meaningless to Peggy, to free Doe so late in her life. But it had great meaning to Doe herself. It had unlocked her heart. All she cared about now was her three grandchildren. That and earning her wage through service in this house.

Doe led Peggy up a wide flight of stairs to the main floor of the house. Everyone lived above the level of the street. Indeed, Doe led her even higher, to the lavish second story, where instead of a drawing room Peggy found herself being led to the porch and, yes, the cane chairs, the pitcher of iced lemonade, the swaying shoo-flies, the slaveboy with a fan almost the size of his own body, and, standing at a potted plant with a watering can in her hand, Lady Ashworth herself.

"It's so kind of you to come, Miz Larner," she said. "I could scarcely believe my good fortune, when I learned that you would have time in your busy day to call upon me."

Lady Ashworth was much younger and prettier than Peggy had expected, and she was dressed quite comfortably, with her hair pinned in a simple bun. But it was the watering can that astonished Peggy. It looked suspiciously like a tool, and watering a plant could only be construed as manual labor. Ladies in slaveholding families did not do such things.

Lady Ashworth noticed Peggy's hesitation, and understood why. She laughed. "I find that some of the more delicate plants thrive better when I care for them myself. It's no more than Eve and Adam did in Paradise—they tended the garden, didn't they?'' She set down the can, sat gracefully on a cane chair beside the table with the pitcher, and gestured for Peggy to be seated. ''Besides, Miz Larner, one ought to be prepared for life after the abolition of slavery.''

Again Peggy was startled. In slave lands, the word *abolition* was about as polite as some of the more colorful expletives of a river rat.

''Oh, dear,'' said Lady Ashworth, ''I'm afraid my language may have shocked you. But that *is* why you're here, isn't it, Miz Larner? Don't we both share the goal of abolishing slavery wherever we can? So if we succeed, then I should certainly know how to do a few tasks for myself. Come now, you haven't said a word since you got here.''

Peggy laughed, embarrassed. ''I haven't, have I? It's kind of you to be willing to see me. And I can assure you that ladies of stature in the United States are not up to their elbows in wash water. Paid servants do the coarser sort of work.''

''But so much more expensively,'' said Lady Ashworth. ''They expect their wages in cash. We don't use much money here. It's all seasonal. The French and English buyers come to town, we sell our cotton or tobacco, and then we pay all the tradesmen for the year. We don't carry money with us or keep it around the house. I don't think we'd keep many *free* servants with such a policy.''

Peggy sighed inwardly. For Lady Ashworth's heartfire told such a different story. She watered her own plants because the slaves deliberately overwatered the most expensive imports, killing them by degrees. Some imaginary shortage of cash had nothing to do with keeping free servants, for the well-to-do families always had money in the bank. And as for abolition, Lady Ashworth loathed the word as much as any other slaveholder. For that matter, she loathed Peggy herself. But she recognized that some limitation on slavery would have to be achieved in order to placate public opinion in Europe and the United States, and all that Lady Ashworth ever intended to allow Lap-Rip to accomplish was the banning of slavery in certain regions of the Crown Colonies where the land and the economy made slavery unprofitable anyway. Lady Ashworth had always had success in convincing Northerners that she was quite radical on slavery, and expected to do as well with Peggy.

But Peggy was determined not to be treated with such contempt. It was a simple matter to find in Lady Ashworth's heartfire some of her more recent mistreatment of her slaves. ''Perhaps instead of wielding the watering can," said Peggy, "you might show your commitment to abolition by bringing back the two slaves you have standing stripped in chains without water to drink in the hot sun of the dockyard."

Lady Ashworth's face showed nothing, but Peggy saw the rage and fear leap up within her. "Why, Miz Larner, I do believe you have been doing some research."

"The names and owners of the slaves are posted for all to see," said Peggy.

"Few of our Northern visitors pry into our domestic affairs by visiting our disciplinary park."

Too late did Peggy realize that the guards at the disciplinary yard—hardly a "park"—would never have let her inside. Not without a letter of introduction. And Lady Ashworth *would* inquire who it was who provided a Northern radical like Peggy with such an entree. When she found that there was no such letter and Peggy had made no such visit, she would think—what? That Peggy was secretly a torch? Perhaps. But more likely she would think that one of the household Blacks had talked to Peggy. There would be punishments for the only two Blacks that Peggy had had contact with: Doe and Lion. Peggy looked into the futures she had just created and saw Lady Ashworth hearing Doe's confession, knowing perfectly well that the old woman was lying in order to protect Lion.

And what would Lady Ashworth do? Lion, refusing to confess, would be whipped and, in the futures in which he survived the whipping, sold west. Doe would be turned out of the house, for even though she had not given Peggy a bit of information, she had proven she was more loyal to a fellow Black than to her mistress. As a free black of advanced age, Doe would be reduced to living from scraps provided by the charity of other slaves, all of whom would be opening themselves to charges of stealing from their masters for every bit of food they gave to Doe.

Time to lie. "Do you think that you're the only . . . abolitionist . . . living in Camelot?" said Peggy. "The difference is that some of the others are sincere."

At once Lady Ashworth's heartfire showed different futures. She would now be suspicious of the other ladies in Lap-Rip. Which of them had exposed Lady Ashworth's hypocrisy by speaking to Peggy, or writing to her, about the Ashworth slaves now being disciplined?

"Did you come to my house to insult me?"

"No more than I came to be insulted," said Peggy.

"What did I do to insult you?" said Lady Ashworth. What she

did not say, but what Peggy heard just as clearly as her words, was that it was impossible for Lady Ashworth to insult Peggy, for Peggy was nobody.

"You dared to claim that you share the goal of abolishing slavery wherever you can, when you know perfectly well that you have no intention of living for even a single day of your life without slavery, and that your entire effort is merely to pacify Northerners like me. You are part of your husband's foreign-relations strategy, and you are as committed to preserving slavery in the New Counties as anyone else in the Crown Colonies."

At last the façade of cheerfulness cracked. "How dare you, you priggish little nobody? Do you think I don't know your husband is a common tradesman with the name of Smith? No one ever heard of your family, and you come from a mongrel country that thinks nothing of mixing the races and treats people of quality as if they were the common scum of the street."

"At last," said Peggy, "you have consented to deal with me honestly."

"I don't consent to deal with you at all! Get out of my house."

Peggy did not budge from her seat. Indeed, she picked up the pitcher of lemonade and poured herself a tall glass. "Lady Ashworth, the need for you to create the illusion of gradual emancipation has not changed. In fact, I think you and I have a lot more to talk about now that we're not lying to each other."

It was amusing to watch Lady Ashworth think through the consequences of throwing Peggy out—an event which would undoubtedly get reported all over the north, at least in abolitionist circles.

"What do you want, Miz Larner?" said Lady Ashworth coldly.

"I want," said Peggy, "an audience with the King."

3

Painted Birds

Jean-Jacques Audubon soon forgot the strangeness of painting from a live bird and concentrated on colors and shapes. Arthur and Alvin both sat in the grass behind him, watching the goose come to life on the paper. To Arthur it was a kind of miracle. A dab here, a dab there, a streak, colors blending sometimes, sharp-edged in other places. And from this chaos, a bird.

From time to time the model grew weary. Arthur jumped up from the grass and spoke to the geese, and soon another took the place of the first, as close a match as he could find. Jean-Jacques cursed under his breath. "They are not the same bird, you know."

"But they're alive," said Arthur. "Look at the eyes."

Jean-Jacques only grunted. For the bird did look alive on the paper. Arthur whispered about it to Alvin, but Alvin's reply gave him no satisfaction. "How do you know he didn't make the dead birds look just as alive in his paintings?"

At last the painting was done. Jean-Jacques busied himself with putting away his colors and brushes, until Arthur called out to him, rather angrily. "Look here, Mr. Audubon!"

Jean-Jacques looked up. The goose was still there, not posed anymore, but still on the ground, gazing intently at Arthur Stuart. "I'm finish with the goose, you can let it go." He turned back to his work.

"No!" Arthur Stuart shouted.

"Arthur," said Alvin softly.

"He's got to watch," said Arthur.

Sighing, Jean-Jacques looked up. "What am I watching?"

The moment Audubon's eyes were on him, Arthur clapped his hands and the goose ran and clumsily staggered into the air. But as soon as its wings were pulling against the air, it changed into a beautiful creature, turning the powerful beats of its wings into soaring flight. The other geese also rose. And Jean-Jacques, his weariness slipping from him, watched them fly over the trees.

"What grace," said Jean-Jacques. "No lady ever dances with so much beauty."

At that Arthur charged at him, furious. "That's right! Them living birds are prettier than any of your damned old paintings!"

Alvin caught Arthur by the shoulders, held him, smiled wanly at Jean-Jacques. "I'm sorry. I never seen him act so mad."

"Every painting you ever made killed a bird," said Arthur. "And I don't care how pretty you paint, it ain't worth stopping the life of any of them!"

Jean-Jacques was embarrassed. "No one say this to me before. Men shoot their guns all the time, birds die every day."

"For meat," said Arthur. "To eat them."

"Does he believe this?" Jean-Jacques asked Alvin. "Do you think they are hungry and shoot the birds for food? Maybe they are stuffing it for trophy. Maybe they are shooting for *fun*, you angry boy."

Arthur was unmollified. "So maybe they're no better than you. But I'd rather cut off my hand than kill a bird just to make a picture of it."

"All these hours you watch me paint, you admire my painting, no? And now you choose this moment and tout á coup you are angry?"

"Cause I wanted you to see that bird fly. You painted it but it could still fly!"

"But that was because of your talking to the bird," said Jean-Jacques. "How can I know such a boy as you exist? I am oughting to wait for some boy to come along and make the bird pose? Until then I draw trees?"

"Who asked you to paint birds?"

"Is this the question you wanted to ask me?" said Jean-Jacques.

Arthur stopped short. "No. Yes. The way you stuffed them birds back in the shop, that showed me you *know* the birds, you really see them, but then how can you kill them? You ain't hungry."

"I am often hungry. I am hungry right now. But it is not the bird I want to eat. Not goose today. What beautiful gooses. You love them flying, and I love them flying, but in France nobody ever sees these birds. Other birds they see, not the birds of America. Scientists write and talk about birds but they see only sketches, bad printing of them. I am not very good painter of people. Most of the people I do not like, and this makes my paintings not pretty to them. My people look like they are dead—etouffé—avec little glass eyes. But birds. I can paint them to be alive. I can find the colors, I see them there, and put them on the paper. We print, and now the scientist know, they open my book, *voilà* the American bird they never see. Now they can think about bird and they *see* them. God lets you to talk to birds, angry boy. He lets me to paint them. I should throw away this gift of God except today, when you are here to help me?"

"It ain't your gift when it's the bird as dies for it," said Arthur Stuart.

"All creatures die," said Jean-Jacques. "Birds live the lives of birds. All the same. It is a beautiful life, but they live in the shadow of death, afraid, watching, and then, boom! The gun. The talon of the hawk! The paws of the cat. But the bird I kill, I make it into the picture, it will live forever."

"Paint on paper ain't a bird," said Arthur Stuart sullenly.

Jean-Jacques's hand flashed out and gripped Arthur's arm. "Come here and say that to my picture!" He forced Arthur to stand over the open sketchbook. "You make me look at flying gooses. Now you look!"

Arthur looked.

"You see this is beautiful," said Jean-Jacques. "And it teaches. Knowing is good. I show this bird to the world. In every eye, there is my bird. My goose is Plato's goose. Perfect goose. True goose. *Real* goose."

Alvin chuckled. "We aren't too clear on Plato."

Arthur turned scornfully to Alvin. "Miz Larner taught us all about Plato, lessen you was asleep that day."

"Was this the question you had for Mr. Audubon?" asked Alvin. "Asking why he thinks it's worth killing birds to paint them? Cause if it was, you sure picked a rude way to ask it."

"I'm sorry," said Arthur Stuart.

"And I think he gave you a fair answer, Arthur Stuart. If he was shooting birds and selling them to a poulterer you wouldn't think twice cause it's nature's way, killing and eating. It's all right to shoot a bird so some family can buy the carcass and roast it up and eat it gone. But iffen you just paint it, that makes him a killer?"

"I know," said Arthur Stuart. "I knowed that right along."

"Then what was all this shouting for?" asked Alvin.

"I don't know," said Arthur. "I don't know why I got so mad."

"I know why," said Jean-Jacques.

"You do?" asked Alvin.

"Of course," said Jean-Jacques. "The gooses do not like to die. But they cannot speak. They cannot, how you say, complain. So. You are the interpreter for birds."

Arthur Stuart had no answer for this. They walked in silence for a while, as the road led them to the outlying buildings and then quickly into the city, the ground turning into a cobbled street under them.

"I think of a question for you, King Arthur," said Jean-Jacques at last.

"What," said Arthur, sounding far from enthusiastic.

"The sound you make, no goose ever make this sound. But they understand you."

"Wish you could have heard him when he was younger," said Alvin. "He sounded just like any bird you want."

"He lost this when his voice change? Getting low?"

"Earlier," said Alvin. He could not explain how he changed Arthur Stuart's body so that the Finders couldn't claim him. Though Jean-Jacques seemed a decent enough fellow, it wouldn't be good to have any witness who could affirm that Arthur really was the runaway slave the Finders had been looking for.

"But my question," said Jean-Jacques, "is how you learn this language. You never *hear* this language, so how to learn it?"

"I *do* hear the language," said Arthur. "I'm talking their language right back to them. I just have a really thick human accent."

At this, Jean-Jacques burst out laughing, and so did Alvin. "Human accent," Jean-Jacques repeated.

"It ain't like the geese talk in words anyway," said Arthur. "It's more like, when I talk, I'm making the sound that says, Hi, I'm a goose, and then the rest of it says things like, everything's safe, or, quick let's fly, or, hold still now. Not words. Just . . . wishes."

"But there was a time," said Alvin, "when I saw you talking

to a redbird and it told you all kinds of stuff and it wasn't just wishes, it was complicated.''

Arthur thought about it. "Oh, that time," he finally said. "Well, that's cause that redbird wasn't talking redbird talk. He was talking English."

"English!" said Alvin, incredulous.

"With a really thick redbird accent," said Arthur. And this time all three of them laughed together.

As they neared Mistress Louder's boardinghouse, they could see a burly man bounding out into the street, then returning immediately through the garden gate. "Is that a man or a big rubber ball?" asked Jean-Jacques.

"It's Mr. Fink," said Arthur Stuart. "I think he's watching for us."

"Or is it Gargantua?" asked Jean-Jacques.

"More like Pantagruel," said Arthur Stuart.

Jean-Jacques stopped cold. Alvin and Arthur turned to look at him. "What's wrong?" asked Alvin.

"The boy knows Rabelais?" asked Jean-Jacques.

"Who's that?" asked Alvin.

"Alvin was asleep that day, too," said Arthur Stuart.

Jean-Jacques looked back and forth between them. "You and you have attend to school together?"

Alvin knew what Audubon must be thinking—that Alvin must be a dunce to have gone to school at the same time as a child. "We had the same teacher," said Alvin.

"And she taught us in the same room at the same time," said Arthur Stuart.

"Only we didn't always get the same lesson," said Alvin.

"Yeah, I got Rabelais and Plato," said Arthur Stuart, "and Alvin married the schoolteacher."

Jean-Jacques laughed out loud. "That is so pleasant! Your wife is a schoolteacher but this slaveboy is the top student!"

"Reckon so, except one thing," said Alvin. "The boy is free."

"Oh yes, I'm sorry. I mean to say, this Black boy."

"Half-Black," Arthur Stuart corrected him.

"Which make you half-White," said Jean-Jacques. "But when I look at you, I see only the Black half. Is this not curious?"

"When Black folks look at me," said Arthur Stuart, "they see only the White half."

"But the secret about you," said Jean-Jacques, "is that deep in your heart, *you know Rabelais!*"

"What does that have to do with Black and White?" asked Alvin.

"It have to do that all this Black and White just make this boy laugh inside. When you are laughing deep down where no one else can see, Rabelais is there. Yes, Arthur Stuart?"

"Rabelais," said Alvin. "Was that the book about the big huge fat guy?"

"So you did read it?"

"No," said Alvin. "I got embarrassed and gave it back to Miz Larner. Margaret, I mean. You can't talk about things like that with a lady!"

"Ah," said Jean-Jacques. "Your schoolteacher began as Miz Larner, but now she is Margaret. Next you will call her 'mama,' n'est-ce pas?"

Alvin got a little tight-lipped at that. "Maybe you French folks like to read nasty books and all, but in America you don't go talking about a man's wife having babies."

"Oh, you plan to get them some other way?" Jean-Jacques laughed again. "Look, Pantagruel has seen us! He is coming to crush us!"

Mike Fink strode angrily toward them. "You know what damn time it is!" he called out.

People nearby looked at him and glared.

"Watch your language," Alvin said. "You want to get fined?"

"I wanted to get to Trenton before nightfall," said Mike.

"How, you got a train ticket?" asked Alvin.

"Good afternoon, Pantagruel. I am Jean-Jacques Audubon."

"Is he talking English?" asked Mike.

"Mike, this is John James Audubon, a Frenchman who paints birds. Jean-Jacques, this is Mike Fink."

"That's right, I'm Mike Fink! I'm half bear and half alligator, and my grandma on my mother's side was a tornado. When I clap my hands it scares lightning out of a clear sky. And if I want a bird painted, I'll pee straight up and turn the whole flock yellow!"

"I tremble in my boots to know you are such a dangerous fellow," said Jean-Jacques. "I am sure that when you say these things to ladies, their skirts fly up and they fall over on their backs."

Mike looked at him for a moment in silence. "If he's making fun of me, Alvin, I got to kill him."

"No, he was saying he thinks you make a fine speech," said

Alvin. "Come on, Mike, it's me you're mad at. I'm sorry I didn't get back. I found Arthur Stuart pretty quick, but then we had to stay and help Mr. Audubon paint a goose."

"What for?" asked Mike. "Was the old colors peeling off?"

"No no," said Jean-Jacques. "I paint on *paper*. I make a picture of a goose."

Before Alvin could explain that the former river rat was making a joke, Mike said, "Thanks for clearing that up for me, you half-witted tick-licking donkey-faced baboon."

"Every time you talk I hear how much of English I have yet to learn," said Jean-Jacques.

"It wasn't Mr. Audubon's fault, Mike. It was Arthur Stuart who made us stay while he talked a goose into holding still. So Mr. Audubon could paint a picture without having to kill the bird and stuff it first."

"Well that's fine with me," said Mike. "I'm not all that mad about it."

"You get more mad that this?" asked Jean-Jacques.

"None of you ain't seen me mad," said Mike.

"I have," said Alvin.

"Well, maybe a little bit mad," said Mike. "When you broke my leg."

Jean-Jacques looked at Alvin, seeing him in a new light, if he could break the leg of a man who did indeed seem to be half bear.

"It's Verily who's about ready to explode," said Mike.

"Verily?" asked Alvin, surprised. Verily Cooper hardly ever showed his temper.

"Yeah, he drummed his fingers on the table at lunch and on the porch he snatched a fly right out of the air and threw it at the house so hard it broke a window."

"He did?" asked Arthur Stuart, in awe.

"I said so, didn't I?" said Mike Fink.

"Oh, yeah, I forgot who was talking," said Arthur.

"Arthur and Mr. Audubon are hungry and thirsty," said Alvin. "You think you can take them in and see if Mistress Louder can get them a slab of bread and some water, at least?"

"Water?" said Audubon with a painted expression. "Do you Americans not understand that water can make you sick? Wine is healthy. Beer is good for you as long as you don't mind making urine all the time. But water—you will get, what you call it, the piles."

"I been drinking water all my life," said Alvin, "and I don't get no piles."

"But this mean you are, how you say . . ." Then he rattled off a stream of French.

"Used to it," said Arthur, translating.

"Yes! Yoost a twit!"

"Used. To. It," Arthur repeated helpfully.

"English is the stupidest language on Earth. Except for German, and it is not a language, it is a head cold."

"You speak French?" Alvin asked Arthur Stuart.

"No," said Arthur, as if it were the stupidest idea in the world.

"Well, you understood Mr. Audubon."

"I guessed," said Arthur. "I don't even talk English all that good."

Right, thought Alvin. You can talk English any way you want to. You just *like* to break the rules and sound like this is your first day out of a deep-woods cabin.

"Come on in and get something to eat," said Mike. "And if you won't drink water, Mr. Odd Bone—"

"Audubon," Jean-Jacques corrected him.

"I hope hard cider will do the trick, cause I don't reckon Mistress Louder has anything stronger."

"Can *I* have some hard cider?" asked Arthur Stuart.

"No, but you can have a cookie," said Alvin.

"Hurrah!"

"*If* she offers you one," said Alvin. "And no hinting."

"Mistress Louder always knows what a fellow's hungry for," said Arthur Stuart. "It's her knack."

Jean-Jacques laughed. "The food I am hungry for has never been served in this whole continent!"

"What do you mean?" said Mike Fink. "We got frogs and snails here."

"But you have no garlic."

"We got onions so strong they make you fart blue," said Mike. "And I tasted a Red man's peppercorn one time that made me think I was a fish and I woke up in the river."

"The food of France does nothing so wonderful. It *taste* so good that every day God send a saint down to Paris to bring him his dinner, but what does he know?"

They continued the bragging contest into the kitchen. But Alvin stopped off in the small parlor, where Verily sat comfortably with a book on his lap. He glanced at Alvin and then back down at the book.

"Oh, you're back," said Verily. "I assumed you had been killed and Arthur sold into slavery." He turned a page. "Next time, perhaps." He said it with no expression at all. Mike was right. Alvin had never seen Verily Cooper so mad.

"I'm sorry," Alvin said.

"All right then," said Verily, setting down the book and rising to his feet. "Let's go." Verily walked toward the door.

"This late in the afternoon?" asked Alvin as he passed.

Verily stopped and looked at Alvin in feigned surprise. "Afternoon? So late? I had no idea."

"I said I'm sorry," said Alvin.

"I'm not like Peggy," said Verily. "I can't see your heartfire off in the distance and assure myself that everything's all right. I just sit here waiting."

"I can't believe this," said Alvin. "You sound like a wife."

"I sound angry," said Verily. "I think it's interesting that in your mind this translates as 'sounding like a wife.'"

"Now you sound like a lawyer," said Alvin.

"But you still sound like someone who thinks his life is so much more important than anyone else's that he can worry and inconvenience other people and all will be made right if he just says 'I'm sorry.'"

Alvin was stunned. "How can you say that? You know that's not how I feel."

"That's not what you *say*. But it's how you *act*."

"Sure, yes, maybe I do act like that. I'm on this journey trying to find out what this knack I have is *for*. I was told once that I'm supposed to build a Crystal City only I don't know what it is or how it's made. So I'm flailing around, changing my mind from day to day and week to week because I don't even know where to begin. Some Tennizy town calling itself Crystal City? Or maybe New England, because one of the wisest people I know tells me that's where I'll learn how to create a city?"

"This is not about whether or not you follow my suggestion," said Verily.

"I know what it's about," said Alvin. "Your knack is as remarkable as mine. On top of that you're an educated man. So why are you wandering all over America, following a half-educated journeyman blacksmith who doesn't know where he's going?"

"That is precisely the question I've spent this whole day asking."

"Well, answer it," said Alvin. "Because if you want to be the center of your own life, then get on with it. Go away. The longer you follow me around the more you're going to get caught up in *my* life, and pretty soon all you'll be is the fellow who helped Alvin Smith build him a Crystal City."

"That's if you succeed in building it."

"Now we're to it, ain't we, Very?" said Alvin. "It's worth it to tag along with me iffen I end up building the damn city. But what if I never figure it out? *Then* what's your life about?"

Verily turned his back on Alvin, but he didn't leave the room. He walked to the window. "Now I see," he said.

"See what?"

"I sat here getting angrier and angrier, and I thought it was because you were delaying our journey and hadn't sent word, and I talked myself into resenting the high-handed way you make decisions, but that was nonsense, because I'm free to leave any time. I'm with you by my own choice, and that includes being patient while you figure things out. So why was I angry?"

"Being angry isn't always for a reason that makes sense."

"Do you imagine you have to tell a lawyer that?" Verily laughed grimly. "I see now that I was really angry because I'm not in control of my own life. I've handed it over to you."

"Not to me," said Alvin.

"You're the one leading this expedition."

"You think just because you're not in charge of your own life right now, I must be in charge?" Alvin sat down on the floor and leaned against the wall. "I didn't give myself this knack. I didn't set the Unmaker to trying to kill me a dozen times over while I was growing up. I didn't cause myself to be born where this torch girl could see my future and use my birth caul to save my life every one of those times. I didn't choose to get all caught up with Tenskwa-Tawa, either—I was kidnapped by a bunch of Reds as was in cahoots with Harrison. And when I do make a choice it's liable to blow up in my face. I figured out how to save Arthur from the Finders but what did it cost him? He can't do the voices anymore, not even the true voices of the birds. I'd give anything to put him back to rights, the way he was. And this golden plow, this living plow I found in the fire, that was the worst mistake of all, cause I don't know how to use it or what *it's* for. But I feel like it's got to make sense. There's got to be some purpose behind it. Some plan. Only I can't see what it's supposed to be. Not the future, not the present, not the past. And Margaret's no help neither, cause she sees too many futures and all she cares about is whether I'm dead, as if there's some future in which I don't die. Verily, you feel like you're getting led around on a string, but at least you can look at the other end of the string and see who's holding it.''

"You," said Verily.

"And you can take it back if you want. You can go your own way. But me, Verily, who's holding *my* string? And how can I get away?''

Verily sank to his knees in front of Alvin and put his hands on Alvin's shoulders, then pulled him into an embrace. "You need a friend, and I'm nothing but a nag, Alvin.''

"You're the friend I need, Verily, as long as you want to be," said Alvin.

They held each other for a long moment, both of them rejoicing in the closeness, and both relieved that they hadn't lost it in the flaring of tempers of two strong-willed men.

"So we stay another night?" asked Verily.

"If Mistress Louder hasn't changed the sheets," said Alvin.

"She hasn't," said Verily. "She said she wouldn't till she saw you ride off.''

"So she knew I wouldn't get away today?''

"She wished," said Verily. "You know she's set her cap for you.''

"Don't be silly. She's twenty years older than me at least, and I'm a married man.''

"Cupid shoots his arrows where they'll cause the most mischief," said Verily.

"She mothers me," said Alvin. "That's all it is.''

"To you it feels like mothering," said Verily, "but to her it feels like wifing.''

"Then let's get out of here tonight.''

"The harm's already done," said Verily, "and she's not going to do anything about it, so why not stay tonight in a familiar bed?''

"And eat familiar food," said Alvin.

"Which I smell right now," said Verily.

"It's not even suppertime," said Alvin.

"How often a woman's love comes out as cookies.''

"One more night in Mistress Louder's house," said Alvin.

"You'll always come back here when you're in Philadelphia," said Verily.

"Why, you think I can't turn away from a good meal and a soft bed?"

"I think you can't bear the thought of breaking her heart."

"I thought I was blind to other people's needs and desires."

Verily grinned. "I believe that the person who said that was in a bit of a snit. A rational person would never speak of you that way."

"So we leave for New England in the morning?" said Alvin.

"Unless Arthur Stuart has another errand for us."

"And Verily Cooper, attorney-at-law, comes along with us?"

"You never know when you might need someone to talk you out of jail."

"No more jails for me," said Alvin. "Next time somebody locks me up, I'll be out before they turn around."

"Don't you think it's ironic that you have no idea what you're supposed to do," said Verily, "and yet so many people have gone to so much trouble to prevent you from doing it?"

"Maybe they just don't like my face."

"I can appreciate the sentiment," said Verily, "but I think it's more likely that they fear your power. Once you made that plow, once you set Arthur Stuart free, it became known that such a man as you existed. And evil people naturally assume that you will use that power exactly as they would use it."

"And how is that?"

"The greedy among them think of gold. What vault could keep you out? Since the only thing that keeps them from stealing is that they can't get into the vaults, they can't believe you won't use the power that way. By the same reasoning, the more ambitious of your enemies will imagine you have designs on public power and prestige, and they will try to discredit you in advance by tarring you with whatever charge they think might be believed. The mere fact that you've been tried taints you, even though you were acquitted."

"So you're saying they don't have any more idea what I'm spose to do than I have."

"I'm saying that your chances of never getting locked up again are remote."

"And so that's why you're coming along."

"You can't build your Crystal City from inside a jail, Alvin."

"Verily Cooper, if you think I'm going to believe that's why you're coming with me, think again, my friend."

"Oh?"

"You're coming along because this is the most exciting thing going on and you don't want to miss any of it."

"Exciting? Sitting here all day in the heat while you watch a Frenchman paint?"

"That's what made you mad," said Alvin. "You wanted to be there yourself to see Arthur talk them birds into posing."

Verily grinned. "Must have been a sight to see."

"For the first couple of minutes, maybe." Alvin yawned.

"Oh, that's right, your life is so boring," said Verily.

"No, I was just thinking that you would have gotten a lot bigger kick out of the way we broke into the taxidermist's shop and set free a bird that wasn't quite dead."

Verily paced around the room, orating. "That's it! Right there! This is intolerable! This is what makes me so angry! Leaving me out of everything fun! This is why you are the most irritating friend a man could have!"

"But Verily, I didn't know when I left the house that anything like that was going to happen."

"That's exactly my point," said Verily. "You don't know what's going to happen, and given what's happened to you your whole life, it is unreasonable—indeed it is unconscionable—for you to presume that any task you set out on will proceed without dangerous and fascinating consequences!"

"So what's your solution?"

Verily knelt before him and rested his hands on Alvin's knees. Nose to nose he said, "Always take me with you, dammit!"

"Even when I have to whip it out and pee into a bush?"

"If I allow any exceptions, then sure as you're born, there'll be a talking badger in the bush who'll clamp his jaws on your pisser and won't let go till you give him the secret of the universe."

"Well, hell, Verily, if that ever happens I'll just have to pee sitting down for the rest of my life, cause I don't know the secret of the universe."

"And *that's* why you've got to keep me with you."

"Why, do *you* know the secret?"

"No, but I can strangle the badger till he lets you go."

"Badgers got powerful claws, Verily. Your legs'd be in shreds in ten seconds. You are such a greenhorn."

"There is no badger, Alvin! This was a hypothetical situation, deliberately exaggerated for rhetorical effect."

"You're spitting right in my face, Very."

"I am with you through it all, Alvin. That's what I'm saying."

"I know, Verily Cooper. I'm counting on you."

4

Stirred-Up

In the cheap boardinghouse where Calvin and Honoré were staying, the kitchen was in the back garden. This was fine with them. Arriving home from a night of carousing, they wanted something to eat but didn't want to call the landlady's attention to their late arrival. This was Camelot, after all, in which men were expected to drink, but only with absolute decorum, and never in a way that would discommode polite ladies.

Most of the food was in the locked pantry inside the house, on the ground floor where the slaves lived. No need to wake them up. The kitchen shed had a little food in it. There was a pot of cheap cooking molasses, some rancid butter, and leftover chickpeas stuck to the pot they had been cooked in. Honoré de Balzac looked at the mess with distaste. But Calvin just grinned at him.

"You're too finicky, Monsieur Haute Société," said Calvin. "This is all we need for a good batch of stirred-up."

"A word that I thank God I am not familiar with."

"It's called stirred-up because you stir it up." In moments Calvin had the stove hot and rancid butter melting in the frying pan. He ladled in some molasses and scraped chickpeas out of the pot, adding them to the mess. Then he stirred.

"See?" he said. "I'm stirring."

"You are stirring side-to-side," said Honoré. "And the mixture is going steadily down in quality. The one thing you are *not* doing is stirring *up.*"

"Ain't English funny?" said Calvin.

"The longer I know you, the less sure I am that what you speak is English."

"Well, hell, that's the glory of English. You can speak it ten thousand different ways, and it's still OK."

"That barbarous expression! 'O. K.' What does this mean?"

"Oll Korrect," said Calvin. "Making fun of people who care too much about how words get writ down."

"Now, writing *down*, that makes sense. The ink flows down. The pen points down. Your hideous mixture should be called 'stirred-down.' "

The butter-and-molasses mess was bubbling now. "Nice and hot," said Calvin. "Want some?"

"Only to ward off imminent death."

"This cures not just hunger but the French disease and cholera too, not to mention making mad dogs whimper and run away."

"In France we call it the English disease."

"That bunch of Puritans? How could they catch a disease of coition?"

"They may be pure in doctrine, but they hump like bunnies," said Honoré. "Nine children to a family, or it's a sign God hates them."

"I'm a-feared I done taught you to talk substandard English, my friend." Calvin tasted the stirred-up. It was good. The chickpeas were a little hard, and Calvin suspected that in the darkness he had inadvertently added some fresh insect flesh to the mix, but he'd had enough to drink that he cared less than he might have sober. "Polite people don't say 'hump.' "

"I thought that *was* a euphemism."

"But it's a coarse one. We're supposed to get into fine homes here, but we'll never do it if you talk like that." Calvin proffered the spoon.

Honoré winced at the smell, then tasted it. It burned his tongue. Panting, he fanned his open mouth.

"Careful," said Calvin. "It's hot."

"Thank God the Inquisition didn't know about *you*," said Honoré.

"Tastes good, though, don't it?"

Honoré crunched up some chickpeas in his mouth. Sweet and buttery. "In a crude, primitive, savage way, yes."

"Crude, primitive, and savage are the best features of America," said Calvin.

"Sadly so," said Honoré. "Unlike Rousseau, I do not find savages to be noble."

"But they hump like bunnies!" said Calvin. In his drunken state, this was indescribably funny. He laughed until he wheezed. Then he puked into the pan of stirred-up.

"Is this part of the recipe?" asked Honoré. "The pièce de résistance?"

"It wasn't the stirred-up made me splash," said Calvin. "It was that vinegar you made us drink."

"I promise you it was the best wine in the house."

"That's cause fellows don't go there for wine. Corn likker is more what they specialize in."

"I would rather regurgitate than let the corn alcohol make me blind," said Honoré. "Those seem to have been the two choices."

"It was the only saloon open on the waterfront."

"The only one that hadn't already thrown us out, you mean."

"Are you getting fussy now? I thought you liked adventure."

"I do. But I believe I have now gathered all the material I need about the lowest dregs of American society."

"Then go home, you frog-eating stump-licker."

"Stump-licker?" asked Honoré.

"What about it?"

"You are very, very drunk."

"At least my coat isn't on fire."

Honoré slowly looked down at his coattail, which was indeed smoldering at the edge of the stove fire. He carefully lifted the fabric for closer inspection. "I don't think this can be laundered out."

"Wait till I'm awake," said Calvin. "I can fix it." He giggled. "I'm a Maker."

"If I throw up, will I feel as good as you?"

"I feel like hammered horse pucky," said Calvin.

"That is exactly the improvement I want." Honoré retched, but he missed the pan. His vomit sizzled on the stovetop.

"Behold the man of education and refinement," said Honoré.

"That's kind of an unattractive smell," said Calvin.

"I need to go to bed," said Honoré. "I don't feel well."

They made it to the bushes along the garden wall before they realized that they weren't heading for the house. Giggling, they collapsed under the greenery and in moments they were both asleep.

The sun was shining brightly and Calvin was a mass of sweat when he finally came to. He could feel bugs crawling on him and his first impulse was to leap to his feet and brush them off. But his body did not respond at all. He just lay there. He couldn't even open his eyes.

A faint breeze stirred the air. The bugs moved again on his face. Oh. Not bugs at all. Leaves. He was lying in shrubbery.

"Sometimes I just wish we could build a wall around the Crown Colonies and keep all those meddlesome foreigners out."

A woman's voice. Footsteps on the brick sidewalk.

"Did you hear that the Queen is going to grant an audience to that busybody bluestocking abolitionist schoolteacher?"

"No, that's too much to believe."

"I agree but with Lady Ashworth as her sponsor—"

"Lady Ashworth!"

The ladies stopped their ambulation only a few steps away from where Calvin lay.

"To think that Lady Ashworth won't even invite you to her soirees—"

"I beg your pardon, but I have declined her invitations."

"And yet she'll present this Peggy person—"

"I thought her name was Margaret—"

"But her people call her Peggy, as if she were a horse."

"And where is her husband? *If* she has one."

"Oh, she has one. Tried and acquitted of slave-stealing, but we all know a slaveholder can't get justice in those abolitionist courts."

"How do you find *out* these things?"

"Do you think the King's agents don't investigate foreigners who come here to stir up trouble?"

"Instead of investigating, why don't they just keep them out?"

"Oh!"

The exclamation of surprise told Calvin that he had just been spotted. Even though some control was returning, he decided that keeping his eyes closed and lying very still was the better part of valor. Besides, with his face covered by leaves, he would not be recognizable later; if he moved, they might see his face.

"My laws, this boardinghouse should be closed down. It brings entirely the wrong element into a respectable part of town."

"Look. He has fouled his trousers."

"This is intolerable. I'm going to have to complain to the magistrate."

"How can you?"

"How can I not?"

"But your testimony before the court—how could you possibly describe this wretched man's condition, while remaining a lady?"

"Dear me."

"No, we simply did not see him."

"Oh!"

The second exclamation told Calvin that they had found Honoré de Balzac. It was comforting to know he was not alone in his humiliation.

"Worse and worse."

"Clearly he is no gentleman. But to be out-of-doors without trousers at all!"

"Can you . . . can you see his . . ."

Calvin felt that this had gone far enough. Without opening his eyes, he spoke in a thick Spanish accent, imitating the slavers he had heard on the docks. "Señoritas, this tiny White man is nothing compared to the naked Black men in my warehouse on the Spanish dock!"

Shrieking softly, the ladies bustled away. Calvin lay there shaking with silent laughter.

Honoré's voice emerged from the bushes not far away. "Shame on you. A writer of novels has a brilliant chance to hear the way women really talk to each other, and *you* scare them away."

Calvin didn't care. Honoré could pretend to be a writer, but Calvin didn't believe he would ever write anything. "How did you lose your pants?"

"I took them off when I got up to void my bladder, and then I couldn't find them."

"Were we drunk last night?"

"I hope so," said Honoré. "It is the only honorable way I can think of for us to end up sleeping together under a hedge."

By now they had both rolled out from under the bushes. Squinting, Honoré was staggering here and there, searching for his trousers. He paused to look Calvin up and down. "I may be a little bit nude, but at least I did not wet my trousers."

Calvin found them, hanging on the hedge, wet and stained. Calvin pointed and laughed. "You took them off and *then* you peed on them!"

Honoré looked at his trousers mournfully. "It was dark."

Holding his dirty laundry in front of him, Honoré followed Calvin toward the house. As they passed the kitchen shed, they caught a glare from the tiny old Black woman who supervised the cooking. But that was as much of a rebuke as they would ever hear from a slave. They went in through the ground floor, where Honoré handed his wet trousers to the laundress. "I'll need these tonight before dinner," he said.

Keeping her head averted, the slave woman murmured her assent and started to move away.

"Wait!" cried Honoré. "Calvin's got some just as bad off as mine."

"She can come up and get them later," said Calvin.

"Take them off now," said Honoré. "She will not look at your hairy white legs."

Calvin turned his back, stripped off his pants, and handed them to her. She scurried away.

"You are so silly to be shy," said Honoré. "It does not matter what servants see. It is like being naked in front of trees or cats."

"I just don't like going up to our room without trousers."

"In trousers wet with urine, you will be disgusting. But if we are both naked, everyone will pretend not to have seen us. We are invisible."

"Does that mean you plan to use the front stairs?"

"Of course not," said Honoré. "And I must lead the way, for if I have to climb three flights of stairs looking at your buttocks I will lose the ability to write of beauty for at least a month."

"Why do you think the cook glared at us?" asked Calvin.

"I have no idea, my friend," said Honoré. "But does she need a reason? Of course all the Black people in this place hate all the White people."

"But usually they don't show it," said Calvin.

"Usually the White men wear trousers," said Honoré. "I am quite certain that the slaves all knew we were asleep under the hedge long before we woke up. But they did not cover us or waken us— that is how they show their hatred. By not doing things that no one commanded them to do."

Calvin chuckled.

"Tell me what's funny?" Honoré demanded.

"I was just thinking—maybe it wasn't you what peed on your trousers."

Honoré pondered this for a few moments. "For that matter, my friend, maybe it wasn't you who peed on *yours*."

Calvin groaned. "You are an evil man, Honoré, with an evil imagination."

"It is my knack."

Not till they got to their room and were changing clothes had Calvin's head cleared enough for him to realize the significance of what the ladies were talking about by the hedge. "A schoolteacher abolitionist named Peggy? That's got to be Miz Larner, the schoolteacher Alvin married."

"Oh, my poor Calvin. You went three days without mentioning your brother, and now you have relapsed."

"I been thinking about him ever since we got that letter from Mother telling about the wedding and how the curse was lifted and all. I wonder if he plans on having seven sons." Calvin cackled with laughter.

"If he has such a plan we must find him and stop him," said Honoré. "Two Makers is more than the world needs already. We have no need for three."

"What I'm thinking is we ought to look up this bluestocking abolitionist Peggy and make her acquaintance."

"Calvin, what kind of trouble are you planning to make?"

"No trouble at all," said Calvin, annoyed. "Why do you think I want to cause trouble?"

"Because you are awake."

"She's going to have an audience with the Queen. Maybe we can slip in with her. Meet some royalty."

"Why will she help you? If she is married to Alvin, she must know your reputation."

"What reputation?" Calvin didn't like the direction Honoré's comments were tending. "What do you know about my reputation? I don't even have a reputation."

"I have been with you continuously for months, my friend. It is impossible you do not have a reputation with your family and your neighbors. This is the reputation that your brother's wife would know."

"My reputation is that I was a cute little kid when anybody bothered to notice that I existed."

"Oh no, Calvin. I am quite sure your reputation is that you are envious, spiteful, prone to outbursts of rage, and incapable of admitting an error. Your family and neighbors could not have missed these traits."

After all these months, to discover that Honoré had such an opinion of him was unbearable. Calvin felt fury rise up inside him, and he would have lashed out at Honoré had the little Frenchman not looked so utterly cheerful and open-faced. Was it possible he had not meant to offend?

"You see what I mean?" said Honoré. "You are angry even now, and you resent me. But why? I mean no harm by these observations. I am a novelist. I study life. You are alive, so I study you. I find you endlessly fascinating. A man with both the ambition and the ability to be great, who is so little in control of his impulses that he pisses away his greatness. You are a tiger studying to be a mouse. This is how the world is kept safe from you. This is why you will never be a Napoleon."

Calvin roared in fury, but could not bring himself to strike Honoré himself, who was, after all, the only friend he had ever had. So he smashed the flat of his hand against the wall.

"But look," said Honoré. "It is the wall you hit, and not my face. So I was not entirely right. You do have some self-control. You are able to respect another man's opinion."

"I am not a mouse," said Calvin.

"No no, you did not understand. I said you are studying to be a mouse, not that you have passed your examinations and are now living on cheese. When I hear you go, squeak squeak squeak, I think, What an odd noise to come from a tiger. I have known few tigers in my life. Many mice, but few tigers. So you are precious to me, my friend. I am sad to hear this squeaking. And your sister-in-law, I think all she knows of you is the squeak, that is what I was saying before. That is why I doubt that she will be glad to see you."

"I can roar if I need to," said Calvin.

"Look at how angry you are. What would you do, hit me? That, my dear friend, would be a squeak." Honoré looked at his own naked body. "I am filthy like a wallowing pig. I will order up a bath. You may use the water when I'm done."

Calvin did not answer. Instead he sent his doodlebug over the surface of his own body, ejecting all the dirt and grime, the dried-on urine and sweat, the dust and ashes in his hair. It took only moments, for once he had shown his doodlebug what to do, it could finish on its own without his directing it, just as his hand could keep sawing without him thinking of the saw, or his fingers tie a knot without him even looking at the string.

Honoré's eyes grew wide. "Why have you made your underwear disappear?"

Only then did Calvin realize that every foreign object had been pulverized and ejected from his body. "Who cares? I'm cleaner right now than you'll ever be."

"While you are using your powers to beautify yourself, why not change your odor? To a flower, perhaps. Not a nasturtium—those already smell like unwashed feet. What about a lilac? Or a rose?"

"Why don't I change your nose to a cauliflower? Oops, too late, someone already did."

"Aha, you are insulting me with cabbages." Honoré pulled the string that would ring a bell in the servants' quarters.

Calvin pulled on some clean clothes—cleanish, anyway—and was just leaving the room when a slave arrived in response to Honoré's summons. Honoré was buck naked now, without even shirttails to conceal nature's modest endowment, but he seemed utterly unaware; and, for that matter, the slave might not have seen him, for her gaze never seemed to leave the floor. Honoré was still specifying exactly how many kettles of hot water he wanted in his tub when Calvin started down the stairs and could hear the Frenchman's voice no more.

Lady Ashworth's door was opened by a wiry old slave in close-fitting livery. "Howdy," said Calvin. "I heard tell that my sister-in-law Peggy Smith was visiting here and—"

The slave walked away and left him standing at the door. But the door was still open, so Calvin stepped inside onto the porch. By habit he sent his doodlebug through the house. He could see from the heartfires where everybody was; unlike Peggy, though, he couldn't see a thing in the heartfires, and couldn't recognize anyone in particular. All he knew was a living soul was there, and by the brightness of it, whether it was human or not.

He could guess, though. The heartfire moving slowly up the back stairs must be the slave who had opened the door for him. The heartfire on the porch above Calvin, toward which the slave was moving, had to be Lady Ashworth. Or Lord Ashworth, perhaps—but no, he was likely to be as close as possible to the King.

He set his doodlebug into the floor of the upstairs porch, feeling the vibration caused by their talking. With a little concentration, it turned into sound. The slave sure didn't say much. "Gentleman at the door."

"I'm expecting no callers."

"Say he sister be Peggy Smith."

"I don't know anyone by such a . . . oh, perhaps Margaret Larner—but she isn't here. Tell him she isn't here."

The slave immediately walked away from Lady Ashworth. Stupid woman, thought Calvin. I never thought she'd be here, I need to know where she *is*. Don't they teach common civility to folks in Camelot? Or maybe she's so high up in the King's court that she didn't need to show decent manners to common folk.

Well, thought Calvin, let's see what your manners turn into when *I'm* through with you.

He could see the slave's slow-moving heartfire on the back stairs. Calvin walked into the house and found the front stairs, then bounded lightly up to the next floor. The family entertained on this level and the large ballroom had three large French doors opening onto the gallery, where Lady Ashworth was studying a plant, pruning shears in hand.

"That plant needs no pruning," said Calvin, putting on the sophisticated English voice he had learned in London.

Lady Ashworth turned toward him in shock. "I beg your pardon. You were not admitted here."

"The doors were open. I heard you tell your servant to send me away. But I could not bear to leave without having seen a lady of such legendary grace and beauty."

"Your compliments disgust me," she said, her cavalier drawl lengthening with the fervor of her opinion. "I have no patience with dandies, and as for trespassers, I generally have them killed."

"There's no need to have me killed. Your contemptuous gaze has already stopped my heart from beating."

"Oh, I see, you're not flattering me, you're mocking me. Don't you know this house is full of servants? I'll have you thrown out."

"Blacks lay hands on a White man?"

"We always use our servants to take out the trash."

The banter was not engaging even a tiny fraction of Calvin's attention. Instead he was using his doodlebug to explore Lady Ashworth's body. In his peregrinations with Honoré de Balzac, Calvin had watched the Frenchman seduce several dozen women of every social class, and because Calvin was a scientist at heart, he had used his doodlebug to note the changes in a woman's body as her lust was aroused. There were tiny organs where certain juices were made and released into the blood. It was hard to find them, but once found, they could easily be stimulated. In moments, Calvin had three different glands secreting rather strong doses of the juices of desire, and now it was his eyes, not just his doodlebug, that could see the transformation in Lady Ashworth. Her eyes grew heavy-lidded, her manner more aloof, her voice huskier.

"Compared to your grace and beauty I am trash and nothing more," Calvin said. "But I am *your* trash, my lady, to do with as you will. Discard me and I will cease to exist. Save me and I will become whatever you want me to be. A jewel to wear upon your bosom. A fan behind which your beauty may continue unobserved. Or perhaps the glove in which your hand may stay clean and warm."

"Who would ever have guessed that such talk could come from a frontier boy from Wobbish," she said, suppressing a smile.

"What matters isn't where a man is from, but where he's going. I think that all my life was leading to this moment. To this hot day in Camelot, this porch, this jungle of living plants, this magnificent Eve who is tending the garden."

She looked down at her pruning shears. "But you said I shouldn't cut this plant."

"It would be heartless," said Calvin. "It reaches up, not to the sun, but to you. Do not despise what grows for love of you, my lady."

She blushed and breathed more rapidly. "The things you say."

"I came in search of my brother's wife, because I heard she had visited here," said Calvin. "I could have left a card with your servant to accomplish that."

"I suppose you could."

"But even on the harsh cobbles of the street, I could hear you like music, smell you like roses, see you like the light of the one star breaking through on a cloudy night. I knew that in all the world this is the place I had to be, even if it cost me my life or my honor. My lady, until this moment every day of life was a burden, without purpose or joy. Now all I long for is to stay here, looking at you, wondering at the marvels of perfection concealed by the draperies of your clothing, tied up by the pins in your hair."

She was trembling. "You shouldn't talk about such . . ."

He stood before her now, inches from her. As he had seen with Honoré's seductions, his closeness would heighten the feelings within her. He reached up and brushed his fingers gently across her cheek, then her neck, her shoulder, touching only bare skin. She gasped but did not speak, did not take her eyes from his.

"My eyes imagine," he murmured, "my lips imagine, every part of my body imagines being close to you, holding you, becoming part of you."

She staggered, barely able to walk as she led him from the porch to her bedroom.

Besides studying the women's bodies, Calvin had also studied Honoré's, had seen how the Frenchman tried to maintain himself on the brink of ecstacy for as long as possible without crossing over. What Honoré had to do with self-discipline, Calvin could do mechanically, with his doodlebug. Lady Ashworth was possessed by pleasure many times and in many ways before Calvin finally allowed himself to find release. They lay together on sheets clammy with their sweat. "If this is how the devil rewards wickedness," murmured Lady Ashworth, "I understand why God seems to be losing ground in this world." But there was sadness in her voice, for now her conscience was reawakening, ready to punish her for the pleasure she had taken.

"There was no wickedness here today," said Calvin. "Was not your body made by God? Did not these desires come from that body? What are you but the woman God made you to be? What am I but the man God brought here to worship you?"

"I don't even know your name," she said.

"Calvin."

"Calvin? That's all?"

"Calvin Maker."

"A good name, my love," she said. "For you have made me. Until this hour I did not truly exist."

Calvin wanted to laugh in her face. This is all that romance and love amounted to. Juices flowing from the glands. Bodies coupling in heat. A lot of pretty talk surrounding it.

He cleaned his body again. Hers also. But not the seed he left inside her. On impulse he followed it, wondering what it might accomplish. The idea rather appealed to him—a child of his, raised in a noble house. If he wanted to have seven sons, did it matter whether they all had the same mother? Let this be the first.

Was it possible to decide whether it would be a boy or a girl? He didn't know. Maybe Alvin could comprehend things as small as this, but it was all Calvin could do just to follow what was happening inside Lady Ashworth's body. And then even that slipped away from him. He just didn't know what he was looking for. At least she wasn't already pregnant.

"That was my first time, you know," he said.

"How could it be?" she said. "You knew everything. You knew how to—my husband knows nothing compared to you."

"My first time," he said. "I never had another woman until now. Your body taught me all I needed to know."

He caused the sweat on the sheets to dry, despite the dampness of the air. He rose from the cool dry bed, clean and fresh as he was when he arrived. He looked at her. Not young, really; sagging just a bit; but not too bad, considering. Honoré would probably approve. If he decided to tell him.

Oh, he would tell him. Without doubt, for Honoré would love the story of it, would love hearing how much Calvin had learned from his constant dalliances.

"Where is my sister-in-law?" Calvin asked matter-of-factly.

"Don't go," said Lady Ashworth.

"It wouldn't do for me to stay," said Calvin. "The gossipy ladies of Camelot would never understand the perfect beauty of this hour."

"But you'll come back."

"As often as prudence allows," he said. "For I will not permit my visits here to do you any harm."

"What have I done," she murmured. "I am not a woman who commits adultery."

On the contrary, Calvin thought. You're just a woman who was never tempted until now. That's all that virtue amounts to, isn't it? Virtue is what you treasure until you feel desire, and then it becomes an intolerable burden to be cast away, and only to be picked up again when the desire fades.

"You are a woman who married before she met the love of her life," said Calvin. "You serve your husband well. He has no reason to complain of you. But he will never love you as I love you."

A tear slipped out of her eye and ran across her temple onto her hair-strewn pillow. "He rides me impatiently, like a carriage, getting out almost before he reaches his destination."

"Then he has his use of you, and you of him," said Calvin. "The contract of marriage is well-fulfilled."

"But what about God?"

"God is infinitely compassionate," said Calvin. "He understands us more perfectly than humans ever can. And he forgives."

He bent over her and kissed her one more time. She told him where Peggy was staying. He left the house whistling. What fun! No wonder Honoré spent so much time in pursuit of women.

5

Purity

Purity did her best to live up to her name. She had been a good little girl, and only got better through her teens, for she believed what the ministers taught and besides, wickedness never had much attraction for her.

But living up to her name had come to mean more to her than mere obedience to the word of God in the Bible. For she realized that her name was her only link back to her true identity—to the parents who had died when she was only a baby, and whose only contribution to her upbringing was the name they gave her.

The name contained clues. Here in Massachusetts, the people mostly hailed from the East Anglian and Essex Puritan traditions, which did not name children for virtues. That was a custom more common in Sussex, which suggested that Purity's family had lived in Netticut, not in Massachusetts.

And as Purity grew older in the orphan house in Cambridge, Reverend Hezekiah Study, now well into his seventies, took notice of her bright mind and insisted, against tradition, that she be given a full education of the type given to boys. Of course it was out of the question for her to enroll at Harvard College, for that school was devoted to training ministers. But she was allowed to sit on a stool in the corridor outside any classroom she wanted, and overhear whatever portion of the lesson was given loudly enough. And they let her have access to the library.

She soon learned that the library was the better teacher, for the authors of the books were helpless to shut her out because of her sex. Having put their best knowledge into print, they had to endure the ignominy of having a woman read it and understand it. The living professors, on the contrary, took notice of when Purity was listening, and most of them used that occasion to speak very quietly, to close the door, or to speak in Latin or Greek, which the students presumably spoke and Purity was presumed not to understand at all. On the contrary, she read Latin and Greek with great fluency and pronounced it better than all but a few of the male students—how else would she have come to the notice of a traditionalist like Reverend Study?—but she began to learn that the professors were rarely as coherent, deep, or penetrating in their thought as the authors of the books.

There were exceptions. Young Waldo Emerson, who had only just graduated from Harvard himself, would have brought her right into his classroom if she had not refused. As it was, she heard every word of his teaching quite clearly, and while he was prone to epigrams as a substitute for analysis, his enthusiasm for the life of the mind was contagious and exhilarating. She knew that Emerson cared much more about being thought to be erudite than actually thinking deeply—his "philosophy" seemed to consist of anything that would be particularly annoying to the powers that be without being so shocking that they would fire him. He got the reputation among the students as an original and a rebel without having to pay the penalty for actually being either.

It was not from Emerson, therefore, but from the library that Purity made the next leap toward understanding the meaning of her name and what it told her about her parents' lives. For it was in a treatise, "On the Care of Offspring of Witches and Heretics," by Cotton Mather that she first came to understand why she was an orphan bearing a Netticut name in a Massachusetts house.

"All children being born equally tainted with original sin from Adam," he wrote, "and the children of fallen parents being therefore not more tainted than the children of the elect, it is unjust to exact from them penalties other than those that naturally accrue to child-

hood, viz. subjection to authority, ignorance, inclination to disobe-
dience, frequent punishment for inattention, etc.'' Purity read this
passage with delight, for after all the constant implication that the
children of the orphanage clearly were not as likely to be elect as
children growing up with parents who were members of the
churches, it was a relief to hear no less an authority than the great
Cotton Mather declare that it was unjust to treat one child differently
from any other.

So she was quite excited when she read the next sentence, and
almost failed to notice its significance. ''To give the children the
best chance to avoid the posthumous influence of their parents and
the suspicion of their neighbors, however, their removal from the
parish, even the colony, of their birth would be the wisest course.''

And the clincher, several sentences later: ''Their family name
should be taken from them, for it is a disgrace, but let not their
baptismal name be changed, for that name cometh unto them from
and in the name of Christ, however unworthy might have been the
parents who proffered them up for christening.''

I am named Purity, she thought. A Netticut name, but I am in
Massachusetts. My parents are dead.

Hanged as witches or burned as heretics. And more likely,
witches, for the most common heresy is Quakerism and then I would
not be named Purity, while a witch would try to conceal what he
was and would therefore name his children as his neighbors named
theirs.

This knowledge brought her both alarm and relief. Alarm because she had to be on constant guard lest she also be accused of
witchery. Alarm because now she had to wonder if her ability to
sense easily what other people were feeling was what the witchy
folk called a ''knack.''

Relief because the mystery of her parents had at last been solved.
Her mother had not been a fornicator or adulteress who delivered
up the baby to an orphanage with the name pinned to a blanket. Her
father had not been carried off as a punishment of God through a
plague or accident. Her parents had instead been hanged for witchery, and given what she knew of witch trials, in all likelihood they
were innocent.

As Waldo Emerson said in class one day, ''When does a God-
given talent cross an imperceptible boundary and become a devilish
knack? And how does the devil go about bestowing gifts and hidden
powers that, when they were granted unto prophets and apostles in
the holy scriptures, were clearly gifts of the Spirit of God? Is it not

possible that in condemning the talent instead of the misuse of that talent, we are rejecting the gifts of God and slaying some of his best beloved? Should we not then judge the moral character of the act rather than its extraordinariness?''

Purity sat in the hallway when he said this, grateful that she was not inside the classroom where the young men would see her trembling, would see the tears streaming down her cheeks, and would think her a weak womanly creature. My parents were innocent, she said to herself, and my talent is from God, to be used in his holy service. Only if I were to turn it to the service of Satan would I be a witch. I might be one of the elect after all.

She fled the college before the lecture was over, lest she be forced to converse with someone, and wandered in the woods along the river Euphrates. Boats plied the river from Boston as far inland as their draft would allow, but the boatmen took no heed of her, since she was a land creature and beneath their notice.

If my talent is from God, she thought, then if I stay here and hide it, am I not rejecting that talent? Am I not burying it in the garden, like the foolish servant in the parable? Should I not find the greater purpose for which the talent was given?

She imagined herself a missionary in some heathen land like Africa or France, able to understand the natives long before she learned their language. She imagined herself a diplomat for the Protectorate, using her talent to discern when foreign ambassadors or heads of state were lying and when they were sincere.

And then, in place of imagination, she saw a boy of twelve or so, dark of skin with tight-curled hair, shoot up out of the river not three rods off, water falling off him, shining in the sunlight, his mouth open and laughing, and in midair he sees her, and she can see his face change and in that instance she knows what he feels: embarrassment to be seen buck naked by a woman, the fading remnants of his boisterous fun, and, just dawning under the surface where his own mind couldn't know it yet, love.

Well I never had *that* effect before, thought Purity. It was flattering. Not that the love of a twelve-year-old boy was ever going to affect her life, but it was sweet to know that at the cusp of manhood this lad could catch a glimpse of her and see, not the orphan bluestocking that so disgusted or terrified the young men of Cambridge, but a woman. Indeed, what he must have seen and loved was not a woman, but Woman, for Purity had read enough Plato to know that while wicked men lusted after particular women, a man of lofty aspirations loved the glimpse of Woman that he saw in good women, and by loving the ideal in her helped bring her to closer consonance, like lifting the flat shadow off the road and rejoining it to the whole being who cast it.

What in the world am I thinking about. This child is no doubt every bit as peculiar as I am, him being Black in a land of Whites, as I am an orphan in a land of families and am thought to be the child of witches to boot.

All these thoughts passed through her mind like a long crackle of lightning, and the boy splashed back down into the water, and then near him another person rose, a grown man, heavily muscled in the shoulders and back and arms, and considerably taller than the boy, so that although he didn't jump, when he stood his bare white buttocks showed almost completely above the water, and when he saw where the Black boy was looking, his mouth agape with love, he turned and . . .

Purity looked away in time. There was no reason to allow the possibility of impure thoughts into her mind. She might or might not be one of the elect, but there was no need to drag herself closer to the pit, thus requiring a greater atonement by Christ to draw her out.

"So much for a spot where nobody comes!" the man cried out, laughing. She heard a great splashing, which had to be the two of them coming out of the water. "Just a minute and we'll be dressed so you can go on with your walk, ma'am."

"Never mind," she said. "I can go another way."

But at the moment she took her first step to return along the riverbank, a coarse-looking man with heavy muscles and a menacing cast to his face stepped in front of her. She couldn't help gasping and stepping back—

Only to find that she was stepping on a man's boot.

"Ouch," he said mildly.

She whirled around. There were two men, actually, one of them a dapper but smallish man who looked at her with a candor that she found disturbing. But the man she had stepped on was a tall, dignified-looking man who dressed like a professional man. Not in the jet-black costume of a minister, but not in the earthy "sad" colors of the common folk of New England. No, he dressed like nothing so much as . . .

"An Englishman," she said. "A barrister."

"I confess it, but marvel that you guessed it."

"English visitors come to Cambridge often, sir," she said. "Some are barristers. They seem to have a way of dressing to show that their clothing cost considerable money without ever quite violating the sumptuary laws.'' She turned around to face the menacing man, unsure whether this Englishman was a match for him.

But then she realized that she had been momentarily deceived by appearances. There was no menace in the rough fellow, no more than in the Englishman. And the other one, the dapper little fellow who was still inspecting her with his eyes, posed no danger, either. It was as if he knew only one way to think of women, and therefore shelved his attitude toward Purity under the heading ''objects of lust,'' but it was a volume that would gather dust before he cared enough to take it down and try to read it.

''We must have frightened you,'' said the Englishman. ''Our friends were determined to bathe, and we were determined to lie on the riverbank and nap, and so you didn't see any of us until you were right among us, and I apologize that you saw two of our company in such a state of deshabille.''

''And what, pray, is a state of Jezebel?''

The dapper little fellow laughed aloud, then stopped abruptly and turned away. Why? He was afraid. Of what?

''Pardon my French,'' said the Englishman. ''In London we are not so pure as the gentlefolk of New England. When Napoleon took over France and proceeded to annex the bulk of Europe, there were few places for the displaced aristocracy and royalty to go. London is crawling with French visitors, and suddenly French words are chic. Oops, there I go again.''

''You still have not told me what the French word meant. 'Cheek,' however, I understand—it is a characteristic that your whole company here seems to have.''

The barrister chuckled. ''I would say that it's yourself that takes a cheeky tone with strangers, if it were not such an improper thing to say to a young lady to whom I have not been introduced. I pray you, tell me the name of your father and where he lives so I can inquire after your health.''

''My father is dead,'' she said, and then added, despite her own sense of panic as she did so, ''He was hanged as a witch in Netticut.''

They fell silent, all of them, and it made her uneasy, for they had nothing like the reaction she expected. Not revulsion at her confession of such indecent family connections; rather they all simply closed off and looked another way.

''Well, I'm sorry to remind you of such a tragic event,'' said the Englishman.

''Please don't be. I never knew him. I only just realized what his fate must have been. You don't imagine that anyone at the orphanage would tell me such a thing outright!''

"But you are a lady, aren't you?" asked the Englishman. "There's nothing of the schoolgirl about you."

"Being an orphan does not stop when you come of age," said Purity. "But I will serve myself as father and mother, and give you my consent to introduce yourself to me."

The Englishman bowed deeply. "My name is Verily Cooper," he said. "And my company at the moment consists of Mike Fink, who has been in the waterborne transportation business but is on a leave-of-absence, and my dear friend John-James Audubon, who is mute."

"No he's not," said Purity. For she saw in both Cooper and Audubon himself that the statement was a lie. "You really mustn't lie to strangers. It starts things off in such an unfortunate way."

"I assure you, madam," said Cooper, "that in New England, he is and shall remain completely mute."

And with that slight change, she could see in both of them that the statement was now true. "So you choose to be mute here in New England. Let me puzzle this out. You dare not open your mouth; therefore your very speech must put you in a bad light. No, in outright danger, for I think none of you cares much about public opinion. And what could endanger a man, just by speaking? The accent of a forbidden nation. A papist nation, I daresay. And the name being Audubon, and your manners toward a woman being tinged with unspeakable presumptions, I would guess that you are French."

Audubon turned red under his suntan and faced away from her. "I do not know how you know this, but you also must be seeing that I did not act improper to you."

"What she's telling us," said Verily Cooper, "is that she's got her a knack."

"Please keep such crudity for times when you are alone with the ill-mannered," said Purity. "I observe people keenly, that is all. And from his accent I am confident that my reasoning was correct."

The rough fellow, Mike Fink, spoke up. "When you hear a bunch of squealing and snorting, you can bet you're somewhere near a pig."

Purity turned toward him. "I have no idea what you meant by that."

"I'm just saying a knack's a knack."

"Enough," said Cooper. "Less than a week in New England

and we've already forgotten all caution? Knacks are illegal here. Therefore decent people don't have them.''

"Oh yeah," said Mike Fink. "Except she *does*."

"But then, perhaps she is not decent," said Audubon.

It was Purity's turn to blush. "You forget yourself, sir," she said.

"Never mind him," said Cooper. "He's just miffed because you made that remark about unspeakable presumptions."

"You're travelers," she said.

"John-James paints North American birds with an eye toward publishing a book of his pictures for the use of scientists in Europe."

"And for this he needs a troop along? What do you do, hold his brushes?''

"We're not all on the same errand," said Cooper.

At that moment the two she had seen in the river came out of the bushes, still damp-haired but fully clothed.

"Ma'am, I'm so sorry you had to see so much horseflesh without no horses," said the White one.

The Black one said not a thing, but never took his eyes from her.

"This is Alvin Smith," said Cooper. "He's a man of inestimable abilities, but only because nobody has cared enough to estimate them. The short one is Arthur Stuart, no kin to the King, who travels with Alvin as his adopted nephew-in-law, or some such relationship.''

"And you," said Purity, "have been long enough out of England to pick up some American brag."

"But surrounded by Americans as I am," said Cooper, "my brag is like a farthing in a sack of guineas."

She couldn't help but laugh at the way he spoke. "So you travel in New England with a Frenchman, who is only able to avoid being expelled or, worse, arrested as a spy, by pretending to be a mute. You are a barrister, this fellow is a boatman, as I assume, and the two bathers are . . ." Her voice trailed off.

"Are what?" asked Alvin Smith.

"Clean," she said. Then she smiled.

"What were you going to say?" asked Smith.

"Don't press her," said Cooper. "If someone decides to leave something unsaid, my experience is that everyone is happier if they don't insist on his saying it."

"That's OK," said Arthur Stuart. "I don't think she knows herself what was on her lips to say."

She laughed in embarrassment. "It's true," she said. "I think I was hoping that a jest would come to mind, and it didn't."

Alvin smiled at her. "Or else the jest that did come to mind was of a sort that you couldn't imagine yourself making, and so it went away."

She didn't like the way he looked at her as if he thought he knew all about her. Never mind that she must be looking at him the same way—she *did* know about him. He was so full of confidence it made her want to throw mud on him just to show him he wasn't carried along by angels. It was as if he feared nothing and imagined himself capable of achieving anything. And it wasn't an illusion he was trying to create, either. He really *was* conceited; his attitude reeked of it. His only fear was that, when push came to shove, he might turn out to be even better than he thought himself to be.

"I don't know what I done to rub you the wrong way, ma'am," said Smith, "other than bathing nekkid, but that's how my mama taught me it ought to be done, so my clothes don't shrink."

The others laughed. Purity didn't.

"Want something to eat?" Arthur Stuart asked her.

"I don't know, what do you have?" she said.

His eyes were still focused on her, slightly widened, his jaw just a bit slack. Oh, it was love all right, the swooning moon-in-juning kind.

"Berries," said the boy. He held out his hat, which had several dozen blackberries down in it. She reached in, took one, tasted it.

"Oh no," said Cooper mildly. "You've eaten a berry, so you must spend one month of every year in Hades."

"But these berries are from New England, not hell," she said.

"That's a relief," said Smith. "I wasn't sure where the border was."

Purity didn't know how to take this Smith fellow. She didn't like looking at him. His boldness bothered her. He didn't even seem ashamed that she had seen him naked.

Instead she looked at Cooper. The barrister was a pleasant sight indeed. His manner, his dress, his voice, all belonged to a man that Purity thought existed only in a dream. Why was he different from other men who dressed in such a way?

"You aren't an ordinary lawyer," she said to him.

Cooper looked at her in surprise. And then his surprise turned to dread.

"I'm not," he said.

What was he afraid of?

"Yes he is," said Smith.

"No," said Cooper. "Ordinary lawyers make a lot of money. I haven't made a shilling in the past year."

"Is that it?" asked Purity. It could be. Barristers did seem a prosperous lot. But no, it was something else. "I think what makes you different is you don't think you're better than these others."

Cooper looked around at his companions—the smith, the riverman, the French artist, the Black boy—and grinned. "You're mistaken," he said. "I'm definitely the better man."

The others laughed. "Better at what?" asked Mike Fink. "Whining like a mosquito whenever you see a bee?"

"I don't like bees," said Cooper.

"They like *you*," said Arthur Stuart.

"Because I'm sweet." He was joking, but Purity could see that his fear was growing greater. She glanced around, looking for the source of the danger.

Smith noticed the way she looked around and took it as a sign, or perhaps just a reminder. "Come on now," said Smith. "Time for us to move on."

"No," said Cooper. Purity could see his resolve harden. He wasn't just afraid—he was going to act on his fear.

"What's wrong?" asked Smith.

"The girl," said Cooper.

"What about her?" demanded Arthur Stuart. He spoke so truculently that Purity expected one of the men to rebuke him. But no, he was treated as if his voice had equal weight in the company.

"She's going to get us killed."

Now she understood. He was afraid of *her*. "I'm not," she said. "I won't tell anybody he's a papist."

"When they put your hand on the Bible and swear you to tell the truth?" asked Cooper. "You'd send yourself to hell and deny that you know that he's Catholic?"

"I am not a *good* Catholic," said Audubon modestly.

"Then you go to hell no matter who's right," said Smith. It was a joke, but nobody laughed.

Cooper still held Purity in gaze, and now it was her turn to be afraid. She had never seen such intensity in a man, except a preacher in his pulpit, during the most fiery part of the sermon. "Why are you afraid of me?" asked Purity.

"That's why," said Cooper.

"*What's* why?"

"You know that I'm afraid of you. You know too much about what we're thinking."

"I already told you, I don't know what anybody's thinking."

"What we're *feeling,* then." Cooper grinned mirthlessly. "It's your knack."

"We already said that," said Fink.

"What if it is?" Purity said defiantly. "Who's to say that knacks aren't gifts from God?"

"The courts of Massachusetts," said Cooper. "The gallows."

"So she's got a knack," said Smith. "Who doesn't?"

The others nodded.

Except Cooper. "Have you lost your minds? Look at you! Talking knowledgeably of knacks! Admitting that Jean-Jacques here is French and Catholic to boot."

"But she already knew," said Audubon.

"And that didn't bother you?" said Cooper. "That she knew what she could not possibly know?"

"We all know things we shouldn't know," said Smith.

"But until she came along, we were doing a pretty good job of keeping it to ourselves!" Cooper rounded on Purity, loomed over her. "In Puritan country, people hide their knacks or they die. It's a secret they all keep, that they have some special talent, and as soon as they realize what it is they also learn to hide it, to avoid letting anyone know what it is that they do so much better than other people. They call it 'humility.' But this girl has been flaunting her knack."

Only then did Purity realize what she had been doing. Cooper was right—she had never let anyone see how easily she understood their feelings. She had held it back, remaining humble.

"By this time tomorrow I expect this girl will be in jail, and in a month she'll be hanged. The trouble is, when they put her to the question of other witches she's consorted with, whom do you imagine that she'll name? A friend? A beloved teacher? She seems to be a decent person, so it won't be an enemy. No, it'll be strangers. A papist. A journeyman blacksmith. A barrister who seems to be living in the woods. An American riverman."

"I'd never accuse you," she said.

"Oh, well, since you say so," said Cooper.

Suddenly she was aware of Mike Fink standing directly behind her. She could hear his breathing. Long, slow breaths. He wasn't even worried. But she knew that he was capable of killing.

Smith sighed. "Well, Very, you're a quick thinker and you're right. We can't just go on with our journey as if it were safe."

"Yes, you can," she said. "I don't normally act like this. I *was* careless. In the surprise of meeting you here."

"No," said Cooper, "it wasn't meeting us. You were out here walking alone. Oblivious. Blind and deaf. You didn't hear Al and Arthur splashing like babies in the water. You didn't hear Mike howling miserable river ballads in his high-pitched hound-dog voice."

"I wasn't singing," said Mike.

"I never said you were," said Cooper. "Miss—what's your name again?"

"She never said," Fink answered.

"Purity," she said. "My parents named me."

"Miss Purity, why after all these years of living in humility are you suddenly so careless about showing your knack?"

"I told you, I wasn't, or I'm not usually, and it's not a knack anyway, it's a talent, I'm simply observant, I—"

"Today," said Cooper. "This hour. Do you think I'm a fool? I grew up in one of the most witch-ridden parts of England. Not because more people had knacks but because more people were watching for them. You don't last an hour if you're careless. It's a good thing you ran into us and not someone you knew. This place is thick with ministers, and you were going to show your knack no matter whom you met."

Purity was confused. Was he right? Was that why she had fled the college, because she knew that her knack could no longer be hidden?

But why couldn't it be hidden now? What was driving her to reveal it?

"I believe you may be right," she said. "I thank you for waking me up to what I was doing. You have nothing to fear now. I'm going to be careful now."

"Good enough for me," said Smith.

"No, it isn't," said Cooper. "Al, I yield to you on most things, but not on something that's going to get us caught up in some witch trial."

Smith laughed. "I've done my time setting around waiting for lawyers. There ain't no jail can hold me or any of my friends."

"Yes, there is," said Cooper. "It's six feet long, and they nail it shut and bury it."

They all looked thoughtful. Except Arthur Stuart. "So what are you going to do to her?" he demanded. "She ain't done nothing wrong."

"She *hain't* done nothing," said Mike Fink.

Arthur looked at the river rat like he was crazy. "How can *you* correct me? You're even wronger than I was!"

"You left out the *h* in *haint*."

"I won't be accused myself, and I won't accuse you," said Purity.

"I think you will," said Cooper. "I think you want to die."

"Don't be absurd!" she cried.

"More specifically, I think you want to be hanged as a witch."

For a moment she remained poised, meaning to treat this idea with the scorn it deserved. Then the image of her parents on a gallows came to her mind. Or rather, she admitted that it was already in her mind, that it was an image that had dwelt with her ever since she made the connections and realized how they had died. She burst into tears.

"You got no right to make her cry!" shouted Arthur Stuart.

"Hush up, Arthur," said Smith. "Verily's right."

"How do you know this?" said Audubon.

"Look at her."

She was sobbing so hard now that she could hardly stand. She felt long, strong arms around her, and at first she tried to flinch away, thinking it was Mike Fink seizing her from behind; but her movement took her closer to the man who was reaching for her, and she found herself pressed against the fine suit of the barrister, his arms holding her tightly.

"It's all right," said Cooper.

"They hanged my mother and father," she said. Or tried to say—her voice could hardly be understood.

"And you just found out," said Cooper. "Who told you?"

She shook her head, unable to explain.

"Figured it out for yourself?" said Cooper.

She nodded.

"And you belong with them. Not with the people who killed them and put you out to an orphanage."

"They had no right!" she cried. "This is a land of murderers!"

"Hush," said Cooper. "That's how it feels, but you know it isn't true. Oh, there are murderers among them, but that's true everywhere. People who are glad to denounce a neighbor for witchcraft—to settle a quarrel, to get a piece of land, to show everyone how righteous and perceptive they are. But most folks are content to live humbly and let others do the same."

"You don't know!" she said. "Pious killers, all of them!"

"Pious," said Cooper, "but not killers. Think about it, just *think*. Every living soul has some kind of knack. But how many get hanged for witchcraft? Some years maybe five or six. Most years none at all. The people don't want to surround themselves with death. It's life that they want, like all good people everywhere."

"Good people wouldn't take me away from my parents!" Purity cried.

"They thought they were doing good," said Verily. "They thought they were saving you from hell."

She tried to pull away from him. He wouldn't let her.

"Let me go."

"Not yet," he said. "Besides, you have nowhere to go."

"Let her go if she wants," said Arthur Stuart. "We can get away from here. Alvin can start up the greensong and we'll run like the wind and be out of New England before she tells anybody anything."

"That ain't the problem," said Smith. "It's her. Very's worried about keeping her from getting herself killed."

"He doesn't need to worry," Purity said. This time when she pulled away, Cooper let her. "I'll be fine. I just needed to tell somebody. Now I have."

"No," said Cooper. "It's gone. You're not afraid of death anymore, you welcome it, because you think that's the only way you can get home to your family."

"How do you know what I think?" she said. "Is that your knack? I hope not, because you're wrong."

"I didn't say you were *thinking* those things. And no, that's not my knack at all. But I'm a barrister. I've seen people at the most trying moments of their lives. I've seen them when they've decided to give up and let the world have its way. I recognize that decision when I see it. You've decided."

"What if I have?" she asked defiantly. "And anyway I haven't, so it doesn't matter."

Cooper ignored her. "If we leave her here, she'll die, sooner or later. She'll do it just to prove she's part of her family."

"No I won't," said Purity. "I don't even *know* for sure that that's what happened to them. I think the evidence points that way, but it's a slender arrow indeed."

"But you want it to be true," said Cooper.

"That's silly! Why would I want that!"

Cooper said nothing.

"I don't hate it here! People have been kind to me. Reverend

Study arranged to let me use the Harvard library. I get to listen to the lectures. Not that it will ever amount to anything.''

Cooper smiled ever-so-slightly.

"Well, what *can* it amount to?" Purity demanded. "I'm a woman. Either I'll marry or I won't. If I marry, I'll be raising children. Maybe I'll teach them to read before they get to school. But I won't be the one who gets to teach them Latin and Greek. They'll get their Caesar and their Tully and their Homer from someone else. And if I don't marry, the best I can hope for is to be kept on as a matron in the orphanage. Children are the only people who'll ever hear my voice.''

"Ain't nothing wrong with children," said Arthur Stuart.

"That's not what she means anyway," said Cooper.

"Don't you dare interpret me anymore!" Purity cried. "You think you know me better than you know yourself!"

"Yes, I think I do," said Cooper. "I've been down the same road.''

"Oh, were you an orphan? As a barrister, did they make you work with children all the time? Did they make you sit outside the courtroom to plead your case?''

"All these sacrifices," said Cooper, "you'd make them gladly, if you believed in the cause.''

"Are you accusing me of being an unbeliever?''

"Yes," said Cooper.

"I'm a Christian!" she said. "You're the heretics! You're the witches!''

"Keep your voice down," said Fink menacingly.

"I'm not a witch!" said Audubon fervently.

"You see?" said Cooper. "Now you *are* accusing us.''

"I'm not!" she said. "There's no one here but you.''

"You're a woman whose world has just turned upside down. You're the daughter of witches. You're angry that they were killed. You're angry at yourself for being alive, for being part of the very society that killed them. And you're angry at that society for not being worthy of the sacrifice.''

"I'm not judging others," she said.

"They were supposed to build Zion here," said Cooper. "The city of God. The place where Christ at his coming could find the righteous gathered together, waiting for him.''

"Yes," whispered Purity.

"They even named you Purity. And yet you see that nothing is pure. The people are trying to be good, but it isn't good enough.

When Christ comes, all he'll find here is a group of people who have done no more than to find another way to be stubble that he will have to burn.''

"No, the virtue is real, the people are good," said Purity. "Reverend Study—"

"Virtue is real outside New England, too," said Verily Cooper.

"Is it?" she asked. "Most people here live the commandments. Adultery is as rare as fish with feet. Murder never happens. Drunkenness can never be seen anywhere except at the docks, where sailors from other lands are permitted—and why should I defend New England to you?"

"You don't have to," said Cooper. "I grew up with the dream of New England all around me. In every pulpit, in every home. When someone behaved badly, when someone in authority made a mistake, we'd say, 'What do you expect? This isn't New England.' When somebody was exceptionally kind or self-sacrificing, or humble and sweet, we'd say, 'He belongs in New England,' or 'He's already got his passage to Boston.' ''

Purity looked at him in surprise. "Well, we're not *that* good here."

"I know," said Cooper. "For one thing, you still hang witches and put their babies in orphanages."

"I'm not going to cry again, if that's what you're hoping for," said Purity.

"I'm hoping for something else," said Cooper. "Come with us."

"Verily!" said Smith. "For pete's sake, if we wanted a woman with us we'd be traveling with Margaret! You think this girl's ready to sleep rough?"

"Ain't decent anyway," said Mike Fink. "She's a lady."

"You needn't worry about my going with you," said Purity. "What kind of madman are you? Perhaps I *am* angry and disillusioned about the dream of purity here in New England. Why would I be any happier with you, who aren't even as pure as we are here?"

"Because we have the one thing you're hungry for."

"And what is that?"

"A reason to live."

She laughed in his face. "The five of you! And all the rest of the world lacks it? Why don't they all just give up and die?"

"Few give up living," said Cooper. "Most give up looking for a reason. But some have to keep searching. They can't bear to live without a purpose. Something larger than themselves, something so good that just being a part of it makes everything worthwhile. You're a seeker, Miss Purity.''

"How do you know all these things about me?"

"Because I'm a seeker, too. Do you think I don't know my own kind?"

She looked around at the others. "If I were this thing, a seeker, why would I want to be with other seekers? If you're still seeking, it means you haven't found anything, either."

"But we have," said Cooper.

Smith rolled his eyes. "Verily Cooper, you know I still don't have a clue what we're even looking for."

"That's not what I'm talking about," said Cooper. "You're not a seeker, Alvin. You already have your life handed to you, whether you want it or not. And Arthur here, he's not a seeker, either. He's already found what *he* wants."

Arthur hung his head, embarrassed. "Don't you go saying!"

"Just like Mike Fink. They've found *you,* Al. They're going to follow you till they die."

"Or till I do," said Smith.

"Ain't going to happen," said Fink. "I'll have to be dead first."

"You see?" said Cooper. "And Jean-Jacques here, he's no seeker. He knows the purpose of his life as well."

Audubon grinned. "Birds, women, and wine."

"Birds," said Cooper.

"But you're still seeking?" asked Smith.

"I've found you, too," said Cooper. "But I haven't found what *I'm* good for. I haven't figured out what *my* life means." He turned to Purity again. "That's why I knew. Because I've stood where you're standing. You've fooled them all, they think they know you but it just means you've kept your secret, only now you're fed up with secrets and you have to get out, you have to find the people who know why you're alive."

"Yes," she whispered.

"So come with us," said Cooper.

"Dammit, Very," said Smith, "how can we have a woman along?"

"Why not?" said Cooper. "Quite soon you're going to rejoin your wife and start traveling with her. We can't camp in the woods our whole lives. And Miss Purity can help us. Our painter friend may be happy with what he's accomplished here, but we don't know anything more than we did before we arrived. We see the villages, but we can hardly talk to anyone because we have so many secrets and they're so reticent with strangers. Miss Purity can explain things to us. She can help you learn what you need to learn about building the City of—"

He stopped.

"The City," he finally said.

"Why not say it?" said Purity. "The City of God."

Cooper and Smith looked at each other, and Purity could see that both of them were filled with the pleasure of having understood something. "See?" said Cooper. "We've already learned something, just by having Miss Purity with us."

"What did you learn?" demanded Arthur Stuart.

"That maybe the Crystal City has another name," said Smith.

"Crystal City?" asked Miss Purity.

Cooper looked at Smith for permission. Alvin glanced at each of them in turn, until at last his gaze lingered on Purity herself. "If you think she's all right," said Alvin.

"I know she is," said Cooper.

"Got a couple of minutes?" Alvin asked Purity.

"More like a couple of hours," said Mike Fink.

"Maybe while you talk and talk I bath in the river," said Audubon.

"I'll keep watch," said Fink. "I fell in enough rivers in my time without getting nekkid to do it on purpose."

Soon Purity, Smith, Cooper, and Arthur Stuart were sitting in the tall soft grass on the riverbank. "I got a story to tell you," said Alvin. "About who we are and what we're doing here. And then you can decide what you want to do about it."

"Let me tell it," demanded Arthur Stuart.

"You?" asked Alvin.

"You always mix it up and tell it back end to."

"What do you mean, 'always'? I hardly tell this story to anybody."

"You ain't no Taleswapper, Alvin," said Arthur Stuart.

"And you are?"

"At least I can tell it front to back instead of always adding in stuff I forgot to tell in the proper place."

Alvin laughed. "All right, Arthur Stuart, *you* tell the story of my life, since you know it better than I do."

"It ain't the story of your life anyway," said Arthur Stuart. "Cause it starts with Little Peggy."

" 'Little' Peggy?" asked Alvin.

"That's what her name was *then*," said Arthur.

"Go ahead," said Alvin.

Arthur Stuart looked to the others. Cooper and Purity both nodded. At once Arthur Stuart bounded to his feet and walked a couple
of paces away. Then he came back and stood before them, his back
to the water, and with boats sailing along behind him, and the summer sun beating down on him while his listeners sat in the shade,
he put his hands behind his back and closed his eyes and began to
talk.

6

Names

Margaret did not waste time worrying about when—or if—her promised audience with the Queen might happen. Many of the futures she found in other people's heartfires led to such a meeting, and many more did not, and in neither case did she see such an audience leading to the prevention of the bloody war she dreaded.

In the meantime, there were plenty of other activities to fill her time. For she was finding that Camelot was a much more complicated place than she had expected.

During her childhood in the North she had learned to think of slavery as an all-or-nothing proposition, and in most ways it was. There was no way to half-permit it or half-practice it. Either you could be bought and sold by another human being or you couldn't. Either you could be compelled to labor for another man's profit under threat of death or injury, or you couldn't.

But there were cracks in the armor, all the same. Slave owners were not untouched by the normal human impulses. Despite the most stringent rules against it, some Whites did become quite affectionate

in their feelings toward loyal Blacks. It was against the law to free
a slave, and yet the Ashworths weren't the only Whites to free some
of their slaves and then employ them—and not all those manumitted
were as old as Doe. It might be impossible to attack the institution
of slavery in the press or in public meetings, but that did not mean
that quiet reforms could not take place.

She was writing about this in a letter to Alvin when someone
knocked softly at her door.

"Come in?"

It was Fishy. Wordlessly she entered and handed Margaret a
calling card, then left almost before the words "Thank you, Fishy"
were out of Margaret's mouth. The card was from a haberdasher in
Philadelphia, which puzzled her for a moment, until she thought to
turn it over to reveal a message scrawled in a careless childish hand:

> *Dear Sister-in-law Margaret,*
> *   I heard you was in town. Dinner? Meet me downstairs*
> *at four.*
>
>   *Calvin Miller*

She had not thought to check his heartfire in many days, being
caught up in her exploration of Camelot society. Of course she
looked for him at once, his distinctive heartfire almost leaping out
to her from the forest of flames in the city around her. She never
enjoyed looking into his heartfire because of all the malice that was
constantly harbored there. Her visits were brief and she did not look
deep. Even so, she immediately knew about his liaison with Lady
Ashworth, which disgusted her, despite her long experience with all
the sins and foibles known to humankind. To use his knack to provoke the woman's lust—how was that distinguishable from rape?
True, Lady Ashworth could have shouted for her slaves to cast him
from the house—the one circumstance in which slaves were permitted to handle a White man roughly—but Lady Ashworth was a
woman unaccustomed to feeling much in the way of sexual desire,
and like a child in the first rush of puberty she had no strategies for
resistance. Where the patterns of society kept girls and boys from
being alone together during that chaotic time, preventing them from
disastrous lapses in self-control, Lady Ashworth, as an adult of high
station, had no such protection. Her wealth bought her privacy and
opportunity without giving her any particular help in resisting temptation.

The thought crossed Margaret's mind: It might be useful to know of Lady Ashworth's adultery.

Then, ashamed, she rejected the thought of holding the woman's sin against her. Margaret had known of other people's sins all her life—and had also seen the terrible futures that would result if she told what she knew. If God had given her this intense knack, it was certainly not so that she could spread misery.

And yet . . . if there was some way that her knowledge of Calvin's seduction of Lady Ashworth might help prevent the war . . .

How bitter it was that the most guilty party, Calvin, was untouchable by shame, and therefore could not have his adultery used against him, unless Lord Ashworth was a champion dueler (and even then, Margaret suspected that in a duel with Calvin, Lord Ashworth would find that his pistol would not fire and his sword would break right off). But that was the way of the world—seducers and rapists rarely bore the consequences of their acts, or at least not as heavily as the seduced and the broken-spirited.

Dinner would be at four o'clock. Only a couple of hours away. Fishy had not waited for a return message, and in all likelihood Calvin wasn't waiting either. Either she would meet him or she would not—and indeed, his heartfire showed him unconcerned. It was only a whim for him to meet her. His purpose was as much to find out who she was as to cling to her skirts in order to get in to see the King.

And even the wish to meet King Arthur contained no plan. Calvin knew Napoleon—this exiled king would not impress him. For a moment Margaret wondered if Calvin planned to kill King Arthur the way he had murdered—or, as Calvin thought of it, *executed*—William Henry Harrison. But no. His heartfire showed no such path in his future, and no such desire in his heart at present.

But that was the problem with Calvin's heartfire. It kept changing from day to day, hour to hour. Most people, limited as they were by the circumstances of their lives, had few real choices, and so their heartfires showed futures that followed only a handful of probable paths. Even powerful people, like her husband Alvin, whose powers gave him countless opportunities, still had their futures sorted into a wider but still countable number because their character was predictable, their choices consistent.

Calvin, on the contrary, was whim-driven to a remarkable extent. His attachment to this French intellectual had shaped his life lately, because Balzac had a firm character, but once Calvin's futures diverged from Balzac's, they immediately branched and rebranched and forked and sprayed into thousands, millions of futures, none more likely than the others. Margaret could not possibly follow them all and see where they led.

It was in Alvin's heartfire, not Calvin's, that she had seen Alvin's death caused by Calvin's machinations. No doubt if she followed every one of the billion paths of Calvin's future she would find almost as many different ways for Calvin to achieve that end. Hatred and envy and love and admiration for Alvin were the one consistency in Calvin's inconstant heart. That he wished harm for Alvin and would eventually bring it to pass could not be doubted; nor could Margaret find any likely way to prevent it.

Short of killing him.

What is happening to me? she wondered. First I think of extortion by threatening to expose Lady Ashworth's sin, and now I actually think of murdering my husband's brother. Is the mere exposure to Calvin a temptation? Does his heartfire influence mine?

Wouldn't that be nice, to be able to blame Calvin for my own failings?

One thing Margaret was sure of: The seeds of all sins were in all people. If it were not so, how would it be virtue when they refrained from acting on those impulses? She did not need Calvin to teach her to think of evil. She only needed to be frustrated at her inability to change events, at her helplessness to save her husband from a doom that she so clearly saw and that Alvin himself seemed not to care about. The desire to force others to bend or break to her will was always there, usually hidden deeply enough that she could forget she had that wish within her, but occasionally surfacing to dangle the ripe fruit of power just out of her reach. She knew, as few others did, that the power to coerce depended entirely on the fear or weakness of other human beings. It was possible to use coercion, yes, but in the end you found yourself surrounded only by the weak and fearful, with all those of courage and strength arrayed against you. And many of your strong, brave enemies would match you in evil, too. The more you coerced others, the sooner you would bring yourself to the moment of your doom.

It would even happen to Napoleon. Margaret had seen it, for she had examined his hot black heartfire several times when she was checking on Calvin during his stay in France. She saw the battlefield. She saw the enemies arrayed against him. No coercion, not even fueled by Napoleon's seemingly irresistible knack, could build a structure that would last. Only when a leader gathered willing followers who shared his goals could the things he created continue after his death. Alexander proved that when his empire collapsed in fragments after his death; Charlemagne did little better, and Attila did worse—*his* empire evaporated upon his death. The empire of the Romans, on the other hand, was built by consensus and lasted two thousand years; Mohammed's empire kept growing after his death and became a civilization. Napoleon's France was no Rome, and Napoleon was no Mohammed.

But at least Napoleon was trying to create something. Calvin had no intention of building anything. To make things was his inborn knack, but the desire to build was foreign to his nature; the persistence to build was contrary to his temperament. He was weak himself, and fearful. He could not bear scorn; he feared shame more than death. This made him think he was brave. Many people made that mistake about themselves. Because they could stand up to the prospect of physical pain or even death, they thought they had courage—only to discover that the threat of shame made them comply with any foolish command or surrender any treasure, no matter how dear.

Calvin, what can I do with you? Is there no way to kindle true manhood in your fragile, foolish heart? Surely it's not too late, even for you. Surely in some of the million divergent paths of your heartfire there is one, at least, in which you find the courage to admit Alvin's greatness without fearing that others will then scorn you for being weaker. Surely there's a moment when you choose to love goodness for its own sake, and cease to care about what others think of you.

Surely, in any heap of straw, there is one strand which, if planted and tended, watered and nurtured, will live and grow.

Honoré de Balzac trotted along behind Calvin, growing more annoyed by the moment. "Slow down, girder-legs, you will wear me down to a stub trying to keep up with you."

"You always walk so slow," said Calvin. "Sometimes I got to stride out or my legs get jumpy."

"If your legs are jumpy then jump." But the argument was over—Calvin was walking more slowly now. "This sister-in-law of yours, what makes you think she'll pay for dinner?"

"I told you, she's a torch. The Napoleon of torches. She'll know before she comes downstairs to meet us that I don't have a dime. Or a shilling. Whatever they call it here."

"So she'll turn around and go back upstairs."

"No," said Calvin. "She'll want to meet me."

"But Calvin, my friend, if she is a torch then she must know what is in your heart. Who could want to meet you then?"

Calvin rounded on him, his face a mask of anger. "What do you mean by that?"

For a moment, Honoré was frightened. "Please don't turn me into a frog, Monsieur le Maker."

"If you don't like me, why are you always tagging along?"

"I write novels, Calvin. I study people."

"You're studying me?"

"No, of course not, I already have you in my mind, ready to write. What I study is the people you meet. How they respond to you. You seem to wake up something inside them."

"What?"

"Different things. That is what I study."

"So you're using me."

"But of course. Were you under some delusion that I stayed with you for love? Do you think we are Damon and Pythias? Jonathan and David? I would be a fool to love you like such a friend."

Calvin's expression grew darker yet. "Why would you be a fool?"

"Because there is no room for a man like me in your life. You are already locked in a dance with your brother. Cain and Abel had no friends—but then, they were the only two men alive. Perhaps the better comparison is Romulus and Remus."

"Which one am I?" asked Calvin.

"The younger brother," said Honoré.

"So you think he'll try to kill me?"

"I spoke of the closeness of the brothers, not the end of the story."

"You're playing with me."

"I always play with everybody," said Honoré. "It is my vocation. God put me on the earth to do with people what cats do to mice. Play with them, chew the last bit of life out of them, then pick them up in my mouth and drop them on people's doorsteps. That is the business of literature."

"You take a lot of airs for a writer who ain't had a book printed up yet."

"There is no book big enough to contain the stories that fill me up. But I will soon be ready to write. I will go back to France, I will write my books, I will be arrested from time to time, I will be in debt, I will make huge amounts of money but never enough, and in the end my books will last far longer than Napoleon's empire."

"Or maybe it'll just seem that way to the folks who read them."

"You will never know. You are illiterate in French."

"I'm illiterate in most every language," said Calvin. "So are you."

"Yes, but in the illiteracy competition, I will concede to you the laurels."

"Here's the house," said Calvin.

Honoré sized it up. "Your sister-in-law is not rich, but she spends the money to stay in a place that is respectable."

"Who says she ain't rich? I mean, think of it. She knows what folks are thinking. She knows everything they've ever done and everything they're going to do. She can see the future! You can bet she's invested a few dollars here and there. I bet she's got plenty of money by now."

"What a foolish use of such a power," said Honoré. "The mere making of money. If I could see into another person's heart, I would be able to write the truest of novels."

"I thought you already could."

"I can, but it is only the imagined soul of the other person. I cannot be *sure* that I am right. I have not been wrong yet about anyone, but I am never *sure*."

"People ain't that hard to figure out," said Calvin. "You treat it like some mystery and you're the high priest who has the word straight from God, but people are just people. They want the same things."

"Tell me this list as we go inside out of the sun."

Calvin pulled the string to ring the doorbell. "Water. Food. Leaking and dumping. Getting a woman or a man, depending. Getting rich. Having people respect you and like you. Making other people do what you want."

The door opened. A Black woman stood before them, her eyes downcast.

"Miz Larner or Miz Smith or whatever name she's using, Margaret anyway, she's expecting to meet us downstairs," said Calvin.

Wordlessly the Black woman backed away to let them come in. Honoré stopped in the doorway, took the woman by the chin, and lifted her head till their eyes met. "What do *you* want? In the whole world, what do you want most?"

For a moment the woman looked at him in terror. Her eyes darted left, right. Honoré knew she wanted to look down again, to get back to the safe and orderly world, but she did not dare to turn her face away from him as long as he held her chin, for fear he would denounce her as insolent. And then she stopped trying to look away, but rather locked her gaze on his eyes, as if she could see into him and recognized that he meant her no harm, but only wanted to understand her.

"What do you want?" he asked again.

Her lips moved.

"You can tell me," he said.

"A name," she whispered.

Then she tore herself away and fled the room.

Honoré looked after her, bemused. "What do you suppose she meant by that?" he asked. "Surely she has a name—how else would her master call her when he wanted her?"

"You'll have to ask Margaret," said Calvin. "She's the one who sees what's going on inside everybody's head."

They sat on the porch, watching bees and hummingbirds raid the flowers in the garden. Soon Calvin began to amuse himself by making the bees' wings stop flapping. He'd point to a bee and then it would drop like a stone. A moment later, dazed and annoyed, it would start to buzz again and rise into the air. By then Calvin would be pointing to another bee and making it fall. Honoré laughed because it *was* funny to see them fall, to imagine their confusion. "Please don't do it to the hummingbirds," Honoré said.

He regretted at once that he had said such a foolish thing. For of course that was exactly what Calvin had to do. He pointed. The hummingbird's wings stopped. It plummeted to the ground. But it did not buzz and rise back into the sky. Instead it struggled there, flapping one wing while the other lay useless in the dirt.

"Why would you break such a beautiful creature?" said Honoré.

"Who makes the rules?" said Calvin. "Why is it funny to do it to bees but not to birds?"

"Because it doesn't hurt the bee," said Honoré. "Because hummingbirds don't sting. Because there are millions of bees but hummingbirds are as rare as angels."

"Not around here," said Calvin.

"You mean there are many angels in Camelot?"

"I meant there are thousands of hummingbirds. They're like squirrels they're so common."

"So it is all right to break this one's wing and let it die?"

"What is it, God watches the sparrows and you're in charge of hummingbirds?"

"If you can't fix it," said Honoré, "you shouldn't break it."

Calvin glowered, then pushed himself out of his chair, vaulted the railing, and knelt down by the hummingbird. He fiddled with the wing, trying to straighten it. The bird kept struggling in his grasp.

"Hold still, dammit."

Calvin held the broken wing straight, closed his eyes, concentrated. But the fluttering of the bird kept annoying him. He made an exasperated gesture, as if he were shaking a child, and the bones of the wing crumbled in his fingers. He took his hands away and looked at the ruined wing, a sick expression on his face.

"Is this a game?" asked Honoré. "See how many times can you break the same hummingbird wing?"

Calvin looked at him in fury. "Shut your damn mouth."

"The bird is in pain, Monsieur le Maker."

Calvin leapt to his feet and stomped down hard on the bird. "Now it's not."

"Calvin the healer," said Honoré. Despite the jesting tone he was sick at heart. It was his goading that had killed the bird. Not that there was any hope for it. It was doomed to die as soon as Calvin made it fall from the air. But even that had been partly Honoré's fault for having asked Calvin *not* to do it. He knew, or should have known, that would be a goad to him.

"You made me do it," said Calvin. He couldn't meet Honoré's gaze. This worried Honoré more than a defiant glare would have. Calvin felt shamed in front of his friend. That did not bode well for that friend's future.

"Nonsense," said Honoré cheerfully. "It was your own wise choice. Do not kill bees, for they make honey! But what does a humming bird make? A splash of color in the air, and then it dies, and voilà! A splash of color on the ground. And where is color more needed? The air is full of bright color. The ground never has enough of it. You have made the world more beautiful."

"Someday I'll be sick of you and your sick jokes," said Calvin.

"What's taking you so long? I'm already sick of me."

"But you like your jokes," said Calvin.

"I never know whether I will like them until I hear myself say them," said Honoré.

He heard footsteps inside the house, coming to the door. He turned. Margaret Smith was a stern-looking woman, but not unattractive. Au contraire, she was noticeably attractive. Perhaps some might think her too tall for Honoré's comfort, but like most short men, Honoré had long since had to settle for the idea of admiring taller women; any other choice would curtail too sharply the pool of available ladies.

Not that this one was available. She raised one eyebrow very slightly, as if to let Honoré know that she recognized his admiration of her and thought it sweet but stupid of him. Then she turned her attention to Calvin.

"I remember once," she said, "I saw Alvin heal a broken animal."

Honoré winced and stole a glance at Calvin. To his surprise, instead of exploding with wrath, Calvin only smiled at the lady. "Nice to meet you, Margaret," he said.

"Let's get one thing straight from the start," said Margaret. "I know every nasty little thing you've ever done. I know how much you hate and envy my husband. I know the rage you feel for me at this moment and how you long to humiliate me. Let's have no pretenses between us."

"All right," said Calvin, smiling. "I want to make love to you. I want to make you pregnant with my baby instead of Alvin's."

"The only thing you want is to make me angry and afraid," said Margaret. "You want me to wonder if you'll use your powers to harm the baby inside my womb and then to seduce me the way you did with another poor woman. So let me put your mind at rest. The hexes that protect my baby were made by Alvin himself, and you don't have the skill to penetrate them."

"Do you think not?" said Calvin.

"I know you don't," said Margaret, "because you've already tried and failed and you don't even begin to understand why. As for wanting to seduce me—save those efforts for someone who doesn't see through your pretenses. Now, are we going to dinner or not?"

"*I'm* hungry," said Honoré, desperate to turn the conversation away from the dangerous hostility with which it had begun. Didn't this woman know what kind of madman Calvin was? "Where shall we eat?"

"Since I'm expected to pay," said Margaret, "it will have to be in a restaurant I can afford."

"Excellent," said Honoré. "I am ill at the thought of eating at the kind of restaurant *I* can afford."

That earned him a tiny hint of a smile from the stern Mrs. Smith. "Give me your arm, Monsieur de Balzac. Let's not tell my brother-in-law where we're going."

"Very funny," said Calvin, climbing over the railing and back onto the porch. The edge of fury was out of his voice. Honoré was relieved. This woman, this torch, she must truly understand Calvin better than Honoré did, for Calvin seemed to be calming down even though she had goaded him so dangerously. Of course, if she was protected by hexes that might give her more confidence.

Or was it hexes she was counting on? She was married to the Maker that Calvin longed to be—maybe she simply counted on Calvin's knowledge that if he harmed her or her baby, he would have to face the wrath of his brother at long last, and he knew he was no match for Alvin Maker. Someday he would have it out with him, but he wasn't ready, and so Calvin would not harm Alvin's wife or unborn baby.

Certainly that was the way a rational man would see it.

Calvin tried to keep himself from getting angry during the meal. What good would it do him? She could see everything he felt; yet she would also see that he was suppressing his anger, so even that would do no good. He hated the whole idea of her existence—someone who thought she knew the truth of his soul just because she could see into his secret desires. Well, everyone had secret desires, didn't they? They couldn't be condemned for the fancies that passed through their mind, could they? It was only what they acted on that counted.

Then he remembered the dead hummingbird. Lady Ashworth naked in bed. He stopped himself before he remembered every act that others had criticized—no reason to list the catalogue of them for Margaret's watchful eye. For her to report to Alvin with, no doubt, the worst possible interpretation. Alvin's *spy*—

No, keep the anger under control. She couldn't help what her knack was, any more than Calvin could, or anybody else. She wasn't a spy.

A judge, though. She was clearly judging him, she had said as much. She judged everybody. That's why she was here in the Crown Colonies—because she had judged and condemned them for practicing slavery, even though the whole world had always practiced slavery until just lately, and it was hardly fair to condemn these people when the idea of emancipation was really just some fancy new trend from Puritan England and a few French philosophers.

And he didn't want to be judged by what he did, either. That was wrong, too. People made mistakes. Found out later that a choice was wrong. You couldn't hold that against them forever, could you?

No, people should be judged by what they meant to do in the long run. By the overarching purpose they meant to accomplish. Calvin was going to help Alvin build the Crystal City. That was why he had gone to France and England, wasn't it? To learn how people were gathered to one purpose and governed in the real world. None of this feeble teaching that Alvin did back in Vigor Church, trying to turn people into what they were not and never could be. No, Alvin would get nowhere that way. Calvin was the one who would figure it all out and come back and show Alvin the way. Calvin would be the teacher, and together the brothers would build the great city and the whole world would be ruled from that place, and even Napoleon would come and bow to them, and *then* all of Calvin's mistakes and bad thoughts would be forgotten in the honor and glory that would come to him.

And even if he never succeeded, it was his *purpose* that counted. *That's* who Calvin really was, and that was how Margaret should judge him.

Come to think of it, she had no business judging him at all. That's what Jesus said, wasn't it? Judge not lest ye be judged. Jesus forgave everybody. Margaret should take a lesson from Jesus and forgive Calvin instead of condemning him. If the world had a little more forgiveness in it, it would be a better place. Everybody sinned. What was Calvin's little fling with Lady Ashworth compared to Alvin killing that Slave Finder? What was a dead hummingbird compared to a dead *man*? Margaret could forgive Alvin, but never Calvin, no, because he wasn't one of the favored ones.

People are such hypocrites. It made him sick, the way they were always pretending to be *soooo* righteous. . . .

Except Balzac. He never pretended at all. He was just himself. And he didn't judge Calvin. Just accepted him for the man he was. Didn't compare him with Alvin, either. How could he? They had never met.

The meal was almost over. Calvin had been so busy brooding that he hadn't noticed that he was almost completely silent. But what could he say, when Margaret thought she already knew everything about him anyway?

Balzac was talking to her about the slavegirl who opened the door for them at the boardinghouse. "I asked her what she wanted most in all the world, and she told me what she wanted was a name. I thought people named their slaves."

Margaret looked at him in surprise, and it took a moment for her to respond. "The girl you talked to has two names," she finally said. "But she hates them both."

"Is that what she meant?" asked Balzac. "That she didn't like her name? But that's not the same as wishing she had one."

Again Margaret looked contemplative for a few moments.

"I think you've uncovered something that I was having trouble understanding. She hates her name, and then she tells you she wishes she had one. I can't decipher it."

Balzac leaned over the table and rested his hand on Margaret's. "You must tell me what you are really thinking, madame."

"I am really thinking you should take your hand off mine," said Margaret mildly. "That may work with the women of France, but uninvited intimacies do not work well with me."

"I beg your pardon."

"And I did tell you what I really thought," said Margaret.

"But that is not true," said Balzac.

Calvin almost laughed out loud, to hear him front her so bold.

"Is it not?" asked Margaret. "If so, I am not aware of what the truth might be."

"You got a look in your eyes. Very thoughtful. Then you reached a conclusion. And yet you told me that you can't decipher this girl's wish for a name."

"I said I can't decipher it," said Margaret. "I meant that I can't find her real name."

"Ah. So that means you *have* deciphered *something*."

"I've never thought to look for this before. But it seems that the two names I had for her—the name her mother called her, which was awful, and her household name, which is hardly better; they call her 'Fishy'—neither of those is her true name. But she thinks they are. Or rather, she knows of no other name, and yet she knows there must *be* another name, and so she wishes for that true name, and— well, as you can see, I haven't deciphered anything."

"Your decipherment is not up to your own standard of under-standing maybe," said Balzac, "but it is enough to leave me breath-less."

On they blathered, Balzac and Mrs. Smith, trading compliments. Calvin thought about names. About how much easier his life might have been if his own name had not been shared with Alvin, save one letter. About how Alvin resisted using the name Maker even though he had earned it. Alvin Smith indeed. And then Margaret— why did she decide to stop being Peggy? What pretension was she nursing? Or was Margaret the true name and Peggy the disguise?

Chatter chatter. Oh, shut up, both of you. "Here's a question," Calvin asked, interrupting them. "Which comes first, the name or the soul?"

"What do you mean?" asked Balzac.

"I mean is the soul the same, no matter what you name it? Or if you change names do you change souls?"

"What do names have to do with . . ." Margaret's voice trailed off. She looked off into the distance.

"I think decipherment happens before our eyes," said Balzac.

Calvin was annoyed. She wasn't supposed to take this seriously. "I just asked a question, I wasn't trying to plumb the secrets of the universe."

Margaret looked at him with disinterest. "You were going to make some foolish joke about giving Alvin the *C* from your name and you could be the one that everybody likes."

"Was not," said Calvin.

She ignored him. "The slaves have names," she said, "but they don't, because the names their masters give them aren't real. Don't you see? It's a way of staying free."

"Doesn't compare with actual freedom," said Calvin.

"Of course it doesn't," said Margaret. "But still, it's more than just a matter of the name itself. Because when they hide their names, they hide something else."

Calvin thought of what he had said to start this stupid discussion. "Their souls?"

"Their heartfires," she said. "I know you understand what I'm talking about. You don't see into them the way I do, but you know where they are. Haven't you noticed that the slaves don't have them?"

"Yes, they do," said Calvin.

"What are you talking about?" said Balzac.

"Souls," said Calvin.

"Heartfires," said Margaret. "I don't know if they're the same thing."

"Doesn't matter," said Calvin. "The French don't have either one."

"Now he insults me and my whole country," said Balzac, "but you see that I do not kill him."

"That's because you've got short arms and you drink too much to aim a gun," said Calvin.

"It is because I am civilized and I disdain violence."

"Don't either of you care," said Margaret, "that the slaves have found a way to hide their souls from their masters? Are they so invisible to you, Calvin, that you haven't ever bothered to notice that their heartfires are missing?"

"They still got a spark in them," said Calvin.

"But it's tiny, it has no depth," said Margaret. "It's the memory of a heartfire, not the fire itself. I can't see anything in them."

"Seems to me that they've found a way to hide their souls from *you*," said Calvin.

"Doesn't he ever listen to anybody?" Margaret asked Balzac.

"He does," said Balzac. "He hears, but he doesn't care."

"What am I supposed to be caring about that I'm not?" asked Calvin.

"What the Black girl said she wished for," said Balzac. "A name. She has hidden away her name and her soul, but now she wants them back and she doesn't know how."

"When did you two figure this out?" asked Calvin.

"It was obvious once Madame Smith made the connection," said Balzac. "But you are the most knowledgeable people I know of, when it comes to hidden powers. How could you not know of this?"

"I don't do souls," said Calvin.

"The powers they bring from Africa work differently," said Margaret. "Alvin tried to figure it out, and so did I, and we think that everybody is born with hidden powers, but they learn from the people around them to use them in different ways. We White people—or at least English people—but Napoleon's like this too, so who knows—we learn to use these powers individually, binding them tightly to some inborn talent or preference or need. A little bit of it we can put outside ourselves, in hexes, but the real power is held in each person. While the Reds, they open their powers to the world around them, becoming less and less alone, more and more tied to the power of nature. It gives them great powers, but cut them off from the natural world and it's gone."

"And Blacks?" asked Balzac.

"They learn to put it into objects, or perhaps they find it there, I don't know. Since I've never done it myself, nor has Alvin, we could only speculate. Some things I've seen in Black folks' heart-fires, though—I could hardly believe it. Yet it's so. Arthur Stuart's mother—she had extraordinary power, and by making something, she gave herself wings. She flew."

Balzac laughed, then realized she wasn't joking or even speaking metaphorically. "Flew?"

"At least a hundred miles," said Margaret. "Not far enough, not entirely in the right direction, but it was enough to save her baby, though her own strength and life were spent."

"This Arthur Stuart, why don't you ask *him* how the power of Black people works?"

"He's just a boy," said Calvin scornfully, "and he's half-White anyway."

"You don't know him," said Margaret. "He doesn't know how the powers of Blacks work because it isn't carried in the blood, it's taught from parent to child. Alvin learned the greensong of the Reds because he became like a child to Tenskwa-Tawa and Ta-Kumsaw. Arthur Stuart grew up with his power shaped into a knack, like Whites, because he was raised among Whites. I think Blacks have a hard time holding on to their African ways. Maybe that's why Fishy can't remember her real name. Someone took her name from her, took her soul, to keep it in hiding, to keep it safe and free. But now she wants it back and she can't get it because she's not African-born, she's not surrounded by a tribe, she's surrounded by beaten-down slaves whose heartfires and names are all in hiding."

"If they got all these powers," said Calvin, "how come they're slaves?"

"Oh, that's easy," said Balzac. "The ones who capture them in Africa, they are also African, they know what the powers are, they keep them from having the things they need."

"Blacks against Blacks," said Margaret sadly.

"How do you know all that?" Calvin asked Balzac.

"I was at the docks! I saw the Blacks being dragged off the ships in chains. I saw the Black men who searched them, took away little dolls made of cloth or dung, many different things."

"Where was I when you were seeing this stuff?"

"Drunk, my friend," said Balzac.

"So were you, then," said Calvin.

"But I have an enormous capacity for wine," said Balzac. "When I am drunk I am at my best. It is the national knack of the French."

"I wouldn't be proud of it if I were you," said Margaret.

"I wouldn't be sanctimonious about our wine, here in the land of corn liquor and rye whiskey." Balzac leered at her.

"Just when I think I might like you, Monsieur Balzac, you show yourself not to be a gentleman."

"I don't have to be a gentleman," said Balzac. "I am an artist."

"You still walk on two legs and eat through your mouth," said Margaret. "Being an artist doesn't give you special privileges. If anything, it gives you greater responsibilities."

"I have to study life in all its manifestations," said Balzac.

"Perhaps that is true," said Margaret. "But if you sample all the wickedness of the world, and commit every betrayal and every harm, then you will not be able to sample the higher joys, for you will not be healthy enough or strong enough—or decent enough for the company of good people, which is one of the greatest joys of all."

"If they cannot forgive me my foibles, then they are not such good people, no?" Balzac smiled as if he had played the last ace in the deck.

"But they do forgive your foibles," said Margaret. "They would welcome your company, too. But if you joined them, you would not understand what they were talking about. You would not have had the experiences that bind them together. You would be an outsider, not because of any act of theirs, but because you have not passed along the road that teaches you to be one of them. You will feel like an exile from the beautiful garden, but it will be you who exiled yourself. And yet you will blame *them*, and call them judgmental and unforgiving, even as it is your own pain and bitter memory that condemns you, your own ignorance of virtue that makes you a stranger in the land that should have been your home."

Her eyes were on fire and Balzac looked at her with rapt admiration. "I always thought I would experiment with evil, and imagine good because it was easier. Almost you convince me I should do it the other way around."

Calvin was not so entranced. He knew that this little sermon was directed at him and he didn't like it. "There's no such secret that the good people know," said Calvin. "They just pretend, to console themselves for having missed out on all the fun."

Margaret smiled at him. "I took these ideas from your own thoughts of only a few minutes ago, Calvin. You know that what I'm saying is true."

"I was thinking the opposite," said Calvin.

"That's what you *thought* you were thinking," said Margaret. "But you wouldn't have had to think such thoughts if that was what you really thought about it."

Balzac laughed aloud, and Calvin joined him—albeit halfheartedly.

"Madame Smith, I could have labored all my days and never thought of a conversation in which someone was able to deliver such a sentence and have it mean anything at all. 'That's what you thought you were thinking.' Delicious! 'You would not think these thoughts if you really thought what you think you thought.' Or was it 'thought you think.' ''

"Neither one," said Margaret. "You are already preparing to misquote me."

"I am not a journalist! I am a novelist, and I can improve any speech."

"Improve this," said Margaret. "You two play your foolish games—Calvin playing at being powerful, Monsieur de Balzac playing at being an artist—but around you here is real life. Real suffering. These Black people are as human as you and me, but they give up their heartfires and their names in order to endure the torment of belonging to other people who despise and fear them. If you can dwell in this city of evil and remain untouched by their suffering, then it is you who are the trivial, empty people. You are able to hold on to your names and heartfires because they aren't worth stealing."

With that she rose from the table and left the restaurant.

"Do you think we offended her?" asked Calvin.

"Perhaps," said Balzac. "But that concerns me a great deal less than the fact that she did not pay."

As he spoke, the waiter was already approaching them. "Do the gentlemen wish to pay in cash?"

"It was the lady who invited us," said Balzac. "Did she forget to pay?"

"But she did pay," said the waiter. "For her own meal. Before you sat down, she wrote us her check."

Balzac looked at Calvin and burst out laughing. "You should see your face, Monsieur Calvin!"

"They can arrest us for this," said Calvin.

"But they do not wish to arrest a French novelist," said Balzac. "For I would return to France and write about their restaurant and declare it to be a house of flies and pestilence."

The waiter looked at him coldly. "The French ambassador engages us to cater his parties," he said. "I do not fear your threat."

A few moments later, up to his arms in dishwater and slops, Calvin seethed in resentment. Of Margaret, of course. Of Alvin, whose fault it was for marrying her. Of Balzac, too, for the cheerful way he bantered with the Black slaves who would otherwise have done all the kitchen work they were doing. Not that the Blacks bantered back. They hardly looked at him. But Calvin could see that they liked hearing him from the way more and more of them lingered in the room a little longer than their jobs required. While *he* was completely ignored, carrying buckets of table scraps out to be composted for the vegetable garden, emptying pails of dishwater, hauling full ones from the well to be heated. Heavy, sweaty labor, filth on his hands, grime on his face. He thought last night's urine-soaked sleep was as low as he could get in his life, but now he was doing the work of slaves while slaves looked on; and even here, there was another man that they all liked better than him.

Calvin returned to the kitchen just as a Black man was carrying a stack of clean plates to put back on the shelves. The Black man had just a trace of a smile on his face from something Balzac had said, and it was just too much after all that had happened that night. Calvin got his bug inside the dishes and cracked them all, shattered them in his arms. Shards sprayed out everywhere.

The crashing sound immediately brought the White chef and the overseer, his short, thick rod already raised to beat the slave; but Balzac was already there, throwing himself between the slave and the rod. And it was, truly, a matter of throwing himself, for the slave and the overseer were both much taller than Balzac. He leapt up and fairly clung to the slave like a child playing pick-a-pack.

"No, monsieur, do not strike him, he was innocent. I carelessly bumped into him and dropped all the plates on the floor! I am the most miserable of men, to take a dinner I could not pay for and now I have break all these plates. It is my back that deserves the blows!"

"I ain't going to whip no White man like a buck," said the overseer. "What do you think I am?"

"You are the arm of justice," said Balzac, "and I am the heart of guilt."

"Get these imbeciles out of my kitchen," said the chef.

"But you are French!" cried Balzac.

"Of course I am French! Who would hire an English cook?"

Immediately Balzac and the chef burst into a torrent of French, some of which Calvin understood, but not enough to be worth trying to hear any more of it. Balzac had taken all the fun out of it, of course, and the slaves were looking at him—sidelong, lest they be caught staring at a White man—as if he were God himself come to lead them out of captivity. Even when Calvin was annoyed and tried to get even a little, it ended up making Balzac look good and Calvin look like nothing.

Lead them out of captivity. God himself. His own thought of a moment before echoed in his mind. Margaret says they've lost their names and their heartfires. She hates slavery and wants it done away. They need someone to get their souls back and lead them out of captivity.

Balzac can't do that for them. What is he? A prawn of a French-man with ink on his fingers. But if I free the slaves, what will Alvin be then, compared with me?

For a moment he thought of striking the overseer dead and getting the slaves to run. But where would they run? No, what was needed was a general uprising. And without souls, the Blacks could hardly be expected to have the gumption for any kind of revolt.

So that was the first order of business. Finding souls and naming names.

7

Accusation

Alvin didn't exactly doze off while Arthur Stuart told the story of his life. But his mind did wander.

He couldn't help hearing how Arthur Stuart's voice didn't change when he spoke. No one else would have remarked upon it, but Alvin still remembered how, when Arthur Stuart was younger, he could mimic other folks' voices perfectly. No matter how high or low the voice, no matter what accent or speech impediment it had, no matter how whispery or booming it might be, it came easily from the boy's mouth.

And then came the Slave Finders, with a sachet containing pieces of Arthur's hair and body taken when he was first born. They had the knack of knowing when a person matched up with a sachet, and there was no hiding from them, they could smell like blood-hounds. So Alvin took the boy across the Hio River, and there on the Appalachee side he made a change in the deepest heart of the tiniest parts of Arthur's body. Not a large change, but it was enough that Arthur no longer matched up with his own sachet. Alvin took him down under the water to wash away the last traces of his old skin. And when he came up out of the water, Arthur was safe. But he had lost his knack for doing voices.

Ain't that the way of it? thought Alvin. I try to help, and I take away as much as I give. Maybe that's how God set up the world, so nobody could get no special advantages. You get a miracle and you lose something ordinary that you miss from then on. Some angel somewhere measures out the joy and misery, and whatever your portion, you get it no matter what you do.

Suddenly Alvin was filled with loneliness. Silly to feel that way, he knew, what with these good companions alongside him. But somewhere down south there was his wife who was also his teacher and his guardian, the bright pair of eyes that watched him from infancy on, even though she was scarcely more than a baby herself when she started. Margaret. And in her womb, the start of the next generation. Their firstborn daughter.

And, thinking of them, he began to seek for them. He wasn't like Margaret, able to leap from heartfire to heartfire with a thought, able to see just by having the wish to see. He had to send his doodlebug out, fast, faster, racing across the map of America, down the coast, passing heartfires of every living thing, through fields and bright green forests, over rivers, across the wide Chesapeake. He knew the way and never got lost. Only in the city of Camelot itself did he have to search, looking for the paired heartfires that he knew so well, that he sought out every night.

Found. Mother and the tiny heartfire of their developing daughter. He could not see into heartfires the way Margaret could, but he could see into the body. He could tell when Margaret was speaking but had no notion what was said. He could hear the heartbeat, feel the breathing, tell if she was upset or calm, but he could not know why.

She was eating. She was tense, her muscles held rigid, her attitude wary. Two companions at dinner. One of them unfamiliar to him. The other . . .

What was Calvin doing across a table from Margaret?

At once Alvin did a closer check on his wife and baby. Nothing interfering with the baby in the womb—her heartbeat was regular, she showed no distress.

Of course not. Why should he even imagine that Calvin posed any threat to his family? Calvin might be a strange boy, plagued with jealousy and quick to wrath, but he wasn't a monster. He didn't hurt people, beyond hurting their feelings. No doubt his fear came from Margaret's constant warnings about how Calvin was going to get him killed someday. If he posed any danger to Margaret or the baby, she'd know long beforehand and would take steps to stop him.

Calvin and Margaret dining together. That bore thinking about. He could hardly wait for Margaret to get some time alone and write to him.

Then he got to thinking about Margaret and how he missed her and what it might be like, the two of them settling down without feeling the weight of the world on their shoulders, spending their time raising children and working to make a living. No Unmaker to be watched for and fended off. No Crystal City to be built. No horrible war to be avoided. Just wife, children, husband, neighbors, and in time grandchildren and graveyards, joy and grief, the rising and falling floods and droughts of the river of life.

"You fall asleep, Alvin?" asked Verily.

"Was I snoring?" asked Alvin.

"Arthur finished his tale. Your life story. Weren't you listening?"

"Heard it all before," said Alvin. "Besides, I was there when it happened, and it wasn't half so entertaining to live through as the tale Arthur makes of it."

"The question is whether Miss Purity wants to be one of our company," said Verily.

"Then why are you asking *me?*" said Alvin.

"I thought you might help us listen to her answer."

Alvin looked at Purity, who blushed and looked away.

Arthur Stuart glared at Verily. "You accusing Miss Purity of lying?"

"I'm saying," said Verily, "that if she believed your story, then she might fear the great power that Alvin has within him, and so she might give the answer that she thinks will keep her safe, instead of the answer that corresponds to her true inclinations."

"And I'm supposed to know whether she's telling the truth or not?" asked Alvin.

"Her heart isn't made of wood," said Verily, "so *I* can't tell if it beats faster or slower when she answers."

"She's the one with the knack to tell what people feel," said Alvin. "Margaret's the one as sees into folks' heartfire. Me, I just fiddle with stuff."

"You are too modest," said Purity, "if what your disciples say is true."

That perked Alvin right up. "Disciples?"

"Isn't that what you are? The master and his disciples, wandering about in the wilderness, hoping to recruit another."

"To me it looks more like a lost man and his friends, who are willing to be lost with him till he finds what he's looking for," said Alvin.

"You don't believe that," said Purity.

"No," said Alvin. "They're my friends, but that's not why they're here. They're fellow dreamers. They want to see the Crystal City as much as I do, and they're willing to travel hundreds of miles to help me find it."

Purity smiled faintly. "The Crystal City. The City of God. I wonder who it is you'll end up hanging, since you can't very well hang witches."

"Don't plan on hanging anybody," said Alvin.

"Not even murderers?" said Purity.

Alvin shrugged. "They get themselves hung no matter where they go."

"Once you have the gallows, you'll find new reasons to hang people from it."

"Why are you being so spiteful?" asked Verily. "New England hasn't added a capital crime in the two hundred years since it was founded. And some former capital crimes haven't led to the gallows in a century. You have no reason to think that a decent society will go mad with the power to kill."

"New England didn't need new reasons," said Purity, "because it had such a fine catchall. No matter what someone did, if you want him dead, he's a witch."

"I wouldn't know," said Verily.

"You said it yourself," said Purity. "Everyone has a knack. They hide it out of fear and call it humility. But if someone wants to kill a man, he only has to detect his knack and denounce him for it. So anyone can be killed at any time. Who needs new laws, when the old ones are so broad?"

"Did you become this cynical in the past few hours?" asked Verily. "Or have you always taken the lowest possible view of human life?"

"Human life is wicked to the core," said Purity, "and only the elect of God are lifted above human wickedness and caught up into the goodness of heaven. To expect wickedness from human beings is the best way I know of to avoid surprises. And when I am surprised, it's always pleasantly."

"Ask her the question and have done," said Alvin.

"And if I say I don't want to travel with you?" said Purity.

"Then we'll travel on without you," said Alvin.

"Doing me no harm?" asked Purity.

Verily Cooper laughed. "Even if we wanted to, Alvin wouldn't let us. When a bee stings him, he puts the stinger back in it, heals it up, and sends it on its way."

"Then my answer is no," said Purity. "People will be looking for me by now. If you want to be safe from inquiries, you'd best let me go and be about your business."

"No," said Arthur Stuart. "You got to come with us."

"And why should I?" asked Purity. "Because you spin a good tale?"

"I told you the truth and you know it," said Arthur.

"Yes," said Purity, softening. "You did believe every word you said. But it has no bearing on me. I have no part in what you're trying to do."

"Yes, you do!" cried Arthur Stuart. "Didn't you get the point of my story? Somebody's in charge of all this. Somebody gave Alvin the powers he's got. Somebody led his family to Horace Guester's roadhouse, so Little Peggy would be in place to watch over him. Why did my mother fly so near to that place, so I'd be there waiting when Alvin came back? And Mike Fink, and Verily Cooper—how did they get to meet up with him? Don't tell me it was chance cause I don't believe in it."

"Nor do I," said Purity.

"So whoever led us to Alvin, or him to us, that's who led you here today. You could have walked anywhere. We could have been anywhere on the river, bathing. But here we were, and here you came."

"I have no doubt that we were brought together," said Purity. "The question is, by whom?"

"I don't know as it's a who," said Alvin. "Arthur thinks God's in charge of all this, and I don't doubt but what God has his eye on the whole world, but that don't mean he's spending extra time looking out for me. I got a feeling that knacks get drawn together. And the power I was born with, it's right strong, and so it's like a magnet, it just naturally grabs hold on other strong people and links them up. It's not like good folks are the only ones as get drawn to me. Seems like I get more than my share of the other kind, too. Why would God send *them* to me?"

Arthur Stuart didn't seem to be swayed by Alvin's argument.

Clearly they'd been down this road before. "God brings some, and the other one brings the others."

"They just come natural," said Alvin, "both kinds. Don't go guessing what God's doing, because them as tries to guess always seems to get it wrong."

"And how would you know they was wrong," said Arthur, "lessen you thought you had a scope on God's will!" He sounded triumphant, as if he had at last landed a blow on the body of Alvin's argument.

"Cause it works out so bad," said Alvin. "Look at this place. New England's got everything going for it. Good people, trying to serve God as best they can. And they do, mostly. But they figured that God wanted them to kill everybody as used a knack, even though they never found out how to tell if knacks came from God or the devil. They just called all knacks witchcraft and went off killing folks in the name of God. So even if they got all the rest of God's will just right, look what they done to Miss Purity here. Killed her folks and got her brought up in an orphanage. It don't take a scope on God's will to know New England ain't got it figured out yet."

"You sound like professors arguing over an obscure point of Latin grammar, when the passage itself is a forgery," said Purity. "Whether I was led to you by God or nature or Satan himself, it doesn't change my answer. I have no business with you. It's here that my destiny lies. Whatever I am and whatever happens to me, my story begins and ends with the . . . with New England."

"With the courts of New England," said Verily.

"So you say," said Purity.

"With the gallows of New England," Verily insisted.

"If God wills," said Purity.

"No," said Verily, "you'll meet the gallows only if *you* will it."

"On the contrary," said Purity. "Meeting you has been the most important lesson of my life. Until I met you, until I heard your story, I was sure my parents could not really have been witches and therefore a great injustice was committed. I didn't really believe that witches existed. But I have seen now that they do. You have powers far greater than God meant anyone but a prophet or apostle to have, Mr. Smith, and you have no qualms about using them. You are going about gathering disciples and planning to build a city. You are Nimrod, the mighty hunter against the Lord, and the city you mean to build is Babel. You want it to lift mankind above the flood and take

men into heaven, where they will be as God, knowing all things.
You are a servant of the devil, your powers are witchery, your plans
are anathema, your beliefs are heresy, and if my parents were one-
tenth as wicked as you, they deserved to die!''

They all stared at her in silence. Arthur Stuart had tears streaking
his cheeks.

Finally Alvin spoke—to the others, not to her. ''Best be on our
way, boys,'' he said. ''Arthur, you run and tell Audubon to dry off
and get dressed.''

''Yes, sir,'' said Arthur quietly, and he was gone.

''Aren't you even going to argue with me?'' asked Purity.

Alvin looked quizzically at her for a moment, then walked away
toward where Mike Fink had gone to stand watch. Only Verily Cooper remained.

''So you admit that what I said is true,'' said Purity.

Verily looked at her sadly. ''What you said is false as hell,''
said Verily. ''Alvin Maker is the best man I know in all the world,
and there's no trace of evil in him. He's not always right, but he's
never wrong, if you understand what I'm saying.''

''That is just what I'd expect a demon to say of his master the
devil.''

''There,'' said Verily. ''What you just said. That's why we're
giving up on you.''

''Because I dare to name the truth?''

''Because you've latched on to a story that can capture everything we say and do and turn it into a lie.''

''Why would I do that?'' asked Purity.

''Because if you don't believe these stupid lies about us, then
you have to admit that they were wrong to kill your parents, and
then you'd have to hate them, and they're the only people that you
know. You'd be a woman without a country, and since you're already a woman without a family, you can't let go of them.''

''See how the devil twists my love for my country and tries to
turn it against me?'' said Purity.

Verily sighed. ''Miss Purity, I can only tell you this. Whatever
you do in the next few hours and days, I expect you'll have plenty
of chance to judge between Alvin Smith and the law of New England. Somewhere inside you there's a place where truth is truth and
lies get shed like raindrops off oil. You look in that place and see
which is acting like Christ.''

''Christ is just as well as merciful,'' said Purity. ''Only the
wicked claim that Christ is only forgiving. The righteous remember

that he denounced the unrepented sin, and declared the truth that everlasting fire awaited those who refused to choose righteousness.''

"He also had sharp words for hypocrites and fools, as I recall,'' said Verily.

"Meaning that you think I'm a hypocrite?''

"On the contrary,'' said Verily. "I think you're a fool.''

She slapped his face.

As if she hadn't touched him, he went on in a mild tone of voice. "You've been made foolish by the harm that's been done to you, and by the fact that the wickedness of this place is so small compared to its goodness. But that doesn't mean it isn't real, and hasn't poisoned you, and won't kill you in the end.''

"God dwells in New England,'' said Purity.

"He visits here as he visits all places, and I dare say he finds much to be glad of in these farms and villages. A garden of the soul. But still aslither with snakes, like every other place.''

"If you plan to kill me,'' said Purity, "you'd better do it quick, because I'm going now to denounce you and send them after you.''

"Then be off,'' said Verily. "They'll either find us or they won't, depending on what Alvin decides. And if they do find us, keep this in mind: All he wants is for people to have a chance at happiness. Even you.''

"My happiness doesn't depend on a witch!''

"Does so,'' said Verily. "But up to now, the witches it depended on were dead.''

Tears appeared in her eyes; her face reddened; she would have slapped him again except she remembered that it did no good. Instead she turned and ran from him into the woods, almost bumping into Alvin and Mike Fink, who were returning along the path. A moment later she was gone.

"I think you lost, Very,'' said Alvin. "Or was that your plan?''

"She's not at her best,'' said Verily. He looked from Mike to Arthur to Alvin. "Well, is it time for us to put on seven-league boots?''

Alvin grinned at him. "Wouldn't you rather we tied you to the mast as we sailed on past the siren?''

Verily was startled. "What do you mean by that?''

"I mean that I saw how you were looking at her. She struck something in you.''

"Of course she did,'' said Verily. "She's been strangled by the need to hide her very considerable knack, and now she finds that her parents were killed for the same cause. She has to distinguish between herself and those who knowingly do witchcraft. She has to draw the line of virtue and stand on the right side of it without denying what she is and what she knows. I lived that life, except that my parents were fortunate enough to stay alive. I understand something of what she's going through.''

"Inconvenient time for her to come to her crisis of faith, don't you think?'' said Alvin.

"Don't make more of this than it is,'' said Verily. "As I told her, if she denounces us the authorities will either find us or not, depending on what *you* decide.''

Mike snorted. "That's an easy one.''

At that moment Arthur Stuart and a dripping, somewhat-dressed Audubon appeared. "She's gone,'' Arthur Stuart said.

"That is good, the way I am dress,'' said Audubon.

"She's gone to report us,'' said Mike Fink, "and here we are jawing.''

"It's up to Alvin whether we run or wait,'' said Verily. "She might not denounce us.''

"But then she might,'' said Mike. "And if she does, let's not be here.'' But Verily and Alvin were looking at each other, deciding some question that the others hadn't heard.

"Is there some reason,'' Alvin asked, "why I might choose to let them find us?''

Still Verily declined to answer.

"To save her,'' said Arthur Stuart.

Now they all looked at Arthur. He looked at Alvin, just as intently as Verily had the moment before. Alvin had the distinct impression that he was supposed to understand some unspoken explanation.

"How would it save her, for us to be caught?'' asked Alvin.

"Because the way she's acting,'' said Arthur Stuart, "she's going to get herself killed. Unless we save her.''

Mike Fink came between them. "Let me get this straight. You want *us* to get locked up and tried as witches so we can save *her*?''

"How would us getting locked up help her?'' said Alvin.

"How many birds can I paint in jail?'' asked Audubon.

"You wouldn't stay in jail long,'' said Verily. "Witch trials are notoriously quick.''

"What is it about a woman that makes *her* life worth the lives of four men and a boy?'' demanded Mike.

Verily laughed in exasperation. "What are you thinking, Mike?

This is Alvin Smith. The Maker of the Golden Plow. How long do you suppose he'd let us wait in jail?"

"You really don't want to leave her behind, do you, Very?" said Alvin. "Or you neither, Arthur Stuart, is that right?"

"Sure is," said the boy.

"That's right," said Verily.

"Goodness gracious," said Mike sarcastically. "Is this love we're talking about?"

"Who's in love?" demanded Arthur.

"Verily Cooper's in love with Miss Purity," said Mike Fink.

"I don't think so," said Verily.

"He must be," said Mike, "because he's let her go off to denounce us to the authorities and he wants us to get arrested because he thinks that'll make her feel bad and she'll change her mind about us and she'll recant her testimony against us and then she'll decide to come along with us. Which is a fine plan, except for the part where we get hung and she kneels at the foot of the gallows weeping her poor little eyes out she feels so bad."

Arthur Stuart looked at Verily, calculation in his eyes. "You think we might change her mind about us by getting arrested?" he asked.

"Mike is wrong, it's not pity I'm counting on," said Verily. "It's fear."

"Fear of what?" asked Alvin.

"Fear of the working of the law. Right now she believes the law is just and therefore we and her parents deserve to die. She'll change her mind quick enough when she sees how witch trials go."

"You've made a pretty long chain out of one link," said Mike.

"Give her a chance," said Arthur Stuart.

Alvin looked at Arthur, then at Verily. Who ever would have thought this man and this boy would be rivals in love? "Might be worth a try," said Alvin.

"If they arrest me they'll take my paintings and destroy them," said Audubon.

"I'll keep you and your paintings safe," said Alvin.

"And if they kill you," said Audubon, "what will happen to my paintings?"

"I won't care," said Alvin.

"But I will!"

"No you won't," said Arthur Stuart. "Cause if Alvin gets killed, so will you."

"That is my point!" cried Audubon. "Let us run away! This

greensong that you speak of, for hiding in the forest while running very fast. Sing!''

"What I got in mind," said Alvin, "is more like a saunter on the riverbank. And remember, all of you—confess to nothing. No witchcraft. No knacks. Don't even admit to being French, John James."

"I ain't going to lie under oath," said Arthur Stuart.

"Don't lie, just refuse to answer," said Alvin.

"That's when they torture you," said Verily. "When you refuse to say yes or no."

"Well, they *hang* you when you say yes," said Alvin, "and I ain't heard of them just letting you go if you deny it."

"If you don't answer, you can die without ever going to trial."

Alvin began to chuckle. "Well, now I get it. You *want* to go to trial. This ain't about Purity or being in love or any such thing. You want to take on the witch laws."

"Well *I* don't," said Mike Fink. "I sure don't have to answer under oath when someone asks me if I ever served Satan."

"It seems to me," said Alvin, "that if you want to have your day in court, Verily, you ought to do it as a lawyer, and not as a defendant."

"And you oughtn't to drag along folks as don't want to stand trial," said Mike.

"Not that any harm would come to any of us," said Alvin.

Audubon threw his arms heavenward. "Listen to him! Alvin has the . . . *hubris.* He think he can save everybody."

"I can," said Alvin. "That's just a fact."

"Then let's stay around and save *her,*" said Arthur Stuart. "We don't have to get arrested to do that."

"I want to do more than save her body from death," said Verily.

"Please don't tell us what more you want to do to her body," said Audubon.

Verily ignored him. "I want her to learn the truth about her parents and about herself. I want her to be proud of her knack. I want her to come join us in building the Crystal City."

"Those are all good things to want," said Alvin. "But just at this moment I have a keen memory of the months I spent in jail back in Hatrack River, and I got to say I don't wish even an hour in such a place for any of this company."

"Yes! The wisdom of Solomon!" cried Audubon.

"Which ain't to say I don't see your point, too, Very," said Alvin. "And as for you, Arthur Stuart, I can see as how a young man like you sees a damsel walking straight to the dragon's lair and he's plain got to draw his sword."

"What are you talking about?" asked Arthur.

"Saint George," said Alvin. "And the dragon."

"The boy will not let me to kill birds," said Audubon, "but *dragons.*"

Mike Fink looked puzzled. "Ain't no dragons around here."

"Fall in line behind me," said Alvin, "and say nothing, and touch nothing, and don't stray from the path I mark."

"So you'll leave her to their mercy," said Verily.

"I promise you, Very," said Alvin, "you'll get everything you want."

Verily nodded. Alvin looked at Arthur Stuart, wordlessly making him the same promise, and the boy also nodded.

They all lined up behind him on the riverbank. Alvin started off walking, then picked up his pace, jogging along, then loping, then flat-out running. At first the others worked hard at it, but then they began to hear a kind of music, not with instruments, not the kind you sing or dance to, but the sound of wind in leaves and birds singing, the chatter of squirrels and the buzz of insects, the high white sizzle of sunlight striking the dew on the leaves, the languid rush of water vapor distilling into the air. The sound of their footfalls merged with the music and the world around them turned into a blur of green, which contained every leaf, every tree, every bit of earth, and made them all one thing; and the runners were part of that one thing, and their running was part of the song, and the leaves parted to let them pass, and the air cooled them and the streams bore them over without their feet getting wet and instead of growing legsore or ribstitched they felt exhilarated, full of the life around them. They could run like that forever.

Then, moments later, the greensong began to fade. The trees narrowed to a strip of wood along the river. Cultivated fields held a muted music, low tones of thousands of identical lives. Buildings broke the song entirely, gaps of silence that were almost painful. They staggered, felt the pounding of their feet on the ground, which was hard now, and the branches snagged at them as they passed. They cantered, jogged, walked, and finally stopped. As one they turned away from the fields and buildings, away from the city of Boston with the tall masts of the ships in the harbor rising higher than the buildings, and faced upriver, to the place through which the song had carried them.

"Mon dieu," said Audubon. "I have flied on angel wings."

They stood in silence for a while longer. And then Arthur Stuart spoke.

"Where's Alvin?" he said.

Alvin wasn't there. Mike scowled at Verily Cooper. "Now look what you've done."

"Me?" said Verily.

"He sent us off and stayed behind to get arrested," said Mike. "I'm sworn to protect him and then you get him to do something like this."

"I didn't ask him to do this alone," said Verily.

Arthur Stuart started walking up the path, back into the woods.

"Where are you going?" asked Verily.

"Back to Cambridge," he said. "It can't be that far. The sun's hardly moved in the sky."

"It's too late to stop Alvin from doing this," said Mike.

Arthur looked back at him like he was crazy. "I know that," he said. "But he expects us to go back and help."

"How do you know this?" asked Audubon. "He tell you what he plan to do?"

"He told all of us," said Arthur. "He knows Verily wants to have a witch trial. So, Alvin's decided he'll be the witch. Verily gets to be the lawyer. And the rest of us have to be witnesses."

"But the girl will denounce us, too," said Audubon.

Verily nodded. "That's right," he said. "Yes, that's right. So the three of you, I want you to wait in the woods until I come fetch you."

"What's the plan?" asked Mike.

"I won't find that out till I talk to Alvin," said Verily. "But remember this: The only charge that matters in a witch trial is, Did Satan rule you? So that's the only question you answer. Nothing about knacks or hidden powers. Just about Satan. You never saw him, you never talked to him or any demons, he never gave you anything. Can you all swear to that truly?"

They all laughed and agreed they could.

"So when it's time to testify, that's the only question you answer. For the rest, you just look stupid."

"What about me?" said Audubon. "I was baptized Catholic."

"You can talk about that, too," said Verily. "You'll see. If I'm half the lawyer I trained to be, none of this will ever come to trial." He joined Arthur on the path. "Come along. It's legal work now. And if everything comes out right, we'll have Alvin free and Miss Purity as a traveling companion."

"I don't want to travel with her!" said Mike. "Look at the trouble she's already caused us!"

"Trouble?" said Verily. "I've been stupefied with boredom in New England. Everything's so peaceful here. Everything runs smoothly, most disputes are settled peacefully, neighbors pretty much get along, people are happy an extraordinary proportion of the time. I'm a lawyer, for heaven's sake! I was about to lose my mind!"

At first Reverend Study was dismissive. "I can understand your being fascinated with the idea of witches, but it's from the past, my dear Purity."

"They bragged about it," said Purity. "I didn't ask them."

"That's just it, you see," said the minister. "They're not from New England, and those from outside tend to mock our stricter adherence to scripture. They were having fun with you."

"They were not," said Purity. "And if you refuse to help me, I'll go straight to the tithingmen myself."

"No no," said Study. "You mustn't do that."

"Why not? A woman's testimony is valid in court. Even an orphan, I think!"

"It's not a matter of—Purity, do you realize the trouble you are heading into with these wild charges?"

"They're not wild. And I know what you're trying so hard not to say—that my parents were hanged as witches."

"What!" said Study. "Who told you such a thing! Who is spreading such slanders!"

"Are you saying it's not so?"

"I have no idea, but I can't imagine it's true. There hasn't been a witch trial in this part of New England for . . . for much longer than you've been alive."

"But the trial wasn't here," said Purity. "It was in Netticut."

"Well, that's a bit of a reach, don't you think? Why Netticut?"

"Reverend Study, the longer we talk, the farther these men will flee. And one of them is a papist, a Frenchman, brought here under false pretenses. They've been pretending he was mute."

Reverend Study sighed.

"I can see you have no respect for me, just like the others," said Purity.

"Is that what this is about? Trying to earn respect?"

"No, it's not!"

"Because this is not the way to do it. I remember the Salem trials. Well, not that I remember them myself, I wasn't even here,

but the shame of that city still endures. So many killed on the testimony of a group of hysterical girls. The girls were left unpunished,
you know. They lived out their lives, however their consciences let
them do it, because it was impossible for an earthly judge to know
which charges were malicious and which were the product of self-
delusion and mob mentality.''

"I am neither a group nor hysterical."

"But such charges do provoke a certain skepticism."

"That's nonsense, Reverend Study. People believe in witchcraft.
Everyone does. They check for it at the borders! They preach—no,
you preach against it in meetings!''

"It's all so confusing. What I preach about is the attempt to use
hidden powers. Even if they exist, they should not be used to gain
advantage over one's neighbor, or even to gain good fame among
one's friends. But the formal charge of witchcraft, that requires allegations of contact with Satan, of maleficence. Depending on who
the interrogators are, there may be questions about witches' sabbaths,
there will be naming of names. These things get out of hand."

"Of course they'll lie about Satan. They never said anything
about Satan to me."

"There. It's not witchcraft, you see?"

"But isn't that just what we expect?" said Purity. "Don't we
expect a witch to lie?''

"That's what happened at Salem!" cried Study. "They started
interpreting denials as lies, as attempts to cover up Satan's penetra-
tion of the community. But later it was discovered, it was realized,
that there had never been any witchcraft at all, and that the confes-
sions they got were all motivated by a selfish desire to save one's
own life, while the only ones hanged were those who refused to
lie."

"Are you saying that you believe the Bible is wrong when it
says we shall not suffer a witch to live?"

"No, no, of course if you actually find a witch, then you must
. . . act, but—"

"I have found a witch, Reverend Study. Please summon the
tithingmen to help me obey the Lord's injunction in the Bible."

Sick at heart, Reverend Study rose to his feet. "You leave me
no choice."

"As they left *me* no choice."

Study stopped at the door and spoke without facing her. "Do
you not understand that many long-pent resentments can be released
by this sort of thing?"

"These men are intruders here. What resentments can anyone have against them? The judges will be honest. My testimony will be honest."

Study leaned his head into the doorjamb and almost whispered his answer. "There *have* been rumors. About you."

Purity felt a thrill of fear and joy run through her body, making her tremble for a moment. Her guess was right. Her parents *did* die for witchcraft, just as she figured. "All the more reason, then, for me to prove myself loyal to the scripture and an enemy to Satan."

"Fire burns all hands that touch it."

"I serve God, sir. Do you?"

"Sometimes God is best served by obeying his more merciful statements. Judge not lest ye be judged. Think of that before you point a finger." Then he was gone.

Purity waited alone in Reverend Study's office. His library, really, it was so stacked and shelved with books. How did he get so many? Had he really read them all? Purity had never had an opportunity to study the titles. Sets of pious literature, of course. Collections of noted sermons. Scriptural commentary. Law books? Interesting—had he thought of studying law at some time? No, it was ecclesiastical law. With several books on the prosecution of witches, the investigation of witches, the purification of witches. Reverend Study might pretend to have no concern with such matters, but he *owned* these books, which meant that at some time he must have planned to refer to them. He had not been "here" during the witch trials in Salem, which were the last held in eastern Massachusetts. That could mean he hadn't been born yet—how long ago were they?—at least a century, perhaps half again that long. But he had been involved in witch trials somewhere. Yes, he knew and cared very much about these things.

She held the book *On the Investigation of Witchcraft, Wizardry, and Other Satanic Practices* but could not bring herself to open it. She heard that they used to torture the accused. But that must not be the way of it today. The laws were strict that a person could not be forced to incriminate himself. Ever since the United States were formed from the middle colonies and put that rule into their Bill of Rights, the same principle had been given force of law in New England as well. There would be no torture.

The book fell open in her hands. Could she help it? It fell open to a particular place which had been well-thumbed and much underlined. How to put the question to a witch who is with child.

Was my mother pregnant with me when she was arrested and tried?

The child is innocent before the law, being unborn and thus untouched by original sin. Original sin inheres to the child only upon birth, and therefore to take any action which might harm the unborn infant would be like punishing Adam and Eve in the garden before the fall: an injustice and an affront to God.

I gave my mother a little longer life. I saved her by being—yes, my very name—by being pure, unstained, untouched by original sin. How many weeks, how many months did I give to her?

Or did she think of this as torture, too? Had my father already been hanged as she languished in prison, awaiting her own trial as she grieved for him and for the child in her womb, doomed to be an orphan? Would she rather have died? Did she wish she didn't have a child?

She should have thought of that before she partook of forbidden practices. "Knacks" they called them in the wicked parts of the land. God-given gifts, that journeyman blacksmith called them, as he attempted to deceive her. But the true nature of Satan's false gifts would soon come clear. The "knacks" these witches use, they come from Satan. And because I know I have never had truck with Satan, then the small talents I have can't possibly be a hidden power. I'm just observant, that's all. I don't turn iron into a golden plow, like the one Arthur Stuart told about—a plow that dances around because it's possessed by evil spirits like the Gadarene swine.

She trembled with uncontainable excitement. Fear is what it felt like, though she had nothing to fear. It also felt like relief, like she was receiving something long waited for. Then she realized why: Her mother named her Purity to help her keep herself unstained by sin. Today she had faced the temptation of Satan in the form of that wandering blacksmith and his troupe of lesser witches, and for a moment she felt such terrible desires. The barrister was so attractive to her, that half-Black imp was so endearing, and Alvin himself now seemed sufficiently modest and self-effacing, and his dream of the City of God so real and desirable, that she longed to join with them.

That had to be how her mother was seduced by the devil! Not understanding, not being warned, she fell into the trap. Perhaps it was Purity's father who seduced her mother, just the way Verily Cooper had been calling to Purity on the riverbank today, evoking strange feelings and longings and whispering inside her mind that this was love. It had to be the devil making her think such thoughts. Married to a witch! Trapped just as her mother had been! Oh my

Father which art in heaven, I thank thee for saving me! I am a sinner like all others, but oh, if thou hast chosen me to be among thy elect, I shall praise thy name forever!

She heard the hurried footsteps on the stairs. She closed the book and replaced it on the shelf. When the door opened, Reverend Study and the tithingmen found her sitting on a side chair, her eyes closed, her hands clasped in her lap, the classic pose of the soul who refused to be touched by the evils of the world.

Reverend Study declined to go with them to catch the witches. Well, too bad for him, Purity thought. Let others of stronger heart do what must be done.

Horses would do little good on the river road. One of the tithingmen, Ezekial Shoemaker, took a group of grim-looking men on horseback to try to block escape downriver, while the other, Hiram Peaseman, kept his men with Purity as they walked the path that the witches must have taken.

"Why are you so certain they went downriver?" asked Peaseman, a stern-looking man who, until now, had always made Purity somewhat afraid.

"They said they were bound for Boston no matter what I chose to do."

"If they're witches, why wouldn't they lie to throw us off?"

"Because at the time," she said, "they thought to persuade me to join them."

"Still don't mean they weren't lying," said Peaseman.

"They told many a lie, I assure you," said Purity, "but they spoke the truth when they said they were bound for Boston."

Peaseman fixed his icy gaze upon her. "How do you know that wasn't a lie as well?"

For a moment Purity felt the old fear come over her. Had she revealed her hidden power?

And then her new confidence returned. It wasn't a hidden power. "I'm very observant," she said. "When people lie, they show it by little things."

"And you're never wrong?" asked Peaseman.

They had stopped walking now, and the other men were also gathered around her.

She shook her head.

"Only God is perfect, miss," said one of the other men.

"Of course you're right," said Purity. "And it would be pride in me to say I was never wrong. What I meant was that if I've been wrong I didn't know it."

"So they might have lied," said Peaseman, "only they did a better job than others."

Purity grew impatient. "Are you really going to stand here, letting the witches get away, all because you don't know whether to believe me or not about which way they were going to walk? If you don't believe me, then you might as well doubt everything I said and go back home!"

They shuffled their feet a little, some of them, and none spoke for a moment, until Peaseman closed his eyes and spoke what was on their minds. "If they be witches, miss, we fear they lay a trap for us, into which you lead us, all unwitting."

"Have you no faith in the power of Christ to protect you?" asked Purity. "I have no fear of such as they. Satan promises terrible power to his minions, but then he betrays them every time. Follow me if you dare." She strode forth boldly on the path, and soon heard their footsteps behind her. In moments they were all around her, then ahead of her, leading the way.

That's why she was last to see why they were stopping not fifty rods along the river path. There sat Alvin Smith on a fallen tree, leaning up against a living one, his hands clasped behind his head. He grinned at her when she emerged from the crowd. "Why, Mistress Purity, you didn't need to come and show me the road to Boston, or to trouble these men to help me on my way."

"He's the chief witch," said Purity. "His name is Alvin Smith. His companions must be nearby."

Alvin looked around. "Companions?" He looked back at her, seeming to be puzzled. "Are you seeing things?" He asked the men: "Does this girl see things what ain't there?"

"Don't be deceived," said Purity. "They're hereabouts."

"Am I remembering aright, or did she just call me a witch a minute ago?" asked Alvin.

"She did, sir," said Peaseman. "And as one of the tithingmen of Cambridge village, it's my duty to invite you back to town for questioning."

"I'll answer any questions you have for me," said Alvin. "But I don't see why I should go back instead of furthering my journey."

"I'm not the law, sir," said Peaseman. "Not the judge anyway. I'm afraid we need to bring you one way or another."

"Well, let's choose the one way and not the other," said Alvin. "On my own two feet, unbound, in free acceptance of your hospitable invitation."

A faint smile touched Peaseman's lips. "Yes, that's the way we prefer, sir. But you'll forgive us if we have to bind you so you can't get away.''

"But I give you my word," said Alvin.

"Forgive us, sir," said Peaseman. "If you're acquitted, you'll have my apology. But we have to wonder if the accusation be true, and if it be, then bound is safer for all, don't you think?''

In answer, Alvin held his hands forward, offering to be bound. Peaseman was not to be tricked, however, and tied Alvin's hands behind his back.

"That's not a good rope," said Alvin.

"It's a good one I bet," said Peaseman.

"No, it won't hold a knot," said Alvin. "Look." He shook his hands lightly and the knot slipped right off the rope.

Peaseman looked dumbly at the rope, which now dangled limp from his hand. "That was a good knot.''

"A good knot on a bad rope is no better than a bad knot," said Alvin. "I think it was old Ben Franklin what said that first. In *Poor Richard*.''

Peaseman's face went a little darker. "You'll do us the favor of not quoting that wizard's words.''

"He wasn't no wizard," said Alvin. "He was a patriot. And even if he were as wicked as . . . as the pope, the words are still true.''

"Hold still," said Peaseman. He tied the knot again, tighter, and then redoubled it.

"I'll try to hold my hands still so it don't slip off," said Alvin.

"He's toying with you," said Purity. "Don't you see this is his hidden power? Don't you know the devil when you see him?''

Peaseman glared at her. "I see a man and a rope that don't hold a knot. Who ever heard of the devil giving a man the power to untie knots? If that were so, how would ever a witch be hung?''

"He's mocking you," Purity insisted.

"Miss, I don't know how I offended you," said Alvin. "But it's a hard enough thing for a traveler to be named for a witch, without being accused of causing everything that happens. If one of these men loses his footing and falls into the river, will that be my doing? If someone's cow sickens somewhere in the neighborhood, will it be blamed on me?''

"You hear his curses?" said Purity. "You'd best all look to your cattle, and step careful all the way home.''

The men looked from one to another. The rope slipped off Alvin's hands and fell onto the ground. Peaseman picked it up; the knot had already loosened visibly.

"I give you my word not to flee," said Alvin. "How would I get away from so many men even if I had a mind to? Running would do me no good."

"Then why did your companions flee?" demanded Purity.

Alvin looked at the men with consternation. "I got no one with me, I hope you can all see that."

Purity grew angry. "You had them, four of them, three men and a half-Black boy who you saved from slavery by changing his nature, and another one a French painter who's a papist pretending to be mute, and a riverman who tried to kill you and you used your powers to take a tattooed hex right off his skin, and the last was an English barrister."

"Excuse me, miss, but don't that sound more like a dream than an actual group of folks what might be traveling together? How often do you see barristers from England with country boys like me?"

"You killed a man with your knack! Don't deny it!" cried Purity, furious, near tears at his obvious lies.

Alvin looked stricken. "Is it murder I'm charged with now?" He looked at the men again, showing fear now. "Who am I supposed to have killed? I hope I'll have a fair trial, and you have some witnesses if I'm to stand for murder."

"No one's been murdered here," said Peaseman. "Miss Purity, I'll thank you to keep silent now and let the law take this man."

"But he's lying, can't you see?" she said.

"The court can decide the truth."

"What about the plow? The Black boy told how this man made a golden plow that he carries with him always, but doesn't show to anyone, because it's alive and his very companions saw it move of itself. If that's not proof of Satanic power, what is?"

Peaseman sighed. "Sir, do you have a plow like the one she describes?"

"You can search my sack," Alvin answered. "In fact, I'd take it kindly if someone would carry it along, as it has my hammer and tongs, which is to say it holds my livelihood as a journeyman smith. It's yonder on the far side of the fallen maple."

One of the men went and hefted the bag.

"Open it!" cried Purity. "That's the one the plow was in."

"Ain't no plow in that sack, gold or iron or bronze or tin," said Alvin.

"He's right," said the man with the sack. "Just hammer and tongs. And a loaf of dry bread."

"Takes an hour of soaking before it can be et," said Alvin. "Sometimes I think my tongs might soften up faster than that old hardtack."

The men laughed a little.

"And so the devil deceives you bit by bit," said Purity.

"Let's have no more of that talk," said Peaseman. "We know you accuse him, so there's no need to belabor it. There's no plow in his sack and if he walks along peaceful, there's no need to tie him."

"And thus he leadeth them carefully down to hell," said Purity.

Peaseman showed wrath for the first time, walking boldly to her and looking down at her from his looming height. "I say enough talk from you, miss, while we lead the prisoner back to Cambridge. Not one of us likes to hear you saying *we* are deceived by Satan."

Purity wanted to open her mouth and berate all the men for letting this slick-talking "country bumpkin" win them over despite her having named him for a servant of hell. But she finally realized that she could not possibly persuade them, for Alvin would simply continue to act innocent and calm, making her look crazier and crazier the angrier she got.

"I'll stay and search for the plow," she said.

"No, miss, I'd be glad if you'd come along with us now," said Peaseman.

"Someone needs to look for it," she said. "His confederates are no doubt skulking nearby, waiting to retrieve it."

"All the more reason that I won't let you stay behind alone," said Peaseman. "Come along now, miss. I speak by the authority of the village now, and not just by courteous request."

This had an ominous ring to it. "Are you arresting *me*?" she asked, incredulous.

Peaseman rolled his eyes. "Miss, all I'm doing is asking you to let me do my work in the manner the law says I should. By law and common sense I can't leave you here exposed to danger, and with a prisoner who can't be tied I need to keep these men with me." Peaseman looked to two of his men. "Give the young lady your arms, gentlemen."

With exaggerated courtesy, two of the men held their arms to her. Purity realized that she had little choice now. "I'll walk of myself, please, and I'll hold my tongue."

Peaseman shook his head. "That was what I asked many

minutes and several long speeches ago. Now I ask you to take their arms and argue no further, or the next step will not be so liberal.''

She hooked her hands through the crooks of their elbows and miserably walked along in silence, while Alvin talked cheerily about the weather, walking freely ahead of her on the path. The men laughed several times at his wit and his stories, and with every step she tasted the bitterness of gall. Am I the only one who knows the devil wears a friendly face? Am I the only one who sees through this witch?

8

Basket of Souls

"What is it that you think you're looking for?" asked Honoré. They had spent the heat of the day on the docks and were dripping with sweat. It was getting on toward evening without a sign of relief from the heat.

"Souls," said Calvin. "In particular, the theft of souls."

They stood in the scant shade of a stack of empty crates, watching as a newly arrived ship was moored to the dock. Honoré sounded testy. "*If* the transaction I saw on the docks has something to do with missing heartfires—which are *not* souls as the priests describe them—then it was not theft at all. The dolls were freely given."

"Sometimes theft doesn't look like theft. What if they think they're lending them, but they can't get them back? What about that?"

"And what if you are getting us in the path of something dangerous? Did you think of *that*?"

Calvin grinned. "We can't get hurt."

"That statement is so obviously false that it is not worth answering," said Honoré.

"I don't think you understand what I can do," said Calvin.

A gangplank was run up from the dock to a gap in the ship's gunwale.

"These are a filthy-looking crew, don't you think? Portuguese, perhaps?"

"If I decide you and I aren't going to get hurt, we won't," said Calvin.

"Oh, so you can read minds like your sister-in-law?"

"Don't have to read minds when you can melt the knife right out of a man's hand."

"But Monsieur le Genius, not all knives are seen in advance."

"I see 'em."

"Nothing ever surprises you?"

Before Calvin could get farther than the first sound of the word *nothing*, Honoré slapped him on the back of the head. Calvin staggered forward and whirled around, holding his neck. "What the hell do you think that proved!"

"It proved that you *can* be harmed."

"No, it proved you can't be trusted."

"You see my point?" said Honoré. "It is when you feel safe that you are most vulnerable. And since you are stupid enough to feel safe all the time, then you are vulnerable all the time."

Calvin's eyes became narrow slits. "I didn't feel safe all the time. I felt safe with *you*."

"But lately we have been together all the time." Honoré grinned again. "You *are* safe from me. I am not the proud owner of any useful knack and I carry no weapon and I am too busy studying humanity to bother harming any individual human. But being safe *from* me does not mean you are safe *with* me."

"Don't lecture me, you French fart."

"You praise me too much. Garlic, wine, onion soup, rich cheese, these combine to make the fart française the best of all possible farts. Voltaire said so."

Calvin didn't laugh. "Look," he said. "Look at that slave. Got nothing to do."

"You have a sharp eye. He is waiting."

"Is he your man?"

"I observe what men *do*. I do not pretend to be able to tell whether two Black men, one seen from behind, the other from the face, both from a distance, and their clothes identical to the costume of half the slaves in Camelot, are in fact the same man."

"You saying it's him?"

Honoré sighed. "I say I cannot tell."

"Then just say it. Don't get into those damned fancy orations."

Honoré ignored him. Staggering and squinting, their backs bent, their eyes searching, the first Blacks were appearing on the deck. "It *is* a slave ship."

"Well we knew that," said Calvin.

"We 'knew' it about three other ships today that had no slaves aboard."

"We knew this was a slave ship because look at the White men on the deck with padded sticks. They wouldn't need those to load crates."

"If only I were as clever as you," said Honoré.

The Black they had been looking at before, who might or might not be the one Honoré had seen taking puppets, came forward with two buckets of water and a basket. His head down, so as not to look any of the White dockworkers in the eye, he said something to the dock foreman, who waved him over to the foot of the gangplank.

"No, you dumb buck!" The foreman's voice carried clear over to where Calvin and Honoré were waiting. "Wait back there! If you start backing them up on the gangplank then they crowd each other right off into the water! Stupid, stupid, stupid." By the time he was through with his list of stupids, the Black man with the buckets had bowed and ducked his head long enough to get to the indicated waiting place.

"He knew," said Honoré.

"What did he know?"

"He knew where to stand," said Honoré. "He was already walking there before the man pointed."

"Why would he get the foreman angry?"

"He got the foreman to think he was stupid," said Honoré.

"The foreman started out thinking he was stupid. They think *all* Black people are stupid."

"Do they?" said Honoré. "They think some are more stupid than others."

The first slaves, hobbled and joined by ankle chains, staggered and clanked down the gangplank, then headed straight for the water. There was a great deal of spilling and quiet cursing from the waterboy. Calvin used his doodlebug to get a closer view. Sure enough, each slave was handing over some small item, made of scraps of cloth and splinters of wood and bits of iron.

"He's our man," said Calvin. "But what made you think those were dolls they were handing over?" asked Calvin.

"I got a good look at only one. It was larger than the others. It was a doll."

"Well the others aren't."

"But they are something, am I right?"

"Oh, they're something all right. Wish I could ask them what it is. How they get powers into those things."

"What *are* they, if they aren't dolls?"

"They're nothing. I mean they don't look like anything. Knotted cloth, strings, threads, iron, wood, bits of this and that. No two alike."

"Ah, for the knack of your brother's wife."

"We'll find out soon enough."

"But is it not ironic that we spend all day watching and waiting, and now that we have found this man, we still have no idea what he's doing, but *she* already knows?"

"What makes you think she knows anything?" demanded Calvin.

"Because she can see into that man's heartfire. She has watched us all day, and the moment we saw *him,* she could hop over and look inside him and know it all."

"Damn," said Calvin, looking at Honoré with annoyance. "Don't go telling me you can *feel* when she's looking at you?"

"I didn't have to *feel* anything," said Honoré. "I knew she would because she was curious. She would see in our heartfires that we were going to search for this man, so she would watch us. Obvious."

"To you."

"Of course to me. I am the world's leading authority on the behavior of human beings."

"In your opinion."

"But you see, I am the kind of man who always thinks he is the best in the world at whatever he does. So are you. It is one of the ways we are alike."

Calvin grinned. "Damn right."

"The difference between us is that I am correct in that opinion."

Calvin's eyes squinted again. "Someday I'm not going to pretend I think you're joking when you say things like that."

"What will you do to punish me, make me wake up under a hedge with a terrible headache and my clothing covered with urine?"

The women were coming down now, naked to the waist and

roped, not chained together, though the ropes had chafed their wrists
and ankles enough to draw blood.

"Your brother's wife already knows the name of this bringer of
water, and where he lives, and what he had for breakfast," said
Honoré.

"Yeah, well, we'll know soon enough."

"Do you think he won't notice two White men following him?"

Calvin grinned wickedly. "Like I said, I can do everything that
needs doing. I can follow him without him seeing us or knowing he
was followed."

"Using your doodoobug?"

"Doodlebug."

"But you do not know all the hidden powers this Black man
might have. How do you know he won't catch your doodlebug and
hold it captive?"

Calvin started to scoff at this idea, but then grew solemn. "You
know, I'd be a fool to think he's not dangerous just cause he acts
dumb around the foreman."

"You are learning to be suspicious! I am proud of you!"

"But my doodlebug doesn't have to ride inside him or anything
like that."

"Good," said Honoré. But he could see that Calvin was worried
now.

Every single one of the newly arrived slaves had something to
give the man. The women were not as trusting as the men. They
didn't have them in their hands or the scant clothing they wore—
they spat these things from their mouths into the dipper. "Some of
them have two," said Calvin. "Two thingamajigs." When there was
something in the dipper, the waterboy always put it into the right-
hand bucket. He was building up quite a collection in there.

Last in line were a dozen or so good-sized children, looking far
more terrified and weak than the adults. None of them had anything
for the waterboy.

"The women who had two," said Honoré.

"Yes," said Calvin. "For the children."

In the midst of serving them, the waterboy clumsily knocked
over the right-hand bucket, spilling water over the hot boards of the
dock. He served the rest of the children from the other one. When
the last was served, they saw why he had spilled the important pail,
for one of the sailors snatched up the bucket that still had water and
dashed it onto the back of the last child. This was uproariously funny
to the White stevedores. While they laughed, the waterboy knelt,

scooped everything out of the other bucket, and tucked it into the small basket he carried.

He wasn't home free, though. The foreman stopped him just as he started away from the dock. "What you got in *that*?" he demanded, pointing at the basket.

"I don't know what my master put there," said the waterboy.

"I know one thing he better put there," said the foreman.

The two men looked at each other in grim silence for a long time, until finally the waterboy grinned and rolled his eyes and reached into the basket. "I so stupid, boss, I so stupid, I plumb forget." He took out a coin and offered it to the foreman.

"Where's the rest?" asked the foreman.

"That all he give me," said the waterboy.

"Come on, Denmark," said the foreman.

"Ah," whispered Honoré. "We have learned his name."

"Better be his name," said Calvin. "He sure as hell ain't no Scandinavian."

"Tell you what," said the foreman. "I'll tell him you give me one penny and see what he says."

"But I give you a shilling," said Denmark.

"You think he'll believe that, if I tell him otherwise?"

"You get me a whipping, that don't get you no more money," said Denmark.

"Get the hell off my dock," said the foreman.

"You a kind man, boss," said Denmark, bowing and nodding as he backed away. Then he turned his back and picked up the buckets again, but before he could stand up the foreman planted a foot on his backside and sent him sprawling on the dock. The stevedores and sailors laughed. But the slaves lined up for inspection by the customs officers, they didn't laugh. And Denmark himself, when he got up from the dock his face didn't show much amusement. But Calvin and Honoré could see how he composed himself, putting on a silly grin before he turned around. "You a funny man, boss," said Denmark. "You always make me laugh."

With exaggerated care, Denmark picked up the buckets without turning his back to the foreman. And he made a show of stopping and looking behind him a couple of times to make sure no one had snuck up to kick him again. His clowning kept the White man laughing even after he was gone.

Through it all, the newly arrived slaves didn't take their eyes off him.

"He is showing them how to survive here," said Honoré.

"You mean get a White man mad? That's smart."

"He is not a stupid man," said Honoré. "He is a clever man. He shows the others that they must act stupid and make the White man *laugh*. They must make the White man feel amusement and contempt, for this will keep Whites from feeling fear and anger."

"Probably," said Calvin. "Or maybe he just gets his butt kicked now and then."

"No," said Honoré. "I tell you I am the authority on human nature. He does this on purpose. After all, he is the one who gathers up their souls."

"I thought you said these weren't their souls at all."

"I changed my mind," said Honoré. "Look at them. The soul is missing now."

They looked at the Blacks in their chains and ropes, while the customs inspectors prodded them, stripped them, checked their body orifices, as if they were animals. They bore it easily. The looks of fear that they had worn as they emerged into sunlight were gone now. Gone also was the intensity with which they had gazed after Denmark as he carried away their tokens, or whatever they were. They really did seem like animals now.

"They been emptied, all right," said Calvin. "They all had heartfires getting off the boat, strong ones, but now they're all slacked back like a fire settled down to coals."

"They knew," said Honoré. "They were ready before they got off the boat. How did they know?"

"Maybe that's one of the things Margaret can tell us later," said Calvin.

"If she ever speaks to us again," said Honoré.

"She'll speak to us," said Calvin. "She's a nice person. So she'll start feeling guilty about sticking us for the price of the meal last night."

"They knew," said Honoré. "And they all consented. They gave away their souls into his hands."

"What I want to know," said Calvin, "is where he keeps them and what he does with them."

"Then we must go to your sister-in-law and ask her, since you are certain she will speak to us."

Calvin glared at him. "I'm already following him. He can't see my bug."

"Or he does not *show* you that he sees," said Honoré.

"I been doing this longer than you have. I *know*."

"Then why are you trembling?" said Honoré.

Calvin whirled on him, backing him against the crates. "Because I'm barely stopping myself from making your heart . . . stop . . . beating."

Honoré looked surprised. "Did you lose your sense of humor under the hedge?"

Calvin backed away, only slightly mollified. "One thing you ain't is funny," said Calvin.

"But if I practice, perhaps I will *become* funny."

"*I'm* the funny one," said Calvin. He backed off, leaving Honoré room to stand without pressing his body against the crates. "Or did *you* lose *your* sense of humor under the hedge?"

"We are both funny fellows," said Honoré. "Let's follow the man with a basket of souls. I have to know what he does with them."

"He's going through a door."

"Where?"

"In Blacktown," said Calvin. "There's junk hanging all over the place. Only one other heartfire in the house." He whistled. "That's *bright*."

"What's bright?" asked Honoré.

Calvin didn't answer.

Honoré leaned closer to him. "It's not fair not to tell me."

Calvin looked at him stupidly. "Tell you what?"

Margaret sat at her writing table, composing her daily letter to Alvin. She never mailed them. She could have, since she always knew where he was and where he was going. But why make him find post offices in every town he visited? Better to wait until the last hours before sundown. Whatever he was doing, he'd pause and let his thoughts turn to her. More to the point, he would send out his doodlebug to watch her. He could not read her thoughts, but he could see how her arms moved, her fingers; he could find the pen, the paper. She dipped it into ink only so that she could look back and see what she had written. She knew that he could see the words she formed on paper as clearly as if he were looking over her shoulder. She would ask questions; when they were half-formed, she would find the answer in his memory.

It was a lopsided arrangement, she knew. She could see his inmost thought, even the feelings he was scarcely aware of himself. She could see his choices unfold before him, could see them narrow again as he chose. He had no secrets from her. She, on the other hand, could keep anything secret that she chose, except for the condition of her body. He could reassure her that the baby was doing well; he could worry about her working too hard. But her thoughts remained closed to him. It hardly seemed fair.

And yet Alvin didn't mind—honestly didn't mind at all, never even seemed to notice. She knew there were several reasons for this. First, Alvin was an open fellow, not given to keeping secrets. He could keep them, of course, but once he trusted someone, he told the whole story, leaving nothing out, whether it reflected badly on him or not. Sometimes it sounded to others like boasting, when the things he had done were quite remarkable. But it was neither boasting nor confession. He simply reported what was in his memory. So it was no burden to him to have her see into his heartfire so readily.

A second reason for his lack of resentment, however, troubled her: He simply didn't care. He didn't mind that she knew his secrets, and he also didn't mind that he didn't know hers. He might be more inquisitive! Did this mean he didn't love her? Did it betray some fundamental selfishness? No, Alvin was generous of spirit. He simply wasn't all that curious about the minutiae of her thoughts. He was content to know what she told him. He trusted her. That's what it was, trust, not a lack of love.

The third reason, and probably the most important, was also the least satisfying. Alvin accepted everything about Margaret as a given, as part of the natural world around him. Though he didn't learn of it till later, she had watched over him through his entire childhood and saved his life many times. She had taught him, disguised as an older spinster schoolmarm. As the sun had shone on him every day, so had her care for him. He took her for granted. Having her inside his mind was as natural as breathing.

I am not even the weather in his life. I am more like the climate. No, more like the calendar. There are holidays, but the rest of the time he loses track, knowing the days will pass one by one whatever he names them.

Mustn't think that way. Write.

Dearest Alvin, I miss you now more than ever. Calvin is such an unpleasant boy, the opposite of you, and yet when I hear his voice it reminds me of yours.

Only the letters were not really written out so nicely. As soon as she saw that he understood, she would cease writing a word and skip ahead. The letter really began more like this: DA, I miss now mor. C is such an unpl boy, the opp of y&yet wh I hear hi voi it rem me of yo.

It was hard to imagine anyone else making sense of these scraps of words, scrawled in a child's printed hand instead of Margaret's elegant script, since printing was easier for Alvin to detect from a distance.

She kept writing: I think you're a fool to stay in that jail a single night. Walk out of it, gather up your companions, and come home. I don't much care for Mistress Purity. She has some good futures but they're not likely, and there's great harm possible, too, if you stay and win her away from New England.

His question: So it can be done?

Yes but . . .

Does she hang if we don't take her?

Margaret knew that a truthful answer would leave Alvin no choice but to stay.

Death isn't the worst thing in the world, she wrote. We're all going to do it, and if she's hanged as a witch it has a very good chance of leading to the repeal of the death penalty for witchery, and a much higher standard for conviction. So her death does much good.

In Alvin's mind she saw the immediate answer but she had known it already, known it without looking, for it was in his character: Let's try to achieve that same end without letting them dangle her.

By telling him the truth she had guaranteed that he would linger in that jail.

She wrote: Wasn't last year's imprisonment and trial enough of that for one lifetime?

He ignored her, and framed a question in his mind: Calvin? What does he want?

To be you, she wrote. Or, failing that, to destroy everything you ever accomplish. He seduced a fine lady by giving her irresistible lust. Can you do that?

His reply: Never thought of that. Want me to?

No!!!! Not while you're not here in the flesh, you torturer.

I'm going to be tortured.

They're just going to run you. You'll enjoy the exercise.

The conversation would have gone on for a while, but there came an urgent knock at her door.

Someone knocking, she wrote.

Then she looked for heartfires just outside her door and found one. Fishy.

"Come in?"

"Two White man downstairs a-see you, ma'am."

Visitors, she wrote.

She looked for heartfires downstairs, but found only one man there to visit her.

Honoré de Balzac, she wrote. Calvin's partner in debauch. Must go down. Tomorrow?

And his answer: Tomorrow. Always. I love you.

Feeling a lump in her throat, Margaret folded up the paper and put it away. There were still many inches on the page to write more letters to Alvin.

Downstairs, Balzac bounded up from his chair. He was as jumpy as a frog on a frying pan.

"Monsieur Balzac," Margaret began.

"You must to help me with Calvin," said Balzac, his excellent English collapsing just a little. "Where is he?"

"I don't know," said Margaret. "He's not here, if that's what you mean."

"But he is here, Madame. He is here but he is not here. Look!"

When she looked where he pointed, she was surprised to see that Calvin was indeed there, sitting on a wooden plank bench, bouncing mindlessly, his eyes staring off into space. How could she not have noticed he was with Balzac when she looked for heartfires before coming downstairs?

Because his heartfire wasn't there. Or rather, it was a mouse-sized heartfire, and there was no future in it, only a sort of numb awareness of the present. As if Calvin were looking at his own actions through peripheral vision.

As if Calvin were one of the slaves.

But no. The slaves of Camelot still had their heartfires. Weak ones, with their true names lost to them, their passions damped and gone, their futures channeled into a few narrow paths. More, certainly, than was left with Calvin. He kept his name, but very little else. And as for future and past, they were a thick fog. Shimmers and shadows appeared, but she could make no sense of them. Most particularly, Margaret could not see anything about where his doodlebug was.

"Let's take my dear brother-in-law out into the garden for our chat," said Margaret.

Balzac nodded, clearly relieved that she had so readily grasped the situation.

The garden lay in the hot deep shadow the house cast in the afternoon. With no one nearby to overhear, Margaret listened as Balzac poured out his story; even as he spoke, she followed the same events in his memory. The day on the docks; the unloading of the slaves; the waterboy named Denmark; the little bits of knotted this-and-that which were handed over or spat into the dipper; Calvin following Denmark with his doodlebug.

"I warned him," said Balzac. "He wouldn't listen."

"He never has," said Margaret.

"Never?" asked Balzac. "I thought you hadn't met him till this week."

"It is my misfortune to be deeply acquainted with everyone I meet," said Margaret. "Calvin is not a prudent man. Nor are you."

"As a pebble is to the moon, so is my imprudence compared to Calvin's," said Balzac.

"When you're dying of the disease that you call 'English' and the English call 'French,' when your mind is failing you, when you are blind and decaying, you will not be able to remember thinking of your imprudence as a slight thing," said Margaret.

"Mon dieu," said Balzac. "Have I heard my fate?"

"A very likely ending to your life," said Margaret. "Many paths lead there. But then, there are also many paths on which you are more prudent with the company you keep."

"What about luck?" asked Balzac.

"I'm not much of a believer in luck," said Margaret. "It wasn't luck that lost our friend Calvin his soul."

"How *could* it be lost, if the devil already had it?" Balzac was only half joking.

"What do I know of souls?" said Margaret. "I've been trying to understand what it is that the slaves in this city have given up. In Appalachee they don't do this, and I wonder if it's because they have some hope of escape. Whereas here, hope is nonexistent. Therefore, to remain alive, they must hide from their despair."

"Calvin wasn't despairing."

"Oh, I know," said Margaret. "Nor did he provide his captor with bits of string and whatnot. But then, those devices may be the Blacks' way of accomplishing what Calvin can do on his own, by his inborn knack: to separate some part of himself from his body."

"I am persuaded. But what part? And how can we get it back?"

Margaret sighed. "Monsieur Balzac, you seem to think I am a better person than I really am. For I am still quite uncertain whether I wish to help Calvin recover himself." She looked at Calvin's empty face. A fly landed on his cheek and walked briefly into and out of his nostril. Calvin made no move to brush it away. "The slaves function better than this," said Margaret. "And yet he seems not to be suffering."

"I understand," said Balzac, "that the better one knows Monsieur Calvin, the more one may wish to leave him in this docile state. But then, you must consider a few other things."

"Such as?"

"Such as, I am no blood kin of this man, and feel no responsibility for him. You, however, are his sister-in-law. Therefore, I can and will walk away from this garden without him. What will you do with the body? It still breathes—there are those who might criticize you for burying it, though I would never speak ill of you for such a decision."

"Monsieur Balzac, you should consider a few things yourself."

"Such as?" Balzac echoed her with a smile.

"Such as, you have no idea how much of our conversation Calvin is overhearing, however inattentive he might seem. The slaves hear what is said to them. Furthermore, there is no place on this earth where you could go that Calvin could not find you to wreak whatever vengeance he might wish to exact from you."

Balzac deflated slightly. "Madame, you have caught me in my deception. I would never leave my dear friend in such a state. But I hoped that a threat to leave you responsible for him might persuade you to help me save him, for I have no idea how to find where his soul is kept, or how to free it if I find it."

"Appeals to decency work much better with me than threats of inconvenience."

"Because you are a woman of virtue."

"Because I am ashamed to appear selfish," said Margaret. "There is no virtue that cannot be painted as a vice."

"Is that so? I have never found a need to do that. Painting vices as virtues, now, that is my expertise." Balzac grinned at her.

"Nonsense," said Margaret. "You name virtues and vices for what they are. That is your knack."

"I? Have a knack?"

"What were the last things Calvin said?"

Balzac held still a moment, his eyes closed. "In Blacktown," he said. " 'Junk hanging all over the place,' he said. Oh, and a moment before that he mentioned going through a door. So perhaps that's inside. Yes, in a house, because I remember him saying, 'Only one other heartfire in the house.' And then the last thing he said was, 'That's *bright*.' "

"A light," said Margaret. "A house with one other heartfire in it. Besides the one belonging to this Denmark fellow. And something bright. And then he was taken."

"Can you find it?" asked Balzac.

Margaret didn't answer. Instead she looked doubtfully at Calvin. "Do you suppose he's incontinent?"

"Pardon?" asked Balzac.

"I'm speculating on the best place to take him. I think he should stay with you."

"Why am I not surprised?"

"If he has trouble dealing with urination and defecation, I believe it will cause less scandal for you to help him."

"I admire your prudence," said Balzac. "I suppose I must also provide him with food and drink."

Margaret opened the purse tucked into her sleeve and handed a guinea to Balzac. "While you tend to his physical needs, I will find his doodlebug."

Balzac tossed the guinea into the air and caught it. "Finding it is one thing. Will you bring it back?"

"That is beyond my power," said Margaret. "I carry well-made hexes, but I don't know how to make them. No, what I will do is find where he is and discover who is detaining him. I suspect that in the process I will find the souls of the slaves of Camelot. I will learn how the thing is done. And when I am armed with information . . ."

Balzac grimaced. "You will write a treatise on it?"

"Nothing so useless as that," said Margaret. "I'll tell Alvin and see what he can do."

"Alvin! Calvin's life depends upon the brother he hates above all other persons on earth?"

"The hate flows in only one direction, I fear," said Margaret. "Despite my warnings, Alvin seems unable to realize that the playmate of his childhood has been murdered by the man who usually dwells in this body. So Alvin insists on loving Calvin."

"Doesn't it make you weary? Being married to such a lunatic?"

Margaret smiled. "Alvin has made me weary all my life," she said.

" 'But' . . . no, let me say it for you . . . 'But the weariness is a joy, because I have worn myself out in his service.' "

"You mock me."

"I mock myself," said Balzac. "I play the clown: the man who pretends to be so sophisticated that he finds kindly sentiment amusing, when the reality is that he would trade all his dreams for the knowledge that a woman of extraordinary intelligence felt such sentiments for him."

"You create yourself like a character in a novel," said Margaret.

"I have bared my soul to you and you call me false."

"Not false. Truer than mere reality."

Balzac bowed. "Ah, madame, may I never have to face critics of such piercing wisdom as yourself."

"You are a deeply sentimental man," said Margaret. "You pretend to be hard, but you are soft. You pretend to be distant, but your heart is captured over and over again. You pretend to be self-mockingly pretentious, when in fact you know that you really are the genius that you pretend to be pretending to be."

"Am I?" asked Balzac.

"What, haven't I flattered you enough?"

"My English is not yet perfect. Can the word 'flattery' be used with the word 'enough'?"

"I haven't flattered you at all," said Margaret. "On every path of your future in which you actually begin to write, there comes from your pen such a flood of lives and passions that your name will be known for centuries and on every continent."

Tears filled Balzac's eyes. "Ah, God, you have given me the sign from an angel."

"This is not the road to Emmaus," said Margaret.

"It was the road to Damascus I had in mind," said Balzac.

She laughed. "No one could ever strike you blind. You see with your heart as truly as I do."

Balzac moved closer to her, and whispered. No, he formed the words with his lips, counting on her to understand his heart without hearing the sound. "What I cannot see is the future and the past. Can I have my freedom from Calvin? I fear him as I fear no other living man."

"You have nothing to fear from him," said Margaret. "He loves you and wants your admiration more than that of any man but one."

"Your husband."

"His hatred for Alvin is so intense he has no real hate left over for you. If he lost your admiration, it would be a mere fleabite compared to losing hope of Alvin's respect."

"And what is that compared to my fleabite? A bee sting? A snakebite? An amputation?"

Margaret shook her head. "Now you *are* reaching for flattery. Take him home, Monsieur Balzac. I will try to find his heartfire somewhere in a house in Blacktown."

9

Witch Hunt

Hezekiah Study could not concentrate on the book he was trying to read, or the sermon he needed to write, or even on the pear he knew he ought to eat. There were several bites taken out of it, and he knew he must be the one who had taken them, but all he remembered was fretful, wandering thoughts about everything. Purity, you young fool. He'll come now, don't you know? He'll come, because he always comes, and because your name is on it, and he knows who you are, oh yes, he knows you, he wants your life, he wants to finish the job he started before you were born.

This is how he spent the afternoon, until at last a breeze arose, rattling the papers pinned under the paperweight on his writing desk. A breeze, and a shadow of cloud that dimmed the light in the room, and then the sound he had been waiting for: the trot-trot-trot of a horse drawing a little shay behind it. Micah Quill. Micah the Witcher.

Hezekiah rose and walked to the window. The shay was only just passing on the street below; Hezekiah caught but a glimpse of the face in profile, from above. So sweet and open, so trustworthy—Hezekiah had once trusted it, believed the words that came out of the shyly smiling mouth. "God will not permit the innocent to be punished," said that mouth. "Only the Lord Savior was foreordained to suffer innocently." The first of a thousand lies. Truth flowed to Micah Quill, was sucked in and disappeared, and emerged again looking ever so much like it used to, but changed subtly, at the edges, where none would notice, so that simple truth became a complicated fabric indeed, one that could wrap you up so tightly and close you off from the air until you suffocated in it.

Micah Quill, my best pupil. He has not come to Cambridge to visit his old schoolmaster, or hear the sermons he now preached on Sundays.

Leaning out his window, Hezekiah saw the shay stop at the main entrance of the orphanage. How like Micah. He does not stop for refreshment after his journey, or even to void his bladder, but goes instead directly to work. Purity, I cannot help you now. You didn't heed my warning.

Purity came into the room, relieved to see that the witcher was not some fearsome creature, some destroying angel, but rather was a man who must have been in his forties but still had the freshness of youth about him. He smiled at her, and she was at once relaxed and comfortable. She was much relieved, for she had feared the torment of conscience it would cost her, to have Alvin Smith, who seemed such a nice man, examined and tried by some monster. Instead the proceeding would be fair, the trial just, for this man had no malice in him.

"You are Purity," said the witcher. "My name is Micah Quill."

"I'm pleased to meet you," said Purity.

"And I to meet you," said Quill. "I came the moment your deposition was sent to me. I admire your courage, speaking up so boldly against a witch so dire."

"He made no threat to me," said Purity.

"His very existence is a menace to all godly souls," said Quill. "You could feel that, even if he uttered no threat, because the spirit of Christ dwells in you."

"Do you think so, sir?" asked Purity.

Quill was writing in his book.

"What do you write, sir?"

"I keep notes of all interviews," said Quill. "You never know what might turn out to be evidence. Don't mind me."

"It's just that . . . I wasn't giving my evidence yet."

"Isn't that silly of me?" said Quill. "Please, sit down, and tell me about this devil-worshiping slave of hell."

He spoke so cheerfully that Purity almost missed the dark significance of the words. When she realized what he had said, she corrected him at once. "I know nothing of what or how the man worships," said Purity. "Only that he claims to have a witchy knack."

"But you see, Miss Purity, such witchy knacks are given to people only because they serve the devil."

"What I'm saying is I never saw him worship the devil, nor speak of the devil, nor show a sign of wishing to serve him."

"Except for his knack, which of course *does* serve the devil."

"I never actually saw the knack, either, with my own eyes," said Purity. "I just heard tales of it from the boy who traveled with him."

"Name the boy," said Quill, his pen poised.

"Arthur Stuart."

Quill looked up at her, not writing.

"It *is* a joke, sir, to name him so, but the joke was made years ago by those who named him, I do not jest with you now."

He wrote the name.

"He's a half-Black boy," she began, "and—"

"Singed in the fires of hell," said Quill.

"No, I think he's merely the son of a White slave owner who forced himself on a Black slave girl, or that's the implication of the story I was told."

Quill smiled. "But why do you resist me?" he said. "You say he's half-Black. I say this shows he was singed by the fires of hell. And you say, no, not at all—and then proceed to tell me he is the product of a rape of a Black woman by a White man. How could one better describe such a dreadful conception than by saying the child was singed in the fires of hell? You see?"

Purity nodded. "I thought you were speaking literally."

"I am," said Quill.

"I mean, that you literally meant that the boy had been to hell and burned there a little."

"So I say," Quill said, smiling. "I don't understand this constant insistence on correcting me when we already agree."

"But I'm not correcting you, sir."

"And is that statement not itself a correction? Or am I to take it some other way? I fear you're too subtle for me, Miss Purity. You dazzle me with argument. My head spins.''

"Oh, I can't imagine you ever being confused by anybody,'' said Purity, laughing nervously.

"And again you feel the need to correct me. Is something troubling you? Is there some reason that you find it impossible to feel comfortable agreeing with me?''

"I'm perfectly comfortable to agree with you.''

"A statement which, while sweet of sentiment, does constitute yet another disagreement with my own prior statement. But let us set aside the fact that you are unable to accept a single word I utter at face value. What puzzles me, what I must have your help to clarify, is the matter of some missing information, and some extra information. For instance, your deposition includes several extraneous persons whom no one else has seen. To wit: a lawyer named Verily Cooper, a riverman named Mike Fink, and a half-Black boy named Arthur Stuart.''

"But I'm not the only one who saw them,'' said Purity.

"So the deposition is wrong?''

"I never said in the deposition that I was the only one who saw them.''

"Excellent! Who else was there at this witches' sabbath?''

"What witches' sabbath?'' Purity was confused now.

"Did you say you stumbled upon this coven of witches as they frolicked naked on the banks of the river?''

"Two of them were bathing, but I saw no sign of anything more dire than that.''

"So to you, when witches cavort naked before your eyes, it is innocent bathing?''

"No, I just . . . I never thought of it as a . . . it wasn't a worship of any kind.''

"But the tossing of the child toward heaven—a Black child, no less—and the way the naked man laughed at you, unashamed of his nakedness . . .''

Purity was sure she had neither spoken of nor written down any such description. "How could you know of that?''

"So you admit that you did not include this vital evidence in your deposition?''

"I didn't know it *was* evidence.''

"Everything is evidence,'' said Quill. "Beings who frolic naked, laugh at Christians, and then disappear without a trace—which part of this experience would not be evidence? You must leave nothing out.''

"I see that now,'' said Purity. "I reckon I didn't know what a witches' sabbath might look like, so I didn't know when I saw it.''

"But if you didn't know, why would you denounce them?'' asked Quill. "You haven't brought a false accusation, have you?''

"No, sir! Every word I said was true.''

"Oh, and what about the words you did *not* say?''

Purity was even more confused. "But if I didn't say them, how can I know which words they are?''

"But you know them. We just discovered them. The fact that it was a pagan bacchanal, with a naked man molesting a naked boy before your eyes—''

"Molest! He only tossed him in the air as a father might toss his own child, or an older brother might toss a younger.''

"So you think this might be incest as well?'' asked Quill.

"All I ever thought was to report what they said of themselves, that Alvin Smith is the seventh son of a seventh son, with all the knacks that such men are prone to have.''

"So you believe the words of the devil concerning this?'' asked Quill.

"The words of what devil?''

"The devil who spoke to you and told you that knacks just happen to come to seventh sons of seventh sons, when in fact witchcraft can only be practiced by those who have given themselves over to the service of Satan.''

"I didn't understand that,'' said Purity. "I thought it was the use of hidden powers that was the crime, all by itself.''

"Evil is never all by itself,'' said Quill. "Remember that when you testify you will take an oath with your hand on the sacred scripture, the very word of God under your hand, which is the same as holding Christ by the hand, for he is the very Word. You will give oath to tell the truth, the *whole* truth. So you must not attempt to withhold any more information as you have been doing.''

"But I've withheld nothing! I've answered every question!''

"Again she must contradict the servant of God even when he speaks the plain truth. You withheld the information about pederasty, about the witches' sabbath, about incest—and you attempted to pretend that this Alvin's hidden powers came naturally from the order in which he was born within his family, even though it is impossible for any such devilish power to come from nature, for nature was born in the mind of God, while witchy powers come from the anti-Christ. Don't you know that it is a terrible sin to bear false witness?''

"I do know it, and I told the truth as I understood it.''

"But you understand it better now, don't you?" said Quill. "So when you testify, you will speak truly, won't you, and name things as they truly were? Or do you intend to lie to protect your witch friends?''

"My—my *witch friends?*''

"Did you not swear that they were witches? Are you recanting that testimony?''

"I deny that they were friends of mine, not that they were witches.''

"But your deposition," said Quill. "You seem to be retreating from that document as fast as you can.''

"I stand by every word in it.''

"And yet you claim these men were not your friends? You say that they pleaded with you to go with them as they continued their wicked journey through New England. Is this something they would ask of a stranger?''

"It must be so, since I was a stranger to them, and they asked me.''

"Beware of a defiant tone," said Quill. "That will not help your cause in court.''

"Am I in court? Have I a cause there?''

"Haven't you?" said Quill. "The only thing standing between you and the gallows is this deposition, your first feeble attempt to turn away from evil. But you must understand that the love of Christ cannot protect you when you half-repent.''

"Turn away from evil? I have done no evil!''

"All men are evil," said Quill. "The natural man is the enemy of God, that's what Paul said. Are you therefore better than other people?''

"No, I'm a sinner like anyone else.''

"So I thought," said Quill. "But your deposition shows that these men called you by name and begged you to go with them. Why would they do that, if they did not count you among their number, as a fellow witch?''

Purity was stunned. How could this have happened? She was the accuser, wasn't she? And yet here she sat denounced by a witcher. "Sir, is it not as likely to be a sign that I was *not* among their number, and that they wished to persuade me?''

"But you do not describe a scene of seduction," said Quill.

"You do not tell us how the devil stood before you, his book open, waiting to write your name in it the moment you say that you consent."

"Because he did not do that," said Purity.

"So it was *not* a seduction, and the devil did *not* entice you to love and serve him."

Purity remembered how she felt in the presence of Verily Cooper, the desires that washed over her when she saw how handsome he was, when she heard the clear intelligence of his speech.

"You are blushing," said Quill. "I see that the spirit of God is touching you with shame at what you have withheld. Speak, and clear your conscience."

"I didn't think it was anything," said Purity. "But yes, I did for a moment feel enticed by one of Alvin's companions, the lawyer named Verily Cooper. I thought of it only as the feelings a girl my age might easily have toward a handsome man of good profession."

"But you did not have those feelings toward a man of good profession," said Quill. "You had them toward a man that you yourself have called a witch. So now the picture is almost complete: You came upon a witches' sabbath, unspeakable incestuous debauchery taking place between a naked man and a naked boy on the riverbank, and another witch caused you to feel sexual desire for him, and then they invite you to join them on their evil passage through New England, and at the end of this you dare to tell me they had *no* reason to think you might go along with them?"

"How can I know what reasons they had?"

Quill leaned across the table, his face full of love and sympathy toward her. "Oh, Miss Purity, you don't have to hide it any longer. You have kept the secret for so long, but I know that long before you were brought to that witches' sabbath, you were keeping your powers hidden, the powers the devil gave you, concealing them from everyone around you, but secretly using them to gain advantage over your neighbor."

Tears started flowing down Purity's cheeks. She couldn't help it.

"Doesn't it feel better to tell the truth? Don't you understand that telling the truth is how you say no to Satan?"

"Yes, I have a knack," said Purity. "I have always been able to sense what a person feels, what they're about to do."

"Can you tell what *I* am about to do?"

Purity searched his face, searched her own heart. "Sir, I truly do not know you."

"Thus the devil leaves you to fend for yourself in the hour of your need. Oh, Miss Purity, the devil is a false friend. Reject him! Turn away from him! Cease this pretense!"

"What pretense? I have confessed all!"

"Again she contradicts me. Don't you understand that as long as you are contradicting me, the spirit of the devil is in you, forcing you to contend against those who serve God?"

"But I don't know what more to confess."

"Who told you the witches' sabbath was to be held there on the riverbank that day?"

"No one told me," said Purity. "I told you, I was walking along the path."

"But is it your custom to walk along the river at that time of day?"

"No. No, I just read something in the library that made me think."

"What was it you read?"

"Something about . . . witchcraft."

Quill nodded, smiling. "Now, didn't that feel better?"

Purity did not know what it was that should have felt better.

"You were thinking of your evil pact with Satan, and suddenly you found yourself walking along the river. Perhaps you flew, perhaps you walked—I hardly think that matters, though it is possible you flew without knowing that you flew—most people fly to the witches' sabbath, often upon a broom, but I will not deny that some might walk. However it happened, you suddenly found yourself in the midst of a debauch so foul it shocked even a hardened witch such as yourself, and you longed to be cleansed of your deep wickedness, for having met souls even more lost than you, you remembered to fear God and so you came back with a story. It was still full of lies and you still left out much, but the key was there: You said the word *witch,* and you named a name. That is the beginning of redemption, to name the sin and repudiate the seducer."

Though many of his statements were not at all the way she remembered it happening, nevertheless, the end of his statement was true. How could she not have seen it before? She was led there, and probably by the devil. And hadn't she be filled with such terrible emotions that they had to warn her to be careful or she'd get herself denounced as a witch? Yes, she was one of them, they recognized her as one of them, and instead of accusing them, she should have accused herself. The beginning of redemption. "Oh, I want to have the love of God again. Will you help me, Mr. Quill?"

He leaned forward and kissed her on the cheek. "Miss Purity, I come to you with the kiss of fellowship, as the Saints greeted each other in days of old. Deep inside you is a Christian soul. I will help you waken the Christian within you, and get shut of the devil."

Weeping now, she clutched his hands within hers. "Thank you, sir."

"Let us begin in earnest, then," said Quill. "In your fear you first named only strangers, people passing through. But you have been a witch for many years, and it is time for you to name the witches of Cambridge."

She echoed him stupidly. "Witches of Cambridge?"

"It's been many, many years since this part of Massachusetts has had a witch trial. Witchery and witchism are thick here, and with your repentance we have a chance to root them out."

"Witchism?"

"The belief system surrounding witchery, which protects it and allows it to flourish. I'm sure you've heard these lies. The claim that knacks are natural or even a gift from God—this clearly is a satanic lie designed to keep people from getting rid of witchcraft. The claim that knacks don't exist—absurdly, that is what many supposedly wise men claim!—that also provides a shelter under which the covens can remain safe to work their evil. It is well known that while many witchists are simply echoing the beliefs of strong-willed people around them, others are secret witches, pretending to disbelieve in witchery even as they practice it. These are terrible hypocrites who must be exposed; and yet often they are the most attractive or interesting of the witchists, keeping you from recognizing their true nature. Can you think of any who speak this way?"

"But I can't imagine any of them are witches," said Purity.

"That's not for you to decide, is it?" said Quill. "Name the names, and let me examine them. If they're witches, I'll have it out of them eventually. If they're innocent, God will preserve them and they'll go free."

"Then let God show them to you."

"But I am not the one being tested," said Quill. "You are. This is your chance to prove that your repentance is real. You have denounced the stranger. Now denounce the snake in our own garden."

She imagined herself naming names. Whom would she denounce? Emerson? Reverend Study? These were men she loved and admired. There was not witchery in them, nor witchism either.

"All I know of witchcraft is my own knack," she said. "That and the men I already denounced."

Suddenly tears appeared in Quill's eyes. "Now Satan fears that his whole kingdom in this land is in jeopardy, and he terrifies you and forbids you to speak."

"No sir," said Purity. "Honor forbids me to name those who are not witches and who to my knowledge have done only good in the world."

"So you are the judge?" whispered Quill. "You dare to speak of honor? Let God judge them; you have only to name them."

Now she remembered Reverend Study's admonition. Why did I ever speak at all? Is this where it always leads? I cannot be considered pure unless I falsely accuse others?

"There are no other witches but myself, as far as I know," she said.

"I ask for witchists, too, remember," said Quill. "Come now, child, don't fall back into the cruel embrace of Satan out of a misplaced sense of loyalty. If they are Christians, Christ will keep them safe. And if they are not Christians, then do you not better serve them and the world at large by exposing them for what they are?"

"You twist everything I say," she said. "You'll do the same to them."

"I twist things?" said Quill. "Are you now *denying* your confession of witchcraft?"

For a moment she wanted to say yes, but then remembered: The only people ever hanged as witches were those who confessed and then either did more witchcraft—or recanted their confession.

"No sir, I don't deny that I'm a witch. I just deny that I ever saw anyone from Cambridge do anything that I might call witchery or even . . . witchism."

"It's not a good sign when you lie to me," said Quill. "I believe you attend a class taught by one Ralph Waldo Emerson."

"Yes," she said, hesitantly.

"Why are you so reluctant to tell the truth? Is Satan stopping your mouth? Or is that how these other witches punish you for your honesty, by stopping up your mouth when you try to speak? Tell me!"

"Satan isn't stopping my mouth, nor any witch."

"No, I can see the fear in your eyes. Satan forbids you to confess the names, and even frightens you into denying that he is threatening you. But I know how to get you free of his clutches."

"Can you drive out the devil?" she asked.

"Only you can drive out the devil within you," said Quill, "by denouncing Satan and those who follow him. But I will help you shake off the fear of Satan and replace it with the fear of God by mortifying the flesh."

Now she understood. "Oh, please sir, in the name of God, I beg you, do not torture me."

"Oh really," he said impatiently. "We're not the Spanish Inquisition, now, are we? No, the flesh can be mortified better through exhaustion than through pain." He smiled. "Oh, when you're free of this, when you can stand before this community of Saints and declare that you have named all of Satan's followers here, how happy you will be, filled with the love of Christ!"

She bowed her head over the table. "Oh God," she prayed, "what have I done? Help me. Help me. Help me."

Waldo Emerson saw the men at the back of the classroom. "We have visitors," he said. "Is there something in the teachings of Thomas Aquinas that I can explain to you, goodmen?"

"We're tithingmen of the witch court of Cambridge," they said.

Waldo's heart stopped beating, or so it seemed. "There is no witch court in Cambridge," he said. "Not for a hundred years."

"There's a witch girl naming other witches," said the tithingman. "The witcher, Micah Quill, he sent us to fetch you for examination, if you be Ralph Waldo Emerson."

The students sat like stones. All but one, who rose to his feet and addressed the tithingmen. "If Professor Emerson is accused of witchery then the accuser is a liar," he said. "This man is the opposite of a witch, for he serves God and speaks truth."

It was a brave thing the boy had done, but it also forced Emerson's hand. If he did not immediately surrender himself, the tithingmen would be taking along two, not just one. "Have done," Waldo told his students. "Sit down, sir." Then, walking from his rostrum to the tithingmen, he said, "I'm happy to go with you and help you dispel any misconception that might have arisen."

"Oh, it's no misconception," said the tithingman. "Everyone knows you're a witchist. It's just a matter of whether you do so as a fool or as a follower of Satan."

"How can everyone know that I'm a thing which I never heard of until this moment?"

"That's proof of it right there," said the tithingman. "Witchists are always claiming there's no such thing as witchism."

Waldo faced his students, who had either turned in their seats to face him, or were standing beside their chairs. "This is today's puzzle," he said. "If the act of denial can be taken as proof of the crime, how can an innocent man defend himself?"

The tithingmen caught him by the arms. "Come along now, Mr. Emerson, and don't go trying any philosophy on us."

"Oh, I wouldn't dream of it," said Waldo. "Philosophy would be wasted against such sturdy-headed men as you."

"Glad you know it," said the tithingman proudly. "Wouldn't want you thinking we weren't true Christians."

They had Alvin in irons, which he thought was excessive. Not that it was uncomfortable—it was a simple matter for Alvin to reshape the iron to conform with his wrists and ankles, and to cause the skin there to form calluses as if they had worn the iron for years. Such work was so long-practiced that he did it almost by reflex. But the necessity to be inactive during the hours when he could be observed made him weary. He had done this before—and without the irons— for long weeks in the jail in Hatrack River. Life was too short for him to waste more hours, let alone days or weeks, growing mold in a prison cell and weighed down by chains, not when he could so easily free himself and get on about his business.

At sundown, he sat on the floor, leaned back against the wooden side wall of the cell, and closed his eyes. He sent out his doodlebug along a familiar path, until he found the dual heartfire of his wife and the unborn daughter that dwelt within her. She was already heading for her writing table, aware through long custom that because Alvin was farther east, sundown came earlier to him. She was always as impatient as he was.

This time there was no interruption from visitors. She commiserated with him about the chains and the cell, but soon got to the matter that concerned her most.

"Calvin's doodlebug has been stolen," she said. "He had sent it forth to follow the man who collects the names and some part of the souls of Blacks arriving at the dock." She told him of Calvin's last words to Balzac before all his will seemed to depart from his body. "First, I must know how much of his soul remains with his body. It is different from the slaves, for he seems to hear nothing and has to be led. His bodily functions also are like an infant's, and Balzac and their landlord are equally disgusted at the result, though the slaves clean him without complaint. Is this reversible? Can we communicate with him to learn his whereabouts? I have searched this city all the way up the peninsula, and find no collection of heartfires and no sign of Calvin's. It has been hidden from me; I pray it is not hidden from you.''

Alvin had no need to write or even formulate his answers. He knew that she could find all his ideas in his heartfire moments after he thought of them and they fell into his memory. The kidnapped doodlebug—Alvin had never worried about that. His fears had always been that something awful might happen to his body while he wandered. But in his experience, his body remained alive and alert, and whenever anything in his environment changed—his eyes detecting movement, his ears hearing some unexpected sound—his attention would be drawn back into his body.

His attention, and therefore his doodlebug. That's what the doodlebug was, really—his full attention. That's what was missing from Calvin. Even when things happened around his body, happened *to* his body, he could not bring his attention back to it. His body was no doubt sending him frantic signals demanding his attention.

The slaves, on the other hand, couldn't possibly have surrendered their attention to the man named Denmark. What they gave up was their passion, their resentment, their will to freedom. And their names.

That was an important conclusion: There was no reason to think that this Denmark fellow had Calvin's name. In fact, what he probably had was a net of hexwork that contained the free portion of separated souls. He might not even be aware that Calvin's doodlebug had got inside. The hexes caught him automatically, like the workings of an engine. The hexwork also served to hide the soulstuff that it contained. Calvin could not see out, and could not be seen inside.

But the hexes could be seen. Margaret could not possibly find them, since she saw only heartfires, and if a man knew how to hide heartfires from her, he could certainly hide his own heartfire so she could not discover the man who knew the secret.

''Is he hiding from me?'' she wrote.

He doesn't know you exist. He's hiding from everybody.

''How could Calvin be captured, when he didn't make the little knotted things the slaves made?''

I don't know the workings of Black powers, but my guess is that each slave put his own name and all his fears and hatred into the knotwork. They needed the knots in order to lift this part of their souls out of their bodies. Calvin needed no such tool.

''They had to do a Making?'' she wrote.

Yes, he thought, that's what it was. A Making. Whether it was the power of Whites or Reds or Blacks, that's what it came down to: connecting yourself to the world around you by Making. Reds made the connection directly—that connection *was* their Making, the link they forged between man and animal, man and plant, man and stone. Blacks made artifacts whose only purpose was power— poppets and knotted strings. Whites, however, spent their lives making tools that hammered, cut, tore at nature directly, and only in the one area that they called their knack did they truly make that link. Yet they did make that connection. They were not utterly divorced from the natural world. Though Alvin could imagine such men and women, never feeling that deep, innate connection, never seeing the world change by the sheer action of their will in harmony with that part of nature. How lonely they must be, to be able to shape iron no other way than with hammer and anvil, fire and tongs. To make fire only by striking flint on steel. To see the future only by living day to day and watching it unfold one path at a time. To see the past only by reading what others wrote of it, or hearing their tales, and imagining the rest. Would such people even know that nature was as alive and responsive as it is? That hidden powers move in the world—no, not just *in* the world, they *move* the world, they *are* the world at its foundation? How terrible it would be, to know and yet not touch these powers at any point. Only the bravest and wisest would be able to bear it. The rest would have to deny the hidden powers entirely, pretend they did not exist.

And then he realized: That's what the witchcraft laws *are*. An attempt to shut off the hidden powers and drive them away from the lives of men.

"At least the witchcraft laws admit that hidden powers exist," wrote Margaret.

With that, Alvin realized the full import of what Verily was attempting. It would be good to strike down the witchery laws, but only if it led to an open acknowledgment that knacks were good or evil only according to the use made of them.

"Verily's strategy is to make the whole idea of witchcraft look foolish."

Well, it *is* foolish, thought Alvin. All the images of the devil that he had heard of were childish. What God had created was a great Making that lived of itself and contained lesser beings whom he tried to turn into friends and fellow Makers. The enemy of that was not some pathetic creature giving a few lonely, isolated people the power to curse and cause misery. The enemy of Making was

Unmaking, and the Unmaker wore a thousand different masks, depending on the needs of the person he was attempting to deceive.

I wonder what form the Unmaker takes to bring this witcher fellow along?

"Some men need no deception to serve him," wrote Margaret. "They already love his destructive work and engage in it freely of their own accord."

Are you speaking of this Quill fellow? Or of Calvin?

"No doubt they both believe they serve the cause of Making."

Is that true, Margaret? Aren't you the one who told me that however much a man might lie to himself, at the core of him he knows what he truly is?

"In some men the truth lies hidden so deeply that they see it again only at the last extremity. Then they recognize that they have known it all along. But they see the truth only at the moment when it is too late to seize upon it and use it to save themselves. They see it and despair. That is the fire of hell."

All men deceive themselves. Are we all damned?

"They cannot save themselves," she wrote. "That does not mean they cannot be saved."

Alvin found that comforting, for he feared his own secrets, feared the place in himself where he had hidden the truth about his own motives when he killed the Finder who murdered Margaret's mother. Maybe I can open up that door and face the truth someday, knowing that I might still be saved from that hard sharp blade when it pierces my heart.

"Calvin's need for redemption is more dire than yours right now."

I'm surprised you want to save him. You're the one who tells me he'll never change.

"I tell you I've seen no change in any of his futures."

I'll search for him. For the hexes that hide him. I can see what you cannot. But what about Denmark? Can't you find him when he walks the streets, and learn the truth?

"He is also guarded. I can find him on the street, and his name is carried with him, so he hasn't parted with that part of his heartfire. Nevertheless, he has no knowledge, no memory of where he takes the knotwork and whom he gives it to. There are blank places in his memory. As soon as he leaves the docks with a basket of souls, he remembers nothing until he wakes up again. I could follow him, with eyes instead of doodlebug. . . ."

No! No, don't go near him! We know nothing of the powers at

work here. Stay away and cease to search. Who knows but what some part of yourself goes forth from your body, too, when you do your torching? If you were captive as well it would be too much for me to bear.

"We are all captives, aren't we?" she wrote. "Even the baby in my womb."

She is no captive. *She* is home in the place she wants most to be.

"She chooses me because she knows no other choice."

In due time she'll eat of the fruit of the tree of knowledge of good and evil. For now, she is in the garden. You are paradise. You are the tree of life.

"You are sweet," she wrote. "I love you. I love you."

His own love for her swept over him, filling his eyes with tears and his heart with longing. He could see her set down the pen. No more words would appear on the paper tonight.

He lay there, sending forth his doodlebug. He found Purity easily. She was awake in her cell, weeping and praying. He stifled the vindictive thought that a sleepless night was the least she owed him. Instead, he entered her body and found where the fluids were being released that made her heart beat faster and her thoughts race. He watched her calm down, and then kindled the low fires of sleep in her brain. She crawled into bed. She slept. Poor child, he thought. How terrible it is not to know what your life is for. And how sad to have found such a destructive purpose for it.

Verily Cooper left Arthur Stuart, Mike Fink, and John-James Audubon in a small clearing in a stand of woods well north of the river and far from the nearest farmhouse. Arthur was making some bird pose on a branch—Audubon discoursed about the bird but it never made it into Verily's memory. It was a daring thing he was going to try. He had never knowingly attempted to defend a man he knew was guilty. And Alvin was, under New England law, guilty indeed. He had a knack; he used it.

But Verily thought he knew how witch trials were run. He had read about them in his mentor's law library—surreptitiously, lest anyone wonder why he took interest in such an arcane topic. Trial after trial, in England, France, and Germany, turned up the same set of traditional details: curses, witches appearing as incubi and succubi, and the whole mad tradition of witches' sabbaths and powerful gifts from the devil. Witchers asserted that the similarity of detail was proof that the phenomenon of witchcraft was real and wide-spread.

Indeed, one of their favorite ploys was to alarm the jury with statements like, "If this has all been happening under your very noses in this village, imagine what is happening in the next village, in the whole county, all over England, throughout the world!" They were forever citing "leading authorities" who estimated that, judging from the numbers of known witches actually brought to trial, there "must be" ten thousand or a hundred thousand or a million witches.

"Suspect everybody," they said. "There are so many witches it is impossible that you don't know one." And the clincher: "If you ignore small signs of witchcraft then you are responsible for permitting Satan to work unhindered in the world."

All this might have had some meaning if it weren't for one simple fact: Verily Cooper had a knack, and he knew that he had never had any experience of Satan, had never attended a witches' sabbath, had not left his body and wandered as an incubus to ravish women and send them strange dreams of love. All he had done was make barrels that held water so tightly that the wood had to rot through before the joints would leak. His only power was to make dead wood live and grow under his hands. And he had never used his knack to harm a living soul in any way. Therefore, *all* these stories had to be lies. And the statistics estimating the number of uncaught witches were a lie based upon a lie.

Verily believed what Alvin believed: that every soul was born with some connection to the powers of the universe—perhaps the powers of God, but more likely the forces of nature—which showed up as knacks among Europeans, as a connection to nature among the Reds, and in other strange ways among the other races. God wanted these powers used for good; Satan would of course want them used for evil. But the sheer possession of a knack was morally neutral.

The opportunity was here not just to save Purity from herself, but also to discredit the entire system of witch trials and the witchery laws themselves. Make the laws and the witnesses so obviously, scandalously, ludicrously false that no one would ever stand trial for the crime of witchcraft again.

Then again, he might fail, and Alvin would have to get himself and Purity out of jail whether she liked it or not, and they'd all hightail it out of New England.

Cambridge was a model New England town. The college dominated, with several impressive buildings, but there was still a town common across from the courthouse, where Alvin was almost certainly imprisoned. And, to Verily's great pleasure, the witcher and the tithingmen were running both Alvin and Purity. A crowd surrounded the common—but at a safe distance—as Alvin was forced to run around in tight circles at one end of the meadow and Purity at the other.

"How long have they been at it?" Verily asked a bystander.

"Since before dawn without a rest," said the man. "These are tough witches, you can bet."

Verily nodded wisely. "So you know already that they're both witches?"

"Look at 'em!" said the bystander. "You think they'd have the strength to run so long without falling over if they weren't?"

"They look pretty tired to me," said Verily.

"Ayup, but still running. And the girl's a brought-in orphan, so it's likely she had it in her blood anyway. Nobody ever liked her. We knew she was strange."

"I heard she was the chief witness against the man."

"Ayup, but how would she know about the witches' sabbath iffen she didn't go to it her own self, will you tell me that?"

"So why do they go to all this trouble? Why don't they just hang her?"

The man looked sharply at Verily. "You looking to stir up trouble, stranger?"

"Not I," said Verily. "I think they're both innocent as you are, sir. Not only that, but I think you know it, and you're only talking them guilty so no one will suspect that you also have a knack, which you keep well-hidden."

The man's eyes widened with terror, and without another word he melted away into the crowd.

Verily nodded. It was a safe enough thing to charge, if Alvin was right, and all folks had some kind of hidden power. All had something to hide. All feared the accusers. Therefore it was good to see this accuser charged right along with the man she accused. Hang her before she accuses anybody else. Verily had to count on that fear and aggravate it.

He strode out onto the common. At once a murmur went up—who was the stranger, and how did he dare to go so close to where the witcher was running the witches to wear them down and get a full confession out of them?

"You, sir," said Verily to the witcher. He spoke loudly, so all could hear. "Where is the officer of the law supervising this inter-rogation?"

"I'm the officer," said the witcher. He spoke just as loudly—people usually matched their voices to the loudest speaker, Verily found.

"You're not from this town," Verily said accusingly. "Where are the tithingmen!"

At once the dozen men who had formed watchful rings around both Alvin and Purity turned, some of them raising their hands.

"Are you men not charged with upholding the law?" demanded Verily. "Interrogation of witnesses in witch trials is to take place under the supervision of officers of the court, duly appointed by the judge or magistrate, precisely to stop *torture* like this from taking place!"

The word *torture* was designed to strike like a lash, and it did.

"This is not torture!" the witcher cried. "Where is the rack? The fire? The water?"

Verily turned toward him again, but stepped back, speaking louder than before. "I see you are familiar with *all* the methods of torture, but running them is one of the cruelest! When a person is worn down enough, they'll confess to . . . to *suicide* if it will end the torment and allow them to rest!"

It took a moment for the surrounding crowd to understand the impossibility of a confession of suicide, but he was rewarded with a chuckle. Turn the crowd; everyone who ended up on the jury would know of what was said here today.

Because the tithingmen were looking away, both Alvin and Purity had staggered and dropped to their knees. Now they both knelt on all fours in the grass, panting, heads hanging like worn-out horses.

"Don't let them rest!" the witcher cried frantically. "You'll set the whole interrogation back by hours!"

The tithingmen looked to their rods and switches, which they used to goad the runners, but none moved toward the two victims.

"At last you remember your duty," said Verily.

"You have no authority here!" cried the witcher. "And I *am* an officer of the court!"

"Tell me then the name of the magistrate here in Cambridge who appointed you."

The witcher knew he'd been caught exceeding his authority, since he had none until the local judge called for his services, and so he did not answer Verily's challenge directly. "And who are

you?" the witcher demanded. "From your speech you're from England—what authority do *you* have?"

"I have the authority to demand that you be clapped in irons
yourself if you cause these two souls to be tortured for one more
moment!" cried Verily. He knew the crowd was spellbound, watching the confrontation. "For I am Alvin Smith's attorney, and by
torturing my client without authority, you, sir, have broken the Protection Act of 1694!" He flung out an accusing finger and the
witcher visibly wilted under his accusation.

Verily was growing impatient, however, for the plan wasn't to
win a petty victory here on the common. Was Purity so tired she
couldn't lift her head and see who was speaking here?

He was about to launch into another tirade, during which he
would wander closer to Purity and stand her up to face him if need
be, but finally she recognized him and eliminated the need.

"That's him!" she cried.

The witcher sensed salvation. "Who? Who is he?"

"The English lawyer who was traveling with Alvin Smith! He's
a witch too! He has a knack with wood!"

"So he was also at the witches' sabbath!" cried the witcher.
"Of course Satan quotes the law to try to save his minions! Arrest
that man!"

Verily immediately turned to the crowd. "See how it goes!
Everyone who stands up for my client will be accused of witchcraft!
Everyone will be clapped into jail and tried for his life!"

"Silence him!" cried the witcher. "Make him run along with
the others!"

But the tithingmen, who reluctantly took Verily by the elbows
because he *had* been accused, had no intention of doing any more
running, now that it had been called torture and declared to be illegal.
"No more running today, sir," said one of them. "We'll have to
hear from the judge before we let you do such things again."

As a couple of tithingmen helped Purity stagger toward the
courthouse, she whimpered when she came near Verily. "Don't
bring me near him," she said. "He casts spells on me. He wants to
come to me as an incubus!"

"Purity, you poor thing," Verily said. "Hear yourself spout the
lies this witcher has taught you to tell."

"Speak no word to her!" cried the witcher. "Hear him curse
her!"

To the tithingmen, Verily wryly muttered, "Did that sound like
a curse to you?"

"No muttering! Keep still!" screamed the witcher.

Verily answered the witcher loudly. "All I said was, to a man with a hammer everything looks like a nail!"

Some people understood at once and chuckled. But the witcher was not one for irony. "A satanic utterance! Hammers and nails! What have you cursed me with? Confess your meaning, sir!"

"I mean, sir, that to those who *profit* from *witch trials,* every word sounds like a curse!"

"Get him out of here with his filthy lies and innuendoes!"

The tithingmen dragged him and Alvin off to the courthouse, to cells far from each other, but they were near each other several times, and though they didn't speak, they traded glances, and Verily made sure Alvin saw him grinning from ear to ear. This is working exactly as I wanted, Verily was saying.

Alone in his cell, though, Verily lost his smile. Poor Purity, he thought. How deeply had this witcher twisted her mind? Was her integrity so tied up in knots that she was no longer capable of seeing how she was being manipulated? Somewhere along the line, she had to realize that the witcher was using her.

Let it be soon, thought Verily. I don't want Alvin to have to wait long in this jail.

Hezekiah Study had already packed his bag for an extended stay with his niece in Providence when he heard the shouting on the common and leaned out his window to listen. He watched the English lawyer embarrass Micah Quill, manipulating the master manipulator until Hezekiah wanted to cheer. His heart sank when Purity denounced the lawyer—and, indeed, she *had* spoken of a lawyer in Alvin Smith's party right from the start—but the lawyer managed to plant seeds of doubt in every onlooker's mind all the same. To Hezekiah Study, it was the first time he'd ever seen the early stages of a witch trial without dread and despair seizing his heart. For the English lawyer was grinning like a schoolboy who doesn't mind the punishment because it was worth it to put the rock through the schoolmaster's window.

He's in control of this, thought Hezekiah.

His better sense—his bitter experience—answered: No one's ever in control of a witch trial except the witchers. The man is grinning now, but he'll not grin in the end, with either the rope around his neck or his decency stripped from him.

Oh, God, let this be the day at last when the people finally see that the only ones serving the devil at these trials are the witchers!

And when his prayer was done, he came away from the window and unpacked his bag. Come what may, this trial was going to be fought with courage, and Hezekiah Study had to stay. Not just to see what was going to happen, but because this young lawyer would not stand alone. Hezekiah Study would stand with him. He had that much hope and courage left in him, despite all.

10

Captivity

Calvin didn't notice, at first, that he was trapped. With his doodle-bug he followed Denmark into Blacktown, the section of Camelot devoted to housing skilled slaves whose services were being rented out, or where trusted slaves who were running errands for out-of-town landlords found room and board. Blacktown wasn't large, but it spilled over its official borders, as one warehouse after another had rooms added on upper floors—illegally and without registration—and where slaves came and went.

It was into one such warehouse just outside Blacktown that Denmark went and Calvin followed. Rickety stairs inside the building led to an attic story filled with an incredible array of junk. Boards, bits of furniture, strap and scrap iron, old clothes, ropes, fishnets, and all sorts of other random items dangled from hooks in the ceiling joists. At first he was puzzled—who would spend the time to bind all these things together?—but then he realized what he was seeing: larger versions of the knotwork that Denmark had collected from the newly arrived slaves.

He was about to return to his body and tell Honoré what he had found and where it was, when suddenly the junk parted and Calvin saw a dazzling light. He exclaimed about it, then moved closer and saw that it was made of thousands and thousands of heartfires, held within a net which hung, of course, from a hook in the ceiling.

What kind of net could hold souls? He moved closer. The individual heartfires were much tinier than those he was used to seeing. As so often before, he wished he could see into them the way torches did. But they remained a mystery to him.

His vision, though, could see what Margaret's never could: He could see the stout web of knotted cords that held the heartfires. On closer examination, though, he saw that each heartfire danced like a candle flame above one of the little bits of knotwork that he and Honoré had watched Denmark collect from the arriving slaves. So the web probably wasn't hexy at all.

With that, Calvin drew back, expecting to return instantly to his body to speak to Honoré. He even started to speak. But his mouth didn't move. His eyes didn't see. He remained where he was, looking at the heartfires with his doodling sight instead of gazing out of his eyes at the street.

No, that wasn't so. He was vaguely aware of the street, as if seeing it out of the corners of his eyes. He could hear sounds, too, Honoré's voice, but when he tried to listen, he kept getting distracted. He couldn't pay attention to Honoré, couldn't focus on what his eyes were seeing. He kept coming back here to the knots and the net, no matter how hard he tried to tear himself away. He could feel his legs moving, as if they were someone else's legs. He could tell that Honoré's voice was becoming agitated, but still he couldn't make out what was being said. The sounds entered his mind, but by the time the end of a word was said, Calvin had lost his hold on the beginning of it. Nothing made sense.

Now with sick dread he realized that Honoré's warning had been well placed. This net was designed to catch and hold souls, or bits of souls, anyway, and keep anyone from finding them. Calvin had sent a bit of his own soul into the net, and now he couldn't get out.

Well, that's what *they* thought. Nets were made of cord; cord was made of threads wound and twisted; threads were spun from fibers. All of these were things that Calvin well understood. He set to work at once.

Denmark Vesey scowled at Gullah Joe, but the old witchy man didn't even seem to notice. White men had been known to step back a bit when they saw Denmark passing by with such a look on his face. Even the kind of White men who liked to goad Blacks, like those men on the dock today, they wouldn't mess with him when he wore that scowl on his face. He only let them push him around today because he had to show the new slaves how to keep White folks happy. But he still felt the rage and stored it up in his heart.

Not that he felt the kind of fury that filled that net of souls hanging up not ten paces away. That's because Denmark wasn't no man's slave. He wasn't even fully Black. He was the son of one of those rare slaveowners who felt some kind of fatherly responsibility toward the children he sired on his Black women. He gave freedom to all his half-Black bastards, freedom and a geography lesson, since every one of them was named for a European country. Few of them stayed free, though, if they once strayed from Mr. Vesey's plantation near Savannah. What difference did it make being free, if you had to live among the slaves and work among them and couldn't leave any more than the slaves did?

It made a difference to Denmark. He wasn't going to stick around on the plantation. He figured out what letters were when he was still little and got hold of a book and taught himself to read. He learned his numbers from his father's cousin, a French student who lived on the plantation to hide out because he took part in an anti-Napolcon rally at the university. The boy fancied himself some kind of hero of the oppressed, but all Denmark cared about was learning how to decode the mysteries that White people used to keep Black folks down. By the time he was ten, his father had him keeping the books for the plantation, though they had to keep it secret even from the White foreman. His father would pat his head and praise him, but the praise made Denmark want to kill him. "Just goes to show your Black mama's blood can't wipe out *all* the brains you get from a White papa." His father was still sleeping with his mother and getting more babies on her, and he knew she wasn't stupid, but he still talked like that, showing no respect for her at all, even though *her* children were smarter than the dim-witted little White weaklings that Father's *wife* produced.

Denmark nursed that anger and it kept him free. He wasn't going to end up on this plantation, no sir. The law said that there wasn't no such thing as a free Black man in the Crown Colonies. One of Denmark's own brothers, Italy, had been seized as a runaway in Camelot, and Father had to lay some stripes on Italy's back before the law would let up and go away. But Denmark wasn't going to get caught. He went to his father one day with a plan. Father didn't like it much—he didn't want to have to go back to doing his own books—but Denmark kept after him and finally went on strike, refusing to do the books if Father didn't go along. Father had him back in the fields under the overseer for a while, but in the end he didn't have the heart to waste the boy's talents.

So when Denmark was seventeen, his father brought him to Camelot and set him up with letters of introduction that Denmark had actually written, so the hand would always match. Denmark went around pretending to be a messenger for his absentee owner, soliciting bookkeeping jobs and copy work. Some White men thought they could cheat him, getting him to work but then refusing to pay the amount agreed on. Denmark hid his anger, then went home and in his elegant hand wrote letters to an attorney, again using his father's name. As soon as the White men realized that Denmark's owner wasn't going to let them get away with cheating him, they generally paid up. The ones that didn't, Denmark let the matter drop and never worked for them again. It wasn't so bad being a slave when your owner was yourself and stood up for you.

That went on till his father died. Denmark was full grown and had some money set by. No one knew his father in Camelot so it didn't matter he was dead, as long as nobody went back to Savannah to try to follow up on something Denmark wrote in his father's name. Not that Denmark didn't worry for a while. But when it became clear that it was all going well, he started to fancy himself a real man. He decided to buy himself a slave of his own, a Black woman he could love and get children from the way his father did.

He chose the one he wanted and had an attorney buy her for him, then went to pick her up in the name of his father. But when he got her home and she found out that a Black man had bought her, she near clawed his eyes out and ran out screaming into the neighborhood that she wasn't going to be no slave to a Black man. Denmark chased her down, getting no help from the other residents of Blacktown—that was when he realized they all knew he was free and resented him for it. It all came down to this, from his woman and from his neighbors: They hated being slaves, hated all White people, but more than anyone or anything else they hated a free buck like him.

Well, let them! That's what he thought at first. But it grew so he could hardly bear the sight of his woman, chained to the wall in his tiny room, cursing him whenever he came home. She kept making dolls of him to try to poison him, and it made him good and sick more than once. He didn't know a thing about poppeting. He'd

spent all his effort learning the White man's secrets and knew nothing about what Black folks did. He came to the day when he realized
he had nothing. He might fool White folks into letting him keep the
results of his own labor, but he was never going to be White. And
Black folks didn't trust him because he didn't know their ways,
either, and because he acted so White and kept a slave.

Finally one day he knelt down in front of his woman and cried.
What can I do to make you love me? She just laughed. You can't
set me free, she said, cause Black folks are never free here. And you
can't make me love you cause I never love him as owns me. And
you can't sell me cause I tell my new master about you, see if I
don't. All you can do is die when I make you a right poppet and
kill it dead.

All that hate! Denmark thought that rage was the ruling principle
of his own life, but it was nothing compared to what slaves felt.
That was when Denmark realized the difference between free and
slave—freedom stole hate away from you, and made you weaker.
Denmark hated his father, sure, but it was nothing compared to his
woman's hate for him.

Of course he had to kill her. She'd laid it out so plain, and it
was clear he wasn't going to change her mind. It was just a matter
of time before she killed him, so he had to defend himself, right?
And he owned her, didn't he? She wouldn't be the first Black woman
killed by her master.

He hit her in the head with a board and knocked her cold. Then
he bundled her into a sack and carried her down to the dock. He
figured to hold her under the water till she drowned, then pull her
out of the sack and let her float so it didn't look like murder. Well,
he had her under the water all right, and she wasn't even struggling
inside the sack, but it was like a voice talking in his mind telling
him, You killing the wrong one. It ain't the Black woman killing
you, it's the White folks. If it wasn't for the White folks, you could
marry this girl and she be free beside you. They the ones she wants
to kill, they the ones you ought to kill.

He dragged her out of the water and revived her. But she wasn't
right after that. It might have been the blow to the head or it might
have been the water she took on and the time she spent not breathing,
but she walked funny and didn't talk good and she didn't hate him
anymore, but everything he loved about her was dead. It was like
he was a murderer after all, but the victim lived in his house and
bore him a baby.

Oh, Denmark, he was a sad man all the time after that. The joy of fooling White folks was gone. He got sloppy with his work, doing it late, and his customers stopped hiring him—though of course they thought it was his White master they were firing. The Black people around him hated him too, for what he done to his woman, and he had to watch all the time to keep them from getting any of his hair or fingernails or toenails, or even his spit or his urine. Cause they would have killed him with that, if they could.

His son Egypt got to be four years old and Denmark prenticed him to a Black harness maker. Had to do all kinds of pretending, of course, that it was a White man who owned the boy and wanted him trained to be useful on his plantation, and it cost nine pounds a year, which was most of what Denmark was earning these days, but the paperwork went well enough, and even though Egypt was treated like a slave, he was learning a trade and there'd come a day when Denmark would tell him the truth. You free, boy, he'd say that day. Egypt Vesey, no man owns you. Not me, not nobody.

When Egypt was gone, the last light went out of the boy's mama. The day Denmark saw his woman drinking varnish, he knew he had to do something. Stupid as she had become, she hated her life and hated him. He agreed with her. Maybe he hated himself even more than she did. Hated everything and everybody else, too. It was chewing him up inside.

That was when he met Gullah Joe. Joe came to him. Little Black man, he suddenly appeared right in front of Denmark when he was in the dirt garden peeing. He wasn't there, and then he was, holding a crazy-looking umbrella all a-dangle with strange knots and bits of cloth and tin and iron and one dead mouse. "Stop peeing on my foot," said Gullah Joe.

Denmark didn't have much to say. Piss just dried right up when Gullah Joe said so. Denmark knew he must be the witchy man they were always threatening him with. "You come to kill me, witchy man?" Denmark said.

"Might," said Gullah Joe. "Might not."

"Maybe you best just do it," said Denmark. "Cause if you don't, what if I kill *you*?"

Gullah Joe just grinned. "What, you hit me with a board, put me in a sack, drown me till I can't walk or talk right?"

Denmark just started to cry, fell to his knees and begged Gullah Joe to kill him. "You know what I am! You know I'm a wicked man!"

"I'm not God," said Gullah Joe. "You gots to go see him preacher, you want somebody send you to hell."

"How come you talk so funny?"

"Cause I not no slave," said Gullah Joe. "I from Africa, I don't like White man language, I learn it bad and I don't care. I say *people* talk real good." Then he let loose a string of some strange language. It went on and on, and turned into a song, and he danced around, splashing up the mud from Denmark's pissing all over his bare feet while he sang. Denmark felt every splash as if he'd been kicked in the kidneys. By the time Gullah Joe stopped singing and dancing, Denmark was lying on the ground whimpering, and there was blood leaking out of him instead of piss.

Gullah Joe bent over him. "How you feel?"

"Fine," Denmark whispered. " 'Cept I ain't dead yet."

"Oh, I don't want you dead. I make up my mind. You be fine. Drink this."

Gullah Joe handed him a small bottle. It smelled awful, but there was alcohol in it and that was persuasive enough. Denmark drank the whole bottle, or at least he would have, if Joe hadn't snatched it out of his hands. "You want to live forever?" Gullah Joe demanded. "You use up all my saving stuff?"

Whatever it was, it worked great. Denmark bounded to his feet. "I want more of that!" he said.

"You never get this again," said Gullah Joe. "You like it too good."

"Give it to my woman!" cried Denmark. "Make her well again!"

"She sick in the brain," said Gullah Joe. "This don't do no good for brain."

"Well then you go on and kill me again, you cheating bastard! I'm sick of living like this, everybody hate me, I hate myself!"

"I don't hate you," said Gullah Joe. "I got a *use* for you."

And ever since then, Denmark had been with Gullah Joe. Denmark's money had gone to supporting both him and Gullah Joe, and to accomplish whatever Joe wanted done. Half Denmark's day was spent taking care of new-arrived slaves, gathering their names and bringing them home to Joe.

The whole idea of taking names came from Denmark's woman. Not that she thought of it. But when Denmark rented the warehouse and brought Gullah Joe and the woman both to live there, Gullah Joe asked her what her name was. She just looked at him and said, "I don' know, master." It was a far cry from what she used to say to Denmark, back before he made her stupid. In those days she'd say, "Master never know my name. You call me what you want, but I never tell my name."

Well, when Gullah Joe asked Denmark what the woman's name was, and Denmark didn't know, why, you might have thought Joe had eaten a pepper, the way he started jumping around and howling and yipping. "She never told her name!" he cried. "She kept her soul!"

"She kept her *hate*," said Denmark. "I tried to *love* her and I don't even know what to call her except Woman."

But Gullah didn't care about Denmark's sad story. He got to work with his witchery. He made Denmark catch him a seagull— not an easy thing to do, but with Joe's Catching Stick it went well enough. Soon the seagull's body parts were baked, boiled, mixed, glued, woven, or knotted into a feathered cape that Gullah Joe would throw over his head to turn himself into a seagull. "Not really," he explained to Denmark. "I still a man, but I fly and White sailor, he see gulls." Joe would fly out to slaveships coming in to port in Camelot. He'd go down into the hold and tell the people they needed to get their name-string made before they landed, and give it to the half-Black man who gave them water.

"Put hate and fear in name-string," he said to them. "Peaceful and happy be all that stay behind. I keep you safe till the right day." Or that was what he told Denmark that he said. Few of the arriving slaves spoke any English, so he had to explain it to them in some African language. Or maybe he was able to convey it all to them in knot language. Denmark wouldn't know—Gullah Joe wouldn't teach him what the knotwork meant or how it worked. "You read and write White man talk," Gullah Joe said. "That be enough secret for one man." Denmark only knew that somehow these people knew how to tie bits of this and that with scraps of string and cloth and thread and somehow it would contain their name, plus a sign for fear and a sign for hate. Even though he couldn't understand it, the knotted name-strings made Denmark proud, for it proved that Black people knew how to read and write back in Africa, only it wasn't marks on paper, it was knots in string.

Besides gathering the names of the newly arrived slaves, Denmark helped collect the names of the slaves already in Camelot. Word spread among the Blacks—Denmark only had to pass along a garden fence with an open basket, and Black hands would reach out and drop name-strings into the basket. "Thank you," they said. "Thank you."

"Not me," he would answer. "Don't thank *me*. I ain't nobody."

Came a day not long ago when they had all the slaves' names, and Gullah Joe sang all night. "My people happy now," he said. "My people got they happy."

"They're still slaves," Denmark pointed out.

"All they hate in there," said Gullah Joe, pointing at the bulging net.

"All their hope, too," said Denmark. "They got no hope now either."

"I no take they hope," said Gullah Joe. "White man take they hope!"

"They all stupid like my woman," said Denmark.

"No, no," said Gullah Joe. "They smart. They wise."

"Well, nobody knows it but you."

Gullah Joe only grinned and tapped his head. Apparently it was enough for Joe to know the truth.

There was one person who wasn't happy, though. Oh, Denmark was glad enough to have a purpose in his life, to have Black people look at him with gratitude instead of loathing. But that wasn't the same as being happy. His woman was still before him every day, lurching through her housework, mumbling words he could barely understand. Gullah Joe saw that his people weren't unhappy anymore. But Denmark saw that the happiest people were the Whites. He heard them talking.

"You see how docile they are?"

"Slavery is the natural state of the Black man."

"They don't *wish* to rise above their present condition."

"They are content."

"The only place where Blacks are angry is where they are permitted to live without a master."

"The Black man cannot be happy without discipline."

And so on, throughout the city. White people came to Camelot from all over the world, and what they saw was contented slaves. It persuaded them that slavery must not be such a bad thing after all. Denmark hated this. But Gullah Joe seemed not to care.

"Black man day come," said Gullah Joe.

"When?"

"Black man day come."

That was why Denmark Vesey was scowling at Gullah Joe today, as the old witchy man carried the basket of name-strings through the knotwork that guarded the place. All these happy slaves. Was Denmark Vesey the only Black man in Camelot who lived in hell?

Gullah Joe pulled the net open and started to pour in the new name-strings. At that moment, cords along the bottom of the net began to pop open, one by one, as if someone were cutting them. Name-strings dropped out, at first a few, then dozens, and then the whole net opened up and the name-strings lay heaped on the floor.

"What did you *do*?" asked Denmark.

Gullah Joe did not answer.

"Something wrong?" asked Denmark.

Gullah Joe just stood there, his hands upraised. Denmark walked through the hanging junk, circling around until he could see Joe's face. He was frozen like a statue—a comic one, with eyes wide and teeth exposed in a grimace, like the minstrels in those hideous shows that White actors did with their faces painted Black.

This wasn't just a net giving way. Someone or something *had* broken open the net and spilled the name-strings onto the floor. If it had the power to do that, it had the power to hurt Gullah Joe, and that's what seemed to be happening.

What could Denmark do? He knew nothing about witchery. Yet he couldn't let anything happen to Joe. Or to the name-strings, for that matter, for the name of every slave in Camelot was spilled here. Yet if Denmark walked within the charmed circle that Joe had shown him, wouldn't he be in the enemy's power, too?

Maybe not if he didn't stay long. Denmark ran and leapt, knocking Joe clear out of the circle. They both sprawled on the floor, leaving a dozen large charms swaying and bumping each other.

Gullah Joe didn't show any sign of being hurt. He leapt up and looked frantically around him. "Get up by damn! A broom! A broom!"

Denmark scrambled to his feet and ran for the broom.

"Two broom! Quick!"

In moments the two of them were standing just outside the circle, reaching the brooms inside to sweep the name-strings outside in great swaths.

"Fast!" cried Joe. "He take apart you broom you go slow!"

Denmark hadn't thought he was going any slower than Joe, but then he realized that the end of the broomstick nearest his body was holding almost still as he levered the broom to sweep out name-strings. No sooner had he thought of this than the broomstick rocketed straight at him like a bayonet, ramming him in the stomach just under the breastbone. Denmark dropped like a rock, the breath knocked out of him. And when he did manage to take in a great gasp of air, he immediately vomited.

A few minutes later, Gullah Joe was bending over him. "You got you air? He not hurt you bad. He no see you, or you dead man."

"Who?" asked Denmark.

"You think I know?"

"You talk like you know everything," said Denmark.

"When I know, I say I know. This one, he a bad devil. He wander like stray dog, come passing through, he see all the names, devil eat name like food, like cake, taste him sweet. He come in my circle and now he get caught, he no come out. So he mad, him! Tear up net. Tear up name, kill me if he can. But I stop him."

"I helped."

"Yes, you knock me down, very smart."

"Why you holding still like that?"

"See me knotty hair? She wiggle, he get inside, he break me in bits."

Denmark had long wondered why Gullah Joe had braided his hair with ribbons and scraps. It wasn't decoration, it was protection—as long as the knotted braids weren't wiggling.

"So that hair keep out the devil?"

Joe flipped his braids boastfully. "Hair, she keep him out of *me.*" Then he pointed at the dangling charms that used to ring the net of name-strings. "These charm, they keep him in my circle." Joe grinned. "It got him."

"What you want him for?" asked Denmark. "Can you ask him for wishes or something?"

Gullah Joe looked at him like he was stupid. "You live White too long, boy, it make you strange."

"I thought maybe it was like a genie or something."

"You no ask devil help you, he help you be dead, that be his help you." Gullah Joe began walking around, looking at the dangling charms hanging elsewhere in the room. "You get me that one, that one, that one."

Denmark, being tall, had no trouble unhooking the charms Joe indicated. Soon they had a new circle created, just like the other one, only when you looked close there were no two charms alike. It seemed not to matter. In a few more minutes they gathered the name-strings from the floor, piled them in another net, and hoisted them off the floor in the midst of the charmed circle.

"Now nobody see them again, they safe, they don't get lost, they don't get found."

"So we beat the devil this time," said Denmark.

Gullah Joe shook his head sadly. "No, he tear one up. He pick that one, he tear her up, he break the string, she name be fly off somewhere.''

"Lost?"

"Oh, she name try to get home, she try so hard." Gullah Joe sighed. "Some name she strong, but she blind, no find the way. Some name see the way, but she no fly, she fade away. This one, she strong, she bright, maybe she get home."

"Which one was it?"

"You think I tell she name? Call that name to *me*? You think I be so bad? No sir. I no say she name, I be pray that name find that girl, she a good one. Why he pick her?"

"Don't ask me," said Denmark. "I don't know why anybody picks anybody."

"No, he go to her, he know her. He know her. That devil, he been walking Camelot street, him. That devil, be maybe him a man. Be maybe him a White man." Gullah Joe smiled. "Be maybe him soul fly, get caught here, but he body be somewhere."

Denmark thought about this. A White man somewhere with his soul trapped outside his body. "You thinking maybe we ought to find him?"

"How much him I catch here?" Gullah Joe asked. "Black people soul, I take name, I take anger, I take sad, all the rest stay body. But the White man, how much he send out, how much he give me?" He went to his table, where a hundred secrets sat in jars and little boxes. He opened one, then another, rejecting each until he found a box with a fine white powder in it. He grinned and picked up a pinch of it between his fingers. Then he walked to the edge of the original circle, where the devil-man was trapped. He parted his fingers as he blew the powder sharply. The fine grey dust quickly filled the exact dimensions of the circle, swirling right up to the edges but never drifting out. Denmark saw a tiny light, like a mosquito with a fire-fly's tail, changing colors as it darted about within the cloud.

"That's him?" asked Denmark.

"He got him power," said Gullah Joe, his voice filled with awe.

"How can you tell?"

"You so far off, you see him, right?"

"Sure, I saw him. Like a firefly."

Gullah Joe laughed. "You so blind! He like a star. Bright star. We got trouble in this circle. He be find a way out. And then he be mad."

"Then let's get out of here," said Denmark. "I don't want him clipping me open like that net."

"No problem," said Gullah Joe.

"You mean you can keep him from getting out?"

"I got my best circle hold him. She strong enough? I don't know. But I don't got no better, so . . . maybe we dead, maybe we safe." Gullah Joe shrugged. "No problem."

"Well it matters to me!" cried Denmark.

"Be maybe you better go," said Gullah Joe, grinning. "You go find out what house got him a man, him eyes open, nobody inside."

"White man?"

"You think Black man break a name-string?" asked Gullah Joe contemptuously.

"Not all Black men be good," said Denmark.

"Black men all be on our side," said Gullah Joe.

Denmark laughed rudely. "That the stupidest thing you said since I know you."

Gullah Joe looked at him oddly. "I know what I know."

"Oh, they on your side now, Joe, cause you got their name-strings in a bag, you keeping them happy. But that don't mean they on your side, you fool. White master got them all so scared they want to please him, like little puppy dogs. They not telling *now* cause what if the White man take their soul? But they ain't on your *side*. They on their master's side."

"You think you the only smart man?" asked Joe, annoyed.

"I seen it a thousand times. Blacks betraying Blacks, each time hoping the master will like them better than the other slaves, treat them good. You watch."

"I be do this long time, lots of year now," said Gullah Joe. "Black people know what I got here, they never turn against me."

"Then how did this White devil find out where you were?"

Joe's eyes grew wide at the question. Then he grinned at Denmark. "You show them the way."

"I did not," said Denmark. "I wore that memory net you made me, nobody find anything about you from me!"

"He no look in your *head,* my net make it empty in there. This devil follow your *feet* till he come in right behind you."

"How do you know that?"

"I know what I know," said Gullah Joe, for about the thousandth time since Denmark had known him. "I see him come in."

"You're lying," said Denmark. "If you seed him come in you would have told me."

"I feel him. I feel him hot eyes looking. I feel them charm dance, I feel them charm shake."

"Then why didn't you stop him?"

Gullah Joe grinned. "Be maybe I think he no find name-string. Be maybe I think circle keep him out."

"Be maybe you full of shit," said Denmark. "You didn't know he was here till the net started popping. He probably followed *you* inside the circle."

Gullah Joe thought about that. "Better us find him body."

"So you ain't going to admit he took you by surprise," said Denmark testily. "You got to keep pretending you see all, you know all."

"I no see *all*," said Gullah Joe. "I see more than you."

"*Some*times."

"You see so good? Then you go out and use you eyes and you mouth and you ears, you find out where they be this empty White man body without no soul."

Denmark laughed bitterly. "That be every White man I know of."

Gullah Joe ignored his remark. "You find him, and then we make him soul go back in him."

"You can do that?"

Gullah Joe shrugged. "Maybe."

"So what if it doesn't work?"

"Then he body die," said Gullah Joe. "Body him not last long time it got no soul in."

"What the hell did you just say?" asked Denmark. "All these slaves, they be dying without their souls?"

"Black people still got they soul!" said Joe impatiently. "Only White man put him soul out like this. Soul no come home, he body, she think she dead, she be rotting."

"So if he don't find his way home, his body's going to die?"

"No, she don't die, him body. That body rot, she turn to bone, she turn to dust, but she still be alive cause that soul, she can't find that body no more, she never go home."

"So he's walking around dead already," said Denmark. "All right then, why look for him?"

"Body rotting alive, that too slow. He do mischief." Gullah Joe grinned and held up a huge knife. "Better us get him out of here."

"How, by killing his body?"

"Kill?" Gullah Joe laughed. "We got to bring him body here, put she inside the circle. Soul go back in body, then he leave my house."

"Won't that make him stronger, to have body and soul together again?'' asked Denmark. ''You want him out wandering around, knowing what we got going here?''

''Maybe that happen if we put him *whole* body in the circle,'' said Gullah Joe, laughing.

''I thought you said—''

''We put in just him head,'' said Gullah Joe. ''Then we all be safe. That soul got to go into that head. But he go in, he drop dead!''

Denmark laughed. ''I got to see that.'' Then his face grew grim. ''Course you know, you talking about killing a White man.''

Gullah Joe rolled his eyes. ''They plenty White man. You find him.''

In the early evening, Margaret took a turn around the block. Hot as it was, she couldn't have hoped to get to sleep tonight if she hadn't taken some exercise. And the air, though at street level it was charged with the smell of fish and horse manure, was not as stale as the air inside the house. Alvin had assured her that most of the time smelly air was still just air and it did no harm to breathe it. Better the smell than the mold indoors. When he tried to tell her all the nasty living creatures that inhabited every house, no matter how clean or well-swept, Margaret had to make him stop. Some things were better not to know.

She was coming back down the long side of the house when she heard the sound of someone whimpering off in the garden. There was but one heartfire there, one she knew well—the slave called Fishy. But Margaret almost didn't recognize her, because her heartfire had been transformed. What was the difference? A tumult of emotions: rage at every insult done her, grief at all that she had lost. And deep down, where there had been nothing at all, now Margaret found it: Fishy's true name.

Njia-njiwa. The Way of the Dove. Or the Dove in the Path. It was hard for Margaret to understand, because the concept was a part of both. A dove seen in the midst of its flight in the sky, which also marks the path of life. It was a beautiful name, and in the place where her name was kept, there also was the love and praise of her family.

''Njia-njiwa,'' said Margaret aloud, trying to get her mouth and nose to form the strange syllables: *N* without a vowel, as a syllable by itself. Nnn-jee-yah. Nnn-jee-wah. She said it aloud again.

The whimpering stopped. Margaret stepped around a bush and there was Fishy—Njia-njiwa—cowering where the foundation of the house next door rose out of the earth. Fishy's eyes were wide with fright, but Margaret could also see that her hands were formed into claws, ready to fight.

"You stay away from me," said Fishy. It was a plea. It was a warning.

"You got your name back," said Margaret.

"How you know that? What you do to me? You a witchy woman?"

"No, no, I did nothing to you. I knew your name was lost. How did you get it back?"

"He cut me loose," said Fishy with a sob. "All of a sudden I feel myself go light. Down on a breeze. I can't even stand up. I know my name's flying only I can't call it home cause I don't *know* it. I thought I was going a-die. But it do come home and then it all come back to me." Fishy shuddered, then burst into tears.

Margaret didn't need an explanation. She saw it now in Fishy's memory. "Every vile thing that your master has done to you. Every insult by every White person. The happy life with your mama that got taken away. No wonder you wanted to kill somebody." Margaret stepped closer. "And yet you didn't. All that fire inside you, and all you did was come out into the garden and hide."

"When she find out I didn't do my work she going a-beat me," said Fishy. "She going a-beat me bad, only this time I don't know if I can take it. She not so strong, ma'am. I take the stick outen her hand, I beat her *back*, how she going a-like that, you think?"

"It wouldn't feel good, Njia-njiwa."

The girl winced at the sound of her name and wept again. "Oh, Mama, Mama, Mama."

"You poor thing," said Margaret.

"Don't you pity me, you White woman! I clean your filth just like all the rest!"

"Good people clean up after the people they love," said Margaret. "It isn't the cleaning that you mind, it's being forced to do it for people you don't love."

"People I hate!"

"Fishy, would you rather I call you by that name?"

"Don't you go saying my true name no more," said Fishy.

"All right, then. How about this? How about if I say I had you helping me today, and I pay your mistress a little to compensate for having taken you away from your duties?"

Fishy looked at her suspiciously. "Why you do that?"

"Because I *do* need your help."

"You don't have to pay for that," said Fishy. "I be a slave, ain't you heard?"

"I don't want your labor," said Margaret. "I want your *help*."

"I don't got no help for White folks," said Fishy. "It be all I can do not to kill you right now."

"I know," said Margaret. "But you're strong. You'll contain these feelings. It's good to have your name back. It's as if you weren't alive before, and now you are."

"This ain't no life," said Fishy. "I got no hope now."

"Now is when your hope begins," said Margaret. "This thing you've done, you and the other slaves, giving up your names, your anger—it makes it safer for you, yes, it makes it easier, but you know who else it helps? Them. The White people who own you. Look at the other slaves, now that you have your anger back. See what they look like to the master."

"I know how they look," said Fishy. "They look stupid."

"That's right," said Margaret. "Stupid and contented."

"I ain't going a-look stupid no more," said Fishy. "She going a-see it in my eyes, how much I hate her. She going a-beat me all the time now."

"I can't help you with that right now," said Margaret. "I'd buy you away from her if I could, but I haven't that much money. I might rent your services, though, so you don't have to spend time with your mistress until you've got these feelings under control."

"I never going a-*control* these feelings! Hate just going a-get bigger and bigger till I kill somebody!"

"That's how it feels now, but I assure you, slaves in other cities, in other places, nobody takes their pride and hides it away, but they learn, they watch, they wait."

"Wait for what? Wait to die."

"Wait for hope," said Margaret. "They don't *have* hope, but they hope for hope, for a reason to hope. And in the meantime, there are many White men and women like me, who hate the whole idea of slavery. We're doing all we can to set you free."

" 'All you can' ain't worth nothing."

Margaret had to admit the truth of what she said. "Fishy, I fear that you're right. I've been trying to do it with words alone, to persuade them, but I fear that they're never going to change until they're made to change. I fear that it will take war, bloody terrible war between the Crown Colonies and the United States."

Fishy looked at her strangely. "You telling me there be White folks up North, they willing to fight and die just to set Black folks free?''

"Some," said Margaret. "And many more who are willing to fight and die in order to break the back of King Arthur, and others who would fight to show that the United States won't get pushed around by anybody, and—why should you care why they fight? If the war comes, if the North wins, then slavery will end."

"Then bring on that war."

"Do you want it?" asked Margaret, curious. "How many White people should die, so you can be free?"

"All of them!" cried Fishy, her voice full of loathing. Then she softened. "As many as it takes." And then she wept again. "Oh, sweet Jesus, what am I? My soul so wicked! I going to hell!"

Margaret knelt beside her, facing her, and dared now to lay her hand gently on Fishy's shoulder. The girl did not recoil from her, as she would have earlier. "You will not go to hell," said Margaret. "God sees your heart."

"My heart be full of murder all the time now!" said Fishy.

"And yet your hand is still the hand of peace. God loves you for choosing that, Fishy. God loves you for living up to your true name."

The movement was slight, but it was real, as Fishy leaned a little closer to Margaret, accepting her touch, and then her embrace, until she wept into Margaret's shoulder. "Let me stay with you, ma'am," whispered Fishy.

"Come with me to my room, then," said Margaret. "I hope you don't mind going along with me in some lies."

Fishy giggled, though at the end it was more of a sob than a laugh. "Around here, ma'am, if folks got they mouth open, if they ain't eating then they lying."

11

Decent Men

So this was what it came to, after all these years at the bar, as lawyer and as judge: John Adams had to sit in judgment in Cambridge over a witch trial. Oh, the ignominy of it. For a time he had been something of a philosopher, and caused an international incident over his involvement in the Appalachee Revolution. He had spoken for union between New England and the United States, daring the Lord Protector to arrest him for treason. He had called for a ban on trade with the Crown Colonies as long as they trafficked in slaves, at the very time that his fellow New Englanders were loudly calling for the right to enter into such trade. There wasn't a question of import in New England since the 1760s that John Adams hadn't been a part of. He had even founded a dynasty, or so it seemed, now that his boy John Quincy was governor of Massachusetts and chairman of the New England Council. And for the past fifteen years he had distinguished himself as a jurist, winning at last the love of his fellow Yankees when he refused an appointment to the Lord Protector's Bench in England, preferring to remain "among the free men of America."

And now he had to hear a witch trial. The toadlike witcher, Quill, had come to see him when he arrived in Cambridge last night, reminding him that it was his duty to uphold the law—as if John Adams needed prompting in his duty from the likes of Quill. "I have not exceeded the law in any respect," said Quill, "as you'll see even from the testimony of the witches, unless they lie."

"God help us if a witch should tell a lie," John had murmured. Quill missed the irony entirely and took the answer as an affirmation. Well, that was fine. John didn't mind if he went away happy, as long as he went away.

John should have died last year, when he got the grippe. He had it on the best authority that the Boston papers had all planned on a double-page spread for his obituary. That was precisely the space devoted to the eulogy of the last Lord Protector to shuffle off his mortal coil. It was good to be considered at a level with rulers and potentates, even though he had never quite succeeded in joining New England to the United States, making it impossible for him to play a role in that extraordinary experiment. Instead he remained here, among the good people of New England, whom he truly loved like brothers and sisters, even though he longed now and then to see a face that didn't look like every other face.

Witch trials, though—it was an ugly thing, a holdover from medieval times. A shame on the face of New England.

But the law was the law. An accusation had been made, so a trial would have to be held, or at least the beginning of one. Quill would have his chance to get some poor wretch hanged—if he could do it without violating the prerogatives of the bench or pushing the powers of the law beyond their statutory and natural limits.

Now at breakfast John Adams sat with his old pupil, Hezekiah Study. I adhere to a double standard, John admitted to himself. Quill's visit to me last night I thought highly improper. Hezekiah's visit, equally intended to influence my judgment in this case, I plan to enjoy. Well, any fool can be consistent, and most fools are.

"Cambridge is not what it used to be," said John to Hezekiah. "The students don't wear their robes."

"Out of fashion now," said Hezekiah. "Though if anyone had known you were coming, they might have put the robes back on. Your opinion on the subject is well known."

"As if these boys would so much as part their hair for a relic like me."

"A holy relic, sir?" asked Hezekiah.

John grimaced. "Oh, so I'm to be called 'sir' by you?"

"I was your student. You gave me Plato and Homer."

"But you wanted Aristophanes, as I recall." John Adams sighed. "You must realize, all my peers are dead. If I'm to have anyone on this earth call me John, it will have to be a friend who once called me 'sir' because of my seniority. We should have a new social rule. When we reach fifty, we're all the same age forever."

"John, then," said Hezekiah. "I knew God had heard my prayer when I learned that it was you and no other who drew this case."

"One judge is coughing his life out into bloody handkerchiefs and the other is burying his wife, and you think this is how God answers your prayers?"

"You weren't due, and here you are. A witch trial, sir. John."

"Oh, now you've knighted me. Sir John." He wanted to laugh at the idea of his ever being the answer to someone's prayer. Since his own prayers seemed rarely to be answered, it wouldn't be quite fair of God, would it, to play him as the prize in someone else's game of piety.

"I know how you feel about witches," said Hezekiah.

"You also know how I feel about the law," said John. "I may disbelieve in the crime, but that doesn't mean I'll have any bias in the handling of the case." Oh, let's stop the pretense that the question has come up casually. "What's your interest in it? Didn't you used to defend these cases, back when you were a lawyer?"

"I was never a good one."

John heard the pain in his voice. Still haunted after all these years? "You were an excellent lawyer, Hezekiah. But what is a lawyer against a superstitious, bloody-minded mob?"

Hezekiah smiled wanly. "I assume you know that the black-smith's lawyer was arrested last night."

Quill hadn't seen fit to mention this little ploy, but John had learned it from the sheriff. "I can see it now. Lawyer after lawyer steps forth to defend this man, only to be accused, each in turn, and locked away. Thus the trial continues till all the lawyers are in jail."

Hezekiah smiled. "There are those who would regard that as the best of all possible outcomes."

John chuckled with him, then sighed. "Don't worry, Hezekiah. I won't have defense attorneys locked up in order to bolster the witchers' case. You shouldn't be talking to me about this, though."

"Oh, I knew what you'd do about that," said Hezekiah. "If Quill thought he could get away with that—well, you'll see when you meet the lawyer. He has Quill by the character!"

"That would be a slippery place to try to hold him."

"No, it wasn't the lawyer. It was another matter I wanted to bring to your attention."

"Bring it in open court then, Hezekiah."

"I can't. And it's not evidentiary, anyway."

"Then tell me afterward."

"Please don't torment me, friend," said Hezekiah. "I wouldn't attempt anything unethical. Trust me enough to hear me out."

"If it's about the case . . . ."

"It's about the accuser. . . ."

"Who will also be a defendant in her own trial."

"She'll not be tried," said Hezekiah. "She's cooperating with Quill. So this can have no compromising effect on an action in court."

"Don't blame Quill for *her*. She came up with this accusation on her own."

"I know, sir. John. But she's not your normal accuser. Her parents were hanged for witches when she was a newborn. Indeed, her father took the drop, as they say, before she was even born, and her mother but weeks afterward. She found it out only a few days ago, and it put her in such a state that—"

"That she brought false accusation against a stranger?" John grimaced. "You have a fleck of yolk on your chin."

Hezekiah dabbed at it with his napkin. "I think the accusation is not false," said Hezekiah.

John glared at him. "I'm glad you didn't say anything to compromise this blacksmith's case."

"I don't mean that it's objectively true, I mean that she's being forthright. Her intent is pure. She believes the charge."

John rolled his eyes. "So how many should I hang for one girl's superstition?"

Hezekiah looked away. "She's not superstitious, sir. She's a sweet girl, good-hearted, and very bright. She's been studying with me, and sitting in on lectures."

"Oh, right. The girl and her professors. That's why Harvard got raided by the tithingmen and half the faculty hauled off for questioning."

"She didn't initiate that, sir. She refuses to accuse any but the original defendants."

"Till that rope-happy ghoul runs her into the ground."

"You should have heard the blacksmith's lawyer accuse Quill of using torture. Out on the common in front of everybody." Hez-

ekiah smiled at the memory. "He held the strings and Quill danced
for the crowd."

John liked the image as much as Hezekiah did, but he was a
judge, and the first skill he had perfected was the ability to remain
solemn and suppress even so much as a twinkle in his eye. "So
you're here to tell me that this girl, this Purity, means well as she
tries to get this young man hanged."

"I mean to say it isn't a case of vengeance for spurned love, or
any such thing as are usually at the heart of witch trials."

"Then what is it? Since we both know . . ." John glanced
around and lowered his voice. ". . . that the one certainty in this trial
is that there *are* no witches."

"The boy was full of brag about some knack or other. All she
knows is what he told her, or someone in his party. But she believed
it. She's doing this because she *must* believe in the law that hanged
her parents. If she did not believe that the law was right, then the
sheer injustice of it would drive her mad."

"Oh, now, Hezekiah. 'Drive her mad'? Have you been reading
sensational novels?"

"I mean it quite literally. She has a deep faith in the goodness
of our Christian community. If she thought her parents were falsely
accused and hanged for it—"

"Who were her parents? Is it a case I . . ." And then, doing the
arithmetic in his head—the girl's age, that many years ago—he realized whose daughter she was. "Oh, Hezekiah. *That* case?"

Tears spilled from Hezekiah's eyes. "What I wanted you to
know, John, was that the one who seems to be the accuser is merely
the last victim of that wretched affair."

John answered gently. "New England is a lovely place, Hezekiah. We have our share of hypocrisy, of course, but generally we
face up to our sins and the frailty of human nature, and confess our
wrongs right smartly. But this one—how did it ever go that far?"

"You didn't see what I saw, John," said Hezekiah.

"No, don't tell me. You need no excuse, my friend. You stood
alone."

"I couldn't . . . I could not . . ."

John laid his hand over Hezekiah's. "Thus we take a good
breakfast and render it indigestible," he said. "Come, now, there's
no blame attached to you."

"Oh, but there is."

"So you're defending her, to make up for it?"

Hezekiah shook his head. "I've looked after her all her life. It's my penance. To stay here, in obscurity. There's blood on my hands. I won't have more. The young lawyer who's languishing in the jail, he's the one. When you let him out, when he defends his friend, see if he doesn't give you a way to resolve the whole matter. All I ask is that you not bring charges against the accuser.''

"This English barrister can do it, but not you?''

"I took a vow most solemnly before heaven.''

"And deprived the New England bar of an honest man. The bench as well. You should be in robes like mine, my friend.''

Hezekiah brusquely wiped the tears from his cheeks. "Thank you for seeing me, John. And for treating me as a friend.''

"Now and always, Hezekiah. Will I see you at the trial?''

"How could I bear that, John? No. God bless you, John. He brought you here, I know it. Yes, I know you think God is a watchmaker who installed an infinite spring—''

"A quotation I never said, though it's much attributed to me—''

"I heard the words from your lips.''

"Stir your memory, and you'll recall that I was quoting the line in order to refute it! I'm no deist, like Tom Jefferson. That's *his* line. It's the only God he's willing to worship—one who has closed up shop and gone away so there's no risk of Tom Jefferson being contradicted when he spouts his nonsense about the 'rational man.' Him and his wall of separation between church and state—such claptrap! Such a wall serves only those who want to keep God on the far side of it, so they can divide up the nation without interference.''

"I'm sorry to have brought your old nemesis into this.''

"You didn't,'' said John. "*I* did. Or rather, *he* did. You'd think that he'd stop getting under my skin, but it galls me that *his* little country is going to be part of the United States, and mine isn't.''

"Isn't *yet*,'' said Hezekiah.

"Isn't in my lifetime,'' said John, "and I'm selfish enough to wish I could have lived to see it. The United States needs this Puritan society as a counter-influence to Tom Jefferson's intolerantly secular one. Mark my words, when a government pretends that it is the highest judge of its own actions, the result is not freedom as Jefferson says, but chaos and oppression. When he shuts religion out of government, when men of faith are not listened to, then all that remains is venality, posturing, and ambition.''

"I hope you're wrong about that, sir,'' said Hezekiah. "Many of us look to the United States as the next stage of the American experiment. New England has come this far, but we are stagnant now.''

"As this trial proves." John sighed. "I wish I *were* wrong, Hezekiah. But I'm not. Tom Jefferson claims to stand for freedom, and charges me with trying to promote some kind of theocracy or aristocracy. But there is no freedom down his road."

"How can we know that, sir?" said Hezekiah. "No one has ever been down this road?"

"I have," said John, and regretted it at once.

Hezekiah looked at him, startled, but then smiled. "No matter how precise your imagination, sir, I doubt it will be accepted as evidence."

But it wasn't imagination. John had *seen*. Had seen it as clearly as he saw Hezekiah standing before him now. It was a sort of vision that God had vouchsafed to him all his life, that he could see how power flowed and where it led, in groups of men both large and small. It was a strange and obscure sort of vision, which he could not explain to anyone else and had never tried, not even to Abigail, but it allowed him to chart a course through all the theories and philosophies that swirled and swarmed throughout the British colonies. It had allowed him to see through Tom Jefferson. The man talked freedom, but he could never quite bring himself to free his slaves. Abolitionists criticized him for hypocrisy, but they missed the point. He wasn't a lover of freedom who had neglected to free his slaves; he was a man who loved to control other people, and did it by talking about freedom. Jefferson had stood naked in front of the world when he tried to silence his critics with the Alien and Sedition Acts almost as soon as Appalachee won its freedom from the Crown. So much for his love of freedom—you could have freedom of speech as long as you didn't use it to oppose Jefferson's policies! Yet as soon as the acts were repealed—after years of hounding Jefferson's enemies into silence or exile—people still talked about him as the champion of liberty!

John Adams knew Tom Jefferson, and that's why Tom Jefferson hated John Adams, because John really was what Jefferson only pretended to be: a man who loved freedom, even the freedom of those who disagreed with him. Even Tom Jefferson's freedom. It made them unequal in battle. It handed the victory to Jefferson.

"Are you all right, sir?" asked Hezekiah.

"Just fighting over old battles in my mind," said John. "It's the problem with age. You have all these rusty arguments, and no quarrel to use them in. My brain is a museum, but alas, I'm the only visitor, and even I am not terribly interested in the displays."

Hezekiah laughed, but there was affection in it. "I would love nothing better than to visit there. But I'm afraid I'd be tempted to loot the place, and carry it all away with me."

To John's surprise, Hezekiah's words brought tears to his eyes. "Would you, Hezekiah?" He blinked rapidly and his eyes cleared. "You see, now, you've moved this old man with your kindness. You found the one bribe I'm susceptible to."

"It wasn't flattery, sir."

"I know," said John. "It was honor. May God forgive me, but I've never been able to purge my heart of the desire for it."

"There's no sin in it, John. The honor of good men is won only by goodness. It's how the children of God recognize each other. It's the feast of love."

"Maybe God *did* bring me here," said John. "In answer to my own prayers."

"Maybe that's how God works," said Hezekiah. "We pray for a messenger from God—who knows but what the messenger also prayed for a place to take his message?"

"What does that make me, an angel?"

"Wrestle with Jacob. Smite his thigh. Leave him limping."

"Once your allusions were all to Homer and the Greek playwrights."

"It's the Bible now," said Hezekiah. "I have more to fear from death than you do."

"But longer to wait before it comes," said John ruefully.

Hezekiah laughed, shook John's hand, and left the table. John sat back down, tucked in, and finished. The meeting had been more emotional than John had expected, or than he cared for, truth be known. Emotions had a way of filling you up and then what did you do with them? You still had to go on about your life.

Except for Hezekiah Study. He had *not* gone about his life. His life had ended, all those years ago, back in Netticut, on the end of a couple of ropes.

And my life? When did it end? Because it has ended, I see that now. I'm like Hezekiah. I took a turn, or didn't take a turn; I stopped, or failed to stop. I should have been something else. I should have been president of a fledgling nation of free men. Not a judge at a witch trial. Not a stout little man eating the dregs of his breakfast alone at table in a boardinghouse in Cambridge, waiting for Tom Jefferson, damn him, to die, so I can have the feeble satisfaction of outliving that bastard son of Liberty.

Oh, Tom. If only we could have been friends, I could have

changed you, you could have changed me, we could have become in reality the statesmen you pretend to be and I wish I were.

Purity could hardly sleep all night. It was unbearable, yesterday, the running, running, running. And yet she bore it. That's what surprised her. She sweated and panted but she kept on and on and on, and all the while she ran there was a kind of music in the back of her mind. As soon as she tried to listen to it, to find the melody of it, the sound retreated and all she could hear then was the throbbing of her pulse in her head, her own panting, her feet thudding on the grassy ground. But then she'd stagger a few steps and the music would come back and it would sustain her and . . .

She knew what it was. Hadn't Arthur Stuart talked about how Alvin could run and run with the greensong he learned from that Red prophet? Or was it Ta-Kumsaw himself? It didn't matter. Alvin was using his witchery to sustain her and she wanted to scream at him to stop.

But she had learned a little between yesterday and today. Quill had taught her. Everything she said got twisted. She had never mentioned Satan, had never even thought of him, but somehow her meeting with Alvin and his friends on the banks of the river had turned into a witches' sabbath, and Alvin swimming in the river with Arthur Stuart had been turned into incestuous sodomy. And she finally realized what should have been obvious all along—what Reverend Study had tried to warn her about—that whatever fault there might be in Alvin Smith, it was nothing compared to the terrible evil that resulted from denouncing him as a witch. What would happen if she cried out what was in her heart? "Stop it! Stop witching me to keep running!" It would only make things worse.

Is this what happened to my parents?

Gradually, as the day wore on, she had begun to notice something else. It was Quill who was filled with fear and rage, his mind alert to take anything that happened and turn it into proof of the evil he was looking for. Quill looked at Purity with fascination and loathing, a combination she found fearful and disturbing. But Alvin Smith, he was as cheerful toward her today as he ever was on the riverbank. Not a complaint toward her for getting him locked up. And yes, he used his witchery, or so it seemed to her, but he did it out of genuine kindness toward her. That was the truth—by her own knack she knew it. He was a little impatient with her, but he bore her no ill will.

Now, as the day of her testimony loomed, she did not know

what to do. If she bore witness against Alvin now, telling the simple truth, Quill would make it seem as though she was holding back. She could imagine the questioning. "Why are you refusing to mention the witches' sabbath?" "There was no witches' sabbath." "What about the naked debauchery between this man and this half-White boy who is said to be as it were his own son?" "They played in the river, that's all." "Ah, they *played* in the river, a naked man, a naked boy, they sported in the river, is that your testimony?" Oh, it would be awful, every word twisted.

Simpler by far to confess to a lesser crime: I made it up, Your Honor, because they frightened me by the riverbank and I wished them to see what it felt like. I made it up because I had just learned my parents were hanged for witchcraft and I wanted to show how false accusations are too readily believed.

She had almost resolved on this course of action when the key turned in the lock and the door opened and there stood Quill, his face warm and smiling, filled with love. To her it looked like hate, and now she could see what somehow had eluded her before: Quill wanted her to die.

How could she have missed it? It was her knack, to see what people intended, what they were about to do. Yet she saw no further than his smile the first time they met, saw nothing but his genuine love and sympathy and concern for her. How could her knack have failed her?

Was it what Quill had said to her, in one of his many rambling discourses on Satan? That Satan was not loyal and did not uphold his disciples?

Why, then, would she see the truth now?

Or was it the truth? Was Satan now deceiving her into thinking she saw hatred where love truly existed?

There was no way out of this circle of doubt. There was no firm ground to hold to. Alvin Smith, who admitted to witchery, was kind and forgiving to her though she did him great harm. Quill, who was the servant of God in opposing witchery, twisted every word she said to make her bear false witness against Smith and his friends. And now he seemed to want her to hang. That was how it *seemed*. Could the truth be so simple? Was it possible that things were exactly as they seemed?

"I know what you're thinking," said Quill softly.

"Do you?" she murmured.

"You're thinking that you want to recant your testimony against

Alvin Smith and make the whole trial go away. I know you're thinking that because everybody does, just before the trial."

She said nothing. For she could sense the malice coming from
him like stink from an untended baby.

"It wouldn't go away," said Quill. "I already have your testimony under oath. All that would happen is that perjury would be
added to your crimes. And worse—having repented, you would be
seen to have returned to Satan, trying to conceal his acts. Indeed,
you already seemed to be concealing the other witches in Cambridge.
You could not have expected to protect your friends and incriminate
only the strangers, could you? Were you that naive? Were you so
caught up in the snares and nets of Satan that you believed you
could hide from God?"

"I've hidden nothing." Even as she said it, she knew the futility
of denial.

"I have here a list of the professors and lecturers at Cambridge
who are known to create an atmosphere of hostility toward faith and
piety in their classrooms. You are not alone in denouncing them—
my colleagues and I have compiled this list over a period of years.
Emerson, for instance, scoffs at the very idea of the existence of
witches and witchery. You like Emerson, don't you? I've heard that
you were especially attentive in spying outside his classroom."

"It wasn't spying, I was given the right to listen," said Purity.

"You heard him," said Quill. "But my question is, did you see
him? At a witches' sabbath?"

"I never saw a witches' sabbath, so how could I have seen him
at one?"

"Don't chop logic with me," whispered Quill. "The syllogism
is false because your testimony has been false. You told me about
one witches' sabbath yourself."

"I never did."

"The debauchery," he whispered. "The crimes against nature."

She looked him boldly in the face, seeing his lust for her blood
so strongly depicted in the fire of his face, the tension of his body
that she would not have needed a knack to detect it. "You are the
one who hates nature," she said. "You are the enemy of God."

"Feeble. I advise against your using that line in court. It will
only make you look stupid and I answer it so easily."

"You are the enemy of goodness and decency," she said, speaking more boldly now, "and insofar as God is good, you hate God."

"Insofar as? The professors have taught you well. I think your answer, despite your attempts to deceive, has to be 'yes' to the question of whether you saw Emerson at a witches' sabbath.''

''I say no such thing.''

''I say that by using professorial language in the midst of a satanic denunciation of my role in God's service, your true spirit, held a helpless prisoner by Satan, was trying to send me a coded message denouncing Emerson.''

''Who would believe such nonsense?''

''I'll say it in a way the court can understand,'' said Quill. He checked off Emerson's name. ''Emerson, yes. One of Satan's spies, caught. Now look at the other names.''

''Coded message,'' she said contemptuously.

''What you don't understand is that your very sneer shows your contempt for holiness. You hate all things good and decent, and your scornfulness proves it.''

''Go away.''

''For now,'' said Quill. ''Your arraignment is this morning. The judge wants to hear you when Alvin Smith makes his plea.''

But she was not fooled. Her knack was too trustworthy for her to doubt what she saw now.

''You're such a bad liar, Quill,'' she said. ''The judge never needs to have a witness at the arraignment. I'll be there because I'm to be arraigned as well.''

Quill was face-to-face with her again at once. ''Satan whispered that lie to you, didn't he.''

''Why would you say that?''

''I saw it,'' he said. ''I saw him whisper to you.''

''You're insane.''

''I saw you looking at me, and in a sudden moment you were told something that you hadn't known before. Satan whispered.''

Had he seen it? Was it his knack to see other knacks working?

No. It was his knack to find the useful lie hidden inside every useless truth. He had simply seen the transformation in her facial expression when she understood the truth about his intentions.

''Satan has never told me anything,'' she said.

''But you already told me about your knack,'' he answered with a smile. ''Don't recant—it will go hard with you.''

''Maybe I have a talent for seeing other people's intentions,'' she said defiantly. ''That doesn't mean it comes from Satan!''

''Yes,'' he said. ''Use that line in court. Confess your sin and then deny that it's a sin. See what happens to you under the law.'' He reached out and touched her hand, gently, caressingly. ''God loves you, child. Don't reject him. Turn away from Satan. Admit all the evil you have done so you can prove you have left it behind you. Live to let your womb bear children, as God intended. It's Satan, not God, who wants you twitching at the end of a rope.''

''Yes,'' she said. ''That much is true. Satan your master wants me dead.''

He winked at her, got up, and went to the door. ''That's good. Keep that up. That'll get you hanged.'' And he was gone, the door locked behind him.

She shook with cold as if it weren't summer with the heat already oppressive this early in the morning. Everything was clear to her now. Quill came here ready to do exactly what he had done— take a simple accusation of the use of a knack, and turn it into a story about Satan and gross perversions. He knew he had to do this because honest people never told stories about Satan. He knew that she would not name others she saw at witches' sabbaths because there were never any such conclaves, and all such denunciations had to be extracted through whatever torture the law would allow. Witchers did what Quill did because if they did not do it, no one would ever be convicted of trafficking with Satan.

This was how her parents died. Not because they really did have knacks that came from Satan, but because they would not play along with the witchers and join them in persecuting others. They would not confess to falsehood. They died because the City of God tried so hard to be pure that it created its own impurity. The evil the witchers did was worse than any evil they might prevent. And yet the people of New England were so afraid that they might not live up to the ideals of Puritanism that they dared not speak against a law that purported to protect them from Satan.

I believed them. They killed my parents, raised me as an orphan, tainted with the rumor of evil, and instead of denouncing them for what they had done to me, I believed them and tried to do the same thing to someone else. To Alvin Smith, who did me no harm.

Purity threw herself to her knees and prayed. O Father in heaven, what have I done, what have I done.

Alvin finished the piss-poor breakfast they served to prisoners in the jail, then lay back on his cot to survey the people that he cared about. Far away in Camelot, his wife and their unborn daughter thrived. In Vigor Church, his mother and father, his brothers and sisters, all were doing well, none sick, none injured. Nearby, Verily was being let out of his cell. Alvin tracked him for a while, to be sure that he was being released. Yes, at the door of the courthouse they turned him loose to go find his own breakfast.

Out on the riverbank, Arthur Stuart and Mike Fink were fishing while Audubon was painting a kingfisher in the early-morning light. All was well.

It was only by chance that Alvin noticed the other heartfires converging on the river. He might not even have noticed them, in his reverie about eating fish just caught from the river, roasted over a smoky fire, except that something was wrong, some indefinable change in the world his doodlebug passed through. A sort of shimmering in the air, a feeling of something that loomed just out of sight, trembling on the verge of visibility.

Alvin knew what he was seeing. The Unmaker was abroad in the world.

Why was the Unmaker coming out in the open with the tithingmen? There had been no sign of the Unmaker lingering around Quill, who was clearly a lover of destruction.

Of course the very question contained its own answer. The Unmaker didn't have to emerge where people served its cause willingly, knowingly. Eagerly. Quill wasn't like Reverend Thrower. He didn't have to be lied to. He loved being the serpent in the garden. He would have been disappointed if he couldn't get the part. But the tithingmen were decent human beings and the Unmaker had to herd them.

Which was, quite literally, what it was doing. Quill had asked them to go searching for a witches' sabbath. They set out with no particular destination, except a vague idea that since Purity had spoken of encountering Alvin's party on the riverbank, that might be a good area to explore. Now, whenever they turned away from Arthur and Mike and Jean-Jacques, they stepped into the Unmaker's influence and they became uneasy, vaguely frightened. It made them turn around and walk quite briskly the other way. Closer to Alvin's friends.

Well, thought Alvin, this looks like a much better game if played by two.

His first thought was to bring up a fog from the river, to make it impossible for them to find their way. But he rejected this at once. The Unmaker could herd them whether they could see their way or not. The fog would only make it look more suspicious-sounding, more like witchery, when they recounted their story later. Besides, fog was made of water, and water was the element the Unmaker used the most. Alvin wasn't altogether certain that his control was

so strong, especially at a distance, that he could count on keeping
the Unmaker from subverting the fog. Someone might slip and die,
and it would be blamed on witchery.

What did the tithingmen care about? They were good men who
served their community, to keep it safe from harm and to keep the
peace among neighbors and within family. When a couple quarreled,
it was a tithingman who went to them to help them iron it out, or
to separate them for a time if that was needed. When someone was
breaking the sumptuary laws, or using coarse language, or otherwise
offending against the standards that helped them all stay pure, it was
a tithingman who tried, peacefully, to persuade them to mend their
ways without the need of dire remedies. It was the tithingmen who
kept the work of the courts to a minimum.

And a man didn't last long as a tithingman in a New England
town if he fancied himself to be possessed of some sort of personal
authority. He had none. Rather he was the voice and hands of the
community as a whole, and a soft voice and gentle hands were pre-
ferred by all. Anyone who seemed to like to boss others about would
simply be overlooked when the next round of tithingmen were chosen. Sometimes they realized that they hadn't been called on for
many years, and wondered why; some even humbly asked, and tried
to mend their ways. If they never asked, they were never told. What
mattered was that the work be done, and done kindly.

So these were not cudgel-wielding thugs who were being herded
toward the riverbank. Not like the Finders who came after Arthur
Stuart back in Hatrack River, and were perfectly happy to kill anyone
who stood violently against them. Not even like Reverend Thrower,
who was somewhat deceived by the Unmaker but nevertheless had
a zeal to pursue "evil" and root it out.

How could Alvin turn good men away from an evil path? How
could he get them to ignore the Unmaker and take away its power
to herd them?

Alvin sent his doodlebug into the village of Cambridge. Into the
houses of families, listening for voices, voices of children. He
needed the sound of a child in distress, but quickly realized that in
a good Puritan town, children were kindly treated and well watched-
out-for. He would have to do a little mischief to get the sound.

A kitchen. A three-year-old girl, watching her mother slice onions. The mother leaned forward on her chair. It was a simple matter
for Alvin to weaken the leg and break the chair under her. With a
shriek she fell. Alvin took care to make sure no harm befell her.

What he wanted was from the child, not from her. And there it was. The girl cried out: "Mama!"

Alvin captured the sound, the pattern of it in the air. He carried it, strengthened it, the quivering waves; he layered them, echoed them, brought some slowly, some quickly in a complicated inter-weave of sound. It was very hard work, and took all his concentration, but finally he brought the first copy of the girl's cry to the tithingmen.

"Mama!"

They turned at once, hearing it as if in the near distance, and behind them, away from the river.

Again, fainter: "Mama!"

At once the tithingmen turned, knowing their duty. Searching for witches was their duty, but the distress of a child calling for her mother clearly was more important.

They plunged right into the Unmaker, and of course it chilled their hearts with fear, but at that moment Alvin brought them the girl's cry for yet a third and last time, so when fear struck them, instead of making them recoil it made them run even faster toward the sound. The fear turned from a sense of personal danger into an urgent need to get to the child because something very bad was happening to her—their fear became, not a barrier, but a spur to greater effort.

For a while the Unmaker tried to stay with them, trying out other emotions—anger, horror—but all its efforts worked against its own purpose. It couldn't understand what Alvin was relying on: the power of decent men to act against their own interest in order to help those who trusted them. The Unmaker understood how to make men kill in war. What it could not comprehend was why they were willing to die.

So the tithingmen hunted fruitlessly in the woods and meadows, trying to find the girl whose voice they had heard, until finally they gave up and headed into town to try to find out which child was missing and organize a search. But all the children were in their places, and, despite some misgivings—they had all heard the voice, after all—they went about their ordinary business, figuring that if there needed to be a witch hunt, tomorrow would do as well as today.

On the riverbank, Arthur and Mike and Jean-Jacques had no idea that the Unmaker had been stalking them.

In his cell, Alvin wanted only to lie back and sleep. That was when the sheriff came for him, to bring him into the court for his arraignment.

*   *   *

Verily had only a few minutes to confer with Alvin before the arraignment began, and always with the sheriff present, so there couldn't be much candor—but such was the rule with witch trials, so no potions or powders could be passed between them, or secret curses spoken. "No matter how it seems, Alvin, you must trust me."

"Why? How is it going to seem?"

"The judge is John Adams. I've been reading his writings and his court cases, both as lawyer and as judge, since I first began the study of law. The man is decent to the core. I had no knowledge of his ever doing a witch trial, though, and so I had no idea of his position on them. But when I came out of jail this morning, I was met by a fellow who lives here—"

"No need for names," said Alvin.

Verily smiled. "A fellow, I say, who's made some study of witch law —in fact that's his name, Study—and he tells me that Adams has never actually rendered a verdict in a witchery case."

"What does that mean?"

"There's always been some defect in the witchers' presentation and he's thrown the whole thing out."

"Then that's good," said Alvin.

"No," said Verily. "That's bad."

"I'd go free, wouldn't I?"

"But the law would still stand."

Alvin rolled his eyes. "Verily, I didn't come back here to try to reform New England, I came in order to—"

"We came to help Purity," said Verily. "And all the others. Do you know what it would mean, if the law itself were found defective? Adams is a man of weighty reputation. Even from the circuit bench of Boston, his decisions would be looked at carefully and carry much precedence in England as well as in America. The right decision might mean the end of witch trials, here as well as there."

Alvin smiled thinly. "You got too high an opinion of human nature."

"Do I?"

"The law didn't make witch trials happen. It was the hunger for witch trials that got them to make up the law."

"But if we do away with the legal basis—"

"Listen, Verily, do you think men like Quill will flat-out disappear just cause witchery ain't there to give them what they want? No, they'll just find another way to do the same job."

"You don't know that."

"If it ain't witchcraft, they'll find new crimes that work just the way witchcraft does, so you can take ordinary folks making ordinary mistakes or not even mistakes, just going about their business, but suddenly the witcher, he finds some wickedness in it, and turns everything they say into proof that they're guilty of causing every bad thing that's been going wrong."

"There's no other law that works that way."

"That's because we *got* witch laws, Very. Get rid of them, and people will find a way take all the sins of the world and put them onto the heads of some fellow who's attracted their attention and then destroy him and all his friends."

"Purity isn't evil, Alvin."

"Quill is," said Alvin.

The sheriff leaned down. "I'm trying not to listen, boys, but you know it's a crime to speak ill of a witcher. This Quill, he takes it as evidence that Satan's got you by the short hairs, begging your pardon."

"Thank you for the reminder, sir," said Verily. "My client didn't mean it quite the way it sounded."

The sheriff rolled his eyes. "From what I've seen, it doesn't matter much how it sounds when you say it. What matters is how it sounds when Quill repeats it."

Verily grinned at the sheriff and then at Alvin.

"What are you smiling at?" asked Alvin.

"I just got all the proof I need that you're wrong. People don't like the way the witch trials work. People don't like injustice. Strike down these laws and no one will miss them."

Alvin shook his head. "Good people won't miss them. But it wasn't good people as set them up in the first place. It was scared people. The world ain't steady. Bad things happen even when you been careful and done no wrong. Good people, strong people, they take that in stride, but them as is scared and weak, they want somebody to blame. The good people will think they've stamped out witch trials, but the next generation they'll turn around and there they'll be again, wearing a different hat, going by a different name, but witch trials all the same, where they care more about getting somebody punished than whether they're actually guilty of anything."

"Then we'll stamp them out again," said Verily.

Alvin shrugged. "Of course we will, once we figure out what's what and who's who. Maybe next time the witchers will go after folks with opinions they don't like, or folks who pray the wrong way or in the wrong place, or folks who look ugly or talk funny, or folks who aren't polite enough, or folks who wear the wrong clothes. Someday they may hold witch trials to condemn people for being Puritans.''

Verily leaned over and whispered into Alvin's ear. "Meaning no disrespect, Al, it's your wife who can see into the future, not you.''

"No whispering,'' said the sheriff. "You might be giving me the pox.'' He chuckled, but there was just a little bit of genuine worry in his voice.

Alvin answered Verily out loud. "Meaning no disrespect, Very, it don't take a knack to know that human nature ain't going to change anytime soon.''

Verily stood up. "It's time for the arraignment, Alvin. There's no point in our talking philosophy before a trial. I never knew till now that you were so cynical about human nature.''

"I know the power of the Unmaker,'' said Alvin. "It never lets up. It never gives in. It just moves on to other ground.''

Shaking his head, Verily led the way out of the room. The sheriff, tightly holding the end of Alvin's chain, escorted him right after. "I got to say, I never seen a prisoner who cared so little about whether he got convicted or not.''

Alvin reached up his hand and scratched the side of his nose. "I'm not all that worried, I got to admit.'' Then he put his hand back down.

It wasn't till they were almost in the courtroom that the sheriff realized that there was no way the prisoner could have got his hand up to his face with those manacles on, chained to his ankle braces the way they were. But by then he couldn't be sure he'd actually seen the young fellow scratch his nose. He just thought he remembered that. Just his mind playing tricks on him. After all, if this Alvin Smith could take his hands out of iron manacles, just like that, why didn't he walk out of jail last night?

12

Slaves

"You must take care of him," said Balzac.

"In a boardinghouse for ladies?" asked Margaret.

Calvin stood there, his unblinking gaze focused on nothing.

"They have servants, no? He is your brother-in-law, he is sick, they will not refuse you."

Margaret did not have to ask him what had precipitated his decision. At the French embassy today Balzac received a letter from a Paris publisher. One of his essays on his American travels had already appeared in a weekly, and was so popular that the publisher was going to serialize the rest of them and then bring them out as a book. A letter of credit was included. It was enough for a passage home.

"Just when you start earning money from your writing about America, you're going to leave?"

"Writing about America will pay for leaving America," said Balzac. "I am a novelist. It is about the human soul that I write, not the odd customs of this barbaric country." He grinned. "Besides, when they read what I have written about the practice of slavery in Camelot, this will be a very good place for me to be far away."

Margaret dipped into his futures. "Will you do me one kindness, then?" she asked. "Will you write in such a way that when war comes between the armies of slavery and of liberty, no government of France will be able to justify joining the war on the side of the slaveholders?"

"You imagine my writing to have more authority than it will ever have."

But already she saw that he would honor her request, and that it would work. "You are the one who underestimates yourself," said Margaret. "The decision you made in your heart just now has already changed the world."

Tears came to Balzac's eyes. "Madame, you have give me this unspeakable gift which no writer ever get: You tell me that my imaginary stories are not frivolous, they make life better in reality."

"Go home, Monsieur de Balzac. America is better because you came, and France will be better when you return."

"It is a shame you are married so completely," said Balzac. "I have never loved any woman the way I love you in this moment."

"Nonsense," said Margaret. "It is yourself you love. I merely brought you a good report of your loved one." She smiled. "God bless you."

Balzac took Calvin's hand. "It does me no good to speak to him. Tell him I did my best but I must to go home."

"I will tell him that you remain his true friend."

"Do not go too far in this!" said Balzac in mock horror. "I do not wish him to visit me."

Margaret shrugged. "If he does, you'll deal with him."

Balzac bowed over her hand and kissed it. Then he took off at a jaunty pace along the sidewalk.

Margaret turned to Calvin. She could see that he was pale, his skin white and patchy-looking. He stank. "This won't do," she said. "It's time to find where they've put you."

She led the docile shell of a man into the boardinghouse. She toyed with the idea of leaving him in the public room, but imagined what would happen if he started breaking wind or worse. So she led him up the stairs. He climbed them readily enough, but with each step she had to pull him on to the next, or he'd just stand there. The idea of completing the whole flight of stairs in one sweep was more than his distracted attention could deal with.

Fishy was in the hall when Margaret reached her floor. Margaret was gratified to see that as soon as Fishy recognized who it was, she shed the bowed posture of slavery and looked her full in the eye. "Ma'am, you can't bring no gentleman to this floor."

Margaret calmly unlocked her door and pushed Calvin inside as she answered. "I can assure you, he's not a gentleman."

Moments later, Fishy slipped into the room and closed the door behind her. "Ma'am, it's a scandal, She throw you out." Only then did she look at Calvin. "What's wrong with this one?"

"Fishy, I need your help. To bring this man back to himself." As briefly as she could, she told Fishy what had happened with Calvin.

"He the one send my name back to me?"

"I'm sure he didn't realize what he was doing. He's frightened and desperate."

"I don't know if I be hating him," said Fishy. "I hurt all the time now. But I know I be hurting."

"You're a whole woman now," said Margaret. "That makes you free, even in your slavery."

"This one, he gots the power to put all the names back?"

"I don't know."

"The Black man who take the names, I don't know his name. Be maybe I know his face, iffen I see him."

"And you have no idea where they take the names?"

"Nobody know. Nobody *wants* to. Can't tell what you don't know."

"Will you help me find him? From what Balzac said, he lurks by the docks."

"Oh, it be easy a-find him. But how you going a-stop him from killing you and me and the White man, all three?"

"Do you think he would?"

"A White woman and a White man who know that he gots the names? He going a-think I be the one a-tell you." She drew a finger across her throat. "My neck, he cut that. Stab you in the heart. Tear him open by the belly. That's what happen to the ones who tell."

"Fishy, I can't explain it to you, but I can assure you of this— we will *not* be taken by surprise."

"I druther be surprise iffen he kill us," said Fishy. She mimed slitting her own throat again. "Let him sneak up behind."

"He won't kill us at all. We'll stand at a distance."

"What good that going a-do us?"

"There's much I can learn about a man from a distance, once I know who he is."

"I still gots a room to finish cleaning."

"I'll help you," said Margaret.

Fishy almost laughed out loud. "You the strangest White lady."

"Oh, I suppose that would cause comment."

"You just set here," said Fishy. "I be back soon. Then I be on your half-day. They have to let me go out with you."

Denmark spent a fruitless morning asking around about a White man who suddenly went empty. He'd knock on a door, pretending to be asking for work for a non-existent White master—just so the slave who talked to him had a story to tell when somebody asked them who was at the door. The slaves all knew who Denmark was, of course—nobody was more famous among the Blacks of Camelot than the taker of names. Unless it was Gullah Joe, the bird man who flew out to the slaveships. So there wasn't a soul who didn't try to help. Trouble was, all these people with no name, they had no sharp edge to them. They vaguely remembered hearing this or that about a White man who was sick or a White man who couldn't walk, but in each case it turned out to be some old cripple or a man who'd already died of some disease. Not till afternoon did he finally hear a story that sounded like it might be what he needed.

He followed the rumor to a cheap boardinghouse where yes, indeed, two White men had shared a room, and one of them, the Northerner, had taken sick with a strange malady. "He eat, he drink, he pee, he do all them thing," said the valet who had cared for their room. "I change him trouser three times a day, wash everything twice a day." But they had left just that morning. "French man, he gots a letter, he pack up all, take away that empty man, now they be both all gone."

"Did he say where he taking the sick man?" asked Denmark.

"He don't say nothing to me," said the valet.

"Does anybody know?"

"You want me to get in trouble, asking question from the White boss?"

Denmark sighed. "You tell him that Frenchman and that Northerner, they owe my master money."

The valet looked puzzled. "Your master dumb enough a-lend them money?"

Denmark leaned in close. "It's a lie," he said. "You *say* they owe my master money, then the White boss tell you where they gone off to."

It took a moment, but finally the valet understood and retreated into the house. When he came back, he had some information. "Calvin, he the sick man, he gots a sister-in-law here. At a boardinghouse."

"What's the address?"

"White boss don't know."

"White boss hoping for a bribe," said Denmark.

The valet shook his head. "No, he don't know, that the truth."

"How'm I going to find her with no address?"

The valet shrugged. "Be maybe you best ask around."

"Ask what? 'There's a woman with a sick brother-in-law named Calvin and she living in a boardinghouse somewhere.' That get me a lot of results."

The valet looked at him like he was crazy. "I don't think you get much that way. I bet you do better, you tell them her name."

"I don't *know* her name."

"Why not? I do."

Denmark closed his eyes. "That's good. How about you tell me that name?"

"Margaret."

"She got her a last name? White folks has a last name every time."

"Smith," said the valet. "But she don't look big enough for smith work."

"You've *seen* her?" asked Denmark.

"Lots of times."

"When would you see her?"

"I run messages to her and back a couple of times."

Denmark sighed, keeping anger out of his voice. "Well now, my friend, don't that mean you know where she lives?"

"I do," said the valet.

"Why couldn't you just tell me that?"

"You didn't be asking where she live, you ask for the *address*. I don't know no number or letter."

"Could you lead me there?"

The valet rolled his eyes. "Sixpence to the White boss and he let me take you."

Denmark looked at him suspiciously. "You sure it ain't tuppence to the White boss and the rest to you?"

The valet looked aggrieved. "I be a Christian."

"So be all the White folks," said Denmark.

The valet, all anger having been stripped from him long ago, had no chance of understanding pointed irony. "Of course they be Christian. How else I learn about Jesus 'cept from them?"

Denmark dug a sixpence out of his pocket and gave it to the valet. In moments he was back, grinning. "I gots ten minutes."

"That time enough?"

"Two blocks over, one block down."

When they got to the door of Margaret Smith's boardinghouse, the valet just stood there.

"Step aside so I can knock," said Denmark.

"I can if you want," said the valet. "But I don't see why."

"Well if I don't knock, how'm I going to find out if she be in?"

"She ain't in," said the valet.

"How you know that?"

"Cause she over there, looking at you."

Denmark turned around casually. A White woman, a White man, and a Black servant girl were across the street, walking away.

"Who's looking at me?"

"They *was* looking," said the valet. "And I know she can tell you about that Calvin man."

"How do you know that?"

"That be him."

Denmark looked again. The White man was shuffling along like an old man. Empty.

Denmark grinned and gave another tuppence to the valet. "Good job, when you finally got around to telling me."

The valet took the tuppence, looked at it, and offered it back. "No, it be sixpence the White boss want."

"I already paid the sixpence," said Denmark.

The valet looked at him like he had lost his mind. "If you done that, why you be giving me more? This tuppence not enough anyway." Huffily, he handed the coin back. "You crazy." Then he was gone.

Denmark sauntered along, keeping them in sight. A couple of times the slave girl looked back and gazed at him. But he wasn't worried. She'd know who he was, and there was no chance of a Black girl telling this White lady anything about the taker of names.

"That him," said Fishy. "He take the names."

Margaret saw at once in Denmark's mind that he could not be trusted for a moment. She had been looking for him, and he had been looking for her. But he had a knife and meant to use it. That was hardly the way to restore Calvin's heartfire.

"Let's go down to the battery. There are always plenty of people there. He won't dare harm a White man in such a crowd. He doesn't want to die."

"He won't talk to you, neither," said Fishy. "He just watch."

"He'll talk to me," said Margaret. "Because you'll go ask him to."

"He scare me, ma'am."

"Me too," said Margaret. "But I can promise you, he won't harm you. The only one he wants to hurt is Calvin here."

Fishy looked at Calvin again. "Look like somebody done hurt him most all he can be hurt till he be dead." Then she realized what she had said. "Oh."

"This name-taker, Denmark Vesey, is quite an interesting fellow. You know that he isn't a slave?"

"He free? Ain't no free Blacks in Camelot."

"Oh, that's the official story, but it isn't so. I've already met another. A woman named Doe. She was given her freedom when she became too old to work."

"They turn her out then?" demanded Fishy, outraged.

"Careful," said Margaret. "We're not alone here."

Fishy at once changed her demeanor and looked down at the street again. "I seen too many damn cobblestones in my life."

"They didn't turn her out," said Margaret. "Though I have no doubt there are masters cruel enough to do so. No, she has a little room of her own and she eats with the others. And they pay her a small wage for very light work."

"They think that make up for taking her whole life away from her?"

"Yes, they think it does. And Doe thinks so, too. She has her name back, and I suppose she has reason enough to be angry, but she's happy enough."

"Then she a fool."

"No, she's just old. And tired. For her, freedom means she doesn't have to work anymore, except to make her own bed."

"That won't be enough for me, Miz Margaret."

"No, Fishy, I'm quite sure it won't. It shouldn't be enough for anyone. But don't begrudge Doe her contentment. She's earned it."

Fishy looked back and became agitated. "He coming closer, ma'am."

"Only because he's afraid of losing track of us in the crowd." Margaret steered Calvin toward the seawall. Out in the water they could see the fortresses: Lancelot and Galahad. Such fanciful names.

King Arthur indeed. "Denmark Vesey is free and he earns his living by keeping the account books of several small businesses and professional offices."

"A Black man know his numbers?"

"And his letters. Of course he pretends that he works for a White man who really does the work, but I doubt any of his clients are fooled. They maintain the legal fiction so that nobody has to send anyone to jail. They pay half what they would for a White man, and he gets paid far more than he needs to live in Blacktown. Clever."

"And he take the names."

"No, actually, he collects them, but he takes them somewhere and gives them to someone else."

"Who?"

Margaret sighed. "Whoever it is, he knows how to shut me out of just that part of Denmark's memory. That's never happened to me before. Or perhaps I simply didn't notice it. I must have skimmed past this man's heartfire before, searching for the taker of names, but because only part of his memory was hidden, I would never have noticed." Then she thought a little more. "No, I daresay I never looked in his heartfire, because he has his name, and so his heartfire burns brightly enough that I would have assumed he was a White man and not looked at all. He was hidden right out in the open."

"You a witchy woman, ain't you, ma'am?"

"Not in the sense that White folks use the word," said Margaret. "I don't do any cursing, and what hexes I have to protect me, those were made by my husband, I do no such work. What I am is a torch. I see into people's heartfire. I find the paths of their future."

"What you see in my future?"

"No, Fishy," said Margaret. "You have so many paths open before you. I can't tell you which one you'll take, because it's up to you."

"But that man, he don't kill me, right?"

Margaret shook her head. "I don't see any paths right now where that happens. But I don't tell futures, Fishy. People live and die by their own choices."

"Not even your own future? Your husband?"

Margaret grimaced. "I did try to get my husband to change his life. You see, on every path where he doesn't get killed sooner, he ends up dying because of the betrayal of his own brother."

Fishy took only a moment to realize the connection. "Be maybe you don't mean *this* brother?"

"No, I *do* mean this brother."

"Then why you not let that name-taker man cut his throat?"

"Because my husband loves him."

"But he going a-kill him!"

Margaret smiled wanly. "Isn't that the strangest thing?" she said. "Knowing the future doesn't change a man like my husband. He does what's right no matter where the road leads."

"He *always* do what's right?"

"As much as he understands it. Most of the time he tries to do as little as possible. He tries to learn, and then teach. Not like Denmark Vesey. He's a man who *acts*." Margaret shuddered. "But not wisely. Cleverly, yes, but not wisely, and not kindly, either."

"He squatting under that tree yonder."

"Now is the time, Fishy. Go to him, tell him I want to talk to him."

"Oh, Miz Margaret, you sure he don't hurt me?"

"He'll think you're pretty." Margaret touched her arm. "He'll think you're the most beautiful woman he's ever seen."

"You joking now."

"Not at all. You see, you're the first free Black woman he's known."

"I not free."

"He bought a slave once. Hoping to make her his wife. But she was so ashamed of being owned by a Black man that she threatened to expose his ability to read and write and tell the authorities that he's a free Black in Camelot."

"What he do?"

"What do you think?"

"He kill her."

"He tried. At the last moment he changed his mind. She's still his slave, but she's crippled. Mind and body."

"You didn't have to tell me that story," said Fishy. "I wasn't going to let him talk love to me. He scare me too bad."

"I just thought you should know."

"Well, you know what? It take away some of my scared, knowing that about him."

It stabbed Margaret to the heart, watching the smiling girl change before she turned around and walked among the Whites promenading on the battery. The smile fled; her eyelids half closed; she bent her shoulders and looked down as she made her way, not directly toward Denmark, but off at an angle. After a short time she doubled back and came to him from another way. Very good, thought Margaret. I didn't think to tell her to do that, but it keeps it from being obvious to onlookers that I sent her to fetch Denmark.

Fishy handled it deftly. My mistress want a-talk to you. What about? My mistress want a-talk to you. No matter what he said, she answered like a parrot. Maybe he knew she was pretending or maybe he thought she was stupid and stubborn, but either way, it got him up and walking, following Fishy's roundabout course as she walked two paces ahead of him. They couldn't walk side by side, or it would seem to White folks that they were promenading, and it would be taken as outrageous mockery. Instead it was obvious she was leading him, which meant they were on an errand for their master, and all was well with the world.

"What you want to talk about?" Denmark asked her, keeping his head downcast. But in the tone of his voice she could hear his hostility toward her.

"You're looking for me," she said.

"Am not," he said.

"Oh, that's right. It's Calvin you're looking for."

"That his name?"

"His name won't give you any power over him greater than what you already have."

"I got no power over nobody."

Margaret sighed. "Then why do you have a knife in your pocket? That's against the law, Denmark Vesey. You have other hidden powers. You're a free Black in Camelot, doing account books for—let's see, Dunn and Brown, Longer and Ford, Taggart's grocery—"

"I should have knowed you been spying on me." There was fear in his voice, despite his best effort to sound unconcerned. "White ladies got nothing better to do."

Margaret pressed on. "You found out where I lived because the valet at Calvin's former boardinghouse led you. And you have a woman at home whose name you never utter. You nearly drowned her in a sack in the river. You're a man with a conscience, and it causes you great pain."

He almost staggered from the blow of knowing how much she knew about him. "They hang me, a Black man owning a slave."

"You've made quite a life for yourself, being a free man in a city of slaves. It hasn't been as good for your wife, though, has it?"

"What you want from me?"

"This isn't extortion, except in the mildest sense. I'm telling you that I know what and who you are, so that you'll understand that you're dealing with powers that are far out of your reach."

"Sneakiness ain't power."

"What about the power to tell you that you have it in you to be a great man? Or to be a great fool. If you make the correct choice."

"What choice?"

"When the time comes, I'll tell you what the choice is. Right now, you have no choice at all. You're going to take me and Calvin and Fishy to the place where you keep the name-strings."

Denmark smiled. "So they still some things you don't know."

"I didn't say I knew everything. The power that hides the names also hides from me your knowledge of where they are."

"That be the truth, more than you know," said Denmark. "I don't even know myself."

Fishy scoffed aloud at that. "This ain't no White fool you can play games with."

"No, Fishy," said Margaret, "he's telling the truth. He really doesn't know. So I wonder how you find your way back?"

"When it time for me to go there, I just wander around and pretty soon I be there. I walk in the door and then I remember everything."

"Remember what?"

"How do I know? I ain't through that door."

"Powerful hexery," said Margaret, "if hexery it be. Take me there."

"I can't do that," said Denmark.

"How about if I cut off your balls?" asked Fishy cheerfully.

Denmark looked at Fishy in wonder. He'd never heard a Black woman talk like that, right out in public, in front of a White.

"Let's hold off on the mutilation, Fishy," said Margaret. "Again, I think Denmark Vesey may be telling me the truth. He really can't find the place unless he goes there alone."

Denmark nodded.

"Well, then. I think we have no further business together," said Margaret. "You can go now."

"I want that man," said Denmark. He glanced at Calvin.

"You'll never have him," said Margaret. "He has more power than you can imagine."

"Can't be that much," said Denmark. "Look at him, he's empty."

"Yes, he was taken by surprise," said Margaret. "But you won't hold him for long."

"Long enough," said Denmark. "His body starting to rot. He be dying."

"You have till the count of three to walk away from me and keep on walking," said Margaret.

"Or what?"

"One. Or I'll call out for you to take your filthy paws off of my body."

Denmark at once backed away. There could be no charge more sure of putting Denmark on the end of a rope without further discussion.

"Two," said Margaret. And he was gone.

"Now we lost him again," said Fishy.

"No, my friend, we've got him. He's going to lead us right where we want to go. He can't hide from me." Margaret made a slow turn, taking in the view. "Today, I think it's worth it to splurge on a carriage ride."

Margaret led Fishy and Calvin to the row of waiting carriages. It took Margaret lifting his foot and Fishy pulling him up to get Calvin's uncaring body into the coach. The moment Calvin was settled in his seat, Fishy started to get down.

"Please, stay inside with me," said Margaret.

"I can't do that."

As if he were part of their conversation, the White driver opened the sliding window between his seat and the interior of the carriage. "Ma'am," he said, "you from the North, so you don't know, but around here we don't let no slaves ride in the carriage. She knows it, too—she's got to step out and walk along behind."

"She has told me of this law and I will gladly obey it. However, my brother-in-law here is prone to get rather ill during carriage rides, and I hope you understand that if he vomits, *I* am not prepared to hold a bag to catch it."

The driver considered this for a moment. "You keep that curtain closed, then. I don't want no trouble."

Fishy looked at Margaret, incredulous. Then she leaned over and pulled the drapes closed on one side of the coach while Margaret closed them on the other. Once they were closed off from public view, Fishy sat on the padded bench beside Calvin and grinned like a three-year-old with a spoon full of molasses. She even bounced a little on the seat.

The window opened again. "Where to, ma'am?" asked the driver.

"I'll know it when I see it," Margaret said. "I'm quite sure it's in Blacktown, however."

"Oh, ma'am, you oughtn't to go up there."

"That's why I have my brother-in-law with me."

"Well, I'll take you up there, but I don't like it."

"You'll like it better when I pay you," said Margaret.

"I'd like it better iffen you paid me in advance," said the driver. Margaret just laughed.

"I meant to say half in advance."

"You'll be paid upon arrival, and that, sir, *is* the law. Though if you'd like to throw me out of your carriage, you are free to summon a constable. You can ask him about having a slave seated in your carriage, too, while you're at it."

The driver slammed the window shut and the carriage lurched forward, quite roughly. Fishy whooped and nearly fell off her seat, then sat there laughing. "I don't know how come you White folks don't ride like this all the time."

"Rich people do," said Margaret. "But not all White people are rich."

"They all richer than me," said Fishy.

"In money, I'm quite sure you're right." And then, because she was enjoying Fishy's delight, she also bounced up and down on her seat. The two of them laughed like schoolgirls.

Denmark felt the knife in his pocket like a two-ton weight. It was a terrible thing he'd been planning to do, killing a helpless man like that, and it was made all the worse by the fact that White lady knew he meant to do it. He was used to being invisible, White people paying him no mind except now and then to give him a little random trouble. But this woman, her idea of trouble was specific. She knew things about him that nobody knew, not even Gullah Joe. She scared him.

So he was glad to get away, glad to wander the streets of Blacktown until he came upon a door and suddenly he knew this was the one, though he couldn't have said how he knew, or why he didn't remember it from before. He set his hand on the knob and it opened easily, without a key. Once he was inside and the door shut behind him, he remembered everything. Gullah Joe. The struggle over the name-strings. No wonder he was supposed to kill that White man! The thing he did, unraveling some poor slave's name and cutting it loose to wander who knows where. . . .

But he did know where. He whooped with laughter. "Gullah

Joe, you won't believe it! I met the Black girl what got her name cut loose by the devil you caught!''

Gullah Joe glared at him. ''Be maybe you not shouting me business so all can hear it in the street, they.''

''She goes by the name Fishy,'' said Denmark, close enough that he didn't have to shout. ''I don't think it was no accident that White boy cut *her* name loose, cause she be rented out to his sister-in-law.''

''I think you telling me you find this White man?''

''I did, but he ain't dead yet.''

Gullah Joe slapped the table hard. Denmark was startled and his jocular mood fell away. ''You lose you courage?''

''She knew I was coming,'' said Denmark.

''A woman, she!''

''She got him down to the battery, all them White folks around, you think I'm going to show that knife, let alone cut a White boy with it?''

''Boy? This White man be maybe him a child?''

''No, he a man, but he be young. Bet he don't shave.'' Denmark remembered how Calvin looked. So empty. Like his woman. That White witch knew all about her.

Against his will, Denmark looked for her. There she was, mending clothes in a corner. She didn't look up. It took all her concentration just to get the needle into and out of the cloth. She used to be hot-hearted like that Fishy girl. Maybe I could have won her over fairly, if I tried. If I set her free. But I had to control her, didn't I? Just like a White man. I was *master*.

''How he be?'' demanded Gullah Joe.

''Who?''

''The devil him body!''

''He pretty far gone, Gullah Joe.''

''Not far enough.'' Gullah Joe glanced over to the circle that contained the captive. Denmark saw that it was twice as thick with knotwork charms as it had been when he left early in the morning.

''He been trying to escape?''

''Be maybe he already escape, him.''

''Well, if he did, wouldn't we know it? Wouldn't you be dead?''

''Be maybe he learn too much,'' said Gullah Joe. ''Look! Look a-that.''

Though there was not a touch of a breeze in the attic, one of the charms suddenly swayed, then bounced up and down.

''He doing that?'' asked Denmark.

Gullah Joe looked at him with scorn. "No, fool, they cock-roaches in the charm, they be making her bounce."

"How can he do that if you got him captive?"

Gullah Joe might have had an answer, but at that moment they both heard the door opening downstairs. Gullah Joe seemed to leap straight up in the air, and Denmark was about to let out an excla-mation when Joe shook his head violently and covered his own mouth with his hand as a sign for silence.

Denmark leaned over close. "I thought you said nobody could get in here."

There were footsteps on the stairs. No effort was being made to muffle them, either. Clump, clump, clump. Slow progress, many feet.

Finally Denmark realized what he was hearing. "It's her," he whispered. "She brought him here."

Her voice wafted up the stairs. "Indeed I did," she said. "Step aside, Denmark Vesey. It's Gullah Joe I need to talk to."

Gullah Joe danced around his desk like a child desperate to pee. Nobody had ever pierced his defenses so easily. No one had ever called him by name when he didn't want them to. Whoever this was had to be so powerful that Gullah Joe hardly knew what charms to try. She had already passed by some of his most powerful ones.

Denmark saw the witchy man's desperation and realized that this situation was definitely not under control.

"Calvin!" cried Margaret. "Can you hear my voice?"

They were near the top of the stairs, now, able to peer around in the attic and see all the hanging charms. The White woman, the White man, and the slave girl Fishy.

Margaret was listening for an answer. To her surprise, it came from the man beside her.

"I hear you," said Calvin. But his voice was soft, his manner distracted.

"I've brought your body near to your doodlebug, Calvin," she explained.

Calvin's mouth mumbled a reply. "Get me out of here," he said, his voice flat.

"Kill him now," said Gullah Joe. "He body, she calling back him soul. Kill him!"

Denmark picked up a much larger knife than the one he concealed in his pocket. "You keep him back," he said to Margaret.

She ignored him completely, and instead began to lead Calvin closer to the large concentration of charms.

"Stop, you! Don't take him there!" Gullah Joe threw a handful of powder at her, but it blew away from her in a sudden breeze and ended up stinging his eyes and making him weep. "How you do that witchery!"

She ignored him, and parted the charms to push Calvin through.

"Oh, yes," said Calvin, now sounding more like himself, though not quite that cocky yet. "This is right. Bring me home."

"Stop him!" screamed Gullah Joe.

Denmark lunged between the charms and the White man, his knife drawn.

Margaret immediately shoved Calvin hard, forcing him and Denmark both to stumble and fall into the midst of the circle that contained Calvin's doodlebug.

Gullah Joe howled in fury and threw himself to the floor.

"I have a problem, here, Margaret."

It was quite likely the thing Calvin would have said. It had his intonation. And it was certainly true. Unfortunately, the voice was coming out of Denmark Vesey's mouth.

"What's your problem, Calvin?" she asked.

"I can't get back into my body," he said. "So I'm glad you tossed in a spare."

"That's not a spare body, somebody's using it," Margaret said.

"You think I don't know that? But I can't get into my own body and I can't talk without I got one."

Margaret walked over to Gullah Joe. "What's wrong? Why can't he get back into his body?"

"Cause she be half-dead, she! Look a-him, he steal my friend body him!"

"Your body is dying," Margaret said to Calvin. "Denmark said something about that before. You're rotting."

"Give back him body!" cried Gullah Joe.

"Then help me get him back into his own body!"

"How I do that!" said Gullah Joe. "He dead man in him grave!"

"He is *not*," said Margaret. "Calvin, you have to heal your body."

"I don't know how," said Calvin. "I never tried to raise the dead."

"You're not dead," said Margaret. "Look, your chest is rising and falling."

"All right, I'm trying, but it's not like a cut finger, I don't know what to—"

"Wait!" Abruptly, Margaret turned around, walked over to Gul-

lah Joe, and dragged him to his feet. "You know!" she shouted.
"Tell me!"

"What I know?" said Gullah Joe, feigning helpless misery.
"You the witchy woman, you break down all this charm, you."

Gullah Joe smiled and shrugged. Margaret recognized the expression, the gesture. It was the way slaves told their masters to go
to hell. She looked into his heartfire and saw many things. But all
his lore was hidden from her.

"You know how to heal him," Margaret said, looking him in
the eyes, her breath on his face. "You've captured souls before, and
you know how to put them back."

Gullah Joe just folded his arms and stared off into space.

"Excuse me, Miz Margaret," said Fishy. She pushed past Margaret and, placing her left hand on Gullah Joe's right cheek, with
her right hand she slapped his other cheek with such force that blood
shot right out of his mouth. "Talk to the nice lady!" screamed Fishy
in Gullah Joe's face. "She be no enemy, you hear me?"

"Him scare me!" cried Gullah Joe, pointing at Calvin on the
floor. "Get him out on that body!"

Fishy laid another slap on him, this time so hard that Gullah Joe
fell over, his arms pinwheeling, his long knotted braids flopping
away from his body. Some charm must have come loose this time,
because suddenly more of his mind opened up to Margaret. She
didn't need him to tell her now. She opened two little jars on Joe's
big table, got two solid pinches of powder, one from each, then
strode to the charm circle where Calvin lay and threw the powder
out over him.

She thought of Antigone as she did it, spreading dirt on her
brother's corpse despite the edict of Creon forbidding it. Am I rit-
ually burying my husband's brother? If I thought Alvin might be
saved by letting him die . . . but I'd lose Alvin. This is his beloved
little brother that he played with half his growing-up years. If he
dies it can't be by my hand, even indirectly. It would destroy my
life with Alvin, and wouldn't necessarily save his. In Alvin's heartfire, which she spent a moment checking, there was no path that did
not lead to Calvin's treachery. As long as the boy is alive, Alvin
isn't safe.

And yet it was for love of Alvin that she didn't let him die. The
powders drifted down onto Calvin's body, got sucked in through his
nostrils, and almost at once he became more animated. He sat up.
"I'm so damn hungry," he said.

Gullah Joe screamed. "No! Go back! Get out of here!"

Calvin rose to his feet. "This the bastard trapped me here out-side my body?"

"It was an accident," said Margaret. "Don't harm him."

Calvin reached up, then winced and stumbled.

"Heal yourself!" cried Margaret again.

Calvin stood there, apparently trying something that no one else could see. "I'm getting better by the second," he said. "Just having my bug back in my body, it's healing me by itself."

At that moment, Fishy screamed. Margaret whirled around, and there was Denmark, knife in hand, staggering toward Calvin, brandishing the blade. Fishy leapt onto his back, tugging on the knife arm, and finally toppling the two of them onto the floor.

In the meantime, Calvin wasn't swaying anymore. He was steady on his feet, and when he turned around to face Denmark, he had the presence of mind to heat the knife so hot that Denmark screamed and flung it from him. "You got into my body!" Denmark screamed at Calvin, but now he was holding his burned hands limply in front of him. "I be wearing your castoff!"

Calvin seemed not even to notice Denmark. It was Gullah Joe he was looking for. "You lousy bastard, you filthy trap-laying witch!" he cried. "Where are you!"

At that moment a seagull started fluttering frantically around the room. Before it could find an open window, Calvin pointed at it and it dropped to the floor. In the instant, the bird disappeared and Gullah Joe lay there where it had been. Calvin advanced toward him, and the look of hate and rage on his face was terrible to behold.

"Calvin, stop it!" cried Margaret. "It was an accident! They caught you in a snare but they had no idea it was you, and when they realized your powers they had no choice but to keep you confined for fear of whatever vengeance you might take."

Calvin regarded her in silence for a moment, then turned back to the circle he had been in. He yanked all the charms from the ceiling until the circle didn't exist anymore. Gullah Joe's weeping was the only sound they could hear. But when Calvin walked over to the lesser circle and began pulling down those charms too, Joe began to shout at him. "Leave that alone! I begging you! You turn them loose like that, some of names never find they way home to they body!"

Calvin paid no attention to him. He tore the charms from the ceiling and then opened the new net, this time by hand, scattering the name-strings all over the attic floor.

"Don't hurt them," Gullah Joe pleaded, weeping. "Stop him, Denmark!"

But Denmark was sitting on the floor, weeping.

"Tear up the name-strings," cried Fishy. "Give the slaves back their anger!"

Calvin looked over at Fishy and smiled nastily. "What good does anger do for anybody?"

Then, savagely, furiously, with the power of his mind alone he unmade all the knotted strings until they lay in tatters. They all watched the seething pile of name-strings as bits of this and that flew upward from the untangling mass. And then all lay still, the bits and pieces commingled.

Now that the deed was done, Gullah Joe stopped remonstrating with Calvin. He looked up toward the invisible sky beyond the ceiling that crouched overhead. "Go home to you body, you! All you name go home!" Then he sank to his knees, weeping.

"What are you crying for," demanded Calvin. He looked at Denmark, too, who was only just beginning to dry his eyes.

"You too strong a wind for me," said Gullah Joe. "Oh, my people, my people, go home!"

Calvin lurched toward him a couple of steps, then fell to the floor. "I'm dying, Margaret," he said. "My body's too far gone."

"He be dying, that save me the trouble of killing him," said Denmark. "All we done for our people, he just undid it all."

"No!" cried Fishy. "He be setting us free! All our rage tied up in that net, that be the bad jail of all. We be slaves then, right down to the heart. Give up ourself so we can hide? From what? The worst thing already happen, when we give you our name-string."

Margaret knelt beside Calvin's body. "You have to heal yourself," she kept murmuring to him.

"I don't know where to start," Calvin whispered. "I'm filled with corruption clear through."

"Alvin!" cried Margaret desperately. "Alvin, look! Look at me! See what's happening here!" She rose to her feet and began forming letters in the air. H-E-L-P. C-A-L-V-I-N. H-E-A-L H-I-M! "Look at me and save his life, if you want him to live!"

"What you do in the air, you?" asked Fishy. "What you waving at?"

"My husband," said Margaret. "He doesn't see me." She turned to Gullah Joe. "Is there something you can do to help all those lost names return home?"

"Yes," said Joe.

"Then take your friend Denmark and go do it."

"What are *you* going to do" asked Denmark sullenly.

"I'm going to try to get my husband to heal his brother. And if he can't, then I'm going to hold Calvin's hand while he lies dying."

Calvin let out a deep moan of despair. "I ain't ready to die!" he said.

"Ready or not, you'll have to do it sometime," Margaret reminded him. "Heal yourself, as best you can," she told him. "You're supposed to be a Maker, aren't you?"

Calvin laughed. Weak and bitter, the sound of that laughter. "I spend my whole life trying to get out from under Alvin. Now the one time I need him, it's the only time he isn't right there under foot."

In the ensuing silence, Gullah Joe's voice came, soft and low. "They do it, them," he said. "They finding the way back."

"Then you'd better go out into the street and spread the word through the city," said Margaret. "They're filled with rage long pent up. You have to keep them from rising up in a fruitless rebellion as soon as all their strong passions come back." They did nothing. "Go!" she shouted. "I'll take care of Calvin here."

Gullah Joe and Denmark staggered out into the street, going from house to house. Already the sound of moaning and singing could be heard all over the city. In Blacktown, they collared every black person they could find and explained it to them as best they could, then sent them out with the warning: Contain your anger. Harm no one. They'll destroy us if we don't keep to that. The taker of names says so. We're not ready yet. We're not ready yet.

Inside the warehouse attic, Margaret and Fishy were reduced to mopping Calvin's brow as he lay delirious in his fever-racked stupor. Body and soul were together again, but only, it seemed, in time to die.

After a while a third pair of hands joined them. A Black woman who moved slowly, hesitantly. Her speech was slurred when she asked a question or two; it was hard to understand her. Margaret knew at once who she was. She laid her hand on the Black woman's hand; on the other side of her, Fishy did the same. "You don't gots to work today," said Fishy. "We take care of him."

But the woman acted as if she didn't understand. She kept on helping them take care of Calvin as if she had some personal stake in keeping him alive. Or maybe she was simply loving her neighbor as herself.

13

Judgment Day

John Adams didn't even bother to seat himself comfortably on the bench. It was supposed to be routine. Quill would read out the charge. The young lawyer for the defense would plead his client guilty or not. They'd be back out the door in a few minutes.

It started right. Quill read the charge. It was the normal collection of allegations of dealings with Satan, and as it became clear it was more a peroration than a simple reading of charges, John gaveled him down. "I think we've heard all the charges and you've moved on to opening arguments, Mr. Quill."

"For a full understanding of the charges, Your Honor, I—"

"I have a full understanding of the charge, as does the defendant," said John. "We'll hear your elaboration of the particulars at a later time, I'm sure. How does the defendant answer to the charges?"

Verily Cooper rose from his chair, his movement smooth, a perfect gentleman. By contrast, the lanky smith seemed to unfold himself, to come out of the chair like a turtle out of its shell. His chains clanked noisily.

"Alvin Smith, how do you plead?" asked John.

"Not guilty, Your Honor."

Alvin sat back down, and John started to announce the schedule for tomorrow, when the trial would begin. Then he noticed that Cooper was still standing.

"What is it, Mr. Cooper?"

"I believe it is customary to hear motions."

"Peremptory motions to dismiss are never granted in witch trials," John reminded him.

Cooper just stood there, waiting.

"All right, let's have your motion."

Cooper approached the bench with several petitions written out in an elegant hand.

"What is all this?" demanded Quill.

"It seems," said John, "that the defendant has some interesting requests. All right, Mr. Cooper. Relieve Mr. Quill's curiosity and read out your motions."

"First, the defense requests that since the prosecution intends to prosecute a witness named in the records of the parish as Purity Orphan on the same evidence as my client, the trials be joined."

"That's ridiculous," said Quill. "Purity is our prime witness and the defense knows it."

John was amused by Cooper's maneuver, and he enjoyed seeing Quill's outrage. "Are you saying, Mr. Quill, that you are *not* planning to try Mistress Purity on the basis of the same evidence?"

"I'm saying it's irrelevant to this trial."

"I believe that Mistress Purity should have the rights of a defendant in this courtroom," said Cooper, "since the evidence she gives here should not then be able to be turned against her in her own trial."

Before Quill could answer, John asked him sharply, "Mr. Quill, I'm inclined to grant this motion, unless you are prepared to grant an irrevocable dismissal of all charges against Mistress Purity that might arise from her testimony in this trial."

Quill was speechless, but only for a moment. It was easy to guess what he was thinking during his hesitation: Was it more important to keep the trials separate, or to be able to try Purity at all? "I have no intention of dismissing on a confessed witch."

John banged his gavel. "Motion granted. Is Mistress Purity in the court?"

A timid, weary-looking young woman rose from her place behind the prosecutor's bench.

"Mistress Purity," said John, "do you consent to a joint trial? And, if you do, do you consent to having Mr. Verily Cooper represent you and Alvin Smith together?"

Quill objected. "Her interests are different from those of Alvin Smith!"

"No, they're not," said Purity. Her voice was surprisingly bold. "I consent to both, sir."

"Take your place at the defense table," said John.

They waited while she seated herself on the other side of Verily Cooper. John gave them a moment or two to whisper together. It was Quill who broke the silence. "Your Honor, I feel I must protest this irregular procedure."

"I'm sorry to hear that you feel that way. Let me know if the feeling becomes irresistible."

Quill frowned. "Very well, Your Honor, I *do* protest."

"Protest noted. Note also, however, that the court takes exception to the practice of deceiving a witness into testifying in someone else's trial, only to find his own testimony used against him in his own trial. I believe this is standard in witch trials."

"It is a practice justified by the difficulty of obtaining evidence of the doings of Satan."

"Yes," said John. "That well-known difficulty. So much depends upon it, don't you think? Next motion, Mr. Cooper."

"I move that because Mr. Quill has openly and publicly violated the laws against extracting testimony under torture, all evidence obtained from interrogation of either of my clients during and after that torture be barred from these proceedings."

Quill bounded to his feet. "No physical pain was inflicted on either defendant, Your Honor! Nor was there threat of such pain! The law was strictly adhered to!"

Quill was right, John knew, according to more than a century of precedents since the anti-torture law was adopted after the Salem debacle. The witchers all made sure they didn't cross the line.

"Your Honor," said Cooper, "I submit that the practice of running an accused person until a state of utter exhaustion is reached is, in fact, torture, and that it is well known to be such and falls under the same strictures as the forms of torture specifically banned by the statute."

"The statute says what it says!" retorted Quill.

"Watch your temper, Mr. Quill," said John. "Mr. Cooper, the language of the statute is clear."

Cooper then read off a string of citations from contract law dealing with attempts to skirt the letter of a contract by devising practices that were not specifically banned but that clearly defied the fair intent of the contract. "The principle is that when a practice is engaged in solely in order to circumvent a legal obligation, the practice is deemed to be a violation."

"That is contract law," said Quill. "It has no bearing."

"On the contrary," said Cooper. "The anti-torture law is a contract between the government and the people, guaranteeing the innocent that they will not be forced by torture into giving false testimony against themselves or others. It is the common practice of witchers to use methods of torture invented after the writing of the law and therefore not enumerated in it, but having all the same pernicious effects as the prohibited practice. In other words, the common practice of running a witness in a witch trial is designed to have precisely the same effect as the tortures specifically prohibited: to extract testimony of witchcraft regardless of whether such testimony is supported by other evidence."

Quill ranted for quite a while after that, and John let him have his say, while the court reporter scribbled furiously. Nothing that Quill was saying would make the slightest difference. John knew that in terms of truth and righteousness, Cooper's position was true and righteous. John also knew that the legal issue was nowhere near as clear. To drag precedents from contract law into witchery law, which was a branch of ecclesiastical law, would expose John to charges that he had wilfully sown confusion, for where would such a practice stop? All the legal traditions would be hopelessly commingled, and then who could possibly learn enough law to practice in any court? It would be an outrageously radical step. Not that John worried about being criticized or censured. He was old, and if people chose not to follow his precedent, so be it. No, the real question was whether it was right to risk damaging the entire system of law in order to effect a righteous outcome in witchery cases.

When Quill wound down, John hadn't yet made up his mind. "The court will take this motion under advisement and announce a decision at a later point, if it isn't mooted by one of the other motions."

Cooper was clearly disappointed; Quill was not much relieved. "Your Honor, even to consider this motion is—"

John gaveled him to silence. "Next motion, Mr. Cooper."

Cooper arose and began a string of citations of obscure cases in English courts. John, having the advantage of the written motion in front of him, enjoyed watching Quill come to realize what Cooper was setting up. "Your Honor," Quill finally said, interrupting Cooper. "Is counsel for the defense seriously suggesting that the interrogator be barred from giving testimony?"

"Let's hear him out and see," said John.

"Therefore, Your Honor," said Cooper, "the interrogators in witch trials, being without exception professionals whose employment depends, not on finding truth, but on obtaining guilty verdicts, are interested parties in the action. There is no record of a witcher in the last hundred years ever finding, upon interrogation, that a person charged with witchcraft was not guilty. Furthermore, there is a consistent pattern of witchers expanding upon testimony; there are only two cases in which charges of Satanic involvement were present in the original testimony, and both those cases were found to be deliberate falsifications. The pattern is clear: All legitimate witch trials begin with no evidence of anything beyond the use of a knack. Testimony concerning Satan only shows up when the interrogator arrives, and then comes into court in only two ways: through the interrogator's own testimony contradicting a witness or defendant who denies that Satan was involved, or through testimony from witnesses who confess to Satanic involvement as part of a confession that is taken as repentance, following which charges are dismissed. In short, your Honor, the historical record is clear. Evidence of Satanic involvement in all witch trials in New England is produced by the witchers themselves and those who, in fear of death, bend to their will and produce the only kind of confession that the witchers will accept."

"He's asking this court to deny the very basis of witchcraft law!" cried Quill. "He's asking this court to contradict the clear intent of Parliament and the Massachusetts assembly!"

John almost laughed aloud. Cooper was audacious in the extreme. He wasn't just trying to get this case thrown out without a trial, he was demanding that John rule in such a way as to make it almost impossible to hold a witch trial ever again. If, that is, John's decision was accepted as a valid precedent.

It came down to this thought: He's giving me a chance to do something brilliant in the last years of my life.

"Your charge is of serious malfeasance on the part of Mr. Quill," said John. "If I were to sustain this motion, I would have no choice but to revoke Mr. Quill's license and institute charges of perjury against him, just to start with."

"I have acted according to the best traditions of my profession!" cried Quill. "This is an outrage!"

"Nevertheless," said John, "these charges are of so grave a nature as to call into question the entire proceeding against Mr. Smith and Mistress Purity. For I have a feeling that if I were to grant either of these two motions, your next motion would be for a strict reading of the witchcraft laws."

"It would, Your Honor," said Cooper.

"Strict reading is what *I'm* asking for!" cried Quill.

"You're asking for a strict reading of the anti-torture law," said John. "The courts have long been aware that a strict reading of the witchcraft law requires that for a conviction there must be evidence not only of the use of hidden powers, but also that such powers originate from the influence and power of Satan."

"That is not a requirement, it is a stipulation!" Quill shouted.

"Do not shout at me, Mr. Quill," said John. "Justice may be blind, but she is not deaf."

"I beg your pardon."

"No matter how it exercises your temper, Mr. Quill, it is long established that a strict reading of the traditional text of the witchcraft laws leads to the conclusion that the involvement of Satan is not stipulated but rather must be proved. That the possession of an extraordinary ability is not prima facie evidence of Satanic involvement, and that this specifically arises from the tradition of ecclesiastical law, which must always leave room for the possibility of a miracle enacted by faith in Jesus Christ and the intervention of heaven."

"Is it the defense's theory that these two witches have been working miracles by the power of Christ?" Quill said it as if it were the most absurd thing ever heard. But then the words hung in the air, unanswered, undisputed, and the effect was the opposite of what Quill intended. John knew that one of the main points taken from the courtroom today would be the possibility that people with the power of God in them might be charged with witchcraft if witchers had their way.

Good work, Mr. Cooper.

"It is the decision of this court that the motions raised by the defense must be decided before the trial can proceed. Therefore, I order the bailiff to send the jury home and to clear the courtroom, lest the discussion of evidence that is about to take place influence the eventual trial. We reconvene at noon. I recommend that everyone take an early dinner, because I intend to resolve these matters before we adjourn this evening."

Bang with the gavel, and John got up from the bench and almost danced back to the robing room. Who would have thought that a nasty little witch trial would suddenly take on such proportions? John had dismissed charges based on faultiness of evidence in both the witch trials he had presided over before, but in those cases it was because of contradiction within a witness's testimony, and it created no precedent. Cooper had created a far more potent situation, in which granting either of his evidentiary motions could destroy the witch laws, making them unenforceable. And given the political climate in New England, there was little chance of a legislature reinstating them, not without strict safeguards that would remove all the little tricks from the witchers' arsenal. What they did in England, of course, might be quite different. But if John knew his son Quincy, the Massachusetts assembly would act immediately and before Parliament even discussed the issue, the law in New England would be established. Parliament would then be in the awkward position of having to repudiate an ecclesiastical law set forth in New England, the place where Christian life was regarded as being most pure. There was a good chance that it could all be ended, right here, today.

John sat in the plush chair, almost lost in the cushions, for it had been designed for larger men than he. He closed his eyes and smiled. God had a role for him to play, after all.

Purity had no idea what Verily Cooper's plan was. All she knew was that Quill hated it, and if Quill hated it, she had to like it. Besides, she could see plainly that Verily Cooper had no ill intent toward her, nor Alvin, though he was in chains because of her. Still, it wasn't easy for her to sit beside these men that she had accused. If she had known when she made her charges where they would lead . . . She tried to explain this to them.

"We know that," said Verily Cooper. "Don't think twice about it."

"Where's the food?" said Alvin. "We only got a little while to eat."

"I don't know why you're helping me," said Purity.

"He's not," said Alvin. "He's trying to change the world."

"Alvin has trouble with authority," said Verily. "He doesn't like it when somebody else is in charge."

"I want somebody to be in charge of getting me something to eat. This table is starting to look mighty tasty."

At that point the bailiff approached and asked them if they wanted to eat down in the jail, separately, or right there at the defense table, with a picnic lunch donated by several of the ladies of Cambridge, including his own wife.

"What extraordinary kindness," said Verily.

The bailiff grinned. "My wife was on the commons yesterday. She thinks you're Galahad. Or Percival."

"Will you thank her for me? For all of us?"

Soon the table was spread with bread, cheese, and summer fruit, and Alvin set to eating like a teenager. Purity had a much harder time working up an appetite, though once she had the taste of pears and cheese in her mouth, she found she was hungrier than she had thought.

"I don't know," said Purity, "why you should ever forgive me."

"Oh, we forgive you," said Alvin. "We more than forgive you. Verily, here, he's downright obsessed with you."

Verily only smiled, his eyes twinkling. "Alvin's feeling out of sorts," he said. "He doesn't like jails."

"Have you been in jail before?" asked Purity.

"He was acquitted of all charges," said Verily. "Proving that I'm a clever lawyer."

"Proving I was innocent," said Alvin. "An advantage I don't have this time."

Only now did Verily show annoyance. "If you think you're guilty, why did you plead innocent?" he said sharply.

"I'm not guilty of witchcraft," said Alvin. "Under a 'strict reading' or whatever. But the things Mistress Purity said about me, well, you and I both know they're true." As if to demonstrate it, he peeled the manacle from his right hand like it was made of clay.

Purity gasped. She had never seen such power. Even hearing Arthur Stuart's account on the riverbank, she had not realized how effortlessly Alvin worked his will with iron. No incantations, no sign of strain.

"Mistress Purity is startled," said Verily.

"What do you think?" said Alvin. "Should I spread some iron on this bread and eat it?"

"Don't be a show-off," said Verily.

Alvin leaned back in his chair and ate a thick slab of bread and cheese—a posture he could not have assumed while manacled. His mouth full, he talked anyway. "I reckon you needed to remember, Mistress Purity, that what you said about me was true. Don't you go blaming yourself for telling the truth."

Purity found herself on the verge of tears. "The whole world's awry," she said.

"True," said Alvin, "but in different ways in different places. Which is what makes traveling worthwhile."

"I know you only mean good for me, both of you. Though you're annoyed with each other. I don't know why."

"Verily Cooper thinks he's in love with you," said Alvin.

Purity didn't know what to say to that. Nor did Verily, who was blushing as he ate a slice of pear. He didn't contradict Alvin, though.

"Not that I don't approve of Verily falling in love," said Alvin, "and my wife tells me you're a good girl, loyal and smart and patient and all the other virtues that a wife of Mr. Cooper has to have."

"I didn't know that I had met your wife, sir," said Purity.

"You haven't," said Alvin. "Don't you remember what Arthur told you about her?"

"That she was a candle."

"Torch," said Alvin.

"We don't hear much about knackery here in New England. Except as it pertains to disposing of the bodies of downer animals."

Verily laughed aloud. "I told you she had a sense of humor, Al."

She allowed herself a small smile.

"Let's just say that Margaret thinks you're worth the trouble of my staying in jail a couple of nights," said Alvin.

"You sustained me while we were running yesterday, didn't you?"

Alvin shrugged. "Who knows how tough you are? At some point, everybody gives in and says what the questioner wants to hear."

"I'd like to think I could withstand torture as well as the next person," said Purity.

"That's my point," said Alvin. "Nobody can withstand it, if the questioner knows what he's doing. The body betrays us. Most people never find that out because they're never asked a question that matters. And those that are, most give the answer the questioner wants without a lick of torture. It's only the strong ones, the most stubborn ones as gets tortured."

"Mr. Cooper," said Purity, "I hope you don't think I'm giving any stock to Mr. Smith's jests about your feelings toward me."

Verily smiled at her. "You don't know me, so I can hardly expect you to welcome such an idea."

"On the contrary," said Purity, "I know you very well. I saw you in court today, and on the commons, too. I know the kind of man you are."

"You don't know he farts in his sleep," said Alvin.

Purity looked at him, appalled. "Everyone does," she answered, "but most people find no need to mention it during meals."

Alvin grinned at her. "Just didn't want this to turn into a love feast. Not while my lawyer here is trying to burn down the barn to kill the fleas."

Verily's face darkened. "It's not 'fleas' when innocent people die, and others become perjurers out of fear."

"How much justice will be done when judges go striking down laws whenever some lawyer gives them half an excuse?"

"That's theory," said Verily. "When the practice of the law leads to injustice, then the law must change."

"That's what Parliament is for," said Alvin. "And the assembly."

"What politician would dare announce that he was in favor of witchcraft?"

The argument might have gone on, but at that moment the door of the courtroom opened and Hezekiah Study came in. He gave no greeting, but stalked down the aisle straight to a chair directly behind the defense table. He spoke only to Verily Cooper.

"Don't do it," said Hezekiah Study.

"Don't do what?"

"Don't take on the witchers," he said. "Try the case. Or better yet, if your client really has the knack he's charged with, shed the chains and begone with you."

Only then did Hezekiah notice the manacle lying warped and deformed in Alvin's lap. Alvin grinned at him and mashed the last hunk of bread and cheese into his mouth all at once.

"Pardon me, sir, but who are you?" asked Verily Cooper.

"This is Reverend Study," said Purity. "He advised me not to charge Alvin with witchcraft. I wish I'd listened to him then."

"You'll wish you had listened to me now," said Hezekiah.

"The law is on my side," said Verily.

"No, it isn't," said Hezekiah. "Nothing is on your side."

"Sir, I know my case, and I know the law."

"So did I," said Hezekiah. "I tried the same strategy."

Now Verily was interested. "You're a lawyer, sir?"

"I *was* a lawyer. I gave it up and became a minister."

"But you lost a witch trial, I take it?"

"I tried to use the strict reading you're going for," said Hezekiah. "I tried to show that the testimony of the witcher was tainted. Everything you're doing."

"And it failed?" asked Verily.

"What do you do," asked Hezekiah, "when the witcher calls *you* to the stand?"

Verily stared at him in silence.

"The witcher can call my lawyer?" asked Alvin.

"It's ecclesiastical law," said Hezekiah. "The law is older than advocacy. There is no privilege unless you're an ordained minister."

"So they called you," said Purity. "But what did you say?"

"I could only tell the truth," said Hezekiah. "I had seen my clients use their knacks. Harmless! A gift of God, I said it, but there was my testimony." Tears flowed down his cheeks. "That's what hanged them."

Purity was weeping also. "What were their knacks?"

"Who?" asked Alvin.

"My mother and father," said Purity, looking at Hezekiah for confirmation.

He nodded and looked away.

"What did they die for?" asked Purity. "What was their crime?"

"Your mother could heal animals," said Hezekiah. "That's what killed her. A neighbor with an old quarrel waited too long, called her too late, and his mule died, so he said that by the power of Satan she cursed the animals of all those who didn't please her."

"And my father?"

"He could draw a straight line."

The words hung there for a moment.

"That's *all?*" asked Alvin.

"On paper. In the soil. Truer than a surveyor. His fences were the marvel of the neighborhood. He won the plowing prize every year at the parish fair. No one could cut so straight a furrow. His wife always made him cut the fabric when she was sewing. People remembered his knack when his wife was on trial, and he admitted it readily, seeing no harm in it, since it neither harmed others nor gave him any advantage. Except at the fair."

Purity could hardly talk for weeping. "That's why they died?"

"They died for envy," said Hezekiah, "and for the bloodlust of the witcher, and for the incompetence and arrogance, the *pride* of their attorney who called himself their friend but dared to put their lives at risk in a larger cause. I could have won them a banishment. They were well-liked and the trial was unpopular. The witcher was willing to dicker. But I had a cause.'' He gripped Purity's hands. "I can't let this man do the same to you! I've spent my life trying to keep you from the same fate, because they marked you, don't think they haven't. Quill knows who you are. Because of you, they couldn't hang your mother until you were born, and the outrage built and built among the people. There was a strong sentiment to break them out of jail. But the witchers called in the authorities and they guarded the hangings. And then they sent you away, so as not to remind the people of the outrage that had been done against you. To this day, God help the witcher who comes through that part of Netticut, because the people know the truth there.''

"Then it was a victory of sorts," said Purity quietly. "They didn't die for nothing.''

"They *died*,'' said Hezekiah. "Their accusers were ostracized until they moved away, but they're still alive, aren't they? The witchers lost a lot of prestige, but they're still in the witch business, aren't they? That feels like dying for nothing to me.''

"It's a different trial," said Verily. "And a different judge.''

"He's an honorable man, bound by law,'' said Hezekiah. "Don't think he isn't.''

"Honorable men aren't bound by bad laws,'' said Verily.

Alvin laughed, a little nastily. "If that's so, how you going to tell the honorable ones from the dishonorable? Who's bound by law at all, since every law is bad at one time or another?''

"Whose side are you on?'' Verily asked testily.

"I'm supposed to build a city,'' said Alvin. "And if I don't build it on law, what am I going to build it on? Even Napoleon makes laws that bind him, because if you don't then there's no order, it's chaos all the way down.''

"So you'd rather hang?''

Alvin sighed and held up the twisted manacle. "I'm not going to hang.''

"But someone will," said Verily. "If not this year then next, or the year after. Someone will hang. You said so yourself.''

"Let witch trials fade out by themselves,'' said Alvin.

"The way slavery's fading?'' Verily answered mockingly.

The door opened again. People were beginning to return. The bailiff came back to clean up the meal. "You didn't eat much,'' said the bailiff.

"*I* did,'' said Alvin.

Hezekiah and Purity still held hands across the railing separating spectators from the court. "Beg pardon," said the bailiff. "She's a defendant now. I don't want to put her in chains, but she's not allowed to touch folks beyond the rail."

Hezekiah nodded and withdrew his hands.

The bailiff left with the picnic basket. Alvin wrapped the manacle around his wrist again. Purity couldn't resist touching it. It was hard again. As hard as iron.

Quill came back into the courtroom smiling.

Purity turned and whispered to Hezekiah. "You're wrong, you know," she said. "It wasn't you that hanged them."

Hezekiah shook his head.

"I never knew them, but I sit now where they sat, though guiltier, because I'm the one who leveled the charge. And I tell you, they knew who their friends were."

"I was no friend to them."

"They knew who their friends were," said Purity, "and I know who their friends were. All may have been outraged, but they let the hanging take place. You alone followed me or found me here. You alone took care to raise me in safety. You gave years of your life to their child. That is a true friend."

Hezekiah buried his face in his hands. His shoulders shook, unable to bear what she had placed upon them. Absolution was a heavier burden, for the moment, than guilt.

Quill rose to his feet the moment John Adams called the court to order.

"Your Honor, I have a motion."

"Out of order," said John.

"Your Honor, I think all can be settled when we call Mr. Verily Cooper to the stand! This is ecclesiastical law and there is no—"

John banged the gavel again and again until Quill fell silent.

"I said your motion was out of order."

"There are precedents!" said Quill, seething with fury.

"On the contrary," said John. "Your motion may be in order when we resume the trial of Alvin Smith and Purity Orphan. But at the moment, this is a hearing on a motion, and in this procedure I am the questioner. There are no sides and no attorneys, only my own pursuit of information to allow me to reach a conclusion. So you will take your seat until I call you for questioning. You are the equal of all other persons in this court. You have no standing to make a motion of any kind. Is that clear to you at last, Mr. Quill?"

"You exceed your authority, Your Honor!"

"Bailiff, bring manacles and leg irons. If Mr. Quill speaks again, they are to be placed upon him to remind him that he has no authority in this courtroom during this hearing."

White-faced and trembling, Quill sat down.

The hearing went quite smoothly for quite a while. John questioned Purity first. She described the nature of the charges she originally made, and then told how Quill had deformed them, turning harmless frolicking in the river into an incestuous orgy, and a peaceful conversation on the riverbank into a witches' sabbath. He asked her about the professors from the college, and she affirmed that she had never mentioned them and only found out they were being questioned when Quill demanded that she denounce them, Emerson in particular.

Then the professors were brought forward, one at a time, to recount the experience of being questioned by Quill. Each one stated that he had been led to believe that others had confessed and implicated them, and that their only hope was to confess and repent. All denied being the one who confessed.

Then John turned to Quill.

"Aren't you going to question *him* first?" Quill said, pointing to Alvin.

"Have you forgotten whose hearing this is?" asked John.

"I just want to hear whether *he* denies the witchcraft charges!"

"You'll find that out in the trial," said John, "since the accused can be called to give testimony against themselves in witch trials."

"You're favoring him," said Quill.

"You're testing my patience," said John. "Put your hand on the Bible and take your oath."

Quill complied, and the questioning began. Quill answered scornfully, denying that he had deceived anyone. "She's the one who talked of Satan. I had to stop my ears, she spoke of him so lovingly. She wanted carnal knowledge of him. She even told me that Satan had instructed her to lie and say I made up the story, but I was not afraid because I knew that in *lawful* courts, my testimony would have greater trust than hers."

John listened to Quill calmly enough, as his testimony grew nastier and nastier. "These professors behave exactly as one would expect a conclave of wizards to behave," said Quill. "I wouldn't have questioned them if the girl hadn't denounced them. She thought better of it at once, of course, and tried to deny it, but I knew what she had told me, and it was enough. They deny that they confessed, but several of them did, as my depositions to the court affirm."

John picked up a pile of affidavits from the bench. "I do have those depositions and I've read them all."

"So you know the truth, and this whole hearing is a travesty."

"If it is," said John, "it follows the script you wrote."

"I wrote no script for *this*," said Quill. "I expected this court to function like a proper witch trial."

"But Mr. Quill, this is not a witch trial. This is a hearing on a motion. You seem unable to grasp that. This proceeding has been entirely proper. And I am ready now with my ruling on the motion."

"But you haven't questioned Alvin Smith!"

"All right," said John. "Mr. Smith, how are you today?"

"Tired of being in chains, Your Honor," said Alvin, "but otherwise in good condition."

"You ever have any dealings with Satan?"

"I'm not sure who you're referring to," said Alvin.

John was surprised. He was expecting a simple 'no.' "Satan," he said. "The enemy of God."

"Why, if Satan means an enemy of God, I've had dealings with a fair number in my time, including Mr. Quill here."

"Your Honor!" cried Quill.

"Sit down, Mr. Quill," said John. "Mr. Smith, you seem to be deliberately misunderstanding my question. Don't try my patience, please. Satan, as generally conceived, is a supernatural being. You've been accused of getting powers from him and obeying his commands. Did you get any hidden powers from Satan, or obey him?"

"No sir," said Alvin.

"More to the point," said John, "did you ever tell Purity Orphan that you had dealings with Satan, or could she ever have seen you in the presence of Satan?"

"If you mean the bright red fellow with the claws of a bear and cloven hooves and horns on his head," said Alvin, "I've never seen him or heard from him. He's never even sent me a note. I have *smelled* him, but only when I was alone with Quill."

John shook his head. "I don't think you're taking this proceeding seriously."

"No sir," said Alvin, "I admit that I am not."

"And why is that? Don't you understand that your life may hinge upon the outcome of this hearing?"

"It doesn't," said Alvin.

Cooper tried to shush him.

"And why do you believe that you're safe, regardless of the outcome of this hearing?"

Alvin rose to his feet and pulled the manacles off his wrists as easily as he might have pulled off mittens. He shook his feet and the ankle braces clanked on the floor. "Because I got the knack I was born with. As far as I know, it's God, not Satan, who creates us, and so whatever knack I have came from God. I try to use it kindly and decently. One thing I never do is try to use my knack to force someone else to do something against their will. But you and my lawyer here, you seem determined to force the people of New England to get rid of their witchery laws whether they want to or not. Mr. Quill is a lying snake, but you don't strike down all the laws just to catch a few liars."

Verily Cooper rested his head on the desk. John, who was trembling at the sight of such obvious supernatural powers, could see that to Verily Cooper this was old news.

Alvin was still talking. "I was willing to stick it out and see how you two twisted up the laws without actually breaking too many of them, but my wife needs me right now, and I'm not wasting another minute here. When I got time I'll come back and you and I can talk this out, Your Honor, because I think you're an honorable man. But for the present, I've got somewhere else to be."

Alvin started toward the door at the back of the court.

Quill jumped to his feet and tried to stop him. His hands slid off Alvin as if he'd been greased. "Stop him!" Quill cried. "Don't let him go!"

"Bailiff," said John. "Mr. Smith seems to be escaping."

Alvin turned around and faced the judge. "Your Honor, I thought this wasn't my trial. I thought this was a hearing on a motion. You don't need me here."

Verily stood up. "Alvin, what about Purity?"

"She ain't going to hang," said Alvin. "By the time you're through, she'll probably be Queen of England."

"Wait just a minute, Alvin," Verily said. He turned to face John Adams. "Your Honor, I ask the court to release my client on his own recognizance, with his promise to appear in court in the morning."

John understood what he was asking, and decided to grant it. The escape would be turned into a legal release. "The defendant's presence not being necessary at this hearing, and with proof positive that the defendant's compliance with his imprisonment up to this point has been entirely voluntary, the court deems him worthy of our trust. Re-

leased on his own recognizance, to appear in court at ten in the morning tomorrow.''

"Thank you, Your Honor,'' said Alvin.

"An outrage!'' cried Quill.

"Sit down, Mr. Quill,'' said John Adams. "I'm ready to rule
on the motion.''

Quill slowly sat down as the door closed behind Alvin Smith.

"Your Honor,'' said Verily Cooper. "I must apologize for my
client's behavior.''

"Sit down, Mr. Cooper,'' said John. "I have my rulings. Mr.
Smith's point was well taken. It is not the place of the court to
destroy the law in order to achieve justice. Therefore both motions
are denied.''

Quill flung his arms out wide. "Praise God!''

"Not so fast, Mr. Quill,'' said John. "This hearing is not over.''

"But you've ruled.''

"During the process of this hearing, I have heard substantial
evidence of misconduct by those officers called interrogators or
witchers. The appointment of these witchers is in the hands of the
ecclesiastical authorities, who have delegated that responsibility to
an examining board of experts on witchery, who are responsible for
making sure that witchers are fully trained. However, the actual license to interrogate and serve as an officer of the court is issued by
the governor upon a swearing-in by a judge. This license is required
for an interrogator to have standing in a civil court and call a witch
trial. The licenses of all witchers fall under the law that governs the
licensing of all government officials not specified in any particular
act. Under that law, your license can be suspended upon a finding
by a judicial officer of the level of magistrate or higher that you
have used your office against the interests of the people of the commonwealth. I so find. Mr. Quill, I hereby declare your license and
the license of all other interrogators in the commonwealth of Massachusetts and in the judicial circuit of New England to be suspended.''

"But you can't—you—''

"Furthermore, I declare all interrogations made under these licenses to be suspended as well. I order that no judicial proceeding
may continue until and unless hearings are held that substantiate the
evidence under the normal rules of evidence in the civil courts,
which are the courts that have jurisdiction over licensing. If you or
any other witchcraft interrogator cannot demonstrate that the evidence you have given in court meets the standard of evidence in the

civil courts, the suspension of your license may not be lifted. And as long as your license is suspended, no officer of the law in New England is permitted to arrest, imprison, confine, arraign, or try any person on the orders of an interrogator; and since the law requires that a witcher be the prosecutor at any witch trial in New England, I order that no witch trial may be held in New England until and unless an interrogator in possession of a valid license is available to prosecute."

The words flowed out of John like water from a spring. He felt as though he were singing. Alvin Smith's point had been well taken. But in the moment when he realized that, for honor's sake, he would have to deny Cooper's clever motions, a new path opened up in his mind and he saw how he could put a stop to witch trials, not by using judicial precedent to destroy the law, but by using another law to trump it.

"I declare this hearing adjourned." He banged the gavel. Then he banged it again. "I call the court to order in the matter of the commonwealth versus Alvin Smith and Purity Orphan. This being a witch trial, we may not proceed without the presence of an interrogator with a valid license. Is there an interrogator with such a license in the courtroom?"

John looked at Quill cheerfully. "You, sir, seem to be sitting at the prosecutor's table. Have you such a license?"

Quill saw the handwriting on the wall. "No, Your Honor."

"Well," said John. "As there seem to be no other candidates for the role of interrogator present, I have no choice but to find that this trial is improper and illegal. I dismiss the charges. The defendants are free to go. Mr. Smith is not obligated to return to court. Court is adjourned."

Quill rose shakily to his feet. "If you think you can get away with this, you're wrong, sir!"

John ignored him and walked away from the bench.

Quill shouted after him. "We'll get new licenses! See if we don't!"

But John Adams knew something that Quill had forgotten. Licenses were issued only on the authority of the governor. And John was pretty sure that Quincy would not issue any licenses until the Assembly of Massachusetts had plenty of time to write a new witch law that eliminated the office of interrogator and required the normal rules of evidence to hold sway, including the right of the defendant not to be compelled to testify. The churches had the right, of course, to hold witch trials any time they wanted, but the maximum penalty in the ecclesiastical courts was excommunication from the congregation. And they used *that* power against people who didn't attend church often enough.

When the door of the robing room had closed behind him, John couldn't help it. He danced a little jig all around the room, singing a childish ditty as he did.

Then he remembered what he had seen Alvin Smith do, and his mood sobered at once.

He sat in the plush chair and tried to understand what he had seen. John had never believed in knacks that defied natural law, but now he realized that he had come to believe this, not because they didn't exist, but because no one would dare to use such powers in New England, where you could hang for it. The witch laws were wrong, not because such powers were wholly imaginary, but because they didn't necessarily come from Satan. Or did they? Had he crippled the witchcraft laws at the very moment when he had proof that they were necessary?

No. Cooper might not have prevailed with his motions, but his point was well taken. It was only the falsified testimony of the witchers that showed any involvement of Satan with knacks. Without the witchers, knacks were just inborn talents. That some of them were extraordinary did not mean that the possessor of such a knack was either evil or good. Nor was there any evidence that the witch laws had ever been used against people whose hidden powers were truly dangerous. It was obvious that if Alvin Smith had not wished to be confined, no jail could have held him. Therefore only those whose knacks were relatively mild and harmless could ever have been convicted and hanged. It was a law that did nothing it was intended to do. It protected no one and harmed many. It would be good to be rid of it.

In the meantime, though, there was Alvin Smith. What a strange young man! To walk away from his own trial because he thought his lawyer was going to get him off by hurting society at large—was he really that altruistic? Did the good of the people mean more to him than his own good name? For that matter, why had he stayed? John knew without asking. Just as Hezekiah had begged him not to let any harm come to Purity, so also had Alvin stayed for the trial specifically in order to link Purity's fate to his own. But no matter what happened, Purity wasn't going to hang. Alvin had the power to see to that.

But that wasn't enough for Verily Cooper. Saving his friend, saving this girl, that wasn't enough. He had to save everybody. John understood the impulse. He had it himself. He had been thwarted in it, and it hurt him to fail. Not like it hurt Hezekiah Study, of course. But at long last, Cooper had brought them both a chance to redeem their past failures. It was a good gift. Cooper might be too clever for his own good, but he used it in a good cause, which was more than could be said for many clever men.

Knacks. Alvin Smith could shed iron like melting butter. What is my knack? Do I have one? Perhaps my knack is just to hold on my course whether it seems to be taking me anywhere or not. Stubbornness. That could be a gift of God, couldn't it? If so, I daresay I've been blessed with far more than my share. And when God judges me someday, he'll have to admit I didn't bury my talent. I shared it with everyone around me, much to their consternation.

John Adams had a good laugh about that, all by himself.

14

Revolt

No sooner was Alvin out of the courtroom than he began to run, long loping strides that would carry him to the river. No greensong helped him at first, for the town was too built up. Yet he was scarcely wearied when he reached the place where Arthur, Mike, and Jean-Jacques were just awakening from their late-afternoon naps. For a moment they wanted to show him what Jean-Jacques had painted, but Alvin had no time for that.

"I was in court and I couldn't pay attention to half that folderol, and my mind wandered to Margaret and there she was, her heart beating so fast, I knew something was wrong. She was spelling big letters in midair. Help. And I looked around her and there was Calvin lying on the floor of an attic in Camelot, and he's in a bad way."

Jean-Jacques was all sympathy. "You must feel so helpless, to be so far away."

Mike Fink hooted with laughter. "Alvin ain't all that helpless wherever he is."

"It means we're going to part company with you, Jean-

Jacques,'' Alvin said. ''Or rather, some of us are. Arthur, you're coming with me.''

Arthur, who had been on tenterhooks waiting to hear the plan, now grinned and relaxed.

''Mike, I'd appreciate it if you'd go on into town and meet Very. He'll have that Purity girl with him, I reckon, or I'll be surprised if he don't. So if you'd tell him that he and you and her and Jean-Jacques here, you should all head for the border of New Amsterdam. I figure we can join up in Philadelphia when I'm done with whatever it is Margaret wants me to do.''

''Where?'' asked Mike. ''Philadelphia's a big place.''

''Mistress Louder's rooming house, of course.''

''What if she don't got room?''

''Then leave word with her where you'll be. But she'll have room.'' Alvin turned again to Jean-Jacques. ''It's been a pleasure, and I'm proud to know a man with such a knack for painting, but I'm taking Arthur and we got nobody to hold the birds still for you now.''

''So what I do now?'' said Jean-Jacques. ''I make you angry when I kill the bird and stuff it. My career is over if I do not kill the bird.''

Alvin looked at Arthur Stuart. ''I got to tell you, Arthur, I got no problem with him killing a bird now and then for the sake of folks studying his paintings.''

Arthur stood there looking down at the ground.

''Arthur, it ain't like I got a lot of time here,'' said Alvin.

Arthur looked up at Jean-Jacques, then at Alvin. ''I just got to know one thing. Does a bird have a soul?''

''Am I a, how you say, théologien?''

''I just—if a bird dies, when it dies, when you kill it, what happens to it? Is it completely dead? Or is there some part of it that . . .''

Arthur stood there with tears beading up on his cheeks. Alvin reached out to hug him, but Arthur pulled away. ''I ain't asking for a hug, dammit, I'm asking for an answer!''

''I don't know about that,'' said Alvin. ''What I see is like a little fire inside every living thing. Humans got a big bright one, most of them anyway, but there's fire like that in every animal. The plants, too, only the fire is spread out all through the plant, not just in one place like it is with the animals. Margaret sees something like that, she says, only she don't catch much more than a glimpse of what's in the animals, like the shadow of a fire, if you get my drift.

Now is that heartfire a soul? I don't know. And what happens to it after a body dies? I don't know that either. I know it ain't in the body anymore. But I know sometimes the heartfire can leave the body. Happens when I'm doodlebugging, part of it goes out of me. Does that mean that when the body's dead the whole thing can go? I don't know, Arthur. You're asking me what I can't tell you.''

"But it might, you can say that, can't you? It might live on, I mean if humans do it, then birds might too, right? Their heartfires may be smaller but that don't mean they'll burn out when they die, does it?''

"I reckon that's good thinking,'' said Alvin. "I reckon if anybody lives on after death—and I think they do, mind you, I just ain't seen it—then why not birds? Heartfire is heartfire, I should think, lessen somebody tells me different. Is that good enough?''

Arthur Stuart nodded. "Then you can kill a bird now and then, if you got to.''

Jean-Jacques bowed in salute to Arthur. "I think, Mr. Stuart, that this was the question you really wanted to ask me from the start. Back in Philadelphia.''

Arthur Stuart looked a little embarrassed. "Maybe it was. I wasn't sure myself.''

Alvin rubbed Arthur's tight-curled hair. Arthur ducked away. "Don't treat me like a baby.''

"You don't like it, get taller,'' said Alvin. "Long as you're shorter than me, I'm going to use your head to scratch an itch whenever I feel like it.'' Alvin touched the brim of his hat in salute to Mike and Jean-Jacques. "I'll see you in Philadelphia, Mike. And Jean-Jacques, I hope to see you again someday, or at least to see your book.''

"I promise you your own copy,'' said Jean-Jacques.

"I don't like this,'' said Mike. "I should be with you.''

"I promise you, Mike, I'm not the one in danger down there.''

"It's a blame fool thing to do!'' said Mike.

"What, leave you behind?''

"Healing Calvin.''

Alvin understood the love that prompted these words, but he couldn't leave the idea unanswered. "Mike, he's my brother.''

"I'm more brother to you than he ever was,'' said Mike.

"You are now,'' said Alvin. "But there was a time when he was my dearest friend. We did everything together. I have no memories of my childhood without him in them, or scarcely any.''

"So why doesn't he feel that way?''

"Maybe I wasn't as good a brother to him as he was to me," said Alvin. "Mike, I'll come back safe."

"This is as crazy as it was you going back to jail."

"I walked out when I needed to," said Alvin. "And now I've got to get moving. I need you to get Jean-Jacques out of New England without getting deported as a Catholic, and Verily and Purity need somebody who isn't ga-ga with love to make sure they eat and sleep."

Arthur Stuart solemnly shook hands with Mike and Jean-Jacques. Alvin hugged them both. Then they took off at a jog, the man leading, the boy at his heels. In a few minutes the greensong had them and they fairly flew through the woods along the river.

"He's coming," said Margaret.

"Where he be, you say?" asked Gullah Joe.

Outside, they heard the sound of galloping horses. The singing and wailing from the slave quarters had grown more intense as the sun set and darkness gathered.

"I can't tell," said Margaret. "He's in the midst of the music. Running. He moves like the wind. But it's such a long way."

"We tell folks what you say," said Denmark, "but this be too hard for them. The anger, it come so fast to them. I hear some talking about killing their White folks tonight in their beds. I hear them say, Kill them the White babies, too, the children. Kill them all."

"I know," said Margaret. "You did your best."

"They be other ones, too," said Gullah Joe. "No name come back a-them. Empty like him. More empty. They die. He kill them."

Margaret looked down at Calvin's body. The young man's breath was so shallow that now and then she had to check his heart-fire just to see if he was alive. Fishy and Denmark's woman were tending him now, so Margaret could rest, but what good did washing him do? Maybe they were keeping the fever down. Maybe they were just keeping him wet. They certainly weren't keeping him company, for he had lapsed into unconsciousness hours ago and all his futures had come down to just a handful that didn't lead to a miserable death here, tonight, in this place.

"Why he no fix up, him?" asked Gullah Joe. "He strong."

"Strong but ignorant," said Margaret. "My husband tried to teach him, but he refused to learn. He wanted the results without practicing the method."

"Young," said Gullah Joe.

"I learned when I was young," said Denmark.

592 *ALVIN WANDERING*

"You never be young," said Gullah Joe.

Denmark grimaced at that. "You right, Gullah Joe."

"Your wife," said Margaret.

Denmark looked at the slave woman he had bought and ruined. "She never let me call her that."

"She never told you her name, either," said Margaret.

Denmark shook his head. "I never call her by no slave name. She never tell me her true name. So I got no name for her."

"Would you like to speak that name? Don't you think that in her present state, she'd like to hear someone call her by name?"

"When she be in her right mind she don't want me to," said Denmark.

"Slavery makes people do strange things," said Margaret.

"I never was a slave," said Denmark.

"You were, all the same," said Margaret. "They fenced you around with so many laws. Who is more a slave than the man who has to pretend he's a slave to survive?"

"That didn't make me do *that* to her."

"I don't know," said Margaret. "Of course you made your own choices. You tried to find a wife in just the way your father did— you bought one. Then you found yourself in a corner. You thought murder was your only hope. But at the last moment you couldn't do it."

"Not the last moment," said Denmark. "The moment after."

"Yes," said Margaret. "Almost too late."

"Now I live with her every day," said Denmark. "Now who own who?"

"All that anger outside—what if they kill? Do you think they're murderers?"

"You think they not?" asked Denmark.

"There has to be something between murder and innocence. I've seen the darkest places in everyone's heartfire, Denmark. There's no one who doesn't have memories he wishes he didn't have. And there are crimes that arise from—from decent desires gone wrong, from justified passions carried too far. Crimes that began only as mistakes. I've learned never to judge people. Of course I judge whether they're dangerous or not, or whether they did right or wrong, how can anyone live without judging? What I mean is, I can't condemn them. A few, yes, a few who love the suffering of others, or who never think of others at all, worthless souls that exist only to satisfy themselves. But those are rare. Do you even know what I'm talking about?"

"I know you scared," said Denmark. "You talk when you scared."

"We're safe enough here," said Margaret. "I'm just . . . what you did to your wife, Denmark. Do you think I haven't thought of doing that to someone? An enemy? Someone who I know will some-day cause the death of the person I love most, the person I've loved my whole life, from childhood up. I know that desperate feeling. You have to stop him. And then you see the chance. He's helpless. All you have to do is let nature take its course, and he's gone."

"But you call your husband," said Denmark. "You wave your arms and make letters in the air. Somehow he see that."

"So I chose to do the right thing," she said.

"Like me," said Denmark.

"But maybe I chose too late," she said.

Denmark shrugged.

"Maybe. It ain't all work out yet."

"All these people thirsting for vengeance. What will they choose? When will it be too late for them? Or just in time?"

A new sound. Marching feet. Margaret ran to the window. The King's Guard, marching in Blacktown.

"Damn fool they," said Gullah Joe. "What we do here in Blacktown? Who we hurt? They scared of *us,* they no remember they gots them Black people hate them, in they house, they wait down the stair, White man sleep, up the stair they go, cook she got she knife, gardener he got he sickle, butler he break him wine bottle, he got the glass, the edge be sharp. When they blood paint the walls, when they body empty, who the Black man put on that tall hat? Who the Black woman wear the bloody dress?"

The images were too terrible for Margaret to bear. She had al-ready seen them herself, in the blazing heartfires of angry slaves. What Gullah Joe imagined, she had seen down ten thousand paths into the future. Until Calvin tore up the name-strings, that future hadn't shown up anywhere. She couldn't predict it. Calvin had the power to change everything without warning. Margaret was unac-customed to surprise. She didn't know how to deal with a situation that she hadn't had time to watch and think about.

She walked away, into a corner of the room. She began to pray.

But she couldn't keep her mind on the words of her prayer. She kept thinking of Calvin. As if she didn't have enough to worry about. Wasn't it just like Cal? Set loose forces that could cause the deaths of thousands of people, and he was going to lie there dying through it all.

594   *ALVIN WANDERING*

As for Gullah Joe and Denmark, she hadn't the heart to tell them, but the likeliest future, whether the slave revolt happened or not, was that the King and his men would be looking for the person who planned the revolt. It had to be a conspiracy. It couldn't be mere chance that in the morning the entire slave population of Camelot was docile, and suddenly by nightfall they were keening and howling in every house. There had to be a plot. There had to be a signal given. It wasn't hard to find slaves who, under torture, would mention the taker of names. And others who would point him out. The mastermind of the conspiracy, that's what they'd call him. They'd call it Denmark Vesey's War, as if it was war to have families murdered in their sleep, and then every third slave in Camelot hanged in retribution, while Denmark Vesey himself would be drawn and quartered, and the pieces of him hung on poles in Blacktown, lest anyone forget.

She hadn't the heart to tell him that. Nor did it matter, in the end, for one thing was certain in Denmark's heartfire: If this happened to him, he would believe that he deserved it, for the sake of what he did to his woman.

Calvin. Again he kept intruding in her thoughts. Something about Calvin. What? He can't heal himself, so what is he good for?

For something that he *does* know how to do.

Margaret got up from her prayer and rushed to Gullah Joe. "You've done this before, Gullah Joe. I've heard the stories, I've seen them in the slaves' memories, legends of the zombi, the walking dead."

"I no do that," said Gullah Joe.

"I know, you don't do it on purpose, but there he is, dead but alive. There must be something you have, something in your tools, your powders, that can wake him up. Just for a little while."

"Wake him up, then he die faster," said Gullah Joe.

"I need him. To save the people he did this to."

"He no heal him own body," said Gullah Joe scornfully.

"Because he doesn't know how. But he can do *something*."

Gullah Joe got up and went to his jars. Soon he had a mixture—a dangerous one, to judge from the way he never let any of the powders touch his skin and looked away when mixing so as not to breathe in any of the dust. When it was mixed, he poured it through a hole in a small bellows, then plugged the hole tightly. Even at that, he wetted down cloths for the rest of them to breathe through, in case any dust got loose in the air.

Then he took the bellows, put the end in one of Calvin's nostrils, then waxed the other nostril closed. "You," he said to Denmark. "Hold him mouth closed."

"No," said Denmark. "I can't do that. That too much like drowning him."

"I'll do it," said Margaret.

"What you tell husband then, this go bad?"

"It's my fault anyway," said Margaret. "I told you to do it."

"I do it, ma'am," said Fishy. "I do this."

Margaret stepped back. Fishy got one hand under Calvin's jaw and the other atop his head.

"I say go, you close him tight the mouth," said Gullah Joe.

Fishy nodded.

"Go."

She clamped Calvin's mouth shut. Calvin feebly resisted, desperate for breath. Nothing came in except a thin stream of air around the nipple of the bellows. Gullah Joe slammed the bellows together just as Calvin inhaled desperately. A cloud of dust emerged from around the bellows. Gullah Joe was ready for it. He picked up a bucket of water and doused Calvin with it, catching and settling the dust at the same time.

Calvin jerked and twitched violently. Then he sat up, pulling away from Fishy's grip, tearing the bellows and the wax out of his nostrils. Then he choked and coughed, trying to clear his lungs.

He looked no healthier. Indeed, patches of his skin were sloughing off, sliding like rotten fruit thrown against a window. But he was alert.

"Calvin, listen to me," Margaret said.

Calvin only choked and gasped.

"The slaves are about to revolt. It has to be stopped. Alvin's too far away, I need your help!"

Calvin wept. "I can't do nothing!"

"Wake up!" Margaret shouted at him. "I need you to be a man, for once! This isn't about you, this isn't about Alvin, it's about doing the decent thing for people who need you."

Some of what she was saying finally penetrated Calvin's hazy mind. "Yes," he said. "Tell me what to do."

"Something to take their minds off their anger," she said. "What we need is a heavy storm. Wind and rain. Lightning!"

"I can't do lightning."

"How do you know you can't?"

"Cause I grew up trying." He looked down at his hand. The

bare bone of one finger was exposed. "Margaret, what's happening to me!"

"You were too long out of your body," she said. "Alvin's hurrying here to save you."

"He don't want to help me, he wants me dead!"

"Stop thinking about yourself, Calvin!" she said sternly. "I need something that feels like a force of nature."

"I can do fires. I can set the city on fire."

As he spoke, a couple of tiny flames danced around on the floor beside him.

"No!" cried Margaret. "Good heavens, are you insane? The slaves will be blamed for setting the fires, it would make everything even worse! Not fire."

"I don't know how anything works," Calvin said. "Not deep enough to change it. Alvin tried to teach me but all I wanted was the showy stuff." He wept again. Margaret had to seize his wrists to keep him from rubbing the skin off his face.

"Get control of yourself," she said. She turned helplessly to Gullah Joe. "Isn't there something—"

Gullah Joe laughed madly. "I tell you! No good this way! Zombi no good! All he think be, I so dead! He be sad, all sad, him."

"What about the water?" she asked Calvin. "I know you and Alvin played with water, he told me. Making it splash without throwing in a stone—that's a game you played. Remember?"

"Big splash," he said.

"Yes, that's right. Make it splash out there. In the river, really big splashes. Slosh the water up on the shore. Make it flood."

"All we did was little splashes," said Calvin.

"Well this time do a big one!" Margaret shouted, her patience wearing thin. If, in fact, she had any patience left at all.

"I'll try, I'll try, I'll try." He cried again.

"Stop that! Just do it!"

She felt someone kneel down beside her. Fishy? No, Denmark's wife. She had a damp cloth. Gently she pressed it against Calvin's forehead. Then his cheek. She mumbled something unintelligible, but the music of it was calm and comforting. Calvin closed his eyes and began trying to make the water in the river splash.

Margaret also closed her eyes and cast about for heartfires near the river. She skipped from one to another, up and down the shore, on the north side of the peninsula and the south. No one was looking toward the water. They were all watching inland, fearful of the howling from the slaves.

Then one of them noticed that the boats were rocking in the water. Masts tipped, then tipped back again. He looked out at the water. Wave after wave was coming, as if from giant stones falling, or perhaps something pulsing deep under the water. Each wave was higher than the one before. They began breaking onto the docks.

More and more people were seeing the waves now, and those near the water began to run farther inland. The waves were coming up onto the streets, forming rivers that flowed over the cobblestones. Farther inland the water came until it was streaming across the peninsula. Ships battered against the dock and began to break into kindling. People ran screaming through the streets, pounding on doors, begging to be let inside.

And the slaves also pounded on the doors. Where a moment before all they could think of was murder and vengeance, now in their ground-floor quarters a new passion had taken hold: to get to the first floor before this flood drowned them. Wave after wave swept through the slave quarters. The howling and singing stopped, to be replaced by a cacophony of panicked cries.

Many of the Whites, seeing the flood, opened the doors and let their slaves, now chastened and afraid, come up to safety. Others, though, kept the doors locked, and more than one discharged a weapon through the door, warning the slaves to stay back.

There were no more thoughts of killing the White families they worked for. Already the slaves were telling the stories that made sense to them. "God be telling us, Thou shalt not kill, or I send a flood like Noah!" "Lord, I don't want to die!" Terror took the place of rage, damped it down, swept it out, drowned it, for the moment, at least.

"Enough," said Margaret. "You did it, Calvin. Enough."

Calvin sobbed in relief. "That was so hard!" He lay back down, rolled over, curled up and wept. Or rather, tried to curl up. As he dragged his legs across the floor, his right foot was pulled away from his body. Margaret gagged at the sight. But Denmark's woman reached down, picked up the foot, and put it in place at the end of the damaged leg.

"He just about dead," said Denmark.

"No," moaned Margaret. "Oh, Calvin, not now, not when you finally did something good."

"That the best time a-die," said Fishy helpfully. "You get in heaven."

Margaret turned again to Gullah Joe.

"No look me, you!" he said. "I do all you say, look what happen!"

"What if he sent out his doodlebug again? Like before? Even if he dies, can't you hold on to it? Keep it from getting away?"

"What you think I be? I a witchy man! You want God, him!"

"You held him captive before. Do it again! Try it!"

Even as she insisted, she could see the paths of the future change. When she finally saw one in which Calvin was still alive at dawn, she shouted at him, "That's it! Do that!"

"Do what?"

"What you were thinking! Right when I shouted."

Gullah Joe threw up his hands in despair, but he set to work, making Denmark and Fishy help him, moving charms into a new circle, then putting an open box in the midst of it. "Tell him go in box. Put him whole self in box."

"Did you understand him, Calvin?"

Calvin moaned in pain.

"Send out your doodlebug! Let him catch it and save it. It's your only chance, Calvin! Send your doodlebug to Gullah Joe, go into the box he's holding. Do it, Calvin!"

Panting shallowly, Calvin complied as best he could. Gullah Joe kept tossing a fine powder into the circle. It wasn't till the tenth throw that he shouted. "You see that? Part him go in! Look a-that!"

Another cast of the powder, and this time Margaret also saw the spark.

"All bright him! Inside, go all inside!"

"Do it, Calvin. Your whole attention, put it inside that box. Everything that's you, into the box!"

He stopped moaning. He rolled onto his back, his eyes staring straight up.

"He's done all he can do!" cried Margaret. "He's exhausted."

"He dead," said Fishy.

Gullah Joe slammed the lid on the box, turned it upside down, and sat on it.

"You hatching that?" asked Fishy.

"Inside circle, inside my hair." Gullah Joe grinned. "This time he no get out!"

"All right, Alvin," Margaret murmured. "Come quickly."

She leaned back against Denmark's wife, who knelt behind her like a cushion. "I'm so tired," she said.

"We all sleep now," said Denmark.

"Not me," said Gullah Joe.

Margaret closed her eyes and looked out into the city again. The water was calm again and the panic had died down, but the revolt was over for the night. Killing had been driven out of the hearts of the Blacks.

But now the thought of killing was showing up in other hearts. Whites were rushing to the palace, demanding that someone find out who started the plot. It had to be a plot, all the slaves starting up at once. Only the miraculous intervention of the waves had saved them. Do something, they demanded. Catch the ringleaders of the revolt.

And King Arthur listened. He called in his advisers and listened to them. Soon there were questioners in the streets, directing groups of soldiers as they gathered Blacks for questioning.

How long? thought Margaret. How long before Denmark Vesey's name comes up?

Long before dawn.

Margaret rose to her feet. "No time for rest now," she said. "Alvin will come here. Tell him what you've done. Don't harm Calvin's body in any way. Keep it as fresh as you can."

Gullah Joe rolled his eyes. "Where you go?"

"It's time for my audience with the King."

Lady Ashworth spent the entire rebellion throwing up in her bedroom. The flood, too. For her husband had found out about her liaison with that boy—slaves who had once been docile now suddenly seemed to take relish in sowing dissension between her and Lord Ashworth. In vain did she plead that it was only once, in vain did she beg for forgiveness. For an hour she sat in the parlor, trembling and weeping, as her husband brandished a pistol in one hand, a sword in the other, one of which he would set down from time to time in order to take another swig of bourbon.

It was only the howling of the slaves that broke off his drunken, murderous, suicidal ranting. This was one house where none of the Blacks wanted to brave a crazed White man with a gun, but he was all for shooting them anyway if they didn't shut up and stop all that chanting and moaning. As soon as he left her alone, Lady Ashworth fled to her room and locked the door. She threw up so abruptly that she didn't have time to move first—her vomit was a smear down the door and onto the floor beneath it. By the time the flood came she had nothing left to throw up, but she kept retching.

With the Blacks terrified and Lady Ashworth indisposed, the only person able to answer Margaret's insistent ringing at the door was Lord Ashworth himself, who stood there drunken and disheveled, the pistol still in his hand, hanging by the trigger. Margaret immediately reached down and took the gun away from him.

"What are you doing?" he demanded. "That's my gun. Who are you?"

Margaret took in the situation with a few probes into his heart-fire. "You poor stupid man," she said. "Your wife wasn't seduced. She was raped."

"Then why didn't she say so?"

"Because she *thought* it was a seduction."

"What do you know about any of this?"

"Take me to your wife at once, sir!"

"Get out of my house!"

"Very well," said Margaret. "You leave me no choice. I will be forced to report to the press that a trusted officer of the King has had a liaison for the past two years with the wife of a certain plantation owner in Savannah. Not to mention the number of times he has accepted the hospitality of slaveowners who make sure he doesn't have to sleep alone. I believe sexual congress between White and Black is still a crime in this city?"

He backed away from her, raising his hand to point the gun at her, until he remembered that she had his pistol. "Who sent you?" he said.

"I sent myself," she said. "I have urgent business with the King. Your wife is in no condition to take me. So you'll have to do it."

"Business with the King! You want him to throw me out of office?"

"I know the ringleader of the slave revolt!"

Lord Ashworth was confused. "Slave revolt? When?"

"Tonight, while you were threatening to kill your wife. She's a shallow woman, Lord Ashworth, and she has a mean streak, but she's more faithful to your marriage than *you* are. You might take that into account before you terrify her again. Now, will you take me to the King or not?"

"Tell me what you know, and I'll tell him."

"An audience with the King!" demanded Margaret. "Now!"

Lord Ashworth finally stumbled into the realization that he had no choice. "I have to change clothes," he said. "I'm drunk."

"Yes, by all means, change." Lord Ashworth staggered from the room.

Margaret strode into the house, calling out as she went. "Doe! Lion! Where are you?"

She didn't find them till she opened the door down to the ground floor. Half soaked in floodwater, the slaves were as frightened and miserable a group as she had ever seen. "Come upstairs now," she said. "Lion, your master needs help dressing himself. He's very drunk, but I have the gun." She showed him the pistol. Then, certain that Lion had no murder in his heart, she handed the gun to him. "I suggest you lose this and then don't find it for a few days." He carried the gun upstairs with him, only dropping it into his pocket at the last minute.

"You sure he don't kill the master?" asked Doe.

"Doe, I know you're a free woman, but can you go to Lady Ashworth? As a friend. No harm will come to you from it. She needs comforting. She needs you to tell her that the man who had the use of her was more than a trickster. He forced her against her will. If she doesn't remember it that way, it just proves how powerful he is."

Doe looked studious. "That a long message, ma'am," she said.

"You remember the sense of it. Find your own words."

King Arthur and his council had been meeting for an hour before Lord Ashworth finally bothered to show up, and it was obvious he had been drinking. It was rather shocking and would have been a scandal on any other night, but all the King could think about was that finally he was here, perhaps he could break the impasse over what to do. Hotheaded John Calhoun was all for hanging one out of every three slaves as an example. "Make them think twice before they plot again!" On the other hand, as several of the older men reminded him, one didn't seize one-third of the city's most valuable property and destroy it, just to make a point.

Lord Ashworth, however, did not seem interested in the argument. "I have someone to see you," he said.

"An audience! At a time like this!"

"She claims to know about the conspiracy."

"We know about it already," said the King. "We have soldiers searching for the hideout right now. If they're wise, they'll drown themselves in the river before they let us take them."

"Your Majesty, I beg you to hear her."

The intensity of his tone, despite his drunkenness, was sobering. "All right, then," said the King. "For my dear friend."

Margaret was ushered in, and she introduced herself. Impatiently, the King got to the point at once. "We know all about the conspiracy. What can you possibly add to what we know?"

"What I know is that it wasn't a conspiracy, it was an accident."

She poured out the story, keeping it as close to the truth as possible without announcing just how powerful Calvin was before, and how helpless he had become. A young White man of her acquaintance noticed a man taking something from each slave that disembarked. It turned out that they were charms that held the slaves' true names, along with their anger and their fear. Tonight there had been an accident that destroyed the name-strings, and the slaves suddenly found themselves filled with the long-hidden rage. "But the flood frightened it out of them, and you'll have no rebellion now."

"Claptrap," said Calhoun.

Margaret looked at him coldly. "The tragedy of *your* life, sir, is that despite all your ambition, you'll never be king."

Calhoun turned red and started to answer, but the King raised a hand to silence him. He was quite a young man, perhaps younger than Margaret and there was an air of quiet assurance about him that she rather liked, especially since he seemed interested in what she had said. "All I want to know," he said, "is the name of the one they call the taker of names."

"But you already know it," she said to him. "Several witnesses have told you about Denmark Vesey."

"Ah, but *we* know about him because of excellent investigative work. How do *you* know?"

"I know that he's innocent of any ill intent," she said.

A man handed the King a paper. "Ah, here it is," the King said. "Your name is Margaret Smith, yes? Married to an accused slave thief. And you're here in Camelot to meddle in our ancient practice of servitude. Well, tonight we've seen where leniency takes us. Do you know how many slaves told us about plans to kill entire White families in their sleep? And now I find that there's a White woman intimately involved with the conspirators."

With sick dread, Margaret saw herself playing the leading role in some nasty futures in the King's heartfire. She hadn't bargained on this. She should have probed into her own future before coming to the King with wild-sounding stories about Blacks giving up their names voluntarily, for safekeeping, and then getting them back suddenly. "You must admit it sounds like a fable," the King explained kindly.

"Your Majesty," said Margaret, "I know that there are those who urge you to punish this revolt with brutality. You may think this is necessary to make your subjects feel secure in their homes, but Your Majesty, extravagant measures like the one Mr. Calhoun proposes will only bring greater danger down upon you.''

"It's hard to imagine a more heinous danger than our servants turning their knives on us," said Calhoun.

"What about war? What about bloody, terrible war, that kills or injures or spiritually maims a generation of young men?''

"War?'' asked the King. "Punishing revolt will lead to *war*?''

"The rhetoric surrounding the issue of whether the western territories of Appalachee will be slave or free is already out of hand. A wholesale slaughter of innocent Black men and women will outrage and unify the people of the United States and Appalachee, and stiffen their resolve that slavery will have no place among them.''

"Enough of this,'' said the King. "All you have succeeded in proving to me is that you are part of a conspiracy that must include at least one of the servants in the palace. How else could you know what John Calhoun's proposal is? As for the rest, when I need advice from an abolitionist woman on affairs of state, you're the very person I'll call upon.''

"Your Majesty,'' said Calhoun, "it's obvious this woman knows far more about the conspiracy than she's letting on. It would be a mistake to let her leave so easily.''

"What I know is that there *is* no conspiracy,'' said Margaret. "By all means, arrest me, if you're prepared to bear the outcry that would follow.''

"If we hang one slave in three, no one will be asking around about *you*,'' said Calhoun. "Now arrest her!''

This last order was flung at the soldiers standing at the door. At once they strode in and took Margaret by the arms.

"She'll confess soon enough,'' said Calhoun. "In treason cases, they always do.''

"I don't like knowing about things like that,'' said the King.

"Neither do I,'' said another man's voice. It took a moment for them to realize that it wasn't one of the King's advisers who spoke.

Instead, it was a tall man dressed like a workingman on holiday—clothes that were meant to be somewhat dressy, but succeeded only in looking vaguely pathetic and ill-fitting. And beside him, a half-Black boy two-thirds grown.

"How did you get in here!'' cried several men at once. But the stranger answered not a word. He walked up to Margaret and kissed her gently on the lips. Then he looked steadily into the gaze of one of the soldiers holding her by the arm. Shuddering, he let go of her and backed away. So did the other soldier.

"Well, Margaret," said the man, "it looks like I can't leave you alone for a few minutes."

"Who are you?" asked the King. "Her foreign-policy adviser?"

"I'm her husband, Alvin Smith."

"It was thoughtful of you to show up just as we've arrested your wife. No doubt you're part of the conspiracy as well. As for this Black boy—it's not proper to bring your slave into the presence of the King, especially one too young to have been reliably trained."

"I came here to try to keep you from making the mistake that will eventually take you off your throne," said Margaret. "If you don't heed the warning, then I at least am blameless."

"Let's get her out of here," said Calhoun. "We've got hours of work ahead of us, and it's obvious she needs to be interrogated as a member of the conspiracy. Her husband, too, and this child."

Margaret and Alvin looked at each other and laughed. Arthur, on the other hand, was too busy gazing at the magnificence of the council room to care much about what was going on. He didn't really notice the King until now, when Alvin pointed him out. "There you are, Arthur Stuart. That's the man you were named for. The King of England, in exile in the Crown Colonies. Behold the majesty of the crownèd head."

"Nice to meet you, sir," said Arthur Stuart to the King.

Calhoun's outrage reached a new level. "You dare to mock the King in this fashion? Not to mention naming a Black child after him in the first place."

"Since you've already got me hanged in your mind," said Alvin, "what harm will it do if I compound the crime?"

"Compound nothing, Alvin," Margaret said to him. "He's been warned that if he takes retribution against this revolt that didn't even happen, killing slaves without reference to guilt or innocence, it will lead to war."

"I have no fear of war," said Arthur Stuart. "That's when kings get to show their mettle."

"You're thinking of chess," said Margaret. "In war, everyone has their chance to bleed." She turned to Alvin. "My message was delivered. It's out of my hands. And your brother needs you."

Alvin nodded. He turned to the company surrounding him. "Gentlemen, you may return to your deliberations. I ran down here from New England this afternoon and I have no more time to spend with you. Good evening."

Alvin took Arthur by one hand and Margaret by the other. "Make way please," he said.

The men blocking his path didn't move.

And then, suddenly, they did. Or rather, their feet did, sliding right out from under them. Alvin took another stride toward the door.

The King drew a sword. So did the other men, though they had to get them from the wall where they hung during the meeting. And two guards by the door drew pistols.

"Really, Your Majesty," said Alvin, "the essence of courtesy is that one must allow one's guests to leave."

Before he finished talking, he already reached out to change the iron in the swords and the pistols. To their horror, the armed men found their weapons dissolving and dribbling into pools of cold wet iron on the floor. They dropped their weapons and recoiled.

"What are you, sir!" cried the King.

"Isn't it obvious?" said Calhoun. "It's the devil, the devil's dam, and their bastard son!"

"Hey," protested Arthur Stuart. "I may be a bastard, but I'm not *their* bastard."

"Sorry we have to be on our way so quickly," said Alvin. "Have a nice future, Your Majesty." With that, Alvin reached down, pulled the lockset out of the massive door, and then pushed gently on it, making it fall away from its dissolving hinges and land with a crash on the floor outside the council room. They walked away unmolested.

The stink of Calvin's dead body filled the attic when Margaret led Alvin and Arthur into the place. Alvin went at once to the corpse and knelt by it, weeping. "Calvin, I came as fast as I could."

"You want to cry," said Denmark, "cry for the dead."

"I already explained to him about holding Calvin's heartfire in the box," Margaret said.

"I can't repair the body without the heartfire in it," said Alvin. "And it can't hold the heartfire until it's repaired."

"Do both at once," said Margaret. "You can do it, can't you, Gullah Joe? Feed the heartfire back into the body, bit by bit?"

"You lose you mind?" asked Gullah Joe. "How many miracle you want tonight?"

"I'll just do my best," said Alvin.

He worked on Calvin's body for three hours. No sooner did he start in on one repair than the one he just completed started to decay again. Working steadily and methodically, though, he was able to get the heart and brain back into working order. "Now," he said.

Gullah Joe slid off the box, carried it close to Calvin's body, and opened it.

Alvin and Margaret both saw the heartfire leap into the body. The heart beat convulsively. Once. Twice. Blood moved through the collapsing arteries. Alvin paid no heed to that problem—it was the lungs he had to repair now, quickly, instantly. But with the heartfire inside the body, it became far easier, for now he could make a pattern and the body would imitate it, passing the information along through the living tissues. A half-ruined diaphragm contracted, then expanded the lungs. The blood that pumped feebly through the body now bore steadily increasing amounts of oxygen.

That was only the beginning. Dawn had fully come before Alvin's work was done. Calvin breathed easily and normally. The flesh had healed, leaving no scars. He was as clean as a newborn.

"What I see this night," said Gullah Joe. "What god you be?"

Alvin shook his head. "Is there a god of weariness?"

Someone started pounding on the door downstairs.

"Ignore them," said Margaret. "There are only two of them. They won't break in until there are more soldiers to back them up."

"How long do we have?" asked Alvin.

"Not long," said Margaret. "I suggest we leave now."

"Is there no rest for the devil?" asked Alvin.

"You a devil too?" asked Gullah Joe.

"That was a joke," said Alvin. "Margaret, who *are* these people?"

"Time enough to explain on the road." Margaret turned to the others. "It's not safe for you to stay here, Denmark, Gullah Joe. Come away with us. Alvin can keep you safe until you're in the North, out of this miserable place." She turned to Fishy and Denmark's wife. "You aren't in the same danger, but why should you stay? We'll take you north with us. If you like, you can go on to Vigor Church. Or Hatrack River." Margaret looked at Gullah Joe and smiled. "I'd like to see what all the knackish folk in Hatrack River would make of *you*."

Denmark tugged at Alvin's sleeve. "What you done for your brother. Raise him from the dead. What about my wife?" He brought her forward.

Alvin closed his eyes and studied her for a few moments. "It's an old injury, and it's all connected with the brain. I don't know. Let's get away from here, and when we're safely in the North, I'll do what I can."

They all agreed to come along. What choice did they have?

"Can't you take all us?" asked Fishy. "All the slave in this place, take us!"

Margaret put her arm around Fishy. "If it was in our power, we'd take them. But such a large group—who would take so many thousands of free Blacks all at once? We'd bring them north, only to have them turned away. *You* we can bring with us."

Fishy nodded. "I know you mean to do good. It never be enough."

"No," said Margaret. "Never enough. But we do our best, and pray that in the long run, it *will* be enough."

Alvin knelt again by Calvin, shook him gently, woke him. Calvin opened his eyes and saw Alvin. He laughed in delight. "You," he said. "You came and saved me."

15

Fathers and Mothers

Mike Fink and Jean-Jacques Audubon waited a discreet distance away as Hezekiah Study led Verily and Purity through the graveyard. The graves were located in a curious alcove in the wall of the cemetery. Purity knelt at her parents' graves and wept for them. Verily knelt beside her, and after a while she reached for Hezekiah and drew him down with her as well. "You're all I have left of them," she said to Hezekiah. "Since I have no memories of my own, I have to rely on yours. Come with us."

"I'll travel with you as far as Philadelphia," said Hezekiah. "Beyond that I can't promise."

"Once Alvin starts talking about the Crystal City, you'll catch the vision of it," said Verily. "I promise."

Hezekiah smiled ruefully. "Will there be a need for an old Puritan minister?"

"No doubt of it," said Verily. "But a scholar like you—I think we'll have to tear you away from the things you can learn there in order to get a sermon out of you."

"My heart isn't much in sermonizing anyway," said Hezekiah. "I'm tired of the sound of my own mouth."

"Then don't listen," said Purity. "Why should we miss out on your sermons just because *you* don't want to hear them?"

They lingered near the graves for some time. Only when they were leaving did it occur to Verily how odd it was to have such an alcove enclosing just those two graves. Otherwise the graveyard walls marked out a simple rectangle.

Hezekiah heard the question and nodded. "Well, you see, when they were buried, the witcher insisted the graves had to be outside the churchyard. Can't have witches in hallowed ground. Then the witchers left, and all the neighbors who knew them and loved them, they tore down the wall at that place, and laid out a new course, and now they're inside the wall of the churchyard after all."

They stood on the south bank of the Potomac, waiting for the ferry to return to their shore to carry them across into the United States—specifically New Sweden, which despite its name was now almost as thoroughly English-speaking as Pennsylvania. A long-legged waterbird swept down into the water, elegant in its graceful passage from a creature of air to a creature of water.

"Too bad Audubon ain't here to tell us what bird that is," said Alvin.

Arthur Stuart took Margaret by the hand. "You were there," he said. "You know. What kind of bird was it that carried me?"

Margaret looked at him in puzzlement. "What do you mean?"

"I remember flying," said Arthur. "Hour after hour, all the way north. What kind of bird was that?"

"It wasn't a bird," she said. "It was your mother. She knew some of the witchy lore that Gullah Joe uses. She made wings and she flew, carrying you the whole way."

"But I saw a bird," said Arthur.

"You were a newborn," said Margaret. "How could you possibly remember?"

"Wings, so wide," said Arthur. "It was so beautiful to fly. I still dream about it all the time."

"Your mother wasn't a bird, Arthur Stuart," said Margaret.

"Yes she was," said Arthur. "A bird in the air, and then a woman when she came to earth."

Alvin remembered now how a question had nagged at Arthur the whole time he was with Audubon, a question that he could never quite frame in a way to get the answer he needed. Now Alvin had

the answer for him. "She *is* waiting for you, Arthur Stuart," said
Alvin. "With wings or without, your mother bird is still alive, waiting for you when the time comes."

Arthur Stuart nodded. "I think you're right," he said. "I feel
her sometimes in the sky, so high I can't see her, but she's looking
down and she sees me." He looked to Alvin and Margaret for re-
assurance. "That's not silly, is it?"

"They'd have to have a thousand angels watching her every
minute in heaven," said Margaret, "to keep your mama from watching over you."

Arthur Stuart nodded. "When I see her," he said, "that's when
I'll find out my true name."

"All names are true on that day," said Alvin. "When we see
each other for what we really are."

Margaret said nothing. She took no comfort in thinking of a day
of resurrection far in the distant future, for she had never seen that
day in any heartfire. All her visions ended, sooner or later, in death.
That's what was real to her.

Real and yet not terribly important. She felt her own swelling
abdomen, where the baby's tiny heartfire was growing. As long as
she had enough time to see this through, to bring this girl into the
world and raise her to adulthood, she'd have no complaint when
death came for her.

The ferry pulled in and the people from the New Sweden side
disembarked noisily. Alvin, Margaret, and Arthur walked back to
where Fishy, Gullah Joe, and Denmark and his wife waited for them.
Fast as they were traveling, news had already reached them of mass
hangings of rebel slaves in Camelot. They feared the worst—John
Calhoun's proposal to hang one in every three. But it turned out to
be only twenty.

Only twenty.

In addition, a warrant had been issued for a scoundrel named
Denmark Vesey, an illegally freed half-Black who had plotted the
whole thing, meeting every slave ship that came to port. Well, that
would never happen again. Blacktown was cleaned out and the laws
concerning the movements of slaves without their masters were going to be tightened considerably. The days of soft treatment were
over for the slaves of the Crown Colonies. They'd learn who was
boss.

Once the stories crossed the Potomac, however, they changed.
The facts were the same, but now the story was told with growing
anger. Even Blacks want to be free, that's what the Northerners said.

Whatever they might have planned, they didn't kill a single White. And now the Crown Colonies are cracking down even harder on these poor souls. Enough. The line had to be drawn. No slavery in the western territories. And no more rights for Slave Finders in the United States. Repudiate the treaty. If the Congress we've got won't do it, then we'll elect one that will. Never again will a human being on northern territory be the property of another man. People might not know it yet, but this was the rumor of war, and soon enough these seeds would bear fruit. Margaret had spent many months trying to forestall it. Now she knew that war was the only hope of ending slavery. Dreadful as it might be, it was a war that had to be fought. And here in New Sweden, the chatter of war was from the right side. It was her people talking.

Overhearing such conversation at a roadside inn, where the whole party could sit at a table together, Black, White, and all in between, led Denmark to lean back in his chair, fold his hands behind his head, and say, "It be good to be home!"

All along the road, Alvin worked steadily at trying to heal the damage to Denmark's wife. Margaret assured him that all her memories were still in her heartfire, somewhere, hidden from Margaret because they were hidden from the woman herself. It was slow, meticulous work, healing only a few nerves at a time, a few tiny regions of the brain. But they could all see the improvement in her. She limped less and less. Her hands became more deft. Her speech became clearer. She remembered more and more.

There came one morning when she woke up screaming from a terrible dream. Fishy was with her, but Denmark soon came at a run. When he entered the room, his wife looked up at him and said, "I dream you try a-kill me!"

Weeping, Denmark confessed his terrible sin to her, and begged forgiveness. "I not that man no more," he said.

That healing, too, would be long and slow.

The journey that Alvin had made in one night, running with the greensong to carry him along, took them more than a week at their leisurely pace. But it ended at last, on a familiar street in Philadelphia. Arthur Stuart recognized the rooming house and ran on ahead. Soon Mike Fink rushed out into the street to greet them, followed more slowly but no less happily by Verily, Purity, and Hezekiah. And when Alvin came into the house, there was Mistress Louder, covered in flour but not to be restrained from hugging him. She immediately adopted Margaret as her favorite daughter, and fussed over the unborn baby so much that Alvin joked that Mistress Louder thought she was the mother.

Alvin and Margaret were given the best room, the one with a balcony overlooking the garden. They sat there that first evening, taking in the peace of their first night together in so long that Alvin marveled aloud that the child had ever managed to get itself conceived.

"Let's not be apart again like that," said Margaret.

"Well, not to point the finger, but you were traveling as much as me."

"Never again," said Margaret. "You won't be rid of me."

Alvin sighed. "I never want to be rid of you, but I also want the baby to be safe. I'll take you home—Hatrack or Vigor Church, whichever you want—but I've got to go to a place in Tennizy calling itself Crystal City."

"Take me with you."

"And run the risk of you giving birth on the road? No thanks," said Alvin.

Margaret sighed. "All this wandering, all this separation, and what have we accomplished? The war is still coming. And you still don't know how to use that plow of yours, or what the Crystal City really is, or how to build it."

"I know a few things, though," said Alvin. "And maybe the main reason for all this travel wasn't the tasks we had in mind. Maybe it was those folks in the other rooms. Denmark and Gullah Joe and Fishy and Denmark's lady—I think we'll get them all to the Crystal City, in the end. And Purity and Hezekiah—I think they'll come along, too."

"And Calvin," said Margaret. "He's changed."

"Couldn't bring himself to travel with us, though."

"I think he's ashamed of what his carelessness set off back in Camelot," said Margaret. "But he's steadier. His heartfire has a lot of paths that lead somewhere. And . . ."

"And?"

She brought his hand up to her mouth and kissed it. "And maybe I have other reasons to look into the future with more hope."

"I reckon now he owes his life to me, somewhat, he's got to think different."

"Well, don't count on gratitude. It's the most fleeting of all human virtues. The change in him has to run deeper than that. I think it was when he raised that wave to stop the slave revolt from happening. Thousands of lives were saved when he did that."

Alvin chuckled.

"Why are you laughing?"

"Well, I was on the road, but I was looking ahead. I saw him trying to make a splash in the water, like the old game we played. But he was so weak, he wasn't up to it, he couldn't concentrate."

"So you did it," said Margaret.

"It wasn't easy even for me," said Alvin, "and I was healthy and experienced."

"Well, don't tell *him* that he didn't make that flood."

Alvin laughed. "And take away his one memory of doing something heroic? Not likely."

They sat a while longer in silence. Then Margaret patted her belly and sighed.

"What?"

"I was just thinking how much my mother would have loved to be here. She set such store by babies. Lost a couple before I came along and managed to live through infancy."

"But your mother *is* here," said Alvin. He reached over and laid his hand on her chest, over her heart. "Every heartbeat, she put it there, she heard those heartbeats in the womb, month after month. She's in your heartfire now, as you were in hers. That doesn't go away just because of a little thing like death."

She smiled at him. "I imagine you're right, Al. You usually are."

He kissed her. They sat there a little while longer, till the mosquitoes drove them back inside. They fell asleep clinging to each other, and even in their sleep they kept reaching out to touch each other, for fear that one might have slipped away in the night. Miraculously, they were still there in the morning, touching, breathing, hearts beating together; heartfires bright; lives entwined.

NORTH AMERICA
POLITICAL FEATURES
National Boundaries
Duchy Boundaries
State/Colony/Territory
Scale of Miles
0 50 100 150 200 250 300

CANADA
(FRANCE)

ACADIA

QUEBEC

WEST ANGLIA

NEW ENGLAND

NEW HOLLAND

WEST HAMPSHIRE

EAST HAMPSHIRE

IRRAKWA

HURON
Fort Detroit

Hatrack River

HIO TERR.

SUSKWA HENNY

Dekane

MASSA-CHUSETTS

Boston

PLYMOUTH

NETTICUT

RHODE ISLAND

PENNSYLVANIA

NEW ORANGE

NEW AMSTERDAM
New Amsterdam

Philadelphia

Luther
NEW SWEDEN

Vigor Church

WOBBISH TERR.

Carthage City

NOISY RIVER TERR.

APPALACHEE

RAPPAHANNOCK

ROANOKE

DUCHY OF VIRGINIA

NEW DOVER

NEW WALES

Franklin

SPENSER

RALEIGH

NEW KENT

DUCHY OF CAROLINA

DRYDEN

CROWN COLONIES

Camelot

DUCHY OF JACOBIA

NUEVA BARCELONA
(SPAIN)

FLORIDA
(SPAIN)